O F
L O V E
A N D
L I F E

OF
LOVE
AND
LIFE

Three novels selected and condensed
by Reader's Digest

The Reader's Digest Association Limited, London

With the exception of actual personages identified as such, the
characters and incidents in the fictional selections in this volume
are entirely the product of the authors' imaginations and have no
relation to any person or event in real life.

The Reader's Digest Association Limited
11 Westferry Circus, Canary Wharf, London E14 4HE

www.readersdigest.co.uk

ISBN 0-276-42995-8

CONTENTS

SUN AT MIDNIGHT

ROSIE THOMAS

All her life, Alice Peel has lived in the
shadow of her famous mother, listening
to tales of how she was one of the first
female scientists to live and work at
Kandahar, a small Antarctic
research station.
From an early age, Alice vowed that
she'd never fall for the lure of such a
bleak and dangerous wilderness.
But now her frail and elderly mother
has one last request—that Alice should
follow in her footsteps.

CHAPTER ONE

IT WAS A WARM, still day. There were pools of deep shadow under the trees and the river reflected the light like a sheet of crumpled tinfoil. Drawn by the day's brilliance, Alice Peel had left her desk on an impulse and walked out into the University Parks. She moved slowly, letting the sun beat on the top of her head and the back of her neck. It was a week-day and it felt odd but distinctly pleasant to be wandering around in the middle of the afternoon. Only a few other figures were dotted against the grass. There was almost another month to go before the students returned and the academic year slipped into gear once more.

When the path reached the river she turned left to follow the curve of the bank. Ahead of her a footbridge and its reflection merged to make an O, the lower half blurred like a winking eye. She listened to the tinny scratching of distant music. The scratching grew steadily louder and a punt rounded a bend in the river. Framed in the bridge's O, it turned watery furrows of pewter and olive-green as it surged closer. A girl was vigorously poling. The punt's four or five passengers lolled on the cushions, laughing up at her.

The girl's T-shirt rode up to reveal a tattoo on her belly. The punt was close enough for Alice to see that the design was a butterfly before she realised that the man sitting on the prow with his back to her was Peter. The thick hair was his, and the faded shirt was the one she had washed yesterday. The unexpected sight of him made her heart jump.

The long craft slid by, stirring the smell of mud and weeds mingled with boat varnish. The voices were loud, raised over the blare of the music.

Peter's head idly tilted, then he caught sight of Alice, already receding on the riverbank. He sat upright. 'Al! Hello, Al!' He scrambled to his feet, windmilling his arms. The punt rocked wildly and he danced barefoot on the slippery wood. She caught a brief glimpse of surprise like a flaw in the ready glitter of his smile.

'Aaaaa-al,' he shouted again. He was already into a jump, the smile still seeming to hang in the air as his limbs hit the water. A plume of glittering spray shot into the air to the accompaniment of shrieks from the punt's passengers. The girl didn't shout. She stood looking back over her shoulder, the pole trailing in her hand.

Peter hauled himself onto the bank. Grinning and dripping, he shook himself like a huge dog. 'Hi,' he gasped to Alice. ''Bye!' he called after the punt as it slid away. Disregarding his sopping clothes, Peter swept her into his arms. A watery kiss landed on her cheek.

'Pete,' she said. She wasn't surprised. The shouting, the impetuous leap into the water, they were all typical of him. But she felt disquiet wrinkling her usual smooth tolerance of his extravagant behaviour. 'Who were they?'

He waved the arm that wasn't attached to her. 'Students.'

'I thought you were teaching today.'

Peter was an artist. He built big cuboid sculptures of tubes and wire and twisted metal that also incorporated found objects like pram frames and tailors' dummies. He didn't sell a lot of his work and he taught an art summer school for extra money.

'We were playing hooky. And I thought you were working. Hey. Since we're both not working, let's go and have tea somewhere.'

'But you're wet.'

'You're dry enough for both of us.' He kissed her again. 'Lovely and dry and warm. Come on. Scones and cream. You know you want to.'

She smiled at him. There was a café near the gates of the Parks. They walked there together, Peter wincing whenever his bare feet encountered a sharp stone.

On the way they met Mark, a sculptor who rented the studio next to Pete's, and they ended up heading to the café together. Alice walked beside Mark and Peter shuffled backwards ahead of the two of them so he could see and talk at the same time. As they passed a builder's skip he noticed a typist's chair with the seat and back support missing. He carried it away with him, spinning the shaft as he talked.

There was a table free in the little row on the pavement outside the café and they crowded round it. Peter took off his shirt and draped it over his salvaged chair skeleton. Steam rose gently from his damp trousers.

When it arrived, Alice poured the tea. The others were talking about art. She half listened to a heated conversation she seemed to have been overhearing ever since she had known Peter. Art always appeared to involve arguments. It was messily subjective. To Pete, one piece of work might be enormously impressive and another might be derivative shit, but Alice could never work out which was going to be which, or if there was any empirical evidence on which to base these opinions.

In the end it came down to a matter of taste, she believed, and there was no measuring or calibrating taste. Science was different. As a scientist herself and the child of scientists, Alice had reason and logic in her blood. Knowledge meant measurement, demonstration, proof.

Sunlight lay across the table. Pete sprawled back in his chair, lanky and at ease, grinning at her. Their life together was made up of a series of small encounters like this one. They met friends, had tea or dinner or went to the pub together. They went to parties and gave their own— were giving one the very next evening, in fact. Peter was gregarious and liked nothing better than to gather a crowd of people around him. It meant that she didn't see a lot of him on his own, but she didn't mind that. She had what she wanted in life.

'Are you an artist?' Mark asked her.

'A scientist. A sedimentary geologist.'

'My God,' he said.

'He's one theory. Not many geologists subscribe to it, though.'

They all laughed. When the scones had all been eaten, they stood up. As they said goodbye, Peter invited Mark to tomorrow's party. Finally Peter shouldered his chair-remnant, and he and Alice headed for home.

The end-of-the-day traffic was heavy, but when they turned into Jericho everything was quiet again. The little red-brick houses with their Gothic touches had been built in the nineteenth century for clerks and the more senior college servants, but lately they had become sought after and very expensive. Alice couldn't have afforded to buy one, not on an academic's salary, and of course Peter wasn't able to contribute anything, but her mother had helped her with the down payment. Sometimes it seemed to Alice that her mother's life was always the vivid, engrossing, three-dimensional backdrop against which her own activities were executed on a much dimmer and smaller scale.

It was cool inside the house. From where she stood in the hallway, as Pete's mouth brushed against the nape of her neck, Alice could see straight through the kitchen doors into the garden.

Pete's hands slid up and cupped her breasts. 'Mmm . . .' he said. 'Come on. Let's go to bed.'

Their bedroom would be cool too, behind white blinds.

A minute later they were stretched out on the white-covered bed. On the bedside table the phone cheeped. Pete swore, but neither of them made a move towards it. After a dozen rings, the answering machine picked up.

'Alice, are you there?'

There was a pause and then an audible tut-tutting of annoyance. 'Well, wherever can you be, at this time of day? I need to speak to you. Give me a ring straight back, won't you?' The voice was brisk.

'Yes, *ma'am*,' Pete murmured. He never voiced any criticism of Alice's mother, the formidable Margaret Mather, but there was not much love lost.

Alice smiled. She would call in and see her parents in the morning.

Margaret Mather sat at the gate-leg table in the large bay window of the house on Boar's Hill. Books and papers and correspondence leaned in haphazard piles on either side of her computer. She had never been tidy, or even faintly house-proud, and the table was littered with dirty plates as well as her sheaves of work. The Persian rugs were matted with cat hair, and the cat itself, a fat white creature with a penetrating smell, lay licking itself on the sofa.

Margaret's husband Trevor worked or read in his small upstairs study with a view of the sloping garden. His room, together with Alice's old bedroom, represented the only ordered area in the entire house.

Margaret was working through the morning's emails. She was in her seventies, but she took to new technology with enthusiasm. Email made her complicated correspondences with friends and with fellow scientists working in her field, marine mammal biology, much easier.

In the 1960s, Margaret had made a series of television films about whales and seals in the seas surrounding Antarctica. She spent many months of the year living down on the ice, even doing most of her own underwater camerawork. She wrote the films' drily lyrical commentaries, too, and narrated them in her strong Yorkshire accent. The series made her and her voice famous.

She was never short of energy. Even after she had become a celebrity she continued her research and maintained her reputation as a serious scientist. Her meticulous work on the breeding patterns of Weddell seals pioneered a subsequent generation of Antarctic studies.

This morning, Margaret was replying to a message from Lewis Sullavan. There had been a succession of increasingly insistent communications from his staff and now there was one from the great man himself.

'My dear friend,' she began, 'I really cannot accept your kind invitation, much as I would like to. The fact is that I am now 77 years of age and I have severe arthritis. However, there remains the alternative proposal. My daughter is very interested in the idea.' Margaret whistled through her teeth as she sat back to review what she had written.

'We'll see, eh?' she said, addressing the last remark to the cat.

She heard a car and looked up. Alice's car drew up outside the front door. Margaret saved her unfinished message to Lewis Sullavan and was hobbling away from a blank screen by the time Alice came in.

'Ah, there you are at last,' Margaret said briskly.

Alice wrapped her arms round Margaret, hugging her close. After a brief embrace, Margaret leaned away, apparently for a better view of her daughter.

Alice's hair was thick and slightly wavy, the same texture and silvery blonde colour as her mother's had once been. Margaret's was white now. They were both slightly built, but Alice seemed to grow taller as Margaret's painful stoop increased.

'How do you feel?' Alice asked.

'I'm grand,' she answered, though the pain was bad today. 'And we're away on holiday in three days, even though we don't do so much here that needs taking a holiday *from*.'

'Come on, you're just going to stay in a nice hotel in Madeira and enjoy being waited on for once. Where's Dad?'

'He'll be down as soon as he realises you're here. I want a word first.'

'Is something wrong? Have you seen Dr Davey?'

'Don't fuss, Alice. I'm perfectly fine.' She sat down, hands folded.

Alice understood that her mother wanted to be invulnerable, to remain as all-capable and all-knowing as she had always managed to be; she despised her own increasing physical frailty, as if it were some moral weakness. In fact, there was nothing weak about Margaret and there never had been. She had been one of the first women scientists to penetrate the male domain of Antarctic research; she had filmed her seals beneath the ice of the polar sea and she had never shrunk from anything just because she was a woman, or a wife, or a mother. Her great energy and single-mindedness tended rather to make everyone around her feel weak by comparison. Recognition of this was one of the strongest of the many bonds between Alice and her father.

'Now, listen to me Alice. I've got a tiptop invitation for you.' Margaret paused for dramatic effect. 'You have been invited to go to Kandahar Station,' she announced grandly.

Alice had never heard of it, so couldn't express either enthusiasm or reluctance. 'What?'

'Lewis Sullavan has *personally* asked you.'

'Lewis Sullavan doesn't know me from a hole in the fence.'

But Alice knew who he was. His media empire had been founded in the 1960s with a stake in one of the early commercial television companies. It had since grown, hydra-headed, and now included newspapers and magazines in the UK and Europe, a Hollywood film company and interests in television companies across the world.

'And if he doesn't know me, why would he invite me out of the blue to go to some station I've never heard of?'

Margaret didn't even blink.

Alice quietly answered the question for herself. 'Because of you.'

For as long as she could remember she had been notable because of her mother's achievements rather than her own. Even her choice of subject had been influenced by her mother. Alice might have wished to become a biologist herself, but she never could, or would, compete with what Margaret had done. Instead, she had chosen geology, her father's speciality. In her teens they had taken camping trips alone together, looking at rocks. These times, when she had had the undivided attention of one of her parents, were among the happiest of Alice's life.

'Go on. Tell me. How do you know this media mogul and what is Kandahar Station?'

'I met him many years ago when I was making my first series for the television.' It was always *the* television, in Margaret's old-fashioned way.

'I didn't know that.'

'It's a very long time ago. Kandahar Station is Lewis's current toy. It's a new research base. Largely funded at present by Sullavan himself, but with some EU support. As you know, he's passionately pro-Europe. The intention is that Kandahar will ultimately offer facilities for European scientists and joint European research initiatives.'

'And where is it?' Alice asked, although she knew the answer.

'Antarctica.'

Of course.

Alice had grown up with the waterfall sound of the word. Margaret was in her forties when her only child was born and most of her polar adventures were already behind her, but to the small Alice, hearing the stories, her mother's doings and those of Scott and Shackleton and the others had run together into a continuous mythology of snow and terrible cold and heroic bravery. She curled up under her warm blankets and shivered, full of admiration and awe. At the same time, Alice made a childish resolution that she would never venture to such a place, and her decision seemed to be endorsed by the fact that her father had never been there either.

More than twenty-five years later, Alice saw no reason to change her mind. 'No,' she said now.

'Alice, it's an honour. Sir Lewis wants to name the laboratory block Margaret Mather House. What do you think of that?'

'It is an honour,' Alice gently agreed. 'Do you think it would be too much for you to go yourself? To see the ice again?'

Margaret's face flooded with longing. 'I would go if . . . if I didn't have damned arthritis and if I wasn't going to be a nuisance and a liability.'

Anyone planning to travel south would have to undergo medical and fitness examinations. Margaret knew she wouldn't pass any tests. And it would be Margaret's idea of misery to feel that she might be a burden.

'So. I want you to go instead. In my place. Lewis has asked for you.'

The imperiousness of her demand grated on Alice. 'I don't think I can do that.' Antarctica was her mother's love, not hers.

Margaret lifted one hand. 'Hear me out. It's not just a PR excursion. You're being offered a place on the base for the entire summer season. Just think. For a geologist to get the chance to go to Antarctica? You can pursue your own research project. You even have the time to do it.'

That much was true. After five years of teaching undergraduates, Alice had a six-month break coming up in which to pursue her own research. She planned to do some field work in western Turkey.

The familiar waves of her mother's enthusiasm and determination pounded against Alice. 'I'm flattered. And I can see it would be a nice media hook for Sullavan.' That was what it was about, of course. Some television footage, articles about the scientist daughter following in the scientist mother's footsteps, another way to promote a very rich man's latest diversion. 'But I have made my plans for the next six months.'

There was a sound of creaking floorboards.

'And now here's your father,' Margaret announced.

Trevor Peel was a small, pink-faced, egg-shaped man. A fringe of feathery white hair clung to his otherwise perfectly bald head. He eased himself round the door, trying from behind the shield of his gold-rimmed glasses to second-guess the temperature between his wife and daughter. He knew about Margaret's invitation and also Alice's likely response to the idea of travelling in her place.

Alice loved her father dearly. He had a sharp mind, but it was coupled with a tolerant disposition. He had lacked the ambition rather than the intellect to reach the front rank himself as a scientist, and he had always devoted himself to encouraging his formidable wife instead. In this they had been an ideal match. All through Alice's childhood, Margaret had often been away but Trevor was invariably there.

15

'You've got a few days to think it over, Alice,' Margaret announced. 'I'll let Lewis know you're considering it very seriously.'

The glance that passed between Trevor and Alice said, *Better try and nip this in the bud.*

Alice drew in a breath. 'Mummy, I don't want to go to Antarctica. It doesn't fit in with my plans.'

'Just give me your reasons why not,' Margaret said.

'Because I am happy where I am,' Alice said gently. Antarctica was an unknown and Alice preferred the known world.

Margaret's eyebrows drew together. 'I don't see what happiness has to do with anything,' she said at length.

No, Alice thought. Her mother understood achievement, as in doing your best and then improving on that. Happiness would come a long way down her list of considerations.

'I'm sorry,' she repeated, thinking: I have disappointed her. It was not a new realisation.

Later, Alice walked in the garden with Trevor. They leaned against the sycamore tree, and Trevor drew a line in the dust with the toe of his shoe.

'Are you sure about not going south?' he asked tentatively.

'Yes, I am. Realistically, what would my study be?'

It was much easier to talk to Trevor like this, not just because he was interested in the scope of her rock investigations but because he listened to what she said, whether it was related to science or not.

'You won't need to apply for funding, as I understand it. You just go, look at something that interests you and Sullavan picks up the tab. That doesn't happen every day, does it?'

Almost all research projects involved time spent in the field, studying rock formations and collecting samples for lab analysis. Expeditions to remote places were expensive to set up and needed complex support.

'What *is* the deal?'

She hadn't given Margaret the opportunity to explain even this much herself, so her mother wasn't the only one guilty of not listening. Sometimes, she thought, we bring out the worst in each other.

'It's a maverick set-up,' Trevor explained, 'as you would expect with anything connected to Sullavan. Kandahar is down at the base of the Antarctic peninsula. It was built in the 1950s for the British Antarctic Survey, who closed it down in the late 1990s. The bay gets iced up in winter and it's difficult to supply as a year-round station. They were on the point of dismantling the site when Sullavan offered to buy it as the base for his pet project: United Europe in Antarctica. Now he's got to get some decent science under way; it probably doesn't matter too much exactly what so long as it has popular appeal. Which is where Margaret comes in.'

And by extension her daughter, neither of them went on to add.

'I see.'

'Not tempted?'

'Not in the least.' Alice smiled. It was easy to sound entirely certain.

Her father put an arm round her and hugged her, then the two of them left the shade of the sycamore tree and walked back to the house.

Trevor and Margaret tried to persuade Alice to stay for lunch.

'No, I've *really* got to go,' Alice said, 'because we're having people round this evening, and I've still got to make the food and buy wine.'

'Can't Peter do something?' Margaret asked.

It wasn't that Alice's parents disliked Peter, more that they didn't understand how he lived a life with no particular plans. The few pieces of his work that they had seen left even Margaret with nothing to say. They believed that art lived on gallery or drawing-room walls and didn't incorporate the contents of builders' skips.

For his part, Peter was always polite to them, but the politeness had a resistance to it that was almost ruder than if he had dispensed with it and just been himself.

'It's easier if I do it. He'll be in charge of the barbecuing. So. Have a lovely time in Madeira.'

Alice hugged her mother as she left.

'Think about Kandahar,' Margaret called after her, as a parting challenge. She believed in having the last word.

It was 5.30 and Alice was lying in a hot bath when Peter appeared in the bathroom doorway. She saw his reflection first in the steamy mirror, then turned her head to smile at him. 'Were you working?'

'I had a mass of invoices, bills. I hate doing all that.'

'I know you do. Pete? I've been asked to spend a season in Antarctica.'

'And?'

And what? she wondered. What if I said, 'I'm going, and I won't be back for six months?' Instead she murmured, 'Well, I said no, of course.'

Pete nodded. That was what he would expect. He was used to her, to her precise ways, to the regularity of their life together that provided a framework for his erratic behaviour.

She closed her eyes as he leaned over and kissed her. But not before she had seen a flash in his black eyes that she couldn't read.

Pete was the one who ended the kiss. 'We're going to have a *great* party,' he said. He didn't ask any more about Antarctica. Alice had said that of course she wasn't going, so there was no need to pursue it.

It was a good party. The house and garden overflowed with different people, painters and writers and lecturers and scientists as well as the old friends Alice had grown up with. Oxford had been her home for most of her life and she loved this bringing together of different elements from within it. Recognising when the party was moving under its own impetus, she gave herself up to the pleasure of it.

Alice's oldest friend Jo was there and her husband Harry. They had brought their three-month-old twins and put them in their car-seat cradles to sleep in Alice and Pete's bedroom.

'Al, I am so knackered,' Jo muttered. She had black rings under her eyes and her flat hair clung to her cheeks. 'They never sleep at the same time. I never get more than an hour. What am I going to *do*?'

'They'll start sleeping better soon.' Alice took her friend's hands and rubbed them between her own.

Then Becky arrived, late. Her current man was a psychologist, an unnervingly handsome Indian who didn't say very much. As always, Becky talked enough for both of them. 'I'm sorry, Al, have we missed everything? The traffic from London, you wouldn't believe. Vijay said we should just move to Oxford. Jo! Come here, baby-mother, give me a hug. God, your boobs are so fabulous.'

Alice and Becky and Jo had been friends since the fourth form. Jo had once said, 'I'm the good girl, Alice is the clever girl and Becky is the star in the firmament.'

Now Jo said, 'I've just got to go up and check on them again. I don't know where Harry is.' She looked as if she was going to cry.

'Harry's in the garden with Pete. I'll go up and make sure they're still fast asleep; *you* sit here and talk to Beck,' Alice told her.

She gave them both a glass of wine and went up the stairs. Loud music came up through the floorboards but didn't seem to bother Jo's babies, asleep in their padded plastic cradles. Alice stooped down to look at one of them, and wanted to touch the tip of her finger to his rosy skin.

She stood up again, almost reluctantly, and walked to the door. From the semidarkness of the bedroom she could see down to the half-landing. Pete was standing in the angle of the stairs, just out of sight of anyone who might be in the hallway. His hand slid slowly down the back of a girl who was pressed up against him, came to rest on her bottom. She was wearing a cropped pink top that exposed a broad expanse of skin above low-slung trousers.

Alice stood completely still. He bent his head and kissed her. She angled herself closer still, the movement eloquent of intimacy and familiarity. The two of them knew one another's bodies.

A second later, the girl ducked away from him. Pete rose up onto the balls of his feet, as if balancing on the brink of something delightful, then followed the girl.

It was just a kiss at a party. It was what parties were for.

But everything about the tiny encounter told her that it was much more than just a kiss at a party.

Becky and Jo both stared at her as she came back.

'Are they all right?' Jo was already heaving herself to her feet.

'They're fine. I just saw Pete kissing some girl on the stairs.'

Becky and Jo looked at each other. 'Which girl?' Becky asked.

Alice glanced around the crowded room. 'That one.' She was standing by the mantelpiece. Midway between her hip bone and her neat belly-button there was a butterfly tattoo.

'Never seen her before,' Becky said.

'She's one of Pete's students.'

'And where is he?' Jo asked in a let-me-at-him way.

Alice forced a smile. 'He'd better keep out of my sight for an hour.'

She drank some more wine and kept talking and laughing, then she danced. She wanted to dance with Pete, but they were never in the right place together.

At 1 a.m. Jo and Harry went home, carrying a baby seat apiece. Becky and Vijay left at two.

The hard-core guests stayed until it was light. She would have liked to be drunk herself, but all she felt was cold. Pete had spent the last hour playing his guitar and singing. Now he was sitting on the sofa, a glass of whisky at his feet.

Alice stood in front of him. 'Pete, come to bed.'

The bedroom was disorientatingly light. They lay down and Pete turned and lay against her, one arm heavy over her hips.

'Who was she?' Alice asked.

'Who was who?'

'The girl with the tattoo.'

'Tattoo? I dunno. All girls have tattoos. 'Cept you.' He laughed into her hair and she shivered with the first wave of longing for an intimacy that was already gone.

'She was with you yesterday. In the punt.'

'Punt? Oh, yeah, her. Georgia.'

Alice lay on her back, watching the ceiling. If he says anything else, she thought, it will be all right. If I have to ask him what he was doing with her it won't be. The seconds passed. Then she realised from Pete's slow breathing that he had fallen asleep.

19

'Your mother's not very well,' Trevor said.

Alice was sitting at her desk in the Department of Geology. As she pressed the phone to her ear, the maps she had been studying lost their definition and ran together in a grey blur. 'What? What's wrong?'

'She's picked up a chest infection. The hotel doctor's a bit worried.'

'How long has she been ill?'

'A couple of days.'

'Why didn't you tell me?'

Trevor sighed. 'You know what she's like.'

Fierce, stubborn, impatient with weakness. Alice knew what her mother was like.

'Are you going to bring her home? Shall I come out there?'

'There's no need for that. Rest and antibiotics are what she needs.'

'Are you sure? I'll call you later and see how she is.'

After Trevor had rung off, Alice tried to turn back to her work, but anxiety nudged at her and in the end she gave up. It was almost lunchtime. She would call in at Pete's studio and tell him about Margaret. They could have a sandwich and a cup of coffee together.

The studio was in an old warehouse at the end of a cul-de-sac. The heavy door hung narrowly ajar, sagging slightly on its hinges. Alice padlocked her bike to a street sign.

She edged round the door and slipped into the studio. It was dim inside after the bright daylight. Pete wasn't working, then. The blinds were drawn. The concrete-floored space smelt of dust and resin, and something familiar scraped at her subconscious in the split second before she identified it. It was music, the same song that had been playing in the punt on the afternoon when Pete jumped into the water.

His latest work in progress loomed above Alice's head. It was a bird's nest of twisted metal and, within the lattice cage, a polystyrene wig block like a blanched head revolved very slowly. The hair at the nape of Alice's neck prickled as she looked around for the source of the music. She took three quick steps to the inner door.

The door led into a boxed-off cubicle with a metalworker's bench at which Pete did his smaller-scale work. The CD player was balanced on the broken typist's chair from the skip outside the Parks. A girl's handbag spilt its contents on the floor. The girl herself was perched on the edge of the cluttered bench, steadying herself with her hands. Her denim legs stretched out on either side of Pete's head.

Pete hadn't heard Alice come in. Just above and to the side of his right ear Alice could see the butterfly tattoo.

The girl looked straight into Alice's eyes. 'Oh, shit,' she said.

20

Alice didn't move. There was a scramble of movements as Peter leapt to his feet and the girl pulled up and zipped her jeans.

Pete said in a thick voice, 'Al, you know, it isn't—'

'It isn't what I think? Is that what you're going to say?'

He held up his hand. 'Georgia, you'd better go.'

Georgia leaned across and pressed a button to eject the disc from the player. When she had tucked it inside her bag, she stood facing Pete with her back to Alice. 'When will I see you again?'

He had the grace to look uncomfortable. 'I don't know.'

'I see. Well, then, I'll call you.' She glanced at Alice. 'I'm sorry, I really am. But all's fair, as the saying goes.' Then she left.

What does one say now? Alice wondered. Pete was waiting, ready to take his cue from her. He looked like a schoolboy anticipating a scolding, half truculent and half defiant.

'I came over because my mother's not well. I'm worried about her. I was thinking we could have lunch. Just a sandwich or something.'

Her words fell into the space between them. Pete's expression changed to one of relief. 'Of course. Where would you like to go?'

'What? No. I don't want to go anywhere. That was before I saw . . . '

He rushed in: 'Al, believe me, it doesn't mean anything.'

'It's just a dick thing?'

His face flushed. 'No. Well, if you want to call it that, yes. I suppose.'

'How many?'

'How many times? For God's sake. She's just a student.'

'I meant how many other women.'

'Alice, please. What do you think I am? I'm with you, I love *you*.'

She stared at him. She wanted to have him put his arms round her and hear him saying that this was all a mistake—not in the guilty, formulaic way that he was saying it now, but in a way that meant she could believe him. And at the same time she knew that this was utterly unrealistic because she would never again be able to believe what he told her.

When he had finished protesting she listened carefully. She thought she could hear a tiny, feathery whisper. It was the sound of her illusions, softly collapsing.

'I'm going back to work now,' she said. 'We'll have to talk about what's going to happen, but I don't want to do it today. If you can't find a place to stay tonight, I'll go to Jo's.'

She was dry-eyed and her voice sounded level, but her stomach churned with nausea and the palms of her hands were wet. Then she turned around and walked out through the studio. The polystyrene head was still gently turning on its thread of wire.

She cycled back to her office, drank a glass of water and called Jo. 'Are you in? Can I drop in after work?'

'Of course I'm in. I'm always in.'

Jo and Harry lived in Headington. Alice cycled slowly up the hill, buffeted by the tail wind from passing buses, her legs feeling like bags of wet sand.

Jo opened the door with one of the babies held against her shoulder. 'Come through,' she said. She led the way to the kitchen. The second twin was in a Moses basket on the table. 'Cup of tea? Wine?'

'I'd love some tea, please,' Alice said. She didn't think she could keep a glass of wine down. 'Can I hold him?'

Jo handed the baby over at once. He frowned and squinted up at Alice, ready to start crying.

'Here, plug this in,' Jo said, handing over a bottle of formula. Alice poked the rubber teat into the baby's mouth and he began to suck. Jo eyed her, then sat down next to her at the table. 'What's up?'

Alice told her. While she was talking the baby's eyelids fluttered and then closed.

'The thing is, I'm not sure that Georgia is the only one. Now I've seen this much, all kinds of other details seem to be falling into place. When he doesn't come home in the evenings, when he goes off for days at a time, I just get on with my work and feel pleased about how . . . how separately productive and mutually in accord we are. In fact, he's probably got half a dozen women on the go, hasn't he?'

She started on a laugh to distance herself from this possibility and then a flicker in Jo's eyes made the laughter stick in her throat.

'What do you know? Jo, please tell me.'

Jo hesitated. 'Harry saw him one night. In a pub near Bicester. Pete didn't see him, because he had his tongue down some woman's throat at the time. That's how Harry put it.'

'Was it Georgia?'

'It didn't sound like her.'

'No. I see.'

'I thought you sort of knew about Pete and that was the way you chose to handle it. Knowing and not knowing.'

'Perhaps,' Alice murmured. Humiliation made her want to bend double, as if she had a stomachache.

'You deserve better,' Jo observed, lifting the other baby out of his basket as he began to cry in earnest.

'Perhaps,' Alice said again.

'Do you love him?'

Yes, she loved him. Or was it actually the idea of him that she loved, the very way his disarray and lack of precision had made an anarchic foil for her own self-imposed orderliness?

'I don't know,' she told Jo now. The realisation that she truly didn't know shocked her.

'What will you do? Tell him to behave or else?'

'It's a bit late for that. I was going to ask if I could stay here until he's moved out?'

Jo said immediately, 'Of course you can.'

Alice made pasta for dinner while Jo bathed the babies and fed them again. Harry came home, his face creased from the day, and they juggled the wakeful twins between the three of them while they ate. Pete rang Alice's mobile every half-hour, but she didn't take the calls. He rang Jo and Harry's number too, and Harry did pick up the phone.

'Yeah, she's here. But I'd leave it for a while, mate, if I were you.'

The calls stopped after that. Before she went to bed Alice spoke to her father in the hotel in Madeira. 'Is she feeling any better?'

'The doctor called in again. We think she might be better off at home, you know, so we're going to take a flight tomorrow.'

'Can you put her on?'

Alice put the flat of her hand against the wall of Jo's spare bedroom, wanting to feel its solidity.

'It's very annoying,' Margaret said into the phone. The words were hers but her voice was almost unrecognisable.

'You'll be fine. Once you're home.'

'Will I?' She asked the question as though she were a child.

'Yes,' Alice said with a tremor in her voice.

In their bedroom, Jo and Harry undressed for bed. One baby was asleep, the other cried every time Jo put him down. They would alternate this routine throughout the night. Jo walked up and down, rhythmically rocking the baby against her.

'She's very precise. Not detached, exactly. But she doesn't waver, or change her mind. If she's decided it's all over with Pete then it's over.'

Harry got into bed. 'Yes? Probably for the best, then.'

'Maybe. I don't know, though. She seemed happy with Pete. He countered that precision in her. Made her more spontaneous. Al's my best friend. But sometimes I think I don't know her at all. I mean, I've never even glimpsed it, but beneath all that cool logic there might be a wild heart beating. Don't you think?'

There was no answer. Harry had plunged into sleep.

Alice went home for a change of clothes. Pete had been there, she could tell from the crumbs on the counter and a single plate and knife in the sink. She registered this much, then dismissed the thought. The latest telephone conversation with Trevor had left a hard knot of anxiety in her chest. Margaret had had a bad night and was suffering breathing difficulties. Alice said that she would meet them at the airport but Trevor had arranged a private ambulance. Margaret would be driven straight from the airport to hospital. 'I'll see you there,' Alice said.

Eventually, after a long time, Trevor called again. They were in the ambulance. Margaret had taken a turn for the worse. Alice drove to the hospital, and found a seat in the A&E waiting area. Half an hour dragged by before a long white car with blacked-out windows drew up. A stretcher was rolled out of the back and lifted onto a trolley. Alice glimpsed her mother's white hair. She ran in pursuit.

Margaret's eyes seemed twice their normal size. Her face was a parchment triangle and there were purple marks like fresh bruises showing through the skin. She was breathing in fast, shallow gasps.

Medical staff crowded into the cubicle. Alice and Trevor retreated to a row of chairs. Trevor's cardigan was buttoned up wrongly. His white hair stood out round his head and Alice wanted to smooth the wrinkles of freckled skin where it suddenly seemed too loose for his skull.

'The flight,' he murmured. 'I thought . . .' He had thought that she was going to die. Having seen her mother, the fear didn't seem irrational.

'The doctor will tell us everything.'

She sat still, holding her father's dry hand and waiting. At last a doctor came to find them.

'Mrs Peel almost certainly has a form of pneumonia,' she said. 'We are X-raying her now and we'll do some blood tests.'

Under her married name, Margaret sounded like a stranger, Alice thought. She was always Margaret Mather, yes, *the* Margaret Mather.

'Can I go to her?' Trevor asked. There was a pleading note in his voice. It occurred to Alice that she had never been properly aware before of how deeply he loved Margaret.

'We'll stabilise her first. It's a matter of making her comfortable.'

They went back to the row of seats and waited. A teenaged girl was pushed past in a wheelchair. She was wearing school uniform, the navy-blue and cerise of Alice's old school.

Once, Alice remembered, when she was eleven or twelve, Margaret had come to the school to show one of her celebrated films.

'I am going to take you all on a journey,' she said. 'To one of the most remarkable places in the world.'

The film's images were already familiar to Alice. There were the rookeries of Adélie penguins on rocky headlands of the Antarctic peninsula. Thousands of birds seethed on a narrow rock margin between mirror-silver sea and steep walls of ice and snow. Margaret and her assistant moved through the dense colony, counting the eggs and the chicks.

There were shots of penguins flipping out of the sea between the ribbed flanks of icebergs, like dozens of tiny missiles, intercut with footage of the birds cruising underwater. Alice knew that Margaret hadn't used an underwater cameraman; she had dived down into the ice-bound sea to film all this herself. She wanted to nudge her neighbour and tell her so.

The applause at the end was loud. The biology teacher thanked Dr Mather for coming to talk to the school. Margaret stood beside him, and she appeared to be made of different materials and coloured more brightly than Mr Gregory. Alice realised now that that was the moment when she understood how sexy her mother was.

Margaret had another lecture to give after her talk to the school and she drove herself away straight afterwards in her green Alfa Romeo with the dented rear wing. Alice was surrounded by a group of girls.

'Your mum's rather amazing,' Becky Gifford said. Becky's own mother was a television actress, and Becky was the most sophisticated and confident girl in Alice's year. She had never noticed Alice before.

'She is a scientist,' Alice answered, wanting to make clear that that was what was most important.

'So are you going to be one as well?'

'Yes,' Alice told her.

It was probably true, Alice thought now, that she owed her friendship with Becky to Margaret and that day.

A nurse came and stood in front of their chairs. 'You can come and sit with her now,' she told them.

Margaret had been moved to a different cubicle, a glassed-in alcove to the side of the department. She was asleep, propped up on pillows with a clear plastic mask held to her face by an elastic loop.

The time passed. A nurse came every half-hour to check Margaret's pulse and temperature. The evening seeped away, and a different nurse performed the observations, which meant that the night staff had now come on. Alice was just deciding that she would make Trevor eat some food when Margaret opened her eyes. They flooded with mute terror.

Her free hand clawed at the mask. She dragged it off her face and hoarsely whispered, 'I'll suffocate.' Her Yorkshire vowels were exaggerated: *soooffocaaate*.

Alice jerked to her feet. 'No, no, you won't,' she soothed.

Margaret's head turned to Trevor and then the other way, until her eyes connected with Alice's. Alice had never seen her mother afraid before, but her face was livid with it now.

'I want you to do something for me.' She said it to Alice. Even now she managed a degree of imperiousness. 'I want . . .' Margaret took a breath. 'I want you to go south. To Lewis Sullavan's station.'

'I can't go anywhere, not when you are ill.'

Margaret's hand twitched. 'I'll be getting over this. But I want you to go, while you can, while you've got the chance. For . . . me. Do it for me.'

Alice understood what she meant, with the clear precision born in the most intense moment of an intense drama. She knew that she would remember this instant and her exact comprehension of her mother's wishes. There would be no denying or forgetting what was intended.

Margaret was looking at the spectre of her own mortality. She wouldn't die here, not yet; her will was too strong for that. But she knew, finally and empirically, that her strength was not infinite. And her intention was that her life would be carried forward for her, out on the ice where she had lived it most intensely, by her only child.

Alice looked at Trevor and saw the mute imprecation in his face. He had never, throughout her life, demanded a single thing of her. All he had done was to love the two of them, his two women.

'Of course I'll go,' Alice said softly.

The fear in Margaret's eyes faded, replaced for a moment by a clear sapphire glimmer of triumph.

'You'll find details. Email, in my email in-box,' Margaret said.

Gently Trevor lifted the plastic mask and fitted it over his wife's mouth. She nodded her acquiescence and her eyes closed again.

At 10 p.m., Alice drove her father home to Boar's Hill. Once they had eaten and she was sure that he had gone to bed, she made up a bed for herself in her old room. She looked across at the old books on the white-painted shelves. There was Shackleton's *South*, and Fuchs and Hillary's *The Crossing of Antarctica*, both of them presents, on different birthdays, from Margaret. It was as if Alice could see straight through the stiff board covers now, into an Antarctic landscape where the reality of Margaret's films and the explorers' stories overlapped with a fantastical realm of ice turrets and rippled snow deserts and blue-lipped crevasses.

Antarctica lay in wait for her, its frozen jaws gaping wide open.

Sleep was out of the question. Alice went downstairs and sat down at her mother's computer screen, clicked NEW MESSAGE and began to type.

She wrote that if it was appropriate, and if her understanding of the present situation was correct, following her mother's serious illness she would be honoured to be considered in her place for membership of the forthcoming European joint expedition to Antarctica.

She attached a list of her scientific qualifications. At the end, against Previous Antarctic Experience, she typed *none*.

She reread her short message, changing a couple of words and adding her correspondence address. Then she filled in the recipient's email address and quickly pressed *send*. The communication went to someone named Beverley Winston, assistant to Lewis Sullavan.

There was nothing else to be done tonight. Alice went back up to bed, and lay still under the familiar covers. She thought of her own bed in the house in Jericho and wondered where Pete was tonight. Only a little time ago they had woken up in the same bed with nothing more than a kiss glimpsed at a party to separate them.

Now there was the prospect of half a world.

Suddenly, beneath her rib cage, Alice Peel felt a sharp stab of anticipation that shocked her with its ecstatic greed.

CHAPTER TWO

WITH THE STEADY approach of summer, the pack ice in the bay was slowly, grudgingly, breaking up. This morning, the ice was a dirty ivory colour, glinting like polished bone. The expanding streaks of water were black and pewter-grey under a matching sky, and a thin veil of ice fog hung over the cliffs that formed the opposite wall of the bay.

James Rooker replaced the engine casing of the skidoo and twisted the ignition key. The machine obligingly coughed and roared, and Valentin Petkov, the glaciologist, glanced back from where he was placing bamboo wands and marker flags out on the ice and gave a thumbs-up.

The field assistant, Philip Idwal Jones, was nearby, coiling a rope. 'Hey. Rook.' The shout carried clearly in the silence. 'Time for a brew?'

Rooker pulled back the cuff of his glove to check his watch. It was midday and they had been out since 8 a.m. Petkov was keen to set up his markers and take the first set of readings. This part of his study, as Rooker understood it, was to do with comparing the speed of travel of the margins of the ice with the centre. If you could call it speed, he reflected, at the rate of millimetres per year.

Phil dropped his rope and took off his fleece cap to scratch at his spikes of black hair. He was only twenty-six but he had been travelling and climbing since he was seventeen. This was his third Antarctic season. As a mountain guide it was his job to assist the scientists in their field work and at the same time to make sure they didn't fall down a crevasse or off a cliff.

'Ta,' Phil said now when Rooker passed him a Thermos of coffee. 'Phew. Warm, innit?'

It was, compared with a week ago when they had first arrived. Daytime temperatures then had hovered around −23°C, with a heavy wind chill. Today it was a mild and summery −5°C.

'D'you think Val's going to take a break?' Phil wondered, looking over at Petkov, who was still zigzagging across the glacier.

The Bulgarian had a rich bass voice and a barrel chest, and a fondness for whisky and jokes whose punch lines didn't always survive the shift into English. There were six different first languages at Kandahar Station, but English was the common tongue.

Phil beckoned to Valentin by waving a mug in a wide arc. He sighed when the scientist cheerily waved back, either not understanding or not wanting to stop work. 'Daft Bulgar. I'll have to take it over there. Give us one of those butties, mate.' Phil took the Thermos and a wrapped sandwich, and headed off across the snow again.

The skidoo had been tending to stall on the way out from the base. Rooker had found and cleared a blockage in the fuel line. He sat on the machine now, leaning back against the handlebars with his feet up on the seat. When he had looked into the radio room this morning, Niki had told him that the warm and windless weather heralded a storm. Nikolai Pocius was the radio operator, a gaunt Lithuanian communications genius. He was probably right, but it was hard to believe it in this moment of perfect stillness.

Apart from the nine people currently occupying the two huts on a small bluff that made up Kandahar Station, the nearest human habitation was at Santa Ana, a Chilean base that lay 120 miles further up the peninsula. The Chileans maintained a snow ski-way for fixed-wing aircraft, and the Kandahar personnel had flown in there and then been transferred by helicopter to Kandahar. In partnership with the Chileans, Lewis Sullavan had leased for the summer season a pair of New Zealand-owned Squirrel helicopters with two Kiwi pilots and a mechanic. The machines and their crews would be based up at Santa

Ana, but they would be available to transport Kandahar scientists out to field locations too remote to be reached by skidoo and sledge. Rooker envied the pilots. He would have liked to fly over the wilderness of glaciers, watching and trying to second-guess the extreme weather, but there was no chance of that. His fixed-wing licence was out of date and he had flown a helicopter only a handful of times.

The silence expanded and thickened around him. In the ten days since they had arrived here, the peace had soothed him. He escaped outside as often as he could.

The hut was crowded. He found it difficult to live at such close quarters with the disparate group that Shoesmith had assembled here. Dr Richard Shoesmith was the expedition leader. Rooker had taken an instinctive and immediate dislike to him, but the rest of them were mostly all right. It was the mass function that he recoiled from. People were always talking, trying to make themselves heard above the hum of the other voices. They wanted to make their mark, all of them. Sometimes the spectacle touched him, at other times he laughed with everyone else, but he found it impossible to join in properly. The layers that protected him had thickened to the point of impermeability.

Some months earlier, Rooker had arrived in Dallas, to be a pilot for an air charter company. The job had fallen through, so he had filled in on a building site for a while, then moved on to Miami, where a friend of his had a small air-freight business. There had been no work for him, so Rooker had gone to Rio, mostly because he had never been before, and then to Buenos Aires. Restlessness gnawed at him and he found himself moving further and further south, as if he was being driven away from the populous centre of the world and out to the margins, where he belonged. He didn't try to swim against the current. He passed through Rio Gallegos and then, because there was still somewhere further south to go, he drifted on down to Ushuaia, the southernmost town in South America, between the tail bone of the Andes and the mountainous seas of the Drake Passage. There he got a job as a foreman on another building site.

He had grown accustomed to being alone. He had left girlfriends behind him, and some good friends—especially Frankie. Frankie was younger than he was. Although he had known her for fifteen years, they had never slept together. He liked that; it made her different. But now she was married to a chiropractor and living in New York State with him and their three children. And by the time he reached Ushuaia, he had stopped looking for company, except for sex or for someone to drink with.

He had been in a bar when he had heard about Kandahar. Dave, a blond New Zealander, told Rooker, 'They're hiring down south, you know.'

The only place south of Ushuaia was the Antarctic continent.

'Yeah? McMurdo?'

McMurdo was the American polar research station down on the Ross Ice Shelf. Rooker had worked there for a brief summer season when he was in his early twenties.

Dave shook his head. 'Nope. It's a new station, some rich guy's bought a redundant base off the Brits and he's tooling it up to be run for, whatchacallit, in Europe? The EU? Sounds kinda interesting.'

It did, Rooker thought. Keep going, that was the idea. Keep going, while some place even further away still beckons.

He remembered now how remote McMurdo had seemed, ringed by the ice. Yet it had been nothing like this. McMurdo could house over a thousand people. It had bars and buses and a constant round of parties, and he looked back on it now as just a more boring and much harsher version of Ushuaia. It had been too populous and insulated for him to feel the powerful presence of the ice. But it was lucky that he had worked that meaningless long-ago season, because it was the magic phrase 'previous experience' that had secured him this job. He had been taken on by Sullavan and Richard Shoesmith to manage transport, and to act as base mechanic and maintenance man.

That was easy enough. Rooker was good with machinery. He had almost five months ahead of him now, and all he had to do was drive the Zodiac, fix skidoos, and keep the water and the generators running. He felt, at long last, that he had travelled far enough. No one would try to reach him or come pushing up against him here, nudging him for reasons or responses. He could keep a distance from the eight other people.

No, he suddenly remembered, it would soon be nine, not eight, because there was another scientist arriving today.

Shoesmith had made one of his ponderous announcements over breakfast: 'As most of you already know, Dr Alice Peel, from Oxford, will be arriving later today. Please make her welcome.'

Jochen van Meer, the station's medical doctor, had raised his thick blond eyebrows and grinned. 'It will be a pleasure.'

Eight, nine, Rooker thought. It made no difference.

The radio crackled in his inner pocket. Shoesmith's voice broke out of the buzz of static. 'Base, this is Kandahar Base, Base to Rooker. Over.'

'Copy you,' Rooker replied.

Everything about Shoesmith, including his radio manner, was irritating. As soon as they met, at the hotel in Punta Arenas before the flight south, Rooker knew that Shoesmith had the English public schoolboy's conviction that what he did was right because it was always done that way. He had confidence, but it wasn't rooted in competence or insight.

The trouble was that his voice, his manner, even his pink, handsome face, reminded Rooker of Henry Jerrold of Northumberland, England, whom he wanted to forget for ever.

Rooker listened to the leader's instructions. While the glaciology team was working, Richard wanted him to come back to base with the skidoo and ferry the French biologist to one of her penguin colonies. After that, the supply ship was due. Rooker was to take the Zodiac out through the loose ice to meet the new arrival and bring her ashore.

'Roger,' he said.

Rooker raced the skidoo back to base. The outward journey had been slow because he and Phil had stopped to test the snow ahead with a long probe wherever there was a shadow or a dip. But now he drove at full speed, the front skis skimming in the safe tramlines of their exploratory journey. Exhilaration curved his mouth into a wide grin.

The base was six miles away. As he came over the last rise, Rooker saw it lying ahead of him in a sheltered bay, two carmine-red dots against a sweep of snow with the pack ice and a tongue of inky water as a backdrop. Escarpments of rock rose on either side, and behind the base the sloping snowfield was crowned with a towering rock outcrop that marked the glacier's margin. At the closed end of the bay, another tongue of the glacier tumbled in vicious blocks and gashes down to sea level.

Rooker swept the skidoo in a circle and left it under a makeshift shelter at the rear of the huts. One of his extra assignments was to build a proper housing, using materials left by the supply ship. The sky had darkened and he noticed that the wind was rising now.

'Ah, there you are,' Shoesmith said superfluously. He was sitting at the oilcloth-covered table in the middle of the living area with a mass of papers spread out in front of him. The only other work area at Kandahar was at the narrow benches in the chilly lab and most people preferred to do their less demanding work in the warmth of the communal area.

At the far end of the room, the base manager, Russell Amory, and Niki were crowded in the kitchen. Niki was peeling potatoes and Russell was making bread. The two men looked like one another's opposites. Niki was immensely tall and cadaverously thin. He had long, unkempt hair and a wispy beard that didn't hide his hollow cheeks. Russell was short, broad and suntanned, and bald except for a band of fuzz above his ears.

'Where is Laure? Is she ready?' Rooker asked.

As if to answer him the Frenchwoman, Laure Heber, emerged from the door of the women's pit room.

'*Merci, Jeem*,' she smiled. '*Tout prêt.*'

31

Laure's shiny dark hair was cut in a tidy bob. She wore pearl studs in her ears and even her fleece tops were flatteringly shaped. Compared with the eight men on the base she was a miracle of personal grooming.

Now she took her windpants and red parka off the hook by the door and said to Rooker, 'Jochen is coming to the rookery as well. He will help with netting the birds. You can take two of us?'

'Sure,' Rooker answered. Laure was tiny. It would mean squeezing up a bit, but he didn't think the big Dutchman would mind that.

On cue, van Meer popped out of the opposite bunk-room door.

Beside the front door was a whiteboard, with a list of surnames and a box beside each name. A tick in the box indicated that you were safely on the base. If you were going beyond the immediate environs you wrote down your destination and estimated time of return. It was Phil's job, and also Rook's as deputy safety officer, to monitor the status of the board. He scribbled 'transport SW rookery' on it and added his initials.

Laure and Jochen followed suit. Jochen picked up a radio from the shelf next to the whiteboard. 'TBC' on the board indicated that they would need return transport, time to be confirmed by radio link.

They had made the fifteen-minute journey to the Adélie penguin rookery several times before. The colony consisted of more than a thousand breeding pairs. As the skidoo crested the rise, the noise burst on them. It was a solid and constant chorus of guttural chirring. There was a flurry of flippers and beaks covering every inch of rock. The smell was as powerful as the noise. One night at the base, after a day's work at the rookery, Laure had buried her face in her gloves and exclaimed 'Parfum de pingouin' with as much delight as if it were Chanel No. 5. She loved everything about penguins, and Rook liked her for that. He could hardly distinguish what the other scientists specialised in. Especially Shoesmith. Shoesmith was the most bloodless man he had ever met.

Laure and Jochen unpacked the equipment. At this stage the task was to map the nest sites and ring-mark some of the birds. Later in the season, once the chicks were hatched and established, Laure would take feather and blood samples from her ringed birds for DNA analysis back in Paris. One of her studies, Rook had learned, related to the amount of heavy metals and toxic elements accumulated in the birds' feathers. The annual accumulation of pollutants could be measured and so provide a precise bio-indicator of new pollution levels on the subcontinent.

This was the gist of what she had told him one night at dinner, in her perfect English. It had become accepted that everyone sat in the same places every night, so now Laure was always on his right and Phil on his left. Shoesmith presided at the table's head, of course.

Rooker would have liked to stay longer out here, watching the penguins, but there was the ship and the new arrival, so he checked the radio link with Jochen and then left them to their work.

As he came over the headland, Rooker saw the supply ship already gliding towards the mouth of the bay. The sea was getting choppy in the wind, with ice rattling and churning in the swell. It wouldn't be an easy journey in the inflatable.

As he passed the radio room at one end of the lab hut, he heard Niki's voice. '*MV Polar Star, MV Polar Star*, this is Kandahar Station. Do you read me. Over.'

The laconic voice of the ship's radio op crackled back. Rook waited until Niki pushed his headset aside and gave him the thumbs up.

Rook tramped to the main hut and exchanged his parka for a huge orange float suit. To fall into these icebound waters without protection would mean death within minutes. Shoesmith was hovering nearby while Russ and Arturo, the precise little Spanish climatologist, pulled on chest-high waders.

'We'll give you a hand, mate,' Russ said.

Rooker took a spare life jacket. The three of them scrambled down the rocks to the floating jetty where the Zodiac was tethered. With Rook aboard, Russ and Arturo waited for a lull, then rushed the black inflatable out into waist-deep water. Rook lowered the outboard and to his relief it fired at the first pull. The Zodiac roared forward, the prow lifting as high as his head as it breasted the waves, and ice and scudding water punched the rubber floor as he headed for the bay mouth.

Alice stood at the ship's rail with her kitbags at her feet. She had spotted the station in the distance—a pair of reddish specks marooned against a vast expanse of hostile emptiness. Then the clouds of snow and fog closed in again to obliterate even that much. The land's desolation made her feel afraid, even though she had been longing for this moment ever since the ship had left Chile. She had been abjectly seasick for three days. Yet now that the moment had come to leave the little ship and the friendly Spanish crew, she was full of misgivings.

Two sailors lowered the flight of metal steps at the ship's side. As the ship rolled, the platform at the bottom plunged under several feet of glassy water, then it rocked up again with spray cascading off it. The sailors ran down the heaving steps as confidently as if they had been a set of stairs in Benidorm. A black dinghy, pitched at a threatening angle, materialised. A big man in orange waterproofs swept the tiller in an arc; the boat crested a wave and landed neatly at the foot of the steps.

One sailor made it fast, the other ran nimbly up the steps again, grabbed Alice's luggage and yelled 'Vamos!' at her. She let go of the rail, half scrambled and half slithered down to the platform and launched herself with a sob of panic onto the dinghy's floor. Her bags tumbled in after her and some nets of more-or-less-fresh vegetables.

The ropes snaked away and the Zodiac roared free. The boatman kicked a red life-vest towards Alice.

'Put that on,' he shouted without taking his eyes off the sea.

She struggled to get her arms through the holes. Her teeth chattered.

The Zodiac and the waves raced each other to the shore. Alice had never been so far from home or felt the effects of distance so acutely. Nor had she ever been so apprehensive of what lay ahead of her.

It had happened with bewildering speed. It was barely a month since she had arrived at Lewis Sullavan's London headquarters to be interviewed by Dr Richard Shoesmith.

'The Polar Office?' said one of the Sullavanco receptionists. 'You'll find it on the fifth floor, if you'll take the lift behind you.'

The lift slid up a glass tube mounted on the outside of the building, and it gave her vertigo. The carpet of the fifth-floor corridor seemed to rise up to meet her as she stepped out of the lift.

'Dr Shoesmith shouldn't keep you too long,' the Polar Office receptionist said.

A secretary brought Alice a cup of coffee while she waited. This was all so mutedly but distinctly high-rent that it made her smile. It couldn't have been further from the dowdy clutter of the Department of Geology, or any other academic institution she had ever known.

When Dr Shoesmith emerged from his inner office, Alice saw a compact man perhaps ten years older than herself. He was good-looking, but there were pale vertical furrows etched between his eyebrows. He looked fit and slightly out of place in the plush Sullavan offices.

They sat down, Shoesmith behind his desk, and Alice to one side and in a slightly lower chair.

'You have no previous Antarctic experience,' he began.

'None,' she said steadily.

He looked through a neat sheaf of documents: some of her published research papers, a copy of her full academic CV, references, all submitted at the request of Beverley Winston, Lewis Sullavan's assistant.

'Hmm. Doctoral studies . . . Lecturer in sedimentology, University of Oxford . . . Proposed area of study . . . mapping, stratigraphic survey and dating of sedimentary rock formations in the vicinity of . . . Yes.' Richard looked up abruptly and his eyes held Alice's. 'Lewis is very eager to have you join the expedition. Perhaps you could give me your own reasons.'

She looked straight back at him. She would have to be honest. 'The enthusiast was originally my mother. She was, is—'

'Yes, I know who your mother is.'

Of course he did. Alice added softly, 'I have thought about it a great deal since the suggestion was first made.'

The truth was that an entirely unexpected desire had taken hold of her. It wasn't to do with geological research, although her academic appetite for the new realm of Antarctic rock was beginning to grow. It wasn't even for Margaret's sake, although of course that was a part of it. It was much more that she wanted to push out from the secure corner of her own life, the place that her crumbled illusions about Peter had left dusty and unpopulated, and to turn disappointment into discovery.

All her knowledge of the south was secondhand. There was none of her own history in it, although its history surrounded her. Now the blank page that it would offer had begun to draw her. No one who went to the ice ever came back unchanged: Alice had heard that often enough, even from Margaret, the arch-unsentimentalist. Probably everyone who found themselves drawn south was on the run from someone, or something, and that included Richard Shoesmith. But she was running towards it too, faster and faster every day. She was ready to be changed.

Richard Shoesmith was waiting for her answer.

'I want to see it for myself.' Knowing that this was not the time to mention running anywhere, she talked about European scientific cooperation, and the unrivalled opportunity to undertake valuable research. The words were measured, but eagerness coloured them and her voice shivered just audibly with absolute longing.

Richard Shoesmith took all of this in. Some of the rigidity seemed to melt out of him. 'It is a chance that any geologist would jump at, Dr Peel. A complete field season, automatic full funding, the opportunity to make your mark as part of a team at a brand-new station. Because of the nature of our present funding, in the selection of personnel for this expedition there is an inevitable element of, how shall I put it, who you are and whom you know?'

Alice said delicately, 'I think we both understand that.'

Because she knew about Richard Shoesmith, just as he knew about her and her mother's reputation. Shoesmith was a famous name, but not by reason of Richard's own achievements. He was a palaeontologist. He held a research post at Warwick and was currently Reader in Palaeontology there. He had done some new work on evolution and extinction of certain cephalopods and gastropods, but he didn't have a big reputation. His grandfather, however, was Gregory Shoesmith.

As a twenty-two-year-old alpinist and gentleman botanist, Gregory had been one of the youngest members of Scott's Terra Nova expedition. He had acquitted himself with quiet bravery and dignity, and Mount Shoesmith, the majestic peak overlooking the Beardmore Glacier, was named after him. Gregory came home from the ice with what was left of Scott's expedition and had almost immediately enlisted. He survived the entire war and was awarded the VC. He was widowed while he was still a young man, then married again in his forties. His second wife had three children and the youngest of these was Richard Shoesmith's father.

This much Alice knew as fact. She also knew by intuition that she and Richard Shoesmith suffered in common the sun-and-shadow effect of their family reputations. For Lewis Sullavan it made perfect sense to have Gregory Shoesmith's grandson leading his first expedition, just as it would to have Margaret Mather's daughter among the scientists. Who you are, as Richard put it, provided them both with enviable opportunities. And the two of them had always to live without the certainty that what they did achieve was on their own merits.

Richard considered for a moment, then seemed to reach a decision. 'Lewis is strongly in favour of your joining us. And I would be happy to accede to that.' Then he surprised her. 'I love Antarctica with all my heart. I've always loved it, first the idea and then the reality. It's the only place, the only thing I have ever known that is always more beautiful than its admirers can convey, more seductive and more dangerous than its reputation allows. You can never forget it, and it never releases its hold on you. I hope that it will come to be just as important to you.'

'I hope so too,' Alice said. And then she smiled. It was her wide, infrequent and startlingly brilliant smile. 'Thank you.'

'Are you free to travel south at this short notice? Most of the members will be at Kandahar by the middle of October.'

A little more than two weeks' time.

'My mother has been very ill recently, but she's recovering,' Alice said. 'I could be at Kandahar in a month's time, if that would be acceptable.'

'There are a number of things you will need to do before you can definitely join us. Medical and dental checkups, and so forth. Beverley Winston will arrange for you to be kitted out with polar gear. Everything is supplied. You will also have to do some basic survival training. We shall be a full-season core of just ten people in all. Six scientists, including yourself, and four support staff.'

She read the list of names that he passed across the desk to her.

Eight people with whom she would spend five months in a hut perched on the white margin at the distant end of the earth.

'Six nationalities,' Richard said. 'Seven, if you count Welsh. This is not a huge Antarctic research station like McMurdo or even Rothera. We shall be pioneers on an old base and we'll set out with no rules except safety regulations. You know your polar history? Of course you do. You know that Amundsen's bid for the Pole was for Norway's sake. Scott wanted the Pole, of course, but the real reason for his expeditions was scientific exploration and discovery. We shall also be there for science's sake.'

Alice understood that Richard Shoesmith was a scientist through and through. Her liking for him grew. 'Yes,' she said.

The meeting drew to a close. They were shaking hands when he asked, 'Are you free for lunch?'

She had arranged to meet Becky in a bar in Clerkenwell. 'I'm sorry. I'm on my way to see a friend.'

He didn't have to ask her to lunch; it wasn't a part of the vetting process. He was asking because he wanted to. They recognised each other. She smiled at him again.

'Of course. Well, then, good luck with your medicals. We'll speak.'

Alice sailed down in the bubble lift and walked out into the damp autumn morning. All her senses were heightened and sharpened with the intensity of anticipation. She was going into the unknown.

Becky was waiting, her legs hooked round a bar stool. 'How did it go? No, I can see. You're really going? My God, Al, you *are*.'

Alice laughed. 'I'm going. For five months. The summer field season. I'll be leaving at the end of October and I'll be back in March.'

She told Becky about Richard Shoesmith, and the tasks she would have to accomplish before she could leave. All the time she was reminding herself that she was cutting loose from everything she knew and heading for a place on which she had always, from her earliest memories, deliberately turned her back.

'What about the house?' Becky was asking.

'Oh, I'll let it for this academic year,' Alice improvised. 'Maybe I'll travel for a couple of months on the way back. It would be a shame not to, wouldn't it? I've never been to South America.'

Becky was looking at her. 'What about Pete?'

'There's nothing much to tell. He moved out.'

'Is that it?'

While Margaret was still dangerously ill, Alice had stayed at the house on Boar's Hill. Pete telephoned again and again, and when she wouldn't speak to him he turned up unannounced at her office one afternoon. She looked up from her desk to see him in the doorway—or a more than usually unshaven, crumpled, wild-haired version of him.

He slumped down on the spare chair. 'I can't sleep. I've lost my appetite. Alice, why are you so fucking empirical about everything? I love you and I miss you; that's all that matters. I want you to come home.'

'Pete. I came to your studio and found you engaged in oral sex with one of your students. I am empirical, if you mean that I base my reaction to you on the results of observation. How else am I supposed to respond to the evidence? "Oh, look, there's Peter with Georgia. What he's doing actually proves how much he loves me."'

'Alice, *please*.' He put his arms round her and tried to draw her against him. It would have been very easy to give way and bury her face in his shoulder and pretend that she believed him. But Alice preferred meagre facts to the most colourful and persuasive elaborations on the truth.

'I want you to move out. I am going to stay at my parents' house until you do. You've got time to find somewhere else, but that's what I want you to do.'

His face changed. 'I see,' he said at last.

To do him credit, he didn't argue any more then. And he packed his belongings and moved out of the house within two days. He left a note on the kitchen table saying that he loved her even if he had a strange way of showing it. Alice threw it into the bin.

'Yes, that's it,' she told Becky now.

'I'm sorry, darling.'

They had ordered some food and now it was put in front of them. Thinking she was ravenous, Alice had asked for seared tuna and glass noodles. The food had a strange metallic taste.

'Alice, are you sure you're all right?'

'Yes, of course I am.' She smiled at Becky. 'I don't need Pete and his antics. I'm off to Antarctica, aren't I?'

'It sounds very uncomfortable and rather dangerous.'

'But I get to look at four-hundred-million-year-old sedimentary rocks that hardly anyone's ever seen before. I'll wear a butch survival suit and learn how to drive a skidoo and rescue myself from a crevasse, and on good days I'll get a turn at cleaning the base kitchen. Dr Shoesmith promised me that.' Her gaiety was convincing to herself, at least.

'Oh, God.' Becky grimaced. 'You will come *back* safely from down there, won't you?'

'I will,' Alice promised.

No one ever comes back unchanged, she remembered.

From the upright chair beside her bed, Margaret saw Alice walk down the ward towards her. She could see even in a second that there was more colour about her, her face had opened like a flower in the sun. The news must be good.

'There you are. What an age you've been, when I'm dying to hear all about it. Sit down.'

Alice kissed her. 'Do you want tea, before I tell you?'

'Don't be so damned annoying. Put me out of my misery.'

'Yes. I'm going. All right?'

Margaret's face sagged briefly with relief. 'Good,' she said firmly.

Alice sat down and Margaret listened intently as she described her hour with Richard Shoesmith.

'I met his grandfather, you know,' Margaret said.

Gregory Shoesmith had been an old man—*just like me, now. Where do time and strength slip away to?*—but he had taken her hand between his two. He said, 'We have been privileged, you and I. We have seen places that we will never forget.' He had known war and too many deaths, and he had lived a long life, but it was the ice that filled his mind.

Alice didn't look surprised. 'You met everyone.'

Margaret was caught up in the teeming mass of her memories. They swirled around her, thicker and faster, like a blizzard. Alice would inherit the memories. It was like handing on your own genes, mother to daughter. Antarctica was what made me, Margaret thought. It will be the making of my child too, and she needs that. Alice has always been reticent, and now she will come into bloom.

Margaret had no fears for her, any more than she had ever had for herself. She thought, I know what it takes to do well down there and you have it, my Alice. You're more like me than you want to admit.

Three hectic weeks had followed. Alice fitted in all the things she had to do, but only just. She went to see Dr Davey, who had been the family doctor ever since she was born.

'You've never had a day's illness in your life, my dear. I don't need to run a battery of expensive tests to know you are in perfect health.'

He ticked a long list of questions, scribbled a paragraph at the end and signed the medical declaration. Alice countersigned it and sent it off to Beverley Winston.

She visited her dentist and had all her fillings checked. She went up to London and at a Sullavan-owned warehouse near the North Circular Road she was issued with her polar kit: a bewildering pile of fleece and Gore-Tex inner and outer garments, all marked with the EU flag and

Sullavanco logo. The massive red outer jacket, with matching wind-pants, had '1st EU Antarctic Expedition' stitched on it. On the front there was a Velcro sticker that read simply PEEL.

She went up to Cambridge for a three-day survival course run by the British Antarctic Survey for their own departing personnel. They all went to lectures about the dangers of frostbite, and glacier travel, and ecological disposal of waste matter. There were practical sessions about mountaineering and survival. At least Trevor had taught Alice the basics of rock climbing on their Alpine holidays together.

The preparations absorbed her attention on one level; on another she observed her own dashings around as if she were a stranger. Even her body felt slightly unfamiliar. She had lost her appetite, and if she sat down to collect her thoughts between work and meetings she found herself on the brink of falling asleep. This she put down to being too busy, to delayed anxiety about Margaret and perhaps a reaction to Peter's absence.

Two days before she left, Jo and Becky gave a goodbye party for her at Jo's house. Alice wore the long johns and balaclava and huge insulated boots from her polar kit, until she got too hot in the crush and discarded them. She was pulling a fleece vest over her head and briefly revealing her black lace best bra, when she looked up and saw Pete.

'I wasn't invited,' he said, 'but I came anyway and Harry didn't turn me away from the door. You look wonderful. You must be excited.'

'Oh, Pete.'

He held out his arms and she hesitated, then let them enclose her.

'Dance?' he asked.

She nodded. They had always moved well together, she thought.

At the end of the evening, when most of the guests had hugged Alice and said goodbye and told her that she must take care to come back safely, Pete was still there. It was time to go home. Jo and Becky and Harry and Vijay gathered in the doorway to wave goodbye. Alice looked back at the tableau they made and framed it in her mind.

'I'll see you home,' Pete murmured.

They went in Alice's car, with Alice driving, but he jumped out at the other end to open the car door. He followed her up the familiar path, took her key out of her hand and unlocked the front door as well. They half turned to each other, hesitating, then Pete tipped her face up to his.

'I wish you'd let me say I'm sorry.'

'You can say it.' Her voice was raw in her throat.

'I wish you'd let me show you I'm sorry.'

Alice lifted her hand. It started as a warding-off gesture but her fingers seemed to melt. Why not? she thought.

'To say goodbye?' she murmured.

There was a flash of triumph in his eyes, quickly extinguished. But you are wrong, the triumph's really mine, she thought.

Afterwards, Pete lay with his head against her heart. I have just taken what I wanted, she thought, without weighing up whether it would hurt him or not. The notion of revenge had never crossed her mind and this didn't feel like it, but there was a symmetry here.

In the morning Pete asked, 'Are you going so far away because of me?'

She smiled. 'No, Pete. I'm going because of me. And partly because of Margaret.'

Peter sighed. 'I'd better get to the studio, I suppose. I'm still working on *Desiderata*, you know.'

The sculpture with the polystyrene head. 'How's it going?'

'There's something mutinous about it.'

'I see.'

It was Pete's turn to laugh. His eyes crinkled and the inside of his mouth was red. 'My lovely Alice. What you see is figures and graphs.'

'So I haven't changed all that much.'

He turned serious again. 'I think maybe you have. *Desiderata* will be finished by the time you come home. I'd like to show it to you. We can talk about it. We're still friends, Alice, aren't we?'

'Yes, we are,' she reassured him.

Margaret had spent a lot of her time in bed since coming home from hospital, but tonight, Alice's last night in Oxford, she was up and dressed. It was a celebration evening.

Trevor raised his glass of wine to propose a toast. 'Here's to my two Antarctic heroines. I am so proud of you both.'

Tomorrow Alice would set off. The unimaginable vastness and the glamour of the ice left her thrilled with anticipation. She wondered if this was how her mother had felt too, and when she looked through the candlelight into Margaret's face she knew for certain that it was.

It was only when the meal was finished and Alice had cleared the table that they saw how tired Margaret was. Trevor blew out the candles and Alice helped Margaret slowly up the stairs.

She sat on the bed and took off her shoes. 'Darling, you're not going south just because of your . . . because of Peter, are you?'

Alice had played it down. She told Trevor and Margaret that she and Pete had just decided to go their separate ways.

'No. I'm going because it seems like a good idea. Whatever happens, it's not very long and then I'll be home again.'

Margaret said, almost to herself, 'It's not a matter of time. Antarctica makes a different dimension altogether. You'll understand me, when you get there. Always, for ever, you see everything in your life through its prism. Through a veil of diamond dust.'

'What's that?'

'Clear air ice precipitation. Below minus forty, ice crystals form by spontaneous nucleation and are deposited usually in short bursts. Storms of glittering points of ice, falling out of a blue sky. It's beautiful.' Margaret lay back against the pillows. 'I will think of you, with diamond dust falling,' she added, with the deepest satisfaction in her voice.

Alice knew that her mother was offering her what had been the best experience of her own life. As a gesture it was at once expansive and profoundly selfish, and thus perfectly expressive of Margaret herself.

'Thank you,' Alice whispered. 'I will think of you too, with diamond dust falling.'

Trevor drove her to the airport for the evening flight to São Paolo, where she would connect with a flight to Santiago and thence to Punta Arenas at the tip of Chile. At Punta Arenas she would embark on a Spanish supply ship for a three-day voyage across the huge seas of the Drake Passage, to the Antarctic peninsula and Kandahar Station.

'How do you feel?' Trevor asked.

'I feel like an impostor. I'm scared that I'm going to turn up down there and someone will tap me on the shoulder and say, "Excuse me, we were expecting Margaret Mather." I'm afraid of letting her down.'

'Never feel that,' he ordered. 'You can never be an impostor.'

'We'll see,' she temporised. She was leaving many things behind but she carried his love with her, a thread as fine and as strong as a spider's silk. 'What was it like, seeing her off all those years ago?'

'I wanted to plead with her not to go. So I was glad, when she disappeared, that I hadn't given way to begging. Then I just waited for her to come back.'

The huts of Kandahar loomed closer through the mist and spray. A jetty broke out of the fog and so did two more orange-suited men, standing up to their chests in water. One of them, extraordinarily, was grinning widely. The engine was cut. The two men hauled the Zodiac through the surf to its mooring, then held out their arms to Alice. She sat up on the pontoon and they lifted her effortlessly over the surf and swung her down on to the icy beach.

'Welcome to Antarctica,' the smaller one said.

CHAPTER THREE

UP ON THE ROCKY bluff a door opened and a shaft of light shone through the icy murk. A moment later, Alice was stumbling into Kandahar Station.

She reached for her sodden hat and pulled it off. Wet hair fell around her cheeks, and sea water dripped off her and puddled on the floor. She glimpsed a big table, laid with an oilcloth, mugs and plates. There were shelves with a clutter of books, CDs and video tapes. The wooden walls were decorated with pictures and maps, all related to Antarctica.

'Hello, Alice,' Richard Shoesmith said. 'Welcome to Kandahar.'

She blinked and tried to compose herself. Her eyes stung and her nose ran. 'I'm very pleased to be here,' she managed to gasp.

'Would you like a cup of tea?' Richard asked.

Laughter at the absurdity of this exchange, as well as relief, welled up inside her. 'I'd love a cup of tea.'

The bigger of the two men who had helped her out of the dinghy squeezed her fingers in a powerful handshake. 'Russ Amory. Base manager.'

The other one was young, slim and black-haired, with a gold stud in his left ear. He shook her hand too. 'Arturo Marenas. Climatologist.'

'Hello, Russ, Arturo. I'm Alice Peel.'

Russell roared with laughter. 'We guessed as much.'

She looked around the room again. There was an L-shaped desk with radio equipment and a computer under one window, and next to the door a row of cupboards and hooks marked with individuals' names. At the opposite end was a metal-topped table, a sink and a big cooker, shelves with saucepans and dishes, a tall, humming refrigerator. The effect was cosy and crowded, but the homeliness didn't disguise the splintering wood of the walls and the chipped and curling lino tiles on the floor. Kandahar hut had been neglected and hastily brought back into service.

The indoor warmth was in sharp contrast with what she saw when she glanced through the window. The shoreline and the sea ought to have been visible, just a few yards away at the foot of the bluff on which the hut stood, but instead there was a faintly luminous, thick white wall.

'Yes, it's snowing a bit,' Richard said at her shoulder. 'Forecast's not so good for the next couple of days. Won't you sit down here?'

Russell sliced a loaf of bread and grinned at her. An immensely tall, cadaverous man came forward and was introduced as Nikolai Pocius.

'Radio operator, me,' he said in a heavy Russian-sounding accent.

She sat down next to Richard, who was at the head of the table. He explained, 'We've got two teams out working in the field this afternoon. Valentin with Phil on the glacier and Laure with Jochen at the rookery. But Rook's gone to pick them up before the weather comes in. I don't know when we'll be able to get outside again, if the forecast's correct.'

Alice was fitting faces to names. There were four people here and two pairs still out at work. So the boatman, the ninth, must be James Rooker. 'What happens while the weather's bad?' Alice asked.

'We wait. Do what lab work we can. Write notes. Do housework. Painting and decorating, if we have a mind to it.'

'Then wait some more.' Arturo shrugged. 'Welcome to Antarctica.'

Richard Shoesmith saw her face and lightly patted her shoulder. 'Don't worry. It's early season yet. There's plenty of time to get out there. We'll be at Wheeler's Bluff in two or three weeks' time.'

Richard had written to her that Wheeler's Bluff would be their first joint objective. It was a long reef of exposed rock that reared up out of the snow 200 miles inland from Kandahar. From their deep field camp at the Bluff, Alice would carry out a survey of the sedimentary layers and collect rocks for analysis and dating, while Richard searched for fossils. His identification of whatever fossilised flora and fauna were present would in turn enable her to date her rock samples with precision.

'That's good,' Alice murmured.

She wasn't worried about the work itself. She was sure that she could do it when the time came. It was just that, in spite of the homeliness of bread and tea, this place was as utterly unfamiliar as if she had landed on another planet.

'Would you like to see where you'll be sleeping?' Richard asked.

'Yes, please.'

The women's room contained two sets of bunk beds, two sets of lockers and hanging cupboards, and a window. One of the lower bunks was taken, and there were books on the nearest locker and photographs pinned to the wall: Laure Heber's belongings. Alice sat down on the other lower bunk. Richard put her kitbags on the floor beside it.

'Welcome to Kandahar,' he said again. He hesitated, then added, 'You've struck a bit unlucky to have heavy weather to begin with. There are difficulties sometimes; when you're cooped up, everyone gets on top of each other. It's only to be expected.' He shot her a sideways glance, tentative, half apologetic. He was giving her an oblique warning.

Yes, Alice thought. There was an edge, a certain wariness, in the atmosphere here. She had felt it already, out in the communal area. And Richard was right, of course. In an isolated, confined environment like this, small events would take on major significance.

'It will be fine. I'll be fine.' Her eyes met Richard's.

'Yes. I'm sure you are your mother's daughter.'

And you, Gregory Shoesmith's grandson.

'I'll, ah, leave you to unpack, then.'

After a few minutes, Alice heard the sound of different voices. More people had come in. She shivered a little, more from loneliness than cold, then unzipped her kitbag and busied herself with unpacking.

Almost an hour had gone by. It was 8 p.m., the outer door slammed again and she heard yet another set of voices. One was a woman's. Alice jumped up from her bed. She stood uncertainly, waiting, until the bunk-room door opened.

A young woman came in. She had bright, slanting eyes and a bell of dark hair, tousled now from her hat. Her cheeks were reddened by the wind. She held out her hand at once, not smiling. Alice shook it.

'You are settled in,' Laure observed. 'My God, you know, it's a blizzard out there. I think we only made it back thanks to Rook. You are welcome to Kandahar Station, Alice.' She pronounced it, of course, Aleece.

There was a loud noise of metal banging against metal. It was time for dinner and Russ was beating a spoon on a tin plate.

The room was unnervingly full now. There was one empty seat left, next to Richard again, and she slipped into it. A hand descended on her arm and she turned her head to meet her neighbour. She saw a full, curly grey-black beard split by a wide smile, a chest that seemed on the point of bursting the zipper of a pair of ancient red salopettes. He looked like Father Christmas's much younger and more dissolute brother.

'You know, these are crazy people,' the man said.

Alice guessed who this must be. 'How do you do, Dr Petkov?'

He bellowed with laughter. 'I love you British. You are always "How do you do? Would you like a nice cup of tea?"'

He was right, Alice thought. Richard and she, that was how they were. Valentin swept an arm round her and kissed her enthusiastically on the mouth. She kissed him right back.

Across the table was a big blond man with thick features. 'Hi,' he said. 'Jochen van Meer. Base medic. The soup's really good. Have some.'

From the other side of Arturo, Nikolai Pocius, the radio operator, poked his skull-head forward. 'He is right. Russ is making it, even though it's my duty day. It is a flavour known as not-Lithuanian soup.'

Someone else gave an ironic cheer and Alice saw a dark-skinned impish-faced boy on the other side of Nikolai. Philip Idwal Jones, the Welsh mountain guide. He winked at her.

Richard had ladled soup into her bowl. Alice lifted a spoonful and tasted it. Jochen and Nikolai were right, it was very good. Then, she noticed something else. A force field of antagonism divided the two ends of the table. In a moment's silence that was broken only by the clinking of cutlery, the separation seemed as obvious as a brick wall.

On one side, Richard Shoesmith's side, were Jochen the doctor, Arturo and herself, with Valentin somewhere on the borderline. On the other were Russell and Nikolai and Phil and, somewhat surprisingly, Laure. Laure was sitting with her head and shoulder inclined towards her neighbour and the swan curve of her long white neck drew Alice's eyes to the man at the far end of the table.

The man was eating with quick, economical movements, his head bent, looking at no one. She saw that his hair was shaved close to his skull and that it might have been white or grey or silver. There was a dark mole on his forehead, just at the point where his hairline came forward in a vee, and his skin was weather-beaten.

At that moment, with her eyes on him, Rooker lifted his head. She expected that he would meet her glance, but he did not. Alice had never seen such a withdrawn expression. James Rooker looked at nothing and nobody, in spite of Laure's seductive posture. All he would see, she guessed, were the images that played behind his own eyes.

She told herself that she had imagined the force field. Antarctica must already be affecting her. There were only ten tired people having dinner in a remote place. It was the sensation of being trapped in this room with the blizzard driving against the windows, that was heating her imagination.

Richard tinkled his spoon against his water glass. 'Not all of you have had a chance to meet her yet, so I want to introduce Dr Alice Peel who has just joined us from Oxford. Welcome to the Joint EU Antarctic Expedition, Alice, and to Kandahar Station.'

The others made a polite murmur and now Rooker's abstract gaze briefly settled on her face. It made her feel uncomfortable. Alice made a little speech about how happy she was to be here and how much she was looking forward to working as part of the team. There was a small patter of applause, not ironic, she thought.

There was boiled ham and mashed potatoes to follow the soup, then tinned fruit salad. Alice had overestimated her appetite and couldn't finish hers, but Valentin obligingly exchanged plates with her.

After the meal she tried to help with the clearing up, but Russell told

46

her that it was Niki's duty day and she would have plenty to do when her own turn came.

Everyone else was reading, writing notes or listening to music on headphones. Alice went to bed. She lay in the dark security of her bunk, feeling loneliness stretched out beside her. The wind sometimes fell to a low growl; at other times it rose to a high-pitched scream that battered at the roof and the walls. She turned onto her back and lay with her eyes open, her fingers laced over her belly. Quite soon, sleep claimed her.

The blizzard lasted for three days. It was impossible to leave the base— even crossing the few yards to the other hut was a serious excursion.

On the first day, Alice thought she would go and talk about their joint geology projects to Richard, who was working in the lab. She put on her parka and a pair of snow boots, and told Russell where she was headed.

As soon as she stepped out of the door, the wind slammed it shut behind her. She took an unthinking step forward as driving snow filled her eyes and mouth. She choked and lifted her arms to shield her face. The sudden movement and an extra-vicious gust of wind made her stagger, and she overbalanced and fell into thigh-deep snow. Coughing and gasping, she floundered on all fours trying to get her bearings.

She had no idea which way to turn. The edge of the bluff was a couple of yards away in one direction; the main hut could only be the same distance away in the other. But she could see nothing. There was just the blizzard, a whirling wall of snow and sea fog, and the wind tearing as if it wanted to strip and flay her. She stood up again and glimpsed the blurred outline of her fall. She retraced the step that led to it and the red-painted wall of the hut loomed ahead. Against the gale, it took all her strength to heave it open. When it yielded she fell inside in a slanting column of snow. She forced the door shut and bent over, panting for breath.

It was almost impossible to believe that the calm, domestic interior existed on the same planet as the wilderness outside. She had been out for one or two minutes. Russ was sitting in exactly the same position at the table, reading an old newspaper. He looked up. Alice's eyes were watering. She didn't know if they were tears of cold or shock.

Russ got up, went to the coffee pot and poured some coffee into a mug. He put the mug on the table and guided Alice to a chair in front of it. 'Rough weather,' he said kindly. 'You're not adjusted yet. Best to stay put until it quietens down.'

'I had no idea,' she whispered when she could speak.

It was true. Every hour that passed seemed to underline the fact that she knew nothing about the place she had come to. Although she had tried to prepare for it, a world of such hostility was completely new to her.

As the second and third blizzard days of idleness crept by, Alice found it hard to occupy herself. Everyone else seemed quite happy. Russell ran the base, overseeing everything from food preparation to the sorting of waste. Laure had her Adélie penguin samples to work on; Arturo and Valentin worked on their data too. Richard was always busy. Jochen van Meer, the stolid Dutchman, was content to read paperback thrillers and watch DVDs. His own scientific study, to do with respiration, nutrition and body weight at extreme temperatures, involved nothing more at present than taking everyone's blood pressure once in a while and enquiring about their appetite.

Whatever the weather, Niki had to spend most of his hours in the radio room. He had a series of schedules to keep with the Chileans and other bases, and with the ships in the vicinity. Alice found it comforting to know there were other people alive and well in this white inferno.

When she tried to think about home and her parents, or Pete, or Jo and Becky, they seemed too far away to conjure up. Each expedition member was allotted thirty minutes of online time every day for personal emails, but when she sat down to write, Alice couldn't describe her feelings of isolation and claustrophobia.

Philip Idwal Jones and the boatman, as Alice still thought of Rooker, were less in evidence than the rest of the team. The four male scientists occupied one of the bunk rooms and the support staff the other. Philip and Rooker seemed to spend most of their days behind the closed door of their room, with Niki whenever he was off duty. Raised voices and laughter were occasionally audible.

Sooner or later, however, the blizzard would be over and she and Richard would head out into the field. They would spend a week alone together, collecting rocks, in contact with base only via a daily radio link. It was an intimidating prospect, but with the walls of the hut pressing closer and closer around her she was longing to get outside.

On the third day of confinement, Alice was rostered for hut duties. It was a relief to have something concrete to do. She cleaned the bathroom, scrubbed the floor of the living area and baked scones for tea, as well as serving up lunch and dinner. As soon as she banged the plate and spoon, everyone flocked to the table. With so few other diversions, they were all inquisitive about whether the new arrival could cook. After her day in the kitchen, Alice was relieved and flattered when her Spanish omelette and spiced beef casserole were both wolfed down.

'Bravo, Alice.' Valentin beamed. 'You turn out to be a true gift.'

Niki said that the weather forecast for the next forty-eight hours was looking much better. As a climatologist, Arturo usually regarded day-to-day meteorological predictions as beneath him, but now he nodded in agreement. 'It will be weather for sunbathing.'

'Or for field training.' Phil winked at Alice. Before she could set off inland with Richard, Alice would have to practise safety and survival techniques, and it was Philip's job to instruct her.

After Alice had cleared away the dinner dishes and put the coffee pot on the table, Phil went to his room and reappeared with a guitar. He had a big, strong baritone voice, trained in a Welsh choir, that filled the hut. Within a minute everyone was singing with him.

Rooker had a good voice too. Looking nowhere, with his black eyebrows drawn together, he sang 'Brown-Eyed Girl', then 'Yesterday' as a duet with Laure. Everyone clapped that one and Laure laughed. She let her head fall, just for a second, against Rooker's shoulder.

'*Laure, s'il vous plaît?*' Jochen said. He beckoned her to dance. She looked as if she would much rather stay put but she didn't refuse.

Richard took Alice's hand. 'Would you like to?' he asked.

'Yes, please.'

He was stiff at first, but then he loosened up. Alice saw him glance around the room, covertly gauging the mood. Understanding and a sudden affection sprang up in her. Richard was shy and he was also anxious because the success of Lewis Sullavan's venture depended mainly on him. It was no wonder that he sometimes seemed ill at ease.

A whisky bottle materialised on the table behind him. Alice had guessed that Rooker and Phil were drinking in their bunk room, and it was obvious that they were several drinks ahead tonight. Now Richard would have to choose whether to make a heavy-handed objection or to let tonight be an exception to his no alcohol rule.

Richard hesitated, then his mouth lifted at one corner and he gave a self-mocking, acquiescent shrug. He leaned across and picked up an empty glass, nodding to the whisky bottle. 'May I?' he asked pleasantly.

'Sure thing.' Jochen poured him a measure.

When everyone had a glass, Richard lifted his drink. 'Here's to the complete team, and to Kandahar, and to cooperation.'

'And to less bullshit,' Rook drawled.

Laure bit her lip.

The wind had dropped completely. After the days and nights of clamour, the silence was thick enough to touch.

Richard flushed, but otherwise it was as if he hadn't heard.

Alice had begun to distinguish undercurrents of tension between several of the expedition members. Valentin often made a mocking little pout at the sight of Arturo's earring or coordinated clothes, and Arturo retaliated by delicately pressing one finger to his ear when Valentin spoke, as if his voice was just too loud. Laure lifted a scornful eyebrow whenever Jochen leaned too close to her or dropped his big hand on her knee, although Jochen never seemed to notice this. But the discord between Richard and Rooker was like a big boulder just under the surface of a fast-flowing stream. For now, the water cloaked it with a glassy skin, but the smallest alteration would expose the jagged edge.

Valentin spoke first: 'The team.' He stood up and drained his glass, everyone else raised theirs and drank, and the moment passed.

Somehow, against the odds, the evening was turning into a party. Everyone was dancing—even Rook. Pent-up energy from the days of confinement burned off in swaying and singing and waving of whisky glasses. When she looked at the clock again, Alice was amazed to see that it was almost midnight.

She had been aware of the door opening and closing, and now Valentin took her by the elbow. 'You will come to look?'

She pulled on the parka he handed her as they stepped outside the hut.

The air was magically still, though the lead-coloured overhead clouds were ragged from the storm. Over the bay, the cloud had thinned away to long streamers of apricot and pale violet, tinged on the underside with jade. The snowfields and glaciers were washed with delicate shades of lavender and faded rose-pink, and the sea rippled with a long streak of molten gold. Alice drew in a breath. The sun just rested on the horizon. It was a perfect orb of brilliant flame-orange. She glanced down at her watch. It was midnight exactly. From now, the beginning of November, until February, there would be no darkness.

'Not bad?' Valentin chuckled.

'Not . . . bad,' Alice murmured. She wanted to have this moment to herself. The unearthly beauty of it struck a shaft straight into her heart.

He nodded and heaved a sigh. After a moment he patted her on the shoulder and stumped away.

Alice clambered down the rocks to the beach. The chunks of ice lapped by waves looked as if they were made of pure silver. She was so entranced that she walked all along the shoreline until she reached the tongue of rocks that marked the boundary of Kandahar Bay. She climbed up to the flat top of the rocky outcrop with its icing of snow and looked down. On the other side lay a perfect crescent of shingle beach, with a dozen penguins standing like sentries on the shelves of rock.

She climbed down, and exchanged a solemn stare with the nearest penguin as she passed by. Over the next rocky outcrop she found yet another

crescent, smaller and more intimately enfolded by rock. She stood looking out to sea. The sun lifted clear of the horizon, a disc of blazing gold.

Alice turned slowly round. At the centre point of the beach's arc she
saw a flight of pale stone steps. They led straight from the shingle up to
the overhang of snow at the clifftop, as precise as if a stonemason had
just chipped them free.

It was a common geological formation, known as a dyke. A column
of hot magma had intruded into a crack in the existing layers of sand-
and mudstone, and differential weathering had sliced it into horizontal
and vertical planes, just like the treads of a staircase. Alice knew all this
as well as she knew her own name, but she didn't think of it. She saw
the pristine steps leading from water to white skyline, and she knew for
certain that this was a remarkable place.

This place was a temple, she thought, with the waves for music and
nature's flawless architecture to contain its spirit. A breath of premonition stirred, coming from nowhere like a cold wind fanning her cheek.

It wasn't that the temple disturbed her, just that its crystalline calm
had opened up a new channel. Somewhere within her there was a
buried fear, but she couldn't grasp what it was. It lay deep, but as she
groped around its outlines she felt sure that when the time came, when
she needed to, she would be able to face it and then reach beyond it.

It was very cold. Alice flapped her arms and stamped her feet to
restore the circulation. She was surprised by the direction her thoughts
had just led her. She didn't believe in signs or warnings. She shivered.
'I'm a scientist,' she said aloud, then turned deliberately away from the
temple steps and scrambled up and over the first rock tongue. She
passed the penguins and scaled the second outcrop. Then she stopped
short. There was a man sitting below her, looking out to sea, directly in
her path to the beach. Even though his back was to her, every line of his
body indicated disconnection, distance, abstraction.

Alice hesitated, but there was no other way to descend. She began to
climb down, moving noisily to announce herself. At last, when she was
almost on top of him, the man looked round. It was Rooker.

'Be careful,' he said in a low voice.

He moved aside a little and she was about to step past when he indicated a rock seat beside him. In silent surprise she sat down.

'Are you warm enough?' he asked.

Alice thought these were the first remarks he had addressed to her,
except for ordering her to put on the life jacket in the Zodiac. Without
waiting for an answer he took the whisky bottle out of the pocket of his
parka, wiped the flat of his hand over the neck and passed it to her.

Alice took a long gulp. 'I didn't mean to disturb you,' she said.

He said nothing, and the silence erased even the echo of her words. There was a force field around Rooker. It made her skin burn under the heavy fabric of her parka.

When he did finally speak, it made her jump. 'You are quiet. I mean, you don't talk all the time. You didn't disturb me.'

'Do you know the steps? Back there?'

He glanced at her. 'Yes. It's a good place.'

She wondered again what it was that turned his face opaque and gave his eyes the look of always staring inwards.

He lifted the bottle to his mouth again. If he was drunk he was intentionally, almost doggedly so. 'Look.'

Alice followed his pointing finger. A supple dark shape at the water's edge. A leopard seal. The cruel wide mouth showed as it propelled itself up the beach. It flopped down to rest, its head pointing out to sea.

'Leopard,' Rook said.

'My mother studied them. She made films for television.' She added quickly, to get it out of the way, 'Her name's Margaret Mather.'

'There's a plaque with that name, waiting to be put up on the lab block, but I wasn't watching much television around the time when your mother was probably making her films.'

He had never heard of her. Alice was pleased to realise it.

'Where did you grow up?' she asked. His accent was an odd mixture that she couldn't quite place.

'All over,' Rooker said shortly. He was getting tired of her questions.

Alice stood up. 'I'm heading back to base. I'll leave you in peace.'

The idea must have amused him, because he laughed. But he stood up too. He was much taller than her. As she turned to go he put a finger on her shoulder and then touched the Velcro label on the breast of her parka. He lifted one black eyebrow. 'Is that an order? Or an invitation?'

She was suddenly aware of a raw sexual challenge that was so direct, and so at odds with his usual inscrutability, that it took her breath away. She stared at him as shock subsided and anger fluttered in her throat, making it harder to speak. 'Neither. It's my name.' She turned her back and walked on up to the base.

The hut was quiet. Philip was sitting in a corner, softly plucking at his guitar. Richard was working on his notes at the end of the table.

The warmth made Alice's cheeks burn. 'It's beautiful outside,' she said.

'Wait until you see the rocks, out at Wheeler's Bluff,' Richard said.

If everything went according to plan they would be out in the field in eight days' time.

In the women's room, surprisingly, Laure was still awake.

'Did you go for a walk?' she asked.

'Yes. Not very far. I haven't got my bearings yet.'

'No,' Laure agreed thoughtfully. And after a pause, 'You like him, don't you? Richard. I mean, you *like* him.'

Alice was startled. 'Laure, I haven't thought about him in that way. It wouldn't be advisable or professional, would it?'

The other woman climbed under the tidy covers of her bunk. 'You English. Why are you so afraid of what you might feel?'

By the time Alice had worked out a deflecting answer, she saw that Laure had retreated into the appearance of sleep. Alice lay down too, and as she waited for sleep, she thanked heaven for the absence of the wind.

A week went by and the weather improved enough for Alice to embark on several days of safety training with Phil Idwal Jones.

The slope was steep and slick with ice. Alice slid downhill, head first, on her back. Her grip tightened on the ice axe held across her chest, then she gathered all her strength and rolled over on top of it. The pick bit into the ice and she clung on, feet slithering down the hill as her headlong descent abruptly stopped.

'Not bad, girl,' Philip shouted.

Alice spread her arms and legs like a starfish and laughed delightedly at the sky. The sun was so bright that it was hard to believe that the temperature was fifteen degrees below zero. She scrambled to her feet and plodded up the slope again.

'If you do trip and fall, at least you stand a chance now of stopping yourself before you get to the cliff edge,' Phil judged.

'Thanks. What's next?'

'I'm glad you asked me that. We're going down a crevasse.'

They spent an hour gripped in the blue jaws of a shallow specimen while Phil showed her how to use a loop of cord to drag herself painstakingly up a rope, in the event that she might find herself dangling at the end of one. It was hard work.

At last she half rolled and half scrambled over the icy lip and lay prone in the snow. 'Will that do?' she begged.

'All right, then,' the Welshman said. 'You can have your dinner now.'

They sat in the lee of the skidoo, passing a flask of coffee between them and rooting through the boxes Russell had handed them. These exhausting, invigorating days of practising survival techniques had been some of the most enjoyable Alice had ever spent. But there was much more to it than that. They didn't often stop to admire the scenery but, however absorbed she was, she saw how the light and the texture of the whiteness changed with every hour of the endless day. There was nothing static or frozen about this place. She tried to look harder, to bring her senses to bear more intently, so that she would miss nothing.

'What are we doing next?' Alice asked.

Phil nodded at the skidoo. 'You've got to learn to handle this.'

'*Yess.*' Alice pounded her mittened fists in delight.

'Don't think you're going to get to drive everywhere, though, or you'll put Rook and me out of a job.'

Rooker. If he remembered asking her whether 'Peel' was an invitation or a command, he hadn't shown it. Sometimes she found herself watching him, but he gave no sign of noticing her scrutiny.

Alice perched astride the big machine while Phil patiently showed her the controls. It took a few circuits before she got the hang of it. But then she found it was as easy as riding a bicycle and five times as fun.

Phil said laconically, 'You're just about OK at the fun part. Let's go back and you can change the plugs and clean the fuel filter.'

'Can I drive us back now?'

'And put me out of a job?'

But he did let her. As they swept down the hill towards the base, Alice saw the little cluster of utilitarian buildings, the brave red standing out against the ice. It looked like home, she thought.

CHAPTER FOUR

THE RED AND WHITE Squirrel hovered briefly, then settled like a roosting bird within the flagged landing square that Rooker and Phil had prepared in the snow. A moment later, the pilot and his number two had climbed down and unloaded a couple of bags.

Alice had been ready to leave since breakfast time. But there had been a series of delays while Santa Ana considered whether the weather was good enough. The flight to take her and Richard out to Wheeler's Bluff had been off and on again twice already, and it was now early afternoon.

The pilot handed over the cargo bags: fresh vegetables from the supply ship that had reached Santa Ana from Punta Arenas, and mail.

The crew came in and lounged at the table, drinking coffee and gossiping with Russ and Niki. One was called Andy, the other Mick.

There was a package from Peter. Alice found a corner and opened it. The letter was short. He told her that he missed her and that he was sorry. Enclosed with the note were two charcoal sketches of herself. She remembered the night he had done them. A Polaroid photograph fell from between the drawings. It was a picture of Pete, standing beside the construction that had been preoccupying him before she left. He was smiling in triumph. The metal ribs and spars with their festoons of found objects reared above him. She noticed that he had incorporated the dismembered typist's chair. 'PS. *Finished it!*' he wrote.

She stared at his familiar features and tried to remember exactly how she had felt about him. And she wondered who had taken the picture.

A hand touched her shoulder. 'Are you ready?'

Richard glanced from the photograph to Alice's face. She saw that the crewmen had stood up and everyone was streaming outside. She hoisted her kitbag and followed them.

Rooker had stripped down the second of the base's two skidoos, and he and Phil slung it beneath the helicopter's fuselage. Richard and Alice handed over their personal kit for stowage. Russell patted her shoulder and told her that when she came back she would be an old hand.

'I don't know about that. But I'll be glad not to be such a no-no.'

No-no was Phil's catch-all word for her, meaning know-nothing. It was politer than fingy, which translated as fucking new guy.

The pilot waved her and Richard into the helicopter. To her surprise Rooker swung in after them.

'You're coming with us?'

'You're going to refit the skidoo yourself?'

The doors were shut, the rotors started spinning, then the helicopter rose and swung in an arc. Alice watched the base sink beneath her and felt her stomach turn over, partly with vertigo and partly with excitement. She was looking forward to the demands of an isolated field camp with a mixture of fascination and apprehension.

The flight took forty minutes. Through the curve of windshield, a white and blue and grey-stippled immensity of space unrolled, crumpled by the chaos of vast glaciers edging to the sea. Alice's eyes were stinging from gazing so hard. A draught of pure adrenaline surged through her. She swallowed and became aware of Rooker looking round at her.

He smiled, an unpractised version, but the warmth did light up his black eyes. 'Yeah,' he said. She felt the click of a connection between them. Her cheeks were suddenly hot.

After a while Andy said, 'See ahead there? One o'clock?'

In the distance there was a long black-and-white ridge of rock, rising out of the tumbled ice and snow like the fin of a great sea creature from the ocean. This was their destination, Wheeler's Bluff.

The helicopter put down on a flat expanse of bare blue ice about half a mile from the cliff. The wind had scoured the snow off the surface here, so the pilot could see exactly what he was settling on. When the engines stopped, the machine almost bucked in the wind.

The men set about the unloading. Alice pulled her weatherproofs round her and ran to help. The pilots wanted to get back in the air and on their way to Kandahar before the weather deteriorated any further.

It took Rooker half an hour to reassemble the skidoo. Covertly, Alice watched him working. He gave the job all his attention, and his movements were quick and precise. At last he jumped astride the machine and turned the ignition key. The engine caught at once, and he drove the skidoo in a tight circle, revving it hard. He dismounted, lifted the casing off the engine and checked it over again. Then he gave the thumbs-up.

Richard and Alice stood back. Rooker glanced at Alice and she thought she read speculation in the look.

'Anything else?' he asked Richard.

Richard ran his eyes over the loaded sledge that would be towed behind the skidoo. 'That's it,' he said.

Rooker sprinted to the helicopter. A minute later the Squirrel lifted off the ice. Alice looked around her. For hundreds of miles there was nothing but ice, wind, rock and Richard Shoesmith.

It was 9 p.m. by the time they had set up camp. They had driven closer to the Bluff, where the rocks afforded some shelter from the wind. The skidoo and unloaded sledge were parked right in the lee of the rocks and protected by a nylon cover. The two yellow pyramid tents were up, openings facing away from the wind, the food boxes and cooking gear stowed inside one and the geological and climbing equipment inside the other. Richard was putting up masts for the VHF radio antennae.

'Time for some food?' Alice asked.

'I'd say so.'

In her tent—the one in which the kitchen had been established—Alice lit the Primus. Richard and she would take turns at being cook for the day. Tonight there would be fried chicken and vegetable rice.

At 10 p.m. Richard finished the prearranged radio schedule with Niki and presented himself at Alice's tent door.

'Dinner is served.' She grinned up at him.

They talked about the rock sections they would make and measure tomorrow. Richard reclined against her mattress. Alice was sharply aware of the tiny compass of their camp and the hostile miles that cut them off from Kandahar. The training she had done at Cambridge and with Phil seemed inadequate to equip her for survival in this harsh, isolated place.

'Can I ask you something?' she said, wanting to admit to some of her anxiety without sounding too vulnerable. 'Why haven't we got a field assistant out here with us? Phil, or Rooker? Isn't that more usual?'

'It's a fair question,' Richard said after a moment. 'It's easier to provision a two-man camp. It also means we're not taking out a man who would probably be more useful back on the base. But you're right.' He sighed. 'Those aren't the real reasons. The truth is that I prefer it like this. Without extraneous people. You and I know what needs to be done and we can do it. It's simpler. It's peaceful. Isn't it?'

And it was. Alice saw, suddenly, how much Richard longed for peace. The expectations of Lewis Sullavan were weighing more heavily on him than she had guessed. Richard wasn't good at defusing the prickles of tension back at Kandahar. He couldn't deal with Rooker's scorn, and all his speeches about teamwork left his little group bemused rather than united. What Richard really wanted was to immerse himself in science, to be left alone with his fossils, and yet some contrary impulse had driven him to take over the leadership role. A sense of obligation to family expectations and history, she thought. *Just like me.*

'I understand,' Alice said quietly. She was suddenly reminded of a photograph she had seen in books of polar history of the interior of Scott's hut at Cape Evans. Halfway down the row of bearded faces was Gregory Shoesmith's. Richard bore a marked physical resemblance, tonight, to his famous grandfather. And Alice could sense how deeply, for the whole of his life, Richard had wanted to be like him as well as look like him.

Richard sat up. 'Don't worry, we'll be quite safe, the two of us.'

Alice tried not to acknowledge that she was not reassured, and dismissed the thought that if Phil or even Rooker had said the same thing it would have been quite different. As she looked at Richard's attractive but closed-in English face, she realised that she wanted to put her hand to his cheek. She didn't even know if he was married, she remembered.

She made tea, then Richard thanked her gravely for a delicious dinner, just as if they were in Gloucestershire, and said good night.

She curled up in her sleeping-bag, drinking tea and thinking. They had a week's work to do out here, the two of them. That was the thing to focus on, not a momentary desire to touch someone because of the furrow between his eyebrows and the anxiety in his heart.

The days in field camp were very busy but they were also peaceful, as Richard had predicted. The weather was good. The wind dropped and the sun shone, and it was surprisingly pleasant to be outside, moving about in the shelter of the rock ridge. The hours flew as Alice measured and drew in her notebook. Wheeler's Bluff was interesting to them both because the rocks encompassed the transition between the Cretaceous and Tertiary periods, and the sedimentary layers were particularly rich in molluscan fossils. Richard had studied the extinction of mollusc species in other parts of the world, and he intended to establish the dates of extinction here and relate them to his earlier studies.

He worked with quiet absorption, moving up and down the rock band, tapping with his geological hammer to extract another promising specimen. When he removed one he took a GPS reading to establish its exact location and sealed it in a marked sample bag.

His industry spurred Alice on. She clambered over the outcrops, chipping at the chunks of rock with her hammer. She made painstaking measurements of the thick sections and wedged herself into cracks and perched on ledges to draw detailed stratigraphical sections. She collected thin sections from the crucial boundary margin, and labelled her samples. Back on the base she would analyse the rock fragments for mineral composition, then make a more precise analysis with all the facilities of her lab in Oxford.

One afternoon they scaled the rock face to reach the top of the Bluff. They put on climbing harnesses and roped up, and Richard led up a hundred feet of puckered and weathered rock. Alice followed, carefully placing her hands and feet, half intrigued by the rock's composition and half terrified by the height and her exposure. As she scrambled over the top, Richard gave her his hand and pulled her up.

'Well done.' He smiled, with his face close to hers. 'And just look.'

She turned and gasped. The pleated whiteness stretched away into infinity, textured with every shadow of blue and grey. It was the most beautiful sight she had ever seen and the most desolate. It was as if she and Richard Shoesmith were the only people in the universe.

They had fallen into the habit, after they had eaten, of talking for an hour before bed. That night, Alice talked about her father. He was often in her mind out here.

'We used to go to Zermatt every summer, just the two of us,' she told Richard. 'Trevor would collect rocks and show me granite and dolerite and quartz and feldspar. He taught me to rock-climb too.' She laughed. 'Although you wouldn't think it. What was your father like?'

'He was a serving army officer.'

SUN AT MIDNIGHT

'Did you see much of him?'

'No. I went to boarding school; holidays were mostly with my mother's parents because my father and mother were always overseas.'

'That must have been hard.'

'What? No, not really. Most of us children at school were in the same boat. At least I had the name. People—boys—were impressed, as if it made me someone. I knew it didn't, though.'

Alice studied his wind-reddened face. 'Did you know your grandfather?'

'I don't have many memories of him. I was only eight when he died. There was his house near Cambridge; my father and mother took me there just a few times. I remember photographs everywhere: Grandfather receiving his polar medal from the King, Grandfather with Scott's widow. There was one of a killer whale that terrified me. The creature's blunt head was rearing up out of a narrow crack between the ice floes and its mouth was wide open, a huge trap lined with terrible teeth. It used to give me nightmares. I'd wake up screaming and I couldn't tell my mother why.' Richard collected himself. 'It's strange, the things that frighten children.'

'I don't think that's strange. It gives me a shiver just to hear you describe it.'

'Yet your mother went diving among them.'

'The thought of Antarctica scared me too. I liked the stories; I just never wanted to come here myself.'

'And yet?'

Alice didn't feel caught out, as she might have done before they had come to Wheeler's Bluff. Richard and she were confiding in each other now. 'My mother wanted me to come because she couldn't travel herself. I agreed because of her, but I feel differently now.'

Richard was smiling. 'Better, or worse?'

'I imagined what it would be like, but this is beyond imagination. I wouldn't have missed it, this, here and now, for anything else in the world.' She felt it passionately but the words' comparative poverty made her blush. She could feel the colour creeping up her face.

'I'm happy to hear that,' Richard said.

He had leaned closer to her in the cramped space and his voice and the look in his eyes told her: He's going to kiss me.

Do I want him to? Alice asked herself. The answer was yes. The wind and the silence that always lay beneath it drummed in her ears.

But he didn't kiss her. You are a scientist out in the field with a colleague, she reminded herself.

'Um, do you have children yourself?'

'No. I was married but I've been divorced for two years.'

59

'I'm sorry.' She could almost feel the layers of diffidence and loneliness in him, like her own sedimentary rocks, except that Richard's layers were the accretions of British upper-middle-class reserve, and stiff-upper-lipness and fear of showing your feelings.

'I know from your CV that you're single and childless.'

His words set up a shiver at the base of Alice's spine. She didn't know why and the lack of a reason was like the whirling blank spot at the centre of her field of vision that heralded a migraine. 'Yes.'

'Who was that in the photograph?'

For Richard, this was a seriously personal question. She had to think for a second. Of course, he had caught a glimpse of the Polaroid.

'That's Pete. My ex-boyfriend. He's an artist.'

'Is he a good one?'

Alice hesitated. 'Not all that good. Does that sound disloyal?'

'I don't think you would ever be disloyal, Alice.' He touched her wrist then, with just the tip of his forefinger. In their profound isolation, it managed to be the most intimate gesture she had ever known.

'Do you miss him?' Richard asked.

'No,' Alice said. They didn't look at each other.

There didn't seem to be anything to add, for tonight. They agreed, before Richard returned to his tent, on a 6 a.m. start.

Alice crawled into her sleeping-bag. Left alone, she did miss Pete. Or not Pete himself but the warmth and reassurance of another familiar body. She turned onto her side and tried to imagine the pressure of his chest against her spine. Within seconds, the body she was imagining was not Pete's but Richard Shoesmith's.

At once she turned over and lay flat on her back. Sleep had begun to flutter like moths' wings at the margins of her consciousness, but now in the tent's twilight it flew away out of her reach. Her thoughts quickened.

What had he said? There was the nauseating blank spot again.

I know from your CV. Was that it? Yes. *You are single and childless.*

The spot contracted to a single blinding point of light.

Very slowly she flexed her fingers. She lifted her hands from her sides and laid them over her stomach. How long? Oh God, how long, and why had she only just thought about it?

She forced herself to reckon up. Not regular, no. She never had been. The pill hadn't suited her and she'd had a coil fitted after she met Pete. Dr Davey had done it for her.

Think. So much else to fill her mind in the last weeks.

It was now—what?—the end of the third week in November. Her last period had been at the beginning of October, when Margaret was ill and there had been the flurry of decisions to make about Kandahar.

That was it. She had bled more heavily than usual and felt tired and cramped, but she had taken some painkillers and paid no more attention. Since then, nothing. Alice's scalp tightened. Nothing, that is, except the night of the farewell party at Jo's house. Going home with Pete.

Her coil had failed. Her period was now more than three weeks late. Therefore, counting from the date of her last period (it was like insisting on a correct punctuation mark, this accuracy, in a torrent of feverish babble), she could be about seven weeks pregnant.

Wait, she thought. Don't jump to conclusions. There could be all sorts of reasons for a missed period: cold, exertion, anxiety. But as she ran her hands over her body she knew, with a woman's certainty that she would have denied only an hour ago, that she *was* pregnant. Her breasts were fuller, and her thighs and hips had acquired a new solidity. Her fingers met over her abdomen. There was a dome where once there had been a hollow. Already? Was that possible? A flood tide of dismay swept through her as she realised that she had no idea.

The hours passed. She lifted her wrist once in a while to see the luminous dial of her watch. Sleep was unthinkable.

At six o'clock, wearily shaking herself, Alice crawled outside to fill a pan with snow for tea. The world that met her eyes was drained of all colour and definition. The Bluff and the ice sheet were invisible behind veils of spiralling snow. A reddish shape lumbered a few feet away from her. It was Richard in his windproofs, already dismantling the radio antennae in preparation for moving camp ten kilometres further east.

While they were eating breakfast, Richard outlined the day's objectives. Alice spooned up the food, thinking of it as fuel. Do what was expected of her, that was all she could hope for today. When the shock had subsided, she would decide what to do.

They loaded the sledge with mounds of gear and the heavy boxes of rock samples. Richard sealed up the bag of their frozen waste and hoisted the lidded barrel that contained it onto the back of the sledge. Everything, even this, was classified as 'retro'—to be flown back to Kandahar and, in the end, shipped out of Antarctica.

Richard took a compass bearing. The Bluff was intermittently visible through the white veil, but not reliably enough to navigate by. They started to move forwards. Alice drove the skidoo; Richard plodded a little ahead through the fresh snow with a long glacier probe in his hand. He stared into the blankness, trying to see a dip or hollow that might betray a big crevasse. After an hour they changed places and after another hour they changed back again.

It was the longest journey Alice had ever known. After four hours they stopped briefly to eat chocolate and drink from the Thermos.

'How much further?' Alice asked, trying to sound as if she were enquiring out of mere curiosity.

'I reckon we're halfway. Are you OK?'

'I'm fine.'

Cold and exhaustion gnawed at her and her leg muscles screamed, but at last, when she had begun to think that the walk would never end, Richard stopped. He extracted his GPS handset from his parka and took a reading. Then, to Alice's joy, he jerked her the thumbs-up signal.

It was windier here than at their first camp. They tried to work quickly, unloading boxes and preparing to set up the tents. By this time Alice was blundering with tiredness. She spread her tent out on the snow, turning aside for a second to pick up the poles. A strong gust of wind licked over the invisible Bluff and snatched at one corner, then sucked it into the air with a flap like a giant bird's wing. She had forgotten Phil's First Rule. Never leave your tent unpegged, even for a second.

She turned to Richard. 'I'm very sorry,' she said tonelessly.

'We'll share.' He pegged his all the way round before sliding in the poles.

At last they were crouching within the shelter of the remaining tent. Alice stirred a pan of chilli and beans while Richard made the scheduled radio contact with Niki, who gave them the weather forecast.

'Put on your warm clothes out there.'

'OK, Kandahar. Thanks for that.'

Alice squatted on her mattress. With both their sleep kits laid out there was no room to move around.

'Good job we travelled today. We may have to sit out a couple of stormy days,' Richard said cheerfully.

The stove and the light of the Tilley lamp and the food they were sharing made the tent an intimate place. But after they had eaten and wiped the plates and drunk some tea, there was no attempt to have their usual hour's talk. There would be no saying good night to close the conversation safely, because they would be lying here side by side.

Alice took off a couple of layers of clothes and squirmed into her sleeping-bag. Richard moved around for a few minutes, then he lay down next to her and turned out the lamp.

In their little bubble of shelter against the snow, Alice wondered how it would be if she raised her voice and said, *I think I am pregnant.* But even the thought made her hot with dismay. It would be to admit that without any warning her life had slipped out of her control—here, of all places, where control was the only way to survive against the elements.

When the pressure of anxiety forced her eyes open, she saw that Richard was watching her. He lifted one hand and touched her hair. Then his fingers moved across her cheek and rested on her mouth.

Last night—only *last night*?—she would have welcomed the caress. But now, with her body still defensive with shock, she flinched.

He withdrew his hand as if she had bitten it and turned onto his back. 'I'm sorry. That was completely inappropriate.' He sounded as stiff as a Victorian uncle. As if Gregory Shoesmith had ventured too far with a fellow officer's sister at a tennis party.

'No, it's me. I mean . . .' Her voice trailed away, was swallowed by the wind. She couldn't tell him, it's not that I don't want you to, didn't want you to, only this is happening and I don't know anything any more . . .

'I understand. One has to be very careful. Out here. It's very easy to cross boundaries that then can't be put up again. If necessary.'

She did understand what he was saying, in his choked-off way. In this place, raw feelings swelled much closer to the surface. 'I know. Richard, I . . .' She was going to tell him that she liked him. Admired him. Fancied him, then. But it sounded too banal.

'Yes. Yes,' he said quickly, so as not to have to hear anything else.

He turned a little on one side and hunched his shoulder. Alice lay still. Almost at once she fell into an exhausted sleep.

In the morning, when she crawled out of the tent and lifted her face, she saw that the heavens were thick with sparkling motes. Tiny pinpoints of ice cascaded out of a clear sky and caught the sun as they spiralled downwards. It was celestial confetti; the beauty of it took her breath away.

Diamond dust, that's what Margaret had called it. 'I'll think of you, with diamond dust falling,' she had said when they parted.

The sound of Richard's voice made her jump. 'We'll get a day's work in. Bad weather's coming,' he called.

They ate porridge, pulled on their windproofs and began on the new section of the Bluff. Alice remembered it, oddly, as a perfect day. Her work soothed her and silenced her racing thoughts.

In the middle of the afternoon, Richard called her over. From a section of black mudstone, residue of the ocean that had once covered this spot, he had hammered out a fossilised mollusc, complete in every detail.

'I don't know what this is. Look at the whorls, there. It's a species I don't recognise.' His voice was hoarse with excitement. He looked like a small boy on his birthday.

His elation caught fire in her too. 'It's a good day.'

That night the wind started again. It was a different wind, which came at them with a roar, then rose to a howl of fury.

As far as Rooker was concerned, sometimes the place was claustrophobic while at others it could be almost companionable, but being there mostly just meant that you did your work, and you let the days slide by. Without Richard Shoesmith's constant interfering presence, life was even more straightforward. Doing things his own way, Rooker began to build the A-frame skidoo shelter on a rock foundation behind the base.

He went at it steadily, mostly alone. That was nothing new, but the empty brilliance of the air and the monochrome landscape provided fewer immediate distractions than he was used to. Or maybe the certainty that he would have to stay here meant that his mind wasn't always working around the question of the next destination, like a tongue around a jagged tooth. Whatever the reason, thoughts and memories that he was adept at suppressing seemed to rise closer to the surface.

It wasn't just that he thought about Henry Jerrold because Richard Shoesmith brought him to mind. He even began to hear her voice in his head, as clearly as if she had crept up behind him.

Darling? Jimmy, darling, is that you?

Once he even whirled round, but all he found was Laure who had brought him an unnecessary mug of coffee.

Her smile glinted at him. 'Won't you have it before it goes cold?'

'No. Thanks,' he said. He turned back and swung the mallet.

One evening he was standing at the locker beside his bunk, folding clothes. His back was to the room and his head was full of voices that he was trying not to hear. Then someone put a hand on his shoulder.

He didn't think about it. He just spun on his heel and pinned the guy back against the wall, fingers and thumbs splayed against his throat.

Phil's alarmed eyes goggled at him.

Rooker let his hands drop. 'Christ. I'm sorry.'

Phil coughed and massaged his neck. 'Remind me not to upset you. Did you think I was Shoesmith? How seriously is this place getting to you, boy?' With his concern his Welsh accent grew stronger.

'I didn't. It isn't. I was thinking about something else. It was just an automatic reaction, all right?' Rooker snapped.

'Why are you so fucking angry? All the time?' Phil said.

'I said I was sorry.'

'Yeah, you did. It doesn't matter. But if you want to explain why a tap on the shoulder makes you go for a man's throat, be my guest.'

Rooker stood still. A feeling of pressure that he recognised as sadness squeezed at his heart.

Phil looked at Rooker as if he was trying to work something out. 'I'm going to bed,' he said quietly.

Rooker put on his parka and went outside. The wind that met him was restless, raising eddies of snow. He walked along the shoreline, wishing he had a whisky flask with him. He passed the place where he had sat with Alice Peel, and climbed over the outcrop that separated it from the little bay with the natural rock steps. As always, being in this tiny amphitheatre of rock and ice quietened his mind. He sat down halfway up the flight of steps and watched the brash ice undulating with the waves.

Memory was a curse. Whenever you stopped moving, it came up on you like a fog. That was why he preferred cold places, where the wind assailed you if you hesitated for too long. Places like this, where to keep moving was to keep warm. To stay alive.

Jimmy, darling, is that you?

He had closed the door carefully, because slamming it always made her headache worse. He found her lying on the day bed in front of the television. 'How was school today?'

'OK.'

'Give me a kiss, then.'

When he leaned over, she smelled of bourbon and talcum powder and indoor sweat. She was watching a movie.

'Do you want some tea?' she asked, but her eyes never left the screen.

He went through into the kitchenette and looked in the fridge. There was a carton of milk and some leftovers that had been sitting there for a couple of days. He ate a bowl of cornflakes instead.

When he had finished, he made a cup of Nescafé with sugar, just how she liked it, and carried it through to her.

'You're a good boy.'

'Why don't we go out for a bit? It's a nice day. We could go for a walk.'

'I can't, not now. Lester's coming round.'

Jimmy didn't say anything, but he thought it. Bloody, bloody Lester. He was always around, these days. He would flutter round her, telling her that she was beautiful but she should make more of herself. He would lift her hair in his ringed fingers and fluff it out, and their two faces would make identical pouting expressions in the mirror.

'I'll go and see if Gabby's home then,' he said.

'All right, darling. Don't be late, will you?' Her voice was vague.

With Gabby Macfarlane he went down to the ponds. Gabby was a thin, watchful boy who had moved down with his family from the North Island. Neither of them had a fishing rod, so they threw stones instead. Further along the bank they found a pile of concrete fence posts waiting to be dug in. It took the two of them to lift one post and totter to the water's edge with it, but when they swung it between them, then let

65

go, it made a huge and satisfying splash. Soon, every post had sent up its oblong coronet of silver-khaki water. After that they wandered home again. Lester was sitting beside her on the sofa, drinking and giggling.

'You are nothing but a troublemaker, Rooker,' Brice, the headmaster, had told him. The farmer had been to the school, and Jimmy and Gabby had been hauled out of class.

Rooker had nodded. It seemed easier, less of a battle all round, just to agree with him. 'Yeah,' he'd said.

It was too cold to sit any longer on the rock step. That was good. He jumped up and began walking, fast, because his nose and hands had gone numb. Keep moving, that was the idea.

In the morning, Phil came out to breakfast wearing a helmet and boxing gloves. He dodged and feinted around Rooker, who looked startled and then laughed, glad that the little Welshman hadn't taken against him.

Rooker blocked a punch. 'Did you bring those with you, just in case?'

Phil shook his head. 'Sullavan supplied them. Leisure activities. There's ping-pong in one of them crates, as well.'

'Is there now?'

Valentin stood at the window yawning and scratching himself. 'You boys will always be arsing around. Meanwhile we have snowfall.'

Niki monitored the weather reports. Today the helicopter had been scheduled to pick up Richard and Alice. But with heavy snow and winds gusting up to fifty knots, there was no flying.

Out at the Bluff, Richard reported that he and Alice had been left tent-bound by the blizzard. They had four days' supply of food left and were rationing themselves in case they should be marooned for longer. At Kandahar itself the wind was less vicious, but Valentin was right. Snow had closed in again.

Rooker and Phil devised a game. They took the ping-pong bats and ball out to the skidoo shelter and played a version of squash. The ball ricocheted around in the confined space as the bats smashed at it. Shed squash caught on. Everyone joined in, and Valentin drew up a competition ladder. Without Richard, and with no outside work to be done, the industrious culture on the base rapidly broke up.

On the fourth day of bad weather, the email from Sullavanco arrived into this relaxed atmosphere like a reprimand.

It announced that Lewis Sullavan planned to make a personal visit to Kandahar in the week before Christmas. He would be accompanied by his assistant Beverley Winston and a media crew. He planned to stay for two days, and then travel on to New Zealand.

'Jesus H. Christ,' Russell groaned. 'It's less than two weeks.'

Niki passed on the news in that evening's radio schedule with the Bluff. Richard's voice fairly crackled out of the receiver in response. Just as soon as the weather eased enough to allow the helo to take off, he would be back, and preparations would be put in hand. In the meantime he would speak to Russell.

Russell came back from the radio room with a long list of instructions. 'You'd think it was Queen Liz herself coming to stay.' He sighed.

Valentin and Arturo were the finalists in the shed squash tournament. Everyone crowded round the shed during a lull in the wind, taking it in turns to peer in through the crack in the door. Then a fierce rally ended in a meaty slap and a howl of agony from Arturo. A second later he lurched out of the shed door with his hands cupping his nose and blood dripping down his chin.

Valentin burst out in his wake. 'He got his silly head in the way. Bat smack in face. I didn't mean to hit him.'

Of course not, Phil and Rooker agreed. 'Shed squash. It's a man's game and a man must take risks,' Phil said solemnly.

In the hut, Jochen had Arturo in a chair with his head back. He shone a torch up each pulpy nostril. 'Could be broken,' he said.

Arturo gave a howl. By the evening he had two swollen black eyes and his nose was obliterated by splints, bandage and sticking plaster.

'I dunno, Artie,' Phil said. 'I can see that it's different all right. But I'm not sure it's an improvement.'

Arturo held up his middle finger, then winced.

The night's weather report indicated that conditions at Santa Ana were improving, with only moderate winds and precipitation. The pilots would assess the situation again in the morning. Richard and Alice were ending their fifth day in the tent, the fourth of their unscheduled extra stay. They were running low on food.

Alice opened her eyes. There was something different happening outside. The tent walls bellied and then grew taut, but slowly. There was no roaring and banging.

Richard was kneeling at the radio box. She studied the outline of his profile as intently as if he were her lover. She did love him, in a way, after the six days that they had just endured together. They had sung songs, recited poems, played cards and talked until it seemed that they had no more memories to share. They had made each other laugh and listened to each other's dream-ridden sleep. But they did not become lovers. That avenue had turned into a cul-de-sac.

Alice hadn't explained why. This news was too momentous, too personal. She had done plenty of thinking instead. There had been moments of pure panic, but these had been balanced by incredulity and joy.

She was pregnant. There would be a baby.

She counted up the weeks and calculated that it would be in early July. It seemed a long way off yet, but the day would come. This unplanned baby was hardly more than an idea, but there could be no destroying it. The thought alone made her draw in her shoulders and hunch her spine to make a protective cage round it.

Alice considered the possibility of making her announcement as soon as they got back to Kandahar. There would be surprise and concern— and a hasty helicopter ride, a flight onwards from Santa Ana to South America and the rest of the long journey home.

For what reason?

Her house was let for the academic year, her role in the Department was on hold, no one expected to see her before the early summer.

If I go straight home from here in March, she calculated, instead of travelling for another couple of months, I will still only be twenty-one or twenty-two weeks pregnant. My body can look after itself for another two or three months, why not? I can finish what I promised to do here.

She didn't want to leave the ice. Not until it was properly time to go. She would not easily give up this savage and beautiful place.

Richard was searching for radio contact: 'Kandahar, Kandahar, do you read me? This is Wheeler's Bluff camp. Do you read me? Over.'

Niki's voice faded in and out through the static, then grew clear. 'Weather window now opening. Helo transport left Santa Ana at o-nine thirty hours. ETA at Kandahar two-zero minutes from now, estimated departure time for Bluff eleven thirty hours. Do you copy?'

Alice gave a little whoop of delight.

En route from Kandahar to Wheeler's Bluff, Rooker listened to the pilots' laconic exchanges through his headset. Though the weather at Kandahar had been fairly calm, out here the visibility was deteriorating. Still, Andy and Mick were relaxed. The helicopter turned in a tight circle and a savage gust of wind made it buck and judder. The Bluff appeared below them, its black back jagged in the surrounding void. Then they caught sight of a tiny orange triangle out in the wasteland. The isolation of this place and the precariousness of the shelter struck Rooker forcibly. A few moments later, the skis settled on the square and they were down.

'Nice job,' Rooker murmured.

Cold and wind assaulted them as they stepped out. Richard and Alice were already dismantling the tent. With barely a word exchanged, all five set to work in a methodical rush to get everything packed away before the weather deteriorated further and left them all stranded.

When it was done, Rooker saw Alice look around her. She looked different, even though her face was masked by her hood and snow goggles. She held her back straighter and there was a different angle to her head. Something has happened to her, he thought.

'Good trip?' he asked when they were airborne again.

'Yes, thank you,' Alice answered. He noticed the flash of her smile.

The red walls at Kandahar looked shockingly bright as the helicopter darted home over the glacier.

The hut door opened and tiny people spilled out, ready to greet them. The helicopter circled once, then dipped to the landing square.

They had been away in the field for thirteen days, but to Alice it seemed much longer. As she climbed to the ground a wash of triumph and joy swept over her. We did it, she thought.

She was sure, now, that she had made the right decision.

At the same time she noticed that Rooker was watching her. He inclined his head in a strange, small nod of collusion.

Suddenly there were people all around them.

'Don't come too close. I stink.' Alice laughed.

'There's hot water for a shower. I made sure,' Laure told her.

'Coffee and fresh doughnuts as well. Come on in,' Russell insisted.

'Hot water? Doughnuts? Have I died and gone to heaven?'

It was like coming home to the warmth of friends. Richard and Alice were swept into the hut on a swelling, confusing tide of voices. Alice sat down at the table and sipped her coffee. The warm, fatty, sugary taste of the doughnut was so potent that she had to close her eyes.

When she opened them again she saw someone who looked a bit like Arturo, except that his eyes were in circles of puffed-out purple bruises, and his nose was a shapeless plum-coloured mass twice its original size.

'Whatever happened?' she managed to ask.

At the same time, Richard stood up, leaning on his arms, and swung his head in Rook's direction. Obviously, much too obviously, he was assuming that Rook must be the culprit. But he can't be, Alice thought. He wouldn't do that to someone who is only half his size.

Rook said nothing. He stared flat-eyed back at Richard.

'My fault entirely. But was an accident, you know. A stupid thing.' It was Valentin who broke the smouldering silence.

'Just a game,' Arturo muttered thickly.

Richard's face twisted. 'A *game*? It looks as though it half killed him. Can't I trust you to behave like reasonable people when I am off base?'

It was the wrong thing to say. A little ripple of protest went round.

Then Richard collected himself. 'Are you all right, Arturo? One of you had better tell me exactly what happened.'

Alice slipped away to the bunk room. A minute later Laure came in.

'He'd be a better schoolteacher than expedition leader,' she said.

'I know. But he doesn't mean it. He just wants very much to do it right, so much so that he does it wrong sometimes.'

Laure regarded her, a shrewd and measuring look. 'I think you don't like him so much, after two weeks with him.'

Alice coloured. 'I do like him. I admire him. I just think he is like a lot of Englishmen. Their inhibitions tangle their tongues.'

Laure gave a graceful shrug. 'Then I am glad to be French. But this way of Richard's is not fair to other people. To Rooker, *par exemple*.'

'I think maybe quite a lot of things in life have not been fair to Rooker. I also think that he can look after himself.'

'Yes.' Laure nodded. 'You are right.'

Alice went and took a shower. She shivered with pleasure as the hot water sluiced over her itchy skin. She pressed her hands over her stomach, noticing how it protruded. And there was no doubt about it, her breasts felt tender to the touch and her hips and thighs were thickening, ready to carry a new burden. She had never felt so connected to and yet so in awe of her own body. It was doing what it was meant to do, almost without reference to her. She was strong. Everything would go well.

After lunch, Richard called for attention. Everyone was present.

'As you all know, Lewis Sullavan and a camera crew will be arriving in four days' time. I don't think I need to explain how important this visit is for Kandahar. Mr Sullavan is our principal funding agent, and we have a valuable opportunity to show him the research work we're doing. The scientists should therefore be ready to demonstrate in breadth and in detail exactly what is involved in the work. The support staff should also be ready to discuss their role on the base. Are there any questions?'

Russell leaned slowly forward. 'The party's going to consist of five people, right? Four men and one woman?'

'That's correct. Lewis Sullavan and his assistant, a two-man television crew and a journalist.'

'So where are they all going to sleep?' Russell asked, ever practical.

'The assistant in the women's room, Mr Sullavan in the scientists' room and the other three men in the support staff's room. Four of us, therefore, will have to move out into tents for the duration. Arturo is injured. Niki should remain in the hut in case there is a communications emergency. Likewise Jochen for medical purposes.'

'In case the old boy has a heart attack, finding himself without an en suite bathroom or room service?' Phil murmured.

'Or if he decides to call up the helo and have himself flown straight out again,' Rooker added.

Everyone laughed, even Richard.

'Volunteers?' he asked. 'I'm happy to give my bunk to Mr Sullavan.'

'Looks like us three, doesn't it?' Phil stabbed his finger at Rook and Russell in turn.

'It's a kind of volunteering,' Russell laconically murmured.

Valentin flung up his arms. 'And I, I give up my place for my leader. I prefer. In tents we have fun. Better than best behaviour inside, I think.'

Alice spent the days that followed unpacking and examining the samples she had collected at Wheeler's Bluff. She read her accumulated emails and wrote back about the field trip. Margaret replied, *Yes, I remember. That was just how it was. Thank you for bringing it back.*

The brief message from Jo was the one she hesitated longest over. *They've started to sleep much better. Four and sometimes five whole hours at night. Can't tell you what a difference it makes.* She wanted to bombard Jo with questions. It would have been the greatest luxury to have a friend to confide in. But she knew that if she was going to keep her pregnancy to herself for another three months it would have to be *entirely* to herself.

Richard spent hours combing through the reference books in an attempt to classify his mollusc. It was a gastropod, a type of periwinkle with a shell in the form of a conical spiral, but in significant aspects it was unlike any of the species that had already been described.

'I think we have got an entirely new form,' he said. His face looked as if a bright light had been turned on under the skin.

Preparations for the visit went ahead. Everyone worked hard. There was a lot of joking and mock-complaining, but the prospect of critical strangers arriving in their midst made them work as a team in a way that none of Richard's speeches had done.

On the scheduled day a radio message from Santa Ana announced that the fixed-wing flight from Punta Arenas in Chile had just landed.

'Not even one hour's weather delay?' Russell said in disbelief. 'Sullavan must have a direct line straight to God.'

'Nah. He *is* God,' Phil corrected him.

In the afternoon, under a fierce sun, they stood waiting. As soon as the helicopter landed, the doors flew open. A man clambered down and walked backwards across the snow with a camera on his shoulder. Another man followed with a recorder and microphone, and a third emerged and stood beside him. There was a pause, then a woman appeared. She was tall, and even in her padded parka looked slender and elegant.

Beverley Winston had skin the colour of milk chocolate and the cheekbones of a goddess carved out of stone. Her lips were a set of perfectly symmetrical seductive curves. She was the most beautiful woman any of them had ever set eyes on.

This vision looked coolly around her, then lifted one hand in a signal as she stood aside. The cameraman began filming: Lewis Sullavan appeared at the door of the Squirrel. He stood still to allow his television crew to film his proprietorial gaze out over the ice. Then he smilingly held out his hand to Richard, who hurried forward. They shook hands.

'Welcome to Kandahar,' Richard said.

CHAPTER FIVE

RICHARD AND ALICE stood close together, smiling to order, just next to the peeling red wall of the lab hut. A sweep of snow was satisfactorily visible behind Richard's left shoulder, but even Laure had not been able to persuade the penguins required by the director to wander into shot.

Beverley Winston came out of the main hut. All the men, who were working to set up the shot or otherwise trying to look busy, stopped what they were doing to watch her.

'We'll be ready for him in a minute, Beverley,' the director said.

Phil and Rooker finished screwing the plaque to the wall of the hut, but no one paid any attention. Wherever Beverley was, her beauty absorbed all the available regard. And when Lewis Sullavan was present, she reflected on him, so that he was bathed in the lustre of having such a creature for his handmaiden. Not that Lewis himself was physically unimpressive. For a medium-sized man with ordinary features, he glowed with supernatural amounts of power and energy.

'What about the flag?' Beverley asked the director now.

'Well, we tried it draped over the plaque so that Lewis could unveil it, but it looked too cheesy, if you know what I mean.'

Cheesy certainly wouldn't do for Mr Sullavan. Beverley nodded briskly. 'We thought that tracking away to it flying up there would be better.'

Eight flags, representing each of the nationals at Kandahar, flew from the poles above the window of the radio room, including the Welsh dragon. Above them a much bigger EU flag fluttered in the stiff breeze.

'Good. We'll do that then.' Beverley went to fetch her boss.

Lewis Sullavan wore the same red parka, complete with the EU and Sullavanco logos, as all the Kandahar personnel, except that his was a subtly more attractive shade. 'Let's do it,' he said, beaming.

The new plaque on the lab hut wall read simply: MARGARET MATHER HOUSE. The sound recordist held up the mike as the director spoke his intro and the cameraman panned over the line of flags.

The camera came in on Lewis. He gave a little speech about Antarctica belonging to the community of the world, and said how proud he was that the operations at Kandahar were being headed up by two scientists whose names were already written in the history books. Alice wondered how Laure and the others would react to the suggestion that as a recent no-no she was capable of heading up anything polar.

When her turn came, she delivered her rehearsed sound bite about Margaret's career as one of the first women to work in Antarctica.

Richard spoke about his grandfather's legend and how proud he was, almost ninety years later, to have followed him south.

Lewis came forward again. He tilted his head at a respectful angle. 'In honour of Dr Margaret Mather, biologist and inspiration to two generations of scientists, this laboratory block is named Margaret Mather House.'

The cameraman closed in to film Alice studying the plaque, which shone like a square of molten gold in the low sun.

She was glad she had kept her secret. If she had blurted it out she would have been on her way home by now. She would have missed this, and with the liquid gold blinding her eyes and the heat of family pride in her blood, she knew it was one those memories you should keep.

Alice traced the line of her mother's name with her mittened fingers. If the baby is a girl, she thought, I'll call her Margaret.

When they gathered for the evening meal, they found that Russell had transformed the mess table with a white cloth, wineglasses and candles.

The soft light flattered the dilapidated room and the chapped faces of the expedition members. In their best approximations of clean clothing, most of the men looked like suntanned polar heroes from another age, burly and invincible behind their dark beards.

Lewis automatically took Richard's place at the head of the table, overthrowing the established order and setting up an immediate alert for where Beverley would place herself. Without a second's hesitation she sat down next to Rooker, the only person who had already taken his usual seat. Jochen van Meer used his weight to push himself in on her other side. There was an almost audible sigh of disappointment from the other men. Sex had flown in and unbalanced them all.

Alice found herself between Philip and Valentin, which suited her fine. She glanced around the table and briefly caught Laure's eye. A smile flickered, their only mutual acknowledgement so far of how unkempt Beverley made them feel. Laure's gaze moved on. She was looking at Rooker, who was now talking to Beverley. Alice wasn't surprised, because Laure was always stealing glances at him. Rooker generally ignored her.

In a room full of men who suddenly seemed unaccountably desirable, Alice also noticed how handsome Rooker was. The dark mole on his forehead, just at the hairline, drew her eyes. His beard was trimmed closer than the other men's and it emphasised the shape of his mouth.

Is that an order, or an invitation?

He had been drunk that night. But the memory of his finger pointing to her name label still made Alice shift in her seat.

It was a convivial meal. Lewis Sullavan held court, turning the blaze of his attention on each of them in turn. He asked Alice if she would let him accompany her in the field tomorrow.

'Certainly.' Alice smiled. They would go up to an outcrop behind the base that she had already mapped. That was planned.

'And what brings you to Antarctica, James?' Sullavan asked suddenly.

'Rooker,' Rooker said.

'Rooker,' Sullavan repeated smoothly.

Rook drained an inch of cognac and set his glass down. He said, 'Money. And it's a place to be.'

'I see from your CV that you are a pilot.'

'I was.'

There was a small silence, but he didn't elaborate.

Lewis laughed. 'You're a bit of a maverick, aren't you? A loner, a chancer. I like that.' He chuckled. 'I recognise the breed.' The implication was that Lewis himself was of the same breed. 'Where are you heading next?'

'I have no idea,' Rooker said.

Beverley lowered her curved eyelids a fraction as she absorbed and stored the information.

Lewis hesitated, then his head swivelled. 'Valentin, my friend. I was in Sofia last week. Is it your home town?'

At midnight, Beverley politely excused herself and stood up. She headed for the women's room, drawing ripples of longing in her wake.

At 1 a.m. exactly, Lewis consulted his watch. 'I think we'd better call it a day. It's another busy one tomorrow.'

The party was over, without negotiation.

Alice wasn't ready for sleep. Her skin buzzed and prickled. Remembering that Russell would be spending the night out in a tent, she murmured to him that she would make a start on the washing-up. The mundane activity of scouring saucepans occupied her attention. She wasn't even thinking about the baby, or the future.

A pair of hands descended on her shoulders. Instead of whirling round she hunched herself forward, protecting her belly.

Richard whispered in her ear, 'I'm sorry. I didn't mean to startle you.'

Very slowly Alice turned to face him. Their faces were only an inch apart in the dimly lit room. The dammed-up sexual tension of the evening threatened to discharge itself. Alice almost melted against him. She shivered with longing to be touched. But the glinting light in his eyes made it easy to resist. There was something wrong.

'Thank you,' he said, 'for being an ally.'

She knew what he was talking about: the antagonism between himself and Rooker that divided Kandahar.

Am I an ally? Of course I am. Does that make me Rooker's opponent?

'You are quite right, of course,' Richard went on. He took a strand of her hair and twisted it between his fingers. She wished he wouldn't. These small gestures of intimacy were more erotically charged than most of the sex she could remember.

'About what?' she managed to ask.

'That it's not a good idea to do this. Not while we are living in this place, while we are working together. But I wanted to kiss you just once. I've wanted to kiss you since the day you came in to the Polar Office.'

Her skin crawled now. 'No. I'm sorry . . .'

He seized her round the waist. Fear trickled icily down the back of her neck. He would *feel* her protruding stomach.

She took a step sideways. A shadow fell across his face, and an expression indicating that he had expected to be disappointed, which told her more about his history than all the information he had given her in the tent out at the Bluff. There had been too many of the wrong expectations placed on him. All his life he had been struggling to make himself fit a predetermined shape.

She forced herself to touch his arm and smile remorsefully. 'I'm sorry,' she repeated. 'You know, it's being here . . .'

'You're right. I've already told you that. Don't worry.' Richard was reassuring her that he wouldn't make demands on her or make public what had passed between them tonight. 'But when we get back to England?'

I'll have a *baby*.

'Everything will be different, Richard.'

The next day, Rooker and Phil took Lewis and Alice on the skidoos up to the rock outcrop. Alice unloaded her pack and hoisted it on her back. They were only a mile from the base but she had a rope, emergency food and an insulated bag to crawl into for shelter if the weather came in.

Lewis waved the safety officers away. 'Alice and I will be just fine.' As they left he smiled at her. 'Just show me what you normally do.'

'Don't step anywhere except where I lead, will you? I've mapped all this section of rock and I know where the crevasses are.'

'No ma'am,' he said.

Alice laid out her geological hammer and compass, and opened her notebook. She planned to make a detailed survey of a section that she had only glanced at in the mapping process. 'The work isn't very interesting to watch, I'm afraid,' she apologised.

She talked as she worked, aware of Lewis standing just behind her shoulder. She measured a sequence of layers and drew them in her notebook, then tapped out a series of samples, and bagged and labelled them. She became absorbed in the work. She wasn't sure how many minutes had passed before she looked round for Lewis. Out of the corner of her eye she caught the red flash of his parka, maybe twenty feet away.

Her sharp cry of warning squeezed out of her throat at the same time as his yell of alarm. As her head jerked fully round, he disappeared from view. A split second later she saw his head and upper body. His arms were akimbo, wedged against the snow. The rest of him had disappeared into a narrow, veiled crevasse.

'Keep still. Don't thrash around.' Keeping eye contact with him, Alice took the ice axe and rope from her pack. Oh, God. She had known the crevasse was there. She should have kept him on a rope. How could anyone keep *Lewis Sullavan* tied on the end of a rope?

She uncoiled the rope, knotted a loop in the end, paid out a length and tied another knot. She passed the shaft of her ice axe through the second knot and drove the whole shaft deep into the soft snow until the pick bit into the rope knot and held it firm. She secured herself to the rope and took a self-locking carabiner off her harness loop.

'Lewis,' she said quietly. He was motionless, his face grey with shock. She snapped the carabiner into the loop of rope and moved carefully over the snow to kneel in front of him. 'Lewis, I want you fasten this into the loop of your harness. Can you do that for me?'

Slowly he reached out his mittened hand and took it from her. His arm was trembling, his face screwed up in an agony of concentration. There was a metallic snap. She had him on the rope now.

'Well done.' Alice smiled to reassure him, although she could hardly breathe. She stepped back to where her axe was buried in the snow and put her boot firmly on the head. She gathered the rope in her mittened hands and braced herself. 'Now. I'm going to haul on this end. Can you pull on that end and try to scramble out?'

He bit his lips, then nodded and clamped his mittens on the rope.

Alice pulled, but it was like dragging a dead weight. Lewis rocked his hips and an inch of his chest emerged, then another. The rope bit into Alice's palms. In a rush, Lewis's torso emerged from the mouth of the crevasse. He got one knee up over the lip, scrabbled wildly, and the other followed. He fell forward on all fours, gasping.

Alice gave him a few seconds' respite, then unhitched the rope from her ice axe, helped him to his feet and led him away to the safety of the rock outcrop. She found the Thermos of hot coffee in her pack, poured a cup and gave it to him. Then she took the radio out of her pocket to call up Phil and Rooker. Her hands were shaking.

'Wait,' Lewis ordered.

She sat obediently, watching him sipping his coffee.

'You did well,' he said after a moment.

'Not really. I shouldn't have let you wander off in the first place.'

Amusement struck cold sparks of light in Lewis's eyes. He was recovering himself. 'Do you think you could have stopped me?'

It was an academic question, Alice thought. 'Are you hurt anywhere?'

'No. I'm not hurt.' He went on, 'It was my fault. I'm sorry. Thank you for keeping your head. I won't forget what you did, but I'd much prefer it now if we continue as if nothing has happened.'

Alice could perfectly well understand why. It was a matter of dignity. 'Of course. Would you like me to call up and say we're ready to head back to the base? Or shall we do some more geology?'

Lewis smiled. 'We could just sit here in the sun and talk.'

'Of course,' Alice said again. She poured more coffee into his cup. He seemed to have recovered with remarkable speed, but at some level he must still be shocked. It was hard to judge how old he was. Somewhere in the early sixties, she guessed. An unroped fall into a crevasse would scare anyone, whatever their age. 'Don't get cold,' she advised.

He pulled the flaps of his fleece hat down over his ears and leaned forward, resting his elbows on his knees and nursing the heat of the coffee. 'You are like your mother,' he said.

'Not very, unfortunately.'

'I don't know about that. You look like she did, in the old days. I loved her, you know,' he said.

There was no wind. Alice hadn't misheard. She stared at him.

'You didn't know.' It wasn't a question. A fleeting glance into the face of death had loosened his tongue. 'She was fifteen years older than me, but I had never met anyone like her.'

'Were you lovers?'

There was a pause. 'Yes,' he said.

Alice turned away. 'Perhaps I don't want to hear this.'

'It only lasted one summer. There was no question that she didn't love your father and you. She was loyal, where it mattered. She was making her second TV series. I was just a beginner in the business and Margaret was like an electric wire. She lit everything up and she had the gift of making everyone she came into contact with shine brightly as well.'

Alice remembered her on the stage at school, how she had looked more vivid than the teachers. 'I see,' she said quietly, wondering whether she really did. There was an explanation now for Trevor's reticence. Perhaps less of a one for his unbroken devotion. 'Were you the only one?' she asked, already knowing the answer.

'I have no idea. I only know that I have never forgotten her. And we have stayed friends over the years.'

Alice wasn't all that surprised, now that this little mineral nugget of the truth glinted at her. Maybe at some level of consciousness she had guessed long ago that her mother had had lovers. 'I see,' she said again. She didn't like to think of the pain that Trevor must have suffered. Sometimes their summer holidays in the mountains had a melancholy edge that she had been too young to understand. Yet Margaret had always come home to him in the end, and there was no doubt that the two of them were happy now, as inextricably entwined as ancient tree roots.

There are many different ways to make a marriage work, Alice reflected. Almost as many as there are marriages.

Lewis had drunk his hot coffee and eaten two biscuits. Warmth and sugar worked to restore his equilibrium. 'It's a long time ago. I was a hungry young man in those days.'

'A bit of a maverick?' She said it without thinking but he nodded, not at all displeased. He was as vain as powerful men always are.

'Yes.' He chuckled. 'Like your friend Rooker. What do you think of him?'

What she actually thought was that there was something about him that required everyone else to take up a position. It was either *your friend Rooker*, or *thank you for being my ally*. And yet Rook himself was absent from all these transactions. He gave no sign of even being aware of them.

She said precisely, 'I think he's dangerous.'

Lewis laughed. He was delighted with this. 'Most interesting men are dangerous. And every interesting woman, take my word for it.'

Alice was chilled. She tried to hide a shiver, but Lewis noticed it.

'I think I shouldn't have blurted out about Margaret and me,' he said.

'I understand,' she told him. And now Margaret Mather House stood here on the windswept peninsula as a footnote to history. She took the radio out again and called up Phil.

In five minutes the two skidoos rounded the corner of the slope and raced up the glacier towards them.

At the last moment Lewis held out his hand. They shook awkwardly.

The base was quiet. The scientists except for Richard were out in the field, and the media crew were on the beach filming Weddell seals.

'Now then, what's next?' Lewis asked.

Richard had scheduled a visit to one of Laure's penguin colonies further down the coast. Rooker was standing by with the Zodiac.

Lewis rubbed his hands together. 'What are we waiting for?'

Rooker drove the Zodiac hard at the shingled beach and Richard leapt out to make it fast. There were so many penguins here that the dinghy's arrival made almost no impression on the hordes of birds streaming up and down the beach. As always, Rooker felt delight at the sight of so much intense and single-minded activity. He stepped into the water in his waders to moor the dinghy. He could see Laure and Jochen working among the rocks above the beach. When he turned back, Richard was helping Lewis Sullavan ashore. The woman assistant, Beverley whats-hername, was next. She stood up too quickly, then almost fell over as a wave slopped against the dinghy. Rooker leaned in and steadied her, then put his arms under hers and lifted her onto the shore. As she murmured her thanks, he could feel the way she was loose against him.

When everyone was safely on the beach, Richard said over his shoulder, 'Wait here for us, Rook.'

It wasn't what Shoesmith said so much as the tone of his voice that made Rooker's fists clench. It was like being eleven years old again.

Uncle Henry Jerrold on the stone steps of the house with blunt-faced stone lions guarding the door, soaked grey light and a ragged grey sky trailing rain. 'Wait here, James.'

So he did, with his coat dripping and his suitcase at his feet.

After she died, there was nowhere for Jimmy to go except back to England. Uncle Henry Jerrold was his family now, and arrangements were made for Jimmy to travel back by ship, retracing the journey he had made with her to New Zealand when he was a baby. He had been too small to remember anything about the first voyage, but he had heard plenty of stories about it. The band leader had played her choice of dance tunes every night, and during the day there had been deck games and fancy-dress competitions. There was a photograph, somewhere, of Jimmy as a little devil, with a tail and a fork and a pair of horns his father had made. He was a mechanic, good with his hands. The photograph had disappeared when people came to clear up the house, after it all happened.

Jimmy travelled on his own, under the care of the nursing sister who ran the ship's infirmary. Uncle Henry was at Southampton to meet him. When the sister handed over her charge, his uncle shook his hand. It was the only time Jimmy could remember touching him.

It was a long train journey up to Northumberland. Jimmy had never seen such rain. Uncle Henry sat next to him, silently reading a newspaper and smelling of wet wool.

Henry was her older brother.

'A good old English snob and stuffed shirt,' she had told Jimmy once, laughing, her mouth wide and lipsticked. 'Not like us, eh?' He had only wondered vaguely what the shirt was stuffed *with*.

He didn't mind Uncle Henry's silence. He didn't want to talk to him either, so that suited them both. When he did speak, it was in a ridiculous voice, blaring and stifled at the same time. His lips didn't move.

'Wait here, James.' A big old door, a stone-slabbed hallway, a cold and silent house. Aunt Eleanor and Uncle Henry had no children.

She said to him once, 'One thing I've got that they haven't, Jimmy, eh? I've got my big boy. I don't need anything else in the world. Not your father, rot him, that's for sure. Not family, either, except for you and me. We're all we need.' She laughed.

Life had a way of turning on you. They didn't have each other any more, because his mother was dead. Uncle Henry and Aunt Eleanor had him now, even though he was the last thing they wanted.

Rooker thought about all this as he watched the penguins going about their business. It wasn't Richard Shoesmith's fault that he looked and sounded like Uncle Henry Jerrold, but just to be in the same room with him brought back memories of the five years he had spent in Northumberland. Five years of rain and routine misery, during which Rooker had taken to a life of rebellion as if he had been born to it. As the son of Annette Rooker née Jerrold, he *had* been born to it. At first he was just mute, and the Jerrolds had taken his silence as insolence. They were expecting gratitude for rescuing him from the orphanage in Dunedin, but none was forthcoming. In time, he had taken up real insolence, defiance, truancy and petty thieving. He had been expelled from two schools.

'You don't care, do you? You don't give a damn,' Henry had once said.

'No,' Jimmy said. It was the truth. What was there to care about?

On the day before his sixteenth birthday he finally walked out. He got a job packing boxes in a Tyneside factory and lodgings in a draughty house belonging to a thirty-year-old divorcée who liked to be kept warm at night. He never went back to the Jerrolds.

'Hi,' a voice said, breaking into Rooker's thoughts. He turned to see Beverley Winston. 'They're cute, aren't they, these little guys?' she added.

Penguins continued to bustle past their feet. He didn't think it was necessary to agree with the obvious.

Beverley was standing close to him, their eyes almost on a level. 'You don't say much.' Her smile was very bright.

'No.'

'Quite a place,' Beverley said. She kept her voice low but he could hear her perfectly, not just what she said but what she was suggesting. He had been amused by her effect on the other men, but now that it was turned on him alone he felt the full force of her allure.

'What happens later?' she asked.

'What do you want to happen?'

She smiled at him. 'I'm sure we can think of something.'

'Yes,' he agreed. 'Why not?' It would be a straightforward transaction and the prospect was enticing.

Russell and Niki collaborated on a second big dinner. Lewis was pleased with the operation of the base and with his brief tour of the science programme. In the morning he would look at Valentin's glacier project and Arturo's weather survey. Beverley slid into her seat next to Rooker and put her hand on his arm when she asked him to pass her the salt. No one had said anything, but it was clear to everyone, except Lewis, that it was a done deal.

'Fuck me,' Phil murmured. His jaw sagged with frank envy and awe.

The other men watched Beverley. Cutlery rattled and the atmosphere prickled with tension. It was a relief when the meal finally ended. Lewis made one of his speeches. He thanked everyone for their work and the warmth of their welcome, and proposed a toast: 'To next year. Antarctica.'

They echoed his words. Next year, Alice thought. Not Antarctica, that's for sure.

81

The generator shed was Rooker's domain. He serviced and maintained the main generator and the back-up, and kept his tools racked along the wall. Washing lines crisscrossed the overhead space where the heat rose from the machinery. The only reason for any of the others to come in here was to collect or hang up laundry, and the lines were bare now.

Rooker leaned against the wall. After a few moments the door opened on to a slice of royal-blue sky. Beverley appeared, wrapped in her parka. They slid together without exchanging a word.

He kissed her, sliding his hands under the parka and her white sweater. Her skin was like satin. Her hands tangled with his clothes, pulling them aside. Rooker looked around and saw an old chair against the shed wall. He sat down, and guided Beverley astride him. She wriggled her jeans down round her hips. A second later they were connected. Rooker forgot everything. He was arching his hips to push higher and harder when the door opened again, admitting the same section of sky. The outlined head and shoulders were unmistakable.

It was Uncle Henry, authoritarian intruder in a child's lonely bedroom.

It was Richard Shoesmith, checking up.

Beverley gave a long sigh. She stood up, not in any great haste, and in one fluid movement hoisted and buckled her jeans. Rooker bundled his clothes approximately into place.

'What's this?' Richard was covering his embarrassment with fury.

Rooker stepped up to him. 'What does it look like?'

Richard's head gave a wobble of outrage that was much too familiar.

Rooker swung his fist and hit him. Richard went down in an untidy heap and lay there.

They all stood in a circle beside the resting Squirrel. Lewis shook hands with each of them. He was the only person on the base who didn't feel the aftereffects of Beverley's play for Rooker and Rooker's assault on Richard. Everyone else was sharply aware of what had happened.

To Alice, Lewis said, 'I won't forget. And give my best wishes to your mother.' To Rooker, 'Get in touch when you're through here. I may have something for you.' And to Richard, 'You're doing a fine job, you and the team.' He gripped Richard's hand in both of his. At such close range he could hardly miss the damage to Richard's jaw and he did an exaggerated double take. 'Hey. What happened here?'

'I took a fall on the ice.'

Lewis swung round to look at Arturo, whose eyes and nose were now shaded in blotches of purple and yellow. 'You people are accident prone, aren't you? I wouldn't want to be in your shoes, Doc.'

Jochen smiled obligingly.

Lewis rubbed his hands. 'Let's go. The dirty old world beckons. I'm sorry to be leaving and I envy you all for being able to stay right here.'

'Sure you do,' Phil murmured as Beverley followed Lewis up the step into the cabin. Everyone watched her rear as she ducked inside.

The rotors sliced the sky and spun into a blur. No one moved as the helicopter lifted off the snow square and buzzed away northwards. It disappeared quickly into a crystalline haze.

Rooker had been looking at an iceberg out in the bay. The berg was the size of a church and the lower sides were an intense sapphire pocked and sculpted into twisted pillars and grottoes. The blue ice was the oldest, hundreds of years old, calved from the heart of the glacier.

Richard swung round to him. 'I want to speak to you.'

With an effort, Rooker took his eyes off the berg. 'I owe you an apology. I shouldn't have decked you,' he muttered.

Richard sagged. The spontaneous admission took the wind out of his intended rebuke. He tried to regain control. 'I won't stand for any more. You're surly, you drink on the base, you're subversive. You can either get yourself into key with the rest of us or get out. Do you understand?'

Rooker stood and listened. It seemed that he had been hearing a version of this speech for as long as he had been able to understand the words. His response had been to shrug and ignore it until, sooner or later, it became easier to get out than to stay. This place, though, was different. He didn't want to leave, because of the silence and the light and the blue-ice cathedral majestically drifting in the bay, and also just because it was so far that there was nowhere else to go.

His mouth hooked in a smile. 'Yeah,' he said.

Richard was watching the iceberg now, too. The wind was driving it aground in the shallow water at the head of the bay. It would remain captive for the rest of the season for them to admire.

At last Richard sighed. Almost to himself he admitted, 'I underestimated the force of it.'

'Of what?'

'Sex. It's the real power in a closed world like this, isn't it? There's no money, no hierarchy to speak of, no distraction apart from work. Then sex unfolds in a blank landscape and it's overwhelming.'

Rooker shrugged. He hadn't noticed that Richard was so smitten by Beverley Winston. Then he realised that he wasn't talking about Beverley. It was the geologist, Dr Alice Peel, with her deceptive mildness and an occasional flash in her eyes that betrayed the opposite. Rooker disliked this thought and the surprise made him consider what Shoesmith had said.

'At least my grandfather never had to take account of *that*.'

'Do you wish you were him?' Rook asked.

'I never could be. I only do what I can here, in my own way.'

The intensity in the words was startling, but Rook only blinked. Indifference was a defence. He didn't want to hear Shoesmith's story, or risk its effects on him. He wanted to maintain his distance, because to be distant was to remain impervious.

Richard turned and made Rooker face him. He held out his hand. 'Shall we declare a truce, then? I don't expect friendship, or even loyalty if that's beyond you, but I do require absolute cooperation.'

Rooker recoiled from this. Shake, like a gentleman. Your word is your bond. It was Uncle Henry incarnate. He stood still for a long, insulting minute while Richard's conciliatory smile slowly congealed. Then he lifted his hand and shook Richard's as if it were a dead snake.

'Good,' Richard said carefully. 'That's good.'

Looking around the table at lunch, Alice noticed that the change that had begun before Lewis Sullavan's arrival appeared complete. The intrusion of people who didn't belong to the group or understand the subtle mechanics of it had forged a team spirit. Everyone was talking and smiling, united by their relief at the departure of the visitors.

Laure was herself again, joking with Jochen; Richard discussed the next month's work schedule. No one mentioned Beverley, but there was an unspoken collective expectation that, in the end, the havoc that her choice of Rooker had caused would become one of the jokes on the base. The episode had improved his standing, but he gave no sign of being aware of this. He was impassive, as always.

It was nine days before Christmas, the beginning of the best time at Kandahar.

The weather was extraordinary. The skies were almost always clear; dozens of rainbows arched delicate filaments against the blue backdrop and rays of pale green and apricot and rose-pink fanned upwards from the horizon, so that it looked as if immense stage footlights played on the sky from somewhere beyond the blocks and crumpled ice tenements of the glacier across the bay. At night, which was night by the clock although no darkness came, the sky to the south of them burned with complex meshed layers of viridian and indigo and scarlet, while the sun hung like a copper ball at the centre of the skein and the glaciers and ice cliffs were splashed with orange and gold and saffron-yellow.

Alice went regularly along the water's edge to the secluded bay where the natural stone steps climbed to the clifftop. She believed that the baby was somehow absorbing the light and colours as it unfurled within her.

She felt as well as she had ever done, and reasoned that if she was well the baby couldn't be otherwise. She ate heartily, and although the work she was doing was hard she didn't find it too much for her.

The boxes of bagged and labelled rock samples slowly filled up. There were other valuable fossil discoveries, but nothing that intrigued Richard as much as the Wheeler's Bluff gastropod. While they worked in the lab hut together, he talked about the paper he would write on it and how it would break major new ground in his field.

She began to be friends with Laure. They talked in the bunk room, when they were changing after work or getting ready to go out again.

'I think I was being stupid.' Laure sighed as she brushed her hair.

'What about?'

'Ah, about Monsieur Rooker. I was dreaming of love.'

'I don't think he's the right character to fit into that particular dream.'

'No. It's so easy to make these mistakes. But he is very handsome, though, and so sexy, don't you think? A bit of a dish?'

Alice laughed again. 'Yes, he's a bit of a dish all right. But not one I want to eat off, thanks all the same.'

'You are right. I think maybe you are always right, Aleece. You are very sensible.'

'Not really,' she said.

Briefly, she thought how luxurious it would be to confide in Laure.

For one thing, it was becoming difficult while dressing and undressing to hide the distinct bulge of her stomach. Alice had calculated that she must be not quite twelve weeks gone. She wouldn't have expected to show yet, but then everyone's body was different. She had been thin before and so perhaps the changes were more noticeable.

But telling Laure was out of the question. If something went wrong—it wouldn't, in her bones she knew it wouldn't—but if it did, she alone must be responsible.

Christmas came.

Richard announced that Christmas Day and Boxing Day would be official rest days. He had another suggestion, too: that there should be an exchange of gifts among the team members. They should each put a present into a sack, and take out a different one. 'You can make something, from whatever you can find on or around the base. Or you can give one of your own possessions, maybe something that has significance for you. Of course, you don't know who is going to receive your present.'

Alice said, 'That's a very nice idea.'

'It's not original,' Richard answered, but he was pleased by her approval.

On Christmas morning everyone slept for an extra hour. Alice and Laure opened their eyes on a silver and gunmetal sea. The fine weather was ending. Someone was playing a recording of Christmas carols on the CD player, and the living area was decorated with tinsel and candles.

The day's eating began with a convivial breakfast of scrambled eggs and smoked fish. Russell produced two bottles of champagne and made Buck's Fizz with concentrated orange juice. Led by Richard they drank a toast to families and friends. Rooker drained his in one gulp, Alice noticed, but he didn't join in the chorus of the toast. He looked more withdrawn today than usual, if that was possible.

After breakfast there was the exchange of team presents. After much thought, Alice had chosen to make someone a present of her treasured copy of *The Rime of the Ancient Mariner*, with reproductions of the Doré illustrations from 1875. She had always loved the poem, and now that she had seen them for herself she thought more than ever that Coleridge's description of the realms of ice was the most chilling she had ever read.

Jochen was the recipient. He looked puzzled by it.

When her turn came to draw a present, Alice reached into the bag and took out the first item her fingers touched. Inside the crumpled paper was a piece of driftwood, rubbed bone-smooth by the waves and curved in a shape that fitted in her two palms. The outlines already suggested the finish, but the wood had been carved with a few extra deep, deft lines that made it into a sleeping, swaddled baby. The piece was beautiful for its simplicity. Alice knew that Rook had done it. She had seen him carving before, his head bent in preoccupation over the wood and the blade of his penknife almost swallowed up in his big hands.

Blood rushed into her face as she looked up. He must *know*. Who else knew? Then her eyes met his hooded glare. Of course he didn't know. How could he have determined that she would pick this gift? It was a coincidence, no more. She composed herself. 'Thank you. It's beautiful,' she said quietly. Some of the darkness melted out of his face.

Afterwards, everyone went outside. There was an assortment of old skis in the store, left behind by the British. Phil and Rooker got the skidoos out of the shelter and fixed tow ropes, and everyone took it in turns to be pulled up the longest slope behind the hut and to ski down again. Everyone except Rooker. He drove the skidoo uphill over and over again, with whooping skiers hanging on to the back.

'I never learned,' he snapped when Alice asked him why.

'You have to try.' She laughed. 'Go on. I'll be your instructor.'

He studied her face for a moment. 'All right,' he said.

He borrowed Phil's skis and boots. Alice walked a little way up the slope with him, took his hands and gently towed him as he ploughed downhill. They did it several times, ascending higher each time. He learned quickly, with a kind of wolfish concentration.

After another half-hour, she drove the skidoo to the top of the slope with Rook wobbling on the tow rope. 'Slowly.' She pointed to the shallowest angle of descent. 'I'll drive alongside.'

He launched himself away, his shoulders rigid with determination.

'Relax. Bend your knees. Keep your hands low,' she shouted after him.

He was gathering speed and she accelerated after him. She told him to lean all his weight on one leg, then on the other. A series of lurching turns developed. 'Hey!' he yelled in unaccustomed delight.

Laure came swooping by. Rooker lost his concentration and plunged forward, crossed his ski tips and somersaulted down the slope.

Alice shot forward to reach him. 'Are you all right?'

He was lying in the snow, a tangle of long limbs and skis and poles. She felt a beat of concern, then she saw that he was laughing. He let his head fall back in a snowdrift and laughed at the sky. She had never seen him look this way, never even heard him laugh with all his heart. The blankness had broken up and he was alive with momentary happiness.

'I can't get up,' he gasped.

She dismounted and flopped down on her knees beside him. She released his bindings, took off the skis and untwisted his legs and arms. To touch him in this unceremonious, affectionate way made her breathe faster and feel grateful for the shield of her goggles. They clasped hands like a pair of drunks and hauled themselves to their feet.

There was powder snow glittering in the close fur of Rook's hair and in his black eyebrows. He shook his head like a dog, the lines of laughter still transfiguring him. 'Again!' he demanded.

Like a child, Alice thought, as if his childhood had been largely unexplored and he had just glimpsed a corner of it. They realised simultaneously that their hands were still linked and quickly let go.

They did it again, faster, and this time he didn't fall.

She bounced up and down on the skidoo pedals and applauded him.

He hesitated, then put his arm round her shoulders and hugged her. 'Thanks. I enjoyed that.'

He was very strong, she could tell from the solidity of him under the folds of his parka. She didn't want him to let go, she realised, but he did.

The wind was twisting little whirlwinds of snow round their feet. They drove the skidoos into the shelter, then climbed the rocks round to the hut door and went in together, laughing.

'Alice just taught me to ski,' Rook announced.

He didn't often volunteer a spontaneous remark. There was a drumming of good-humoured applause and an ironic cheer from Jochen. From his place across the room, Richard looked at them. There was a beat of silence before the general talk and laughter started up again.

Dinner was a success. Russell carved the turkey that Lewis Sullavan had brought with him, and the team fell on it. After the plum pudding there was an Antarctic quiz, set by Niki. Everyone enjoyed it and competition was intense. Arturo won, by one point from Russell. Phil brought out his guitar, and after they had done all the carols they could come up with from each nationality, they sang old Beatles hits.

Then it was time for dancing. The room grew hot and the windows ran with condensation. Rook watched the dancing with a full glass in his hand. After a while, Alice sank down in a chair next to him.

'This is one of the nicest Christmases I've ever had,' she told him.

'Is it?' He was surprised. He didn't have much idea of what Christmas would be like for people who came from ordinary families.

When she was still alive there had been parties. Always a gathering of odd people who didn't want to go home, or didn't have homes to go to. In the later years, when the drink had got the better of her, Jimmy used to haul her to her bed while she muttered and clawed at him. The very last year there had been Lester.

At Uncle Henry's there was church, which smelt of fir boughs for the day, as well as damp and mice. His uncle and aunt gave Jimmy books, when he wanted toy weapons and television and his mother back.

Alice was saying something to him. Her face was a bright, still oval in the jigging room.

'What?' he asked abruptly.

Her expression changed, becoming uncertain. 'I was just asking if you have a family. I'm sorry, I didn't mean to sound intrusive.'

He remembered the skiing lesson and didn't wanted to reject her friendliness now. 'It's all right. I don't have a family. Some . . . friends, but no wife or children.' The words felt unused in his mouth, rusty. He should have been in touch with Frankie, he thought. He could have sent her and the kids an email at least. Alice was still looking at him and he could feel the happiness in her like heat radiating from a fire. An answering smile seeded itself in him. He wanted to go on talking and it was an unusual sensation. 'I've never celebrated Christmas. My mother died when I was a kid in New Zealand and then I lived with relatives until I was old enough to move on. I don't mean I never did partying or seasonal excess.' Her mouth curved in response to this. 'But no tree or sack of presents.'

'We had the sack of presents tonight. I liked your carving very much.'
'How do you know it's my carving?'
'I put two and two together.' She smiled. 'Shall we dance?'

They stood up, and with his hand at the small of Alice's back he drew her close to him. She moved two or three steps in his arms, then seemed to collect herself and draw back to leave a hair's breadth of empty space between them. But still a kind of electricity danced in the air.

The next day was grey inside, with most people nursing hangovers. Outside, the wind battered the hut walls, driving the blizzard so that no one could go out for exercise or to escape the atmosphere. Alice saw that Rooker claimed his half-hour of Internet time for once. His face was dark and closed-in again. He didn't look directly at her, or anyone else.

The blizzard lasted for another five days. Then, on New Year's Eve, the wind lessened. The familiar landscape outside the hut was blunted with heavy layers of new snow.

Throughout the early evening, as the midnight hour in the various countries of Europe came and went, the expedition members wished each other a happy new year while thinking of their families and friends.

This time next year, Alice thought, where will I be?

It was then, standing at the window and looking out at the shifting vista of ice and water, that she felt it. It was a movement inside her, like being gently nudged by another person, a small featherlike stroke, only it came from within. The baby was moving.

She was amazed, flooded with awe at its presence as a new being, but at the same time she knew her calculations were wrong. Fourteen-week foetuses moved, but you couldn't feel it. This baby was older than that.

CHAPTER SIX

THE SUPPLY SHIP was due to reach Kandahar on January 5, but it was delayed for two days. At last the *Polar Star* glided past the ice cliff at the eastern end of the bay. Rooker and Phil were ready in their orange float suits. The Zodiac zipped across the waves to the ship's side.

Alice stood watching from the hut door. The last week had been a torment of indecision. Even now, at this last minute, there was still time for her to say that she would have to leave with the ship.

She couldn't take her eyes off it. It was a lifeline and a sentence of execution all in one. It could remove her from her present dilemma, but to allow it to do so would mean the end of her Antarctic life.

Stay, a siren voice whispered in her ear.

Through Russell's binoculars she watched the ship's captain descend the metal steps. A minute later the dinghy, wallowing a little under the weight of its cargo, circled away and ploughed back towards the shore.

Richard and Russell and Arturo drank coffee and chatted in Spanish to the captain. The rest of them unloaded supplies. At the end of the visit, everyone strolled back down to the jetty.

'Who's coming? All aboard for civilisation,' the captain joked in English as Rooker waded out to bring the dinghy close in to the jetty for him.

Alice's inner voice muttered, *Wait, I am. I'm coming with you.*

'No takers,' Richard responded.

The captain beamingly shook everyone's hand. 'If you cannot be persuaded to leave now, we see you in March.'

Polar Star was scheduled to return on March 15, before the bay iced for the winter, to take them all back to Chile.

Alice was rooted to the beach. There was a chorus of goodbyes as Rook opened the throttle. Alice swallowed hard against the mixture of emotions rising in her throat. It was done.

Staying here was the most irresponsible thing she had ever done, no question. She would be here for two more months. If she was already as much as twenty weeks pregnant—how this had happened she had yet to work out—it would be a much closer-run thing than she had originally allowed for. But she would still be back home in good time.

Richard and Laure and the others walked back up to the hut, but Alice stayed put. As soon as the Zodiac turned away from her flank, the ship began steaming out of the bay. Rooker hauled the dinghy up the beach and made it secure to the concrete mooring block. As he trudged back to the hut, she found herself alongside him.

'Rook? You don't always use your Internet time and I wondered . . . I've got some research . . . if, you know, I could trade some time? Do your kitchen duty, maybe, in return?'

He gave her a glare as cold as a skua's. Alice quailed, wishing she had never raised the subject. She was allowing herself to admit that she was interested in him, but he frightened her, too. There was a rawness under the layers of his self-containment.

He jerked his head. 'Have it. I don't need to trade anything with you.'

That was all. There was no sign of the intimacy that had sprung up between them at Christmas. Rooker had retreated within himself again.

'Thanks,' she murmured, but it was to empty air.

Extra time to check a couple of websites, that was all she needed. She scribbled her name in the access diary immediately above Rook's.

She typed and clicked, then read quickly as the pages came up.

From 14 weeks fluttering movements may be felt, but the first 'quickening' is typically experienced at 18–22 weeks. The sensations she now regularly felt were hardly flutters, more like firm nudges.

At 15 weeks you will be beginning to show . . . Beginning? Hardly.

The measurement from pubic bone to fundus (the upper part of the uterus) will approximately equal the number of weeks you are pregnant. 20cm = 20 weeks. That was much more helpful.

She logged off and went to the bunk room in search of Laure. 'Laure, do you have such a thing as a tape measure?'

'What is that? Ah, I know. No. I am sorry.'

In the end Alice stretched a piece of twine from her pubic bone to the top of her bulge. Then she laid the length of twine against her geologist's steel measuring tape and read 18.5cm. It was maddeningly imprecise but, in any case, now the ship had gone there was nothing to be gained from knowing the dates. She must trust to luck and her body.

In Oxford it was a raw and damp January. Margaret sat at her table in the window, rubbing her aching knees and checking her in-box for Alice's bulletins. Alice's journey was making her feel young again, even if it was only for brief moments. Margaret smiled as she read her messages, nodding in recognition and approval.

'She seems happy enough down there, do you think?' Trevor commented, anxiously reading over her shoulder.

'I knew she would be. I told her it would suit her, didn't I?'

Margaret didn't notice that Alice wrote almost nothing personal. Her daughter was a scientist: it was the science that mattered. It was Trevor's private opinion that there was too little of Alice in them.

Photographs of the hut-naming ceremony had arrived from the Sullavanco Polar Office. Margaret arranged them on the windowsill in front of her desk table. Now when she looked up from her screen she could see the carmine-red walls of Margaret Mather House and Alice smiling in her weatherproofs. Lewis was standing next to her.

That same day, Lewis Sullavan was in the news.

He had added a small chain of resort hotels in Bali and Thailand to his empire, but this had been of interest to no one until a bomb exploded near the swimming pool of one hotel on Ko Samui. A young British couple had been killed and half a dozen other people injured. The bombing was the work of a tiny protest organisation claiming to act on behalf of the very young Thai girls and boys who worked in the sex trade at the resort. There was no direct connection to Lewis Sullavan, but the fact that his company owned the hotel was reported in rival newspapers. He responded by calling a press conference to express his grief and sympathy for the dead and injured and their families, and to say that he was now taking steps to dismiss all staff at his hotels who had ever had anything to do with providing prostitutes of any age for guests.

Margaret and Trevor sat watching the television news. Margaret was fidgeting with her wedding ring.

'Sordid business,' Trevor said.

At Kandahar, the news arrived late and in fragmentary form. Then an email memo to Richard arrived from Beverley Winston. In view of recent unfortunate events it would be most opportune if Mr Sullavan's beneficial work for the EU in Antarctica could be given an extra highlight. Some of the film footage from the recent visit might be released early, before the season's end. And any major scientific discoveries would, of course, receive their proper wide coverage.

Richard rubbed his chapped face, his eyebrows knitting with anxiety.

Phil scowled over his mug of tea. 'Sullavan can't come over all righteous and pretend not to have known what goes on in those resorts of his. It's the way the world goes round—rich old tourists, hungry young kids, it's a fact of life. And our Beverley can't come on all proper, either, because she wasn't averse to a bit on her Antarctic awayday, was she?'

Most of the others were nodding in agreement. Niki grinned.

'Unless I'm mistaken, she wasn't under age,' Rooker drawled. 'And I'm certainly not.'

As Alice had guessed it would, the Beverley Winston affair had turned into a joke among the other men.

'So we're going to have our mugshots in the papers to make Sullavan look good again,' Russell remarked.

But they were so far away, down here on the edge of the ice, that the teeming events of the warm world seemed hardly to touch them.

Only Richard was really concerned. His anxiety to make Kandahar a success that would improve Lewis Sullavan's reputation led him to step up the work rate on the station. He took to supervising the progress of the research more closely. His interference annoyed everyone, and the atmosphere on the base turned sour again.

Another ripple produced by the bomb explosion was that Richard decided the gastropod discovery was so important that he had to look for similar or related specimens in other sections of the fossil-bearing strata of Wheeler's Bluff. He told Alice that they would be making another big trip into the deep field, to last two weeks again.

'Is something wrong?' he asked as she digested this information.

'Nothing at all,' Alice said hastily.

What was wrong was that she was gripped by anxiety about the dangers of the deep field. Pregnancy seemed to be sapping her courage. If anything happened to Richard when they were alone far out on the ice, she doubted that she could deal with it properly. And if *she* were to be the victim, she wondered if Richard would be decisive enough to take action. He might be too determined to make a find at all costs that would satisfy Lewis's desire for positive publicity.

The unwelcome realisation that she didn't have proper confidence in him worked under her skin, chafing and scraping. 'I think we should take a field assistant with us this time,' she ventured.

She could read each successive thought in his eyes. He knew she didn't trust him. And they wouldn't be alone together. And they couldn't take the safety officer away from the base for two weeks because the personnel remaining at Kandahar would need Phil's support. That only left Rooker.

'Why is that?' Richard demanded.

'With an assistant, we'll be able to work more efficiently. We'll have more time if we don't have to handle camp routine.'

It sounded convincing, in a way.

And so it happened. When Richard told her Rooker would be accompanying them, her heart made a startling leap into her throat.

The new camp was further along the Bluff to the southeast of the first ones and was even more exposed and inhospitable. The great crest of black rock was broken up by glaciers and winds roared down the chasms of ice, to shriek and batter around the two tiny tents that lay in their path.

The work was the same as on the first field trip, but Richard was even more driven and dogged in his searching of the fossil-bearing layers. They trudged through the snow and climbed through the bands of rock, measuring and noting and chipping out samples. Rooker drove the skidoo and hauled the sledge. He was very strong, seeming almost unaffected by the wind and cold. Alice felt safe with his dark bulk close at hand. She was less conscious of the vast hostile distance from camp to base than she had been on the last trip. The work itself was unceasing but it had become familiar. Alice got used all over again to never taking off any clothing except the outer windproofs. She was glad of her baggy fleece layers because no one could have any idea of her shape underneath them.

Their work might have been the same, but the atmosphere was not.

Richard and Rooker were working and living in close proximity, and sleeping in the same small tent. It was evident from every remark and every gesture that they loathed each other. Richard's anxiety was making him impatient and autocratic. Rooker did what he was told, but in a silence that was more scathing than words. Alice tried to smooth over the hostility by being cheerful, but she was hampered by the knowledge that she was the cause of at least some of the trouble.

The intimacy that she had shared with Richard at the last camp was gone. I was a fool, she thought, to have let even that much happen.

She hadn't understood, then, that the longing for intimacy was a reaction to the harshness of the ice. It was the human instinct, in this overwhelming place, to draw close round the saving spark of sexual warmth, like hands cupping a match.

Rooker didn't seem to feel it. But Alice often looked up and caught him watching her. Richard noticed it too and his frown deepened.

There was the twice-daily radio link with Niki at Kandahar. One evening Russell reported that Jochen had stomach pains and had spent the day resting in his bunk.

'Really? I hope he'll be fit tomorrow. His study's not progressing that quickly as it is. Over.'

'He's the doctor and I'm base manager,' Russ's voice crackled back, 'and between us we judged that he's not well enough to work. Over.'

'Of course. Yes. Well, give me another update in the morning.'

'He's losing it,' Rooker said later to Alice. He was helping her wipe plates and rinse cooking pots. After the evening meal, Richard had taken to getting straight into his sleeping-bag to write notes and read.

'Losing what?'

'Sense of proportion. Control. He'll get worse before we get off the ice.'

Alice started to contradict him, then gave up the attempt. Richard's diligence was sliding into obsessiveness. He would announce an 8 a.m. start and then brusquely order them to hurry up if they weren't ready to leave camp at 7.45. He would begin a search of one section of rock, only to notice that another site a hundred metres away looked more promising and insist that they shifted to that. Alice did her best to be patient but Rook grew increasingly mutinous.

As he became less reasonable, Richard's physical resemblance to his grandfather increased. He was too impatient to eat properly because stopping for food meant that no work was being done. His cheeks were hollow under the rough spikes of his beard and his eyes sunken.

'Don't judge him too harshly,' Alice said to Rook.

He poured whisky from a flask and handed her the tin mug. She took a long gulp and thought back to the last field trip, when she and Richard had been living and sleeping side by side. It seemed a long time ago. She was afraid now of what might happen to Richard, and as her anxiety had grown her reliance on Rooker steadily increased.

He reclined opposite her, drinking whisky straight from the flask. 'Why does he care about that jackass Sullavan or the European Union?' he mused. 'Do the job, yeah, if you must. But not like that.'

'He is so driven because of who he is. He wants more than anything to live up to his grandfather's name.'

Rook gave a derisive laugh. 'We all act the way we do because of who we are. That's no justification. We are out here, the three of us. We have a degree of responsibility for one another. Shoesmith won't live up to his grandfather's name because he can't and his trouble is that he knows it. He isn't a hero. It's not his fault. He's a neat-minded, anxious man who's afraid to be ordinary just because his name isn't Jones or Brown.'

'You may be right,' Alice agreed.

'I am right. And in a place like this our ordinary leader's longing to be extraordinary makes him dangerous.'

A small icy fingertip, colder than the wind that worried at the tent, touched the nape of Alice's neck. 'He's not a fool,' she said sharply.

'Oh, no. It would be much simpler if he were.' Rooker took a swig of whisky. 'And what are *you* afraid of, Alice?'

He was taunting her, she thought. She considered the question seriously, because a straight answer wouldn't be what he was expecting. 'I used to be afraid of disappointing my mother. Rather similar to Richard, you see, which may be why I feel more forgiving of him than you do. I deliberately turned my back on what she valued so that there would be a lesser risk of exposure. But coming down here has changed that.'

'I see,' he said.

'And you?' she countered.

'Nothing. Nothing's important enough.' He yawned. The conversation was finished and the shutters came down over his face.

In the morning's radio link, Russell reported that Jochen was worse. The doctor's self-diagnosis was appendicitis.

'You'd better advise Santa Ana,' Richard responded.

'Niki called in this a.m. The helo is standing by but the forecast's for winds gusting up to fifty knots.'

'Thank you, Kandahar. Keep me posted.'

It was a long, bleak day. Alice worked doggedly in Richard's wake. The sight of Rook's bearlike bulk trudging ahead of her was the counter-balance to Richard's increasingly frenzied darting.

They reached camp again only just in time for the evening's radio link. The news was that the helicopter had managed a landing and had immediately flown Jochen back up to Santa Ana, where a fixed-wing flight would take him on to Punta Arenas.

'Now we have no doctor on the base,' Richard muttered, once he had signed off. 'The problem I'm facing now is whether to bring down another medic for the last month of the season. It's a very costly option. I'll have to consult the Polar Office. I wonder if Niki can patch me through to London from out here.'

This turned out not to be possible. Richard had to decide between heading back early to Kandahar, where most of his team were caught without medical cover and with only one safety officer, or staying on at the Bluff to pursue his fossils.

'If we can only uncover one or two more Gastropoda. Just one specimen would do,' he kept repeating.

Alice suggested, 'Let's do another day's work, wait for Niki to give us the response from the Polar Office tomorrow evening, then decide. There's nothing to be done now; it's midnight in London.'

Richard nodded, repeating the plan as if he had come up with it him-self. 'And that means a prompt start in the morning, please.' He spoke brusquely to Rooker, as if he had been late every morning of the trip.

'Aye aye, sir.' Rook lifted one hand to his temple in a lazy salute.

The next evening Niki passed on a message from Beverley Winston. Lewis was in Ecuador and could not immediately be contacted.

'Meanwhile we sit here and wait,' Richard fumed. It was, in any case, only another four days before they were scheduled to return.

They woke up to a howling wind and a blinding wall of blown snow. From the mouth of Alice's tent the other tent was barely visible and the snow igloo that sheltered the latrine barrel was completely obscured.

'No leaving camp today,' Rooker announced.

Richard put his dish of porridge aside. 'We'll give it an hour, then see.' After two hours he said, 'Right. It's clearing. Let's move.'

'It isn't doing anything of the kind. I'm safety officer here. No one leaves camp.'

'We're going to work. It's six hundred yards to the nearest section of the Bluff. We'll head there.'

'No.'

'Alice?' After nine days of avoiding eye contact, Richard looked straight into her eyes. *Choose*, he silently challenged her.

She crawled to the tent door and stared out. It did seem that the wind was relenting. Through the whirl of snow she could just make out the outline of the igloo, ten yards away. Almost anything would be better than a day confined to the tents in this atmosphere of rancid dislike. She picked up her parka from her pile of damp, filthy belongings and began to pull it on. Rooker's hand shot out and clamped round her wrist.

'Don't be a fucking idiot.'

'Let go, Rook. I'm going to work.'

He glared at her, then gave a sharp hiss of exasperation. 'I'm sorry. You've got less sense than I gave you credit for.'

He let go and turned away, and she was surprised by how uncomfortable it felt to have disappointed him.

'I'm not coming with you. I'll stay here with the radio.' Rooker tossed a hand-held radio to each of them. 'Call in every thirty minutes.'

'I will make a note in the log of your refusal to accompany us,' Richard said.

'For Chrissake, Shoesmith, this isn't 1913. Write whatever you like in your fucking logbook. I'd do it before heading out into that blizzard, though, because you might not get the chance to do it later.'

As soon as they were under way, Alice knew that it had been a mistake to leave camp. The skidoo seemed to be suspended in a dense white vacuum in which up and down were meaningless. She knew they must be moving forward because the tracks were turning, but there was no view ahead, no landmark to steer by, only blankness. Richard was navigating by compass bearing. They were crossing the glacier towards the Bluff, moving parallel to the crevasses that had become familiar in the last few days, but ahead and to the side was only the unbroken wall of blowing snow. At any moment they might plunge sickeningly into a cleft in the ice. She had seen it happen to Lewis on a clear sunny day.

The skidoo engine stopped. Ahead, the black contours of the Bluff were just visible through the blizzard clouds. They attempted to work, although it was clear from the outset that there was no point. The wind tore the pages of their notebooks and threatened to snatch instruments out of their hands. Richard pressed himself against the snow-plastered rocks and began sweeping them bare with his parka sleeve. As soon as a patch of fossil-bearing rock was exposed, the snow obliterated it again, but he tried to shelter the section with his body. He chipped at the rock with his hammer. There was no hope of labelling a sample bag; he dropped the chunks of rock loose into the pocket of his parka.

Alice watched in dismay, anxiety swelling in her chest.

After thirty minutes she was frozen. The skin of her lips was welded to the ice building up in the layers of fleece and Gore-Tex covering her mouth. With infinite difficulty she extracted the radio from her inner pocket and tried to huddle in on herself to call Rooker. Her lips tore painfully as she tried to speak.

'I read you.' His voice was steady.

'We're trying to work. Visibility nil, conditions deteriorating. Over.'

'Are you coming in? Over.'

'I'll try to make him.'

Alice tottered the few steps to Richard and thumped him on the back. She signalled *Let's go back*. He held his splayed hands up at her to signal *Ten more minutes*. She knew what he was thinking. This minute, or the next one, he might make the great find.

She hunkered in beside him, counting the time away.

He had had long enough now. She grabbed his shoulder, pulling him away from the rock face. *OK*, he signalled. He took out the compass to get the reverse bearing for their journey back to the camp. The wind assaulted him; he dropped the compass. In an eye-blink the instrument hit the ground, then began to slide, skidding out of sight down the small slope to the glacier. It was gone for good.

Two things, Alice thought, her numb brain slowly working. GPS reading, get their position. Then call Rooker. He had the back-up compass.

The GPS unit was in her inner left pocket. She gripped it hard and punched the buttons. As the system searched the skies for satellite signals, she stared at the screen through veils of snow. Then a green message flashed at her: WEAK SIGNAL. The unit could not get a fix accurate enough to pinpoint their position. In zero visibility and without a compass, the 600 yards back to camp might as well be 600 miles.

Now the radio. 'Rook? Rooker, do you copy? *Please*, do you copy?'

'Alice. Report please. Over.'

She blurted out what had happened.

'Listen to me. Don't move. Take what shelter you can against the rocks. Huddle together. Monitor the GPS. I'm coming to get you. Over.'

'Thanks.'

I'm coming to get you. The simplest words, Alice thought, but lovelier than the most beautiful poem ever written.

She hauled at Richard, pulling him down into an angle between rock and slope. There was a tiny diminution of the wind here.

She didn't know how much time passed. Time and her heartbeat slowed together. Then she became aware of a noise that wasn't the wind.

It was whistling and the banging of metal on metal, coming closer.

She struggled to her feet. 'Here!' she yelled. 'Rook-er. Rook-er. Here!'

There was a red blur, just visible through a momentary lull in the blizzard. Alice ran forward to where she had glimpsed the red parka, but there was nothing—only snow and wind.

Then the clanging was beside her, right at her shoulder. She whirled round and saw Rook. He had a whistle between his teeth and was banging two metal saucepans together. The Kandahar meal signal.

Half an hour later, Alice was crawling into her sleeping-bag. Her teeth were chattering and she shivered as if her bones were going to crack.

Richard had barely spoken and nor had Rooker, but Richard was regaining his composure. 'That was well done,' he told Rook now.

'I can't say the same for you. You could have died out there, which is up to you, but you were risking the life of another team member as well as your own . . .' He spat out the words.

'That's enough, Rooker,' Richard snapped. 'I'm going to radio Kandahar for an up-to-date forecast and then make a plan of action.'

After he had gone to the other tent, Rook glanced at Alice, now huddled up silently with her head on a pile of damp clothing. He put his warm hand inside the mouth of her sleeping-bag to feel the temperature of her neck. With his other hand he stroked back her hair.

'You'll warm up soon, then you can go to sleep. None of us is going anywhere for a couple of days, whatever Shoesmith's plan may be.'

As the storm continued, Richard became even more withdrawn. He spent most of the time in his own tent, so Alice and Rooker were thrown together. He was a good listener, she discovered. She told him about Oxford, and Trevor and Margaret. She described Pete and *Desiderata*, and Rooker laughed at the sound of the sculpture. She promised to show him the Polaroid picture of it when they got back to Kandahar.

'I can't go on doing all the talking,' she said suddenly. 'I don't know anything about you. Where did you grow up?'

For a cold moment she knew he was going to snap at her and retreat behind the shutters. But instead he told her that when he was a small boy he had emigrated with his parents from England to New Zealand. His mother had come from a landowning family in Northumberland, and his father had been an actor and a singer. He had left his wife and son not long after they had settled, and neither of them had seen him again. His mother had died about seven years later, Rook added abruptly.

'Then what happened?'

He had been sent back to England, to live with his mother's brother and his wife. A childless couple, who didn't like children very much.

'That must have been hard.'

'It was.' He laughed shortly. 'Do you know what? Everything that Richard Shoesmith says and does reminds me of Uncle Henry Jerrold.'

'I see,' Alice said. She didn't really, but it was at least a partial explanation for Rook's animosity.

On the evening of the third day the wind died away. Twenty-four hours later, the Squirrel was buzzing down towards the familiar contours of the bay. As she looked down at the tiny red huts, Alice felt almost drunk with relief and exhilaration. Luck was still with her. She had risked another expedition to the Bluff and survived with her secret intact.

CHAPTER SEVEN

By the end of February, the bay was solid with ice, a full month earlier than the year before. Blizzards alternated with days of eerie calm. The sun sank lower over the glaciers and the skies flared with lurid refractions of multiplying suns and rainbows. Cold stalked the Kandahar people whenever they left the fragile shelter of the huts. Winter was opening its jaws wider as the sun deserted them.

The bay had frozen almost overnight. The stranded berg was now just a bigger ziggurat that tilted out of a plateau of similar spikes and shards, all trapped until the next spring's thaw would set them free again.

The ship obviously wouldn't be able to enter the bay when it returned in the middle of March; it would take an icebreaker to achieve that. They were faced with a choice of making their way out on foot, over the sea ice to open water, or of bringing in the helicopter to ferry them and their belongings to the ship's side.

'Will we be able to get out?' Alice asked Phil as they stood looking out at the bay. A slow pulse of anxiety was beginning to beat in her.

Phil said thoughtfully, 'I should think so. Mind you, it wouldn't be the first time that a summer team had had to overwinter because they got trapped. It'd be a nuisance, but on the other hand it wouldn't be the end of the world. Six months or so on short rations, that's all.'

Alice made an effort to control her feelings, but a flutter of panic threatened to overtake her. They couldn't, must not, be caught here for a whole winter.

Richard called a meeting. He looked around at all of them, his eyes slightly glassy. 'We will be leaving here on March 15, on schedule. I guarantee you that. In the meantime I ask you to give Kandahar your best effort. We've got less than one month left. We need some results to show for our first season. We need to publish, get ourselves talked about.'

Russell and Phil exchanged sceptical glances. How could Richard guarantee a departure date?

If anyone was depressed, Alice decided, it was the expedition leader. His polar expedition had not delivered any antidote to his self-doubt, or even any properly notable scientific discoveries. It was not exactly her field, but she was beginning to wonder if the gastropod was as important as he wanted it to be.

Without Jochen, the hut was emptier and quieter, and the ebbing and flowing tides of irritation were less predictable. Russell and Valentin were experienced enough to be automatically loyal to Richard as the leader, and Alice had her own reasons, but the others hardly disguised their resentful dislike of him. Niki's Baltic melancholy cast a lengthening shadow, whereas Phil's constant flippancy grated in a different way. Rooker's sardonic silences were unnerving, and without Jochen to pay her attention, Laure was becoming increasingly subdued.

Alice attracted her own share of disapproval. Pregnancy was beginning to make her physically clumsy and also forgetful. She forgot to write her name and destination on the board when she went out, and Rooker scolded her for her carelessness. When she tried to hide her lapses by making herself as inconspicuous as possible, she realised that everyone else thought she was just being lazy.

She had lost much of her appetite, but to provide an explanation for her increasing girth she tried to make it look as if she ate a lot. She loaded up her plate at every meal, then slipped the food back.

Jochen was not going to be replaced. Richard discussed the possibilities with the Polar Office. It seemed that it was not worth the expense of sending another medic all the way down to Kandahar for what would now be a stay of just over three weeks.

Richard repeated, 'March 15. What do we need a doctor for between now and then? We can hardly get out of the hut door.'

When she did venture outside into the short-lived twilight, Alice stood on the sea ice and stared up at the hut, perched so precariously on the rocks that the smallest puff of wind might lift it and carry it away. Their existence here was so fragile. It was hubris, she thought, to imagine that they or anyone else could outwit the forces of Antarctica.

Some emails came from Peter. She hadn't heard from him since Christmas and now here were three at once. They were all imploring.

Are you going to be angry with me for ever? I don't know what I can say or do to make it up, Al, but the truth is that I love you. I'm waiting for you to come home so I can tell you in person. Will you let me? Please answer this.

xxx always P

It was Pete's child she was carrying. Did he have a right to know what she was doing and the risks she was running? She didn't think he did. After the accident of conception, the baby was hers. When she got home she would tell Pete what was happening, and if he wanted it they would negotiate for him to have some share in its future.

Her fingers rested on the keyboard while she reflected on what to tell him now. She looked down briefly at her bruised, chapped knuckles and the broken nails. It was like seeing someone else's hands grafted on to her own wrists. When she came to think about it, the arms didn't feel like her own either, nor did the rest of her heavy, pregnant body. The other Alice, the familiar one who had been a scientist and Peter's girl-friend and part of a trio with Jo and Becky, had gone and someone who would be a mother had crept into her skin in her place.

Disorientation made her shiver. Home was far away and getting there was a series of obstacles. Nothing was normal any longer. The only thing that was still real was Antarctica itself, that giant white mouth. She understood why the old explorers had found it so difficult to extricate themselves and why Margaret had never really escaped its thrall. Its raw power was such that it made the world beyond seem pale and slight.

Dear Pete, I was very glad to hear from you. I'm not angry, and I miss you too. [All this was the truth.]

I'll be back in Oxford in about a month's time, earlier than I planned, and I'd like to see you then, of course. I do know you love me and I love you too, in a way, but it's not enough on either side, nor in the right way, for me to say what I think you want to hear. I'm sorry if this hurts you. I'll call you as soon as I am back.

Much love, Al

After she had sent the bleak message, Alice took out the Polaroid of Pete and *Desiderata*. Loneliness and regret wrapped round her as she reflected that they wouldn't be bringing up their child together. That together-ness couldn't happen, she was certain, but she still yearned for it.

She couldn't go to bed yet. She needed to talk to someone. She put the photograph away and went to find Rooker. She found him in the empty radio room. He was reading, rocking gently in Niki's chair.

He looked up. 'Hi. Has something happened?'

'No. Do you have anything to drink?'

'Sure.' He poured whisky from a flask into a cup and gave it to her. 'Go on,' he said after a minute.

'What?' Then she smiled. It was cosy in here. 'I haven't come to say anything. You tell *me* something,' she added recklessly.

Rooker put down his book. It occurred to him, startlingly, that talking to Dr Alice Peel—telling her something, even—was a much more appealing option than reading any more of it.

'Where shall I start?' The words came out without premeditation.

'What about . . . when you were growing up. In New Zealand, before you went to live with Uncle Henry Jerrold?'

He was utterly amazed that she remembered all this. He had almost forgotten that he had mentioned it, in the tent out at Wheeler's Bluff.

He began to tell her about the first thing that came into his head, his friend Gabby Macfarlane.

Gabby's home was a couple of miles outside town. It was a very clean and orderly house, but it didn't feel all that comfortable. Mr Macfarlane was a square, blocky man with a red face like a slab of meat. When he came in, his wife and children would go quiet. Once, Jimmy saw Mr Macfarlane hit Gabby in the face twice with the back of his hand, blows that made his head crack and jerk sideways as if his neck would snap, but Gabby never uttered a sound.

Apart from when his father was around, Gabby was an inspired wrongdoer. Jimmy and he had recognised each other almost at first glance, and they fell into a life of crime. They stole sweets and toys, and sometimes things they didn't need or even want, like nail brushes.

Gabby and he liked setting fires, too. A match tossed on rags soaked in petrol from the can that Mr Macfarlane kept in the tractor shed made a *whump* and a wall of pure flame out of a pile of rubbish.

Gabby had three older sisters. One day he and Jimmy squirmed on their stomachs through the toetoe grass to a place where the two bigger ones were sunbathing in their knickers. Jimmy gazed through the screen of grass stalks at Joyce's pale splayed legs and the way the bones of her hips poked up to make a kind of cradle of the flesh that spanned them. He thought how much he would like to rest his head in that cradle and then felt embarrassed to connect this hot unwieldy tenderness with Joyce Macfarlane, who had frizzy hair and spectacles.

That day was the first time he went home and found Lester there.

'Jimmy,' she said to him, waving her glass and slopping some of the contents down the front of her silky blouse, 'this is my friend Lester Furneaux and he's a designer.'

The man looked coldly at him, and they both knew that they were rivals for her affection and attention.

Lester. There had been years when he had been able to stop every avenue of thought leading back to him, so why did he intrude now?

'What happened to Gabby Macfarlane?' Alice Peel asked.

In the light cast by the small desk lamp, her face was luminous. She wasn't prying, she was just interested. He could see the faint down on her rounded cheek. The memory of Joyce Macfarlane came back to him, and he felt the same unworded tenderness that was distinct from and much less resistible than lust. He was going to lift his hand and put it over hers, without making any calculation about what might happen next.

The radio gave out a loud burst of scrambled noise. Instead of touching Alice's hand, Rook picked up Niki's headphones and pulled them over his head. The static shriek resolved itself into a human voice as he hastily adjusted the frequency.

'Vernadsky, Vernadsky, I read you. This is Kandahar. Over.'

Vernadsky was a Ukrainian station on the peninsula. Rooker listened intently to the torrent of Russian-English, then lifted the headset from one ear. 'Go and get Niki. Our leader will want to hear this as well.'

Alice knocked on the doors of the bunk rooms and woke the two men. Niki took his seat and the rest of them waited behind him. Richard frowned at the gabble of Russian.

'Ship? There's no ship. What are they talking about?'

But there was a ship.

Richard shook his head. He took the handset from Niki. 'Vernadsky, this is Dr Shoesmith. Thanks for the kind offer. Much appreciated. But we'll stay on base until our scheduled departure day. Over.'

The radio operator's voice sounded startled in response. 'Weather conditions and the latest forecast indicate increasing difficulty . . .'

'Thanks again, Vernadsky. We have information. Out.'

Rook's hand shot out and grabbed Richard by the wrist. He dropped the handset. 'Call up again,' Rooker ordered.

'I beg your pardon?'

'You heard.' He stooped for the handset and thrust it into Richard's hand. 'You're the expedition leader. The Ukrainians are making room on their relief ship to take all your personnel to safety, leaving in two days. It's still a manageable trek out over the ice. Make the right decision.'

Richard was white to the lips. 'I have already made my decision. We stay here until our scheduled departure. There's work to be done. We couldn't be ready to leave in forty-eight hours' time, in any case.'

'We could be ready in *four* if it were a matter of life and death.'

Silence bled through the room.

'It isn't. It's a matter of duty,' Richard said softly. 'And you'll do yours, Rooker, along with everyone else.'

Rooker got up and walked away.

Alice met Richard's eyes. 'Why don't we leave with the Ukrainians, while we can?' she asked.

His lips tightened. 'It's what we have to do, Alice. It's our job to finish our work, to close down the base properly when the time comes and not to run away at the first sign of difficulty like rats off a sinking ship.'

She held his gaze. 'It's an accident of the weather. You're not Captain Scott. You're not your grandfather, but that's because you don't have to be, not because you haven't got it in you. The pioneer days have long gone. We're a party of scientists. We could go home in two days, do our analyses and write up our results. Who's expecting so much? Lewis?'

Richard slowly shook his head. 'Who? Ourselves, of course. Oneself. Are you afraid of staying here, Alice?'

'No.'

It was a lie. As she stood there her stomach jutted out like the prow of a ship. She knew she must be further along than she had calculated. She must have already been pregnant when she had spent her last night in Oxford with Pete. How many months?

She didn't care about duty or honour or science. She cared about life. The life she was carrying inside her. She was afraid to put it in further jeopardy. 'I would like to leave on the Ukrainian ship.'

He brushed the words aside. 'We will all leave together as planned on the *Polar Star*. We'll negotiate the ice by skidoo or be lifted out by helicopter, which contingency we have planned and paid for.'

In the morning, Rooker insisted that everyone convene round the mess table. 'You all know what this is about,' he said calmly. 'We can leave here on the Ukrainian ship. I think we should take a show of hands.'

A pulse twitched at the corner of Richard's mouth. 'I am the leader of this expedition,' he said again. There was a crack in his voice. Alice felt so much sympathy that she could hardly look at him.

Rook ignored him. 'Round the table, then. Russ?'

'Stay till *Polar Star* comes.' The base manager's dry Kiwi voice was unemphatic. Russell's loyalty to the expedition leader was unshaken.

'Arturo?'

'I am able to wind up my studies in time. I go with Ukrainians.'

Laure looked exhausted and faintly tearful. 'Me also.'

'Niki?'

'Ukrainians.'

'Four of us in favour so far, so . . .'

'Just wait a minute, mate.' It was Phil who interrupted him. There was no sign of his usual chirpy grin. 'It's eighteen days to finish the job, right? I don't like pulling out early. I'm for staying put.'

'That's the considered view of our safety officer?' Rooker's voice grated with sarcasm. 'Valentin?'

'I stay. Same reasons as Phil. I think there is no need to hurry away.'

Four all. It was Alice's turn and there was an uncomfortable silence.

'I vote to go out on the Ukrainian ship,' she said clearly.

Rooker leaned back in his chair. 'That's a majority,' he said to Richard. It was as if there were only the two of them in the room.

Very slowly, Richard got to his feet. 'I remain the leader of this expedition and what I say goes. Lewis Sullavan has provided the funding; I control our budget. *Polar Star* is paid for; an entirely unnecessary Ukrainian evacuation is not. We stay here until the agreed date for our departure.'

There was a stubbornness in him that Alice couldn't help but admire, even now. But she was summoning up all her courage to tell them the truth, to blurt out why the Ukrainian ship would have to come.

Before she could open her mouth, Rook sprang up and leapt across the room. His hands went to Richard's throat and he shook him as if he were a child's doll. Russell and Valentin ran at him and tried to haul him off while Phil wrestled an outraged Arturo. Niki's fists swung. Suddenly there was a melee of men and overturning chairs. Alice and Laure stared at each other. This was what all their high-minded European collaboration and teamwork had come to—a brawl over the breakfast table.

The fight was over as quickly as it had begun. Richard spoke out of pinched lips. 'You're relieved of your duties, Rooker.'

Rooker laughed. He seemed genuinely amused.

Looking from one face to another, Alice found that her confession had died in her mouth. She couldn't—*could not*—pipe up now and tell them that she was pregnant and needed to go home. That would be to place her concerns in direct opposition to Richard's. That would oblige him to choose publicly between her requirements and his own overwhelming need.

She would rather almost anything than have to witness his choice.

No. She would have to stay put and pray that her luck would hold.

There was a wary stillness on the base until the Vernadsky ship left. After two days, Niki reported that the Ukrainians had closed their station for the season and were aboard ship en route for Ushuaia. Richard acknowledged the information with a mechanical nod. The rest of them looked at each other, mutely reflecting on the extra degree of their isolation. They depended now on the arrival of their own ship, ice permitting, or on the air support of the Chileans at Santa Ana.

The weather deteriorated. The snow was so thick that there might as well have been no light, because there was no visibility. Alice completely understood the old description of a serious blizzard as 'white darkness'.

The frozen bay became a pearly blank plain with no beginning or end. Only the berg stood out, intermittently visible during the ragged gaps in the weather. The penguins deserted the Kandahar rocks and began their exodus towards the distant sea margin. Without the little birds' constant bustle, or the glimpses of seals basking on the ice or whales blowing in the deeper water, the sense of isolation deepened. The wildlife and the sun were retreating, leaving the human interlopers to the mercy of winter.

The baby moved around much less now. When Laure was out of the bunk room, Alice slid her hands over the mound of her stomach.

Are you there, baby? We're going to be fine, you and me. Wait and see.

Once, Laure opened the bunk-room door, startling her. Alice hunched her back and pulled more clothes round her body.

'What were you saying?' Laure asked doubtfully.

'Nothing,' Alice answered. Now her room-mate thought that she rambled on to herself. It didn't matter. They were all retreating into eccentricity in their different ways, as the light dwindled. As the food supplies began to run low, meals became fragmentary, eaten at different times, and they passed by each other silently.

One night, Alice was reading in her bunk by the light of her head torch when she became aware that something was not quite right. The room was unusually cold. She padded in her thick socks to touch the electric wall heater. The panels were cold. She clicked on the main light switch; nothing happened. She realised that it was the absence of the generator's constant low murmur that had first caught her attention. There was no electrical power because the generator was off.

She dragged on some more layers of clothes. She opened the bunk-room door and closed it behind her with a soft click. Someone was moving around the hut. The walls flickered with a soft, unfamiliar light.

'Hello?' Alice said.

There were lit candles all around the room. A dark figure turned and his huge shadow reared up the wall. She knew who it was.

'Richard, what are you doing? Why is the generator not running?'

'We have to economise on fuel, you know.' Richard's face was all raw bones and black hollows. The hair prickled at the nape of Alice's neck.

She heard another footstep behind her and whirled round. 'Valentin,' she breathed in relief. 'The generator.'

He was frowning. 'It has broken down? We must fix. The freezer will be off. I have to preserve my ice core samples.' Valentin's first thought was for his glaciology study. The freezer in Margaret Mather House was full of the neat sections he had drilled out of the heart of the glacier. Alice remembered that Laure's penguin blood samples were stored there too.

'I switched off the generator to save fuel,' Richard murmured.

The other men had woken up now and they came out of the bunk rooms. Their shadows swept over the walls as the candle flames shivered. The room was crowded with giant spectres.

Someone shouted, 'Shoesmith, what in Christ's name d'you think you're doing?' Rooker was large, angry and reassuringly three-dimensional. He was already scrambling into his weatherproofs. He and Phil headed outside, followed by Valentin. The blast of cold air made them all shiver.

Arturo held Richard by the arm and guided him to a chair. He gave no sign of a protest. No one looked at anyone else. Seconds crumbled away. After a few minutes they heard a stuttering roar as the generator fired up again. The lights blinked on.

Richard lifted his head. 'I do apologise,' he said quietly. 'That was an overreaction. But it is important, you know, if we can't leave here. We must conserve fuel. An airdrop might not be possible for weeks.'

The realisation finally and properly dawned on Alice. We may well be stranded here for the polar winter.

The Ukrainian ship had gone; miles of sea ice would separate them from *Polar Star* when it finally did arrive. Helicopters didn't take off in weather conditions like these. It wasn't that they might die or even go really hungry, because they had walls and a roof to shelter them, and fixed-wing flights from Santa Ana would drop fuel and food supplies on the ice even though they could not land. A few months of isolation would be a grand inconvenience for the others, but it would mean something entirely different for her. Ripples of panic began to wash through her.

Russell was putting mugs of tea on the table. Valentin came banging back from the lab hut. 'No defrosting yet, lucky to say.'

Rooker and Phil returned, stamping their feet.

Richard repeated his apology. 'I should not have closed down the generator. Tomorrow, as a group, we will make contingency plans for rationing fuel and food.'

Alice lifted her head and straightened her spine. Right or wrong, foolish or criminally insane, she had brought herself to this point and all that mattered from now on was survival. There was no question but that they would survive, the two of them. For now, there was no point in doing anything more than she had already done. She would wait quietly, to see if the ship or the helicopters came in good time.

You wait too, baby.

Richard concluded, 'Thank you for restoring the power tonight. Rooker, you've got your job back. Let's try to work together, shall we?'

When the next all-too-brief break in the succession of blizzards came, Rooker and Phil took the skidoos across the sea ice to attempt to find the margin beyond which the water would be navigable.

The daylight subsided rapidly into darkness, and Phil and Rooker were still not back. Niki reported that they were in radio contact, but return progress in darkness over the snow-blanketed ice was painfully slow.

Alice was tortured by anxiety. At last a smear of torchlight was visible in the distance, swaying in the blackness. 'They're back,' she cried.

The two men were exhausted. Phil's fingers were frozen into claws and the tips were blackening with frostbite.

It was nine miles over the ice to the closest point where they judged the ship might be able to follow leads inwards through the pack ice. These were conditions almost unheard-of for the early part of March. The frozen ice was extending fast. By the time the ship did arrive, navigable water might easily be twelve or fifteen miles distant.

'So if we get a clear weather spell we'll do it by helicopter shuttle,' Richard said. 'It's only in the worst case that we'll have to go out over the ice. I'll ask the Polar Office if they can get the ship in earlier.'

To save fuel, the main generator was turned off every night at 10 p.m. ('We're not short of freezer capacity,' Richard had said, jerking his chin at the white outdoors. The men had dug an ice cave behind the lab hut and consigned the lab freezer contents to it.) Everyone piled on extra layers of insulation and retired to their bunks to keep warm, but tonight Alice was too restless. She lit a couple of candles and paced the main room, wearing most of her clothes except her windproofs.

A man's shadow loomed over the wooden wall ahead of her. She turned with her heart leaping into her mouth and saw Rooker.

'So you can't sleep either,' he said. He produced the inevitable bottle and poured Scotch into two mugs.

She drank, then took a breath, with the spirit still scalding her throat. 'Rook, I've got to get back to England.'

'This is Antarctica, not Spain or somewhere. There's no *got* to.'

Shockingly, she felt her face begin to crumple. Tears burned at the back of her eyes. Rooker saw and with his thumbs he stroked the tears away from under her eyes, surprising her with his gentleness. Then he took her face between his hands. 'I've watched you. You're strong and you're brave as well. It's only waiting. What do you fear?'

She was ashamed to tell him her secret, with all its soft womanishness and the attendant implications of wilful miscalculation. She stepped away from him instead. 'I'm sorry,' she said in a different voice. 'The uncertainty gets to us all in different ways, doesn't it? I think I'll go to bed. Thanks for the whisky.'

'Good night,' he said.

Beverley Winston and the Polar Office responded to Richard's request that in view of the extreme weather conditions the relief ship might come to bring them out earlier than scheduled. Unfortunately, she noted, the ship's programme was already determined and to change its itinerary would cost an estimated minimum of $25,000. In view of the fact that it would only make a few days' difference to the planned date, Mr Sullavan judged that this would be an excessive expenditure.

Russ let his disgust show. 'A few days? Does he really not understand that a single day can make the difference down here?'

'Lewis Sullavan's an amateur. He wanted a polar station, but now he's finding out that his toy's too expensive.' Rooker was scathing and no one tried to contradict him.

The last week came. The base was stripped down ready to be closed up, although it seemed impossible that they would actually be leaving. The helicopters had been on the ground at Santa Ana for more than two weeks. The blizzards followed one upon the other with hardly a break between, and fifty- and sixty-knot winds screamed down from the glacier.

On March 12, the *Polar Star* left port to make its way across the Drake Passage and down to the peninsula. The same night Alice was lying sleepless and cold in her bunk. There was a wind, but for once the sky was clear. She heard the small noises of someone moving around in the hut, but after a while everything went quiet again. But then she sensed something else. She sat upright, groping for her torch. Then she coughed.

Smoke. The room was full of smoke.

She couldn't see anything. No light. No generator, of course.

'Laure,' she shouted. 'Laure, wake up!'

The other woman stirred and groaned. '*Qu'est-ce que c'est . . .?*'

110

'Get up!' Alice yelled. 'Fire!'

They were both coughing in the rolling, blinding smoke.

Torch. Find the torch. Breathe some air. Low down. Better. Air clearer down here. She groped and found her torch. The wreathing, acrid smoke was so thick that the light was just a dim blur. Alice took two steps and heaved open the door of the bunk room.

The scene beyond brought a scream into her mouth. There was a wall of flame where the main room lay and there were figures silhouetted against it, spraying a fire extinguisher, which Alice could see was useless. She slammed the door again. There was no escape that way.

They were both choking. Alice hunted for something with which to break the window. Fighting for sight, she hammered with a shoe, then threw it aside; the thick glass would never shatter under its feeble impact.

'*Attends, j'ai mon piolet*,' Laure shrieked. She squirmed under her bunk and dragged out her kitbag. Inside was an ice axe. Alice grabbed the shaft and swung at the glass. Cold, clean air flooded into the room.

'*Oh merci, merci*,' Laure sobbed.

Alice chopped a bigger hole in the glass and padded the jagged shards with clothes. Now that they were about to escape she was aware of the intense cold waiting outside. 'Throw everything out. Anything warm.'

A cascade of blankets and clothes and towels rained down on the snow, followed by a shower of boots and shoes.

There was no time to rescue anything else. They perched on the chair together, and Alice held on to Laure's shoulders as she squirmed over the padded glass and dropped the few feet to the ground. Alice swung her legs over the padding and launched herself forward. She felt a sharp scrape along her arm as she fell and a jarring crack as she hit the ground. Laure helped her to her feet. Above their heads, dense billows of black smoke poured out of their bunk-room window.

Already shivering, they fought their way into as many layers of clothing as they could pile on. Flames were dancing out of the hut door, and as they stopped in their tracks to gaze in horror, the front windows blew out in the heat. A fat column of fire escaped and leapt towards the sky.

There were other figures, stumbling through the snow. Alice counted. Four . . . five. Where were the others? She knew at once that it was Richard and Rooker who were missing.

She turned in a full circle. 'Rook?' she screamed.

A flower of fire was blooming round the nearest window of the lab hut. The narrow neck of ground between the two huts was engulfed by a wall of flame. There was no question of passing that way. She ran back in the direction she had come, to circumnavigate the main hut. On the far side was the window of the scientists' bunk room. Smoke poured out but she couldn't see any flames. Alice ran forward. There were two heads at the window, still inside the hut.

'Rooker,' she yelled. 'Get out!'

It looked as if they were fighting. Richard's arms were raised; Rooker's were locked round him. They lurched. Rook was dragging Richard towards the window but Richard was pulling away. Alice hoisted herself so that she was leaning into the room through the broken window.

'Climb out!' she screamed. '*Richard*.'

Somehow, through the din, the sound of her voice registered on him. He swung his head in her direction as the door of the bunk room dissolved in a blast of heat. Richard gave a rending cry but he could only retreat. The two men flung themselves at the window. Alice rolled aside as Richard thudded down, pushed out of the window by Rooker. An instant later Rooker himself landed beside them.

'Move,' he ordered.

They were up and running, all three of them, away from the fire. Flames forked through the window from which they had just escaped. There was an indrawn breath, an instant of silence, then an explosion. The hut and everything in it was finished.

Richard gave another cry. 'The gastropod,' he said.

Alice couldn't speak. A fossil? A *fossil* didn't matter.

She turned to Rook. He didn't move. His lips were drawn back from his teeth. He looked as if he was seeing a ghost.

The lab hut was properly on fire now, too. Three figures were darting around it, aiming the jets of fire extinguishers at the blaze. Slowly, Rooker collected himself. He took long, unsteady strides, as if he were wading through water, towards the second fire. Alice moved to follow him but Richard dragged at her arm.

'It was in my locker,' he groaned. 'In *there*.'

Alice found her voice. 'I don't care. I care about . . . living things.' Science didn't matter. History didn't matter. Suddenly she thought of Peter. She could remember him saying to her, 'What would you rather have, the human gene code mapped or one life saved that's precious to you?' Shocked by his lack of gravitas, she had claimed science.

Alice shook her head and struggled through the snow to where the others were huddling upwind of the lab hut. Laure held out her arms and they clung to each other for comfort. For the first time in weeks Alice didn't try to hold her body apart. They were all together in this, whatever came; keeping her secret wasn't important any longer.

The extinguishers had temporarily contained the blaze, but the wind and the tinder dryness of the wooden construction were against them. They needed water, but for all the snow that surrounded them there was none to be had. Niki broke away from the group. He ran to the rear of the lab hut and smashed the back window. He was going for the radio equipment. Without radio contact they were truly stranded.

'The pipeline,' Russell shouted.

The base water supply came from an as-yet unfrozen glacier lake high up the hill behind the huts. The insulated piping was disinterred and taken apart, and water trickled out. Seconds later they had formed a chain. Buckets, jerry cans and old paint tins were filled and thrust from hand to hand. They worked like machines. Nobody spoke. In a pall of smoke, Niki and Phil hauled metal boxes with trailing festoons of flex from the broken window and ran with them to the safety of the generator hut.

At first it seemed that the fire was steadily gaining on them. The front wall of the hut was a mass of flames and Margaret's brass name plaque vanished. Then slowly it became apparent that they were holding their own—because the wind had dropped.

'Keep at it,' Rooker yelled back up the line.

They worked grimly for another half-hour. Without the wind blowing sparks across from the main hut, it seemed that the shell and the back half of the lab hut were safe. The wreckage of the main hut was still burning, but with a less ferocious appetite. The snow all around it was blackened, littered with the belongings that had been salvaged. Margaret Mather House loomed in a wreath of smoke, half destroyed.

Alice searched for Rook. He was staring into the smouldering core of the old hut with horror in his eyes. A stab of cold prompted her to look down at her hands. The left one was caked with dried blood. As she gazed at it a dribble of fresh blood ran down from her sleeve.

The others stood in exhausted silence too, gazing at the devastation.

The blood dripped from Alice's fingertips and pocked the snow. 'We should try to get under cover,' she said.

They gathered up the salvaged clothing and equipment and carried it up to the generator hut. It was plain that there wouldn't be enough room for everyone because the field supplies and camp equipment were stored there. The only other intact structure was the new skidoo shelter, so Phil drove the skidoos out and they ducked inside. They squeezed together in a double row and sank down with their backs to the sloping walls. Russell lit a Tilley lamp, and they huddled together, shivering.

Richard raised his head. He said in a flat voice, 'Niki? Can we make radio contact?'

'I don't yet know. I must have daylight.'

Richard continued his muttering. 'Making contact with Santa Ana is the first priority. Until then, shelter, warmth, hot drinks, food.'

'There's the field supplies and Primus stoves,' Russell offered.

'All right. Yes. We'll use those. And we'll wait until daylight.'

It was as if, Alice thought, none of this night's events had come as a surprise to him. Dismay rushed down her spine. It must have been Richard who had started the fire, accidentally or otherwise. He had been lighting candles again, trying with his distorted logic to conserve fuel. What was he thinking? That this was what Antarctica did—it drove you to the edge of the ability to survive and then cruelly tipped you over?

Anger surged through Alice. 'Why are we just *sitting* here? We've got gas and food.' She began to scramble to her feet.

Rooker had shaken off his reverie of horror, whatever had caused it. His glance leapt at hers and for an instant their eyes locked. 'I'm going for the supplies,' he said. The shed door opened on a curtain of smoke.

'Look at you,' Laure cried. She eased back Alice's sleeve and revealed a long gash in her forearm. Alice gazed at it in surprise.

'Needs a stitch or two, I'd say.' Phil's warm Welsh voice seemed to come from a distant place. But the medical supplies were all gone.

Rook came back with a Primus, a set of camping pans and some boxes of dried field rations. Russ crawled outside to the pipeline and a minute later there was the smell of gas and the hiss of blue flame.

'We've got fourteen two-man days,' Rooker reported.

Enough food, just about, for three days for all of them.

'Gas?' Valentin asked.

'Four cylinders after this one.'

Russ and Phil exchanged looks. It would take a lot of gas to cook for nine people.

Arturo kneeled upright and began opening the ration boxes. He found a set of packet soups and poured the contents into the pan of water. 'It will be enough,' he said calmly.

Gratefully, they drank the hot soup. Valentin and Niki murmured to each other in Russian. Russell was silent and sombre, and Phil gazed into space. It was Arturo who had handed the soup mugs round with a smile of encouragement. Rooker looked as if he were sitting at the mess table on any ordinary night. Alice reflected that his impassivity must have been developed in childhood as a form of self-defence. So what could he have seen in the hut flames that transfixed him with such horror?

She wanted to go and kneel beside him, to take his huge hands between hers and rub warmth into them both, but she couldn't do it with seven pairs of eyes on them.

114

Everyone else hungrily finished their soup, but Richard hadn't even picked up his.

'You do not want?' Arturo gently asked.

Seeming to rouse himself, Richard reached out one hand, but the fingers were tightly curled and he couldn't grasp the handle.

'Let's have a look,' Phil demanded.

Richard made to withdraw but Phil caught his wrist and turned the hand palm-up. It was burned and blistered raw, with the seared flesh curling and hanging in loose shreds. Phil drew in a breath and reached for the other hand. It was the same.

'I was trying to save my gastropod,' Richard said in the strange flat voice. 'But Rooker came and dragged me out.'

They had looked as if they were fighting, Alice remembered. 'It's a fossil,' she repeated in a high, hard voice. 'It's not worth a life.'

Rooker had risked his for Richard. Awe and admiration and another feeling, hot and wild, flooded through her. She wanted to look at Rooker but she dared not.

'We'll have to try and dress those,' Phil muttered. He was staring around at the puddled floor and the crowded bodies. 'What's clean?'

'I know,' Laure cried. She began pulling off her parka, then the layers of down and fleece beneath. The innermost layer was a white long-sleeved vest with a tiny frill of lace. Without hesitation she stripped that off too. Her bra was underwired, pale-pink and lacy.

'Christ. My first sight of a real live woman in her bra in five months and I'm busy ripping up her vest for bandages,' Phil said.

Valentin laughed, and a second later they were all wildly giggling. Richard only stared blankly at them.

Laure scrambled back into her outer clothes. Water was boiled and allowed to cool, then she and Russ did their best to clean Richard's burns and wind strips of bandage round them. While the attention was on this, Alice dared to turn her head and at once met Rooker's eyes. To her surprise he smiled, a smile full of warmth and understanding.

Rooker wasn't afraid. And if she was with him, she realised, she didn't fear anything either.

'Aleece, now you,' Laure said.

They sponged away the blood and dirt, then tightly bound her arm.

There was nothing left for them to do but try to sleep. Alice felt the baby languorously move. Relief that it was unaffected by the night's exertions made her want to jump up. She clambered over the legs and torsos to reach the door and half fell out into the darkness.

Russell and Phil had put a half-barrel in the loose snow a few yards

115

past the shelter. As she used it she heard the start of a distant low moaning that steadily rose in volume. It was the wind getting up. Some bad weather was coming in the wake of the brief lull.

She plodded back towards the shelter with the wind already tugging at the loose flaps of her parka. Rooker was standing in her path.

'If you're looking for the bathroom . . .' She smiled, pointing back the way she had come to cover up the wild leap of her heart.

His answer was to put his hands inside her hood and cup her face. 'You came for me. The hut was on fire and you came to look for me.'

So he knew she had been searching for him, not Richard. That was good. 'You did the same for him,' she said quietly.

He bent his head so that his mouth came even closer. He shielded her from the wind, and blotted out the sky and the iron-hard glitter of the stars. 'You can't know how much that means to me.'

'I was afraid . . . I was so fearful that you might be hurt.'

The truth of this seemed enormous, swelling up and washing over her. *I feared that the smallest part of you might be hurt or damaged, that you might be taken away before I had even the chance to tell you so.*

He kissed her, holding her in a tight lock, as if he expected her to run away. But Alice stood on tiptoe to reach closer to him, greedily and blindly kissing him back, and everything else in the frozen world stood still as if time itself had frozen too.

She didn't know how long they stayed locked together, buffered by all their clothes. At last he raised his head, still holding her face between his warm hands.

'Thank you,' he said in a voice she had never heard him use before.

She suddenly remembered his exquisite driftwood carving of a baby. It had been in her locker, with the Polaroid of Pete and *Desiderata*. 'Your Christmas carving. It's gone.'

'I'll do you another,' he promised. They were only inanimate things.

He took her left hand, gently because of her gashed arm, and led her back to the tin shelter. The Tilley lamp had been turned out, and in the darkness Alice patted with her hand and discovered Laure's shoulder. She slid into a space alongside her. Rook folded himself into the draughty slot between Alice and the door. They settled in a sitting position with their backs against the ridged wall, shoulders and hips touching, hand searching for, then clasping, the other's. Alice couldn't even think of sleep. Her heart was knocking too hard, and disbelief and desire and wild excitement chased each other through her thoughts. She wished that she could hear what he was thinking. There would be time, she promised herself, when all this was over.

Alice opened her eyes. She had drifted into sleep at some point and every inch of her body ached with cold and from lying on the hard floor, although someone had tucked a blanket round her. Rook.

Wincing, she twisted her head to look for him, but the only other person in the shelter was Laure. She lay fast asleep with her knees drawn up to her chest and her head in Alice's lap. She stirred and abruptly came to full consciousness.

'Aleece?' she breathed. She turned to gaze up, her ear pressed hard against Alice's belly. Alice saw confusion, speculation and amazed certainty widening the other woman's eyes. Laure had heard the rapid tick-tick of the baby's heartbeat. Now she slipped her hand under Alice's parka and explored the taut dome of her belly. '*Ce n'est pas possible. Tu es . . ?*'

Alice slowly nodded.

'*Mais, personne sait pas?*'

'No,' Alice agreed.

Laure's hand came up to her mouth. 'My God. *You* did not know?'

'Not when I arrived, no.'

'And now we are trapped, and there is no doctor and no good shelter, and what if we must stay here for the whole winter?'

Alice took Laure's hand and reassuringly squeezed it. 'The baby won't come yet. They'll get the helo in in a couple of days and we'll be on the ship and back in the world in no time.' A wild, reckless happiness was singing under her skin. With the memory of Rook and last night in her head it was as if she had found something she had searched for all her life. Nothing could touch her now.

Laure rocked back on her heels. She stared at Alice in utter disbelief. 'I thought you were cool and sensible. But you are not. You are crazy.'

There was the sound of banging outside the tin door. It swung open and Phil and Russ crawled into the shelter. Alice just had time to raise one finger to her lips in a stern, forbidding gesture to Laure.

'He's lost it. Just totally lost it,' Phil was saying. 'He's marching around like a robot, giving orders, then dropping to his knees in the ashes and scrabbling with his bandaged hands for some fossil.'

Russell's mouth set in a line. He said, 'I reckon maybe Richard is having some kind of a mental breakdown.'

Alice set a pot of water on the gas. She thought that they had probably all guessed as much. She sprinkled porridge oats into the water.

The next arrival was Richard himself. Snow and ash were mixed in his beard, and his lips were cracked and bloody under the soot. He wedged the mug of porridge that Alice gave him between his knees. With the fingertips of his right hand he could just about manipulate a spoon.

Arturo came in. 'It is not the best weather for putting up radio antennae,' he said. Of all of them, Alice thought, apart from Rook, Arturo was handling this best. He sat down in front of Richard and took the mug from him. As if it were the most natural thing in the world, he began to feed him spoonfuls of porridge. Afterwards Arturo wiped the remnants from his beard as if Richard were a child. 'You were awake all night. You should sleep now,' he advised him. 'You will work better after sleep.'

Richard nodded his head. Obediently he turned sideways and curled himself up under a blanket.

The first batch of porridge was finished. Alice went for more water, but as soon as she was outside the blizzard assaulted her. She could just discern the struggling shapes of Rook and Valentin. Bent almost double against the wind, they were fighting to re-erect a pole for the antennae. As soon as they raised it to the vertical and tried to anchor it with guy lines, the pegs tore loose and the pole toppled again.

Rooker didn't see Alice until she grabbed at his arm. 'Let me help,' she yelled.

'No. We'll have to wait until the wind drops.'

'Come and get some hot food.'

Laure had made more porridge, and Rooker and Valentin ate. Richard was buried under his blanket and Arturo was nodding off too. A heavy silence spread until Niki pushed his way in.

'What d'you reckon?' Russell asked.

'I think, maybe,' he answered. Phil gave a little whoop of satisfaction and Laure clapped her mittened hands. 'And since we have not made this morning's radio schedule with Santa Ana they will know now that we have some problem. But for making contact I must of course have antenna in place, and for now . . .' His shrug was expressive.

Time passed very slowly. Their confinement was miserably uncomfortable, and they had no books, not even a pack of cards. Food was strictly rationed. They ate an evening meal of soup and two crackers apiece.

Alice sat quietly, occasionally shifting her weight on the hard floor. It was peculiar to think of happiness in connection with their present plight, or to feel ambivalent about the idea of rescue, but each minute that slipped away brought closer the moment when she might have to part with Rook. Even though they hadn't exchanged a single private word throughout the day, he was still close enough to touch. She felt his nearness prickle her thin skin through the foul layers of her clothes.

Richard went outside before the light faded and in his absence they agreed in low voices that all they could do was keep a watch on him. Phil went out too, ostensibly to stretch his legs.

When Richard came back, the state of his hands told them that he had been sifting through the debris again.

The night was even longer and more painful than the day, but the Tilley lamp was blown out and Alice and Rooker were able to sit with their hands linked.

No one slept very much. The talk murmured between them.

'In the village where I come from, in the mountains in northern Bulgaria, the houses all are carved in wood,' Valentin said. 'It is a picture. The lakes are full of fish, and the wild honey . . . ah.'

Laure whispered, 'When I was a small girl, our family holidays were every year in Arcachon, near Bordeaux. In this place there is the biggest sand dune in the world. I remember slip-sliding from the top to the bottom, and near the foot of it there is a small seafood restaurant. Here you can eat *soupe de poisson* that is the best I have ever tasted.'

Phil gave a deep sigh. 'A long day's climbing. The rock hot from the sun, jelly legs, a big thirst on. Sit down outside the pub and take the first pull on the first pint of the night. That's the best taste in the world.'

'Rook?' Laure said out of the dark.

'No,' he said. Nothing else. Alice held on to his hand.

The second morning's weather was no improvement on the first. In the generator shed a makeshift radio table had been rigged up and Niki had reassembled the radio components. After three missed schedules with Santa Ana there would now be concern, but until the wind decreased and the visibility improved there was no chance that they would mount an air reconnaissance.

They ate the last of the porridge and some chocolate.

Richard told them about his grandfather's march with Captain Scott and his raggle-taggle teams of ponies to the foot of the Beardmore Glacier, beneath Mount Shoesmith, where the ponies were finally butchered to feed the dogs on the onward journey. 'My grandfather shot his pony after a day on soft snow. He wrote in his diary that Samuel enjoyed his last feed and, until the last days when the severity of the constant blizzards wore him out, he had pulled with all his heart.'

They all listened in silence. Richard sat with his head thrown back against the shed wall. There were tears in his eyes.

As the light faded again, the wind seemed to give a sigh of exhaustion. An hour after that there was no more banging and battering against the hut walls. The men filed outside to try to erect the pole.

'Are you all right?' Laure demanded as soon as they were alone.

'I'm fine,' Alice said. There were strange ripples of pressure chasing across her belly. Braxton Hicks practice contractions, she remembered from her website reading. It was very early to be having them.

Alice scrambled outside to see if she could help. They were working by torchlight, digging a pit for the pole and clearing snow for ice screws to secure the guy wires. Another pole was raised against the generator hut. Phil and Rook climbed up on the hut roof to ravel a cat's cradle of loops between the two poles. Niki was already at the table inside the hut. There was a series of crackles interspersed with flat silences.

Niki's long fingers minutely tuned the signal. He began calling, 'Santa Ana, Santa Ana, this is Kandahar Station. Do you read me? Over.' The airwaves were a buzz of interference. 'Santa Ana, Santa Ana. Kandahar Station, do you read me? Over.' Nothing came back but scribbled noise.

Niki was patient. 'I will keep trying. What more can we do?'

Valentin and Russ and Phil hovered in the hut. Richard broke away as if he couldn't listen any longer. He blundered back to the skidoo shelter, and Arturo patiently followed him.

Alice and Rooker stood outside in the billowing snow. Now that they had the opportunity, there was too much to say. Rooker was remembering trying to drag Shoesmith away from the fire. His skin crawled with fear. Fire was the worst thing he could think of. Fire and Lester.

Then he had looked up and seen Alice at the window, heard her shouting his name. She had come because of him, not Richard, and that flash of grateful recognition set off a chain of realisation.

He *wanted* her, this stocky, determined little English scientist with her quiet voice that made you listen. Not just her unseen body, although he desired that too. He wanted to touch her and learn about her and hear her talking just for him, and the wish had been in him from almost the beginning, when she had stumbled over him out on the rocks. He had been drunk in an attempt to forget himself and her stillness had been like a cool hand on his burning head. She was courageous and stoical and clear-minded, and yet he sensed there were undercurrents of passion in her that ran like molten precious metal. Out of all the women he had known over all the years, he had never met one like her.

He had been angry with Shoesmith partly because he was jealous.

It had seemed that she might favour *him*, of all people.

But she came back to the burning hut for his sake. She had kissed him, and he had tasted smoke and tears on her skin, and they had sat for two endless and still too-short nights with their hands joined.

Rooker smiled down into her eyes.

Alice saw his face with the frown and the cynical glare melted away. There was just him and she felt a beat of wondering love.

'I am afraid of fire,' he confessed.

'You don't fear anything else. What is it about fire?'

He was very still. After what seemed like a long time, he said, 'A friend of my mother's died in a fire.'

Jimmy came home from school one afternoon to find his mother and Lester both wearing bathing caps. The rubber caps were poked full of holes and there were hanks of gluey hair sticking out. They were even wearing the same lipstick, smudged from boozing.

'We're highlighting our hair, darling. Blonde streaks,' she said.

Lester tilted his head and kiss-pursed his lips. He rested his rubber-gloved fists on his snake hips. 'What do you think, darling?' he cooed.

He was always in the house nowadays. Every evening: watching TV, drinking and giggling, painting her toenails, dressing her up.

'Fuck off,' Jimmy spat at him.

'Jimmy, don't be rude. Come on, sit down with us and have a chat. Tell me about'—her eyes flicked to Lester and back again—'school.'

'Is there anything to eat?' Jimmy asked.

'I expect so, darling. Have a look in the fridge, eh?'

Jimmy knew that there was no point, but he went anyway. Then he sat in his bedroom, staring out of the window. There was a science test tomorrow, but he made no attempt to open his school bag. After a while he stood up again and went along to the bathroom to pee.

Behind him, the door slid open. He looked in the mirror and saw Lester.

Lester was smiling, a big wet smile of pleading and fake friendliness that turned Jimmy's stomach. 'Hey, Jim. Hey, there?' he said softly. There was the funny look in his eyes that always came when he was drunk.

Jimmy whirled round, but as he tried to wriggle past Lester caught hold of him, and then his wet mouth was pressed to Jimmy's. His sloppy tongue probed between his teeth. Jimmy bit hard and then, as Lester recoiled, he brought his knee up between his legs. Lester folded up and slid to the floor, gasping. Jimmy stepped over him and walked to the kitchen. There was a two-thirds-full bottle of whisky next to the bread bin. He stuffed it into the pocket of his coat.

'Lester? Le-ess?' his mother called blurrily from the sofa.

Jimmy walked out of the back door. The tight, hot feeling in his chest made him want to smack his fist against the nearest fence. He walked down the river path and sat on a log. He unscrewed the cap of the whisky bottle and took a long swallow. Later he tried to cry, but his eyes stayed dry and prickly. He sat there until it got dark, thinking of Lester in his house with his mother. Disgust at the memory of Lester's tongue rose in his throat, fighting with the whisky fumes. Jimmy stood up abruptly. The path rose under his feet and tipped him sideways so that he almost fell into the river, but he staggered and managed to right himself.

Lester lived in a caravan beyond a row of farm outbuildings at the edge of town. Jimmy and Gabby had played around outside when they knew Lester was out. They had also snooped through the outbuildings. There was an old petrol-driven lawn mower in one of them, and a mouldy shelf with jerry cans and tins and canisters on it. One of the bigger cans was almost full of petrol.

Jimmy yanked the stuffing out of some old cushions that were piled in the corner of the end shed, and fed all of it through the letter box low down in the door of Lester's caravan. Then he poured petrol in on top. He lit a match and poked that in as well.

There was an immediate huge *boom* followed by a whoosh of flame that came licking out of the slot. It was a cold night and Jimmy had his woolly gloves on. He snapped them off and shoved them into the fire. As he walked away he heard the flames whipping and cracking.

He took the back route home. He expected to find the two of them sitting where he had left them, but the house was utterly silent.

'Mum?' He clicked the light on in the living room and saw her lying asleep on the couch.

Lester wasn't anywhere in the house. Jimmy left his mother where she was and crept silently to bed.

There was a police investigation into Lester Furneaux's death, but no one was ever arrested for setting the fire. There was some question of whether the petrol had actually been stored in the caravan, and whether Lester might have fallen asleep and left a cigarette burning. He was known to drink heavily. Queers like him were not popular or welcome in Turner, South Island, in the 1950s.

Two months later, Mrs Annette Rooker committed suicide by pulling a one-bar electric fire into her bath. She left a short note saying that she felt too lonely to go on. She apologised to her son, Jimmy, and wrote that his uncle, Henry Jerrold, would look after him. He was to be a good boy in England.

Alice was looking at him. She was waiting and listening, but not wanting to force him to say something he preferred to keep back.

'Are you cold?' he asked, just to fill the moment.

She shook her head quickly. 'Rook, I want to tell you something.'

Then there was a huge yell from the generator hut. The door flew open. 'We've got 'em!' Phil bawled.

CHAPTER EIGHT

SANTA ANA HAD been trying to contact Kandahar for thirty-six hours. But they had assumed that the prolonged radio silence was due to a technical malfunction, never imagining a disaster on the scale of the fire.

Niki's headset was clamped to his head and the mike to his lips. 'Some minor injuries only,' he was repeating. 'But the hut is gone. We are seriously short of food and gas. Shelter is limited. Over.'

They were going to be rescued. Everything would be all right, in spite of the risks Alice had taken. At first she felt a hot surge of relief, but after the first seconds her euphoria was dampened by a wave of sadness. She would be leaving the ice, probably for ever. And what about Rooker? Where and how could they ever be together beyond Kandahar?

The first news was that *Polar Star* had arrived and was waiting for them out in open water. There was a cheer at this. Richard had seized the mike. He impatiently gestured for quiet. He was telling the Chilean expedition leader that he needed the helicopters to be ordered out as soon as possible, to lift the Kandahar personnel to a point out on the ice margin from which the *Polar Star*'s Zodiacs could reach them.

The Chilean leader's response was concerned but conservative. He was not prepared to risk both helicopters in a hazardous mission—one would have to remain at Santa Ana as a safety back-up. The Squirrel only carried four passengers so it would have to make three return journeys to the ship, unless some people made the difficult journey out over the ice by skidoo. The immediate weather forecast was bad, he said, so it was unlikely in any event that the pilots would be able to leave for at least another twenty-four hours.

It was arranged that they would maintain four-hourly radio contact.

'Good luck,' Santa Ana said in signing off.

Everyone was smiling and clasping hands, and patting Niki on the back. 'Top man, Nik. Antarctic hero, in fact,' Phil crowed.

Richard nodded. 'It's good,' he kept repeating, but the group's relief and elation didn't seem to touch him. Alice watched him duck outside and after a minute she followed.

'Richard?'

He looked round briefly. 'I've failed,' he said.

'No, you haven't. No one's hurt, we did our work, we completed the season. The fire was an accident, it's one of those things that just happen.'

If you light dozens of candles in a wooden hut where the atmosphere is so dry that it crackles with static electricity, she thought, and she knew he could hear her thinking it. Richard said no more, but as she studied his face she saw the depths of his misery and self-disgust.

'All that matters is the power of the human spirit,' she whispered fiercely. 'You of all people should know that. Scott and your grandfather and the others on that expedition were beaten to the Pole and five of them died, but their heroism and will to survive is what the world remembers.'

'Don't ever speak of this and my grandfather in the same breath,' Richard begged her.

Alice cast around for something positive she could offer him. All the scientists' notes and papers had been burned, their laptop computers and Arturo's weather records and Jochen's incomplete human physiological data. Valentin's ice-core sections had survived along with Laure's penguin samples, buried in the ice cave, but she felt that this comfort was too meagre to offer. Their own rock samples were unaffected by a mere fire, although they were of little scientific value since all the plastic sample bags and labels had melted. Richard's hours of scratching through the debris had not uncovered the lost Gastropoda.

It suddenly came to her that there was one thing she could say that might make a difference. 'You are still expedition leader. Lead us. Lead us out of here,' she challenged him.

For a moment it seemed that he hadn't heard. But then he straightened up and lifted his head. 'Yes,' he said.

Alice became aware that there was one other person loitering outside in the searing cold, while the others had squeezed back into the shelter. It was Rooker. He would not deal well with being made to feel jealous, now or ever. The thought reassured her rather than the opposite. Richard swung past Rook without even looking at him.

'We should get some food while there's some left,' Alice said.

'You were going to tell me something.'

She took a breath, an opportunity to consider. 'I will,' she assured him. The helicopter would lift them across the barrier of ice to the ship and safety. That would be the time to tell him, not here and now outside a hut full of ears and eyes.

'Is that a promise?' He didn't smile and his expression was wary. He had been told too many things in his time that were not good news.

'Yes,' Alice said.

The forecast for the next afternoon and evening was for light winds and improving visibility. Niki had spoken by radio to the captain of *Polar Star*. The ship lay fourteen miles northwest of Kandahar, in open water beyond the unseasonal ice. When the helicopter was ready to begin the evacuation, the ship would nose deeper into the pack to bring the Zodiacs within range of ice solid enough for the Squirrel to land on.

'They wait for us,' Niki confirmed, nodding in satisfaction.

When he came back with filled water canisters, Russell announced that the water supply was slowing to a trickle, either because the pipeline was freezing up or because the glacier lake itself was turning to ice.

'We've only got a few more hours to go,' Rook rallied them. There were just two full camping canisters of gas left. Without running water, they would have to melt snow for drinking. The gas wouldn't last long under those circumstances.

Reluctantly, they settled as best they could for the third night in their cramped shelter. Alice half lay and half sat propped against the icy wall between Laure and Rooker. Rooker's arm came round her shoulders and she let her face rest against him.

An hour passed. Rook's grip on her loosened. He had fallen asleep. Alice tried to relax her limbs but they were knotted with cold. She was shivering. She told herself: Don't be afraid now, when we are about to escape.

A bigger shudder swept over her, crawled inwards from her knees and elbows, intensified and found a focus in her belly. It turned into a definite knot of pain that made her gasp. Her eyes widened. As abruptly as it had come, the pain faded away again.

No, she thought. This can't be.

Cramp. Indigestion. Food poisoning. Surely one of those?

Long minutes passed; maybe ten or more. Her shoulders finally sagged and her clenched fists uncurled.

Then it came again. An insistent wave that tightened until she stared, then rolled away and left her prickling with sweat and horror.

Breathe. Think. If this was the onset of labour, what did that mean?

The birth of a baby, several weeks premature, in this place?

No doctor, no medical supplies, no heat, severely limited water.

Polar Star was just a dozen or so miles away. Wait, hope. Daylight and the helicopter would come. It became a mantra as she sat and stared at the whirling infinity of darkness. Daylight, the helicopter.

The radio shift changed. Rooker and Valentin yawned and crawled out into the painful cold, Niki and Arturo bundled back in their place. When the others come back, she calculated, there will be just four more hours until dawn. Then she would beg Phil and Russ to radio Santa Ana and call for the helicopter to leave at first light. If the weather was right.

The contractions intensified by stealthy bounds. It became as much as she could do not to cry out as the latest one reached its height. Droplets of cold sweat stood out on her forehead.

The intervals were now much less than ten minutes.

She heard the sound of boots kicking the ice outside the door, then Valentin's head appeared. The shift was changing. Where was Rook?

Phil and Russell blundered over the recumbent bodies and made their exit. A big shadow slipped in after them. Rook, thank God.

Another contraction started. This time there was no beginning to it, no time to prepare herself. The pain caught her full on and she cried out. Rooker took hold of her shoulders; Laure reared up and snapped on her head torch. The beam shone full in Alice's face. '*Aleece!*'

The other sleepers were muttering and stirring. Alice realised how bad she must look from the way Laure sucked in her breath so sharply.

'What?' Rooker demanded in a new, raw voice. 'Alice?'

'She is pregnant,' Laure hissed. 'That is *what. Dîtes-moi, Aleece. Vite.*'

'It has started,' Alice said wearily.

Through his hands that were still supporting her, she felt the physical impact of these two pieces of information on Rooker. His body jolted as if he had been punched in the diaphragm.

'What's that? She cannot be pregnant. It's not possible.' Richard's loud, shocked voice sawed through her head.

'She is,' Laure said curtly. She was kneeling over her, gentle hands trying to loosen her clothes.

Rooker drew Alice closer so that she rested against him. 'Radio Santa Ana for help. Tell them just to get here,' he said over her head. Niki was already moving.

Richard spoke: 'Rooker, I suppose this is your doing, is it?'

'Shoesmith.' Rooker's voice was low, but there was a note in it that made everyone in the shelter breathe in. 'This is nothing to do with me, you piece of shit. Even if it were, it's none of your business. So keep the fuck out of it. If you so much as try to touch her, I will rip you to pieces.'

Richard seemed to shrivel. 'She can't give birth to a baby here,' he babbled. 'This is a scientific research station.'

'Or was. Until you burned it down,' Rooker said.

Phil bumped in through the doorway. The habitual merriment had drained from his face. 'Nik and Russ are trying to raise Santa Ana. Alice, can you . . .?' But the question faded away as he looked from her to Rooker and Laure. He whispered, 'I don't know what to do with her. I've only got mountain first-aid training.'

126

'She is going to be fine,' Rooker said.

Alice struggled to sit upright. She wanted to move. 'Let me,' she muttered to Rook and he understood at once.

He helped her to roll onto all fours. The door of the shelter stood ajar, and beyond it there was black emptiness. She crawled towards the ebony slice of pure air. Rooker supported her and they broke out of the shelter together. As she stood upright the cold seared her throat.

'What do you need?'

'I want to move around. It's . . .' Another contraction took all her attention. But it was easier, better when she was moving around than lying inert and helpless in the smelly hut.

'I'm here,' he said calmly. 'Hold on to me.'

Laure materialised at her other side. Another arm came round her waist. They took one and then two small steps in the greasy snow.

A round head bobbed at the door of the generator shed. Russell called out, 'Santa Ana say that they'll be airborne as soon as they can. *Polar Star*'s standing by as well.'

'Aleece?' Laure urgently whispered. 'Can you tell me how many weeks you think you could be?'

'I worked it out. You know, when I realised. I thought by now, twenty-six. But I must have been wrong. Two months wrong, probably. It could be . . . Perhaps thirty-four weeks. *Oh . . .*'

They stopped their pacing and two pairs of arms supported her as the claws of pain dug in again.

'What does that mean, Laure?' Rook demanded.

'I am not certain. I am only a biologist. But I believe that a baby at thirty-four weeks has a chance to survive. It will be small, but if there are no breathing difficulties and it can be kept warm . . .'

There was a second's silence.

Rooker placed himself squarely in front of her. 'We'll get you out to the ship. There's a doctor on *Polar Star*, oxygen, everything. Alice, I promise.'

The grey light of the rapid polar dawn was flooding towards them over the snow. Alice held on to Rooker's hands and looked into his eyes. She could feel the slow vice grip of another contraction beginning. The need for reassurance, *his* reassurance, made her ask him in a voice that was hardly more than a gasp, 'How do you know?'

Rooker didn't move. He bent his head so he could see her better. He felt a pressure to speak that was too strong to resist. He had to tell her something he had never told anyone else.

He saw Alice's face beginning to screw up in a mask of concentration as the pain flowered yet again. If he didn't speak now, this minute, it might be too late and all the blocked avenues and dead ends of the past would come together to make one huge impenetrable dark obstacle, and that would be his life, and there would never be the light and the sunshine that he was stumbling towards in this polar dawn.

'I know, because I love you,' he said.

'Ah, *ah*.' Alice threw her head back and moaned aloud.

'Breathe, Aleece. Breathe big, like this, *whoo whooooo*,' Laure gabbled.

'Because I love you,' Rooker repeated. The words were like a foreign language, scratchy and unwieldy on his tongue, but he had uttered them.

Alice was smiling a wide, drunken smile and her face was wet with tears. 'I love you too,' she whispered. 'Don't leave me.'

Memories punctured Rooker's absorption in this shining moment and all the old black shadows came flooding in on him. 'I won't leave you,' he murmured. 'Not until you and the baby are safe.'

Richard unfolded himself from the skidoo shelter. 'What's happening? What's happening?' he demanded.

'What do you think? We are taking care of her,' Laure snapped.

Valentin came and draped his huge parka over the top of Alice's.

Phil brought his sheepskin hat, the warmest any of them owned, and awkwardly pulled it down over her cap. 'I don't know what to do,' he repeated. To be caught without practical resources was hard for him.

'Thank you, thank you,' Alice dazedly muttered. The familiar faces swam in and out of her sightline. She was grateful but her body was taking over; all her attention becoming fixed on the huge task at hand. 'Walk,' she begged, and they resumed their small, shuffling steps.

Niki burst out of the generator hut with his headset askew. 'They are airborne, just now,' he yelled.

The time passed, a long unmeasured crawl, as the helicopter steadily flew south towards Kandahar.

Alice stared down through the fog of agony. Nothing could have prepared her for this. Her vision blurred, then cleared again. She could suddenly see in minute detail. Between her feet there were snowflakes and crystals, tiny prisms and intricate facets more opulent than the most precious jewels, silvery furrows that trapped blue and amethyst shadows. It was a miniature Antarctica that held all the variety and wonder of the harsh immensity that had seduced her.

Antarctica, Antarctica.

The syllables formed a new mantra, rolling and tapping in her head as she tried to breathe instead of drowning in the infinite sea of pain. She was moaning and sobbing, beyond any shred of pride or dignity.

Once she caught sight of Valentin biting the knuckles of his own hand, and there was Arturo, watching with his arms wrapped round himself as if for protection against this raw femaleness. Russ and Phil grimly waited; Niki was on the radio. Richard stood to one side, alone.

'Listen,' Phil yelled.

Alice's head drooped but the others' jerked up in unison. It was the unmistakable distant buzz of the helicopter.

Rooker allowed himself a backward glance, over his shoulder towards the sea ice and the distance that shrouded *Polar Star*.

What he saw, what he didn't see, almost stopped his heart.

There was no berg visible in the bay. There was no bay at all, just a wall of thick grey sea mist, stealthily rolling in on them. Moist, cold air that would condense and turn to a layer of ice on whatever it touched.

Ahead, in the direction of Santa Ana, the sky was clouded but the air was still clear. A black dot had materialised against the greyness. As they gazed upwards, their exposed faces stinging from the whirl of ice crystals whipped up by the blades, the mist was already billowing over the ruins of Kandahar. The machine hovered, then slowly sank to the ground.

The pilot leapt out. It was Andy. 'How is she?'

'I think not long,' Laure said.

Rooker hoisted Alice towards the helicopter. He knew there wasn't even one second to spare. 'Let's go,' he was shouting.

Alice found herself in the rear seat of the Squirrel. A different feeling swept over her. 'Need to push.' She thought she was saying it aloud, but the words didn't escape her mouth. 'Help me.'

Andy shouted, 'I can't take off now. Look at the mist.'

Laure had had one foot on the door sill, ready to scramble in after Alice. Now she hesitated, then slowly stepped back down to the ice.

Rooker ran to Andy. 'Get in now. Fly it.'

Andy swept his hand towards the mist. 'It would be suicide . . .'

'I'll fly it myself,' Rooker shouted.

He swung round and made for the Squirrel. Richard and Andy grabbed his arms but he shook them off like flies. A second later he was buckling himself into the pilot's seat.

'Stop him,' Richard howled at the Kandahar people. But without any conferring a collective impulse had taken hold of the team. It was Richard they moved in on. Valentin and Phil pinioned his arms, the others blocked his path. Richard struggled but he was outnumbered. The astonished pilot stood aside, his mouth hanging open.

Inside the Squirrel, Rooker deliberately slowed his mind to make a series of cold calculations. Ice. It was ice that could kill them, just as always. The helicopter had been on the ground for no more than three or four minutes, but already the thick, wet mist was beginning to freeze on the fuselage and blades. Once the Squirrel was iced up, takeoff would be impossible. He had to get airborne right now, fly Alice to the ice margin and get her into the *Polar Star*'s Zodiac, then bring the Squirrel back to Kandahar. The mist was thickening, but he rated his chances higher than Andy's. He knew the terrain around the base more intimately.

Fly. He could fly; it was in him, his first instructor had told him so.

'*Rook*.' There was raw desperation in her voice.

'I'm going to pilot us.'

'Do you know how to?'

'Of course I do.'

He ran his eyes over the instruments and controls. Yes. Switch on batteries and fuel pump, check voltage, start up both engines. The blades shivered and obediently spun. He gave the engines a thirty-second warmup, accelerating towards flying speed, then raised the collective lever. The machine lifted as if it were tiptoeing on the snow. The skids were free. Rooker accelerated and lifted into a low hover. They were airborne.

The helicopter swung in a tight circle and headed out over the sea ice. Rooker needed every particle of concentration for flying and navigation by instruments alone. It was like being airborne in a bowl of milk. At 110 metres a dirty-yellow glimmer began to suffuse the milk. A few seconds later they rose out of the fog bank into thin sunshine. Fourteen miles to the northeast somewhere lay *Polar Star*.

Rooker lifted the pilot's headset and pulled it over his head. At once Niki's thick voice filled his ears with directions. It was good. He was dead on course for the ship.

'The Zodiac is launched. They look for you on the ice,' Niki said.

Rook had a second's respite now to look over his shoulder to Alice. Her eyes were starting, and her face was shiny with sweat and tears.

'It's coming. Help me.'

'Hold on.'

'I can't. Stop. Please, stop.'

The wind was getting up. Below them, the mist was streaming in thin tatters. Rooker caught a glimpse of the ridged pack ice far beneath. He eased the Squirrel back into a descent. The ice loomed up to meet him. He searched desperately for a smooth trough between the ragged frozen waves. Then he caught sight of a flat grey saucer, little more in diameter than the Squirrel itself. Hardly able to breathe, he hovered, and with a wordless prayer put the helicopter down. The ice surface held.

Alice was making low noises in her throat. He told her to lie back across the rear seats and bend her knees. Struggling in the awkward space, they dragged down her torn windproofs and soaked underlayers.

Rooker shouted into the headset mouthpiece, 'Polar Star, Polar Star?'

He could see the baby's head. It was wet and black, and netted with blood and mucus. Alice was staring and pushing.

A Spanish voice broke in on him: 'NZ two-zero, do you read me? What is happening, please?'

'The baby is being born. I can see the head.'

'OK. Listen to me. Let her push. Put your left hand on the baby's head, use your right hand to support the mother's tissues underneath.'

It was the Polar Star's doctor. Rook did as he was told but he could see that Alice's body knew what to do. She had stopped groaning and the terror had faded out of her eyes. Now there was a fierce light of absolute determination. Through his hands Rook felt the clench of muscles as the baby's head was born. He cupped his hand to support and protect it, gazing down in wonder at the tiny features.

Here was a new person, a whole new life beginning in this instant.

He had never known anything so natural and simple, yet so momentous. He had to stare even harder to keep his tears from blinding him.

'Is it there?' Alice whispered.

'I can see its face.'

'Again,' she panted, then gave a long wail of triumphant effort.

Gently, Rooker eased out the slippery hunched shoulders and the folded limbs. The baby lay in his two palms, wet with blood and amniotic fluid. She opened her deep, dark eyes and gave a tiny ragged cry.

'It's a girl.'

'Margaret,' Alice said. They were both weeping.

Rooker lifted the tiny creature and laid her on Alice's belly, then stripped off his parka and fleece jacket and tucked it over them.

Alice was laughing as well as crying. 'Meg,' she was murmuring.

Rook looked for the helicopter's emergency survival kit. He broke the seal, tore off the lid and shook out the silvery folds of an insulated bivouac shelter. He wrapped that over and round the baby as well.

'The baby's born,' he said into the headset. 'What do I do now?'

The doctor advised him how to deliver the placenta, and Rooker did as he was told. 'Don't try to cut the cord,' the voice ordered. So he wrapped the baby and the cord and the afterbirth in a warm bloody muddle against Alice's body. 'Now you fly them out to us,' the doctor said. 'Good luck.'

Rooker quickly leaned over Alice. 'You did well. Are you ready?'

'I'm ready.' Her face was soft and beautiful, and full of trust.

'Good. Let's go.'

He opened the door and clambered down onto the pack. He couldn't try to lift off again without checking to see how much ice had formed on the Squirrel. And what he saw next made his throat close and his hands shake. There was a dark, serpentine thread winding through the ivory and grey monotony of the pack ice, a little crack through which water came welling up. The weight of the Squirrel had depressed the flat floe and the sea water had flooded up over the skids. And now it had frozen over them in a thin, glassy layer of pure menace.

He climbed back into the pilot's seat, shivering. All he could do was use the engine power to break the seal of ice and pray to God that both skids came free at the same time. If one came loose before the other and the machine tilted by more than fifteen degrees, the blades would strike the ice and send them all cartwheeling into oblivion.

Rooker raised the collective lever and the machine trembled and tried to lift off. At once it began to list to the left, and he hastily lowered the lever again. The right skid was now free but the left was still solid. The only option left to him was to try again with less power but more yaw. He swallowed hard and gave the left pedal almost full deflection as the engine screamed. Suddenly the trapped skid tore free of the ice, and the machine lurched and tilted crazily as he fought to regain control.

'What's happening?' Alice screamed.

It was another five seconds before he could answer her. They were airborne. When he did speak his voice was almost steady. 'Nothing to worry about. Not the easiest takeoff.'

He flew onwards. Then suddenly, in the distant grey water, he saw the *Polar Star*. There was a black smudge down on the ice margin, surrounded by half a dozen tiny orange specks. 'Look,' he said and pointed.

He set the Squirrel down for the second time, a safe distance from the open water. The sailors were already running towards them. Big gloved hands lifted Alice and the baby in their silver blanket, and laid them gently on the unfurled canvas of a stretcher.

'Rook,' she called, twisting her head to see him. 'Come back quickly.'

He couldn't meet her eyes. 'You'll be safe now.'

They reached the black rubber side of the Zodiac. Alice fought to free one arm and caught Rooker's wrist. She pulled his hand to her mouth and kissed it.

A wave of terrible emotion flooded over him.

He remembered the moment of purity and innocence amid the panic as the baby was born. He wanted to pull her into his arms, and tell her the truth and never have to run or hide or fight ever again. He wanted to hold her and the baby, and keep them safe from whatever the world could do. Most of all he wanted to tell her the truth.

'You will come as soon as you can? Rook? *Answer me.*'

He took a deep, burning, painful breath. 'Alice. I can't follow you. It isn't right. You don't know me. You don't know what I've done. A man died because of me. I am a murderer.'

There wasn't even a beat. 'I don't care,' she screamed. 'I don't care what or who you are. I love you.'

But it was too late. They prised her hands away from him, then lifted her stretcher and placed it in the bottom of the Zodiac. The boatman immediately opened the throttle and the Zodiac nosed away. Rooker couldn't see anything of her, but he didn't take his eyes off the dinghy until it reached the ship's side and was winched up onto the deck of *Polar Star*. Only then did Rooker finally, slowly, turn away.

He strapped himself into the pilot's seat and pulled on the headset, making himself think of nothing but what must be done to make a safe return to Kandahar. Batteries, fuel pump. Start up both engines. The Squirrel's blades spun again. 'NZ two-zero, airborne,' he muttered.

When the cord was tied and cut, and Alice had been stitched, and Meg had been examined and warmed and wrapped, the doctor gave her back to Alice to hold. For what seemed a very long time, suspended between awe and amazement, Alice studied her. Shock and relief made the breath catch in her throat as she held the white bundle close.

'I think all right, both of you, to put you on the aeroplane,' the doctor pronounced at last.

Alice lifted her head to stare at him. She realised that she could hear the throb of the ship's engines. 'Where are we going?'

'To Santa Ana,' the doctor said, staring a little. 'And then, I think they make you a flight to Santiago. We have no facility on the ship . . .'

'*Santiago*? Wait. The pilot . . . the helicopter pilot. Where is he? I have to speak to him. I thought the ship would wait for the other people to come aboard from Kandahar . . .'

The doctor shook his head. 'I will find someone to tell you.'

The ship's first officer knocked and came in. He told Alice that the helicopter had landed again at Kandahar.

'Thank you,' she managed to whisper, over the disablement of relief.

The man twinkled at her. 'You are VIP, I think. We have urgent radio instructions from the big man: we are straight to Santa Ana and a special plane for you and the baby, all the way to hospital in Santiago.'

The big man. It must be Lewis Sullavan. 'And the others?'

The officer almost shrugged. 'Another ship. Maybe one, two days. But by then you will be in a safe place. By order.' He patted her hand.

Alice let her head rest against the pillows. 'Please will you thank everyone for me? The sailors on the Zodiac and the radio operator and the captain. Everyone,' she repeated.

The officer patted her hand again. 'It is not every day,' he murmured.

When he had gone, Alice shut her eyes. She could hear Rook's voice, a desperate low exclamation, *I am a murderer.*

She had answered, *I don't care what or who you are. I love you.*

That was the simple truth.

The ship took her to Santa Ana, and as the second day of Meg's life dawned they went ashore in the Zodiac again. Alice refused a stretcher and walked the few metres to the base, carrying the baby wrapped in ship's blankets. All she could think of was how to contact Rooker.

'Please try to raise them,' she begged Miguel, the radio operator.

The Chilean expedition leader was explaining that a Dash-7 chartered by Lewis Sullavan was on its way from Punta Arenas to collect her. Sullavan had sent a radio message. Would she like to read it?

Sullavan sent his congratulations and his best wishes for both Alice's good health and the baby's. She was to allow him the privilege of making arrangements for them from now on. Professor Peel and Dr Mather were being informed of her whereabouts, and she would of course be able to speak to them from Santiago. In the meantime, so that she could rest and recover, it would be simpler if she were to let Sullavanco do any talking that might be necessary.

What talking? Alice wondered in surprise, before she put the message aside. All that mattered were her daughter and the radio connection to Kandahar. The minutes crawled while she drank tea and waited.

Miguel's head came round the door. 'If you like to talk . . .'

Alice stumbled forward.

Niki's voice greeted her. 'You are well, and lucky, I hear.'

She gasped, 'Nik . . . oh, Nik, are you all right, all of you?'

'A little cold, a little hungry, but not so bad. *Polar Star* will come back or maybe another ship, but first we must have no mist in order to fly.'

Alice tripped over the words in her anxiety. 'That's good, I mean, not good that you're still there. I'm sorry I took the ship away and everything. Nik, please, I need to speak to Rooker. Is he there? Over.'

'He is waiting here.'

In her mind's eye she saw the generator hut. And Rook's face.

'Alice. Can you hear me?' His familiar voice sounded remote.

'I'm here. Tell me. Was the flight back all right? Over.'

'It was less eventful.'

'Rook. Thank you for everything you did.' The words were so dry and colourless. She could only pray that he knew what lay behind them. She said urgently, 'When you get out of there, will you come to England?'

There was a static silence and she glanced in dismay at Miguel before Rook's voice finally cut in. 'I told you something, do you remember?'

'I don't care, it doesn't matter. All that matters is now. *Please*.' She couldn't contain the explosion of sobs.

'It matters to me. Look after Meg, and yourself. Goodbye, Alice.'

'*No*,' she howled. Miguel's hand uncertainly patted her shoulder.

A second later Niki's voice came back again. 'Santa Ana, Santa Ana. Weather report, please.'

She handed over the mike. Two hours later they were in the air. The plane swept her away from Rooker and Antarctica.

Her room in the private hospital in Santiago was full of flowers, all from Sullavanco. In the car from the airport she had seen huge trees in the city parks, skyscrapers shining with glass and steel, lines of traffic, shop windows crowded with goods. She had forgotten that the ordinary world held so much variety, and noise and relentless activity.

Her doctor at the Clinica Providencia was a woman called Cecilia Vicente. She gave Meg a thorough examination. She weighed only just over four pounds but she was in good health. It was Dr Vicente's opinion that she had been delivered about five or six weeks before full term.

'We will watch her carefully, but I am not very worried about this little girl,' she announced. 'Now let us take a look at her mother. Would you like to tell me how you came to give birth in Antarctica?'

Alice did her best to explain. At the end the doctor said, 'I see. I suppose this makes some sense.' The first time Alice had bled might have been caused by the implantation of the embryo, and the second, much heavier loss a little more than a month later had almost certainly been a threatened miscarriage. 'But here we are. Your daughter is a determined creature. She is born with determination in her bones, a true survivor.'

Yes, Alice thought. She will be Margaret's granddaughter in all that.

'How do you feel?' Cecilia asked.

As far as her body and her immediate circumstances were concerned, Alice was fine. She was exhausted and the cut on her arm was slightly infected. She had perineal stitches that made it agony to sit down and her breasts ached, but the wounds would heal. Meg was going to be all right. She had much to be grateful for, but she was not all right.

Images from the helicopter journey and the birth and the events before and after kept going round and round in her head. The more they repeated themselves the more she realised how desperate it had all been. Meg might have been born dead, or strangled by the cord, or she herself might have haemorrhaged. They might have crashed in the mist. She was only just comprehending the risks Rooker had taken for her sake. The more she thought about it the more she longed for him and the bigger the vacuum of his absence became. She had to learn to be a mother and go home to a life that could never be the same as the one she had known. How was she going to do any of this without him?

'Bewildered,' was what she finally said.

The doctor put her hand over Alice's. 'Where is the baby's father?'

'He is in England. But we are not together.'

'Does that mean you are alone?'.

'I have parents, good friends.' She paused. How to tell anyone who had not been with them in Antarctica about Rooker? 'There is someone, the man who flew us out to the ship and delivered my baby. But he is not a person you can . . . put reins on.'

Dr Vicente nodded. 'You have had a shock. A physical shock, of course, but also an emotional one. You are too suddenly a mother, but I believe there has always been a denial in you about this child, or you would not have been able to keep it so far to the back of your mind that you allowed yourself to become trapped on your base. Am I right, Alice?'

She thought about the past: Oxford. Science. The unexpected birth of an unplanned baby was the antithesis of everything that had happened in her life before. Alice turned her head to gaze at Meg, asleep in the crib. Devotion shone through her confusion, and the doctor saw this.

Alice said, 'Yes. You are right.'

'And so it will take a little time for you to adjust. I have seen many, many mothers with their newborn babies. I think, I believe, all will be well for the two of you.'

Later that day the telephone rang beside her bed.

'Alice? Is that you?' From halfway across the world her mother's crisp voice was instantly recognisable. 'I must say, I would have preferred a little more warning before becoming a grandmother.'

'I know. You'll have some knitting to catch up on.'

This was such an outlandish idea that they both burst into laughter, and everything was all right.

Then Trevor came on. 'Ali, I am concerned about you,' he said.

'Don't be. Meg is beautiful and I'm longing to show her to you. I'll be home soon and we can talk then until we're hoarse.'

'What about Peter? He rang this morning, frantic for news.'

'How does Pete know? Did you tell him?'

'Darling, it's not a secret. In fact, you should get ready to be famous.'

'*What?*'

'You're in Sullavan's paper this morning. The baby's hit the headlines as the First European Citizen of Antarctica and you are Dramatic Snow Birth Heroine. Or some such,' he concluded drily.

Alice realised her naivety. Lewis's generosity with planes and clinics was double-edged, of course. The first season at Kandahar had ended in disaster. A heart-warming human-interest story laced with helicopter action and heroism was exactly the publicity that Lewis needed.

Later, when Alice was dozing, the phone rang again.

'This is Beverley Winston.'

Don't even think about jealousy. To be jealous of other women where Rooker was concerned would be to condemn herself to a life of agony. And that was if she were ever to see him again. *I will*, she resolved.

Beverley asked in a friendly, concerned way about the flight from Kandahar and the birth. Alice thought for a second, then answered her questions. If there were going to be stories about her in Lewis's newspapers and magazines, they might as well be factually accurate. Her voice only grew warmer when she described what Rooker had done.

'Yes. Very daring, but perhaps not the most advisable course of action, on the face of it. To make off with a company-leased helicopter in conditions considered too dangerous by the authorised pilot.'

This time Alice didn't think. 'To hell with the company,' she said.

'Well, now, I won't disturb you any more,' Beverley said after only a second's delay. 'If I might just beg you to let us take all the responsibility for dealing with media requests?'

'It's no big deal, surely? She's by no means the first baby to be born inside the Antarctic circle.' It was true that Argentinian and Chilean babies had been born in remote southern communities.

'She is the first European on a European base, and she is Margaret Mather's grandchild.'

Of course.

'Beverley, there is something I would really like you to help me with.'

'What's that?' The suggestion of a bargain quivered between them.

'Where is Rooker now? And the others? Where can I reach him?'

She would trade her story for information. Beverley briefly weighed this up, then murmured, 'They were all lifted out of Kandahar this morning and transferred to another ship. They are at sea now, I gather.'

So they were all safe. 'The ship's name? And I'm sure that the Polar Office must have an address where he can be reached?'

'The best way to handle it would be an exclusive interview with a young journalist, the one I am thinking of is very good and totally sympathetic, and some lovely mother and baby pictures.'

'The ship? And an address?'

'It's the *Southern Mariner*. And I do believe Rooker gave us an address down in Ushuaia, and a reference from, ah, a building company. I don't have either to hand, I'm afraid.'

Alice smiled, though her jaw ached with the tension of this exchange. 'I'd be so glad if you could get them for me. Then I don't see why there should be a problem about an interview and a couple of pictures.'

For two days, Alice struggled to establish ship-to-shore contact with the *Southern Mariner*, but it didn't have a satellite telephone.

On the third day, Alice and Meg were discharged from the Clinica Providencia. Cecilia Vicente came to wave them off.

Dr Vicente said, 'I will not wish you luck because I do not think you need it. But I do wish you happiness.'

Their eyes met. 'Thank you,' Alice said.

Santiago International Airport was crowded. Alice stood with Meg in her arms, obsessively watching the departure boards. The *Southern Mariner* must be putting into port very soon. There was an obscure flight scheduled to Patagonia, and Alice was certain that she would be able to take a connecting flight from there to Ushuaia. She could go right now and search until she found Rooker.

But Meg gave a small snuffling whimper. Alice massaged the tiny back with the flat of her hand. To go looking for him would mean flying her premature baby to distant places, in a chase that might not even lead her to him. She hesitated for one long, painful moment. Then she turned round and boarded the overnight LanChile flight to Madrid. At the end of it she found a Sullavanco PR woman named Lisa, waiting to whisk them through to London, Heathrow.

Alice cupped the back of Meg's bonneted head and held her own head high as they walked towards Arrivals.

'Ready?' Lisa smiled.

As they emerged, the sudden blaze of camera flashes almost blinded her. There was a babble of voices shouting out her name, a television crew, and in the midst of it all a brief glimpse of Trevor and Margaret. Alice's eyes filled with tears at the sight of them.

'Dr Peel is very pleased and relieved to be home,' Lisa called out. 'Nothing else at this time. Thank you.'

'Let's see the baby!'

'Alice, did you plan to do this?'

'What's her name?'

Lisa wheeled them away from the press. 'That's all,' she said firmly.

The crowd fell aside and Trevor and Margaret emerged. Margaret scooped Meg out of Alice's arms and gazed down into the puckered crimson face. Then she lifted her up to the cameramen.

'Her name is Margaret.' She beamed.

They were swept to a waiting limo. Margaret and Trevor and Alice breathlessly toppled into the back with Meg somewhere between them.

'I want to go home,' Alice sobbed, as if she were a child again herself.

'That's just where we're going,' Margaret said firmly.

The bare twigs of the trees on Boar's Hill were thickening with buds and the hawthorn hedges showed a wispy veil of green. Alice felt utterly disorientated. As she carried Meg across the path to the front door and into the house, she could still feel the thick heat of Santiago in her veins and behind her eyes lay the contradictory white vistas of Antarctica.

'I'll make a cup of tea,' Trevor said.

Alice and Margaret went upstairs. In Alice's bedroom lay a Moses basket with a blue quilted lining, a pile of tiny garments and four packs of Pampers, and a stuffed penguin made of black and white plush.

'Jo brought the baby things over. She sends her love. And Peter came with the penguin. To make her feel at home, he said.'

'Oh,' Alice said uncertainly. Another wave of bewilderment threatened to overwhelm her. She put Meg down in the basket.

Margaret held out her arms and suddenly they were clinging together. It was rare for them to hug each other, but now it seemed not so fraught with risk. They stood for a long time.

In the end Alice laid her cheek on the red felt crown of her mother's hat and Margaret told her not to crush it, and then she said that with the windburn and the white goggle marks Alice looked like a real polar explorer. She put her hands up to cup Alice's face and asked her why she hadn't come home as soon as she knew that she was pregnant.

'I wanted to finish what I had started. I learned that from you.'

'And why didn't you tell anyone?'

'Because I didn't know what to say. And because I thought the only person to take responsibility for what I *had* decided should be me.'

Margaret frowned. 'I am not sure that was entirely logical. But ordinary logic doesn't work down south, does it? I remember that.'

Later Alice took a nap in her own bed, with Meg in her basket alongside, but she woke up the instant the baby began to whimper. She undid her dressing gown to start feeding her again.

She thought about Rook and the words he had blurted out. *I am a murderer.* What did he mean? He *wasn't* a murderer, she would have wagered her own life on it, but what was it that lay in his past like a dark obstacle between them? All her instincts still told her to fly south and search until she found him and uncovered the truth. But she could no longer do whatever she wanted whenever she wanted it, because her rhythms must now become the baby's. She began to understand why Jo had been hit so hard by motherhood and she longed to talk to her, but there was another call that had to be made first.

She phoned him on the number he had left with Trevor. 'Pete?'

There was a silence, then his words rushed at her. 'You're home. Al, my God, Al. Why didn't you tell me? Why? She is mine, isn't she?'

'Yes, she's yours.'

'My God,' he said again, now in a whisper. 'How is she?'

'She is perfect.'

'I'm on my way. I'll be there in half an hour.'

Alice was sitting on the sofa, with Meg at her breast, when he whirled in. Peter stopped short. For once, he couldn't find a word. He had chunks of plaster sticking to his jeans and his hair was thick with dust. Alice felt her heart quicken with affection at the sight of him, but that was all. He was a good man, but he wasn't the one she wanted.

He touched one fingertip to Meg's nearest cheek and the baby sighed. 'My God.' Pete breathed again. 'I can't believe it.'

'I know. A whole person, not me, not you, but herself.'

Pete found a seat beside them. 'What do you want?' he asked at length. 'I'm here, you know. I'll do whatever you like.'

She knew what he was offering. She took his hand. 'I don't want anything,' she whispered. 'But thank you.'

'Marry me.'

'No. I can't do that. But it means so much that you asked me.'

'D'you know what you're saying, Alice?' he shouted. 'I am her father.'

'I know you are. You can see her whenever you like, share her with me, take responsibility for her sometimes if that's what you want. But asking me to marry you involves me as well, and I don't want to.'

Peter studied Alice's face. 'You have changed,' he said slowly. 'What has happened? It's something big, isn't it?'

Alice searched for words. 'Pete . . . I honestly didn't know I was pregnant when I went south. When I worked out what was happening, I intended to come back here in good time for the baby to be born. To tell you about it, give you time to prepare yourself, to decide how much or how little you wanted to be involved. That was the plan.'

'Instead?'

'I miscalculated. The ice came early, I missed a chance to leave when I could have done, then there was a fire on the base. In a matter of hours, every way out was closed. It was stupid of me. I'd been there all those weeks and seen the weather, and I *still* hadn't understood how quickly you can come to the edge. Then the baby came. A man called Rooker flew us out. She was born halfway between the base and the ship.'

'I read about it. My daughter, the first European citizen of Antarctica.' There was an edge in his voice. He was hurt and she understood that.

'I'm sorry,' she whispered again. 'I was selfish, and I did put her and other people in danger. It wasn't until . . . until I stood holding her in the airport in Santiago that I began to understand what *a mother* means.' She chose her words with care. 'I promise you that from now on she is and always will be the most important person in the world to me.'

Not the only person.

'I don't know how much danger you were in, Al. I don't think I even want to know. What matters is that you are both safe and well now. But that's not all, is it?'

'No. I fell in love.'

Peter exhaled a long breath. 'A man called Rooker?'

It was Alice's turn to breathe harder now. 'Yes.'

'You know what? I always guessed that when you did fall in love properly it would transform you. And it has.'

'I loved you,' Alice said humbly.

'In a way, yes.' He tucked Meg's blanket round her and added abruptly, 'I've got to go now. There's always going to be a connection between you and me, Al. She's here, between us.' Then he stumbled for the door. 'I'll see you soon,' he called over his shoulder.

Trevor came and poured Alice a cup of coffee.

'Can I tell you about something?' she asked.

'I hope you will.' Trevor sat down in Pete's place.

Beginning at the beginning, Alice told him the story of Kandahar and Rook. The only thing she didn't mention was what Rooker had told her at the end. 'Now I've got to take care of Meg. But I also know that Rooker and I belong together. It's elemental. Does that make any sense?'

Trevor nodded. 'I know what it's like to feel the way you do now.'

She thought of Margaret with Lewis Sullavan, and probably others too, and yet Trevor and Margaret had made it through their painful times. You couldn't harness Rook, but there were many different ways of being together, and maybe Rooker and she could find their own.

She *had* to find him and tell him that whatever was in his past they

141

could confront it together. How long before she could go to him?

Trevor's hand was resting on her arm and he felt the electric impulses flickering under her skin. This burning, passionate creature was a different daughter from the cautious, reflective one he had known. He was happy that she had caught fire and he was full of apprehension for her.

CHAPTER NINE

ROOKER GLANCED BRIEFLY around the bare room. His former landlady, Marta, had let him have his old room back for two nights after the *Southern Mariner* docked in Ushuaia. She had also stored his few surplus belongings while he was at Kandahar. The bookcase was now empty and there was nothing in the cupboard except a few twisted coathangers. He hoisted his two bags and tramped down the stairs.

'So, where you heading?'

'North. Somewhere warm. I've seen enough snow for a while. Marta, thanks for looking after my stuff and for the room.'

'*De nada*. As you can see, there is no people fighting for it.'

Winter was closing in on the town. For three or four months the flame of life would barely glimmer down here.

'*Adios*, Rook,' Marta said.

He leaned down and kissed her. 'I'll send you an address, when I've got myself fixed up somewhere,' he promised.

It was bitterly cold outside. Rooker walked quickly downhill, his breath clouding round his head. Once he hit the main street he would thumb a ride out to the airport, or he might even take a five-dollar ride in a cab. He had money, a whole season's money from working at Kandahar, and a seat booked on the evening flight up to Buenos Aires.

The other Kandahar personnel would all have left town by now, heading back to their homes and families. Rooker needed to travel alone.

The plane banked sharply after takeoff. Rooker remembered the desperate helicopter journey across the ice from Kandahar. He slid out his flask and made a silent tribute. To you, Alice Peel. Then he drank.

His thoughts resumed the course they had been following for days.

The birth of a baby. He had never dreamed that a tiny, wet, hot body delivered into his hands, and a woman's face contorted with pain and then elation, could etch themselves so deeply into his mind. But Meg was another man's child. Apart from the accident of her birth, he hadn't the remotest claim on her. He couldn't contaminate her absolute innocence with his presence, let alone his history. No: Alice and Meg belonged together, in a safe place, a long way from the marginal territories that he occupied. He loved Alice but he must let her go.

She had said things to him that he would treasure—*I love you, don't leave me*—but it would be too much to expect her to look at him in the same way once she was safely back in England and among friends. What could Alice Peel want, or need, from him?

He didn't want to diminish those memories by demanding more and being refused, however gently. He loved her but he must let her go. His thoughts went on, round and round, following the same course.

In Buenos Aires it was hot, and at first Rooker felt his bones ease in the benign warmth. But after Antarctica the air tasted acrid with pollution. He flew on up to Cuba and sat for three days in a bar in Havana Vieja. There was the same aimlessness with which he had originally drifted south, but the emptiness was far harder to bear.

In the end he moved on to Mexico City, where he rented a room and looked half-heartedly for some casual work in the construction business. In yet another bar one night a young girl slid into the seat beside him and asked if he was looking for a friend.

He answered in English, 'Yes, but not the kind of friend you mean.'

The girl smiled. 'Me drink?'

He had a bottle on the table beside him. Rooker shrugged and poured whisky into a second glass. They sat for a few minutes in oddly companionable silence, watching the eddying of the crowds.

'You like to?' the girl asked, making a small suggestive movement.

'No,' Rook said shortly. She was pretty, but he couldn't imagine touching her. He couldn't imagine anything except Alice.

The girl prepared to move on. But before she went she leaned across him. 'You know, everyone have friend some place. Even you, mister.'

Immediately, Rook thought of Frankie.

The morning after her return to Boar's Hill, Alice was woken at five in the morning by Meg's crying. She sat groggily up in bed and fed her. As the dawn probed between the folds of her old curtains, a wave of longing for Antarctica and for Rooker swept through her. She ached with loneliness for him and for what she had left behind.

Later, Trevor came in with a pot of tea on a tray. He brought the newspapers too. There was a big picture of their arrival at Heathrow in the *Oxford Mail*. SOUTH POLE MUM HOME, the caption read inaccurately. There were pictures and brief stories in the national tabloids, too. Most mentioned the joint European Antarctic initiative. Lewis would be pleased.

Between feeds, Alice telephoned the Polar Office. She identified herself and heard the note of avid curiosity in the woman's voice as she answered, 'Oh *yes*. Dr Peel. How can I help you?'

Alice said, 'I'd like to speak to Mr Sullavan, if possible. To thank him.'

'Of course, Dr Peel. I know that he's eager to speak to you too, but he *is* involved in a series of meetings in Toronto today.'

'I understand. Perhaps you could just leave that message? Oh, and one other small thing. May I have James Rooker's contact details, please?'

'I'm *so* sorry. We can't give out—'

'You see, I didn't have a chance to thank him properly. For what he did,' she added delicately.

'Yes.' There was a pause. 'Dr Peel, I know that Mr Sullavan is *particularly* hoping that you'll want to tell your story personally.'

'We-ll,' Alice said, trying to sound as if she was too preoccupied to give the idea proper consideration. 'Beverley Winston did mention it,' she added vaguely. Another meaningful silence ensued.

'So maybe I could just make an appointment for the journalist to pop in to see you and the babe, and have a chat about it all?'

'If I could just clear my mind first. I owe such a debt to James Rooker.'

'I *could* take a very quick peek at the records. For the interview, though, shall we say tomorrow at two p.m.? And a photographer?'

'All right, yes.'

A moment later, Alice was noting down a telephone number and an address in Ushuaia. She dialled. At length a woman's voice answered. With her heart hammering in her chest Alice asked to speak to him.

'Rooker? No.' She couldn't properly decipher the rapid Spanish that followed but the meaning was clear enough.

'But he must have left a forwarding address? He can't have just gone.'

She heard the other woman's laugh, a wheezy exhalation of breath without merriment in it. 'I think you don't know Rooker,' she said.

You don't know me. You don't know what I've done. I am a murderer.

But she *did* know him. She knew him better than she had ever known anyone. She knew in every fibre of herself that he was not what he claimed. He had a black place in his past and he believed it must be hidden from her. To disappear was his solution.

'There must be something.'

'He say that he will send address when he fix up somewhere.'

Alice was thinking that she didn't have so much as a snapshot of him. The fire had consumed her exposed film, her diary, the Christmas wood carving, every scrap of physical evidence that he had ever existed.

She gave her name and telephone number to the Argentinian woman. When she had to hang up she felt as if a lifeline had snapped.

From upstairs, as she tended to Meg for the rest of the day, she heard the phone continually ringing. Margaret and Trevor fielded the calls.

I'll get a routine organised, Alice thought, remembering that Jo had somehow managed all this with *two* of them. She found herself shaking her head in empathetic astonishment.

So far, the evenings had seemed to be Meg's quietest time. Alice carried her downstairs in the Moses basket and put her in a corner of the dining room. Margaret ran her finger down a list of telephone messages while Trevor served up portions of grey-knobbed cauliflower cheese.

'Now then. Jo called twice, Becky called once. They're coming to see you tomorrow. Er . . . let's see, Peter rang again. And Dr Davey's going to drop in. One of your Kandahar colleagues rang.' Alice's head jerked up. 'A Frenchwoman. I wrote down her name and number . . . here it is. Laure Heber. I haven't bothered listing the journalists. Oh, and there was a call from Lewis Sullavan. I think you were sleeping.'

Alice put down her knife and fork. Lewis had instinctively liked Rooker. Surely he would help her to find him? 'What did he say?'

'Best wishes and so on. Hopes to be able to see you before too long.'

'Where was he calling from?'

'I don't know. I didn't ask,' Margaret answered.

Alice glanced at her father. He was eating his dinner with apparent appetite, unconcerned at the mention of Sullavan's name.

This is what time and age do, she thought. Passion and pain are both dulled, then they fade away altogether and leave acceptance in their place. The contrasting urgency of her need for Rooker made her shift and double up in her chair as if she were in pain.

Margaret stared at her over the top of her glasses. 'Are you all right?'

'Yes, thank you,' Alice made herself answer.

Jo and Becky arrived in the middle of the following morning. They enveloped Alice in hugs and questions and exclamations, and up in her bedroom they leaned over the Moses basket.

Becky gripped Alice's wrists and studied her face. 'Why didn't you tell anyone about all this, not even Jo and me?'

'Yes, why didn't you?' Jo demanded. 'We're your friends, aren't we?'

'You are. I didn't know, I didn't realise until weeks after I got there. And then it . . . seemed both too late and too soon to leave, and so I decided just to stay. I thought there was plenty of time.'

As she explained that once she had made the decision to stay on the ice it had seemed essential to take the entire responsibility herself, Alice had the strange sensation that there were two separate worlds spinning round her. There was Oxford; that took in the Department of Geology, her parents, Pete, all their friends and the rhythms of a life that had once seemed to offer everything she wanted. And there was another world, a much emptier place where the wind blew and the horizons were cracked with ice, but it was where Rooker was. The two places would never merge. She could choose one or the other, but not both.

Jo and Becky were both staring at her.

She blinked, realising that she had stopped talking. 'Sorry. I can't seem to make my brain work properly.'

Jo steered her to the bed. 'I know how you feel. It's as if your entire existence has been whisked away. You can't finish a sentence, you can't even get dressed in the mornings. In your case you haven't even got Pete around. That's not to say he wouldn't be with you if he could, by the way. He's been on the phone nonstop to Harry and me. "I'm the father, I ought to be there." Et cetera. Listen. It may feel like it, but it's not going to be this way for ever. Look, Beck and I bought you some things.'

In the carrier bags that Becky had brought upstairs, there were candy-striped sleepsuits and tiny pink socks and a hat like a strawberry, and a white toy polar bear. Alice had tears in her eyes as she unwrapped them.

'Polar bears live in the Arctic,' she sniffed.

'Don't be so bloody pedantic. And Al, you know what? It's OK to have a good cry if you want to.'

Noisy, racking sobs suddenly burst out of her.

Her friends exchanged anxious glances. Becky put a clump of tissues into her hand. Meg snuffled and began to howl too. Jo rocked the baby to soothe her and Becky massaged Alice's hands while she cried and cried.

Alice looked down through the blur of tears at the little pile of baby clothes and bright frills of tissue paper and ribbon. Kandahar had been a life stripped bare, reduced to a matter of survival, too stark for decoration. That was what Rook was for her. He was elemental and essential. The only thing that mattered was where he was now.

At last, the sobs came with less violence. Alice gasped for breath and lifted her head. Then she took Meg gently out of Jo's arms and held her against her heart.

Jo stood up. 'Pete's said he's sorry. You think he doesn't mean it but he does. Let him take care of you both, be a proper family.'

Becky shook her head at her, but Alice knew that Jo was offering her her own version of happiness. 'No,' she murmured. 'I can't do that.'

'So who is he?' Becky asked. She had understood what Jo had missed.

There was a small, weighted silence, then Alice said, 'Rooker.'

There was a pause while the other two placed him among the jumble of names and anecdotes that Alice had included in her emails, and in the garbled press reports of the birth and rescue.

'The pilot. Who took you out? Delivered Meg on the way?'

'Yes.'

Jo whistled. 'That's quite a story. You fell in love with him.'

In spite of everything, Alice smiled. 'It's not a story. It's the truest thing I've ever known. Somehow he saved us.'

'Does he love you?' It was Becky who asked this.

'He did then.'

'Where is he now?'

Alice's eyes met hers. 'I don't know. He seems to have disappeared. And I don't know how to find him.' There was an ache and an emptiness in Alice's voice that discouraged any more questions.

'Antarctic Drama Mum,' Jo said in a bemused voice.

Alice hand suddenly flew up to her mouth. 'Oh, my God. The journalist. And the photographer. Two o'clock. What time is it now?'

Jo looked at her watch. 'Coming up to one.'

'What journalist?' Becky demanded.

'*quoted* magazine. Writer and photographer. Coming here. Heartwarming exclusive story. I promised Lewis Sullavan's people. If I do this he'll have to help me to find Rooker, won't he?'

'*quoted*? You're going to be in a photo spread in *quoted*?' It was Lewis's most popular and successful news and gossip title. Even Alice had occasionally leafed through it. 'Look at you.'

'What do you mean?'

'I mean that Lewis Sullavan won't want Antarctic Drama Mum actually *looking* as if she's just spent six months in somewhere godforsaken like Antarctica and then given birth in a helicopter, will he?'

'Before crying for a solid hour.'

'Are they sending hair and make-up?'

'I don't think so.'

'What kind of a magazine is this? I'll just have to do what I can.'

They set to work. Jo ran downstairs for ice for an eye mask and Becky began tugging at her hair. Alice submitted. She didn't care about how she looked for *quoted*'s photographer, but it was a way for her old friends to draw her temporarily back into the circle.

They were not ready to acknowledge that she might not be the same old Alice any longer, and it was too soon for her to try to explain what had changed her. Perhaps no one would ever fully understand that, except Rooker himself. And Margaret.

The photo shoot gave them something to fix on.

Becky blotted out the windburn with matte foundation and erased the black lines under Alice's eyes with Touche Eclat. They plucked her eyebrows, and applied coats of lash thickener and a hint of kohl. Jo squeezed something from a tube and scrubbed it over her mouth.

'Ouch. Mind the baby. What's that stuff?'

'Lip exfoliant. Your mouth's all chapped.'

'I know that. *Ow*.'

'Give me my goddaughter.'

'What?'

'Well, aren't I? Isn't she?'

'Beck, of course you are, if you want to be. Wait, though. We'd better ask Pete what he thinks.'

They stopped for a moment, acknowledging that there were currents here that would require careful navigation.

Becky quickly nodded. 'Of course. You're right.'

Jo said briskly, 'What shall we dress the First European Citizen in? The stripes? And a clean nappy, to start with. I'll do it.'

At five minutes to two, Becky held up the mirror.

Alice stared at her glossed and tweezed reflection. 'Who am I?'

They held each other's hands and laughed. 'Drama Mum.'

Margaret's wobbly gate-leg table was pushed aside to make room for the photographer to set up his lights. Alice sat on the sofa with Meg in her arms. The journalist turned on her recorder.

'What was it like to be a pregnant woman in Antarctica?'

Alice sighed. If this was going to be the price, she would pay it.

'I went south as a scientist. I made a mistake, two mistakes if you like, in not knowing that I was pregnant in the first place and in staying on at Kandahar once I discovered it. But anyone, man or woman, can make a wrong decision. I stayed because I was proud to be part of the EU team at Kandahar. We made a good beginning. I was very lucky to be with everyone who was there, both as professionals and as people. Now I'm very relieved that we are all safely home again.'

Or safe somewhere, wherever he is.

Two weeks went by. At the end of that time, the issue of *quoted* magazine appeared with its upbeat version of Meg's birth and the European scientists' eventual escape from the burnt-out shell of their base. The fire was described as a dramatic accident and the survivors as polar heroes.

'We weren't heroes,' Alice said with a sigh when she read the article. 'Except for Rooker.'

'Yes, maybe that Rooker. Any news of him?' Margaret asked.

'No. None.'

Trevor's concerned gaze rested on his daughter.

The end of April came, and then it was early May and the weeping willows along the river in the University Parks were in leaf.

After some negotiations, Alice's tenants agreed to move out of the Jericho house a month early. It would be a relief to be able to take Meg home. The Boar's Hill house had begun to seem very crowded, and too small for Margaret and Alice to occupy together.

'I need to get on with work. But I do need to see my granddaughter at least every other day,' Margaret fretted.

'You will see her. She *is* your granddaughter,' Trevor soothed her.

Alice did everything she could think of to locate Rook.

The Polar Office grew resistant to her calls for more information. In the end, they gave her all the contact details they had, for all the expedition members. There was nothing in Rooker's file except the Ushuaia address and a reference from an Argentinian building company. She spoke to a personnel officer in Buenos Aires and an American architect, who could tell her nothing except that Rooker had worked last winter as a site manager at a hotel development in Ushuaia.

Rooker had worked at McMurdo, too. After much effort she got through to an official. Yes, a James J. Rooker had been employed on the base in the 1970s. There was no further data now available.

Russell was at home with his wife and children in Dunedin, New Zealand. 'Christ, Alice, how are *you*? And the baby?'

It was an effort to keep the tremor of urgency out of her voice as she asked the question.

'Rook? Nah. Haven't a clue. I know he once lived up in Christchurch, though. I'll ask around a bit, see if anyone knows anything.'

'Thank you, Russ. *Thank you.*'

Laure was back in her lab. She was working on the penguin blood samples that they had managed to salvage from the snow cave. 'Yes, I am working, of course . . . No, I am so sorry I have no contact for Rook. I think if he wants, he will know where to find you.'

Valentin was in Sofia, Jochen was in Den Haag and Arturo was in

Barcelona. They were all eager to hear news, but none of them had any information about Rooker. Niki was still travelling somewhere in South America. Phil was in North Wales, teaching climbing.

'Jesus. That was an epic and a half. I'll remember the way that bloody helicopter lifted off in a whiteout until my dying day. But if Rooker's such a fucking mix-up that he doesn't want to be found, what's there to say? I liked him, but I'm not sure that he's a prospect, if you want the truth . . . What? . . . Yeah, 'course I will. Whatever I can.'

Richard, she learned, was away in Greece. He was said to be resting and recuperating, and had not left a contact address.

Through a local history society she established that there had been a Northumberland family called Jerrold, and eventually she tracked down a young solicitor in Morpeth whose father had looked after their affairs. He told her that Henry Jerrold had died in the 1980s and his wife ten years later. There were no living relatives, and although there had been a sister who had emigrated to New Zealand in the fifties, she had predeceased her brother and he had no record of her having had a child.

Alice trawled the Internet, but nothing ever came up linked to any version of his name. She had an eerie sense that he might never have existed. The trail had gone dead and she had only one prospect left.

Two days before Alice was due to move back into her own house, a big car turned in at the gate and Lewis Sullavan stepped out. When Margaret came out to greet him, he held her hands in his and kissed her.

'It's good to see you, Maggie. You don't look any different.'

Her face glowed. 'It's twenty years, my dear. Of course I look different. Come in. Here's Trevor, now.'

The two men shook hands. Trevor quickly removed his from Lewis's grasp and replaced it in his pocket, but otherwise he was affable. He and Margaret showed Lewis into the living room.

'I've come to tell you,' Lewis said as he sat down, 'promise you, that next season both the main house and Margaret Mather House will be rebuilt. I think we shall get extra funding from Brussels to support the work.' That was how he would present it. There was no fading or failure in Lewis's world. Everything moved forward. 'And of course there is the miracle of your granddaughter. A new birth, a rebirth for a science station. It's rather marvellously appropriate, when you think of it.'

Alice came down the stairs with Meg in her arms. She presented the baby to Lewis.

He peered down at her, adopting the right genial expression. 'She is almost as beautiful as her mother and grandmother.'

'Thank you,' Alice said.

'I have brought you a small present.' In Lewis's briefcase there were two identically sized gift-wrapped packages. One was an album into which someone had pasted all the Sullavanco press cuttings relating to Meg's birth. In the second album there were photographs. 'The cameraman who came with us was a good stills photographer too,' Lewis said.

Alice slowly turned the pages. The pictures lifted a blindfold. Everything, every detail spread out again in her mind's eye. The old hut, its red walls glowing in the low sunlight. Clouds hanging over the glacier. Their tiny camps out at the Bluff and the vast desert of whiteness.

There were pictures of the expedition members, too. Phil sitting astride a skidoo. Laure, with a hundred Adélie penguins standing sentinel at her feet. Richard, with the ghost of his grandfather in his features. And Rook. He was standing bareheaded at the door of the lab hut. He wasn't smiling, but there was the premonition of a smile round his eyes. Of course he existed. Here he was, whole and complete.

'I didn't have a single picture. They were all burnt,' she managed.

For the rest of the short visit, Lewis talked about his plans for the next Antarctic season and the personnel he hoped to attract.

'No use asking a new mother.' He laughed.

'No. What about Richard?'

'I don't know that he would want to lead another expedition.'

'And Rooker?'

Lewis laughed again. 'That would be to repeat himself. It would go against all the man's instincts. Some of the other personnel may rejoin.'

Five minutes later a mobile phone purred discreetly. Lewis looked at his watch. The visit to Boar's Hill was over.

Alice followed him to his car. 'Do you know where he is?'

Lewis was too all-knowing even to miss a beat. 'No, I don't.'

'Will you help me to find him?'

'That was the bargain, I think? Your cooperation with a little publicity, our cooperation over addresses and other details?'

Alice met his eye. 'That's right.'

He smiled once more. 'I remember the crevasse, Alice. It's me who owes you the favour, rather than vice versa. I'll do what I can.'

June came, and the Oxford streets turned black and white with students in exam clothes. Two weeks later it was party dresses and champagne bottles for the week of the summer balls. And then the University sank into the torpor of the long vacation.

One morning, Alice put Meg into her buggy and pushed her through the streets towards the Parks. Jo and the twins were waiting for her at the café where all those months ago she had had tea with Pete and Mark the sculptor. Afterwards, they steered the babies under the trees beside the river. Jo was talking about preschool. Alice tried hard to listen and make the right responses, but Jo suddenly stopped and faced her.

'You're not listening.'

They were at the curve in the river where Pete had leapt out of the punt and swum ashore. In the past weeks he had often looked in to see Meg. He was generous with presents and offers of money: *Desiderata* was now the centrepiece of an exhibition of his work at a London gallery. From another of their friends, Alice heard that he had begun to console himself with a girl with long red hair. He's a good man, she judged, as she always did at this point. He just doesn't have the longest attention span.

'I am listening,' Alice protested. 'But—music and movement? Isn't it a bit early?'

Jo had turned into a committed mother. There was no investment in the twins' future that she would not make if it lay within her power. 'I don't think it *can* be too early, do you?' she said.

They walked on, through the tunnel of trees. Alice felt the tendrils of familiarity wrapping round her ankles and calves, anchoring her in this place that had once been hers and no longer was. Trapping her.

The roots of her dissatisfaction didn't just lie in her longing for Rooker. If he had sent her a single word, just a sign, she could have gone on waiting. Perhaps he had just been the agent of change, a way of knocking the scales from her eyes that was almost as cruel as it had been wonderful. But I *can* see now, she thought. All my life I have been bending and conforming, doing what I ought rather than what I could. I've applied myself to science and closed my eyes to art; I have rejected fantasy and adopted reason. What was I afraid of?

I can't do it any longer. No one who goes to the ice comes back the same person. What can I do instead?

A vertiginous space opened at her feet and she almost stumbled.

'Have you put her name down for the nursery?' Jo was asking. 'The waiting list's endless and you'll need some childcare, won't you, when next term starts?'

'Yes.' Or no.

At the gates they hugged each other, and Alice stood for a minute to watch her old friend as she walked away. Then she walked the familiar route back to the house in Jericho.

The house was sunny and silent. Her first action after settling Meg was to check her voice-mail. She always did it, always hoping.

The first of the two new messages was from Margaret, wanting to know if she was bringing Meg up to see them later that day. Alice skipped to the second message, resolving to call her mother later.

The next voice was familiar. 'Hello, Alice. This is Richard Shoesmith.'

He gave the date, and the exact time of his call, as precise as always. He said that he was back in the country and was coming to Oxford on a brief visit. He hoped to look her up, if she could spare the time.

Alice wrote down the number he had given and dialled it. She left a message saying that she would look forward to seeing him.

Richard was wearing a tie and carrying a briefcase.

'Come in.' Alice said, and stood back to make room. The hallway was narrow and they skirted round each other clumsily.

Richard followed her into the living room, where Meg sat in her chair in the middle of the floor. 'So. Here she is,' he said, lowering himself into an awkward crouch beside Meg, as if to shake hands with her.

Alice stooped too. 'This is Richard. Hmm? He knows all about the snow and the ice.' She unbuckled the seat straps and swung the baby onto her hip. 'Would you like a cup of tea, or maybe a glass of wine?'

'Oh, just tea. Tea would be perfect.'

He followed her into the kitchen. 'How are you?'

'I'm fine,' Alice said, as she filled the kettle.

The last time we saw each other, she thought. The blur of pain and panic, Rook lifting her into the helicopter. Richard with Valentin and Phil holding his arms. *Stop him*, Richard had shouted.

The spectres of what-if rose in front of her all over again. Gratitude for their escape flooded through Alice. She put her free hand out and caught Richard's arm. She longed to talk, now, about what they had been through together, but his handsome face was stiff, closed, with only a flicker of wariness in the corners of his eyes.

'Good. That's good. It was quite an escape we had, wasn't it? You especially. But here we are. What about your work and so on?'

Alice blinked, but already she understood.

Richard's recuperation in Greece had been a process of sweeping up, locking away chunks of bleeding memory. It was all out of sight now and he would bend his attention back to a rigidly ordered world: palaeontology and university administration. He would no longer dream of living up to his grandfather, because he couldn't. That dream lay in pieces.

Her heart lurched with sympathy for him, but she withdrew her hand. 'I'm not doing much work at the moment, because of Meg. And how are you?' she asked gently.

'I'm pretty well. Needed a rest, you know.'

'Of course.' It was the opposite of what she wanted but she found herself playing his game. She wondered why he had come here.

'Do you want to go back to the ice?' she asked at last, looking at Meg rather than at him.

With an effort, he answered, 'I did my best. I . . . wish it had turned out otherwise, of course. No. I won't be doing another season.'

'That's a shame.'

'Ah. Yes. Well, there it is. Now, I've a little present to give the baby.'

He retrieved his briefcase and brought out a rectangular box. Alice opened it and found a kaleidoscope. She put it to her eye and turned the drum. The beads were chips of blue and silvery glass, and the mirrors multiplied them into the form of a snowflake.

'Thank you, it's beautiful. I'll keep it safe until she's old enough to appreciate it.'

He looked at his watch.

'Richard, do you remember the camp out at the Bluff? The first one? We talked a lot, then.' Exchanging histories, recognising one another in the straitjackets the past imposed.

'Yes.'

'If you want to talk any more, about Kandahar or anything, I am here.'

'Thank you,' Richard said. She knew that he wouldn't talk to her. It was quite likely that they would never see each other again.

He gathered himself together. He was meeting an American palaeontologist. He mentioned the man's name and asked if she knew him.

Alice shook her head. All the way to the front door she didn't ask what was uppermost in her mind, but as he was mumbling a formal goodbye she caught his arm again. 'Have you heard anything from Rook? Have you any idea where he might have gone?'

She saw the flash of pain in his eyes clearly enough now, and realised why he had come. Sadness and sympathy bled through her once more. She had begun to be attracted to him and then she had rejected him. He had been hurt, she now understood, more deeply than she had realised.

'I don't know anything about Rooker,' he said. 'I hope you find what you're looking for.'

'And you,' she called after him as he headed down the path. If he heard, he didn't look back.

Alice sank down on the bottom stair and rested her chin in her hands.

Richard and she were moving in opposite directions. He was retreating and she was admitting to herself what a different world really meant. She wanted to be the person she had been at Kandahar. She knew for certain now that Meg and she would have to leave Oxford. The first imperative was to try to find Rooker; after that she had no idea. All she did know was that she must do something, very soon, or the tendrils would wrap round her and hold her for ever. She would be like Richard, always keeping a version of herself hidden in case the daylight fell on it.

A similarity struck her. Rooker had his cupboard too, with painful truth swept up and locked away inside. The truth had something to do with *I am a murderer*, of course. That was the place to start. Exactly how to go about it was still a mystery.

In the end it was Russell who gave her the answer. He telephoned one morning at 6 a.m., when Alice was changing the baby's nappy. 'Alice? Sorry if it's the middle of the night. Got a bit of info for you.'

'Go on, Russ.'

'There's a little place called Turner, between here and Christchurch. I've got a mate here in Dunedin who's interested in genealogy, who grew up about twenty miles from Turner. I was round there a few days ago, taking back a cement mixer I'd borrowed. I asked him how you set about finding a person's history, just out of interest more than anything, and he asked me for a name. I gave him Rook's, since I'd been talking to you. Seemed to ring a bell with him,. Anyway, to cut a long story short . . .'

Please, Alice silently begged.

'. . . he came up with something. Sad story, in the local paper. He'd seen it in the archives. Woman called Rooker, committed suicide, not long after a friend of hers died in a fire in a caravan. It was burned out one night with him inside it. She'd been questioned, but it doesn't sound as though she was a suspect. Quite a big story, for this part of the world.'

The hair stood up on the nape of Alice's neck. Fire. *A friend of my mother's died in a fire.*

'My mate sent me a photocopy of an article. Here it is, 1967. It mentions that she had one son. Must be our Rooker, by my calculations.'

'Could you scan it and email it to me, Russ? Everything you've got?'

'Will do.'

By that evening she had it in her hand. Almost a full page of the *Turner & Medfield Clarion*. By coincidence almost the same information reached her two days later, in a fax marked 'From the office of Lewis Sullavan'.

There it was. The other side of the world. She and Meg would go to Turner, New Zealand, and try to find out what had happened long ago to the child, James Rooker. There was only the smallest chance that any thread would lead onwards from there, let alone to wherever Rook was now, but Alice was sure that this was where the key to the cupboard lay.

Rooker and Frankie drove in her battered VW up to the lake shore. It was a two-hour journey and the three children in the back seat were sticky and squabbling.

'Stop that, Jackson. Leave your sister alone.'

Jackson sulked. Frankie's daughter Corinna caught Rooker's eye and gave him a sly, turned-in smile exactly like her mother's.

'When will we be there?' the little girl asked.

'Twenty minutes.' Frankie sighed. 'Please God.'

At last they turned into the parking lot.

They set off down a track, the two older children racing ahead. Rooker carried the folding chairs and the cold box and a plaid blanket. Frankie was holding Sammy's hand, her head bent as she listened to whatever her youngest was urgently telling her. Rooker wondered what it would be like to be locked into a family like this, instead of just visiting.

They reached the shore. It was a wide crescent of shingly sand backed by rough grass. There was a stone jetty, with boats moored along it.

Frankie stood with her fists on her hips, smiling at him. 'You don't say much, Rook, do you? But you know, I'm still pretty pleased you came by.'

Jackson clamoured, 'Can we go in a sailboat now, Rook?'

'I need a beer first.'

'Awww.' But all three children were already running towards the water. Rook unfolded the chairs and set them in place.

Frankie took a can of beer out of the cooler and put it into his hand. 'What's with you?' she asked, her tolerance shaded by exasperation.

Rook sat down, burrowing his feet into the pebbly sand. In the two days since he had arrived at the house in upstate New York, this was about the first word that he and Frankie had had alone together.

'How bad is it?' she pressed him.

Frankie had seen some bad times, that was true. There were times when he had been drinking that he was glad he couldn't recall himself. The children were silhouetted against the glittering water. Rooker closed his eyes on a sudden clutch of pain.

'What happened to you, down at the South Pole?'

Automatically he corrected her, 'We weren't anywhere near the Pole.' Then he added, 'A woman had a baby down there, can you imagine that? I delivered it.' He was surprised. Once the first words were out, he felt a dam ready to break behind his tongue. There was a huge weight of water, words, history, waiting to pour out of him.

'Go on,' Frankie said softly.

He told her what had happened. He tried to explain about the innocence and how amazed he had been to hold it in his hands. Meg's birth had made him feel used up and polluted, with the dirt of a lifetime ingrained in the pores of his skin and the furls of his brain. It was too late to clean up. All he could do was keep away from them.

'Rooker, you aren't seeing straight. You've lived tough, but you're no worse than most people who've been in this world four decades or more. What's so bad in the past that you think you're going to pollute a newborn just by being near to her?'

He wouldn't tell Frankie what. There was only one person he might have told. 'She was so tiny. Folded, crimson, wet. And yet as soon as she took a breath she was a complete being. It was as though I had never seen anything in my life before. And after I had seen it, nothing really mattered except the two of them. Look at me. In the long term, how much better will it be for Alice and Meg if I'm not there?'

They were watching the two bigger children as they ran in the shallow water, sending up glittering cages of spray.

'But children don't judge you, or ask for your history. They take you as you are. Mine do, don't they, and you let them? How you know that you *are* doing the right thing by giving these people up. Did you ask the mother if she wanted you to be quite so nobly considerate?'

It was more than two years since he had last seen Frankie, but even so he counted her as his closest friend. He had come up here to find her, hadn't he, in the end? He had told her some of the truth; he should listen to her now. If he didn't, there was nowhere else to turn.

'No, I didn't ask.'

'Do you love her?'

'Jesus, Frankie. I don't know. It doesn't matter now.'

'I think it does matter. Maybe it matters more than anything. Do you?'

'Yes.'

'Does she know?'

'Yes.'

Frankie drained her beer. 'Does she love you?' she asked at last.

'Perhaps. I would have to find that out.'

Frankie let her arms hang over the arms of the chair. 'Then *find* out.'

'I might discover she's gone back to Meg's father. I might screw things up for her in a hundred different ways. Or she might see things differently, now we're not on the ice any longer.'

'Is that how little you think of her?'

Shamed, Rook murmured, 'No.'

Jackson and Corinna were trying to coax Sammy into the water. They each took one of his hands and swung him between them.

Frankie snapped, 'Go to England, Rook. You think you're strong but you're not. You'll never be really strong either, not until you've had the courage to make yourself vulnerable, and if you don't do it soon you'll be so stiffened up that you'll never be able to. *Listen to me*, you asshole.'

She shouted these last words, leaping to her feet and pushing him so hard that his flimsy chair overbalanced. Corinna let go of Sam's hand and he slid into the water. Frankie was already sprinting across the strip of sand as Rooker sat up. She swept Sammy into her arms, and the other two children clung to her as she strode back again.

Corinna was blue-lipped and her teeth were chattering. Rooker wrapped a towel round her and rubbed her dry.

'Rook, c'n we go in a boat now? You said,' Jackson called out from inside his towel.

They stayed late at the shore and it was already dark as they made their way home. All three children were asleep and Frankie stared into the oncoming lights as Rook drove.

She put her hand on his arm. 'Rooker?'

'Yeah.'

'Are you going?'

He sighed. 'I don't know.'

Two days later he was still at Frankie's place. A weight of uncertainty pressed on him. On the third evening he helped Frankie to carry in the grocery bags after she came back from the store.

'I've got something to show you,' she said. She took the rolled-up baton of a magazine out of one of the bags and pitched it at him. Rook picked it up, and it fell open at a big picture. He stared down into Alice's face. She was holding Meg on her lap.

'That's her, isn't it?'

Rook felt a hammering inside him. 'Yes.'

'So, are you going to England?'

All he could see was Alice's face; he could hear nothing but her voice in his ears. 'No,' he said wretchedly. 'How can I?'

Frankie's husband went out that evening to a football game. Once the children were in bed, Frankie and Rooker curled up on the sofa together in front of the television. A glint of light on her cheek caught his eye and he saw that she was crying.

'Frank? What's the matter?'

'I want . . . I want. I want you to be happy. Go to England, find your Alice. Why can't you? It's as if you've made up your mind not to be happy. If she loves you, what right do you have to make *her* miserable?'

Was that true? he wondered. Had he decided on the day that Lester died that happiness was not for him? Rooker let his head sink forward until their foreheads touched. Frankie's hot tears ran over his thumbs.

'I love you,' she whispered.

He nodded slowly. Their faces were pressed together; his eyes were closed now. The dam holding back the buried words was close to breaking. Tears forced themselves between his eyelids and he clenched his teeth to hold everything in place. He loved Frankie too. Like a sister.

'Go to England,' she begged him. 'Do it for me.'

That she should be so generous, so full of concern for him and not herself, made him cry properly. He kissed her forehead and she clung to him.

It was a moment before he could speak. 'I'll go,' he promised at last.

'You're crazy,' Jo protested. 'What about Meg?'

'All Meg needs is me. And I will be there with her.'

They were in the house in Jericho and Jo was helping Alice to clear cupboards ready for it to be let yet again.

'What about your research, your students? They used to mean everything to you and now it's as if nothing except Rooker means anything at all. You're uprooting your baby, carting her off to the middle of nowhere . . .'

'It's New Zealand,' Alice said mildly, 'to begin with. Not Outer Mongolia. I have to do my best to find him; if I sit and do nothing, my life here will be diminished by more than I'm prepared to accept. You have Harry, a family, you've made commitments and it isn't a capitulation to be here.'

'You could have Pete. You could be a family.'

Alice closed a cupboard door with a click. 'That isn't what I want.'

Margaret was much more difficult to deal with. 'New *Zealand*? You can't, Alice, and that's flat. Not running after some safety officer who—'

'Would it be different if he were a scientist?' Alice asked.

'Not at all.' Although Alice didn't think that was quite the truth. 'You've got a child now, you have responsibilities.'

Didn't you? Alice wanted to ask. But that would not have been fair. As a child she had had Trevor, they both had, always. It was Trevor's constancy that had enabled Margaret's unpredictability.

'I'm not abandoning her,' she said quietly. 'Where I go, she goes.'

'What will you do about money?' Margaret asked.

Alice had resigned her teaching and research post. 'I've got the rent from the house. Some savings. I'll have to be careful, that's all.'

Margaret shrank. Tears came into her eyes. 'I'm not that well, Alice. You know I'm not. When am I ever going to see Meg?'

'Often,' Alice comforted her. 'I'll make sure of it.'

Pete tried cajoling, then anger and outrage, and finally threats. 'You can't take her without my consent. I won't let you do it.'

Alice took his two hands. 'Don't do this to us,' she begged at last. 'Not when we could stay friends.'

'Oh, Christ.' There was real pain in his voice. 'She's my daughter.'

'Pete, she'll always be your daughter. For the rest of your life and hers.'

He lifted his head. 'Yes. Make sure you bring her back to me.'

Becky said, 'I think you are doing the right thing. I don't want you to go, but that's for selfish reasons.'

'It is the right thing,' Alice agreed.

CHAPTER TEN

'I WOULD LIKE Alice Peel's address, please.'

'I'm afraid we can't give out expedition members' personal details, Mr Rooker. The Polar Office will forward any communications, of course.'

He was standing in a midtown phone booth, his bag at his feet, waiting to pick up the express bus for JFK. He still wasn't sure whether or not to go to England. Prickles of indecision ran down his spine like beads of sweat. In spite of his promise to Frankie, it would be easy—too easy—to find a way not to do it.

'Could I speak to Beverley Winston?'

'Just a moment, please.'

'Hello.' The low voice was warm, and sweet as molasses.

'Hello, Beverley. This is James Rooker.'

'This is a surprise.'

'I might be going to London.'

Beverley laughed. 'And?'

'I'd like to see Alice Peel, but the Polar Office won't bend the rules. It's like dealing with some Brit secret society that I'm not eligible to join.'

That touched a chord, as he had intended it to do. After a fractional hesitation she said, 'I know. It's comical, isn't it? Wait a minute.'

Rooker leaned against the glass, breathing in the scent of dirt. He heard a keyboard clicking.

'I've got it.'

The only telephone number listed belonged to Alice's parents, but the address was hers: 32 Cranbrook Street, Oxford.

Rooker said goodbye to Beverley and lifted his bag. Ten minutes later the bus swung out into the late-afternoon Manhattan traffic.

At the airport he tried to decide whether or not to board the London flight. After the lonely weeks of travelling, Frankie's generous goodwill had unshackled him. Frankie liked him, loved him, even, and she trusted him to be around her kids. Meg would grow up, like Corinna. He wanted to see that happening and he wanted to share it with Alice.

For how many years, Rooker thought, had he hated the sound of *we*, for all the obligations and restrictions and the potential for disloyalty and bitterness that could be contained in a single syllable?

Ever since she had failed him, he supposed. It hadn't been her fault; he didn't blame her. All he felt now was the soft ache of sympathy. But now there was a chance that *we* might mean himself and Alice and her daughter. If Alice would allow it. If he hadn't already spent too long wandering the world, ruled by fear and self-disgust, instead of believing that love might take root and flourish, even for him.

When the BOARDING sign flickered against his flight, Rooker got up and walked uncertainly to the gate.

Trevor arrived in good time to drive them to Heathrow for the evening's flight to Auckland, via Singapore. Twenty-five hours of travelling and then a stopover in Auckland before flying on to Christchurch. Meg's carry-seat was strapped in the back of the car; their two suitcases were loaded in the boot.

'All set?' Trevor asked.

Alice stood back and looked up at her house. It was clean, closed up, waiting for the new tenants. 'All set,' she answered.

She put the keys in her pocket. They would drop them off at the lettings agency on their way out of town. They headed east, and the home-bound traffic whirled past them in the opposite direction.

The centre of Oxford was a tangle of one-way streets and pedestrian zones. Rooker fumed in his hire car as another massed party of Japanese blocked the road. At last he was turning into Cranbrook Street. His chest felt hollow round the drumbeat of his heart. His mouth was dry with anxiety as he counted off the house numbers: 26, 28, 30.

There was a young man standing on the path in front of number 32.

'I'm looking for Dr Peel.'

161

'I'm afraid you've missed her.' The man stepped hastily back as Rooker advanced on him.

'What do you mean?'

'She is travelling abroad. I'm just the letting agent.' His back was against the porch now. He shrank as Rooker loomed over him.

'I have to know where she has gone. It's very urgent.'

The man faltered, 'New Zealand, I believe. But . . .'

Where? The white light of instant comprehension exploded painfully behind Rooker's eyes. Their paths had crossed. He had arrived just too late because she had set off to look for him. It dawned on him in the same second that he must reach her. He knew with absolute certainty that without her there was less than nothing in the world.

'When?'

'An . . . hour or so. She dropped these keys in . . .'

Rooker's mind was tearing away, leapfrogging hours and miles. Wait. He had her parents' telephone number. 'Phone. I need to telephone.'

The man swallowed. 'You can use my mobile.'

Rooker took the miniature device and stabbed out the numbers. A woman's voice answered.

'My name is James Rooker. I need to speak to Alice.'

There was a beat and then, 'I am afraid she's gone. She's at the airport.'

'Do you have the flight number?'

'Wait a moment.' The voice was cold. Alice's mother didn't approve of him. It didn't matter now. He could try to reintroduce himself later. The only thing that mattered at this instant was reaching her.

'Here it is. Singapore Airlines. SQ 328. Terminal Three. Ten p.m.'

Rooker waved his hand at the agent. The man was sweating, he noticed, but he obligingly produced a pen from his pocket.

'Thank you. Does she have a mobile with her?'

'No.' The voice turned sharper. Of course, because he was at the root of all this. 'Her father is driving her. But his telephone is still here.'

'Thank you.' He would just have to retrace his steps to Heathrow. Rooker tossed the little phone back to its owner.

As he accelerated away, he saw the agent mopping his face in relief.

Alice and Trevor were at the check-in desk as it opened. Afterwards they went and drank tea. Trevor put his hand over hers. 'This is what you want, isn't it?'

Alice nodded. Not the flying and the lonely distance and the weight of uncertainty, but to be doing something that would connect her to him instead of waiting and fading in a life that no longer fitted her.

'You will come home if you can't find what you're looking for?'

'Of course I will.' But she didn't want even to consider that possibility, because it left too much aching space that didn't have Rooker in it.

'I love you,' they told each other at the terminal doors. Trevor tried to smile, then turned abruptly away.

Alice watched him go, torn between the old familiar and the new desire. When she could no longer see him, she turned back into the endless cycle of the airport.

Rooker weaved his way through the fast traffic. The road signs and the miles flashed past. 'Wait for me, wait for me,' he muttered. The first sign for Heathrow whirled at him and then the second. He was almost there. Fifteen minutes later he was at the airport turnoff. He slammed the hire car into the terminal car park and ran.

The airport was packed. He stood at the top of an escalator and scanned the crowds. She was here. She was here *somewhere*. DEPARTURES, a sign informed him.

Alice wheeled Meg towards the DEPARTURES barrier. There was a long crowded slope, divided into aisles by chrome handrails, leading to boarding controls. People flowed around her, some of them walking backwards, in tears, eyes fixed on those they were leaving behind. There was a bored man behind a tall desk, holding out his hand for her boarding card.

Rooker pushed through the crowds and sprinted past shops. The aimless surges became a steady slow tide, creeping towards DEPARTURES. He reached a chrome rail and a slope leading downwards. The press was thickest here. He stared down at the sea of heads.

She was there. *There she was*. He could see her dark head.

She was at the desk, boarding card in hand.

'Alice,' he roared. 'Alice, Alice.' The airport stilled for a second.

He was aware of a flowering of faces as people turned to stare at him.

Someone was calling her name. It was his voice. She turned.

It was Rook. Blood rushed to her head, hammered in the chambers of her ears. He vaulted over a rail, and pushed his way through the crowd.

It *was* him. He reached her and caught her in his arms. Their mouths met blindly. She tasted and smelt the familiarity, the strangeness, the solid manifest reality of him, after months of waiting and wishing.

'It is really you, isn't it?' Her mouth suddenly curved against his, warm with amazement and delight.

163

'It is. You can't escape,' he answered. He held on to her and to Meg's buggy as they pushed their way back up the ramp.

When they reached a quieter place, he propelled her aside and took her face between his hands. 'Why are you going to New Zealand?'

He had to hear it from her, spoken in her voice.

She looked down, seeing the top of Meg's head. 'I'm going to Turner. Russ found a newspaper report from the *Turner & Medfield Clarion*.' She had the print-out of it in her hand luggage. 'It's your family, isn't it?'

'Yes.'

'I thought if I went there I might find a link and I could follow the chain and in the end it would have to lead me to you.' Tears ran down her face and he tried to smooth them away, wordless, amazed that she was prepared to do this much. 'Where have you been?' she whispered.

'Cuba. Mexico. New York State. Oxford. It doesn't matter where. Forgive me. Running away, then running to get here.'

'Oxford?'

'I flew in this morning, drove straight to your house. I missed you by about an hour.'

Alice said in a quiet clear voice, 'You told me that you are a murderer. What does that mean?'

The time had come to tell the secret that Rooker had never confessed to another living soul. He looked blankly at the throngs of people. 'Can we go somewhere?'

'There's a place just up here.'

The tables were messy with spilt drinks and food debris. Alice moved two tall paper cups, a plate of cold chips. They sat down close together, their heads almost touching, Meg's buggy drawn up beside them. He held her wrists in his hands, as if to restrain her when she tried to run.

He closed his eyes. 'Fire,' he managed to say.

Alice waited, but he seemed lost for what to say next.

'Why did your mother do what she did?' she gently prompted.

He took a deep breath. 'She was an alcoholic. I was used to that; we could have managed. I looked after her when she needed it; she was a good mother in the in-between times. She was funny and clever and good company. I didn't feel deprived. I was luckier than some of my friends.' Gabby, for instance. 'Then Lester arrived.'

'Was he her lover?'

'No.' Rooker turned his head away. 'He tried to be mine.'

'How old were you?'

'Twelve.' The dam was cracking. Words started to spill out of him. 'I didn't know he was there, Alice. I swear to you. He was at our house, drinking. He'd just come on to me, not for the first time, and I was disgusted. I hated him and I wanted to hurt him, but I didn't want him to *die*. I stole a bottle of Scotch and drank as much of it as I could, then I went round to his caravan and set fire to it.'

The flood broke loose now. He talked faster and faster.

'I didn't know he was in there. And after he was found dead, no one had seen me, my mother couldn't remember anything. I just told everyone flatly that I'd been in bed all the time. Then I waited, wanting them to find out the truth, because it was too much of a secret to keep. But no one tried very hard. He drank, he was a queer, he was a misfit in Turner. But what it meant, as well as a man being dead because of me, was that my mother lost her friend. He was grown up, he was someone to tease her and keep her company and listen to her grief. I didn't understand that; I thought she shouldn't need anyone but me. She didn't survive very long after Lester died. I suppose she felt too lonely. In the end she just got into the bath and pulled the electric fire in after her.' He hesitated, but only for a second. 'I came home from school and found her.'

Rooker stared straight ahead, not seeing Alice or the crowds. He saw only his mother, the last image he had suppressed. Tears filled his eyes.

Alice stood up and went round the table to him. She wrapped her arms protectively round him and cupped his head against her ribs. 'You are not a murderer,' she whispered. 'You never were a murderer.'

They stayed still. Rooker wept openly and Alice held him close.

At last he was able to speak again. He felt empty, but calm. If Alice were to reject him now, he thought, it would hurt him deeply. But it would not be the end of him.

'Now you know,' he said simply. 'What shall we do?'

They looked into each other's eyes for a long moment. Alice found that she was smiling. 'I don't care. As long as we are together.'

His grasp tightened. 'Don't go to New Zealand.'

'Come with me,' she countered. The flight wasn't full, they had told her that at check-in. 'We can go back to Turner together. The three of us.'

She didn't think for a moment that what Rook had just told her would be the end of the darkness for him. But if they went back together and turned over the stones of his memories, maybe they could lay a solid foundation for the future. Because her future, and Meg's, did lie with Rooker. She was as certain of that as anything she had ever known.

Light suddenly kindled in Rooker's eyes. It was simple.

Everything was simple. They had each other.

'Wait here.' He grinned.

'Oh, no. Wherever you go, I'm coming with you.'

A flight attendant leaned over the occupant of the seat next to Alice's. 'I wonder,' he murmured to the gap-year backpacker, 'if you would be willing to exchange seats so that this family can travel together?'

Rooker felt a jolt of amazement at the word, then a sense of happiness taking root that he had never known before.

'Sure.' The boy shrugged indifferently.

The plane took off and London dwindled beneath them. Alice and Rooker sat with their hands linked, not speaking, knowing how much talking there was still to do. Rags of cloud blotted out the orange bloom of the city as they climbed. They were airborne, in their jet capsule, suspended between what had been and whatever was to come.

Rooker released Alice's hand for a moment and fumbled in his pocket. He brought out a small curl of red Velcro fabric and dropped it into her palm.

One-handed, because Meg lay in her other arm, Alice unfurled it. It was a name label from an EU Antarctic Expedition parka.

PEEL, it said.

ROSIE THOMAS

'You get to a point in your life when the needle swings and you think, "Now, it's my time".' For Rosie Thomas the time came when she reached her fifties, her two children were adults and she found herself on her own after her marriage had ended. Rosie had long had a passion for travel and adventure and was now able to indulge that and, as a writer, combine it with her research.

For her latest novel, *Sun at Midnight*, Rosie spent a month on a tiny Bulgarian research station in Antarctica, and one of the first questions I asked her was how she had managed to secure a place there. 'Very easily, in the end,' she told me. Having tried the British and American stations without success, she eventually contacted a cruise line who supplied her with the SatNav phone number of the Bulgarian base. 'I rang the number and a crackly voice answered, "*Da.*" I launched into my spiel about who I was and what I wanted and the voice replied, "Come next week. Bring malt whisky."'

That was on a Wednesday and, by the Sunday, Rosie had packed and was ready for six weeks in Antarctica. She flew to Ushuaia and spent a week on a supply ship getting to the base. 'As the ship pulled into the bay, I saw this tiny, tiny, red speck and realised that that was where I was going. I suddenly thought: I am absolutely mad. I don't know these people, I don't know their language, and there's no getting out until the ship returns in a month's time. But the Bulgarians were so friendly and welcoming that the time I spent there

was some of the happiest of my life. The weather, the scenery, the wildlife: it's so magnificent and puts life into perspective. It was a real porthole of joy.'

When we met, Rosie was in the midst of writing her next novel, which is set in Cairo. 'In the book there is a "lost in the desert scene" because I got lost in the Fish River Canyon in Namibia and nearly died,' she told me. 'My partner, Theo, and I hired a local guide and set off. But on the second day, our guide fell behind and we never saw him again.' Finding themselves alone in hostile terrain, with little water, little food and no map, Rosie and Theo decided to follow the river, but as it ran in great oxbow loops with huge strips of land in between, they were often forced to make their way inland. 'One afternoon,' Rosie explained, 'we lost the river completely. I was following tracks of what I thought were human footsteps, walking faster and faster with my head down. Theo kept saying, "these are leopard tracks", but I wouldn't listen. The canyon walls were getting higher and higher, and the sun was more and more concentrated, but I pressed on wilfully. Then I went round a corner and there was a blind wall, a dead end. It was a defining moment for me. I thought, This is where it is all going to end. I really felt that I was going to die.' Eventually, the pair found their way back to the river, walked for a further two and a half days, and finally staggered into town.

So, after her death-defying experience in Namibia, will Rosie be less adventurous in future? 'Perhaps, for the moment. But who knows once ideas for the next book come along.'

Jane Eastgate

The one you really want

As Nancy makes preparations
for the perfect Christmas, her
hopes and dreams are shattered
when she discovers that her
husband has been buying
expensive jewellery for
someone else.
Meanwhile, her best friend,
Carmen, is settling down to yet
another solo Christmas, when she
finds an unexpected visitor on
her doorstep . . .

Chapter 1

'GO ON, YOU CAN SAY IT,' Nancy offered, because it was so obviously what Carmen was longing to blurt out down the phone. Five-year-olds had more self-control than Carmen.

Five hundred miles away in London, Carmen replied innocently, 'I wouldn't dream of saying I told you so. We all know what happens to best friends who do that. You're the one who married Jonathan, so it stands to reason you thought he was the bee's knees. If I'd told you then what part of a bee I thought he was, you'd have hated me. That's why I pretended to like him.'

Nancy smiled to herself, thinking that she really should be crying. 'And that's why you don't have a Bafta. You may have tried to pretend, but it didn't fool anyone.'

'Ah, but I didn't tell you I thought he was an idiot,' said Carmen, 'and that's the important thing. You didn't feel as if you had to stick up for him the whole time, you didn't always have to defend him, d'you see, because if I had told you, you wouldn't have taken a blind bit of notice anyway. And we'd have ended up falling out.'

'Would we?' Nancy couldn't imagine falling out with Carmen. They'd been inseparable since they were eight.

'It wouldn't have been easy. Anyway, that's why I didn't. Which is why we're still friends,' Carmen said cheerfully. 'Are you sure you're all right?' she added.

Was she? Nancy suspected that she was in a mild state of shock. It was Christmas morning, after all. Christmas was such a happy day, in her experience, that it was quite hard to take in what had happened.

'I'm great,' said Nancy, because the last thing she wanted was Carmen

171

worrying about her. 'Mum's going to be here soon to give me a hand.'

'And you're really not going to tell her?'

Nancy closed her eyes. 'Completely ruin her Christmas, you mean? You know how Mum feels about Jonathan. She'd be distraught.'

'OK, you're the boss.' Mischievously Carmen said, 'Off you go, back to peeling the parsnips like a good little wifey. Ever tried them poached in honey and arsenic?'

'If I had, I wouldn't be here to tell you, would I?' Belatedly, Nancy said, 'Are you all right?'

'Me? I'm wonderful.'

Nancy felt guilty, because if anyone deserved to have a big fuss made of them over the Christmas period, it was Carmen. When your husband had died three years ago—and, unlike herself and Jonathan, Carmen had been totally devoted to Spike—you were entitled to be depressed. 'Well, look after yourself. I'll call you tonight when I get a chance.'

'Can't wait. And don't forget,' Carmen said chirpily, 'the honey disguises the taste of the arsenic.'

Had it only happened this morning? Was it really less than three hours ago that her world had tilted and begun to crumble? Nancy, her breath misting up the bedroom window of their four-bedroomed detached house, gazed out over the frosty garden, sparkling iridescent in the sunlight like one of those glitter-strewn Christmas cards. The sky was an unseasonal shade of duck-egg blue, and in the distance, beyond Kilnachranan, the mountains rose snow-peaked and dramatic.

And down in the garden on the stiff white grass stood the cause of her current torment. Her Christmas present from Jonathan. It was all thanks to this . . . *thing,* that her life was about to change in a pretty major way.

The card had arrived ten days ago, among half a dozen others. The sound of Christmas cards *phflummping* through the letterbox onto the mat was a thrilling one, because you never knew who might have sent you a card. Prince William perhaps, or Bono from U2 . . . and, incredibly, there *had* been an intriguing-looking envelope among the rest; an expensive cream one addressed in handwriting she hadn't recognised.

Nancy had cast aside the others and ripped open the mystery envelope. The picture on the front of the card was a snow scene of an Edinburgh street. The rank of shops depicted in the painting rang a bell. Cavendish Row, that was it. Opening the card, Nancy read the printed inscription inside: 'Christmas and New Year greetings to a valued customer, from all at Rossiter and Co., Fine Jewellers'. To personalise the card, there was a formless squiggle of a signature at the bottom.

Tuh, so much for being sent a card by someone exciting.

What's more, Nancy thought crossly, Jonathan's surprise had now been ruined. He'd clearly paid a visit to Rossiter's on Cavendish Row and bought her something expensive for Christmas. They were unlikely to send classy greetings cards to every Tom, Dick and Harry who just needed a new watch battery and had popped into the shop. Except it hadn't occurred to the not-so-clever people at Rossiter's that cards sent to the home of a married male customer stood a good chance of being opened, completely innocently, by his wife. And since the whole point of Christmas presents was that they should be a fabulous surprise . . .

Well, that was what she'd thought ten days ago. Gripping the window ledge, Nancy gazed down at her present. Having disposed of the greetings card in the dustbin, she'd spent ages practising her surprised-and-delighted face, because that was how she'd planned to react when she opened the satin-lined jewellery box on Christmas Day. Instead, that morning Jonathan had steered her across the bedroom, instructed her to close her eyes, then pulled open the curtains with a flourish.

'Ta-daaa! You can open your eyes now,' Jonathan had proclaimed, and Nancy had obediently opened her eyes, mystified as to why he would have wanted to put the jewellery box containing her Christmas present out on the windowsill.

Except, of course, he hadn't.

'It's a lawn mower.' It had taken her a good few seconds to get the words out.

'The sit-on kind,' Jonathan had informed her with pride.

'It's . . . it's . . .'

'You just wait, you won't know how you ever managed without one. This takes all the effort out of doing the grass. Trust me'—he had slipped his arms round Nancy and kissed the back of her neck—'you're going to love it.'

It had taken a little while for all the implications to sink in. When they finally did, Nancy had felt like the slow girl at school, the last one to get the punchline of a joke. If Jonathan hadn't bought some jewellery from Rossiter's for her, then he must have bought it for someone else.

Hadn't he?

Nancy frowned. Could there still be an innocent explanation for what had happened? One that simply hadn't occurred to her? And if there was no innocent explanation, who could Jonathan be seeing? Not his secretary, surely. The whole point of a mistress was getting one prettier and younger than your wife. Tania looked like a potato in a pashmina.

A car toot-tooted outside, bringing her back to earth. Rose, her mother, was rattling up the drive in her green Mini. Car, not skirt.

OK, forget the unfaithful husband and the all-but-over marriage. It was Christmas Day. On with the show.

'Darling!' Rose threw her arms round her beloved only daughter. 'You look beautiful! Merry Christmas!'

'You too, Mum.' Nancy hugged Rose in return. Her mother was only in her late sixties, but there was always the worry that this year might be her last. That was why she couldn't tell her about Jonathan's philandering— OK, alleged philandering. It would break her heart.

'Where's that lovely son-in-law of mine?' Rose was peering hopefully past Nancy into the house. 'I've got bags of presents here—they weigh an absolute ton.'

'Jonathan's gone down to the pub to meet Hamish and Pete. Pre-lunch drinks.' Nancy had been delighted to be shot of him for a while. 'He'll be back by two o'clock. Let me carry the bags inside. Oh, Mum, you are naughty, you've brought far too many presents.'

'Rubbish, I enjoy buying them.' Following Nancy inside, Rose heaved a sigh of pleasure. 'Such a gorgeous house. You're so lucky, darling. Can you believe how lucky you are?'

Hastily changing the subject, Nancy said, 'The turkey's in the oven. I've done the potatoes and the bread sauce, but the rest of the vegetables are still—'

'How did I guess they would be?' Rose had been arranging the Christmas presents under the tree. Straightening, she beamed. 'Don't worry, darling, I'm here now. We can have a glass of sherry and a chat while we're doing it all. You can tell me everything that's been going on.'

Nancy had to turn away so as not to let Rose see the tears in her eyes. Did other 28-year-olds tell their mothers everything that had been going on in their lives? Maybe they did. But Rose always saw the best in people; there was a kind of innocence about her.

'Now, parsnips. Carrots. Oh, my word, asparagus—that must have cost a fortune.' Rose, surveying the vegetable basket, was torn between delight and horror at the thought of how much the bundles of fresh asparagus must have cost. 'Right, I'll make a start on the carrots.'

Swallowing the lump in her throat, Nancy watched her mother deftly peel and chop the carrots. Rose McAndrew, four feet eleven inches tall and weighing less than seven stone with all her clothes on. Widowed thirteen years ago, she lived alone in a tiny, pin-neat, rented flat in Edinburgh, still worked part-time as a cleaner in an old people's home and was a prodigious knitter. Every spare second was spent producing, at lightning speed, soft knitted toys which she then donated to a charity shop supporting a children's hospice. There was no one better.

Turning, Rose said happily, 'And what did Jonathan get you for Christmas?'

Nancy swallowed. 'A lawn mower. The kind you sit on. It's out in the garden.'

'A sit-on lawn mower? Oh, my word, how marvellous! You'll be able to ride around on it like the Queen. What fun!'

Forcing a smile, because she was unsure how often the Queen actually rode on a lawn mower, Nancy said, 'I know.'

'That's Jonathan for you, isn't it? So original. He always knows exactly the right thing to buy.'

Other people might have mothers in whom they could confide every detail of their lives, but Rose needed to be cosseted and protected from details that would upset her. Nancy knew she couldn't tell her the truth.

It was six in the evening when Carmen Todd let herself back into her empty house. She'd been helping out at the shelter for the homeless in Paddington all day, serving up plates of Christmas dinner and pouring endless mugs of steaming hot, conker-brown tea. Now, reaching her bedroom, she stripped off her bleached blue sweatshirt and old jeans and chucked them into the laundry basket.

In the bathroom, Carmen switched on the power shower and examined her face in the bathroom mirror while she waited for the water to heat up. Her short black hair was tousled and spiky and her dark brown eyes stood out against the pallor of her skin.

The doorbell rang just as she was about to climb into the shower. Hesitating, Carmen wondered who on earth it could be. She certainly wasn't expecting any visitors. But not answering the door—or at least not speaking into the entryphone—was beyond her capabilities. Hurriedly wrapping a parrot-blue velours dressing gown round herself, Carmen padded through to the hallway and pressed the button on the speaker.

'Yes?'

'Carmen Todd, this is the police. Open the door, please, we have a warrant to search the premises.'

Breathless with disbelief, Carmen said cautiously, 'Rennie? Is that you?'

'Of course it's me! Open the door this minute, woman, before my feet freeze to the pavement.'

'Oh, sorry!' Hastily Carmen buzzed him in and opened the door. Thrilled to see him, she hurled herself into his arms. 'I thought you were in Alabama or Mississippi or somewhere . . .'

'Somewhere with lots of vowels,' said Rennie, hugging her hard in return. 'I know, we were. Well, Illinois, same difference. They had to cancel the rest of the tour. Dave's been hitting the bottle again and Andy's snorting coke like a human Dyson. Neither of them were capable of doing their stuff on stage, and seeing as there was a drying-out clinic handy, Ed packed them both off there. So that's it, I flew back last night. Thought I'd come and see how you're doing. Now, stand back and let me take a good look at you.'

Ditto. Smiling, Carmen took in the almost shoulder-length dark hair, the deep tan, a wicked grin and those glittering, dark green eyes that always looked as though they were ringed with eyeliner—except they weren't, that was just Rennie's impossibly thick eyelashes. He was wearing a tan leather jacket, crumpled cream jeans, a faded brown polo shirt and the kind of hideous brass-buckled belt that only a cowboy would wear. And he was looking lean and fit, as ever. For as long as Carmen had known him, he'd exuded an air of health. The whites of his eyes were a clear blue-white, his tongue raspberry pink, his stomach washboard flat. The cowboy belt let the overall effect down badly, but if Rennie liked something, he wore it, and that was that.

'Stunning as ever,' he pronounced at last, his brown hands on Carmen's shoulders. 'Anyway, I thought this was a respectable street.'

'It's a dressing gown! It's completely done up,' Carmen protested.

'I'm not talking about you, I'm talking about the street. I thought it was supposed to be dead posh around here.'

What with his touring commitments, combined with the fact that he'd spent the majority of the last three years out of the country, Carmen forgave him. Just.

'Actually, it is dead posh.'

'Sorry, it's gone downhill since I was here last. Rear-admirals, QCs, the silver-spoon brigade—more pompous gits than you could shake a stick at in the good old days. Call the police as soon as look at you, they would. Answer the door to a stranger? You must be joking.'

Patiently Carmen said, 'Is there a point to this, or is it just a general off-the-cuff rant?'

'Sweetheart, of course there's a point.' Heading through to the kitchen, Rennie opened the fridge and seized a bottle of Veuve Cliquot. 'OK to open this?'

She hesitated. The bottle had been there for over two years. She'd bought it on the first anniversary of Spike's death, along with several packets of paracetamol and Nurofen. The plan had been to spend the night at home alone, just for a change, and give herself until midnight to carefully think things through. If, when the clock chimed twelve, she decided there was no point in carrying on, she would finish the bottle of champagne then swallow the painkillers.

At eleven o'clock, with the bottle chilling nicely in the fridge, she had opened a writing pad and begun to compose a suicide note.

By midnight the wastepaper bin was piled high with scrunched-up sheets of paper. Mortified, Carmen had discovered that suicide notes weren't as easy to write as she'd recklessly imagined. Everything she put down sounded ridiculous when she tried reading it aloud. Furious with herself, she'd ended up leaving the unopened bottle in the fridge and making herself a cup of tea instead. Since flushing the painkillers down the loo would have been nothing but a criminal waste, she'd stacked them in the bathroom cabinet. The champagne she'd left in the fridge, however, as a salutary reminder.

What the hell. Carmen gestured at the bottle. 'Good idea. I'll get the glasses.'

'And I'll get back to my point,' said Rennie, 'which is that I arrived here two hours ago. You were out.'

'I was helping out at the homeless shelter.'

'That explains the smell.' Rennie had never been one to keep his innermost thoughts to himself. Catching the look on Carmen's face he grinned and said, 'OK, OK, and it's very noble of you to do your bit, but I'm just telling you, you do smell.'

The trouble was, she knew he was right. Exasperated, Carmen headed for the bathroom. 'Open the bottle. I'll be back in five minutes.'

Helpfully Rennie said, 'Want a hand?'

'You're hilarious. Go and sit down in the living room. And don't eat all my Thornton's truffles.'

As she shampooed her hair and soaped her body in the steaming shower, Carmen marvelled at Rennie's attitude to life. He had more energy than anyone she'd ever known, working hard and playing harder, always joking, incapable of not flirting with practically any girl who happened to cross his path. And, being Rennie, an awful lot crossed his path.

Rennie Todd, her brother-in-law. Spike's younger brother. Apart from their smiles, no two brothers could have been less alike. Closing her eyes as rivers of shampoo cascaded down over her face, Carmen pictured Spike, her beloved husband, with his sparkling grey eyes, dark blond hair and tendency towards pudginess. Whereas Rennie crackled and fizzed with energy, Spike had always been the quieter, calmer member of the band. He'd thought more deeply about things, written songs with profoundly meaningful lyrics. Rennie, Carmen was fairly sure, had never had a profound meaningful thought in his life.

And he was still alive, that was another significant difference between the pair of them. Rennie was dazzlingly alive and Spike was dead.

Out of the shower, Carmen towel-dried her hair roughly and wrapped herself back up in her dressing gown. With a bit of luck she now smelt of Jo Malone tuberose rather than Eau de Shelter.

In the living room, Rennie had made himself entirely at home. Stretched out across the navy sofa, he was busy finishing off a tube of Pringles, flicking through TV channels and chatting on his mobile. Grinning across at Carmen, he said into the phone, 'Sorry, darling, have to go now, the nurses are bringing my grandmother in to see me . . . hello, Granny, you're looking well . . . OK, I'll give you a ring, bye now.'

'Thanks a lot.' Carmen snatched the remote control from him, because Rennie could flick channels for England and it drove her insane.

'Sorry.' He grinned up at her, unrepentant. 'Her name's Nicole, but the lads call her Clingfilm. She was desperate to spend Christmas with me. I had to come up with a decent excuse.'

It wasn't only where TV programmes were concerned that Rennie had the attention span of a gnat.

'Couldn't you just have told her you were visiting your tragic old sister-in-law? Wouldn't that have been boring enough?'

'You're joking. Nicole was a huge Spike fan. She'd have wanted to come along and meet you,' said Rennie. 'That's why I invented a granny-in-a-nursing-home in Stockton-on-Tees. That's better.' He sniffed approvingly as Carmen shoved his feet to one side and sat down. 'Same stuff Spike used to buy you.'

'It's my favourite,' said Carmen. 'Unlike some people, I don't get bored of something after three days and rush off to try something new.'

'Touché. And if I wanted a big lecture I could have stayed in Illinois and listened to my manager. Anyway, it's Christmas and we mustn't bicker. Guess what I did this afternoon when I came here and discovered you were out?'

This was one of those completely unanswerable questions. Carmen gave a lazy shrug. 'Who knows?'

'Sat down on your front step.' Rennie raised his eyebrows at her, miming outrage. 'Now, bearing in mind that this *is* Fitzallen Square in the very *poshest* part of Chelsea, I fully expected to be harangued by retired brigadiers, ordered out of the square by SAS troops swinging down from helicopters—I'll never understand why Spike wanted to live in a place like this.'

He did, though. It had been that very air of pompous gentility that had attracted Spike, and the thought of sending the residents into a panic at the prospect of sharing their elegant Georgian square with a member of a heavy rock band like Red Lizard. The sunny, seven-bedroomed property, arranged on four floors and immaculately renovated throughout, was the last place anyone had imagined they'd choose to settle. But it had appealed to Spike's sense of humour. He'd bought the £5 million house as a joke, but within a few months he and Carmen had both fallen in love with it.

'So the SAS swooped in,' said Carmen.

'No, they *didn't*. That's just it. One of your neighbours opened their front door and asked if they could help me. I told them you were out, and said I'd wait on the step until you came back. So they said I couldn't possibly wait outside and why didn't I come over and join them for a drink? Well, at this point, *obviously*, I thought I must be having some kind of hallucination. What were these posh people thinking of?'

'OK, calm down. In that case I'll hazard a guess that it wasn't the Brough-Badhams at number sixty-two.'

Brigadier Brough-Badham and his wife, the Honourable Marjorie, had been so horrified when they'd first heard, four years earlier, who their new neighbours were to be, that they had started a petition. Neither of them had ever spoken a word to these deeply undesirable residents; the brigadier bristled his moustache and his wife looked down her anteater nose at Carmen whenever they passed each other in the square.

'It was your other neighbour, the one on this side.' Rennie jerked his thumb to the right. 'Number fifty-eight.'

'Funny name for a neighbour.'

'Been reading Christmas cracker jokes again?' Digging her in the ribs, Rennie said, 'I can't believe you've never met him. What a great bloke. When he invited me in, I thought you must know each other but he says not. He reckons you've been hiding from him.'

'I have not,' Carmen protested with a fraction too much denial. 'He only moved in three months ago. Our paths haven't crossed, that's all.'

This was true. More or less. Well, not counting the couple of times she'd seen her neighbour climbing out of his car and had ducked away from the window before he could catch a glimpse of her and wave.

'His name's Connor O'Shea,' said Rennie. 'I thought you might have known that, after he pushed that note through your door inviting you to his housewarming party.'

Bugger. The blood rushed to Carmen's pale cheeks.

'So you see, it rather looks as if you *have* been hiding from him.'

'Don't start nagging,' she said self-consciously.

'Come on,' Rennie argued. 'Sweetheart, it's been three years now. The old Carmen would have jumped at the idea of a party.'

'But I'm not the old Carmen, am I? I'm the new Carmen now. And it's not as easy as you're making out.' She paused and watched him expertly remove the cork from the bottle of Veuve Cliquot.

'Great new neighbour. Friendly invite to a housewarming. I don't see the problem.'

'Well, you wouldn't, would you? Because you're you.' Carmen sipped the champagne. 'But I was married to Spike and now I'm not. He's gone and I'm the one that's left. Whenever I meet new people and they find out who I am, all they want to talk about is Spike and what it was like being married to him. They think I'm lucky, because he left me everything in his will, which is pretty weird because I don't feel lucky. So that's why I didn't go to the housewarming party.'

'OK, now I get it,' said Rennie. 'That's why you spend all your time at that damn shelter. Nobody there has any idea that you live in a place like this, that you were married to Spike Todd. They think you're just a normal girl in jeans and a sweatshirt who travels there on the tube.'

'So what does he do, this neighbour of mine?' Carmen was keen to change the subject.

'You see? You're no different to anyone else. Connor O'Shea, big friendly Irish guy in his thirties—how has he managed to make enough money to live next door to you?'

Carmen punched him. 'That's not what I'm asking.'

'Of course it is. Admit it, you're dying to know,' said Rennie. 'He's just bought a house in Fitzallen Square. He drives a Bentley. He has an apartment in New York and a villa in the South of France. So what do you reckon, could he work in the paint department of B&Q? Behind the counter at the post office on Finchley High Street? School caretaker?'

'Right, that's it. I don't want to know,' said Carmen. 'So don't tell me.'

'Fine. Just making a point,' Rennie said innocently. 'Could be a bank robber, come to think of it. Someone big in the East End gangland underworld thingy. Did he look a bit shifty to you, when you were secretly peeping down at him from your bedroom window?'

Bugger, was this another of Rennie's inspired guesses or had that bloody neighbour of hers spotted her and let on to him?

'East End? I thought you said he was Irish.'

'Ah well, begorrah, of course he *said* he was Irish.' Rennie adopted the most appalling Dublin accent. 'But that could just be a cover, couldn't it? A front to steer people away from the truth.'

'You don't have to stay here, you know. You could always go back to your Irish Cockney gang leader and spend the rest of the evening there.'

'He's already invited us. He's got a house full of friends and family. We're welcome over there any time this evening,' said Rennie.

Taking another sip of champagne, Carmen wondered whether this would be a good time to meet her mystery neighbour. Probably, with Rennie here, it was the ideal opportunity. She knew she should be making more of an effort. But, in an odd way, Fitzallen Square's air of reserve—OK, downright unfriendliness—suited the way she'd been feeling. Once you started smiling and saying hello to your neighbours you ran the risk of falling into conversation with them. And from then on you really were on the slippery slope to getting entangled with the kind of people you really didn't want to be entangled with.

'Not tonight,' said Carmen. 'I'd rather just stay here. What time do you have to leave?'

'Charming. Trying to get rid of me already?'

'No!' She hit him on the head with the empty Pringles tube. 'Just asking a perfectly normal question. You turn up out of the blue, you eat my Pringles—if you're hoping for a Christmas dinner, you're out of luck, because I didn't buy any proper f—'

'Hey, calm down, I'm not on the scrounge for a free meal. I came here to see you. And your Pringles obviously.'

'There's another tube out in the kitchen.' Carmen was glad to see him, glad he was here. Deep down, she'd been dreading spending Christmas evening on her own. She'd volunteered to stay on at the shelter but they had told her, kindly, firmly, that she had worked long enough.

They spent the next couple of hours catching up on all the news, drinking, eating and intermittently flipping through the channels on TV. A festive re-run of *Fatal Attraction* prompted Carmen to tell Rennie the story of Nancy and the Christmas card from the jewellers.

Predictably, Rennie shook his head and tut-tutted. 'What an amateur. Number one rule when you're buying anything like that, always pay in cash. And always, *always* give a false address. Ouch.'

'It's not funny. You're single, he's married. Nancy is my best friend and that bastard's cheating on her, I just know he is.'

Looking around the living room, with its complete absence of Christmas decorations, Rennie said, 'If she's your best friend, why didn't she invite you up there for Christmas?'

'She did. I said I couldn't miss my shift at the shelter.'

'And the real reason is?'

'I can get a bit mopey at this time of year. I didn't want to inflict my moods on other people.' Carmen wriggled herself into a more comfortable position on the sofa. 'Plus, I never did like Jonathan.'

'But what if your friend Nancy's got it all wrong? She doesn't know for sure that her husband's fooling around, does she?'

The phone rang. Hastily swallowing a mouthful of Viennese truffle, Carmen snatched it up before Rennie could get in first and say something hideously embarrassing.

'Hi, it's me.' Nancy's voice was hushed and strained.

'And?' Carmen's heart went out to her.

'Mum's just gone up to bed. I don't want her to overhear me. God, what a day. All this pretending everything's fine is exhausting.'

Carmen, who knew all about putting on a brave face and pretending everything was fine, said, 'Where's Jonathan?'

'Out.'

'What? It's Christmas night!'

'I know. He came back from the pub at two o'clock and we had a nice afternoon. Well, nice for Mum,' Nancy amended. 'I mean, everything was like normal, as far as she was concerned. Then at eight o'clock Jonathan got a call on his mobile. He said it was his friend Hamish, having trouble getting his new computer fixed up. So off he went to help, but that was three hours ago and now his phone's switched off, and I'm a bit worried that when he does get home I might punch him.'

'OK, sshh,' Carmen said soothingly as Nancy's voice rose. 'How long is your mum staying with you?'

'Until tomorrow night. That's another thing,' Nancy burst out. 'This afternoon Jonathan told me we've been invited to a Boxing Day party at the pub. Well, I said no because I knew Mum wouldn't be too keen. So Jonathan said fine, me and Mum could stay at home if we liked, but he didn't see why he should miss out on a bloody good party. Oh God.' Nancy took a deep breath, steadying herself. 'It's just awful. What's Mum going to think if he disappears again?'

'Tell her,' said Carmen.

'I can't, I just can't. She'd be so upset.' Nancy sounded close to tears.

'She's your mother.'

'Exactly!'

'Take her home at lunchtime and go on to the party afterwards.'

'How can I do that?' Nancy let out a wail. 'She's all excited about staying with us until tomorrow night!'

'OK, so all three of you have to go to the party.' Carmen was fast running out of options.

'I know, I know we will. But I keep having this horrible thought,' said Nancy. 'What if Jonathan's girlfriend is there? That could be the reason he's so determined to go.'

'Well—'

'Hang on, I can hear a car!' There was the sound of a curtain being swished back, then Nancy hissed, 'It's Jonathan, he's home. I have to go.'

'OK, good luck . . .' but the line had gone dead. 'She's all on her own,' Carmen said defensively, because her eyes were starting to glisten.

'She's not on her own, she's got her mother and her husband there with her. I bet she wishes she *was* on her own.'

'You're all heart,' said Carmen.

'I'm not so bad.' Grinning at her, Rennie said, 'I've got hidden depths.'

As he took out his mobile, Carmen eyed it suspiciously. 'Who are you ringing now?'

'Calling a cab.'

'Where are you going?' Her stomach contracted. Now that Rennie was here, she didn't want him to leave.

'The Savoy.'

'You can stay here if you want.' Carmen prayed she didn't sound as needy as she thought she sounded.

'I know.' Rennie winked to show he'd been teasing her. 'I am staying here. But I'm already booked into the Savoy. I need to get over there and pick up my stuff.'

'Here, cup of tea. Happy Boxing Day.'

Hmm? From the depths of sleep, Carmen heard the clink of china and smelt toothpaste and soap. Her eyes snapping open in disbelief, she saw that Rennie had brought her a cup of tea. Not only that, but it was still pitch-black outside. He was even wearing aftershave.

'Oh my God,' squeaked Carmen, catching sight of the alarm clock. 'It's four o'clock in the morning!'

'I know, blame it on the jet lag. Now drink your tea,' Rennie said bossily, 'and chuck a few things into a case.'

'What's going on?' Carmen eyed him with suspicion.

'I didn't bring you a Christmas present. So this is it. We're going on a little trip.'

The trouble with Rennie was he had absolutely no concept of the words 'little trip'. Last night he'd been talking about Australia and she'd mentioned that it was somewhere she'd always wanted to visit.

Cautiously, Carmen said, 'How are we getting there?'

'Plane. Don't worry, I've already booked the tickets.'

Oh God, it was Australia!

'I don't know where my passport is.' She rubbed her eyes.

'Come on, where's your sense of adventure?'

'Gone walkabout.' Then Carmen saw that he was laughing at her.

'You don't trust me at all, do you? I wasn't actually planning to whisk you off to the Australian outback.'

'Where then?'

'Thought we might try the Edinburgh outback instead. See what Boxing Day parties are like up there.' Rennie ruffled her hair. 'Give your friend Nancy a bit of moral support.'

Nancy nearly fainted when she answered the front door at ten thirty on Boxing Day morning and found Rennie Todd standing on the doorstep.

'Rennie? Good grief, what are you doing here?'

The last time she'd seen him had been at Spike's funeral. And now here he was, looking even more like a rock star than ever in the out-of-context environment of her front doorstep. His long hair gleamed, his diamond earring glittered in the sunlight and he was ridiculously tanned.

'I came to see Carmen,' said Rennie.

'What? But she isn't here!'

He frowned. 'Yes, she is.'

'Honestly, she isn't.' As Nancy shook her head, Jonathan came up behind her to find out what was going on.

'Who is it?'

'Carmen's brother-in-law.' Embarrassed to say his name, Nancy gestured awkwardly towards Rennie. 'He's looking for Carmen. I'm just explaining she isn't here.'

'Look, I'm sorry, but she is,' Rennie insisted, reaching over and yanking Carmen into view.

'*Waaaahhhh*,' shrieked Nancy, hugging her. 'I only spoke to you last night!'

'It was Rennie's idea. We caught the eight o'clock flight.'

'But you said you couldn't come up because you have to work!'

'I made her see sense. They already had plenty of volunteers for today.' Rennie grinned. 'Carmen isn't as indispensable as she likes to think. Hi, I'm Rennie.' He nodded at Jonathan, who was still standing behind Nancy. 'I've heard all about you.'

Oh God, thought Nancy, please don't.

'Actually we've met before.' Leaning past Nancy, Jonathan shook his hand. 'I was there at the wedding.' When Rennie looked blank, he added, 'Carmen's wedding . . . when she married your brother.'

'Oh, right. Sorry, I don't remember you. Never mind, we're here now.' Rennie flashed his dazzling smile. 'All the way up from London. You can invite us in if you like.'

'I can't believe it,' Nancy whispered. 'You're actually here. You don't know how much better that makes me feel.' Lowering her voice still further, she added, 'Does Rennie know?'

Nodding, Carmen said, 'It's OK, he won't say anything.'

'Come through and say hello to Mum,' Nancy said, raising her voice again. Happily she dragged Carmen through to the kitchen, with Rennie following on behind.

Rose flung herself at Carmen in delight. 'What a surprise! It's lovely to see you again.' Having patted Carmen's face, Rose turned and said, 'And I don't think we've met before.'

Stepping forward to drop a kiss on each of her soft powdered cheeks, Rennie grinned. 'If we had, I'd definitely have remembered. I'm Rennie. Mmm, you smell gorgeous, like a Hollywood goddess. It's like kissing Greta Garbo.'

He'd always known how to charm the opposite sex.

'Ah, get away with you!' Flushing with pleasure, Rose playfully slapped his hand. 'Greta Garbo's dead.'

'It's like kissing Greta Garbo at the height of her beauty.' Rennie was undeterred. 'When she starred in *Queen Christina*. That's one of my all-time favourite films.'

'Truly?' Rose's face lit up. 'Greta Garbo's my all-time favourite actress. I watched *Queen Christina* on the television just the other week.'

'I've got it on video,' said Rennie. 'And *Ninotchka*.'

'Well, who'd have thought it? You, another Garbo fan! And with hair like yours,' Rose marvelled. 'I mean, I know it's one of those music things, but does it really have to be that long?'

'*Rose*,' hissed Jonathan, coming into the kitchen. 'He's our guest.'

'So's Rose,' Rennie said easily. 'Which means we can both say whatever we like. Now, we've sprung ourselves on you, so would you let me take you all out to lunch, to make up for it?'

'We can feed you!' Rose looked deeply offended; on the worktop behind her stood bowls of chopped carrots, potatoes and onions. 'There'll be more than enough casserole for everyone.'

Under his breath Jonathan murmured, 'There's enough for everyone in Kilnachranan.'

'But wouldn't lunch out be more of a treat for you? How about the Kincaid Hotel in Edinburgh?' said Rennie.

Jonathan said, 'Bit short notice. I wouldn't think you'd get a table.'

'Oh, they'll find one for me. Suzy Kincaid's an old friend.'

Clearing his throat, Jonathan said, 'That sounds great. The thing is, we've been invited to a party this afternoon. Seems a bit rude to let your friends down because you've had a better offer. Maybe I should give the lunch a miss.'

'Right, better idea,' said Rennie. 'We'll have Rose's casserole for lunch and book a table at Kincaid's for dinner this evening. Then you lot can go to your party this afternoon.' He paused as if the thought had just occurred to him. 'Actually, would they mind if you brought along a couple of extra guests?'

'Great. Of course you can come along.' Jonathan nodded.

'OK with you, Miss Garbo?' Rennie turned to her to double-check. 'You don't mind if we gatecrash?'

'I'd be delighted.' Beaming up at him, Rose said, 'Right, I've a casserole that needs putting together.'

'Go on, you two.' Shooing Carmen and Nancy towards the kitchen door, Rennie said, 'I know you're dying for a proper gossip. I'll stay in here and let Queen Christina show me how to make a casserole.'

Outside, bundled up in fleeces, Nancy said, 'Who'd have thought it? My mum and Rennie Todd, getting on like a house on fire.'

'Ah well, that's Rennie for you. He has the knack. It's a good job Rose isn't twenty years younger.' Carmen's mouth twitched. 'You wouldn't risk leaving her alone with him in the kitchen—oh my God, here it is!'

They had rounded the side of the house. There, ahead of them on the frosted lawn, stood the lawn mower.

'Exhibit A, m'lud,' said Nancy. 'The vehicle the defendant was driving when she ran over her husband.'

'And mowed him to death, chopping him into a million pieces.' Carmen, arms outstretched and fingers wiggling, mimed little bits of Jonathan flying across the garden. 'Well, you wouldn't have to scatter his ashes. Cut out the middle man, that's what I say.'

This was how they had always dealt with emotional crises. Ever since their schooldays, they had learned that poking fun at their various predicaments—and at the members of the opposite sex who had invariably been the cause of them—was their coping mechanism of choice.

'It would make the garden grow,' said Nancy, her nose prickling with the cold. She paused, then said, 'Thanks for coming up.'

'What are you going to do?'

'Get today over with, hope nothing awful happens at the party this afternoon. Once Mum's gone back to her flat, I can ask Jonathan what he's playing at. See what he has to say for himself.'

'And if he's seeing someone?' Carmen raised her slanting eyebrows.

'I leave him.'

'OK. And if he denies it?'

'I don't know.' Nancy felt a bit sick.

Carmen gave her arm a squeeze. 'Rennie and I have rushed up here like the cavalry. I don't want you to feel pressurised into doing something drastic, just because we're here.'

Nancy patted Carmen's icy hand. 'It's just so ironic, isn't it? Everyone was horrified when you and Spike got together. Nobody gave your marriage a chance. And look how happy the two of you were.'

'We got such a kick out of proving everyone wrong.' Carmen smiled. 'Unlike you and Jonathan.'

'I know,' Nancy said wryly. 'Fairy-tale stuff. Jonathan was such a catch, what had I ever done to deserve someone so handsome, so wealthy, with such a good job?'

'NANCY!' Above them, the bedroom window was flung open and Jonathan stuck his head out. 'Where's my blue Ralph Lauren shirt?'

Nancy tilted her face up. 'No idea. Hanging up in your wardrobe?'

'It isn't there. That's why I'm asking you what you've done with it.'

'Used it to mop the kitchen floor,' Nancy murmured under her breath. Raising her voice, she said, 'In your gym bag?'

'Shit.' Jonathan reappeared seconds later holding the offending shirt. 'I wanted to wear this this afternoon.' He looked hopeful. 'If you quickly washed it, couldn't you iron it dry?'

'Wear the white one,' said Nancy. 'That's washed and ironed.'

Heaving a sigh, Jonathan gave up and closed the bedroom window.

'You're a cruel and heartless woman.' Carmen tut-tutted. 'Fancy not rushing up there to wash and iron his shirt.'

'I know.' Nancy felt oddly liberated. 'Just plain selfish, that's me.'

The Talbot Arms, on the outskirts of Kilnachranan, was festooned with multicoloured Christmas lights and from the sound of things, a riotous party was already in progress.

'We needn't stay for long,' Nancy reassured her mother.

'Don't be such a spoilsport,' said Jonathan. 'It's Boxing Day. This lot will still be going at midnight.'

Nancy looked at him. Now that she was fairly sure he was having an affair, everything he said or did seemed significant. The amount of effort he had put into his appearance could mean something. Why, after six years of wearing Eau Sauvage aftershave, had he recently switched to the new Calvin Klein? Was it to match his underpants?

'Will it be mainly young people?' wondered Rose.

'There's Nora who does the food. She's around your age,' said Jonathan. 'If you wanted, you could give her a hand in the kitchen.'

'Sorry,' said Rennie, putting his arm round Rose's shoulders as they made their way up to the front door of the pub, 'she won't have time for skivvying in the kitchen, she's going to be far too busy dancing with me.'

Nancy was on edge, Carmen could tell. She was smiling and greeting people she knew, but there was a hint of brittleness to her smile. Luckily, nobody was paying her much attention. Everyone was far more interested in nudging each other and whispering that that was Rennie Todd.

It was always amusing, watching other people's reactions to celebrities. Rennie, on his best behaviour for Nancy's sake, was handling the situation well. He was great at remembering people's names—just as well, seeing that Jonathan was currently proudly introducing him to Hamish, Pete and a whole host of drinking friends—and excellent at pretending to be interested when they all regaled him with stories of how they had once been in a band that could have made it, if only the record companies had had the sense to offer them a record deal.

'It's a tough business,' Rennie agreed sympathetically. 'We spent a couple of years doing the pub circuit down south. One night we played to an audience of six, and two of them were passed out drunk.'

'Still, you got your lucky break in the end.' Hamish evidently still felt it was unfair.

'We did, we were lucky,' Rennie agreed good-naturedly. 'Hey, let me get you another drink. Rose, how about you? Hamish, this is Rose, my new girlfriend. Rose, say hello to Hamish.'

'**A**nd to think you were worried about your mother,' Carmen murmured an hour later.

'I know.' Nancy smiled, though her eyes continued to dart restlessly around the pub. 'D'you think that could be the one, over there?'

Jonathan was chatting to a girl in a red top and a PVC miniskirt.

'Wouldn't have thought she was his type.' Then again, Carmen supposed, it was hard to know what kind of girl Jonathan might go for. Any one of them here could be a potential Other Woman. Plus, they could have got it all wrong and she wasn't here at all.

'I'm going to give Nora a hand with the food,' said Nancy. 'Have a chat with her, see if I think she knows anything.'

Carmen gave her hand a reassuring squeeze.

When Nancy had disappeared into the kitchen at the back of the pub, Carmen made her way over to the bar where Hamish was now quizzing Rennie about how it felt to play to an audience at Wembley. Rose, chatting away to a dark-haired woman in her late thirties, was admiring her dress.

'Monsoon,' Carmen heard the woman tell Rose. 'A few sequins always brightens things up, don't you think?'

'I've never had anything sparkly like this.' Rose was stroking the sleeve. 'Always too worried about the dry-cleaning bills, I suppose. But this is beautiful. Oh, my word, and so is *that*.' Reverently she pointed to the brunette's right hand. 'Look at this ring!'

From where she was standing, Carmen saw three things. Firstly, despite being in mid-conversation at the time, Rennie stopped speaking. Secondly, six feet away, Jonathan turned his head and glanced across at the brunette. Thirdly, and most damningly of all, the brunette dimpled with pleasure and, for just a fraction of a second, she met Jonathan's gaze and smiled at him.

'Haven't seen that before!' Grabbing her hand, Hamish bellowed, 'Bloody hell, Paula. Bit of a rock, isn't it? Where did that come from?'

'My Auntie May bought it for me for Christmas. It's not real,' said Paula. 'Cubic zirconium.'

'Thought you'd got yourself a secret admirer,' said Hamish jovially. 'Right, who's for another drink?'

Having extricated himself from the crowd, Rennie said in a low voice, 'Is it a fake?'

Carmen's jaw was tight. 'How would I know? I'm no expert. But I saw the way she looked at Jonathan.'

'Right, don't say anything to Nancy just yet. Leave this to me.'

Within minutes, Rennie was flirting with the brunette whose name was Paula. It was a talent he'd never needed to hone; flirting came as naturally to him as breathing. Aware that Nancy was still in the kitchen and Carmen was sitting on a stool over at the bar watching him, he found out that her name was Paula McKechnie and that she was thirty-five and divorced with no children. He also learned that she worked in an art gallery in Edinburgh, was currently single and adored Thai food.

'Tell me,' said Rennie confidentially, 'd'you ever meet a complete stranger and find you just . . . click with them?'

Paula regarded him playfully. 'I suppose it's been known to happen.'

Rennie pulled an apologetic face. 'I think it may be happening now. What are you doing tomorrow night?'

'Um . . .' Clearly flattered, Paula said, 'Why are you asking?'

'Well, I'm staying at the Kincaid Hotel for a few days. If you could suggest a good Thai restaurant, I thought maybe you and I could check it out. I'd love to take you out to dinner, get to know you better.' Rennie paused, a hesitant smile on his lips.

During the course of their conversation he had been aware of Jonathan standing a short distance away, talking about rugby with his friends but clearly paying close attention to what was going on in the vicinity. Paula, also aware of this, said, 'Um, the thing is, it's a bit—'

'Sorry, forget I asked. No problem.' Rennie began to back away.

Paula, terrified that she was about to miss her chance, whispered in a frantic undertone, 'No, look, give me a call tomorrow.' Turning away from Jonathan, she scrabbled discreetly in her fake Louis Vuitton handbag for a card and thrust it into his hand. 'There's my number, but it's better if you don't tell anyone. You know what people can be like . . .'

As smooth as any pickpocket, Rennie slid the card out of sight.

'You'd rather keep it between us.' He nodded understandingly.

There was no sign of Nancy. Carmen was still on her stool watching them intently. Beckoning her to join them, Rennie said cheerfully, 'Hey, Carmen, over here. Got something to show both of you.'

Paula giggled. 'What is it?'

'Bring the bottle with you,' Rennie added as Carmen slipped down from the stool.

Obediently Carmen picked up the almost empty bottle of Frascati.

'OK, little trick I learned.' Pushing up his sleeves, Rennie rubbed his hands together and waggled his fingers like Paul Daniels.

'Magic,' Paula exclaimed with delight. 'I love magic!'

Carmen, sensing something was up, said, 'Rennie's full of tricks.'

'If I can remember how to do it.' He paused, then held out his hand to Paula. 'Right, give me that ring of yours.'

Entranced, Paula slid it off her finger and passed it over. 'Don't make it disappear, will you? Auntie May'll go mad.'

'I won't make it disappear,' Rennie promised. Taking the bottle in one hand and carefully eyeing the level of the wine, he raked the ring down the side of the bottle. The scratch in the glass was clearly visible.

'Is that it?' said Paula.

'Better tell Auntie May to take your ring back to the shop and complain. This isn't cubic zirconium,' said Rennie. 'They've only gone and sold her one with a real diamond in it instead.'

'OK.' Paula leaned forward confidingly and lowered her voice. 'Someone gave me the ring for Christmas. I know it's a real diamond. I just didn't want everyone else to know.'

'Having an affair with a married man, making sure his wife doesn't find out,' said Rennie. 'Can't be easy.'

Paula's jaw tightened. She looked at him for a couple of seconds then briefly shook her head. 'It isn't. Can I have my ring back now?'

But Rennie was studying it. 'Know what Jonathan bought Nancy for Christmas? A lawn mower.'

He watched the colour drain from Paula's face.

'Did he?' Her voice was neutral.

Carmen said, 'Rennie, I—'

'I'd say you got the better deal,' Rennie continued. Maybe this wasn't how they'd planned it but he was buggered if he'd stop now. 'It's Jonathan, isn't it?'

Paula looked as if she'd stopped breathing. '*What?*'

'Come on, don't give me that. You're having an affair with Jonathan Adams, right under his wife's nose, and now you've been caught out—'

'Rennie,' hissed Carmen, jabbing him hard in the ribs, and this time he did stop. But it was too late. Turning, he saw Rose standing behind him holding a tray of baked potatoes. Shit, shit. From the expression on her face, she'd heard everything. Rennie mentally braced himself for the crash of the metal tray dropping to the ground.

'Is this true?' whispered Rose.

Shaking his head, Rennie put a hand on her arm. 'Rose, I'm so sorry.'

Ignoring him, Rose stared at Paula. *'Is it true?'*

Paralysed with horror, Paula glanced helplessly across at Jonathan, but he was too busy laughing at the antics of the local curling team, who were dancing along to the jukebox, to notice.

'Outside,' Rose hissed.

'Wh-what?'

'Outside. Now.' Passing the tray of baked potatoes over to Carmen, Rose nodded at the door. 'Without drawing attention to yourself.'

Carmen put down the tray and looked at Rennie. 'Nancy's going to kill you.'

'That's if her mother doesn't kill Paula first.'

They followed Paula and Rose out of the pub. It was four o'clock, already dark outside, and snow had begun to fall. Illuminated by the misty orange glow of the street lights, Rose McAndrew was giving the trembling younger woman a piece of her mind.

'. . . you're going to listen to me and pay attention. My daughter's a good girl. She deserves so much *better* than this. Her husband may be a despicable idiot, but for some reason, Nancy worships him and I won't have her hurt. If you think it's clever to steal a married man away from his wife, well, then you're as stupid as he is. Men like that aren't worth stealing, trust me.'

'But—' began Paula.

'No buts,' Rose interjected icily. 'It's over. You aren't going to see Jonathan again and Nancy is never going to find out what her pathetic apology for a husband has been up to behind her back.'

'Actually, it's OK. I already know.' Stepping out of the shadows, Nancy saw everyone turn to stare at her. When she had emerged from the kitchen to find her friends and her mother missing from the pub, nobody appeared to know where they might have gone. She had pushed open the front door and heard Rose outside the pub berating someone, and astonishment had rooted her to the spot. But rather than Jonathan's affair, it was her mother's reaction that was confounding her.

She'd never heard her mother like this before, hadn't known she was capable of such a rant. Even more astounding was the discovery that Rose didn't adore Jonathan and worship the ground he walked on.

Everyone was still gazing at her, Nancy realised, waiting for her to say something else.

'I know,' she said again, trembling half with the cold and half with emotion. 'But, Mum, how on earth did *you* find out?'

'I was in the right place at the right time.' As shocked as Nancy, Rose said, 'But I can't believe *you* know. Oh, darling, why didn't you *tell* me?'

'I didn't want to spoil your Christmas. I knew you'd be upset.'

Rose shook her head in disgust. 'Upset? I'm not upset, I'm livid!'

At that moment Jonathan appeared in the doorway. Taking in the situation at a glance he said, 'Why is everyone out here?'

'You may be stupid, Jonathan,' Rose retorted, 'but you aren't brain-dead. Even you must be able to work it out.'

Overwhelmed by the transformation in her mother, Nancy glanced across at Paula, shivering in her sequin-strewn dress. As she reached up to brush snowflakes from her face, a diamond glinted on her right hand. Watching her watch Paula, Rennie said by way of explanation, 'That's the Christmas present.'

How had he found this out? Nancy couldn't begin to imagine.

'Cheating on your wife.' Rose eyed Jonathan with disdain. 'That is so low. How could you? My daughter adores you—'

'Mum, it's OK. I'm going to leave him.' A lump sprang into Nancy's throat, because she couldn't believe she was telling Rose this. Except her mother wasn't actually looking that heartbroken.

'Really? Truly? Oh, darling, thank God!' Clasping her thin fingers together, Rose said anxiously, 'Are you sure?'

'Absolutely sure.' Nancy's smile had gone wobbly with relief. 'I thought you were mad about Jonathan. I thought you'd be devastated.'

'Sweetheart, I've known for years that he wasn't good enough for you! I wouldn't trust him further than I could toss a caber.'

'Look, this is ridiculous,' Jonathan blustered. 'You can't talk about me as if I'm not even here! So what are you trying to make out, that something's been going on between me and Paula?'

'Lies, lies. See what I mean about him being pathetic?' Rose shook her head with contempt. Turning back to face the rest of them she said brightly, 'Brrr, I'm getting a bit chilly. Shall we go now?'

Grinning at Nancy and Carmen, Rennie said, 'Whatever you say, Rose. You're the boss.'

'Wait,' Jonathan called out as they were about to leave. Paula had already scuttled back inside. 'How did you find out?'

Comforted by the feel of Rennie's warm hand against the back of her neck, Nancy said, 'If I told you that, it would spoil the fun. When it's time to start cheating on Paula, you'd make sure it didn't happen again.' She paused and added more cheerfully than she'd imagined possible, 'This way, it just might.'

'How are you doing?' murmured Rennie at dinner that night.

'D'you know, I haven't the faintest idea.' Nancy was touched by his concern; he was a virtual stranger, after all.

'You're in shock,' Rennie told her. 'Hey, but you did the right thing.'

They were in the restaurant of the Kincaid in Edinburgh; Rennie had insisted on booking them into the hotel and treating them to dinner. Following their departure from the Talbot Arms, the four of them had returned to Nancy and Jonathan's house and helped Nancy to pack.

'You don't need to leave,' Carmen had reminded her. 'Why should you have to be the one to go?'

'I'd rather.' Nancy hadn't needed to think about it. The house had always felt more like Jonathan's than hers. He paid the mortgage, the property was in his name, and he'd invariably had the final say when it came to decorating or buying furniture.

Nodding at the waiter, who was wondering if they'd like their glasses refilled, Rennie speared a scallop and said, 'What if he wants you back?'

From across the table, Rose put down her own fork and said, 'She'll tell him to take a running jump. Don't worry, I'll make sure of that.'

Nancy smiled, she couldn't help it. 'Mum, why didn't you ever tell me how you felt about Jonathan?'

'Well,' Rose said. 'To be fair, Jonathan did seem all right to begin with.

It was a while before I decided I really didn't like him. But you were about to be married and you wouldn't have thanked me for telling you. You might have cut me out of your life.'

'Oh God, I wouldn't—'

'Well, I wasn't going to take that risk.' Rose shrugged and calmly buttered a roll. 'Far simpler to pretend to adore him. Anyway, it's over now, and that's the best Christmas present I could have asked for. You have the whole of your life ahead of you. You're young and beautiful and you can do anything you want.'

Nancy prayed she wasn't about to start crying. The suddenness of it all had knocked her for six. 'I don't know what I want to do. I don't know what I *can* do.' A mental image of herself serving behind the counter of Burger King sprang to mind. Hastily she pushed it away.

'Hey, you don't have to worry about that. Give yourself time to think about it,' said Rennie.

Feeling panicky and helpless, Nancy said, 'But I don't have anywhere to live.'

'Now you're being daft,' Rennie said forcefully. 'You can come and stay with us.'

'Of course you can,' Carmen joined in. 'It'd be great to have you in London.' Turning her attention to Rennie, she raised her eyebrows and added pointedly, '*Us?*'

He looked mystified. 'What?'

'You just said *us*.'

Rennie shrugged. 'The rest of the tour's been cancelled. I'm free for the next couple of months.'

'So that's settled, is it?' Carmen sounded rattled. 'Last night you asked if you could stay for a few *days*.'

Nancy, watching her reaction, wondered what this was all about.

'And since then I've decided you could use the company.' Evidently treating Carmen's reaction as a challenge rather than an insult, Rennie said, 'I did promise Spike that I'd keep an eye on you.'

'You liar!' Carmen blurted out. 'That's rubbish. He didn't ask you anything of the sort.'

'OK, maybe he didn't. But it was one of those unspoken things.'

'I don't need keeping an eye on.' Carmen was defensive. 'I'm fine.'

Turning his attention to Rose, Rennie said easily, 'Any Christmas decorations in your home?'

'In my flat, you mean?' Startled, Rose said, 'Well, of course there are.'

'When I turned up at Carmen's place yesterday, there was nothing,' said Rennie, his tone conversational. 'Not a strip of tinsel in sight.'

Rose looked at Carmen, as shocked as if Rennie had just announced that she was the star attraction in a lap-dancing club.

'Oh, pet. Not even a tree?'

'This is ridiculous,' Carmen blurted out. 'There's more to Christmas than decorations, you know! Just because I was too busy to put any up doesn't make me—'

'Actually, don't worry about me,' Nancy said hurriedly. 'I think I'll just stay here in Edinburgh.'

'You will not,' declared Carmen, her eyes flashing. 'You're staying with me. And that way I won't need a . . . a childminder to keep an eye on me, because I won't *be* on my own, will I?'

'Oh, sweetheart,' Rose flapped her hands consolingly, 'he didn't mean it like that.'

'Yes, I did. That's exactly what I meant,' said Rennie. 'And how's Nancy supposed to cheer you up when she's just getting over her own marriage break-up? The two of you would make a fine pair, living like a couple of hermits, each as gloomy as the other. Hey, don't look at me like that,' he told Carmen more gently. 'I'm trying to help here. You both need cheering up and I can do that, it's what I'm good at.'

'He has a point,' Rose said hesitantly.

'Thank you, Rose.' Rennie nodded with satisfaction, beckoning the waiter over. 'We'd like a bottle of Veuve Cliquot please.'

'I hate being cheered up,' Carmen grumbled. 'Insane people, whooping and clapping like orang-utans.'

'OK, if I promise not to behave like an orang-utan, will you let me stay?' He had hold of her hand now and was looking soulful.

Carmen, struggling not to laugh, said, 'Just don't expect to be waited on hand and foot, OK? I know what you're like.'

Dark green eyes glittering, Rennie blew her a kiss across the table. 'No problem, we'll have Nancy there to do all that.'

'Sir, your champagne.' The waiter arrived, holding a bottle that was cloudy with condensation and wrapped in a white napkin.

'Perfect timing.' Rennie grinned up at him. 'We've got something to celebrate.'

'And no singing in the middle of the night,' Carmen warned. 'I hate it when you do that.' To Nancy she added, 'He's not remotely house-trained, you know.'

Nancy began to wonder what she might have let herself in for.

'I can't help it. I need the love of a good woman,' said Rennie.

'Tuh,' Carmen snorted. 'From what I hear, you've had the love of a thousand good women. What you need is a slave.'

Chapter 2

CONNOR O'SHEA MAY HAVE moved over from Dublin eleven years ago, making his home in London, but his Irish accent was as strong as ever. He fully intended to keep it with him for life. It suited him, went with his personality and had the desired effect when it came to the opposite sex. In all fairness, what more could you ask of an accent than that?

Sadly, the person currently on the other end of the phone was male and far more interested in moaning on about staffing problems.

'. . . and Savannah's complaining that the staff T-shirts are too tight. She wants me to order some in size eighteen. I told her it was her fault for being such a whale.'

OK, now he really did have to interrupt. 'Neville, order the T-shirts and stop giving Savannah grief.' From the living-room window, Connor idly watched a taxi pull up outside.

'But she's so fat! It's just . . . ugh.' You didn't need to be able to see Neville to know that he was shuddering with revulsion. Neville was as fastidious as he was fit, and as fit as he was gay.

'Now, you know as well as I do that people go to fitness clubs for different reasons. Some of them are like you. They have bodies like yours and they enjoy keeping themselves in peak physical condition. And then there are the other clients, the kind who just want to be a bit fitter than they are. Women carrying a bit of extra weight know perfectly well that they're never going to look like most of our instructors, but it boosts their confidence no end when they see someone like Savannah taking a class, because she might be a big girl but she's fit as well. And bloody attractive. They enjoy her classes because they can aspire to be like her. Half of them wouldn't attend a class run by a seven-stone stick insect. So just go ahead and order the T-shirts, will you?'

Pressing the OFF button on the phone, Connor wondered why on earth he'd ever asked Neville to manage the Islington branch of the Lazy B. The ethos of the chain of Lazy Bs was that there was more to life than physical perfection.

Anyway, who was that, climbing out of the taxi? Ha, the Invisible Woman. Smiling to himself, Connor watched her pay the driver—thanks to her brother-in-law he now knew that her name was Carmen—and waited to see if she would glance up at his window as she made her way into the house next door.

She didn't glance up. Absently scratching his chest and wondering if it was time for his next cigarette—he was attempting to ration himself to one every two hours—Connor moved away from the window and headed for the fridge instead. A wedge of Cambozola would hit the spot.

OK, he was a disgrace. He freely admitted it. Ten years ago he had opened the original Lazy B in Oxford. His dream had been to create a gym crossed with a really great pub, with the emphasis on enjoyment and socialising. In his time he'd visited plenty of fitness clubs that reminded him of laboratories—cool, clinical places full of sleek modern fittings, featuring obsessive fitness freaks. If there was anything to drink, it was a healthy drink. If there was anything to eat, it was bound to include salad. Which was fine for the fitness freaks, but not so fine for the majority of people who might—in a burst of enthusiasm—join one of these clubs but would, after the first few weeks, find increasingly feeble reasons not to attend. The drop-outs, as Connor had termed them, needed more of an incentive to keep turning up, month after month. And, OK, maybe they'd be socialising more than they'd be exercising, but even a bit of exercise was better than no exercise at all.

Ten years on, the business was going from strength to strength.

The doorbell rang as Connor was wrestling with the wrapper on a packet of Scotch eggs. Heading for the front door, he wondered if it was his neighbour, popping round to introduce herself.

It wasn't his neighbour.

'Dad! Yay, you're here!' Blonde hair flying, Mia threw her arms round Connor, knocking her baseball cap off in the process.

Astounded, he hugged her back. 'I don't believe it. Am I on *This Is Your Life*? Is Michael Aspel hiding behind a postbox?'

'Sorry, it's just me. Come on, then,' Mia said bossily, 'invite me in. It's freezing out here.'

Connor's heart swelled with love for his daughter. 'What a fantastic surprise. Why didn't you let me know you were coming?'

'Duh, because then it wouldn't have been a fantastic surprise, would it?' Reaching down for her cap and kicking the front door shut behind her, Mia beamed at him and wriggled her backpack off her shoulders. 'But I'm glad you weren't out. I'll have a cup of tea and a fried egg sandwich . . . ooh, and I'd love a bath afterwards, my feet are killing me.'

'We're out of eggs,' said Connor.

'No, you aren't, I've brought some.' In the kitchen, Mia unzipped her backpack and pulled out a canary-yellow fleece jacket. Unwrapping the fleece, she triumphantly produced an egg box. 'Present from Mum.'

Wryly, Connor accepted the gift. This meant they were the most organic, free-range eggs imaginable, both inside and out. He just knew they'd be smeared with chicken poo, feathers and bits of straw.

'Great. You fry the eggs, I'll make the tea.'

Mia, not fooled for a second, said cheerfully, 'Coward.'

Connor filled the kettle. He leaned against the worktop and watched his daughter briskly scrub the eggs she'd carried with her all the way from Donegal. It was almost impossible to believe that Mia was sixteen; not so long ago she'd been a strong-willed four-year-old in dusty orange dungarees. And look at her now, taller than ever, wearing distressed black jeans, pointy black boots and a black-and-yellow striped mohair sweater that made her look like a bee on stilts. Her shoulder-length streaky blonde hair was tied back with a pink band and the only make-up she wore was mascara.

Mia, his beautiful daughter. She was the most important person in his life, yet discovering her existence had caused him untold pain. Anger too. Was it any wonder that Mia was strong-willed, when she had Laura as her mother?

Laura had been running one of those hippy shops in Dublin when Connor first met her. He was a hormone-fuelled seventeen-year-old, still at school and working part-time in the bakery next door to Laura's shop. With her waist-length blonde hair, embroidered cheesecloth dresses and bewitching smile he had naturally been attracted to her. Fascinated by her beliefs in crystals, her air of mystery and, OK, her glorious figure, Connor had taken to dropping into her joss-stick-scented shop.

When Laura had started inviting him upstairs to her tiny flat above the shop, he had felt as if he'd won the lottery. Sex was a revelation, better than he'd ever imagined, possibly because Laura, at twenty-seven, was an experienced woman of the world. In her bedroom, which smelt of patchouli and jasmine, she introduced him to the joys of lovemaking and taught him how to give pleasure as well as to receive it.

Their clandestine relationship had lasted three months. Connor was dumbstruck when Laura calmly announced one day, out of the blue, that she was leaving Dublin, giving up the lease on the shop and moving to a smallholding in Donegal.

He felt as if his air supply had been cut off.

'What? But . . . why?'

'I want to be self-sufficient.' Laura stroked his chest; they were in bed together at the time. 'I'll be growing my own vegetables, tending sheep and goats, spinning my own wool—it's going to be fantastic.'

'But I love you,' he blurted out, and Laura smiled.

'You don't. You love having sex with me. I'm ten years older than you are. I know what I want to do with my life and now I'm moving on to the next stage.' Reaching over, Laura planted a warm kiss on his mouth. 'Life's a journey, right? And it's time we went our separate ways.'

Of course, Laura had been right. He'd missed her to begin with, but life went on and he turned out to be less heartbroken than he'd imagined. After a while he started seeing someone else, a pretty eighteen-year-old called Niamh, who was studying law at Trinity.

And that would have been that, had it not been for a chance meeting almost five years later.

Connor's girlfriend at the time—a beautician by the name of Clodagh—had been invited to the wedding of an old school friend in Donegal. Unwillingly, Connor had found himself forced to go along with her. If truth be told, he was on the verge of finishing with Clodagh—but she had insisted, booking them into a nearby country hotel for a long weekend as an incentive. Arriving there on Friday morning, Clodagh announced that she had booked both of them into the health and beauty spa for the entire afternoon. It was at that moment that Connor knew for sure that their relationship was over.

'I don't want any of that stuff,' he told Clodagh.

Bewildered she said, 'Why not? You'd love it.'

'I promise you, I wouldn't.' Connor reached for his jacket. 'You go ahead. I'll see you back here at six.'

It was a hot sunny day in July. Wandering through the town, he had come across a small Friday market with stallholders selling a variety of cheeses, sausages, vegetables, pottery and hand-woven baskets. Feeling hungry, Connor stopped off at a small pub selling food and sat at one of the tables outside to drink his pint of Guinness, and enjoy a plate of ham and eggs with fried potatoes.

Idly, he watched a small girl in orange dungarees fighting a losing battle to persuade her dolls to sit upright. The girl's blonde hair hung loose down her back. Her T-shirt was purple, her feet bare and she was kneeling on the pavement arranging the four shabby stuffed dolls along the top of an upended packing crate. Like spinning plates, every time she reached the fourth doll one of the others would topple over. Amused, Connor realised that the girl was talking to the dolls, threatening to get very cross indeed if they didn't all sit up *straight*.

'Now behave, or I'll give you a smack,' she declared bossily. The first doll promptly keeled forward and landed face down on the pavement.

Picking it up, the girl said, 'Did that hurt? Well, serves you right.'

'I think she hit her teeth,' said Connor and the girl looked over at him as if he were mad.

'She hasn't any teeth. She's a doll.'

Tempted to get competitive, Connor almost asked why she was bothering to speak to the dolls then, seeing as they didn't have any ears either. But since arguing with a small child in the street wasn't entirely dignified, he said, 'You're right, I'm sorry,' and took a gulp of Guinness instead. Reaching for a cigarette, he was about to light it when a stallholder to his left suddenly rose from her seat in order to serve a customer. As she moved forward, her long purple skirt swirled round her legs and in that split second Connor recognised her. He stared at Laura as she piled courgettes into a brown paper bag.

He was looking at his first love. How incredible to see her again now. Realising that the cigarette was still dangling unlit from his lips, he wrenched it out and rose to his feet.

'Laura!'

Laura turned as the customer wandered along to the next stall. Their eyes met and the first thought that flashed through Connor's mind was that she didn't seem nearly as delighted to see him as he was to see her.

'Laura. Great to see you. You're looking . . . um, fantastic.' This wasn't exactly true. With her long hair in a plait, her thin, weather-beaten face and droopy clothes, she looked like a woman who lived off the land. She was thirty-one, but looked forty.

'Hello, Connor. Nice to see you too.' Laura devoted herself to reorganising the sacks of vegetables around her stall.

'How's the self-sufficiency thing going?' said Connor.

'Oh, pretty good. Hard work of course, but it's what I—'

'Mum, can I have a drink?'

Looking down, Connor saw the small girl in the orange dungarees poking her head round the side of the stall.

'In a minute, darling. I'm busy.'

'This is your daughter?' Amazed, Connor said, 'Hey, that's grand news. Congratulations.'

'Thanks. Mia, go and play with your dolls.'

'They're stupid. I hate my dolls.' Puffing out her cheeks, the girl said, 'I'm thirsty.'

'Why don't I fetch her something from the pub?' Connor suggested, because Laura was looking agitated. 'A Coke or something?'

Mia gazed up at him, her eyes like saucers. From Laura's expression you'd think he'd suggested buying her daughter a bourbon on the rocks.

'She doesn't drink that rubbish. I'll get her some water in a minute. Well, it's been nice to see you again—'

'Mia. That's a pretty name,' said Connor. 'How old are you, then?'

'Three,' Laura said hurriedly.

'I'm *not*.' Mia was indignant. 'I'm four.'

Four. The answer was one thing, but the expression on Laura's face was what really made Connor take notice. Why would she lie?

Why indeed?

Feeling light-headed with disbelief, Connor said carefully, 'When's your birthday, Mia?'

Mia gave it some thought. Finally she said, 'When I get my presents.'

Connor looked down at the small girl in front of him, with her huge grey eyes, her button nose and determined chin. Switching his gaze to Laura, he said in a low voice, 'Is this . . .? Is she . . .?'

Except he already knew that she was.

One of the neighbouring stallholders was persuaded to look after Mia and keep an eye on Laura's stall.

Laura took Connor down a series of narrow side streets, away from the market. As he followed her, a million thoughts raced through his brain. A baby, my God, not even a baby, a walking talking four-year-old girl. I'm a father, I've been a father for the last four years . . .

This was mindblowing, almost too much to take in. Yet even as Connor was digesting the information, he was aware that he wasn't reacting with the sense of horror that overcame some men faced with the prospect of unexpected fatherhood. He knew instinctively that he was incapable of turning his back on Mia. He didn't even want to. She existed, she was his own flesh and blood. He couldn't wait to see her again, get to know her, discover what she was like.

They finally reached a small park. Laura sat down on the grass and said, 'I'll get a crick in my neck if I have to look up at you.'

Connor lowered himself to the ground near her and sat crosslegged, facing her.

'She's my daughter,' he said evenly.

Laura nodded. 'Yes.'

'You should have told me.'

'No,' said Laura.

'Yes! I would have stuck by you,' Connor exclaimed. 'OK, I know I was young, but I'd never have left you in the lurch! You didn't need to move away, we'd have coped somehow, between us we could have—'

'Connor, I know you would have stuck by me,' Laura said gently. 'You were a dear, sweet boy. But I didn't get pregnant by accident, you know. You see, I wanted a baby.'

Bombshell number two.

'A baby,' echoed Connor, 'but not a partner?'

'The baby was the most important thing.' Laura was calmer now, regaining control. 'Of course, if I'd met the perfect man I wouldn't have turned him down. But I met you instead and you were just a boy. I'd never have dreamed of landing you with the responsibility of a child. On the other hand, I couldn't have asked for a better father for my baby. You were tall, you had a great physique, you were healthy and bright and kind . . . let's face it, genetically you were perfect.'

Stunned, Connor said, 'Is that what I was? A sperm donor?'

'Oh, Connor, don't make it sound horrible. I wanted a baby with your qualities. Can't you think of that as a compliment?'

'So what happens now?'

'Nothing happens,' said Laura. 'Nothing's changed. You're free to walk away, forget you ever saw us.'

'Jesus, I don't believe I'm hearing this!' Anger welled up inside him. 'I didn't give you an old sweater, Laura! We've created a human being here. You can't seriously expect me to just walk away from my daughter as if she doesn't exist!'

'Connor, you're twenty-one years old. You had a teenage crush on me and we had fun, but we don't love each other. Mia and I are fine as we are, just the two of us. If I tell her you're her father, how is she going to feel in a few years' time when you decide you can't be bothered to see her any more? She'd be devastated.'

'She wouldn't be,' Connor said patiently, 'because I'd never do that to her. But you don't believe me, so how about a compromise? We won't tell Mia I'm her father. I'll just be a friend of yours. That way, she'll have a chance to get used to me.' He paused, keeping a straight face. 'And then it won't come as too much of a shock on her fiftieth birthday when we do tell her the truth.'

'Mia? Come here, darling, and say hello to a friend of mine. His name is Connor,' Laura said when they got back.

'Hi.' Connor crouched down on the pavement, so that he was level with Mia. 'It's very nice to meet you.'

Close up, he saw that the tips of her long eyelashes were golden, like his. Her eyes were silver-grey and watchful. His daughter. He was actually looking at his *daughter*. It was an emotional moment to be—

'Like a box,' said Mia.

'Um . . . sorry?'

She abruptly turned away, disappeared behind the stall and reappeared moments later carrying an empty cardboard box. 'Like a box,' Mia explained, plonking it down on the pavement and pointing. 'There's a corner. There's another corner.'

'Very good. Nearly the same.' He hid a smile. 'But I'm Connor.'

Mia gazed at him, unimpressed. 'I know.'

'Connor's coming to see us on Sunday,' Laura said brightly. 'He'll be coming over to our house. That'll be nice, won't it?'

'Yes.' Obediently Mia nodded. 'You know dandelions?'

'I do.' Connor waited to hear what profound remark might follow.

'They're yellow.'

'You know cows?' said Connor.

'Yes.'

'They go moooo.'

He so longed to make his daughter laugh. Instead Mia shot him a look of disdain.

'But cows aren't yellow.'

Hmm.

'Don't they have yellow cows where you live?' Connor looked dismayed.

'No. Cows aren't yellow, *ever*. Do you like biscuits?'

'Er . . . yes.'

Mia nodded. 'And me.'

'Here.' Taking pity on him, Laura passed over a slip of paper. 'That's our address, and a map of how to get there.'

Connor looked at it. Had she just made this up, plucking a false address out of the air and inventing a map to go with it?

'Don't worry.' Guessing what was running through his mind, Laura smiled. 'That's definitely where we live.'

It was Mia's tenth birthday. Connor said, 'Mia, sit down, I've got something to tell you.'

Mia was wearing purple shorts teamed with a lime-green T-shirt and grubby trainers. Obediently coming to sit next to Connor on the sofa, she hugged her tanned bony knees, spectacularly grazed from a recent fall from the apple tree, and said, 'What is it?'

Connor took a deep breath. Since Mia was a past master at coming straight to the point, he'd decided to take a leaf out of her book.

'The thing is, you know your father.'

'What?'

Oh God, he was messing it up already. The whole point was that she *didn't* know her father. Great start, Connor told himself, well *done*.

'Well, it's . . . um, me.' He pointed to his chest. 'I'm your father.'

A slow smile spread across her face. 'I thought you probably were.'

Connor wondered if she'd understood.

'You thought I was probably your father?' When Mia nodded calmly, he said, 'How? Why?'

'Well, why else would you keep coming to see us? I'm ten now, and you've been visiting us for years. But you aren't Mum's boyfriend,' Mia patiently explained. 'You play Monopoly and tennis with me. When Mum's boyfriends are here, they never want to do stuff like that. They always tell me to go out to play.'

Shaking his head, Connor marvelled at the logic. 'But you never said anything.'

'I did once. I asked Mum, but she said no, you were just a friend. So I left it after that. But I still thought I was right.'

'And now?' Carefully, Connor asked, 'Is it OK? Are you happy about it?'

'Of course I'm happy! I love being right!'

'Happy birthday, sweetheart!' As Mia flew into his arms, Connor picked her up and swung her round.

'*Aaaarggh*,' cried Laura, because Mia's turquoise shirt had billowed up to reveal a tattoo of a dolphin peeping above the low-slung waistband of her faded jeans.

Plonking his daughter down in order to see what Laura was pointing at, Connor said, 'I expect it's only one of those transfer things, it'll wash off in a day or two.'

'Actually it isn't.' Mia beamed with pride. 'It's a proper one.'

Appalled, Connor said, 'But you're only *sixteen*.'

'Exactly. I'm practically a grown-up.' Patting her stomach with pride, Mia said, 'But it's so sweet, Daddy, that you don't know the difference between a transfer and a real tattoo.'

'Sixteen,' Connor groaned.

'Calm down, Dad. Honestly, you're such a dinosaur. You know, I'm officially old enough to get married.' Mischievously Mia said, 'Thank your lucky stars I haven't done that.'

Connor winced at the memory. At least there hadn't been any more tattoos in the last eight months. None that he knew about, anyway. Then he winced again, because his mouth had just caught fire.

'Oh, sorry,' said Mia. 'Bit hot for you?'

Through watering eyes, Connor saw that his daughter was calmly eating her way through a plate of fried eggs on toast, swimming in a pool of flame-red chilli sauce.

Pointing to the relatively modest dash of sauce on his own plate, he said, 'A *bit* hot for me? Where did you get this stuff?'

'There's this brilliant deli in Dublin. It's called Scotch Bonnet sauce. Here, have some water.'

Having downed the water in one, Connor gingerly checked his teeth hadn't fallen out. 'So how long are you staying, then?'

Mia put down her fork. 'Well, the thing is, I've been considering my future. Mum and I were having a chat about it the other day and basically I've spent the last sixteen years living in a self-sufficient smallholding in the wilds of Donegal. Which has been great, in its way, but I feel I need a change of environment.'

This was a more convoluted answer than Connor had been expecting. He nodded to show that he was still listening.

'I mean, at my age I should be expanding my horizons, discovering new people and places, experiencing new stuff—'

'If you ever, *ever* take drugs, I'll—'

'Oh, give me a break, Dad, drugs are for losers. Anyway, so like I said, Mum and I have had a really good talk about it all and the thing is, how about if I came here and lived with you?'

The chilli was probably still burning but Connor was no longer aware of it. 'When?'

Mia spread her yellow-and-black striped arms and said encouragingly, 'Well, here I am, so how about now?'

'And where would you go to school?'

'I'm not going back to school. A-levels are meaningless these days. I'd rather get a job, start building a career. Mum and I talked it all through.'

'What kind of work did you have in mind?' Connor didn't doubt for a moment that she had something in mind.

'Well, I thought I'd train to become the next national chilli-eating champion.' Mia grinned, trawled an index finger through the pool of chilli sauce on her plate. 'Actually, I'd like to come and work for you.'

'And your mother's happy about that?' Connor had to ask, although it certainly sounded as though Laura and Mia had covered all the angles.

'Mum's great. She understands how I feel. It's time to find out how it feels to live in the middle of *somewhere*.' Mia gazed anxiously at him. 'As long as you're happy about it too.'

Happy? He'd spent the last few years dreaming about this day.

'I'm happy.' Connor's heart expanded with love for his beautiful, strong-minded daughter. He smiled. 'I can't imagine anything nicer.'

'Yay!' Jumping up from the table, Mia hugged him. 'Thanks, Dad. OK if I have my bath now?'

The phone rang fifteen minutes later. Sounding strained, Laura said without preamble, 'It's me, Laura. Listen. Mia's disappeared. I don't know where she is. Has she spoken to you at all? Oh God, the school rang and told me she hasn't been in—'

'Whoa,' Connor broke through the stream of jerky sentences. 'Mia's here. She turned up an hour ago.'

'*What?*' Relief was replaced within a split second by irritation. 'Connor, did it not even occur to you that I'd be out of my mind with worry? You should have phoned me!'

'I thought you knew. Mia kept saying you were happy for her to leave school and come and live with me.'

'Oh, for crying out loud, are you serious? *Leave school?* She's supposed to be at school this minute! Put her on,' Laura ordered.

'She's in the bath.' Connor realised he'd been well and truly set up.

'Send her back, then,' said Laura firmly. 'She can't do this, she's only sixteen. Just tell her she can't mess around like this, and send her back.'

'I love this house.' Wet-haired and wearing an oversized T-shirt emblazoned with the words TREAT ANIMALS WITH COMPASSION, Mia reappeared forty minutes later. 'You have no idea what a luxury it is to run the bath taps and know that hot water is going to come out. And dry yourself in real fluffy towels instead of horrible ancient ones—'

'Why don't you give your mum a ring, just to let her know you've arrived safely,' Connor suggested.

Mia's eyes flickered guiltily away from him. Then she straightened her shoulders. 'OK, Dad, here's the thing. I lied.'

'Here's another thing,' said Connor. 'I know.'

'Oh.'

'Laura just rang. She was worried sick.'

'I'm sorry. I'm really sorry,' Mia blurted out. 'I did try to talk it through with her, but she wouldn't listen, and I'd *much* rather be here.'

'She wants you to go home.' Connor saw her wince. 'And I want you to promise never to lie to me again.'

'I won't.' Miserably, Mia shook her head. 'Lie, I mean. Oh God.' She buried her face in her hands. 'Do I have to go back?'

'No.'

Mia's head shot up. 'What?'

'I persuaded Laura to let you stay.'

'*Really?*'

'She's not happy about the school thing,' Connor warned.

'Well, I already knew that, we've been over it enough times. But I'd rather build a career,' argued Mia. 'I mean, in the old days getting a degree meant something to employers, but these days *everyone* has a degree and it just seems . . . well, what's the big deal? Can they do a job?'

Luckily for her, Connor was in agreement. He'd interviewed more than his fair share of clueless graduates in his time. Instinct told him that Mia would achieve whatever she set out to do, workwise.

'I said pretty much the same. That's why we're going to give it a go.'

'Daddy, you're a genius.'

'I know.'

'Shall I phone Mum now and apologise?'

'Might be an idea,' said Connor.

'Then I'll get dressed and we'll set off.'

Bemused, Connor said, 'Set off where?'

Mia shook her head in despair. 'Come on, Dad, keep up. To the Lazy B, of course. I want to make a start on my job.'

Chapter 3

NANCY FELT IT WAS ALL WRONG. The ease with which she'd got over Jonathan was actually embarrassing. One minute she'd been married in Scotland. Now she was down here in London and single again. The least she could have had the decency to do was lose her appetite. But instead of moping around feeling depressed, she was loving every minute.

Rrrrrinnnnggg went the doorbell, and Nancy jumped. Bugger, if that was Rennie she was in trouble.

Hastily wiping her hands on a yard of kitchen roll, she bundled everything into a bowl and hid it in the tumble drier in the utility room. The object she'd spent the last two hours working on she shoved out of sight in the oven, which thankfully wasn't switched on.

Rennie's ability to lose his keys—or walk out of the house without them—was going to get him into the *Guinness Book of Records*.

But it wasn't Rennie.

'Hi! I'm Mia Corrigan. I just moved in next door.' The bright-eyed girl in khaki combats looked about seventeen, which Nancy couldn't help thinking was too young for their neighbour. 'I arrived yesterday afternoon. The thing is, I thought I'd pop over and say hello anyway, but I'm trying to make a Yorkshire pudding. I've done all the egg-beating business and now I find out there isn't any flour in the house. I was wondering if you had any to spare?'

Khaki combats. Long silver earrings. Small dolphin tattoo just visible beneath the vest. It was such an unlikely question that Nancy almost burst out laughing.

'Um . . . yes.'

'Great! Can you lend me a bit? These houses might be the bee's knees, but they aren't what you'd call handy for the shops. Well, not the sort of shops that sell plain flour,' Mia Corrigan amended. 'Of course if it's shoes you're after, costing thousands of pounds, we're spoilt for choice. Sorry, am I talking too much? My mum says I talk for Ireland.'

The girl might be sparky and vivacious, but she was *way* too young for Connor O'Shea. Nancy had glimpsed him leaving for work yesterday morning and knew from Carmen and Rennie that he was in his thirties. How could Mia's mother allow her to move in with a man at her age?

'Now that's what I call a proper food cupboard.' Mia nodded approvingly as Nancy opened the cupboard and located the plain flour. 'You should see ours. Hopeless. When I opened it, I found a CD player and a rugby shirt.' Shaking her head in despair she said, 'Let me tell you, things are going to change. Give me a week there and that kitchen won't know what's hit it.'

Realising that Mia had hoisted herself onto a kitchen stool, Nancy said, 'Would you like a cup of tea?'

'Love one, thanks.' The girl beamed at her. 'I don't know your name.'

'Nancy.'

'Nancy. That's a great name! Well, it's a pleasure to meet you.' Mia watched as Nancy made the tea, then she reached across the table and peeled something blue off the surface. 'What's this? Play-Doh? Hey, I didn't know you had kids! If you ever need a baby sitter—'

'I don't have children. And this is my friend Carmen's house,' Nancy explained. 'I'm just staying here for a while.' Then, because it was almost five o'clock and she really wanted to get the job finished before Rennie came back, she headed over to the tumble drier and took out the mixing bowl she'd bundled inside earlier. Mia, to her credit, didn't bat an eyelid. Next, opening the oven door and retrieving the cake on its silver board, Nancy carried it over to the table.

'Wow,' said Mia. Realising that the Play-Doh wasn't Play-Doh after all, she popped the little wodge of rolled icing into her mouth. 'And I mean, seriously, *wow*. Did you actually make that yourself?'

The birthday cake was an edible plate of chicken Madras with three-colour pilau rice, complete with edible fork, side orders of mango chutney and cucumber raita, and with extra pickled chillies on top.

'It's for Rennie, Carmen's brother-in-law. He's staying here too,' Nancy explained, 'and it's his birthday tomorrow. Chicken Madras is his favourite meal.'

'That is so cool! How much of it can you eat?'

'The whole lot. It's sponge underneath.'

'I can't believe it won't taste of curry! It's just the cleverest thing I've ever seen. Is this how you make your living?'

Nancy smiled. 'It's just a hobby. Look, I'm about to make the hot towel. Pass me that knife and I'll show you how it's done.'

Twenty minutes later, the front door opened and shut as they were putting the finishing touches to the folded hot towel. Rennie yelled out, 'Anyone at home?' and with commendable presence of mind Mia swung into action. By the time he reached the kitchen, everything was hidden once more.

Nancy, hastily wiping icing sugar from the table, said, 'Hi. This is Mia, she's just moved in next door.'

'Hi there!' Clutching her stone-cold mug of tea, Mia eyed him with undisguised curiosity. 'You're the music guy, yeah? Nancy's just been telling me. Sorry, I should probably recognise you.' She pulled an apologetic face. 'No offence, but it's not really my kind of music. I'm more of a Dolly Parton girl.'

Rennie grinned. 'I wouldn't say no to Dolly Parton myself. Nice to meet you, anyway. Just moved to London?'

'Just,' Mia agreed chattily. 'I'm brand new! But isn't this great, having friendly neighbours? It makes all the difference. I don't know a soul in London, apart from my dad.'

'And Connor,' Nancy reminded her. 'You know him as well. That makes two people.'

The corners of Mia's mouth began to twitch.

'I can't wait to tell him this. Did you really think he was my boyfriend? I'm sixteen,' said Mia, grinning broadly. 'Connor's my dad.'

Nancy blushed at her mistake and Rennie, roaring with laughter, flung an arm round her shoulders.

Watching with interest, Mia said, 'How about you two, then?' She turned to Rennie. 'Is Nancy your girlfriend?'

Spluttering with fresh embarrassment, Nancy said, 'No I am not!'

Mia was unperturbed. 'You get on well, though. Look at you.'

'I'm a hopeless case,' said Rennie. 'She wouldn't be interested in someone like me.'

'Why not? You're about the same age, aren't you? You're good-looking,' said Mia with alarming directness, 'and you seem pretty normal.'

Gravely, Rennie said, 'I'm mad, bad and dangerous to know.'

'And I only split up from my husband two weeks ago,' Nancy blurted out. As if Rennie would be remotely interested in her anyway.

Mia said saucily, 'Nothing like a new man to get you over the old one,' then shook her head and said, 'Sorry, sorry, shouldn't be making light of it. But you don't seem like a woman whose marriage just hit the rocks. Are you in bits?'

She's sixteen, thought Nancy. I'm being interrogated about my private life by a sixteen-year-old. For heaven's sake, any minute now she might start counselling me, doling out helpful sixteen-year-old advice.

She was saved from this indignity by the phone. Rennie, answering it, chatted briefly before passing the phone over. 'It's Rose, for you.'

Excusing herself from the kitchen, Nancy spoke to her mother for fifteen minutes. By the time she was finished, Mia had left with her bag of flour and Rennie was leaning against the worktop frowning at the instructions on a packet of boeuf bourguignon.

'It says "do not microwave". That's outrageous. Why would anyone buy a ready meal they can't microwave?' Perplexed, he gave the packet a shake. 'What would happen if I did?'

'You can't. It's in a foil container. You'd blow the microwave up.'

'Bloody hell. Forty minutes.' Tut-tutting with irritation, Rennie crossed the kitchen and switched on the oven. 'Mia had to get back to make her Yorkshire pudding. What's up?' Glancing over at Nancy, he saw that she was looking distracted. 'Something to do with Jonathan?'

'Hmm? Oh, no, not him.' Nancy frowned. 'It's Mum. She's lost her job. The old people's home has been sold to a property developer. She says she knew about it weeks ago, she just didn't want to worry me. She was hoping to find another job, but people aren't interested in taking on a sixty-eight-year-old. I just can't imagine my mum not working,' Nancy went on. 'And she needs the extra money, it makes all the diff—'

'What?' said Rennie as she skidded to a halt mid-syllable.

'Out of the kitchen.' Snatching the foil container from him, Nancy shooed him towards the door. 'I'll do that. Go and have a shower or something.'

'I must smell terrible,' said Rennie with a grin.

The moment he'd sauntered out of the kitchen, Nancy hared over to the oven and rescued the cake. Thankfully the oven hadn't had time to get hot enough to do any damage. Exhaling with relief, she waited until the boiler fired up—bless him, Rennie really was having a shower—and carried the cake carefully up to her room.

Rose wasn't the only one who needed a job. Gazing out of the bedroom window, Nancy knew that she had to sort out her own life. Staying here in London, just coasting along, wasn't something she could do indefinitely. If she moved in with her mother, they could manage the rent on the tiny flat more easily. Perhaps she could get a job in a department store in Edinburgh.

Nancy saw Carmen, bundled up against the cold, heading up the road towards the house. Tapping on the window, she caught her attention and waved. Rosy-cheeked and swamped by her navy coat and pink scarf, Carmen looked up and waved back, and Nancy thought how much more cheerful she'd seemed since Rennie had been staying here. He was good for her, teasing her and making her laugh. Nancy suspected that Carmen would miss Rennie dreadfully—and far more than she realised—when it was time for him to go.

Carmen was still in the hall pulling off her gloves and unwinding the scarf from round her neck when the doorbell rang. She opened the door and gazed enquiringly at the stranger on the doorstep. 'Yes?'

'Oh. Hi.' The stranger on the doorstep, perhaps taken aback by her tone, said, 'Joe James.'

'And?' There was a bag slung over his left shoulder. Was he trying to sell her something?

Hurriedly he fumbled in the pocket of his jacket and produced a letter. As he offered it, Carmen wondered if she'd been a bit brisk.

'I'm here to see Rennie Todd. I do have an appointment. For six o'clock. Um,' he consulted his watch, 'I'm a bit early. I can wait out here, if you prefer.'

'No, that's fine. Come on in.' Feeling guilty, Carmen ushered Joe James past her into the house. The letter-heading bore the name of some charity she hadn't heard of, called Top of the World. 'Come through to the living room and I'll find Rennie for you.'

'He's in the shower.' Overhearing her on the landing, Nancy banged on the bathroom door and shouted, 'Rennie, someone here to see you.'

'Joe James,' Joe called up politely, 'from Top of the World.'

'Joe James,' Nancy relayed through the bathroom door. She listened to Rennie's muffled response, then came downstairs. 'He'll be with you in ten minutes. Can I get you a drink?'

'Coffee would be great. Thanks. I don't want to put you out,' said Joe.

'Not a problem.' Nancy disappeared into the kitchen.

In the living room, Joe sat down on one of the sofas and said, 'Sorry to be a nuisance.'

'You're not a nuisance,' Carmen lied, because she was obliged to keep him company now until Rennie appeared. He had put a holdall next to his feet, into which he could stuff all manner of household objects.

'It's really kind of Rennie to see me. We sent out loads of letters to celebrities. Hardly anyone else bothered to reply.'

'What kind of charity is Top of the World?'

'A really small one. We help sick children do what they want to do, arrange trips and treats for them. You can make a child's day without spending thousands of pounds. And when you see the looks on their faces . . . well, it's just fantastic.'

Charmed by his uncomplicated enthusiasm, Carmen relaxed. 'And you work full-time for the charity?'

'Crikey, no, I just do as much as I can in my spare time. I'm a plumber in real life.' Joe pulled a face. 'Not very glamorous, I'm afraid.'

'But useful.' Carmen found herself warming to him. 'My dad was a plumber. He loved his work, helping people in a crisis.'

'That's the good bit. You're their saviour when you turn up to mend a broken boiler or fix a burst pipe.' Joe's eyes danced. 'They're delighted to see you. They treat you like their new best friend. Then, when you send them the bill, they ring you up and bellow, "*How much?*"'

Laughing, Carmen thought what nice eyes he had, how open and honest his face was. His hair was short and trendily tousled, and he was wearing a blue polo shirt and cream chinos.

Rennie, hair still wet from the shower, burst into the living room holding two mugs of coffee.

'Honestly, you can't get the staff these days. Nancy's just made me carry these through myself. I mean, doesn't she know who I am?'

'You're a spoilt rock star who has to learn that not everyone else is your servant,' said Carmen.

'She's so bossy,' Rennie complained to Joe. 'Has she been bossing you around too?'

'No, she's been fine.' Overwhelmed, Joe jumped to his feet, took the coffee mugs from Rennie, put them down on the table and shook his hand. 'Joe James. It's great to meet you.'

'OK if I stay?' said Carmen.

'See? Bossy *and* nosy.' Sitting down, Rennie winked at her. 'Of course you can stay.'

Rennie drank his coffee and listened to Joe explaining the aims of Top of the World. In his holdall, he'd brought along T-shirts for Rennie to sign, which would then be auctioned. Rennie agreed to create an original design that would be printed onto more T-shirts and baseball caps.

'I've got a couple of tour jackets and a pair of leather trousers as raffle prizes,' said Rennie, 'but they're not back yet from the dry cleaners. When I finish the designs I'll courier everything over to you. By Wednesday, is that OK?'

'Brilliant. We're holding a fundraising ball,' Joe explained to Carmen. 'On Saturday night. It's going to be fantastic. But don't worry about getting a courier'—he turned his attention back to Rennie—'I can pop round and pick the stuff up. It's no trouble.'

'You've got a meeting with your accountant on Wednesday morning,' Carmen told Rennie. 'I'll be here.'

'Great. Wednesday morning.' Nodding eagerly, Joe gazed at Carmen and she thought again how nice he was.

'Well, if that's all.' Rennie rose to his feet and glanced at his watch. 'There's somewhere I have to be by seven thirty.'

'You big durr-brain,' Carmen exclaimed, when Nancy told her what she was planning to do. 'I love having you here. You don't have to go back to Edinburgh just because you're scared about outstaying your welcome. If you want to stay here for the next five years, that's fine by me.'

'Really?' Nancy was incredibly touched.

'Really.'

'And me,' said Rennie, drawn to the kitchen by the smell of frying onions and garlic. 'It's much nicer having me in the house too.'

Carmen rolled her eyes, then batted his hand away with a wooden spoon as he tried to pinch a mushroom.

'It's much noisier, I'll give you that. And don't even look at that grated cheese. I'm making a Spanish omelette.'

'And there was me, thinking that getting flirted with by charity boy might have cheered you up.'

'He wasn't flirting with me. Stop going on about it or I'll send you back to the Savoy.'

'The thing is, I'd love to stay,' said Nancy, 'but I'm worried about Mum. Maybe I should go up and see her. She never moans or complains but I hate the thought of her worrying, all on her own.'

'Why don't we invite her down here?' said Carmen. 'Would she do that, do you think? Come and stay for a week or two?'

'Great idea.' Stealing a mushroom while she wasn't looking, Rennie said, 'Someone to be on my side for a change. Me and Rose against you and Nancy. We can gang up on each other.'

'Really? Are you sure you wouldn't mind?' Nancy was searching Carmen's face for clues.

'It was my idea, wasn't it?'

'I'll give her a ring now.' Hugging Carmen, Nancy said, 'She's never been to London before. Not once in her life.'

'It'll be like Crocodile Dundee visiting New York.' Rennie grinned. 'When she steps off that plane she won't know what's hit her. I'll book her onto a flight with easyJet.'

'She doesn't like taking things from other people,' Nancy warned him. 'She's very proud.'

'Fine. Tell her to make me a chicken casserole and bring it down with her.' Rennie shrugged. 'Then we'll call it quits.'

As it turned out, Rennie never did get to see his chicken Madras birthday cake. A call from his manager in New York had him throwing a few things into a case at midnight and catching a cab to Heathrow.

'It's Jessie, she isn't coping well,' Carmen explained the next morning when Nancy came downstairs to find Rennie gone. Dave, Red Lizard's drummer, was evidently having a rough time in rehab. Jessie, his highly strung wife, was finding it hard to manage without him and had taken to her bed with a bottle of vodka.

'Shouldn't she be in rehab too?' said Nancy.

'Yes, but you have to want to go. If anyone can persuade her, it's Rennie,' said Carmen. 'She trusts him. Anyway, he's going to do his best to sort her out and hopefully be back by the weekend. Right, I'm off to work. Shall I pick up a takeaway on the way home?'

'Lovely.' By the weekend, Rennie's cake would be stale. Realising that she may as well just throw it away, Nancy tried hard not to feel miffed.

'Indian?' said Carmen.

Nancy, feeling she'd had enough of chicken Madras and three-coloured rice, said, 'I'd rather have a Chinese.'

Carmen was glad to have Rennie out of the way for a few days. His teasing remarks about Joe James weren't what she needed right now. It was bad enough feeling the first flickerings of attraction for another man and discovering that you'd completely forgotten how to behave, without having to put up with Rennie's nudge-nudge attitude. For someone with so much experience of the opposite sex, he could be incredibly school-boyish when it came to taking the mickey out of his sister-in-law.

Anyway, it was Wednesday morning and the good news was that he was thousands of miles away. The bad news was that here she was in her bedroom, wondering what to wear. God, it was like being fifteen again.

How about the striped jeans and Nancy's lacy turquoise top?

By the time the doorbell rang at ten o'clock, Carmen had a plan. She told herself it wasn't a plan, but deep down she knew it was.

'Hi! I didn't realise it was raining! Come inside, all the stuff's in the kitchen. What a filthy day. How are you?' Gabbling, she led the way.

'I'm great. Nice to see you again.' Joe followed her into the kitchen. When she turned, Carmen saw that there were raindrops caught in his hair. He was wearing a weatherproof navy jacket and faded denims. And he was smiling at her as if he really was glad to see her again.

'Now, Rennie had to fly to the States on Monday night, but I've got everything here. Leather trousers and tour jackets,' Carmen patted the holdall Joe had brought along with him on Monday evening, then the envelope lying next to it. 'And he faxed his designs over last night. They're in that one.'

'Brilliant. We're really grateful. Actually, I was wondering if . . . No, nothing, it's OK.' Joe shook his head.

Breathless, Carmen said, 'Actually, I was going to ask you something too. We've had a bit of a problem recently with one of our showers. Sometimes the water goes cold for no reason. I was wondering if your company could take a look at it for us?'

'Could be that it just needs a service.' Joe shook his head slowly. 'But then we get that awkward thing, don't we? My boss sends you a bill, you think it's too high and start to think you've been ripped off.'

'I wouldn't,' protested Carmen.

'Well, I'm sorry, but I can't take that risk.' Smiling slightly, Joe said, 'On the other hand, you could let me take a look at the shower now, then the company wouldn't have to send you a bill.'

'I can't do that.'

'Yes, you can. It might just be a valve sticking. I could fix that in a flash. My boss would be none the wiser and you'd be so grateful I might even end up asking the question I didn't have the courage to ask just now.'

Oh wow! This was thrilling, just so thrilling.

'OK,' Carmen said shyly.

'Give me two minutes,' Joe told her, heading back to the front door. 'I'll just get my toolbox out of the van.'

Carmen perched on the edge of the corner bath and watched Joe expertly dismantle the shower. Now, seeing him minus his jacket, she was able to admire the way the muscles rippled in his forearms.

'So what's it like, having Rennie Todd as a boss?' Joe reached for a screwdriver. 'You seem to get on pretty well together.'

'We do. Well, most of the time. But he isn't my boss.'

Joe looked surprised. 'He's not?'

'Rennie's my brother-in-law.' She was able to say it now, without worrying that her voice might go wobbly. 'I was married to Spike.'

'Oh my God, I didn't realise. I'm so sorry.' Mortified, Joe put down the screwdriver. 'I thought you were his personal assistant or something. I'm really embarrassed now.'

'Don't be. To be honest, I quite like people not knowing who I am.'

Reassured, Joe said, 'Still, it must be nice, staying here in his house.'

'Actually, it's my house,' said Carmen. Oh well, in for a penny, in for a pound. 'Rennie's staying here with me.'

'Bloody hell.' Joe's gaze took in the Italian marble bronze and cream bathroom. 'You mean all this is yours?'

Embarrassed, Carmen saw it through his eyes. 'Spike bought it. But when we first started going out together, we didn't have any money,' said Carmen. 'We lived in a really grotty flat in Edinburgh. But we were just as happy. Maybe happier,' she added, because those were the days before Spike had begun to experiment with drugs.

Joe picked up a pair of pliers. 'You must miss him terribly.'

'I do. But it's been three years. I'm getting better.' Hearing the phone begin to ring, Carmen rose to her feet. 'I'd better answer that.'

Rennie had forgotten to cancel the appointment with his accountant. By the time Carmen had finished explaining to him that Rennie was out of the country and apologising on his behalf, Joe had come downstairs.

'All done,' he said easily, rolling down his sleeves as Carmen hung up the phone. 'Good as new. The valve just needed a good clean.'

'You must let me pay you. Now that you know I can afford it.'

'Not a chance.' Joe smiled. 'On the house.'

'Well, thanks.' Feeling brave, Carmen said, 'But now you have to tell me what it was you were about to say earlier.'

'Oh, that. I can't.'

'Fair's fair. You promised.'

'Did I? OK.' Joe paused, running the fingers of his left hand through his dark hair. 'When I came over here on Monday evening I thought you were fantastic. I really felt we, you know, clicked? And all day yesterday I couldn't stop thinking about you. So I decided I'd ask you out. Then, I wondered if you'd like to come to the charity ball with me on Friday night, and I thought wouldn't it be great if you did, we'd have such a brilliant time together . . .' He stopped. 'I thought you were Rennie Todd's PA. But you're Spike Todd's widow. You're way out of my league.'

He would feel uncomfortable because the fact that she had money did make a difference. The way Joe was looking at her made Carmen want to start tearing up twenty-pound notes on the spot. It was the first time in three years that she'd experienced the crackle and spark of physical attraction. Realising she was on the brink of not seeing him again, she blurted out, 'Please ask me to the ball! Nobody else has to know who I am. I'd just really like to go,' she concluded helplessly. 'With you.'

There, now she'd made a complete and utter fool of herself.

'OK.' Putting his hands up, Joe broke into a smile. 'I'd like to go with you too. You've made my day.'

You've made my year, Carmen thought happily. He really had. Thank goodness Rennie wasn't here to tease her about it.

Chapter 4

YOU CAN LEAD A HORSE to water but you can't make it drink. Similarly, you can introduce your daughter to your girlfriend but you can't make them like each other. From the safety of his office, Connor watched Sadie head over to reception to ask Mia a question. Both of them were smiling—well, baring their teeth at each other—but the body language said it all.

Sadie Sylvester was twenty-six and Connor liked her a lot, although sometimes he wasn't entirely sure why. Her hair was a riotous mass of ringlets dyed a vivid shade of magenta. She was curvy, voluptuous and terrifyingly fit. When she'd started working at the Lazy B four months earlier, teaching aerobics and dance classes, he'd found himself drawn to her devil-may-care manner and sexy, slanting eyes.

All in all, Sadie and Mia had quite a lot in common. It would have been nice if they could have hit it off. But this hadn't happened. Connor shuddered at the memory of their first meeting on the evening Mia had moved in. Mia had given him a blow-by-blow account of it. Sadie, having decided to drop round on a whim—he suspected she liked to check up on him—had rung the doorbell at ten o'clock. Her hackles had risen instantly at the sight of Mia, whose version of pyjamas was a skimpy white vest top and low-slung cotton shorts.

'Who are you? What are you doing here? Where's Connor?'

Instantly offended by Sadie's unfriendly manner—and her hair was pretty offensive too—Mia bristled.

'You must be my father's girlfriend. Nice to meet you too. Dad's having a bath.'

'Oh, right. I'll come in. He didn't tell me you were visiting.' Sadie followed Mia into the living room, then made herself comfortable on the sofa where Mia had been sitting.

Sweetly, Mia said, 'I'm not visiting. I've come to live with my dad.' She watched with satisfaction as Sadie's lip-glossed mouth dropped open.

When Connor arrived downstairs shortly afterwards, Sadie sprang up from the sofa and marched him into the kitchen.

'What's going on? Is this really going to happen?' Incensed, Sadie had bombarded him with questions. Having a teenager hanging around the place didn't fit in with her plans at all.

'Hey, don't get worked up,' Connor told her. 'It'll be fine, you'll see.'

'How can you say that?' Sadie rolled her eyes in disbelief. 'This is going to change everything. We won't have any privacy! And what does she plan to do with herself all day? Go to school? Get a job?'

'She already has a job. At the club,' said Connor.

Sadie's nostrils flared. 'At *our* club?'

'*My* club. I've started her on reception. I think she'll do well.'

Sadie, sensing a change of direction was called for, ran her fingers lightly down the gap at the front of Connor's towelling dressing gown.

'I came over here to see you. I thought we'd make love on the sofa.'

'Well, we can't. Mia's watching a documentary about battery farming and it doesn't finish until midnight.'

'Fine. I'm adaptable.' Smiling for the first time and sliding both hands inside the dressing gown, Sadie said playfully, 'We'll go up to your room. Do it the old-fashioned way, use the bed.'

Connor shook his head. 'We can't. It would look so obvious.' Gently removing her hands from inside his dressing gown, Connor said, 'It's her first night here. Come into the living room and we'll all watch TV.'

'Oh, please. Sitting down together to watch a documentary about battery farming isn't my idea of a wild time. Sex is my idea of a wild time, but I'm not allowed to have sex with my boyfriend because our uninvited guest might know what's going on and be embarrassed. No, don't worry about me. I'll leave you and your daughter to enjoy your battery hens.'

When Sadie had left, Connor rejoined his daughter on the sofa.

'Dad, I've got to say this.' Mia tucked her arm companionably through his. 'I'm an easy-going person. I like most people I meet. But that girlfriend of yours is something else. You could do so much better.'

Connor was reminded of why he drank. When he had a beer in his hand, he was happy. And when he had Sadie in his bed he was happy too. She was wildly sexy.

'We'll see,' he told Mia. 'She's not as bad as you think. And anyway'— Connor decided he had to remind his daughter who was the parent around here—'it's my life, not yours, and I'm not going to be running it to suit you. So give Sadie a break, OK? You never know, you may end up the best of friends.'

Now, watching them square up to each other across the reception desk, Connor acknowledged that this was unlikely to happen. Having Mia and Sadie both working here was, he already knew, a big mistake. But Sadie was a damn good instructor with a devoted following. And Mia was attacking her job with relish, impressing everyone—apart from Sadie—with her enthusiasm, cheery manner and eagerness to learn. At this rate she was shaping up to be a dream employee. Her plan was to work her way up to club manager.

Sadie's dark eyes were flashing now, her magenta corkscrew ringlets starting to bounce ominously. As their voices began to rise, Connor left his office and headed over to the desk.

'Ah, good.' Spotting him, Sadie said frostily, 'Back me up here, would you? Just tell your daughter to do as she's told.'

'Excuse *me*.' Mia had no intention of being intimidated. 'What's—'

'Girls, shhh.' Luckily the reception area was empty, but Connor was keen to avoid a squawking match. 'Let's sort this out, shall we?'

Nancy, back from the shops, thought she was hallucinating when she glanced through the railings bordering the garden in the centre of Fitzallen Square. It was a dark grey afternoon and the air was thick with fog, but the small, bundled-up figure sitting on one of the wooden benches beneath a dripping ash tree looked uncannily like her mother.

Nancy made her way through the gate and peered more closely at the solitary figure.

'Mum! Is that *you*?'

Rose, her transparent Pacamac crackling as she pushed the hood down, waved and called back, 'Yoo hoo, darling. Hello!'

Nancy hugged her tightly; it was so good to see her mother again, even if it was like hugging a cellophane-wrapped sweet. Rose even smelt comfortingly familiar. Nancy shook her head in disbelief.

'You're not supposed to be here yet! Rennie booked you onto the four o'clock flight. I was going to meet you at the airport.'

'I know you were, darling. That's why I thought I'd save you the trouble, so you didn't have to trudge all that way.' Beaming, pink-cheeked with the cold, Rose said, 'I looked up the easyJet website on the internet and found out the flight times. Then I rang them and they were able to swap me onto the earlier flight.'

'Website? *Internet?*'

'Sweetheart, I'm not senile. It's a marvellous system,' Rose confided. 'They have computers at the local library, and the librarians are wonderful at showing you how to use them.'

Nancy, her brain in a whirl, said, 'So how *did* you get here from Stansted?'

'Och, it was simple! I just asked a really nice man how I should go about it, and he showed me where to catch the train to Liverpool Street. Then I met *such* a nice family on the train and they explained the whole underground system to me. So when we reached Liverpool Street I worked out which tube station was nearest to here.'

Whatever next? Nancy marvelled. Would Rose be announcing that she'd applied to run the London marathon? Become a weather girl?

Speaking of weather . . .

'What are we still doing out here? Come on, let's get inside. We'll put the kettle on and get you warmed up. How long have you been waiting?'

'Not long at all, pet. I've been sitting here enjoying the gardens.' Having bent to gather together her motley collection of bags, Rose straightened and broke into a broad smile. Thinking she was smiling at her, Nancy was startled to hear her mother call out, 'Bye, sweetheart. Bye, Doreen. See you again. Hope that leg's better soon.'

Spinning round, Nancy saw a man in his thirties with long blond hair heading towards them with a mongrel on a lead. From the depths of his parka, the man called back, 'Bye, Rose, lovely to meet you,' in a light, unmistakably camp voice that sent a shiver of alarm down Nancy's spine.

'Mum,' she hissed when the couple had trotted off damply down the path, 'that wasn't a woman. It was a *man*.'

'What? I'm not with you, pet.'

'You called him *Doreen*.' His name was probably Darren, and Rose had, embarrassingly, misheard him.

Looking amused, Rose said, 'Dear me, his name's Zac and of course he's a man. Doreen's the name of his little dog. She managed to get her leg caught in a drain cover yesterday, that's why she's limping. Now, are we going to have that cup of tea or not?'

Rennie, phoning from New York, insisted on speaking to Rose when he heard she'd arrived safely.

'Oh, yes, I'm having the time of my life,' Rose assured him. 'Everyone in London is so friendly and welcoming.'

'Did you bring me that casserole?' teased Rennie.

'No, pet, I didn't. I was worried about turbulence on the plane. But I'll make you one as soon as you come back,' Rose promised. 'And Carmen's hankering for flapjack, so I'll be doing some of that.'

'Is Carmen there? I'll have a quick word with her.'

'She's upstairs, pet, getting herself all ready for her big date.'

In New York, Rennie's eyebrows went up. 'Big date? Who with?'

'Oh my, let me think, what's the name of Carmen's gentleman friend?' Brightening, Rose exclaimed, 'Ah yes, got it now. Joe.'

'Joe?' echoed Rennie. 'She's actually going out on a date with him?'

'She's very excited,' Rose confided. 'All over the place, bless her heart.'

'I'm having the best time of my life,' Joe whispered in Carmen's ear and she felt herself flush with happiness as his arms tightened round her. They were slowly circling the dance floor as the band played an old Mariah Carey number.

'Me too,' said Carmen. She'd enjoyed herself, and she'd enjoyed being here with Joe. In his company she felt relaxed, normal, desirable again. It was like coming out of hibernation.

'Sheila took me to one side earlier,' Joe confided, 'and told me we made a lovely couple.' Sheila, big and matronly, had organised the raffle at the ball. 'She said we look perfect together.' He paused then added, 'I can't believe that this time last week I hadn't even met you.' He stopped dancing. 'We are going to see each other again, aren't we?'

A lump sprang into Carmen's throat. To think that she'd been worried about tonight being a let-down, that Joe might realise he'd made a mistake. Slowly she nodded. 'I'd love to see you again.'

'OK, I know it's way too soon to be saying this, so I won't.' His breath warm against her cheek, he murmured, 'But right now I'm *thinking* it wouldn't take much for me to fall in love with you.'

Heavens. This was like a Hollywood film.

'Is that scary?' whispered Joe, beginning to dance again as the music changed to George Michael's 'Careless Whisper'. His fingertips, drawing light circles on her back as they moved together in time with the music, were making her skin tingle in the most delicious way.

'Very nice scary,' said Carmen with a surge of happiness.

Joe's dark eyes softened. 'That's good enough for now.'

Rennie arrived back from New York on Sunday morning and reached Fitzallen Square at midday. Any fantasies of opening the front door and being greeted by the welcoming smell of a home-cooked roast dinner were dashed when he bumped into Nancy and Rose in the hallway. Rose was bundled up in a woollen coat, thick knitted scarf and hat.

'You naughty boy, you'll catch your death of cold,' she scolded, eyeing Rennie's crumpled T-shirt and jeans. 'Are you hungry? Shall I make you something to eat before we leave?'

'That would be great. Roast lamb, roast potatoes, carrots, leeks, parsnips, Yorkshire pudding and gravy, please,' said Rennie. Then, catching the worried look on her face he said, 'Rose, I'm joking. You're here on holiday, not to wait on us hand and foot! What have you been doing anyway?'

'Seeing all the sights. Oh, it's been marvellous.' Rose's eyes lit up. 'We went to see Downing Street yesterday, and Madame Tussaud's—what a place that was, all those marvellous people looking so *like* themselves. And Buckingham Palace. And the London Eye. We're just off out again now, to visit the zoo at Regent's Park. Why don't you come with us?'

Fond though he was of Rose, Rennie couldn't imagine anything more awful. Standing in the freezing cold watching penguins swimming around in even icier water wasn't his idea of a good time.

Rennie nodded. 'Thanks, but I'll just stay here. Maybe take Carmen out to lunch.'

'Carmen? She's not around,' said Rose. 'She went out earlier, with Joe.'

'Joe again? You're kidding. What have I missed?'

'Loads.' Nancy's tone was playful. 'Carmen's in love. We've hardly seen her since Friday night.'

Rennie wondered how he felt about this. Carmen? Were they serious?

'Your leather trousers raised four hundred pounds, by the way. And the four jackets went for five hundred and fifty each.'

'Has he been . . . staying here?' In deference to Rose, Rennie phrased it as delicately as he knew how.

Rose looked shocked. 'Of course not! He's been the perfect gentleman. Drives her home, kisses her good night on the doorstep.'

Well, that was something.

'She's come over all dippy,' said Nancy. 'Like a teenager. If she isn't out with Joe, she's talking about him. I swear she counts the minutes before she'll see him again.'

Rennie knew he should be pleased that Carmen was returning to the land of the living at long last. He wished he could *feel* more pleased.

'Well, that's . . . great. Now, you two go off and enjoy yourselves.'

When Rose and Nancy had left, Rennie hauled his case upstairs. His mobile beeped, signalling the arrival of yet another text.

'Where r u? Fancy meeting up? Call me! Miss u loads. Luv Caz. xxx'

Caz was a 28-year-old medical physicist, with the best figure in Finsbury Park. And he had the rest of the day free. Rennie replied to her text with a brief: 'See you at your place in an hour.'

But he couldn't bring himself to raise much enthusiasm at the prospect. As he stood beneath the shower, vigorously shampooing his hair, Rennie recalled Nancy's comments about Carmen, and how she had been counting down the minutes before she would see Joe again. He honestly couldn't remember *ever* counting down the minutes before meeting up with a girlfriend.

Maybe love just wasn't his thing, Rennie thought as he reached for the shower gel. He'd never been in love, not properly. He suspected it had something to do with the thrill of the chase. Or, in his case, the abject lack of it. Whenever he visited a bar or a nightclub, pretty girls approached him, offering him their phone numbers before you could say floozy. Where was the sense of hard-earned achievement in that?

Rennie sluiced the last of the foaming gel from his body, stepped out of the shower and towelled himself dry. Maybe he should ring Caz and cancel. Was it fair to take advantage of her? Wouldn't he be happier stretched across the sofa, watching *Casablanca* or *Citizen Kane*?

But Caz would think *that* was unfair. More than anything else, she wanted to see him—and sleep with him—this afternoon. She would be upset if he let her down now. Wearily, Rennie dragged a clean pair of jeans and a fresh shirt out of his wardrobe. He'd spend the afternoon with Caz and be home early.

Buttoning his denim shirt, Rennie wondered what time Carmen would be back. Tonight he'd have a serious talk with her and find out exactly what was going on between her and Joe James.

'Yay, you're still awake,' Carmen said cheerfully, letting herself into the house at two thirty in the morning and discovering Rennie making his tenth cup of coffee in the kitchen.

Of course I'm still awake, Rennie thought crossly. I've been waiting for *you*.

Aloud he said, 'And what on earth time do you call this? Where have you been? And why's your shirt on inside out?'

Carmen grinned and gave him a hug. 'Yes, Mum, no, Mum, sorry I'm late, Mum. We were having such fun I didn't notice the time. And my shirt isn't on inside out.'

'I should hope not.' Rennie wondered if she could tell that he was sounding jokey but deep down he actually meant it.

'How was New York? How's Jessie?' Having poured herself a glass of water, Carmen perched on the nearest stool. Her eyes were sparkling.

'Jessie's OK. She was just going through a bad patch. Her sister's with her now. So what's happening with you and this chap?'

This time Carmen's whole face lit up. 'We just clicked. He's so . . . great. We never stop talking. That's what we've been doing today. And no, I haven't slept with him yet,' Carmen went on, because it was so transparently obvious what Rennie wanted to ask her. 'We're taking things slowly. People jump into bed together all the time and it means nothing. We want it to be extra special.'

Rennie, who had spent the afternoon in bed with an ecstatic Caz, having completely meaningless sex, helped himself to a Jaffa cake.

'So you might be seeing him again then?'

Carmen pulled a face at him. 'Of course I'm seeing him again. Tomorrow night, in fact.'

'Bet you can't wait.'

'I can't.' She beamed, immune to his teasing.

'You'll be counting the minutes,' said Rennie.

'Right, I'm shattered, I'm off to bed.' Yawning widely, Carmen headed for the kitchen door. Then she paused and gazed seriously at Rennie. 'And yes, I *will* be counting the minutes. I feel as if I'm allowed to be happy again. That's a good thing, isn't it?'

Rennie softened, unable to begrudge her a bit of much-deserved happiness. 'Definitely a good thing.'

'And it's all thanks to you,' Carmen went on happily. 'If you hadn't agreed to help the charity, I'd never have met Joe.'

Rennie waited until she'd gone before exhaling and saying, '*Bugger.*'

Rose was a firm believer in the benefits of the great outdoors. Why be stuck inside when you could be outside breathing in great lungfuls of fresh air? Besides, venturing out into the square enabled you to interact with the outside world, to nod and smile and exchange a few cheerful words with pleasant-looking passers-by.

Not that all of them fell into this category. Yesterday a rigid-looking couple—husband and wife, presumably—had taken the path that led past Rose's bench. The man, in his sixties or thereabouts and with a military air to him, had narrowed his eyes suspiciously at the sight of her. Rose had set down her knitting and smiled at them perfectly politely, but the pair had remained hatchet-faced.

'Morning,' Rose called out as they drew level. 'Beautiful day, isn't it?'

'Hrrmmph,' the man snorted in reply. His wife, averting her thin face, behaved as though she hadn't noticed Rose's presence.

And they had marched on by, not looking very cheerful at all. Feeling sorry for them, Rose had picked up her knitting and smiled to herself. *Separate Tables*, the film that had earned lovely David Niven an Oscar, that was what the couple reminded her of. They'd have fitted right into that hotel dining room, sitting stiffly and in silence in the background.

Rose took a packet of homemade fudge out of her bag and popped a square into her mouth. She gazed around her with satisfaction, listening to the birds twittering in the branches of the ash trees overhead. It might only be Tuesday, but already she regarded this bench as *her* bench.

Reaching the end of a row, Rose heard a rustling noise from the bushes to her left. Next moment there was a yelp of pain and the sound of frantic whimpering. Jumping to her feet, she headed over to the bush and saw a pair of terrified brown eyes peering out at her.

'Doreen, Doreen!' shouted a voice, and the young man called Zac rounded the bend in the path. When he saw Rose on her knees, he broke into a trot.

'She's in here,' Rose told him, attempting to part the spiky branches.

'Oh, Doreen, you are hopeless,' Zac chided, reaching Rose's side and tut-tutting at the little dog's predicament. 'Come on, baby, sshh, keep still, let me just untangle you . . .' Bravely he plunged in, ignoring the vicious thorns, separating the branches until there was enough of a gap to ease Doreen through. 'There, you silly thing, you're safe now.' Leaning back on his heels, he pulled Doreen onto his lap and soothingly stroked her ears. 'Thanks.' He turned to Rose. 'She's a bit too intrepid for her own good. I spend my life having to rescue her from ridiculous places.'

'She has an enquiring mind,' said Rose. 'That's not such a bad thing. Och, look at her wee nose, that's what made her yelp.'

There was a small scratch just above Doreen's nose. Zac gently wiped away the beads of blood and kissed the top of her trembling head.

'And she's not the only one in the wars. Look at you.' Rose tut-tutted, pointing to a deep scratch on his wrist that Zac had sustained while plunging fearlessly to the rescue.

'I'll live,' said Zac.

'But you might drip blood on your clothes.' Rising to her feet, Rose said, 'I've got an Elastoplast in my bag. Come on, let's sort you out.'

As they reached the bench, Doreen began to snuffle excitedly. Opening her capacious bag, Rose said, 'She can smell the fudge. OK if she has a piece?'

'Homemade,' marvelled Zac. 'My word, it's like meeting Mary Poppins.' Clipping Doreen back on her lead, he accepted two pieces of fudge, one for himself and one for Doreen, then allowed Rose to place the Elastoplast over the scratch. Shaking his head, he said, 'This fudge is phenomenal. And you knit as well.' His gaze fell upon the hastily abandoned heap of knitting on the bench. 'What's it going to be? May I see?'

Rose had never before had interest expressed in her knitting by a member of the opposite sex. Holding up the work in progress, she said, 'It's a bit of an experiment, I'm just seeing how it works out. My daughter Nancy wanted a kind of light lacy jackety thing to wear over a long yellow dress she has.'

'Where's the pattern?' asked Zac, studying the front of the knitted jacket and picking the already completed back and sleeves out of the carrier bag on the bench.

'I'm not using one.' Intrigued by the attention he was paying to the frilled, pointy-edged sleeves, Rose said, 'I'm just making it up as I go.'

'Clever.' Zac ran his fingers along the edge of the sleeve, assessing the neatness of the stitches. She had chosen a thin, silky two-ply thread in pale silvery-yellow; the effect she was aiming for was more like lace than knitwear. He had nice hands, Rose noted; long-fingered and sensitive.

'Is your wife a knitter?' Rose said eagerly.

'I'm not married.' Zac gave her a quizzical look. 'Nor likely to be.'

'Oh, now, don't be such a pessimist! You never know who might be just around the corner,' Rose encouraged him.

Zac grinned. 'Actually, I'm interested in knitting. I design knitwear. I have my own shop, just round the corner in Levine Street.' Proudly he added, 'I'm a clothes designer.'

'Really?' Rose cast a dubious glance at his lime-green jacket, mustard-yellow sweatshirt and bizarre black-and-white trousers.

Sensing her doubt, Zac said good-naturedly, 'I'm quite successful. Well, in a minor way.'

Rose hurried to reassure him. 'Oh, I'm sure you are! I didn't mean—'

'It's OK. Listen, I employ outworkers to knit for me. I don't know if that's something you'd consider.' Zac was still fingering the intricate sleeve of the jacket. 'But if you think you might be interested . . .'

Rennie, glancing out of the window, called out, 'Take a look at this.'

Nancy was emptying the dishwasher in the kitchen. Hurrying through to the living room, she followed Rennie's pointing finger.

Below them, Rose had emerged from the gardens across the street, chattering animatedly to a long-haired man with a small dog. As Nancy and Rennie watched, the three of them set off along the pavement.

'How many times have I told her not to speak to strangers.' Nancy heaved a sigh. 'And does she take a blind bit of notice?'

'Want me to go down and bring her back?'

There were con artists around, Nancy knew, who specialised in tricking old ladies into handing over all their money. Heading over to the chair where Rose had left her handbag, she reassured herself that her mother's purse, credit cards and cheque book were all still here.

'Don't worry. We saw him there the other day, walking his dog.' Why that should make a difference, Nancy didn't know, but somehow it did. 'Mum was chatting to him then. The dog's called Doreen,' she remembered. 'I think she'll be safe. He looks too clean to be a mugger.'

'Here we are, home sweet home.' Zac pushed open the door. 'Well, shop sweet shop. Small but perfectly formed. Jacintha, could you be an angel and take Doreen upstairs? She's gasping for a drink.'

Jacintha, with her glossy chestnut hair and painstakingly applied make-up, looked like one of those 'It' girls, thought Rose. Pushing her copy of *Tatler* to one side, she clicked her French-manicured fingers at Doreen and disappeared through the door at the back of the shop.

Rose gazed around with interest. From the outside the shop was small, painted sugar-almond pink and bore a sign above the window with *Zac Parris Designs* inscribed on it in grey and silver lettering.

Inside, the shop space itself was perhaps ten feet wide and twenty feet long with silver-grey walls, fuchsia-pink carpet and lots of gauzy iridescent netting forming a draped and tented ceiling, from the centre of which hung an ornate pale pink and white chandelier. Rose, who had never seen a shop resembling it in her life, exclaimed, 'My word, it's like one of those TV programmes, isn't it? You know, where the people decorate each other's living rooms. It's just beautiful, like a fairy palace! It's the kind of thing that lanky long-haired one would produce, have you seen him? With all the freckles. My friend Morag thinks he's . . .' Rose lowered her voice and half mouthed the words, 'one of those *homosexuals*.'

Hearing a sound like a cross between a laugh and a cough, Rose realised that Jacintha had rejoined them.

'Sorry, listen to me wittering on.' Rose turned her attention to Zac's designs, sparsely displayed on narrow racks against the walls. There was only one of each item. 'Is this the kind of thing you'd be after?'

The sweater was of nubbly oatmeal-shaded lambswool with ivory satin facings round an asymmetric neckline. Extraordinary, thought Rose, blanching as she glimpsed the ornately inscribed price tag.

'My clientele expect individual designs. They don't want to find someone else wearing an identical outfit,' Zac explained. 'That one was knitted by a woman in Devon,' said Zac. 'I send her my drawings. She makes up the garment. Do you think you could do that?'

Rose, who had been knitting incessantly for the last forty years, said, 'That's like asking me if I know how to breathe. So I'd be able to post the garments off to you, would I? Only I don't live in London, you know, I'm just down here on holiday for a couple of weeks.'

'That's fine,' said Zac as the phone on the desk began to ring. 'We'd have to have a trial run, of course. If I give you a sample of work, could you do it in the next day or two? Jacintha, can you answer that, please?'

Jacintha, who had just finished painting her nails, flapped her hands then picked up the phone and said tetchily, 'Hello, Zac Parris Designs, how may I help you? Oh, right. Hang on.' She held the phone out to Zac. 'For you.'

Whoever it was on the other end caused Zac to flush red. Excusing himself, he slipped through to the workroom and closed the door. Jacintha, rolling her eyes in despair, declared, 'Zac's latest no-hoper.'

'Oh.' Another prospective home-knitter, Rose guessed, who had failed the test. Well, she wouldn't do that. Watching Jacintha carefully turn the pages of the magazine, she said brightly, 'He's nice, isn't he?'

'Who, Zac? He's OK.'

Heavens, such enthusiasm. Rose said, 'You must enjoy working here.'

This made Jacintha smile. Gesturing towards the spare chair, upholstered in baby-pink satin, she said, 'Have a seat. Zac could be gone for some time. Shall I tell you why I handed in my notice here last week?'

Startled, Rose said, 'Um, only if you want to, pet.'

Maybe Zac had made some kind of unwanted pass at her.

'Men,' said Jacintha.

Oh dear.

'I mean, what's the main reason for coming to work in the first place? To meet *men*,' Jacintha exclaimed, because Rose was looking blank. 'My friend Shona married her boss, for crying out loud. Now they live in this fantastic five-bed detached on Primrose Hill. And what do *I* do?' Jacintha demanded, her eyebrows arching up into her hairline. 'I chose to come and work in a shop where you meet no men at all!'

Rose was bemused. 'None? What, never?'

'Well, there's the postman, I suppose. And the fat bloke who waddles in to fix the computer when I've spilt coffee in it. Anyway, I'm out of here.' Jacintha nodded with satisfaction. 'I've got a job with a PR agency in Soho. Loads of men, non-stop partying—ha! I can't wait.'

Nancy blew on her icy hands and hung back as Rose tapped on the door of Zac Parris Designs. It was nine twenty-five in the morning and the door was locked, but there were lights on inside. She couldn't believe she'd allowed her mother to drag her here—she was twenty-eight years old, it was *embarrassing*.

'Ah, there he is,' Rose exclaimed happily as Zac appeared in the shop and unlocked the door. 'Morning, pet, I've brought you the sample you wanted. And this is my daughter, Nancy. The one I was telling you about.'

'Of course, come along in.' Zac was smiling but his eyes were shadowed as if he hadn't had much sleep. 'Coffee's on if you'd like some. My word, you were quick. I wasn't expecting to see you today.'

'Och, it was no trouble.' Rose coloured with pride as he lifted up the sample she'd done for him. 'I'm a fast worker. Well, what d'you think?'

Nancy watched him expertly scrutinise the stitching of the strappy, swingy top he'd sketched for her mother to copy.

'You're a pro,' said Zac. 'It's perfect. Now, I'd pay you on average sixty pounds per item. Forty for something smaller, like this. Up to eighty for anything more intricate. Are you happy with that?'

Rose nodded vigorously. 'That sounds wonderful. I can't believe you'd pay that much!'

Zac looked amused too. 'Good. In that case we have a deal. Now, how about that coffee?'

'Where's Jacintha?'

'Oh, she'll roll in at some stage. Mornings aren't her forte.'

Zac was obviously gay. Nancy, observing his camp manner and flamboyant hand gestures, realised that this detail had escaped Rose entirely.

'Well, she's going now. Off to a new job in Soho.' Rose fixed her gaze on Zac. 'She tells me you haven't found anyone to replace her yet.'

'I haven't.' Zac was busy fiddling with the coffee machine and setting out little silver cups. 'Do you take sugar?'

'The thing is, my daughter needs work. She'd be perfect.'

Zac paused, spoon in hand, and spun round to look at Nancy. Under the impression until now that her mother had already suggested her for the job, Nancy realised that he'd had no idea.

'Um . . .' said Zac.

'You wouldn't regret it,' Rose went on proudly. 'She's punctual, efficient, good at dealing with people. She wouldn't sit around painting her nails and reading magazines, either.'

'Mum—'

'And she could start as soon as you like,' Rose went on encouragingly.

Right, that was enough.

'Mum, stop it,' Nancy blurted out. 'I can sort this out myself, OK? Let me speak to Zac. Why don't I see you back at the house?' And strangle you then, she added silently.

'Good idea.' Rose nodded and looked pleased with herself, evidently satisfied that her matchmaking skills had paid off. 'You two have a nice chat, get to know each other.'

'I'm so sorry,' Nancy groaned as soon as the shop door had clanged shut. 'It's OK, you don't have to give me the job. I had no idea she was going to spring it on you like that. Here, let me do that,' she added, because Zac was making a complete pig's ear of trying to spoon sugar into his coffee. His hands were shaking, Nancy saw as she re-sugared, stirred and handed him the silver cup. 'Are you OK? You look a bit . . .'

'Overwrought? Knackered? It's OK, you can say it.' Gesturing for her to follow him, Zac led the way through to his work studio behind the shop. 'Here, take a seat.' Zac hastily gathered up a mass of fabric swatches and gestured for her to occupy the red-velvet-upholstered two-seater sofa. 'Rose is a nice lady. If she thinks you'd be good at the job, you probably would be.' He paused and took a gulp of scalding hot coffee. 'She tells me your marriage just broke up.'

'My husband was cheating on me.' Nancy decided that if he could be blunt, so could she.

'Yeah. Well, I know how that feels.' Zac managed a wry smile.

Sympathetically she said, 'Did it just happen?'

'*Just* happen? It's *always* happening.' Zac heaved a heartfelt sigh and perched on the velvet arm of the sofa. 'It happened again last night.' He shook his head dejectedly. 'Story of my life. I get it wrong every time.'

'I only got it wrong once,' said Nancy, 'but it was a pretty big once. And now I'm five hundred miles from home,' she added, 'staying with my friend Carmen. She's trying to persuade me to move in for good.'

'Aren't you the lucky one,' said Zac. 'I meet someone, they move in with me and then the next weekend they pack their bags and move out.'

As Doreen pattered down the stairs and into the workroom, Zac held out his arms to the little dog. 'Just as well I've got you, sweetie pie, isn't it? At least you'd never leave me.' Giving Doreen a cuddle, he said hopefully, 'Were you devastated when you and your husband broke up?'

'I thought I would be. And I know you probably want me to say yes, but I wasn't.' Nancy struggled to explain. 'It was a huge shock at first, but then I kind of felt . . . well, relieved.'

'So if he turned up on your doorstep this afternoon and begged you to take him back?'

'I wouldn't. It's over.'

'You're so strong.' Zac sighed and stroked Doreen's silky ears. 'I wish I could be like you.' Brightening, he said, 'You can be my role model. Stop me being such a hopeless pushover. Give me pep talks every morning.'

'Hang on,' said Nancy, 'does that mean you're offering me the job?'

'Of course.' Zac sounded surprised.

'But . . . don't you have other people to interview?'

'No.' Zac looked faintly embarrassed. 'To be honest, I kind of hoped Jacintha might come up with someone.' Brightly he added, 'But I'd much rather have you! And Rose did say you'd be perfect for the job.'

Nancy rolled her eyes. 'She's my mother. She thinks I'd be perfect for the Olympic relay team, for the position of Chancellor of the Exchequer *and* to represent the country in the Eurovision song contest.'

'Blimey. If you can do all that,' said Zac cheerfully, 'you can definitely handle working here. How soon can you start?'

Rennie was still asleep when the doorbell rang. Groaning, he rolled over in bed and covered his head with a pillow.

Rrrrinnggg.

God, he hated doorbells. They could seriously damage your health.

But since he was now awake, and appeared to be the only one in the house, he may as well answer it. Naked, carrying his jeans in one hand, he made his way downstairs and pressed the intercom. 'Yes?'

'Um . . . is that Rennie Todd?' It was a girl's voice.

Rennie paused. 'Who is this?'

'Look, I'm sorry,' the girl sounded nervous, 'but I need to speak to you about, um, Carmen. It's important.'

Rennie heaved a sigh and climbed into his jeans. Opening the front door, he saw a girl with ash-blonde hair pulled back from her face in a ponytail. She was pretty, in her mid-twenties, and huddled up against the cold in a red leather jacket, black trousers and high-heeled boots.

'Carmen isn't here.' Rennie shivered as the icy wind blasted his chest.

'I know. I wouldn't be here if she was.'

Briskly, he said, 'Is this going to be quick?'

'Um . . .' The girl shook her head apologetically. 'Not that quick, no.'

Typical. No chance of getting back to sleep then. In which case, caffeine was called for.

'You'd better come in. Coffee?'

'Thanks.' The girl followed him through to the kitchen. 'Sorry if I woke you up.'

'Let's just hope it's worth it.' Filling the kettle, Rennie said, 'So what's your name?'

'Tina.'

'And you know Carmen from where?' It occurred to Rennie that she might be something to do with the homeless shelter.

'I don't know Carmen, I just know *of* her. I'm Joe James's ex-girlfriend.'

'Oh.' Bloody hell, this was all he needed. A jealous ex, come round to stir up trouble.

'No.' Tina was evidently able to read his mind. 'It's not what you think. I just need to warn you about Joe.'

'Shouldn't you be talking to Carmen?' He plonked two mugs of coffee on the table.

'I don't want her to know this is coming from me.' Tina said. 'She'd tell Joe and he'd go mental. I don't want you to tell her I've been here.'

Frowning, Rennie said, 'But Joe gave you this address?'

'No, he didn't. I knew it was Fitzallen Square, because he mentioned it before he came round the first time to see you. When I turned up this morning, I thought I might be able to guess which house it was.' Looking embarrassed, Tina smiled and said, 'I sort of expected yours to be the house with all the groupies queuing up at the front door.'

Gravely, Rennie said, 'Sorry. The groupies don't get here until midday. So how did you find us?'

'Asked the postman.'

Oh well. Rennie nodded and began peeling the silver foil off a KitKat he'd found in the fruit bowl. 'Carry on.'

'Joe is only with Carmen because she's rich,' Tina said bluntly. 'He's after her money.'

'Did he tell you that?'

'We went out together for almost a year. Last week he dumped me. And yes, I was upset.' Tina shrugged. 'I'm being honest here, OK? I thought we'd stay together, get engaged, the whole thing. Anyway, yesterday I rang Joe and told him I'd found his car insurance and MOT certificates in my bag, from when we'd been to the post office to tax the car. He dropped round at lunchtime to pick them up. He was so pleased with himself, he couldn't help bragging about him and Carmen, and how crazy she is about him.' Tina paused, then went on, 'He said his life was about to change, big time. He boasted that he was going to persuade Carmen to help him set up his own plumbing business. He said twenty grand would be nothing to her, she wouldn't even miss it. Which I think is a pretty crappy thing to say, even if it *is* true. And I think Carmen deserves to know what he's up to. There, now I've said it.'

'You want me to tell Carmen,' Rennie said slowly, 'so that she'll finish with your ex-boyfriend. And then what? You can have him back?'

Tina shrugged. 'Maybe. I can't give Joe twenty grand because I don't have any money. But I still love him.'

'Carmen isn't going to believe me.'

'Fair enough. I'm not asking you to tell her so that she'll dump Joe. I'm just suggesting you warn her, so that when he does start dropping hints about twenty grand solving all his problems, she'll stop and think it through before whipping out her diamond-studded cheque book.'

Chapter 5

THE WEATHER HAD TAKEN a dramatic turn for the worse. Pewter-grey clouds loomed and icy rain began to pelt down as Nancy prepared to leave the house. By the time she reached the pavement, the rain had turned to hail, hammering onto her umbrella with the force of gunfire. Shuddering as a car swished past, sending a wave of water over her feet, Nancy wondered just how desperate you had to be for a haircut to venture out in a hailstorm. Well, *this* desperate, clearly. Anyway, she needed highlights as well as a cut. A new job definitely merited new highlights.

'Oh my God,' shrieked Nancy as she turned and saw the bicycle careering straight towards her. The cyclist, having completely lost control, hit the kerb with a metallic crunch, shot over the handlebars and landed against her chest with a lung-crushing thud.

Whoomph, Nancy promptly lost her footing and went over backwards. The cyclist, a teenager wearing an anorak and spectacles streaming with sleet, crashed down on top of her. Clearly horrified he yelped, 'Sorry, sorry', and scrambled to his feet. Nancy, still on the ground, gazed open-mouthed in disbelief as he ran to retrieve his bike from the gutter, leapt onto it and pedalled furiously away.

She hauled herself into a sitting position and gingerly examined her grazed hand. Her umbrella was bowling merrily across the road and her handbag—oh, *perfect*—had burst open in a puddle.

'It's OK, don't move,' called a voice behind her. Carmen's neighbour, Mia's father, crouched beside her and said, 'Shall I call an ambulance?'

Nancy shook her head. 'I'll be all right. Nothing broken.'

'That bloody idiot,' Connor said in disbelief. 'I saw it happen from the window.' He held out his hand. 'By the way, I'm Connor.'

'I know. Mia's dad. Nice to meet you.' Solemnly they shook hands. He was getting drenched, Nancy realised.

'Well, this is stupid. Like trying to pretend it isn't raining at some posh garden party. Think you can stand up?' said Connor.

Nancy nodded and allowed him to help her to her feet. She began to tremble as shock belatedly set in.

'OK,' Connor murmured, leading her to the railings. 'Just wait here a second while I fetch your stuff.'

He was wearing a blue and white rugby shirt and dark blue corduroys. Nancy leaned feebly against the railings and watched him gather together everything that had exploded out of her bag, including a box of tampons, two packets of Maltesers and a lipstick that had rolled into the gutter. He then raced up the road to collect her umbrella.

'Come on,' said Connor, when he returned, 'let's get you inside.' His front door was open and he helped her up the steps into his house.

'Really, you don't have to—'

'Hey, don't spoil my big moment. I've never come to the aid of a damsel in distress before. When I was a kid I always wanted to be a superhero,' Connor confided. 'I used to dream about rescuing people from burning buildings, saving their lives.'

'That's so noble.' Nancy smiled at him, picturing him as a boy.

'Actually, it wasn't. I wanted to rescue them so they'd be eternally grateful and give me some fantastic reward. Remember *Charlie and the Chocolate Factory*? I especially wanted to save Willie Wonka's life, so he'd give me his factory and I'd have a lifetime's supply of sweets. Now, shall I help you off with your coat?'

Nancy discovered that her hands were still shaking too badly to unfasten her belt. Feeling stupid, she stood there like a child while Connor did it for her.

'I can't manage a factory full of sweets, I'm afraid. But you're welcome to the packet of orange TicTacs in my bag.'

Connor grinned and something inside Nancy went *twaannggg* as she looked at him properly for the first time and realised how attractive he was. OK, maybe not take-your-breath-away good-looking like Rennie, but attractive in a down-to-earth way. Connor O'Shea looked rumpled and lived-in and . . . well, just downright *nice*.

Oops, she was still gazing at him. Right, stop it. '*Ouch*.'

'Sorry.' Having peeled off her wet coat, Connor had gently pushed back the sleeve of her favourite olive-green sweater. Flinching, Nancy saw the nasty graze that ran the length of her forearm.

'Hang on, let me get the first-aid kit,' said Connor. 'I think we're going to have to amputate.'

He had such a fantastic voice, lazy and humorous and with that impossible-to-resist Dublin accent.

'Can I keep the arm as a souvenir?' Nancy watched as Connor, having fetched the kit, began to clean her forearm with antiseptic lotion.

'Now that's what I call thrifty. You could mount it on a plaque,' he said approvingly. 'Hang it on your wall. Great conversation piece, and so much cheaper than an oil painting.'

'And when the novelty's worn off, I could sell it on to Charles Saatchi.' Nancy caught his eye and felt that jolt of attraction again. He smelt gorgeous, he had a sense of humour and she just loved the way his eyebrows moved when he smiled, as if they had a life of their own.

'There, all done. Anything else need looking at?'

'I'm fine.' Nancy carefully rolled the sleeve of her sweater down over the bandage. 'Thanks. How can I ever repay you for saving my life?' Reaching for her bag, she said, 'Here, take my TicTacs. I want you to have them.'

Was she making a complete twit of herself? It was so long since she'd flirted with anyone that she couldn't remember how it was done. Nancy ordered herself to get a grip. Here she was behaving like a twittering teenager just three weeks after the end of her marriage.

'Listen,' Connor interrupted her thoughts, 'what are you doing tomorrow night?'

Nancy's heart began to palpitate.

'Sorry? Um . . . nothing planned.' Feeling herself going red, unable to believe this was all happening so fast, she said, 'Why?'

'How about coming round for a drink,' Connor suggested, 'and we can get to know each other properly. Without the smell of antiseptic.'

'Love to. Sounds great!' As she said it, Nancy wondered if that was too eager. But he'd asked her, hadn't he? What was wrong with saying yes?

'Around seven, then? You, Rennie and Carmen?'

Oh.

'Fine!' Nancy smiled extra brightly to hide her disappointment.

'Always good to get to know your neighbours,' Connor said easily. 'I haven't met Carmen yet, not even to say hello to. Here, give me your hand.' Reaching for her left wrist, he dabbed carefully at her upturned palm with a tissue. 'Maybe I should put a dressing on this one as well.'

'What's going on?'

Startled, Nancy twisted round on her chair to find herself being stared at by a girl with wild magenta curls and a beautiful but none-too-friendly face. She was wearing a white shirt that presumably belonged to Connor, and nothing else.

'This is Nancy, one of our neighbours. She had a bit of a run-in with a cyclist,' Connor explained. 'Nancy, this is my girlfriend Sadie.'

Sadie nodded briefly, in acknowledgment. Nancy, attempting a friendly smile, felt as if she'd just stepped into a lift shaft without noticing the lift wasn't there.

'Connor, it's gone four o'clock.' Sadie said shortly. 'We have to be at the club by five.' The implication was clear as her narrowed gaze fixed on Connor's fingers round Nancy's wrist: *put her down.*

'I need to leave too.' Glad that she was no longer shaking, Nancy pulled her hand free and rose to her feet. 'Thanks for the first aid.'

'Thank *you* for making a lifelong fantasy come true.' Connor grinned, oblivious to the effect his words were having on trap-mouthed Sadie. 'Now, don't forget, seven o'clock tomorrow.'

'Absolutely.' Nancy wondered if she could manage to break both legs before tomorrow afternoon. 'See you then.'

Carmen didn't cry, or shout at him, or call him hideous names, but Rennie knew she was thinking them.

'Sweetheart, I'm sorry. I just thought it was only fair to warn you,' said Rennie. 'Don't shoot the messenger.'

Carmen looked at him as if he were her worst enemy. 'But who *is* the other messenger? I have a right to know who's saying this stuff about Joe.'

'I can't tell you. They made me promise. But they're on your side.'

Except he was hurting her now, Rennie knew that. He'd just told her that the man she was besotted with was stringing her along.

'Right, well, thanks.'

'Just bear it in mind,' said Rennie. 'He might be on the level, but—'

'Yes, yes, I get the message, you think Joe is a con artist. I'll make sure I hide my credit cards and never take my eye off my purse.'

'That's not what I meant,' Rennie shot back. 'OK, fine, just forget I said it.'

'How can I forget it?' howled Carmen. 'You *have* said it! Tell me who told you!'

'No.' He was emphatic.

'No? Oh, and why not? Maybe because they don't exist?'

'*What?*' said Rennie.

Carmen jabbed an accusing finger at him. 'It's what *you* think, but you know I won't take any notice if it's just you, so you've come up with this mystery visitor instead.'

Mia rolled her eyes. 'Single.'

'Hooray,' said Rennie. 'Maybe she'd like to save my life.'

'Men, honestly.' Mia tut-tutted. as they watched him go. 'No help at all. How am I supposed to get rid of Sadie?'

'Arsenic?' Nancy suggested.

Mia squeezed her arm. 'Wouldn't that be great? Honestly, it's so unfair. Why can't Dad go out with someone lovely like you? You could join the Lazy B,' said Mia, ever hopeful. 'Act like you're interested in Dad.'

'Look, I'd love to help,' said Nancy, draining her glass of wine and feeling the warmth spread, 'but I couldn't pretend to be interested in your father.' At least this much was true. 'And Sadie would definitely deck me.'

'Oh well, I'll think of something. Maybe what we need's another drink.' Grabbing a fresh bottle of wine, she refilled Nancy's glass, then deftly emptied the rest of the bottle into her empty drink can. 'Cheers!'

By ten o'clock the dancing was in full swing. Connor pulled Nancy energetically onto the dance floor, not realising what he'd done until he saw her flinch and bite her lip.

'Oh God, I'm *sorry*.' Hitting his own forehead in despair, he reached for her wrists and examined the angry grazes on her palms. 'What an idiot I am. I completely forgot.'

Nancy smiled, the twin explosions of pain slowly receding as Connor made his apologies. It wasn't easy to behave in a natural friendly manner when you were aware that his girlfriend was watching you like a kestrel watches a baby shrew.

But Connor, oblivious to Sadie's glares, pulled Nancy into an ungainly bear hug and said in her ear, 'I'm glad you came tonight.'

Behind Connor, she could see Mia giving her the thumbs up.

'I'm glad we came along too,' Nancy told Connor.

'But it's . . .' he frowned at his watch, 'gone ten, and still no Carmen. Are you sure she's coming?'

Nancy wasn't sure at all. Carmen was barely on speaking terms with Rennie. Upon hearing about the party, she had announced that she was working at the shelter until nine and *might* come along later.

'Maybe not,' Nancy admitted. 'She . . . um, might have to work late.'

'Sounds like a dodgy excuse to me. I'm starting to wonder if we're ever going to meet her.'

'Of course you'll—'

'Whoops, sorry,' trilled Sadie, 'didn't mean to step on your foot! Now, have you two finished chatting, because I'd quite like to dance with my boyfriend. This is our favourite song, isn't it, darling?'

Shania Twain was belting out of the speakers. Connor, looking bewildered, said, 'Are you sure?'

But Sadie had already inveigled herself in front of him, gyrating her hips. Making her escape before the ringlets could whip her across the face, Nancy headed over to Mia and a couple of girls from the Lazy B.

'Got your marching orders, then,' observed the taller of the girls, whose name was Therese.

'Take it as a compliment,' Jess, the shorter girl, consoled Nancy. 'She doesn't get nearly as het up when Connor's talking to someone ugly.'

'But that's the thing,' said Therese. 'Connor chats to everyone as if he fancies them. It's just his way. I mean, he doesn't *mean* to do it, he just can't help it.'

Well, that tells me, thought Nancy. So much for thinking that the way Connor had been talking to her might have been in any way special.

Jess said, 'Sadie's going to have her work cut out keeping that jealousy of hers under control. She's mad about Connor. God, look at the way her boobs are jiggling.'

'Whose boobs are jiggling?' Rennie joined them, swigging from a bottle of Pils. 'Oh, right. Implants.'

Mia's eyes widened with delight. 'Are you serious? Is that a boob job?'

Rennie said, 'Trust me, I'm an expert.'

'Ha!' Mia took another gulp from her Lilt can. 'Fabulous.'

'Sshh.' Jess gave her a nudge. 'If Connor marries her, she'll be your stepmum.'

Mia spluttered. 'No, no, he can't do that. I won't let him.'

'My cousin said that when her dad started seeing this hotshot magazine editor,' said Therese. 'They couldn't stand each other. My cousin couldn't *believe* her dad had such terrible taste. When she found out they were thinking of getting married, she threatened to run away.'

'What happened?' Mia was eager for tips.

'They got married. The hotshot editor gave up her job and had four kids in five years.'

Mia looked horrorstruck. 'What did your cousin do?'

'Ran away from home. No other choice. Moved into a disgusting bed-sitter in Clapham.' Therese gave Mia's arm a comforting pat. 'So you see? It could be a lot worse. Count your lucky stars Sadie isn't pregnant.'

This was *seriously* serious. Mia couldn't believe it hadn't occurred to her before. How many women, desperate not to lose the man of their dreams, 'accidentally' became pregnant? God, zillions. And Sadie was how old? Thirty-three? Her biological clock was probably clanging away inside her surgically enhanced chest. She'd do anything to hang on to Connor. She knew he wouldn't leave her high and dry, because Connor would never renege on his responsibilities.

It all made sense. Mia slipped out to the kitchen and found Rose loading the dishwasher.

'Oh, pet, are you all right? Headache?'

Feeling hot, and unaccustomed to drinking, Mia pressed her head against the cold metal of the upright freezer. She nodded. 'Headache.'

'Hang on, I've got painkillers in my bag.' Rose scuttled off and Mia took the opportunity to refill her can with chilled Frascati.

'Here we are!' Rose was back, clutching her handbag. Rummaging through the contents, she found a packet of painkillers and popped a couple out of their casings. 'That's it, sweetheart. They'll perk you up.'

As Mia knocked back the painkillers and sluiced them down with Frascati, wine dripped down the front of her purple top. Rose promptly whisked a tissue from a mini-pack in her bag and handed it to Mia.

That was the thing about handbags, you kept your whole life in them. A thought was unfurling in Mia's brain. A woman's handbag was capable of telling you an awful lot about its owner. And Sadie's handbag was currently hanging on a hook in the cupboard under the stairs.

'Still feeling a bit poorly, pet? Whoops-a-daisy.' Rose caught Mia's arm as she swayed and almost toppled over. 'Why don't you go upstairs and lie down for a few minutes?'

Mia nodded vigorously. 'Have a little rest. Oh, yes. Good idea.'

The hall was empty. Everyone was in the living room singing and dancing along to Abba's 'Waterloo'. Honestly, old people could be so sad sometimes; Mia hoped she wouldn't end up like that.

She opened the under-stairs cupboard and saw Sadie's bag hanging from one of the coat hooks. Most people kept theirs with them but Sadie had been paranoid about drink being spilt on her precious pale-blue suede Prada. Mia's fingers itched to open it but, pressing though her need was, she was aware that it wasn't the height of good manners to go rooting through your dad's girlfriend's personal private things.

If, on the other hand, she accidentally nudged the straps and the bag *happened* to fall open on the floor, well, that would be OK, wouldn't it?

Double-checking that the coast was still clear, Mia gave the handbag straps a casual nudge. Then, when that didn't dislodge the straps, she lifted them over the coat hook and let the bag drop to the floor.

The sound of footsteps made Mia jump. She froze as someone in stilettos tip-tapped across the parquet floor between the living room and the kitchen. Hastily, Mia slid into the under-stairs cupboard and pulled the door almost shut behind her. Moments later the doorbell rang, giving her another shock.

Her dad called out, 'I'll get it,' and Mia heard him emerge from the living room. As he passed the under-stairs cupboard she glimpsed him through the one-inch gap in the door.

Then . . . *click* went the door as Connor closed it. Mia, inside the cupboard, was abruptly plunged into darkness. How she was going to get out again she had no idea; there was no handle on her side of the door.

Oh well, look on the bright side, at least she had privacy now. Her dad was opening the front door; she could just about hear him greeting some late arrival or other. Feeling about in the dark, Mia located the light switch. As light flooded the interior of the cupboard, she smiled down at the handbag on the floor.

'**H**ey,' Connor exclaimed with delight, 'we meet at last.'

Carmen, finding herself being hugged then enthusiastically kissed on both cheeks, felt ashamed of herself. Rennie and Nancy had both told her that Connor O'Shea was a thoroughly nice man.

'There. Now we know each other.' Connor eventually released her. 'I was beginning to think you were avoiding me.'

'I was.' Dimpling, Carmen said, 'Sorry, don't take it personally. I was avoiding pretty much everyone.'

'No need to apologise. Rennie told me about your husband. You've been through a rotten time.' Connor helped her out of her coat. 'And neighbours can be tricky. It's like meeting new people on the first night of your holiday, realising after twenty minutes that you can't stand the sight of them and having to spend the next fortnight hiding.'

He *was* nice. Grateful to him for understanding, Carmen said, 'It's been a rough three years, but I'm back to normal now. Well, normal-ish.' Since marrying Spike, had her life ever really been normal?

When Mia had embarked on her search, she'd had her hopes pinned on finding a diary in Sadie's bag, with any luck containing incriminating entries along the lines of: *Still two-timing Connor—let's hope he never finds out!* or: *Help, I'm pregnant and George has dumped me. Never mind, I'll tell Connor he's the father.*

The problem was, there was no diary in the bag. Mia rifled through the various compartments examining old receipts, a perfume atomiser, keys, pens, three packets of chewing gum and a hairbrush.

She opened Sadie's pink-and-blue striped make-up bag. Mascara, foundation and eyeshadows, three different lipsticks and . . . oh now, what was this?

Bingo!, Mia thought triumphantly, zipping the make-up bag back up. Perfect. Jumping to her feet, she cracked her head against the cupboard's sloping roof. Ooch, never mind, let me out now. She knocked on the door and heard voices—was it still Dad?—outside in the hall.

'**H**i,' said Mia, swaying slightly and clutching her drink can. She beamed. 'Thanks. You must be Carmen.'

Taking the can from her, Connor sniffed it then took a swig of luke-warm Frascati.

'Mia. My daughter,' he told Carmen. 'Drunk.'

'Tiddly,' Mia corrected him, wagging a finger. 'Relaxed.'

'Relaxed enough to shut yourself in a cupboard,' Connor observed.

'Ah, but you're going to be jolly glad I did.' Looking determined, Mia said, 'Dad, I need to have a serious talk with you. About condoms.'

Carmen did her best to keep a straight face. The look of horror on Connor O'Shea's face was fabulous.

'OK. Maybe some other time.' Connor began to steer Mia towards the living room. 'You don't even have a boyfriend.'

'I know I don't have a boyfriend, *duh*. But *she* does.'

They'd reached the door to the living room. As Mia pointed an accusing finger at Sadie, the CD playing on the sound system chose that moment to come to an end, plunging the room into silence.

'*What?*' said Connor.

'Condoms, Dad. You have to use them, every time. I'm *serious*,' Mia insisted as he started to smile. 'She thinks if she gets pregnant, you'll marry her. It's the oldest trick in the book!'

Carmen saw that Sadie Sylvester was shaking her head in amused disbelief, exchanging glances with her co-workers.

'It's *true*,' Mia insisted.

Everyone was staring. Sadie said, 'Connor, isn't it time your daughter went to bed? Then we could all enjoy the party in peace.'

Connor put his hand on Mia's shoulder. 'I think that might be a good—'

'Dad, get off, she's taking you for a fool!' With the air of a conjuror magicking a rabbit out of a hat, Mia stuck her hand down the front of her khaki vest and drew out a folded piece of paper. Triumphantly she unfolded the page torn from a magazine. 'This article is titled, "How I bagged my man!" and it's written by a girl who was desperate not to lose her boyfriend. He kept saying it was way too soon to think about settling down with one woman, but she knew how much he loved kids so she came off the pill without telling him. When she got pregnant he realised he loved her and asked her to marry him. She says, "I know it was a high-risk strategy, but it worked like a charm. My husband's always telling me how glad he is that our darling daughter came along when she did. Of course, he still doesn't know I did it on purpose, but sometimes the end result justifies the means!"'

Everyone was agog as Sadie stalked across the room and snatched the magazine page from Mia's grasp.

'Where did you get this?'

'Cupboard under the stairs. Your handbag accidentally slipped off its hook and everything fell out onto the floor.'

'And my make-up bag accidentally unzipped itself, I suppose.' White with fury, Sadie turned to Connor. 'This is too much. I've had it up to here with your precious daughter.'

'I'm just trying to protect my dad,' Mia retaliated.

'You're a poisonous little witch! You rummaged through my hand-bag.' Sadie's eyes were sparking like fireworks. 'And then you have the nerve to accuse me of planning to trap your father into marrying me. Well, let me tell you, the last thing I want is a baby. Especially when there's a chance I might end up with one like you.'

'So what were you doing with that article hidden away in your bag?' Mia demanded heatedly.

'Therese?' Sadie glanced across the room, to where her co-workers were clustered. 'Why don't you tell Mia what's wrong with your father?'

Startled, Therese said, 'My dad? He's got Parkinson's Disease.'

'Thank you.' Returning her attention to Mia, Sadie said evenly, 'Therese is worried sick about him. So when I was flicking through a magazine yesterday and happened to come across an article about a revolutionary new treatment for sufferers of Parkinson's, I thought Therese might like to see it.' Turning over the ripped-out page, she showed the relevant section to Connor then handed it to Therese. 'Here you are. It might help your dad.'

'Th-thanks,' stammered Therese.

'Don't mention it.' Marching back to where Mia was standing, Sadie said, 'So there you go. I hadn't actually noticed the article on the other side of the page. Feel free to apologise any time you like.'

Mia stood her ground. 'Just because you wriggled out of it this time? I'd rather stick pins in my eyes than apologise to you.'

'Could someone put some music on please?' said Connor, keeping himself between the two warring girls like a boxing referee.

THE ONE YOU REALLY WANT

'No, *don't.*' Sadie turned to glare at a thin, nervy looking male guest who'd had the temerity to make a move towards the CD player. 'Let's sort this out once and for all, shall we? I'm your girlfriend,' she told Connor, 'and she's your daughter. Clearly, you have a choice to make here. One of us has to go.'

Carmen held her breath, enthralled. Sadie was looking confident. Mia was looking . . . actually, she was looking a bit green around the gills.

Connor turned to Mia and said evenly, 'What you did was very, very wrong. I'm ashamed of you.'

Mia said nothing. Sadie preened and looked smug.

'Sweetheart.' Taking her hand, Connor said, 'I'm sorry.'

Sadie gave his fingers a triumphant squeeze. 'You don't have to apologise. She's the one who should be doing that. Oh, darling—'

'No, what I mean is, *I'm sorry.*' Connor shook his head. 'I know Mia's behaved appallingly, but she's still my daughter.'

Crack went Sadie's hand across his face. What with her being so fit, it must have hurt, but Connor didn't even flinch.

'She's going to ruin your life,' Sadie spat, 'and you're just going to stand back and let her do it.'

'I'm not—'

'Well, I feel sorry for you. I'm out of here.' Addressing Mia, Sadie said icily, 'Is there still enough money in my purse to pay for my taxi home, or did you help yourself to that too?'

Pale and swaying, Mia turned abruptly and shot out of the room.

Sadie's upper lip curled with derision. As she headed for the door she hissed at Connor, 'You're making the biggest mistake of your life.'

Mia hadn't had time to close the bathroom door. Nancy found her crouched next to the lavatory. She ran a white flannel under the cold tap, then wrung it out and handed it to Mia. 'Feeling better now?'

'Much. I'm not that great at drinking.' She pressed the cool flannel to her forehead and exhaled with relief as Nancy helped her to her feet. 'That feels nice. Has she gone?'

'Oh, yes. Didn't you hear the front door flying off its hinges?'

'Dad's going to hate me. I suppose I should be sorry, but I'm not.' Perched on the side of the bath, Mia watched as Nancy squeezed toothpaste onto her pink glittery toothbrush.

'You went a bit over the top.'

'I know. I don't make a habit of snooping through people's handbags, honestly. And I'm not out to ruin Dad's life either, but she was just such a nightmare, wasn't she? He'll end up thanking me for it.'

245

'Hmm.' Much as she agreed with Mia's verdict on Sadie Sylvester, Nancy couldn't help feeling she was being overly optimistic.

'I mean, I do *want* him to be happy,' Mia went on, between vigorous bouts of tooth-brushing. 'I'd just love it if he met somebody nice. Like you.' She caught Nancy's startled eye in the mirror above the basin. 'What d'you reckon then? Think you could fancy my dad?'

'Look, it doesn't work like that,' Nancy said helplessly.

'Of course it does! Trust me, I've got a real feeling about this.' Reaching for a towel, Mia wiped her mouth. 'The two of you could be great together.'

'Right, that's enough.' A voice behind them caused both Nancy and Mia to wheel round. Nancy winced at the sight of Connor in the door-way. Just how much had he heard?

'Excuse my daughter. Thanks for keeping an eye on her.' Connor nodded briefly at Nancy, his expression grim. 'I'll take over now.'

'I'll leave you to it.' Relieved to be escaping, Nancy edged her way out of the bathroom. 'See you . . . um, later.'

Chapter 6

CARMEN WAS CLEARING the tables after lunch at the shelter, carrying piles of plates through to the kitchen where Nick and Annie were ploughing through a mountain of washing-up.

'Carmen, stick up for me,' Nick pleaded as Carmen began scraping left-over shepherd's pie into the bin. 'Annie's making fun of my wardrobe again.'

Annie shook her head at him. 'I'm not making fun of your wardrobe, I'm making fun of the clothes you keep in it. Carmen, explain to Nick that real men don't wear Mr Blobby T-shirts.'

Carmen smiled; she really liked Nick and Annie, and enjoyed their bickering arguments. Annie was short, bouncy and in her early twenties. Nick, tall and endlessly cheerful, sported lots of dark hair that seldom saw a hairbrush. He thought it was funny when strangers visiting the shelter mistook him for one of the homeless rather than a volunteer helper. He and Annie lived together in a flat just round the corner.

'Some of your T-shirts aren't too bad,' Carmen said diplomatically—'but maybe it's time to let Mr Blobby go.'

'Have him put to sleep, more like,' said Annie.

Carmen said, 'My boyfriend's got a pair of purple socks with goldfish on them. He only wears them to embarrass me.' Well, it had only happened once, but it was nice to be able to join in on the anecdote front.

'Shows he doesn't take clothes too seriously,' said Nick. 'Good for him.'

Annie turned to Carmen. 'How long have you been seeing your chap?'

'Not long. Early days. But, you know, it's going well.'

'That's great.' Annie was genuinely pleased. 'What's his name?'

'Joe. He's a plumber.'

'You two must definitely come along to our next party then,' said Annie. 'We'd love to meet him.'

Nick, dumping a just-washed baking tin into her hands, said, 'But only if he's wearing his purple goldfish socks.'

'**O**h, and could you write Tasmin Ferreira in the appointment book for four o'clock tomorrow afternoon? She's coming in for a second fitting,' Zac called through from the workroom. 'Doreen, sweetie, go and see Nancy. Tell her I'd love a cup of tea, white, two sugars.'

Nancy smiled as Doreen came trotting into the shop. It was only Wednesday, but already she knew she was going to enjoy working here. Zac was fun, gossipy and indiscreet, filling her in on all the background details of his clients. The website brought in a fair amount of business and she was kept busy replying to emails, answering the phone and chasing up orders for new and original materials.

The phone rang as Nancy was dropping tea bags into two cups.

'Zac?' She covered the receiver with one hand. 'It's your father.'

A mixture of emotions crossed Zac's face as he put down the taffeta bodice he was currently working on and came through to take the phone. Perching on the edge of the desk in his lemon-yellow trousers and pink V-neck merino wool sweater, he said, 'Hi, Dad, how are you?'

Not in a camp way at all.

Nancy, making the tea, was unable to avoid listening to Zac's half of the conversation, which swung from carburettors to football, then to central heating systems and finally gardening.

'OK, Dad, you look after yourself now,' Zac said eventually, with genuine affection in his voice. 'I'll be down to see you next weekend.'

The tea was no longer as hot as it might have been, but Nancy gave it to him anyway. For the past ten minutes Zac had sounded so completely heterosexual that it almost came as a shock when he took a slurp and said, 'Ooh, yum, just what I needed!' in his normal voice.

Catching the look on her face, Zac waggled his free hand in embarrassment. 'OK, you don't have to say it, I know how pathetic I am. The thirty-five-year-old male who can't tell his father he's gay. I'm sorry, but if you start lecturing me, I shall have to sack you.'

'I wasn't going to. I'm the one who couldn't tell her mother her husband was having an affair, remember?' Pushing the biscuit tin towards him, Nancy said comfortingly, 'Have a Hobnob.'

'He's retired now.' Zac heaved a sigh. 'But he worked on the docks for forty years. Mum died when I was twenty. I love my father, but he's a man's man. He wouldn't understand. And I don't want to upset him.'

'Really, you don't have to explain. I think it's nice that you care so much about him. Where does he live?' said Nancy.

'Weston-super-Mare. I'm all the family he has. Every two or three weeks I go down there for the weekend. Put on my proper manly clothes,' Zac said with a wry smile, 'and my butch manly voice, and we spend our time together doing manly things like stripping car engines.'

'He never remarried after your mum died?'

'No. There've been a couple of lady friends. One lasted almost two years, but it fizzled out last summer.'

'Does he ever ask when you're going to settle down and make him a grandfather?' Nancy was curious; surely Zac's father must suspect by now that something was amiss.

'I invented a girlfriend.' Zac bit into a biscuit. 'Samantha, her name was. We had an on-off relationship for eight years. Long-distance too,' he mumbled through a mouthful of Hobnob. 'I told Dad she was working in Australia. Anyway, it did the trick. When Sam and I broke up a couple of years ago I was devastated. She was the love of my life. Going to take me a long time to get over her—ooh, I'd say a decade at least.'

The things we do to protect our parents, thought Nancy as he crunched happily on his biscuit. She swung round on her chair as the bell above the door went ting, and saw Rennie enter the shop. Zac, spotted him too.

'Oh *my*,' Zac murmured, clearly impressed.

'What are you doing here?' said Nancy.

'I used to be a big star.' Rennie shrugged tragically. 'But these days I'm nothing but a lowly errand boy. Rose has finished her latest creation and she sent me down here with it.' He handed the plastic carrier bag over to Zac and said, 'Hi, I'm Rennie.'

Zac looked as if he'd forgotten how to breathe, let alone open a carrier bag. 'I know who you are. Good to meet you. Zac Parris.'

'Why couldn't Rose deliver it?' said Nancy.

'She's cleaning the outsides of all the windows. She's supposed to be down here on holiday,' Rennie marvelled, 'and she never stops.'

Zac was gazing at him, lost in admiration. His eyes travelled speculatively over Rennie's lean, hard body. 'I'm working on something at the moment that would be perfect on you.' Zac blurted the words out in a rush. 'Double-breasted jacket, black-and-white stripes, leather-trimmed velvet lapels. If I make one up for you, would you wear it?'

Rennie hesitated. He looked at the supermarket carrier bag containing the green and gold cobwebby cardigan Rose had completed this morning. 'Would it be knitted?'

Zac frantically flapped his hands. 'No, *no*. Look, let me whizz it up. If you hate it, fair enough. If you love it, just tell people where it came from. Can't say fairer than that, can you?'

'Absolutely not. Start measuring,' said Rennie with a grin.

Carmen may not have forgiven Rennie for the below-the-belt comments he'd made about Joe, but they'd turned out to be unfounded and it was probably about time they put the awkwardness behind them.

Besides, Nancy had taken Rose off to the West End to see *Miss Saigon*—Rose was a sucker for a musical—so she didn't have much choice.

'Looking good, Mrs Todd,' said Rennie, handing her a mug as she appeared in the kitchen.

There was a tea bag still floating in it, Carmen discovered, but it was the thought that counted. It was Rennie's way of saying he was sorry. Glad that Rennie had realised he'd been wrong, she did a quick twirl to show off the bronze silk dress she'd bought specially for tonight.

'You scrub up pretty well,' Rennie told her. 'Where are you off to?'

'Joe's taking me out to dinner. At Passione.' Carmen's chest tightened for a moment, in case Rennie made some snide comment like asking who'd be paying for the meal. Much to her relief, he didn't.

'Great place. You'll love it. You aren't drinking your tea.'

Obediently Carmen took a sip of tea. The tea bag slooshed against her upper lip and her teeth shrivelled in dismay at the strength of the brew. At that moment, thank goodness, the doorbell rang.

'That'll be my minicab.' Carmen grabbed her bag and coat. 'Aren't you off out tonight?'

'Not until later. Now you have a brilliant time.' Helping her into her long black coat, Rennie said, 'You'll dazzle everyone in the restaurant.'

'Thanks.' Touched by the compliment, Carmen gave him a quick kiss. 'Just . . . remember what I said the other night.'

Carmen froze. 'About what?'

'I'm not going to say it, because I don't want us to have another falling out. But you know what I mean.' As he spoke, Rennie carried on fastening the buttons on her coat.

Carmen slapped his hand away, hard.

'I don't believe this is *happening*. You *had* to say it, didn't you? You just had to stick the knife in and spoil everything!'

'I *didn't* say it.'

'You bastard, you bloody selfish bastard!' Seething with the unfairness of it all, furious with herself for having been taken in and thinking that Rennie actually might have been admitting he'd made a mistake, Carmen whacked him again on the shoulder.

'I'm not being selfish,' Rennie protested as the doorbell rang again. 'I'm trying to protect you.'

Storming out to the hall, Carmen yanked open the front door and yelled, '*Two seconds*,' at the waiting driver, who almost fell off the step.

'Right, I've had enough of you,' she bellowed at Rennie. 'I mean it, more than enough. I'm sick of the sight of you, and I'm *extra* sick of you meddling in my life. You can pack your things and get out. *Now*.'

'OK.' Placatingly, Rennie held up his hands.

'I *mean* it,' Carmen repeated, her heart thudding against her ribcage like ominous footsteps. 'You've gone too far this time. When I come home tonight I want to find you *gone*.'

Passione, on Charlotte Street, was divine. Having determinedly put Rennie out of her mind, Carmen concentrated instead on enjoying the evening. And how could you not enjoy it, with food like this? Better still, she was here with Joe, who was being funny, sweet and attentive.

'That's it,' Carmen sighed, patting her stomach and sitting back in contentment. 'I'm full. I couldn't eat another thing.'

'Just coffee.' Joe signalled to the waiter for two espressos and reached for the half-empty bottle of wine. 'And we'll finish this.'

'I don't think I've even got room for any more wine.'

'You have to,' he protested as she half-heartedly attempted to cover her glass. 'It's a special night. I've got something to celebrate.'

'You have?' Carmen was interested.

'I made a big decision yesterday. Well, it's something I've been planning for a long time,' said Joe, 'but making plans is one thing. Acting on them, carrying them out, is another matter. I've handed in my notice.'

Carmen's eyes widened. 'Why?'

'Because nobody ever got rich working for someone else's company.

I'm a bloody good plumber. It's always been my dream to have my own business. So that's what I'm going to do, set up on my own. It just makes sense, don't you think? This way, the more hours I put in, the more money I'll make.'

'I think that's fantastic,' Carmen exclaimed. 'It makes *perfect* sense.'

'So many people dream of doing this, but they're too afraid to take the leap,' Joe went on eagerly. 'But that's the beauty of plumbing, there *is* no risk. It's a win-win situation. Everyone needs plumbing and heating engineers. Give me a few years and I'll be the plumbing king of London.'

'Well, good for you.' Carmen gave his hand an encouraging squeeze. 'When do you start?'

'As soon as I've got everything sorted out. You see, I need a decent van, plus a computer of course, and then I had this *other* brilliant idea this afternoon.' Gazing into her eyes, Joe said, 'How about if you and I were partners? You know, went into this together?'

'What?' Carmen laughed. 'I'm not a plumber.'

'You don't need to be. I mean a business partner. Well, more of a sleeping partner really,' explained Joe. 'You wouldn't have to *do* anything, just put up some of the money we'd need to get this thing up and running. It would save all that faffing around, getting bank loans and stuff. So what d'you think?' He gazed at her intently. 'How does that sound? Great idea or what?'

Carmen's face was frozen; she couldn't tell if she was still smiling or not. There was a buzzing sound in her ears and she felt sick.

How did it sound? Like Rennie, whispering in her ear: *See? Told you.*

'I . . . don't know, Joe.' Was she as white as she felt? With difficulty Carmen cleared her throat. 'Um, how much?'

'Twenty thousand, that's all.' He smiled and stroked her wrist. 'Cheer up, you look terrified. It's not scary, it's an adventure!'

It wasn't an adventure. It was her worst nightmare come true. The waiter brought their bill at that moment and Joe took out his credit card.

'Can we go halves?' Carmen began searching for her bag, but he shook his head.

'No way. Let me do this.' He waited until the waiter had departed. 'Now, what do you say?'

The quicker she said no, the quicker they could change the subject and move on. Taking her courage in both hands, Carmen said as cheerfully as she could, 'Joe, to be honest, I think it'd be easier if you just got a bank loan. Thanks for offering me the . . . opportunity, but—'

'You're saying *no*?'

In that split second, Carmen saw something alter behind his eyes, a shift of emotion that sent a chill down her spine.

'But like you said, you can get a loan from the bank.' She watched Joe's hand leave hers, retreating like the tide. 'That's what banks are for!'

'Oh yes.' Joe's mouth narrowed. 'With their endless interrogations and forms to be filled in and petty bloody rules and regulations. Jesus, that's what I thought we'd try to avoid.'

Carmen realised that he was waiting for her to say, 'Oh, all right then, I'll put up the money.' Instead she shrugged and reached for her glass of wine.

'You don't trust me,' Joe blurted out suddenly. 'Is that it?'

'No.' She shook her head, feeling sicker than ever. 'It's not that. I just think it's better if you go to the bank.'

'But you've got all that money sitting there doing nothing.' Joe was bewildered. 'Piling up, earning interest, making *more* money. And it's not as if you even earned it yourself. You were just lucky enough to marry the right bloke. Twenty grand would be a drop in the ocean as far as you're concerned, I really can't believe you're *being* like this. I feel so stupid.' Joe shook his head. 'I thought what we had was special. I thought you liked me.'

Ditto, Carmen thought miserably, aware that people at neighbouring tables were beginning to nudge each other.

'I do like you.'

'Enough to let me pay for dinner,' Joe said bitterly. 'Oh, yes, that's absolutely fine, isn't it, even though you know I can't afford it. But when it comes to you having to dip into *your* precious bank account—where are you going?'

'Home.' Jerkily, Carmen pushed back her chair. Rummaging in her purse, she took out all the money and threw it onto the table. 'There, that should cover dinner. Bye, Joe. It's been an education knowing you.'

'No, wait, I'm sorry.' Appalled, Joe jumped up too. 'Don't go, I didn't mean it! Carmen, please, I *love* you!' he yelled desperately as she stumbled past startled waiters and neighbouring tables.

Rennie was making a hopelessly cack-handed attempt at ironing his favourite shirt when he heard the front door open. He was due to meet up with a group of friends at a new bar in Soho and had rather hoped that Nancy and Rose would be back from their trip to the theatre before he left—Rose was a spectacular ironer who could always be relied upon to exclaim, 'Will you look at what you're doing to that poor shirt? Here, give it to me, pet, *this* is how it should be done.'

Now, congratulating himself on his excellent timing, he assumed a helpless expression and waited for Rose to come bustling into the kitchen and whisk the iron from his incompetent male grasp.

Except it wasn't Rose.

'You're still here,' said Carmen accusingly.

'I wasn't expecting you back so soon. I've booked a room at the Savoy,' Rennie lied. Pointing to the furiously steaming iron, he said, 'As soon as I've finished this, I'll pack my things.'

Carmen's gaze alighted on the cornflakes packet open on the table.

'What's that doing out?' She was still furious with him.

'Sorry, I had some cornflakes. I was hungry,' said Rennie. 'I'll—'

Zzinnggg went the packet as it whistled past his head. Ducking, Rennie heard it hit the wall behind him. Cornflakes showered in all directions. Carmen gazed around wildly, seized the biscuit tin and hurled it after the cornflakes packet. The lid pinged off, sending biscuits bouncing to the floor.

'OK, stop,' Rennie ordered as Carmen grabbed the tea caddy and flung it wildly at the door. '*Stop*.' His voice rose as she reached for the sugar bowl, because sugar was definitely no laughing matter.

'*No*,' bellowed Carmen, hurling the sugar bowl across the kitchen and watching with grim satisfaction as it smashed against the fridge.

Racing across the kitchen, Rennie grabbed her arms and cornered her.

'Let go of me.' Carmen was wriggling like an eel. 'I hate you.'

'Look, the kitchen didn't do anything wrong.' Refusing to release his grip, Rennie nodded at the cereal-and-sugar-strewn floor. 'I'm the one who upset you and I'm going, I promise. You're right, I should have kept my opinions to myself. You can do whatever you like with Joe. Run off and marry him, if that's what you—'

'It's over, OK?' Carmen's tone was venomous.

'Fine, I know. I'll call a cab and pack my things.' As he took a cautious step back, cornflakes and biscuits crunched under his feet.

'It's over between me and Joe, you idiot.' Carmen swallowed hard before meeting his gaze. 'You were right and I was wrong.'

Over. *Thank God for that*. 'What happened?'

'He wanted the money.' Carmen's eyes were blazing. 'Twenty thousand pounds, just like you told me. *Bastard*.'

'Who's the bastard? Him or me?'

'Him.' Her face crumpled as the realisation sank in. 'Oh shit.'

'Absolutely.' Rennie nodded. 'He *is* a shit.'

'Not him. Your shirt.' She was pointing behind him.

'How can it still be steaming? I switched the steam off,' said Rennie.

It was Carmen's turn to march across the kitchen. As she lifted the iron from the shirt, she said, 'That's not steam, you berk. It's smoke.'

The phone on the worktop began to ring. Carmen froze.

'I'll get it.' Answering the phone, Rennie said briskly, 'Yes?'

'Is that him?' whispered Carmen.

'Yes, she's here.' Rennie's green eyes narrowed.

Carmen felt her stomach disappear. As she held out her hand, she saw that it was trembling. 'Let me speak to him.'

Joe sounded distraught. 'I'm sorry, I'm so sorry. Please . . . forget about the money. Sweetheart, you mean everything in the world to me.'

'I think you mean I meant all the money in the world to you.' Shaking all over, Carmen hung up.

Thirty minutes later, changed out of her smart bronze dress into her old white dressing gown, and with her make-up brutally scrubbed off, Carmen took a sip of the brandy Rennie had poured for her.

The Dyson went quiet in the kitchen. 'All done.' Rennie came into the living room and sat down next to her on the sofa. He pulled her bare feet companionably onto his lap. 'Feeling better now?'

Carmen marvelled at the question Was thirty minutes as long as Rennie took to get over the end of a relationship with someone?

'I've been thinking. It's not as if he asked me to *give* him twenty thousand pounds,' Carmen blurted out. 'What if it was innocent and I overreacted? He does so much for charity.' This was what had been bothering Carmen. To her mind, someone who gave hours of their spare time fundraising for a charity *had* to be a good person.

'So does Jeffrey Archer,' said Rennie.

'Who was it who told you about Joe?' She had been certain that Rennie had invented the mystery visitor. Now she knew he hadn't.

Unexpectedly, Rennie said, 'She made me promise not to tell you while you were seeing Joe. He mustn't know.'

Carmen nodded; she just wanted this to be settled once and for all.

'Joe's ex-girlfriend. He dumped her when he met you. Her name's Tina,' said Rennie. 'She wants him back. But the reason she came here was to let you know the truth. Joe boasted about you, about what he was planning to do. She thought you deserved to know.'

Swallowing the remains of the brandy in her glass, Carmen took a deep breath and said, 'I feel stupid and made a fool of, and I really hate it that you warned me and I refused to believe you. But it isn't the end of the world.'

She picked up the phone and punched out the number for directory enquiries. 'Oh, hi, I'd like the number of the Savoy Hotel in London, please . . . Yes, can you put me through?'

Rennie said, 'Why don't we have another drink?'

'Hello, could you tell me if Rennie Todd has a room booked for tonight? No? OK, thanks very much. Bye.'

'I booked under a false name,' Rennie protested when Carmen looked at him. 'I'm a celebrity, we have to consider security, I have *stalkers* . . .'

'You sad, deluded old man.' Carmen gave his arm a sympathetic pat. 'Whoever in their right mind would want to stalk you?'

'Don't worry. I'll go.'

'Oh, shut up. You know you won't.'

'I just feel I could be more useful here,' said Rennie. 'You need looking after. It's my mission in life to get you through this episode.'

'Plus you get bored in hotel rooms,' Carmen reminded him. 'You're hopeless at being on your own. You buy houses and sell them again without even moving into them. You're a hopeless case.'

'I've got a few of those upstairs. Still want me to go and pack them?'

'Oh, give it a rest.'

Rennie knew he'd won. Life was great here with Carmen, Nancy and Rose. He planted a kiss on Carmen's cheek. 'You love me really. And you aren't stupid.' Forcing her to look at him, he said, 'You'll meet someone else and fall in love.' Something tightened in Rennie's chest. 'At least you know it's possible now. You've turned a corner. You're on your way back to the real world.'

'Turning a corner's one thing,' Carmen pulled a face. 'But that would be turning into you. Oh, here they are.'

Rose and Nancy were back.

'Good show?' said Rennie.

'Heaven! The most wonderful thing I ever saw.' Rose, her eyes pink-rimmed, exclaimed, 'I've never cried so much in all my life!'

'Women.' Rennie shook his head. 'I'll never understand them.'

We need to talk,' said Jonathan.

'Isn't that what we're doing now?' Nancy was interested and relieved to discover that the sound of his voice did absolutely nothing for her.

'I mean properly.' He paused and cleared his throat. 'Face to face. I could . . . come down to London, if you want.'

'What for?' Nancy checked her watch; she really had to leave for work.

'To sort this out. Decide what we're going to do.'

'Get a divorce. It's simple enough, isn't it? There's no need for you to fly down,' said Nancy. 'I'll find a solicitor, tell him to—'

'Look, I don't want a divorce.' Hurriedly Jonathan went on, 'I'm not with Paula any more. It's over. Paula was just a bit of—'

'A floozy?' guessed Nancy.

'A bit of fun, I was going to say. But I suppose that's not right. She was just *there*,' Jonathan said weakly. 'Nancy, listen to me, I still love you! I made one tiny mistake,' Jonathan groaned, 'and I'm *sorry*.'

'Well, that's incredibly generous of you, but the answer's still no. Because I don't love you and I definitely want a divorce.' Re-checking her watch, Nancy said, 'Look, I'm sorry, but I do have to go now.'

'It's Rennie Todd, isn't it?' Jonathan shouted. 'You're letting him screw you! I'm telling you now, you're kidding yourself if you think he's serious. He's sleeping with you because you're there, willing and available.'

'Bit like you and Paula then.' Nancy couldn't resist it.

Jonathan made a noise like an old-fashioned kettle coming to the boil. Rennie, choosing that moment to wander into the kitchen, yawned and said, 'I don't know about you, but I could use a cup of tea.'

'Is that him?' roared Jonathan. 'He'll dump you, you do realise that?'

'Thanks, Jonathan, but you don't need to worry about me. I can look after myself.' As she said it, Rennie raised his eyebrows enquiringly and Nancy nodded, grinning.

'Sweetheart,' said Rennie, 'aren't you cold with no clothes on? Here, let me warm you up.'

'I have to go,' Nancy said hastily, cutting Jonathan off in mid-splutter.

'Sounds a bit agitated,' observed Rennie.

'He thinks we're having an affair.'

'Serves him right. Before you know it, he'll be deciding he wants you back.'

'He already has.' Taking a last gulp of lukewarm coffee Nancy said, 'Just now. I turned down his generous offer.'

'Hey, that's great.' Rennie sounded genuinely pleased. 'Good for you. Fancy a quickie to celebrate?'

'Sorry, late for work already.' Smiling, Nancy grabbed her handbag and inwardly marvelled at how fantastic she felt. Turning down Jonathan had done wonders for her self-esteem. Maybe one day an attractive man would make her an offer along the lines of the one Rennie had just suggested and actually mean it.

Wrenching open the front door, she unexpectedly came face to face with the attractive man she had secretly hoped might be the one to make that offer. Almost cannoning right into his chest, Nancy jumped and let out an undignified yelp of surprise.

'Sorry, sorry.' Connor held out his hands and steadied her, which did nothing to calm her frantically racing heart. 'Didn't mean to give you a fright. I was just about to ring the bell.'

'Caught me by surprise.' Clutching her chest, Nancy took deep breaths and tried not to notice how gorgeous he was looking. OK, maybe not gorgeous—Connor was too scruffy for that—but irresistible all the same. 'Um, did you want to see Rennie?'

'You, actually.' Apologetically Connor said, 'But I can see it's not a good time, you're rushing off to work. I don't want to make you late.'

Which was like plonking a gift-wrapped present into a six-year-old's arms, then snatching it back and saying, 'Don't open it yet.'

'You're here now. I'm not going to be late.' The big lie tripped effortlessly off Nancy's tongue.

'OK, this won't take two minutes. It's actually Mia's idea,' Connor admitted, following Carmen into the hall. 'The thing is, my secretary's eight months pregnant and she's starting her maternity leave on Friday. We're holding a party at the club. I was going to buy a cake, then Mia told me about the one you'd made for Rennie.'

'Hi.' Emerging from the kitchen, Rennie said interestedly, 'What cake?'

'Hey there.' Connor greeted him with a cheerful nod. 'The one Nancy made for your birthday. The curry cake.'

'*Curry cake?*'

'It's OK.' Nancy waved her hands, embarrassed. 'I made a cake for your birthday but you flew over to New York so you didn't get it. It didn't taste of curry, OK? It was a normal sponge cake inside, decorated to look like a plate of chicken Madras and rice. I threw it away.'

'Bloody good job,' declared Rennie. 'Whatever were you thinking of?'

'Mia said it looked fantastic,' Connor added supportively.

Feeling cross and a bit stupid, Nancy glared at Rennie. 'It *was* fantastic. But don't worry, I won't be making you another one.'

Raising his eyebrows in apology, Connor said, 'Hey, I'm sorry, I didn't come here to cause trouble.'

'No, *I'm* sorry.' Rennie shook his head with genuine regret. 'Misunderstanding. I'm really touched. You shouldn't have thrown it away.'

'It would have been stale by the time you got back. Look, forget it, no big deal.' Nancy turned abruptly to Connor. 'So you want me to make one for your secretary, is that it?'

'Well, that was the idea . . . I mean, I'd pay you of course,' Connor added hastily. 'But if you're too busy, that's fine, I'll just buy one from—'

'I have to go to work now.' Feeling hot, frazzled and ashamed of herself for behaving like a teenager in a strop, Nancy said, 'Of course I'll do you a cake. Just leave me a note listing the kind of thing you want.'

257

Chapter 7

NICK, PICKING UP a potato peeler and joining Carmen at the sink in the kitchen at the shelter, said conversationally, 'I used to be married to Shirley Bassey, you know.'

'That's nothing,' Annie airily retaliated as she chopped carrots. 'My first husband was Sylvester Stallone.'

Carmen smiled absently, struggling to pay attention to their banter.

'Miles away,' Nick tut-tutted, waving a hand in front of her face.

Distracted, Carmen said, 'Hmm?'

'Heyyy, she ain't even listenin' to meee,' Nick protested. He mimicked the low-pitched Stallone drawl.

'Oh, shut up, Nick, give it a rest, will you?' Annie rolled her eyes. 'Carmen's not in the mood, OK?'

Carmen turned and caught Annie silently mouthing something at him, but Nick continued to look baffled.

'It's OK,' said Carmen, because someone had to put him out of his misery. 'I'm having a bit of an off-day, that's all. Joe and I broke up.'

'Oh. Hey, I'm sorry.' Nick looked at Annie. 'How did you know?'

'I'm a girl.' Annie was scornful. 'We have this thing called intuition. I'm sorry too,' she told Carmen. 'What a rotten thing to happen.'

Touched by their concern, Carmen said, 'Thanks. I'll live. I just found out he wasn't . . . well, as honest as I'd thought.'

'Honesty's important.' Annie was sympathetic. 'You don't want to be involved with someone you can't trust.'

Nick winked at Carmen and said, 'In that case, your bum looks enormous in those jeans.'

Carmen loved the way they bickered together, like a couple who'd been married for fifty years.

'One other hint,' Annie told Nick. 'Never say that to a girl with a sharp chopping knife in her hand. Or you could really live to regret it.'

The heavens opened as Carmen left the shelter at five thirty. Skulking in the doorway with hunched-shouldered commuters bustling past, she realised that her black woollen coat would soak up the rain like a sponge, and that today was the day she'd forgotten her umbrella.

Bugger it, thought Carmen, today was the day for a cab. But even the cab drivers, it turned out, were against her. Evidently they were less inclined to stop for someone huddled in an oversized coat on the steps of a shelter for the homeless.

'Ugh,' shivered Nick, joining her five minutes later and shuddering as the icy rain hit him in the face. 'What are you still doing here?'

'Waiting for it to ease off before I head for the tube,' Carmen lied.

Nick shook his head. 'It's not going to stop for ages. How about a coffee at Giacomo's?'

Inside the warmth of the friendly Italian cafe, Carmen's coat began to steam gently. By the time Nick arrived at their table with two cappuccinos, her feet had begun to thaw out.

'Proper coffee.' Nick inhaled appreciatively. 'Nothing like it.' He paused. 'Hey, I'm sorry if I put my foot in it earlier.'

'You didn't,' Carmen assured him. 'I'm fine, really. I thought Joe was special. Turns out he wasn't. That's all, no big deal.'

'But it still hurts. When I was nineteen I was absolutely crazy about my girlfriend,' said Nick. 'Until I came home early one day and caught her in *our* bed with *my* sociology lecturer.'

Carmen knew she mustn't laugh. 'That's . . . tragic,' she managed finally. 'How long ago did you meet Annie?'

'Two years ago? Maybe a bit more than that.'

Annie had left work early. Glancing at her watch and realising that it was already gone six, Carmen said, 'Should you give her a ring?'

Nick shrugged, unconcerned. 'I'm old enough to be out on my own.'

'I know you're *old* enough.' Carmen rolled her eyes in despair. 'But what if Annie's cooked dinner and is expecting you home by six?'

'Whoa, whoa. For a start, Annie's the world's worst cook, so any opportunity to miss one of her terrible meals is a bonus. And secondly,' Nick said, dodging as Carmen took an indignant swipe at him on Annie's behalf, 'she won't even be at home. She's out with her boyfriend.'

Carmen froze in mid-swipe. *Boyfriend?*

'Sorry?'

'They've gone to the cinema to see the new Richard Curtis comedy.'

Bemused, Carmen said, 'Don't you . . . um, mind?'

Half smiling, Nick put down his empty cup and said, 'Annie can do what she wants. She isn't my girlfriend.'

'She isn't?' Carmen was confused. When had they broken up?

'I'm not Annie's boyfriend,' Nick carried on. 'We share a flat. We aren't a couple.' He chuckled. 'Me and Annie. Wait till she hears about this.'

'You *act* like a couple,' Carmen protested. 'You talk about the TV shows you watched last night, you throw parties—'

'That you never come to,' said Nick.

'I'm sorry. Next time I will.' Carmen nodded to show she meant it.

'Come along then.' Nick pushed back his chair and stood up. 'Dinner party. Our place. Before you have time to change your mind.'

What time do you call this?' Rennie demanded when Carmen arrived home. 'It's two o'clock in the *morning*. You haven't seen *him*, have you? The pilfering plumber?'

'Of course I haven't.' Carmen peeled off her coat. 'And you know where I was. I left a message on the answering machine. Nick from work invited me back to his place for dinner. We talked for ages, and it was great. Then his flatmate Annie came home with her boyfriend.'

'Hang on.' Rennie frowned. 'I thought Nick and Annie were a couple.'

'Nooo,' Carmen said scornfully. 'Just flatmates.'

'So this Nick bloke, what's he like?'

'Nice. Oh, don't look at me like that.' Carmen flapped her hands in protest. 'I don't fancy Nick. He just bought me a coffee to cheer me up after I told him it was all over between me and Joe.'

'Does he know who you are? That you live in this house?'

'*No.* Nick and Annie are just people I work with. I've never told anyone at the shelter who I was married to or where I live.'

'D'you think they might resent the fact that you're loaded?'

'No, of course they wouldn't. They're not like that,' Carmen said defensively. 'It's just . . . easier this way. Like this morning, Annie was having a moan about their electricity bill and we were talking about what we'd do if we won the lottery. You see?' She spread her hands. 'We wouldn't be able to do that stuff if they knew I lived in a house like this.'

Rennie nodded. 'I think you're right.'

'Don't say you're actually agreeing with me?'

'Just this once. Don't worry, I won't make a habit of it.' Reaching into the fridge, Rennie took out a bowl of left-over apple crumble.

'I'll share that with you,' said Carmen.

'It's fattening.' Rennie looked like an eight-year-old being asked to give away half his sweets.

'Good. That's why I like it.'

'Actually, we've got a bit of an emergency situation. Our supplier's threatening to leave the country.' Rennie searched through the cutlery drawer, handed Carmen a teaspoon and a small bowl, and kept a dessert-spoon for himself. 'Rose told me it's time she headed back to Scotland.'

'Go on then,' said Carmen at lunch on Sunday. 'You ask her.'

'Me?' Rennie was helping himself to the world's best roast potatoes. He raised his eyebrows. 'Now?'

Startled, Rose realised that they were all looking at her. 'Ask me what?'

'We don't want you to go back to Scotland,' Rennie told her. 'But if you *want* to go, we can't stop you.'

Rose put down her knife and fork. Her expression softening, she said, 'That's sweet of you, pet. I've had a wonderful holiday down here.'

'You don't have to leave,' said Rennie. 'We'd love it if you'd stay.'

'Oh, but—'

'Rose, we don't know how we'd manage without you,' Carmen chipped in. 'You're taking care of us. If you think you might like to stay, we'd pay you, of course, to carry on doing everything you've been doing. You could give up your flat in Edinburgh. It's up to you.'

Rose gazed at them, then asked Rennie, 'Is this another of your jokes?'

'No.' Rennie smiled, because only Rose could think it might be. 'We love you. None of us want you to leave.' Teasingly he added, 'Plus, we think we may starve to death without you.'

'Mum?' said Nancy. 'So what d'you think?'

Rose was unbelievably touched. Had they any idea how much she loved being here, *being useful*. 'I'd love to stay.' Her voice quavered with emotion. 'If you're sure you want me.'

'Oh, we do,' Carmen said, grinning.

'All done.' Nancy held out the box containing the cake as Connor opened his front door. It was six o'clock on Friday evening and pregnant Pam's leaving party at the Lazy B was due to start at eight.

'Bring it on inside. Here, let me give you a hand.' As he took the pink-and-white-striped box from her, Connor's hands brushed against her own and a zapping sensation shot up Nancy's arms.

'Yay! Let's see it.' Mia, clearing a space on the table said bossily, 'Come on, Dad, take the lid off.'

'Hey,' said Connor, removing the lid and studying the cake. 'That's amazing. You've done an incredible job.' He put an arm round her shoulders. 'You're a clever old stick, aren't you?'

Stick? Clever old *stick*? What kind of an endearment was that?

'Ignore him.' Sensing her alarm, Mia said consolingly, 'It's just one of those stupid things Dad says.'

Connor turned to Nancy. 'I'm sorry, I just meant you were clever. You don't look a bit like a stick. Anyway, we'd better be getting ready.' He nodded at Mia. 'D'you have it?'

Mia patted her jacket pockets, found what she was looking for.

Embarrassed, Nancy said hurriedly, 'I told you. I don't want money.'

'It isn't money,' said Connor.

'Here.' Mia handed Nancy a card. 'Now you're a member of the Lazy B.'

Overwhelmed, Nancy took the card. 'You don't have to do this.'

'Hey, wasn't I saying just the other day that you should come along to the club?' Mia, whose idea it had been, was looking delighted with herself. 'Come with us tonight,' she exclaimed. 'We'll be leaving here in half an hour. I can give you the guided tour, introduce you to people. And you'll see Pam getting her cake. Fancy that?'

Nancy hesitated, glanced at Connor to see his reaction.

'Of course you must come with us, Nancy.' Connor clutched her arm. 'That's a great idea. How about it then, are you free?'

Nancy was having trouble concentrating. Gathering herself, she said, 'I'm free.'

'Great.' Connor looked pleased.

Mia winked at her and Nancy blushed, suspecting that she and Connor had both just been set up. Mia was clearly a girl with a plan.

It was ten o'clock and the bar at the Lazy B was bursting at the seams, Pam was still having her photograph taken with her much-admired cake and Nancy had met practically everyone who worked at the club.

Rejoining her now, Mia said, 'Pam's shattered, I'm just going to call a cab for her. Have you seen Dad?'

'One of the members lost their locker key. He went to find the master,' said Nancy.

'I haven't even had time to show you around the rest of the club.' Mia knocked back her glass of orange juice and checked her watch. 'I had no idea there were going to be so many people here. So, you and Dad getting on OK?'

There was that knowing look again. Honestly, did Mia have any idea how embarrassing it was to be in this situation, set up by a meddling sixteen-year-old?

'I'm having a nice time. And you don't have to show me around,' said Nancy because Mia was clearly busy. 'I can do that any time.' Glancing down at her shoes she added, 'Maybe when I'm wearing something more appropriate.'

Mia disappeared to call the taxi firm and Nancy sipped her drink, shifting from one pencil-thin high heel to the other. Her feet were starting to hurt now. Four-inch stilettos wouldn't have been the ideal choice for exploring a fitness centre anyway. Sitting down and giving her aching feet a rest would be nice but a quick scan of the room revealed only one free seat, so Nancy headed in the direction of the bar instead. Within seconds, she smelt the overpoweringly heavy scent Sadie wore.

'I know what you're up to,' Sadie announced. 'Getting all friendly with Mia. Offering to make cakes for Connor. Wheedling your way—'

'Actually,' Nancy turned to face her, 'I didn't offer to make the cake. Connor asked me to.'

'And now you're here, at Pam's leaving party. My God, talk about infiltration.' Sadie shook her head in mock admiration. 'And I hear you've joined the club. Don't you worry that you might be making a bit of a fool of yourself?'

Cruel accusations were always painful to hear, Nancy discovered, particularly when there was more than a smidgen of truth in them.

Aloud she said, 'I don't know what you mean,' and saw Sadie's glossy red mouth curl with disdain.

'Oh, come on. Your husband had an affair, am I right? He's found someone else and you're desperate to do the same. My God, I bet you couldn't believe your luck when you found out you had Connor living next door to you. I mean, I'm not saying I *blame* you—but there's such a thing as being too obvious.'

Oh hell, did it really show that much? Her heart thumping unpleasantly, Nancy said, 'Connor's just a friend.'

'Of course he is. As far as *he's* concerned,' Sadie drawled. 'The trouble is, your marriage hit the rocks and your confidence has taken a battering. So when a man comes along and starts being nice to you, you think it's because he's romantically interested. Whereas in reality, that's just Connor's way. It means *nothing*,' she emphasised, her eyes glittering. 'So don't be fooled into thinking you're special, because you're not.'

The gym was more or less deserted; almost everyone had by this time given up exercising and gravitated towards the party downstairs. Nancy, clutching her impractical shoes, padded barefoot past the darkened aerobics studio—where she *wouldn't* be joining the classes run by Sulphuric Sadie—and began investigating the fitness equipment.

One of the rowing machines was occupied by a fit-looking student type with a Walkman clamped to his ears. Nancy made her way over to the running machines and cross-trainers. A middle-aged woman was puffing and panting her way up some kind of never-ending ladder.

'It's a Stairmaster,' she said breathlessly, greeting Nancy with a cheerful smile and sensing her bemusement. 'Ghastly, of course, but does wonders for your bum. Thinking of joining the club, then?'

'Well, yes.' It was such a relief to talk to someone friendly again. 'I mean, I already have.'

'Oh, you'll love it. This is a great place. I was always joining gyms then giving up on them, but here's different. Have you met Connor yet?'

'Um . . . yes. Actually, he's my next-door neighbour.'

'Is he really? I say, lucky old you!' The woman beamed, her legs still pumping away. 'Connor's a gem, isn't he? Half the women who come here are in love with him—whew, that's it, time's up!' Heaving a noisy sigh of satisfaction, she hit the STOP button and jumped down from the Stairmaster. 'Fifteen minutes, that's my lot. Now I can go and have a lovely glass of wine as a reward. Maybe see you in the bar,' she said happily as she headed off for a shower.

Nancy spent some time wandering around, investigating the various scary-looking machines, then spotted a corridor that wound past the glass-fronted dance studio and off to the left. It led to the back stairs. A spiral staircase winding down to the ground floor. Still clutching her shoes, Nancy began to descend the staircase, pausing only when she heard a voice she recognised.

Then a second voice.

She was almost directly above Connor's office, Nancy realised, glancing out of the window and getting her bearings. And the door to the office was open, enabling her to overhear every word of Connor's conversation with Mia.

'. . . you just can't go around ordering people to do things because *you* want them to happen.' Connor was sounding exasperated.

'I'm not ordering you, I'm just suggesting you invite her out to dinner,' Mia wheedled. 'Come on, Dad, I know she'd say yes. You'd have a great time.'

Barely a quarter of the way down the spiral staircase, Nancy froze. A waft of smoke drifted up the stairwell, indicating that Connor had just lit a cigarette.

'Mia, give this a rest, will you? It isn't going to happen. Nancy's a nice person, I like her as a friend, but that's as far as it goes. For one thing, she's only just separated from her husband. And even if I *did* fancy her rotten, I wouldn't get involved because women in that situation are just too . . . vulnerable. It wouldn't be fair on Nancy, or on me.'

Nancy was barely able to hear him now; the buzzing in her ears was so loud she felt as if she'd been dragged underwater. What if she fainted and toppled down the staircase, landing in a heap outside Connor's office? Oh God, how was she going to get out of here?

'You don't fancy her at all?' Mia sounded accusing. 'I thought you *did*.'

'And you're only sixteen,' Connor retaliated, 'which just goes to show how much you know. Listen, Nancy's self-confidence has taken a knock. If I can make her feel that little bit better about herself, I will. But basically, there are some girls you fancy and some you don't, and nothing anyone can do will change that. I'm not interested in Nancy, OK? She's not my type and she's never going to be my type, so can we please close this conversation and head back to the party?'

Nancy forced her legs to move. Clinging to the banister, she crept silently back up the spiral staircase.

'I'm getting really cross now,' Mia grumbled. 'I gave Marcus my Dolly Parton CD two hours ago and he *still* hasn't played it. Why do we have to listen to this boring old rubbish anyway?'

'It's not boring old rubbish, it's U2.' Connor found it hard to believe his own daughter had such tragic taste in music. 'And you're on your own with Dolly Parton.'

'But she's great! If Marcus would just *play* the CD, you'd—'

'We'd still hate it,' said Nancy, 'and there's nothing you can do to make us change our minds.'

With a wounded expression, Mia said, 'I thought you were my *friend*.'

'I am.' Nancy checked her watch. 'But you can't force me to like Dolly Parton.'

'Well said.' Delighted, Connor clapped her on the shoulder.

Just like Mia can't force you to like me, thought Nancy. Aloud she said, 'And now I have to go.'

'Oh, stay a bit longer,' Mia begged. 'If you hang on for another hour we can share a cab.'

'Thanks, but I'll head off now. It's been great. Bye.'

As Nancy headed for the exit, she held her head high. On the outside she was serene and in control. Nobody was going to know how she felt.

'What are you doing?' Mystified, Nancy found Carmen stretched out across the navy sofa, sucking a pen and poring over a copy of *Time Out*.

Carmen pulled the end of the pen out of her mouth with a *plop* and said, 'Moving.'

'*What?*'

Sitting up, Carmen showed her the adverts she'd circled in 'Apartments to Let'. 'I've made a few appointments. Will you come along with me after work tomorrow? Take a look at them?'

Nancy peeled off her coat and plonked herself down on the sofa next to Carmen. 'Why?'

Rennie, lying on his side on the floor watching *Citizen Kane*, said, 'She hates us all.'

'Not *all* of you.' Carmen stretched out one foot and prodded his jutting hipbone. 'Only the ones who won't let you watch what you want on TV because they just have to watch ancient films on video.'

Taking a closer look at the ads Carmen had ringed, Nancy said, 'Clerkenwell? Are you serious?'

'She's barking,' said Rennie, earning himself a kick.

'Shut up,' Carmen told him, 'it's something I have to do.' She turned to Nancy. 'After the Joe thing. I never want to go through that again.'

'But you aren't really moving out?' Nancy was worriedly reading the ads for one-bedroomed flats in unglamorous locations.

'Of course not. Not properly moving out. But . . . OK, it's like with Nick and Annie from work.' Carmen waggled her hands and said falteringly, 'I don't want them to know where I live, in case it, you know, spoils things between us. But I've been to their flat three times now,' she hurried on, 'and it's about time I invited them back to mine.'

'So you're going to rent one and pretend it's where you live?'

'Somewhere really grotty and horrible,' Rennie said with relish.

'I've lived in cheap flats before.' Carmen was defiant. 'So have you.' Carmen turned back to Nancy. 'So will you come with me tomorrow?'

'Of course I will.' Nancy understood why Carmen needed to do this.

Sixteen B, Arnold Street, was the third flat they visited and Carmen knew at once that this was the one.

'Yes,' she said, gazing with satisfaction around the living room. 'This is it. It's perfect.'

Nancy was gazing worriedly up at the ceiling. 'Are you sure?'

They were in a quiet backstreet of Battersea and the landlord had assured her that the neighbours kept themselves to themselves. The first-floor flat comprised a tiny kitchen, an even tinier bathroom, one bedroom and a living room that looked out over the street. The decor was tatty, with floral wallpaper peeling at the edges, and the furniture was mismatched and shabby. But there was a new white bathroom suite, and the kitchen was reasonably clean.

Nancy was still peering in fascination at the multi-stained ceiling. 'It's like a map of Europe up there. Look. And there's a mushroom!'

It wasn't a mushroom, it was a frilly-edged patch of fungus.

'I'll give the whole place a proper clean,' Carmen said happily. 'It'll be great.' She went through to the kitchen, where the landlord was reading an old *Evening Standard* and smoking a cigarette. 'I'll take it.'

He yawned. 'Five hundred deposit and first month's rent in advance.'

Carmen nodded and signed the rental agreement. She handed over the money in cash and watched as the man wrote out a receipt. She saw that his name was Mr Sadler. He lived downstairs and seemed entirely uninterested in his new tenant, which suited Carmen down to the ground. He passed her the front-door keys and they shook hands.

'And keep the noise down,' he said tetchily. 'You don't look noisy, but you never can tell. I don't want any trouble. No police, no ambulances screaming up the street.' He wagged a plump warning finger at her and repeated, 'I won't have trouble in this house. Got that?'

'Got it. I'll be the quietest tenant you ever had. There won't be any trouble,' said Carmen. 'I promise.'

'He thinks you're married and having an affair,' said Nancy. 'That's why he went on about police and ambulances. He's worried that your jealous husband might find out and come storming round with a shotgun.'

They had found a table in the Queen's Head, a traditional working-class pub on the corner of Arnold Street. Carmen, tearing open a packet of smoky bacon crisps with her teeth, said, 'If Spike could see what I was doing, he'd laugh his head off. Do you think I'm barking mad?'

'Not really.' Innocently Nancy said, 'Why don't you tell me a bit more about Nick-from-work? The Nick you thought wasn't single, but now it turns out he is. And he's just a really nice person you enjoy being with.'

'He is. I do. He's a *friend*,' Carmen protested. 'You have an evil mind.'

'Excuse me, can we just cast our minds—evil or otherwise—back a bit? Remember when we used to walk through the park on our way home from school and Spike Todd used to try to run us over on his pushbike? And he used to tease you about your haircut?'

'Witch,' said Carmen.

'And the next thing we knew, he's got you riding around on the back of his bike and you're laughing together and going to his house to listen to him play his guitar,' Nancy continued remorselessly. 'But when I asked you what was going on, you said, "Oh, nothing, Spike's just a *friend*."'

'I've finished my drink.' Carmen held up her glass. 'Your round.'

'So would Nick be *that* kind of friend?'

'Shut up. I'm embarrassed.'

Nancy pulled a face. 'Let me tell you, you don't know the meaning of the word embarrassed. I had Sadie at the club last night telling me what a show I've been making of myself over Connor.'

'Oh well, don't take any notice of *her*.' Carmen gestured dismissively with her bag of crisps. 'She's just jealous. She's been dumped by Connor

JILL MANSELL

and isn't happy about it, that's the only reason she had a go. But he's a free agent now, and you get on brilliantly with Mia, so there's absolutely *no* reason why you and Connor—'

'OK, I haven't told you the other embarrassing thing that happened last night. I overheard him and Mia talking in his office. Mia was saying pretty much the same thing. It isn't going to happen.'

'But—'

'No, really. I heard what Connor said.' Nancy shuddered at the memory and glugged down her wine. 'He doesn't fancy me and that's that. As far as Connor's concerned, I'm just a *clever old stick.*'

Oops, she hadn't meant to raise her voice that much. The pub had fallen silent. Even the group of teenagers clustered around the pool table had stopped playing. Obligingly, one of them called over, 'Don't worry, love, I'd give you one.'

Over at the bar, a middle-aged man said, 'I wouldn't say no to being beaten by a stick.'

Carmen looked at Nancy. 'Shall we not bother with that other drink?'

Naturally, everyone went, 'Ooh,' and 'Ow,' and hilariously clutched their backsides as Carmen and Nancy squeezed their way past them.

On the pavement outside the pub, Nancy exhaled slowly and said, 'Thank goodness we went there. I feel so much better now.'

'They were just having a bit of fun.' Carmen gave her arm a squeeze. 'I'm sorry about Connor.'

'Life goes on.' Nancy had already mentally steeled herself. 'It would've been nice, but never mind. Anyway, ready now?'

'Ready for what?'

'To admit that there might secretly be a bit of a spark going on between you and Nick?'

Carmen smiled. 'OK. Maybe a bit of one,' she agreed, blushing under the streetlamp. 'But what am I turning into? Not a single hint of a man for three years, and now all of a sudden I'm turning into Zsa-Zsa Gabor. First Joe, now Nick . . . I mean, is it my hormones, d'you think? Are they rampaging out of control?'

Winding her purple scarf round her neck, Nancy said, 'I think they're just waking up after a long, long sleep. I think it's great news.'

At lunchtime, Zac took Doreen out for a walk. Upstairs in his flat, Nancy heated the cartons of wild mushroom risotto from his favourite delicatessen and put together a salad. She enjoyed their lunches in Zac's kitchen. When summer came, they would eat out on his roof terrace. For a single man with no family money behind him, Zac had a beautiful flat.

By one thirty he and Doreen were back. Nancy served up the risotto and said, 'May I ask a really impertinent question?'

Zac grinned. 'I love impertinent questions.'

'It's about this place. Your dad worked on the docks. You've told me yourself how hard it can be to keep a business like yours afloat. But you have the shop and this flat, and we're in the middle of poshest Chelsea—'

'So you're wondering how the heck I manage to pay the bills,' Zac finished for her. 'Well, that's easy. I'm actually a high-class prostitute.'

'No, you're not.' Nancy pulled a face at him. 'You're too ugly.'

'Flattery'll get you everywhere. OK,' Zac admitted, 'I was left money when my godmother died. She was my mother's best friend and didn't have any family of her own. Wanda, her name was. She was a stylish lady, liked fashion, encouraged me when I told her I wanted to become a designer. Of course that was when I was thirteen.' He broke off another piece of bread and fed it to Doreen. 'So there you go, that's how I managed to afford the down payment on this place. All thanks to my fairy godmother—ooh, let me phone Sven before I forget. He's twenty-five, blue eyes, white-blond hair, teeth to die for. You should see him, he looks like a model. We met in a bar last night and just clicked.'

Nancy watched him key in Sven's number, listen expectantly for a few seconds then visibly deflate when the answering service kicked in.

'Hi, you, me here!' Zac adopted his buoyant, haven't-a-care-in-the-world manner in order to leave a message. 'All set for tonight? Pick you up at eight. OK? See you later, alligator!'

Nancy helped herself to more risotto.

'Was that all right?' Zac raised anxious eyebrows at her. 'Not too over the top? Just nice and casual?'

'Maybe leave out the alligator next time,' said Nancy.

'Oh God, does it make me sound ancient?'

'You aren't ancient. Stop being such a worry-guts.'

'It's just that his phone's switched off. Why would his phone be switched off?' Zac checked his watch. 'It's quarter to two.'

'He probably went to the cinema. Now, are you going to finish that risotto or shall I?'

'Is this a fashion statement?' Nick nodded at Carmen's hair as she arrived at the shelter on Wednesday morning. 'Those turquoise bits. Mainly at the back.' Helpfully Nick pointed them out. 'I like them.'

'Oh.' Patting her head and feeling the stiffened spikes, Carmen said, 'I've just moved into a flat in Battersea. Been redecorating.'

'Really? Hey, you should have said. I'm a demon with a paintbrush.'

'Demon being the operative word,' Annie chimed in. 'He can't bear the thought of wasting paint, so anything left over has to go *somewhere*. Which is why our bathroom ceiling is red.'

'Ignore her, she has no sense of adventure. Much left to do, or have you finished?'

'Well, I've done the bathroom and the kitchen.' Guessing what was coming, Carmen pretended she hadn't. 'Still got the living room and bedroom to go.'

Nick said easily, 'So you could do with a hand? I'm free tonight.'

A warm Ready Brek glow spread through her stomach. 'If you're sure, that'd be . . . great.' It *would* be great. She hadn't left the turquoise paint streaks in her hair on purpose, but if she'd thought of it she would have.

'Right, that's settled.' Nick rubbed his hands together in let's-get-painting fashion. 'We'll go straight to your flat from here.'

'I can't believe we've done four walls in less than three hours.' Perched on the stepladder, Carmen gazed down at Nick. 'Now you're the one with paint in your hair. Pistachio green.' Tapping his head with her brush she added playfully, 'And parma violet.'

'Big mistake. *Big* mistake.' Nick sighed as he gripped each side of the ladder. 'Never think you can get away with *anything* like that when you're the one stuck up there like a parrot on a wibbly wobbly perch.'

'Waaah,' squealed Carmen as he gave the stepladder an experimental shake. Instinctively her arms shot out and she slithered down, half stumbling against Nick's chest.

'See what I mean? Now you've got paint on your nose.' Nick's mouth twitched as he wiped the bridge of her nose. 'And you're all speckled, like an egg. Blimey, was that your stomach rumbling?'

'You must be hungry too.' Carmen was conscious of how close to each other they were. 'How about a takeaway?'

Nick was gazing down at her. Carmen felt her heart leaping. All of a sudden she was unable to utter a single word. The silence lengthened between them as she waited for Nick to slide his fingers through her hair and kiss her. He wanted to, she knew he did. And she definitely wanted him to, so why wasn't it happening?

Then she realised that Nick was deliberately leaving it up to her. She had to be the one to make the move. OK, well, she could do that. Reaching up, breathing in the mingled smells of peppermint and paint, she brushed her mouth against his. Then pressed more firmly, before relaxing into the kiss.

Oh *yes*.

Finally, Nick pulled away. Smiled. 'So. I've wanted to do that for quite a while.'

Recklessly Carmen said, 'Me too.'

'It might have been more romantic if you could have stopped your stomach rumbling.'

'I know. Sorry about that. We'll get a takeaway.' Nodding decisively, Carmen wiped her hands on her paint-spattered shirt. 'There's an Indian just around the corner in Donovan Street.'

When the doorbell went, Carmen jumped as if a spider had just crawled out of her cleavage. Who on earth was that?

'Nervous,' Nick observed with amusement. 'Don't tell me you forgot to mention your jealous husband.'

Downstairs Carmen found Nancy on the doorstep, pink-cheeked with the cold and clutching a plastic food container. 'Surprise! Thought you might be hungry.'

'Or you thought you might be nosy.' Carmen wasn't fooled. When she'd rung Nancy earlier to tell her she would be coming straight here from work, she had added that Nick would be giving her a hand tonight.

'Nosy? Me? How can you even think that? Is he here?'

'No. Left an hour ago.'

Nancy's face fell.

'Yes, he's here.' Breaking into a grin, Carmen ushered her into the cramped hallway. 'Just don't be too obvious, OK?'

'I'll be wonderfully discreet. You've got paint on your nose, by the way.'

Remembering the tender way Nick had attempted to wipe it off, Carmen said happily, 'I know.'

Upstairs she said, 'This is Nancy, my oldest friend. Nancy, this is Nick.'

'Hi,' Nancy beamed. 'I come bearing shepherd's pie. Carmen told me she was so busy painting last night she forgot to eat.'

Carmen knew at once they'd get along. Nick had an easy-going air about him. Viewing him as if she were Nancy, she saw the messed-up hair, big nose, kind eyes and execrable dress sense.

'Shepherd's pie, my favourite. And to think we were about to grab a takeaway.' Nick beamed. 'I'm even more pleased to meet you now.'

'You've done all this.' Nancy gazed around the room. 'It's looking great.'

'Wait until tomorrow, we'll be in the bedroom then.' Realising too late what he'd just said, Nick hastily backtracked. 'I mean, um, decorating it.'

Sensing the chemistry in the room, Nancy hid a smile. 'I'm just going to stick this in the oven. There's apple crumble too.'

'Can it get any better? Annie's going to be so jealous. I'd better wash all this stuff before it goes solid.'

Nancy watched him lope through to the bathroom with the rollers, trays and paintbrushes. Nudging Carmen, she whispered, 'He's *nice*.'

Carmen's eyes were bright with long-overdue happiness as she clutched Nancy's arm and whispered back, 'I *know*.'

When his brother had died three years ago, Rennie had taken care of Carmen. During the first few days, when she had been paralysed with grief, he had moved into the house in Fitzallen Square and dealt with everything. The funeral had needed to be arranged, a task that had been beyond Carmen. When the initial shock and numbness had begun to wear off, Carmen had been tortured by the thought that she should have been able, somehow, to prevent Spike's death. Night after night Rennie had sat up with her, rocking her in his arms, comforting her and allowing her to weep the worst of the overwhelming feelings of guilt out of her system. He had loved his brother too. Their grief had been shared. But, back then, he'd known that Carmen was the one who most needed support. And he had given it to her, to the best of his ability.

It was a habit that had stuck. Now, three years later, Carmen was back on her feet and capable of living her own life again. A normal life, with all that entailed. Rennie, lying on his bed smoking a cigarette, knew that he should allow her to make her own decisions, her own mistakes.

He'd already interfered once, with Joe—whom he'd never entirely trusted—and that had turned out to be the *right* thing to do. Rennie sighed. And now, hot on the heels of Joe, she was plunging into a new relationship from which he was entirely excluded.

The phone rang in his jeans pocket. Levering it out and exhaling a plume of smoke, Rennie said, 'Yes?'

'Hi! Sheryl!'

He frowned. 'Excuse me?'

'It's Sheryl, remember? Last night at the Met Bar?'

Taking another drag of his cigarette, Rennie recalled the bouncy blonde who had approached him at the bar.

'Right. I remember. And?'

'I gave you my number.' Sheryl sounded as if she was pretending to pout. 'I've been waiting all day for you to ring, but you haven't.'

Clearly the shy and retiring type.

'So?' Sheryl demanded when he didn't reply. 'Fancy meeting up?'

'You gave me your number. I didn't give you mine.' Rennie frowned. 'How did you get hold of it?'

Giggling, Sheryl said, 'Your phone was on the bar next to your drink. I just had a quick peep.'

Bloody hell. 'Wouldn't you class that as an invasion of privacy?'

'Look, I really fancy you,' said Sheryl. 'And I promise you, I'm a great lay.' Persuasively she added, 'Everyone says so.'

Rennie blew a series of smoke rings up at the ceiling. Then he sighed. 'Not interested, thanks. Don't call this number again.'

'But—'

'Goodbye.' He hung up.

Silence. Stubbing out his cigarette, Rennie stood up and went over to the window. It was a grey, cold day and he had just turned down the opportunity to spend the afternoon in bed with a girl whose immodesty knew no bounds.

There was nobody out in the square this lunchtime. The house was empty too. Carmen and Nancy were both at work. Rose, no longer a visitor to Chelsea but a bona fide resident, had trotted off to get herself registered at the local health centre. From there, she was heading over to Battersea to inspect Carmen's new flat.

Now, resting his hands on the window ledge, Rennie wondered what had been the point of turning down an offer of wild sex from an attractive admirer. How else was he going to spend the rest of the day?

Twenty minutes later, Rennie checked his phone and rang a number. 'Hi, it's Rennie. Can we meet up?'

Chapter 8

ANNIE WAS TIDYING UP in the kitchen and Carmen was mopping the floor when Nick headed through to the recreation room and made his way over to where Harry, a regular visitor to the shelter, had found a quiet corner to read. Another chair, pushed against the wall, was occupied by a new visitor. Grubby and dishevelled, with rheumy grey eyes and a matted beard, he was probably in his forties, and smelt strongly of beer. Since arriving he had smoked several cigarettes and silently observed the goings-on in the recreation room. Nick was used to this kind of behaviour. New visitors were always welcomed but never interrogated.

Taking an empty chair between Harry and the new visitor, he said easily, 'So how are you doing, Harry? Chest better now?'

Harry nodded and carried on reading his Mills & Boon.

'Good book?'

'Very good. Driving narrative. Plenty of emotional tension.'

'Excellent.' Nick watched Harry's hands begin to tremble as he closed the battered paperback. 'Ever thought of writing a book yourself?'

'Oh, I have. I mean I *did*,' Harry said quietly.

Intrigued, Nick said, 'You actually wrote a book?'

'Several.'

'Harry, that's fantastic. I'm impressed.'

But Harry simply shook his head. 'No need to be impressed.'

'Hey, you're wrong,' Nick insisted. 'Just *writing* a book is an achievement in itself. It doesn't matter if you don't get published, you've still—'

'I did get published, though. That was the problem.' Harry turned his head to look properly at Nick. 'I wrote a novel and sold it to a publisher. The editor took me out to lunch and told me how fantastic the book was. He said that I had a glittering new career ahead of me.'

Nick waited, didn't speak. He'd never heard Harry say so much before; today was evidently the day for unburdening himself.

'My wife was so excited,' Harry went on eventually. 'The publisher had offered me an advance. It wasn't huge, but decent enough. We both decided I should give up my job in the Civil Service and write full-time.'

This time the silence was more prolonged. Nick finally said, 'So the first book was published?'

Harry nodded, first examining the cracked spine of the Mills & Boon, then his blackened nails.

'It was. But it barely sold at all. We were disappointed, but the publisher explained that this often happened with a first novel. Anyway, I had the second novel finished by then, so we pinned all our hopes on that.' Leaning forward on his chair, Harry wearily rubbed his face. 'Except the publisher didn't like it. He suggested changing it and I tried to do as he asked, but six months later he rejected the rewrite. By this time we'd remortgaged the house. For the next year I struggled with another book, but the publisher didn't want that one either. They dropped me. My wife left me three weeks later. Then the house was repossessed. That's when it all became too much for me. I'd failed at everything. Lost everything.' He paused. 'That was six years ago.'

Nick shook his head. 'That's a rotten thing to happen, Harry. I'm sorry. But you could have a go at writing again. No pressure on you this time. Just write because you want to, not because you have to.'

Harry shrugged. 'I don't think so.' Wiping his nose with a handkerchief he said gruffly, 'Thanks, anyway. I've never told anyone before.'

'I'm glad you did.' Nick gave his arm a brief, reassuring squeeze. 'And, Harry, if there's ever anything I can do to help, just let me know.'

'Thanks.' Harry nodded.

'Now, why don't I get us a nice cup of tea?' Turning to the newcomer, Nick wondered what his story was. Heavy drinking, presumably, leading to problems with his family . . . divorce . . . losing contact with the kids . . . 'How about you, cup of tea?'

There were tears in the man's eyes, Nick saw; hearing Harry's story had evidently brought back to him how much he himself had lost.

Then again, you could never guess.

'No, thanks.' The man cleared his throat and gazed fixedly across the room. clearly unwilling to be drawn into any form of conversation.

'OK. Just tea for you and me then, Harry.'

As she rounded the corner into Fitzallen Square, Rose couldn't remember when she'd last been happier. Working to brighten up Carmen's little flat had been a pleasure rather than a chore. Now she was heading home—*home!*—to cook dinner for everyone and this evening she would sit watching TV with Nancy and Rennie, and crack on with her knitting.

Alerted by the sound of footsteps, Rose saw Brigadier Brough-Badham making his way along the pavement towards her.

As he reached Rose, without slowing down or sparing her even the briefest of glances, he said curtly, 'Get rid of him.'

Astounded, Rose whirled round to gaze at his departing back. Indignantly she shouted, 'Get rid of *who*?'

But Brigadier Brough-Badham carried on walking.

Having assumed he was referring to Rennie—who, at a guess, had either said or done something disreputable again—Rose realised her mistake less than a minute later. The man sitting on the front step of the house, leaning against one of the white pillars, was what Brigadier Brough-Badham would no doubt term as *undesirable*. His hair was dirty and straggly, Rose saw as she approached.

To be polite, Rose said gently, 'Are you waiting for someone, pet?'

The man gazed blearily up at her. Finally, in a hoarse voice, he said, 'Yeah. I'm looking for Carmen.'

Carmen got the shock of her life when she arrived home an hour later and recognised one of the new visitors to the shelter sitting at her kitchen table. Almost jumping out of her skin, she saw the dinner plate in front of him, the half-full mug of coffee, the grubby grey woollen scarf hung over the back of the chair.

Her heart palpitating wildly, Carmen hung back in the doorway. Oh God, this was seriously creepy. What was he doing here? How had he known where she lived? And what on earth did Rose think she was doing, allowing him into the kitchen and feeding him beef stroganoff?

'Hi, sweetheart,' Rose said gaily. 'Hungry?'

Hungry? Was Rose out of her *mind*?

'What's going on?' Carmen addressed the man. 'Have you been following me?'

'No.'

'Then how did you find out where I *live*?'

'God, I'm good,' drawled the man, sitting back in his chair and peeling off his beard. 'I should be an actor.'

'You bastard!' shrieked Carmen as Rennie pulled off his wig and broke into a broad grin. He still looked so hideous she could barely take it in. As she watched, he popped out the soft contact lenses with their ageing pale grey lines around each iris.

'Here, clean yourself up.' Delighted with her part in the subterfuge, Rose was at the ready with a pack of wet-wipes. 'That's not really dirt on his face, pet,' she consoled Carmen. 'It's all make-up. Isn't it clever?' she went on admiringly. 'He certainly fooled me.'

'Fooled Carmen too.' Baring grotesquely stained teeth at her, Rennie dragged off the holey brown sweater he'd been wearing, to reveal one of his own T-shirts underneath. 'Better now?'

'Bastard.' Carmen was tempted to hit him. 'Your teeth are revolting.'

'I wanted false ones but it was too short notice. Remember Lisa?'

Carmen nodded. Lisa had worked as a make-up artist.

'I rang her this morning.' Rennie sounded pleased with himself. 'Went round to her house and got her to grubby me up. It has its good points. Had a whole carriage to myself on the tube.'

'I'm not surprised. You smell like a brewery,' said Carmen.

'Splashed half a can of beer over me for that authentic, reeking-of-alcohol touch. Nice job, don't you think?' Advancing towards her, Rennie leered, 'Come over here and give me a kiss.'

'Hang on, hang on.' Holding up her hands to ward him off, Carmen said, 'What made you do this?'

Still smiling lasciviously, Rennie bared his hideous brown teeth. 'Wanted to see where you worked, find out what you do all day.'

'Oh, don't give me that. You came to spy on Nick!'

Rennie instantly conceded defeat. 'OK, is that so terrible? You said I mustn't come to the flat because I'd be recognised. But it's OK for Nancy and Rose to go there. Why did Nancy turn up at the flat last night?

Because she was dying to meet Nick. And I wanted to meet him too, but I wasn't allowed to,' he said simply. 'So I did it the only way I could.'

'You wanted to spy on him,' Carmen repeated evenly.

'I just wanted to see what he was like.'

Carmen sighed and sat down opposite him. Warily she said, 'Fine, so now you have. And?'

'Dodgy clothes. But I liked him and I'm pretty sure he's on the level.'

'Of course he's on the level.'

He rolled his eyes. 'Don't be so touchy. I'm on your side. Nick's a decent bloke. If you marry him, will I be invited to the wedding?'

'Not a chance,' said Carmen as Rose brought her a plate of stroganoff and rice.

'Could I just lurk at the back of the church if I dress up as a tramp?'

'Still no.' Carmen smiled sweetly at him. 'And do you think you could go and brush your teeth now? They're starting to make me feel sick.'

Nancy's muscles didn't know what had hit them. Her calves were on fire, her lungs were close to bursting and there was barely enough strength in her neck to keep her head from flopping onto her chest.

But in the weirdest way she was actually enjoying herself.

Yes. Two miles. Triumphantly slamming the flat of her hand onto the Stop button, Nancy felt the blissful slowing of the treadmill as it began to wind down. She clung to the side bars, panting and perspiring.

After a shower, Nancy made her way back through to the bar. Spotting Mia taking a break, she carried her coffee over to join her.

'Hey.' Mia put down the magazine she'd been engrossed in and gazed approvingly at Nancy's yellow track suit. 'You're looking fit.'

'Looking fit, feeling knackered.' Stirring her cappuccino, Nancy said, 'Knackered, but smug. I'm enjoying it.' She flinched as she reached forward for her coffee cup. 'Ouch. Maybe it's easier to just hold the cup rather than keep picking it up and putting it down.'

'Speaking of picking up.' Mia's eyes danced. 'What d'you think of Cyanide Sadie's latest victim?'

Nancy knew all about this. The whole club had been buzzing with the news that Sadie had taken up with Antonio, the club's new personal trainer. With his shaven head, liquid brown eyes and sinuous body he strongly resembled a seal. Instantly, upon his arrival at the Lazy B, he had attracted a great deal of fluttery attention from the female members of the club. Antonio was twenty-three, single and super-fit.

Sadie had wasted no time getting in there first. Within a few days they had become an item. Mission accomplished.

'He certainly seems to have cheered her up,' said Nancy.

'Hmm.' Mia smirked.

'What? Isn't that a good thing?'

'She wouldn't be quite so cheerful if she'd seen the way he was flirting with me this morning.'

'What? So what did you do?'

'Ha! Flirted back at him of course.'

'You flirted with Antonio?' Astounded, Nancy said, 'Do you like him?'

'*Duh*. He's way too old for me. But it's going to have Cyanide Sadie foaming at the mouth with fury.'

'It's over between Sadie and Connor,' Nancy protested. 'You don't have to hate her any more.'

Checking her watch, Mia knocked back the rest of her milkshake. 'Are you joking? It's her mission in life to get me the sack.'

For a moment, Nancy almost felt sorry for Sadie. It was obvious that Mia had no intention of backing off. As Nancy left the club ten minutes later, Mia was swinging her blonde hair and doing her flirty thing across the desk with Antonio.

Outside, as Nancy turned left and began to make her way towards the tube, Connor's conker-brown Bentley pulled alongside the pavement. The passenger window slid down.

'Hi!' Eyes sparkling, Connor leaned across from the driver's seat and beckoned her over. 'Hop in and I'll give you a lift.'

Oh God, difficult, *difficult*. Why did he have to be so nice? Why couldn't she make herself not like him?

'No, thanks, I'm fine.' Nancy shook her head, frantically searching for a feasible excuse. 'Um, I've got my return ticket for the tube.' As Nancy spoke, a lorry blasted its horn behind Connor, making her jump.

'Come on, you're holding everyone up.' Leaning across still further, Connor swung open the passenger door. 'They all think you're a hooker now, haggling over the price.'

More horn-tooting. Oh, for heaven's sake. Hastily clambering into the car, Nancy couldn't help thinking that with her trainers, old jeans and wet hair escaping from her baseball cap, she'd be a low-rent hooker.

'Off out anywhere this evening?' Connor said as he pulled away.

'No.' The cold night air had dried out Nancy's lips; she fumbled surreptitiously in her bag for her stick of lipsalve.

'Only I've been invited to the opening of a new restaurant on the King's Road. Fancy coming along?'

Yes.

'No, thanks,' said Nancy, as casually as she knew how.

'No?' Connor pretended to look hurt. 'I'm not that awful, am I? Come on, don't be mean, you can't let me go on my own. There might be girls there after my body. Pestering me, pawing me.'

'And that would be a tragedy.'

Pulling up at a red traffic light, Connor said, 'What's that smell? Kind of fruity.' He sniffed the air. 'Peachy?'

'Apricot lipsalve,' said Nancy.

'Really? Does it taste like apricots?'

Oh Lord, how was he proposing to find out? She knew she couldn't handle being kissed purely in the spirit of investigative research.

'Hey! What are you doing?' Startled, Connor jerked his head away.

'Sshh, keep still. You wanted to know how it tasted.' Willing her hand not to shake, Nancy carefully applied the stick of lipsalve to his mouth.

'Mm. Mmm. Hey, this is *fantastic*.' Smacking his lips together with relish, Connor peered at his reflection in the rear-view mirror. 'Does it make me look like a girl?'

It was colourless lipsalve. 'More like a big old rugby-playing transvestite,' said Nancy. 'And the lights have gone green.'

'Come with me to this opening night.'

'No.'

'Why not?'

Because I fancy you so much I can't stand it, and you don't feel the same way about me.

'I just feel like an early night, that's all.'

For a few minutes Connor drove in silence. As they approached Fitzallen Square he said, 'Have I done anything to upset you?'

Yes.

'No.' Her fingernails dug painfully into the palms of her hands.

'So we're still friends.' Connor pulled up outside their adjoining houses and switched off the engine.

'Still friends.' And *only* friends, Nancy thought with a sigh of resignation. Just good friends and nothing more.

'Well, I'm glad to hear that.' Connor relaxed visibly. 'I'd hate to think I'd done something awful.' Glancing up at the lit windows of Carmen's house, he said, 'Hey, maybe Rennie'd like to be my date.'

'**M**um, could you do me a massive favour?'

Never happier than when she was helping others, Rose said at once, 'Of course I can, pet. What is it?'

'I'm at the Chinese takeaway around the corner from Carmen's flat.' Nancy was sounding frazzled. 'The thing is, I've lost my credit card, but

I think I know where it might be. I used it this morning to book theatre tickets over the internet and I *think* I might have left it on Zac's kitchen table, because I was borrowing his laptop. But if I didn't leave it there, I'll have to ring the card people and get it cancelled.'

'Oh, you'd need to.' Rose, who didn't trust credit cards one bit, immediately began to worry. 'Shall I ring Zac and ask him if your card's there?'

'I already tried. No answer. He must be out.' Lowering her voice Nancy said, 'Hang on, I'm just moving into the street so I'm not overheard. OK, this is why I need a favour. Could you take my spare key and go over there? Let yourself in through the shop, switch off the burglar alarm and just shoot upstairs to the kitchen. Zac won't mind. Then you can ring me from there and let me know if you've found the card.'

'OK. Give me the number for the alarm and I'll go straight away.'

Rose was in the hallway, pulling her gloves on, when the front door opened. Rennie, back from a day of meetings with his manager and agent, was wearing a sea-green shirt, faded jeans, and a thin gold chain round his neck in place of a scarf. How he'd never succumbed to pneumonia, she couldn't imagine.

'Rose. Are you sure they've offered you a job at Spearmint Rhino?'

Rose enjoyed being teased by Rennie. The infamous pole-dancing club had featured on last night's news.

'Cheeky boy. There's a baked ham in the fridge if you're hungry.'

'Where are you going?'

Rose explained about the missing credit card, concluding, 'I'll be back in half an hour.'

'It's late,' said Rennie. 'Come on, I'll give you a lift.'

In Rennie's black Mercedes it took only a couple of minutes to reach Levine Street. Zac's shop was in darkness as Rennie pulled into a free space across the road.

'I won't be long,' said Rose.

'I'll come with you.' Rennie hopped out of the driver's seat.

In the shop doorway Rose peeled off her gloves and took the key from her pocket. Once inside, she found the alarm easily enough and keyed in the code. Phew, done. Now she could relax.

'Hey, how about this?' Rennie was gleefully holding a silver shift dress decorated with huge purple lip-prints against himself. 'Does it suit me?'

'Put that down,' Rose scolded. 'Zac doesn't want your grubby fingerprints all over his clothes.'

Rennie raised a playful eyebrow. 'I think you could be wrong there.'

Rose did her best not to blush. When Nancy had told her that Zac was that way inclined, she'd been shocked. It was one thing seeing people on the TV who were gay, but somehow it had never occurred to Rose that she might know a homosexual in real life. Frankly, if she weren't so fond of Zac she might have felt a bit funny about it.

As they climbed the staircase Rose noted with approval that before leaving the flat Zac had left a couple of lights on in order to deter burglars. The kitchen was to the left, with the door closed. Hearing a faint scuffling noise, she realised that Zac had left Doreen at home.

'Honestly, what a hopeless guard dog,' Rose chided. 'Not a single bark.' Raising her voice before opening the door in order not to startle the little dog, she called out, 'It's all right, sweetheart, only me!'

The next moment her heart leapt into her throat as the door was abruptly yanked open. With her fingers already closed round the door-handle, Rose found herself yanked along with it. Catapulting into the kitchen, she collided with Zac who looked petrified.

'*Rose!* What's going on?' he gasped.

There was a frying pan clutched in his right hand. Her own heart racing, Rose clasped her chest and stammered, 'I thought the flat was empty . . . Nancy told me you were out.'

'I could have killed you.' Zac's face was chalk-white and his hands were trembling violently. 'I thought you were a burglar. If you hadn't called out I'd have hit you over the head with this.'

Wobbly with relief that he hadn't swung the frying pan at her, Rose said, 'Oh, I'm so sorry. Could I sit down for a bit, get my breath back?'

'Um . . . well, I was just on my way out.' Zac shifted awkwardly.

'Sit down, Rose.' Taking charge, Rennie steered her towards the kitchen table and pulled out one of the chairs. 'Nancy rang you, but there was no reply.' As he said it, Rennie's gaze flickered from Zac to the silver mobile phone lying on the table. 'She tried your mobile too, but it was switched off. Where's Doreen?'

'What? Oh, in the bedroom. Having a sleep.' Wiping his perspiring hands together, Zac blurted out, 'I still don't know what you're *doing* here.'

Rose's forehead pleated apologetically. 'Nancy's lost her credit card. She thought she might have left it here in the kitchen. Have you seen it?'

'No.' Wildly Zac shook his head. 'Credit card? No, definitely haven't seen it. Sorry. Right, was that all? Only I really do have to go out!'

Rennie, sauntering over to the far side of the table, where a slew of papers and magazines were scattered, began picking up each one in turn and flicked through them. Nothing. Then he moved Zac's laptop, which lay open and switched off. The credit card, which had slid beneath the laptop, was revealed.

Clasping her hands, Rose exclaimed, 'Oh, thank heavens, there it is!'

281

Zac looked relieved too. Relieved, thought Rennie as he passed the card over to Rose, but still downright twitchy.

'OK if I use the loo before we head off?' Sliding past Zac, Rennie made his way swiftly across the kitchen.

'No!' yelped Zac, lunging after him. 'No, that's not the bathroom—'

Too late, he caught up with Rennie as he pulled open the door.

'*Oh God*,' Zac groaned, slumping against the fridge.

'Sorry, my mistake.' Rennie beamed at him over his shoulder. 'I thought it was a bathroom. Turns out it's a broom cupboard. And you'll never guess what else you've got in here.' He opened the door more widely and Rose's mouth dropped open as Brigadier Brough-Badham emerged from the broom cupboard.

'Oh, my *goodness*,' Rose gasped. 'He lives next door to us,' She spluttered. 'This is just . . . well, *extraordinary*. Whatever is he doing here in your flat, Zac?'

Bracing herself the next morning, Nancy let herself into the shop. Doreen came trotting over, her tail wagging eagerly, and she scooped the little dog up into her arms. At least someone was pleased to see her.

Through the open door leading into the workroom, Nancy could see Zac with his back to her, pinning a swathe of blue velvet round his tailor's dummy. She called out casually, 'Hi, Zac. Everything OK?'

He stopped pinning and turned to face her. Said flatly, 'They told you.'

Maybe not that casual then.

'Sorry.' Nancy moved towards him, feeling horribly responsible and clutching Doreen like a security blanket. 'It's all my fault. I sent Mum over here last night. As far as I was concerned, the flat was empty.'

'Great timing. Put the coffee on, will you?' he said wearily. 'I suppose we'd better talk.'

'We don't have to.' Nancy shook her head. 'If you don't want to.'

But Zac gave her a pitying look. 'Of course I don't *want* to, but we certainly *do* have to. Geoffrey's your neighbour. How do you suppose he's feeling now? If his wife finds out, this'll kill him.'

Geoffrey. It was hard enough to believe that Brigadier Brough-Badham *had* a Christian name, let alone that it was Geoffrey. The thought of Zac and him together was, frankly, mind-boggling.

'There are plenty of gay men who are married. Especially the older ones,' said Zac. 'Geoffrey had his army career to think of. His family. He did his best to fit in. You have no idea how difficult his life has been,' he added defensively. 'And now this. If Marjorie gets to hear about it, I don't know what he'll do.'

'She doesn't know?' Appalled, Nancy said, 'We won't tell her. That's a promise. Truly, we won't breathe a word.'

'*You* might not,' Zac said soberly. 'But what about Rennie? He blurted everything out to you, didn't he?'

Hot with embarrassment, Nancy recalled her and Carmen's arrival home last night. Rennie, greeting them at the front door, had practically dragged them over the threshold exclaiming, 'Quick, quick, get in, you are not going to *believe* this!'

'He did,' she admitted, 'but only because the brigadier's always hated us so much.' Hastily Nancy added, 'But Rennie would never tell Marjorie. That would just hurt *her*. Rennie isn't malicious.'

Zac said seriously, 'Geoffrey couldn't bear it. That's the truth. It would destroy both of them.'

'Don't worry.' Nancy vowed to speak to Rennie. 'And tell Brig—um, Geoffrey not to worry either. Really.'

'And the moral of this story is,' Zac grimaced, 'if your phone rings, answer it. We weren't in bed or anything, by the way.'

'I didn't think that,' Nancy lied, flushing as the unthinkable mental image of Zac and Geoffrey in bed together flashed through her mind.

'OK, stop *picturing* it. Just sit down and I'll tell you the whole story.'

'I don't want to—'

'It's kind of relevant,' Zac said evenly, 'seeing that if it wasn't for Geoffrey, I wouldn't have this shop.'

'I've always been hopeless with men. Well, you know that.' Zac gestured sadly with his hands. 'It's all over between me and Sven, by the way. He chucked me yesterday, texted me to say he's met someone else.'

'Oh, I'm sorry.' Nancy winced in sympathy.

'Don't be. I'm used to it by now. Anyway, I met Geoffrey eight years ago. I was coming out of a gay bar in Soho and he invited me to go for a drink. I wasn't some kind of gigolo,' Zac said defensively. 'I mean, I know he's twenty years older than me, but we really seemed to hit it off, you know? We talked for hours. He told me he was married. The thing with Geoffrey is, he's so buttoned up on the outside, but inside, deep down, he's just another desperately unhappy man who hasn't been able to live the kind of life he was meant to live.'

'So you started . . . um, seeing each other.'

'For about a year,' Zac agreed. 'And I did love him, but the age thing was always a problem. After a while the physical side fizzled out, but we stayed good friends.'

Nancy gestured around the shop. 'And this place?'

'I was struggling to get my own business up and running. The banks wouldn't loan me enough to set up anywhere decent. I didn't ask Geoffrey to help me,' Zac said fiercely. 'He'd always encouraged me, been there for me during the hard times. Then one day he saw the For Sale sign up outside this place. He rang and told me to come and take a look. So I did, but it was obviously way out of my price range. I mean, Levine Street in Chelsea, was he mad? But the next day Geoffrey gave me an envelope with a cheque inside, for more money than I'd ever seen.' Tears filled Zac's eyes. 'I couldn't believe it. Geoffrey didn't want anything in return. He just told me he wanted to make my dreams come true. Remember when you asked me about this place? And I told you my godmother left me the money when she died? That was a lie.'

'Well, the truth would have come as quite a shock.' Bemused, Nancy said, 'But what about his wife? Didn't Marjorie notice all this money missing from their bank account?'

'She's independently wealthy.' Zac shook his head. 'They have separate accounts. Separate beds, separate everything.'

No wonder they'd always looked so miserable. Glancing up, Nancy saw a baby-blue MG pulling up outside the shop—double-parking because its owner didn't believe in searching for a parking space.

'Lysette's here for her fitting.' She clasped Zac's hand. 'Don't worry about Rennie, I'll speak to him. He won't breathe a word.'

Carmen wondered if this was how Richard and Judy felt, working and living together and never tiring of each other's company. It was practically how she and Nick were nowadays. Apart from the evening before last, when Nancy had mislaid her credit card, they had been spending all their time together and it felt . . . well, fantastic. Last night they had gone ten-pin bowling with Annie and her boyfriend before heading back to Battersea for a boisterous game of Monopoly. When Annie and Jonathan had left the flat just before midnight, Nick had slowly removed her clothes and made love to her, and she had given herself to him entirely, wondering if it was possible to feel happier than this.

And now, this morning, here they were on their way into work together, swaying in unison on the packed tube train, and Carmen couldn't help feeling sorry for her fellow commuters because none of them was as filled with such indescribable joy as she was. Were people covertly glancing her way, nudging each other and whispering, 'Look, see that girl over there, did you ever see anyone *glow* like that?'

'I hate to tell you this,' Nick whispered to her, 'but you're starting to scare people.'

Carmen squirmed with pleasure as his breath tickled her ear. 'Why?'

'That smirk on your face. You look like a spaniel who's just heard a really smutty joke.'

'I do not.' Reaching under his jacket at the back and pinching his bottom, Carmen murmured, 'Anyway, it's all your fault.'

'Excellent news. I'm delighted to hear that I'm capable of making you smirk like a spaniel. I shall be adding this talent to my CV.'

He bent his head and kissed her on the mouth, and Carmen had to hang on to the handrail for dear life as her knees turned to noodles.

Chapter 9

'YOU'RE OFF AT SIX, aren't you?' said Antonio. 'Come out for a drink with me after work.'

Mia was beginning to realise that maybe she hadn't done the wisest thing. 'Think before you flirt' was a maxim to which she hadn't adhered and over the past couple of weeks Antonio had become keener and keener. It had been fun at first, but now she didn't know how to make it stop. And if Antonio and Sadie were to break up, that would leave Sadie on her own again. What if she decided to get back with Connor?

'Antonio, I can't. You're with Sadie.' She wished he wouldn't give her that soulful, baby-seal look.

'No problem.' Antonio raised his hands. 'She's got classes until ten.'

'I couldn't go behind her back,' Mia said firmly.

'OK, fine. You want me to finish with her, is that it?'

'No! I think you should stay together.'

'But I like you better.' Antonio's tone was persuasive. 'Sadie's too old for me.'

Snap. Aloud Mia said, 'I'm only sixteen. You're too old for me.'

'But you're so mature for your age,' Antonio persisted.

And you're so immature for yours, thought Mia.

'My dad's very over-protective. He'd go bananas.' Trapped behind the reception desk, she wondered why the phone couldn't come to her rescue and start ringing. 'Thanks for the offer, but I can't. You should stay with Sadie.'

Antonio looked like a baby seal about to be beaten to death with a club. 'I can't believe you're saying that.'

In all honesty, Mia couldn't either. But the time had come to backtrack furiously. 'You're perfect together. Everyone says so,' she lied.

'You think?'

'Definitely. God, Sadie's an amazing woman. You're lucky to have her.'

Glancing to the left, Antonio blanched and began to sidle away. Mia followed the direction of his gaze and saw that the door to the ladies' cloakroom was open. Sadie was standing there, listening to every word.

'Right,' Antonio said hastily. 'Well, I've got a client waiting upstairs.'

Sadie watched him go, her face rigid. Turning, she eyed Mia stonily and gripped the handles of her bag so tightly her knuckles were white. 'I don't know what you think you're playing at,' she hissed.

Nancy had been fascinated by the sight of a plump, tousle-haired blonde in a pristine pale yellow track suit occupying the exercise bike next to hers. For forty minutes the blonde had sat there without exercising at all. Not a single revolution of the pedals, not a single calorie burned. Instead she had remained engrossed in a copy of *Heat* and munched her way through two Wagon Wheels and a bar of Caramac. Looking up and catching Nancy glancing enviously at the half-eaten bar, she'd generously offered her a piece.

'Go on, have some. Best stuff in the world.'

'I haven't had a Caramac for years,' said Nancy. 'I didn't know they still made them.'

'If they ever stopped making Caramacs, life truly wouldn't be worth living. Bugger.' Having checked her watch, the blonde girl reluctantly closed her magazine and slid down from the unexercised bike. 'Speaking of life not being worth living, it's time for my class.'

Waving goodbye, Nancy watched her head for the aerobics studio. It was seven o'clock which meant the girl was booked into Sadie's advanced class. No wonder she'd been conserving her energy.

Fifteen minutes later Nancy was at the bar ordering a coffee when she heard a strange wheezing sound behind her.

'Oh God, my legs, my *lungs*,' panted the tousle-haired blonde. Grabbing a stool, she attempted to clamber onto it. An unlit cigarette dangled from her lips. 'That was the longest, most completely hideous thirty minutes of my life. Have you got a light?'

There was a box of Lazy B matches on the bar. Nancy struck one and held it to the girl's cigarette. 'Fifteen minutes, actually.'

'Bloody hell. It felt more like fifteen hours.' The girl ordered a large vodka and tonic from the barman and inhaled smoke right down to her toes. 'Never, *ever* again.' Holding out a trembling hand she said, 'I'm Tabitha, by the way.'

'Nancy.' Sympathetically Nancy shook her hand. 'First time?'

'First and last.' Tabitha grimaced. 'My darling boyfriend thought I needed to lose some weight so he bought me a year's membership.'

'Well, at least you can tell him you gave it a go.'

'Actually, we've broken up since then. He was one of those controlling types.' Tabitha took another contented puff of her cigarette. 'But I knew the membership had cost a bomb so I thought I may as well come down here and check the place out. Bought this in Harvey Nichols this morning, specially.' Proudly she indicated the pale yellow track suit. 'I felt quite fit and healthy, just looking at myself in the mirror. But, to be honest, I can't see me getting into this fitness lark at all.'

'You never know.' Nancy's tone was encouraging. 'You might start to enjoy it.'

'I know what I'm like.' Stubbing out her cigarette, Tabitha glugged back her vodka and said, 'I bet I never come back here again. That's how these places make their money, isn't it? From the one-visit-wonders. Oh, I say, who is *that*? Does he work here?'

Tabitha's eyes had lit up. At the far end of the bar, Connor was joking with a crowd of squash-playing regulars.

Nancy's heart swallow-dived. 'That's Connor. He owns the place.'

'Now that's my kind of man,' Tabitha said. 'Is he as nice as he looks?'

No, he's vile. 'Yes,' Nancy reluctantly admitted.

'Single?'

'Yes.'

'Hey, maybe this place isn't so bad after all.' Having finished her drink and been on the verge of leaving, Tabitha now settled herself back onto her stool. 'Do you know him to talk to? Could you introduce me? Shall we just go over and say hello? Oh God, do I look a mess?'

Dutifully surveying her, Nancy felt like one of the ugly sisters watching Cinderella walk off with Prince Charming. Tabitha was looking radiant, pink-cheeked from her recent exertions and glowing with anticipation.

'You look fine.' Nancy forced a smile.

Who knew, Tabitha might turn out to be just what Connor had been waiting for. Maybe she was just his type.

It was Sunday afternoon. Carmen checked the oven where the fish pie was bubbling away under the grill. She'd made it herself, because it was one of Nick's favourite meals: cod and prawns, layered with sliced potatoes, mushrooms, tomatoes and a rich cheese sauce.

As she wiped down the worktops, Carmen heard the front door open and bang shut downstairs, signalling Nick's return from the off-licence. Smiling to herself, she marvelled at the way her life had altered out of all recognition in the last couple of months. Rinsing out the cloth, Carmen turned to greet Nick as he squeezed into the tiny kitchen.

'Valpolicella.' He waved the bottle at her triumphantly. 'I know it's red but it was on special offer. Three ninety-nine.'

'Red's fine,' Carmen assured him, because a special offer was a special offer. And even though he'd been gone for just ten minutes she gave him a hug. 'Dinner's nearly ready.'

Nick's grey eyes crinkled at the corners. 'So, time for a quickie first? Or would you prefer a slow one afterwards?'

'You mean I have to choose? Tuh, you can tell you're not eighteen.'

He raised an eyebrow. 'Is that a challenge?'

'For you, obviously. Oh well, serves me right for getting involved with a man past his prime—oooh!' squealed Carmen as he grabbed her arms and began pulling her out of the kitchen and into the bedroom.

'I should turn off the oven,' Carmen giggled as he tipped her onto the bed and yanked off her navy sweater and jeans.

'Making feeble excuses already? Shame on you.' Stepping out of his trousers, Nick tossed them dramatically to one side like a magician.

'What's that noise?' Carmen tilted her head.

'Oh dear, *more* excuses?' Tut-tutting, Nick shook his head. 'Getting desperate now. Let me guess—burglars have broken in—'

'No, I'm serious.' Sliding out from under him as he made a playful lunge towards her, Carmen said, 'I *can* hear something. Listen.' She pressed a finger to his lips and sat up. 'It's like someone taking a shower.'

Nick listened. 'Hygienic burglars?'

Leaping off the bed, Carmen raced across the bedroom in her bra, knickers and woolly socks.

'If there are burglars in your shower,' he called after her, 'you'll frighten the life out of them.'

'Oh oh *oh*,' shrieked Carmen, skidding to a halt at the entrance to the living room. Water was cascading down from the ceiling, drenching the carpet and furniture.

'Bloody hell,' exclaimed Nick, behind her.

'Stop it!' Carmen waved her arms helplessly at the cracked ceiling. 'How do we make it stop? Oh no, look at the walls! Look at my sofa!'

'Where's the stopcock?' Nick gazed around wildly, moving forward then grimacing as his bare feet sank into the sodden carpet.

Darting into the bathroom, Carmen seized a turquoise bath towel and wrapped it round herself. As she galloped downstairs, the door to her landlord's living room was flung open.

'What the bloody hell have you been doing?' he roared. 'There's water coming through my ceiling!'

Incensed, Carmen shouted back, 'You think there's water coming through *your* ceiling? You should see it coming through *my* ceiling. The tank's burst up in the loft or something. Where's the stopcock?'

Mr Sadler let out the kind of groan that suggested it wasn't the first time this had happened. Carmen recalled the patchy stains on her living-room ceiling—the ones she and Nick had painted over.

'Stopcock. Right,' he sighed, ambling into his flat. Carmen followed him through to the kitchen and watched him turn off the stopcock in the cupboard under the sink.

'What do I do about my living room?' Carmen demanded.

'Go and save what you can.' Straightening up with difficulty, Mr Sadler took his mobile out of his trouser pocket and began punching out a number. 'My brother's a plumber, I'll get him over here right away.'

Carmen said pointedly, 'Is he the one who fixed it last time?'

Mr Sadler grunted and reached back under the sink with his free hand, pulling out a box of household candles. 'Better take some of these. I'll have to turn off the mains if we don't want to be electrocuted.'

Upstairs, Nick wrapped his arms round Carmen. 'We'll get the place fixed up again, don't you worry.'

'Everything's ruined,' Carmen said sadly, as the drips fell steadily from the ceiling.

'It's only water. The carpet will dry out and I managed to save the TV.' Nick's tone was consoling. 'It's in the bedroom.'

'Mr Sadler's brother's on his way round to fix it. Probably with gaffer tape and Uhu.' Carmen pulled a face. 'We're not going to have electricity either. It's going to be pitch black and freezing in here by tea time.'

'Hey, don't worry.' Tenderly smoothing her damp spiky hair, Nick said, 'You can come and stay with me.' He gave the turquoise bath towel a playful tug. 'Better go and get dressed.'

'Bet you're glad you came over.' Carmen smiled ruefully. 'No heat, no light, no sex.'

'We still have homemade fish pie.'

By the time Carmen had finished dressing and had packed a holdall to take to Nick's flat, he had served up their meal and was sitting at the dining table solemnly holding Carmen's purple and white striped umbrella over his head as water continued to drip from the ceiling.

Joining him, Carmen leaned over for a kiss.

'We'll have to share the umbrella,' said Nick. 'Come on, eat up before it gets cold.'

Several minutes later there was a knock at the door.

'Plumber's here,' Mr Sadler bellowed as Carmen pushed back her chair and splashed across the carpet to let them in.

'Right, the hatch leading into the roof is in the living room,' Mr Sadler was telling the plumber. Turning to face Carmen he indicated that she should move out of the way to allow the ladder through. 'All right, love? Water stopped dripping now? My brother couldn't make it—he had tickets for the Arsenal match—so I called a number out of the Yellow Pages. Whoops, mind your back.'

Carmen looked at Joe James, behind him. Joe looked at Carmen, evidently confused. Time either stood still or sped by, she was too shocked to be able to tell which.

'Carmen,' said Joe.

'Well, well, what about that?' Mr Sadler nodded jovially. 'Know each other, do you?' Nudging Joe he added, 'Does that mean I get a discount?'

Carmen felt as if her head were full of the expanding insulating foam that got pumped into wall cavities. She watched Joe haul his stepladder and toolbox into the living room and plonk them down. He stared at Nick, sitting surreally at the table and holding the striped umbrella.

'I'm sorry,' said Joe, 'but I really don't get this. What are you doing in a place like this?'

Numbly Carmen said, 'I just moved in a couple of weeks ago. Joe, could we chat privately for a—'

'Joe?' Nick picked up the name. 'Is this the ex-boyfriend you were telling me about?'

Joe's expression tightened. Defensively he said, 'What have you been telling people?'

'Look, *nothing*,' Carmen pleaded, 'but if we could just have a private word in the kitchen—'

'This doesn't make sense.' Joe shook his head. 'What's happened to Fitzallen Square? Why aren't you there any more?'

Why can't you keep your big blabbering mouth *shut*, Carmen longed to flash back at him.

'Fitzallen Square?' Now it was Nick's turn to look perplexed. 'You didn't tell me about this! You mean you rented a room in one of those mansions? Or were you actually living with some mega-rich bloke?'

He was joking, but Carmen couldn't bring herself to smile.

'Hang on, who are *you*?' demanded Joe.

'I'm Carmen's boyfriend.' Nick remained calm. 'Why? D'you have a problem with that?'

Joe replied with a smirk, 'I reckon you're the one with the problem, mate, if you don't know where Carmen's been living up until now.' He turned to Carmen. 'Did you sell it?'

Carmen said nothing.

'Sell what?' demanded Nick, putting down the umbrella.

'Her house in Fitzallen Square.' Joe was by this time enjoying himself. 'Bloody great wedding cake of a place, five storeys high, pillars outside, the lot.' Returning his attention to Carmen, who was finding it increasingly hard to breathe, Joe said, 'Or have you rented it out to some Arab prince or something? I don't get it, though. Why would you give up a place like that for a dump like this?'

Indignantly Mr Sadler said, 'Excuse *me*.'

'And forget to mention it to your new boyfriend,' Joe continued silkily, his eyes not leaving Carmen's chalk-white face.

The room fell silent, apart from the steady drip of water. Finally Nick said in disbelief, 'You own a house in Fitzallen Square?'

'Yes.' Carmen nodded slowly. 'I do.'

'But how? How *can* you?'

'She's loaded, mate.' Having realised that he'd put the cat well and truly among the pigeons, Joe said triumphantly, 'But she never told you. Funny, that. Probably terrified you might ask her to lend you a fiver.'

'Is that true?' said Nick.

Carmen felt like a cornered animal. 'Of course it isn't true!'

'So why did you never tell me you were loaded?' Nick's expression was stony. 'Because you didn't trust me?'

'No!' Floundering, Carmen babbled, 'I just . . . I just couldn't . . .'

'Fine.' Nick rose abruptly to his feet. 'Thanks for that. Bye.'

The door slammed shut behind him and he was gone.

'You *bastard*,' Carmen yelled at Joe.

'Am I? What, for telling the truth?' Joe shrugged, then broke into a broad, satisfied grin. 'Hey, I've just thought of something. If you'd lent me that twenty grand, I wouldn't still be working for this outfit.' Patting the company logo on his jacket he said, 'And your guilty secret would have been safe, because I wouldn't have been sent round here today.'

He was despicable. And Nick had every right to be upset with her. Carmen raced out of the flat. Outside, it had begun to pour with rain. She caught up with Nick at the end of the street, and tugged hard at the sleeve of his sodden sweater.

'Nick, please, it isn't how it sounds. You have to listen to me.'

JILL MANSELL

'Do I? I think you'll find it's exactly how it sounds.' Nick regarded her grimly, pushing his dripping wet hair back from his face. 'No wonder you've kept so quiet about yourself. Where did the money come from?'

'I was married to Spike Todd.' Carmen's teeth were chattering with cold and fear. 'From Red Lizard,' she elaborated. 'They're a rock band.'

'And you divorced him,' said Nick, clearly none the wiser. 'But the settlement bagged you a house in Fitzallen Square.'

'I didn't divorce him. He died.' Part of Carmen marvelled that Nick genuinely didn't know. The other more shameful part wondered if the fact that she was a tragic young widow might work in her favour and earn her some much needed sympathy.

'When?' Nick wasn't looking remotely sympathetic.

'Three years ago. From a drugs overdose.' Carmen blinked rain from her eyes. 'He was an addict.'

'How much is this house worth? The one in Fitzallen Square.'

He was interrogating her. Carmen knew how important it was to be honest now. 'I don't know. Six million, something like that.'

'Mortgage?'

'No.'

'And how much money d'you have besides that?'

'I suppose . . . about the same again.'

'So this whole thing between you and me—I suppose it's all been some kind of sick joke?'

'No!' Horrified that he could even think that, Carmen took a step towards him but Nick moved smartly out of reach.

'OK, I'll ask you again. Why didn't you tell me?'

'I liked Joe. I trusted him.' Defiantly Carmen said, 'But I was wrong. All he cared about was getting his hands on my money.'

'And you thought I was the same.'

'I *didn't*.' Despairingly, Carmen willed him to understand.

'But you weren't one hundred per cent sure,' said Nick.

'Well . . . I suppose so.' She didn't know how to explain the fear Joe had instilled in her.

'You think I'm a gold-digger.' Nick's fury was chilling.

'No, I don't think that! I was going to tell you,' Carmen pleaded.

'No, you weren't. You rented a flat in Battersea and let me help you decorate it.' His voice rising, Nick said, 'And when you aren't slumming it in a rented hovel in Battersea you live in a Chelsea mansion. You've known me for over a year and you still couldn't trust me enough to tell me the truth. I don't want to see you again,' he said icily, 'and I'm certainly not interested in your big fancy house.'

292

Leicester Square was awash with film fans undeterred by the grim weather. As Rennie and Karis made their way along the red carpet, flash-bulbs popped and microphones were eagerly thrust out. Karis, who had begged Rennie to accompany her to the premiere, was having the time of her life posing for photographs in a hot-pink dress split to reveal skimpy silver knickers. Rennie, accosted by a journalist with a micro-phone, explained that yes, he was taking a few months off, no, he and Karis were just good friends and of course he was looking forward to seeing the film tonight, he wouldn't have missed it for the world.

Oh well, only two of those were lies. Karis was harmless enough but he wouldn't class her as a good friend. And the film was by all accounts a prize turkey. Still, he'd been telling the truth about taking time off.

'Rennie, this way.' Rejoining him, Karis intertwined her fingers with his so they could be photographed together for a gossip magazine.

'Are you two an item?' another journalist asked hopefully.

'Just good friends.' Karis dimpled suggestively as she said it, implying with the aid of less than subtle body language that away from the spot-light they were actually at it like rabbits. Rennie wondered what on earth he was doing, preparing to watch a film he knew he didn't want to see, in the company of a girl he didn't particularly want to be with, being asked inane questions by inane—

'Switch it *off*,' hissed Karis.

Taking out his phone, Rennie answered it more to annoy Karis than for any other reason. The caller number wasn't one he recognised.

'Yes? Who is this?' Rennie ignored Karis's frantic hand signals to end the call *this minute*.

'Right, well, I'm the landlord of the Queen's Head in Arnold Street. In Battersea.' Raising his voice to be heard above the babble of voices, the man said, 'I managed to get your number from a girl called Carmen.'

'And?' Faintly irritated, Rennie wondered what Carmen thought she was playing at, giving out his phone number to complete strangers.

'Rennie, put that bloody thing away.' Karis gave him a pointy-elbowed nudge. 'People are trying to *take our photograph* here.'

'. . . lot to drink. So, um, maybe you should come and get her.'

What?

'Hang on, I missed that.' Batting away Karis's hand, Rennie frowned. 'Are you saying Carmen's there at the pub? Who's she got with her?'

'No one. That's why I'm calling you.'

'And she's been *drinking*?' Carmen had never been much of a drinker. Rennie wondered if this was a wind-up, someone's idea of a huge joke.

'Enough to float a battleship. And buying rounds for everyone in the pub.' The landlord said wryly, 'I must be mad, I suppose, ringing you and asking you to take her away. But I reckon she needs to get home. She's up on the pool table right now, doing her Christina Aguilera impression.' He sighed. 'Again.'

'Carmen would never do that.'

'Hang on. Listen.'

Rennie listened as the landlord angled the phone—presumably—in the direction of the pool table. He heard a voice that was unmistakably Carmen's bellowing out, 'Because I'mmmm *beeeyooo-deefulll* . . .'

Shit.

'Rennie, what are you *playing* at?' Losing patience, Karis grabbed the sleeve of his jacket and tried to drag him forwards.

'I'll be right there,' said Rennie.

'I should bloody well think so,' Karis huffed.

'Thanks, mate,' said the landlord.

Rennie ended the call and said, 'Right, I'm off.'

Karis stared at him. 'You're *what*?'

'Leaving,' Rennie repeated. 'Sorry, it's an emergency. Have to go.'

'But what about me?' squealed Karis, beginning to panic. 'You're my partner! I can't go in and watch the film on my own!'

For a couple of seconds Rennie scanned the crowd of waving, cheering film fans lined up behind the barriers. Spotting a slightly gawky but presentable-looking young lad in his early twenties, he strode across and said cheerfully, 'Hi. Want to see the film?'

Aghast, Karis watched as Rennie, along with a couple of security staff, helped a gangly youth over the barrier and brought him over to where she was standing.

'This is Dave,' said Rennie, indicating that Karis should shake hands with the bespectacled youth. 'He'd love to watch the film with you.'

'But . . . but . . .' Karis was gazing in horror at Dave's navy polyester jacket and perspiring upper lip.

'Sweetheart, you'll have a great time. Dave, take good care of her.' Giving Karis a hasty kiss on the cheek, Rennie said, 'Just think, this could be the start of a truly beautiful friendship.'

'Not between you and me, you rotten bastard,' Karis bellowed after him as he hurried off.

Music was still blaring out as Rennie pushed his way into the Queen's Head in Battersea. Carmen and a dreadlocked Wyclef Jean lookalike were arm in arm on top of the pool table, swaying recklessly as they sang along to 'Cry Me A River'.

Rennie walked over to the pool table. 'Carmen? Time to go home.'

'Cry me a ri-verrr,' Carmen wailed into her microphone.

'Come on, sweetheart. That's enough now.'

'Heyyy! Rennie's here,' shouted Carmen, almost losing her balance.

'See what I mean?' said the pub landlord, materialising at Rennie's side. 'She's just bought another eight bottles of champagne.'

'Don't worry your pretty little head about it.' Carmen wagged her finger at the landlord. 'I've got *loooaaads* of money. Hey, Rennie, come on up here and sing with us, we're doing great!'

All around them, people were knocking back champagne from an assortment of wine glasses, tumblers and pint mugs.

'Carmen. Let's go.' Reaching up, Rennie managed to prise the microphone from her hand and seize her by the wrist. 'Now just climb down onto this chair, good girl, and down again . . . that's it, excellent. OK, let's get out of here, shall we? I've got a car waiting outside.'

'You're no fun,' Carmen grumbled, stumbling against him. 'I only gave the landlord your number so you could come down here and join in. We've been having the best time, you know.' She waved and blew kisses at random. 'See you all again soon . . . missing you already—'

Outside the pub, the cold night air hit Carmen like a brick and feeding her into the waiting car was like trying to fit an eel into a shoebox.

'I say, this is posh . . .'

In his hurry to rescue Carmen, Rennie had been forced to commandeer one of the stretch limos outside the cinema. The driver now turned and gave him a doubtful look.

'Not going to be sick, is she?'

'I'm never sick,' Carmen loftily proclaimed.

'Just take us to Fitzallen Square,' said Rennie.

'Oh, look, all my friends have come out to say goodbye.' Carmen waved pointlessly through the blacked-out windows at the gaggle of regulars who had congregated on the pavement to gawp.

'What happened?' Rennie said bluntly as the limousine pulled away from the kerb.

Carmen wilted, rubbed her hands across her face and slumped back against the seat.

'A pipe burst. The flat got flooded.'

'And?'

Her eyes closed, Carmen said, 'Joe James arrived to fix it.'

'Ah.'

'Nick's gone. It's all over.' She took a deep shuddery breath. '*Again*. I knew he wasn't like Joe, but I carried on anyway and now I've lost him.'

Good, Rennie found himself thinking, and wondered why. Aloud he asked, 'Did you explain why you did it?'

'He wasn't interested. As far as Nick's concerned, I thought he was a gold-digger. He's the most honest, decent person and I didn't *trust* him.'

If he was that honest and decent, thought Rennie, he'd surely understand why Carmen had done what she had.

'Do you want me to speak to him?'

'No point. Oops, head's gone spinny.' Swaying against him, Carmen mumbled, 'He's never even heard of Red Lizard.'

The chauffeur turned into Fitzallen Square and Rennie murmured, 'Never mind. Nearly home now.'

'Thanks for coming to fetch me.' Carmen leaned her head against his shoulder. 'I knew I was getting a bit drunk.'

The limo pulled up outside the house. Rennie paid the driver and helped Carmen out of the back seat.

'Nancy and Rose are out. They're gone to the theatre.'

'I know. The pub landlord tried to ring them earlier, didn't get any reply. That's why I gave him your number.' Carmen looked at Rennie, evidently noticing for the first time that he was wearing a smart suit. 'You weren't doing anything special, were you?'

'Nothing special at all. Come on now, let's get you inside.'

Rennie settled Carmen on the sofa with a duvet and a coffee before going upstairs to change. By the time he headed back to the living room in jeans and an old black T-shirt, he fully expected Carmen to be asleep.

Instead she was clutching the phone, gazing into space.

'I just rang Nick. He wasn't kidding when he said he didn't want to see me again.' Shifting over so that Rennie could sit down, Carmen said, 'He doesn't want me working at the shelter any more.'

'What a tosser.'

'Oh God, what am I going to *do*?'

'Easy. Find someone who deserves you,' Rennie said bluntly. 'Because you can sure as hell do better than him.'

'Right. Silly me for asking.' Carmen raised her slanting dark eyebrows. 'And who exactly do you suggest this time? How about Prince William? He wouldn't let it bother him that I've got a few bob in the bank. Or Hugh Grant, maybe? Or . . . ooh, I know, *Hugh Hefner*.'

Or me.

Rennie didn't say it aloud. He kept this renegade suggestion to himself, firmly packed down somewhere deep inside his chest, in the place he had kept it hidden for the last two months. Since Christmas night, in fact, when he had realised the extent of his feelings towards Carmen.

'Why are you looking at me like that?' Carmen demanded irritably.

'Prince William's too young. Hugh Grant's too st-st-stuttery. Hugh Hefner wears too many dressing gowns.'

'You're so critical.'

'I know you. I know you better than almost anyone else on this planet.' And I love you, Rennie silently added, because it was true.

'Oh God,' groaned Carmen. 'What's going to happen to me?'

'Hey, you'll be fine.'

'Give me a hug.' She turned to him, craving reassurance and comfort.

He put his arms round her and she rested her head against his chest. 'Mmm. You smell nice,' she mumbled.

'Carbolic.' Rennie stroked her spiky hair and wondered what Carmen would do if he kissed her. Not that he could allow himself to do it.

Drowsily Carmen said, 'Want to watch a film?'

'Fine. Any favourites?'

'You choose.'

Easing himself away, Rennie sorted through the pile of DVDs next to the TV. Having selected one, he sat back down and settled Carmen comfortably against him once more before pressing PLAY on the remote.

Carmen, her eyelashes beginning to droop, mumbled, 'I'm quite sleepy now.'

'Go ahead. You can even snore if you like.'

'You're such a gentleman.'

I could be, thought Rennie as her eyelids fluttered shut. If you'd just give me the chance to prove it.

Chapter 10

'MORNING, SWEETHEART. How are you feeling?'

'Ancient.' Nancy pulled a face.

'You're in your prime,' Zac chided, reaching behind the workroom door and producing a lavishly wrapped present. 'Happy birthday!'

'You really shouldn't have,' Nancy lied happily, tearing into the gauze and the lilac embossed paper.

'Classic gay guy trick. Wrap fabulously, it makes up for a crap present.'

'Oops, you made a mistake,' said Nancy. 'You accidentally gave me a good one instead.' She separated the mounds of tissue to reveal a squashy, pyramid-shaped shoulder bag made from soft purply-blue leather striped with pink and green velvet and dotted with multi-coloured twisted leather butterflies. She gave Zac a hug, overwhelmed. 'In fact it's better than good, it's amazing. I don't know why you don't—'

'Stick to bags and give up the clothes?' Zac aimed a playful swipe at her head. 'Cheeky wench. I know how you feel about my collection.'

Yes, but I'm *right*, thought Nancy. Zac's bags were divine with a quirky charm of their own.

'Never mind. I love it. Thank you so much.' She kissed Zac on both cheeks. 'Are you still OK for tonight?'

Rennie had booked a table at the Tipsy Prawn in Mayfair.

'Try and stop me,' said Zac. 'I hear the waiters are out of this world.'

'Eight o'clock. Now, whose turn is it to make the coffee?'

'Yours.'

'But it's my birthday,' Nancy said smugly. 'I'm twenty-nine. Plus I'm too busy admiring my lovely new handbag.'

'I don't know.' Zac scratched his head in despair. 'One of us is the boss here. I just wish I could remember who.'

The Tipsy Prawn, a riot of red and gold decor teamed with saucy waiters and chandeliers the size of dustbin lids, was already packed by eight o'clock. Nancy, greeting everyone as they arrived, wondered just how much of a masochist you had to be to welcome the object of your affections and his new girlfriend along to your own birthday party. Then she felt guilty, because Tabitha was great and she genuinely liked her.

Anyway, she hadn't had much choice tonight. Rennie had invited Connor and Mia, and Mia had been the one to suggest that Connor brought Tabitha along too. Nancy knew that Mia was keen to encourage the budding relationship, both because she liked Tabitha and because it meant Connor wouldn't be tempted to drift back to Cyanide Sadie.

'Oh, let me see that,' Tabitha exclaimed. 'Where did you get that bag?'

'It's one of Zac's.' Nancy gave first Tabitha, then Connor, a kiss. 'You can shower him with praise when he gets here; he'll love that.'

'Now, are we ready to sit down?' Rennie was busy being in charge. 'Mia, you're over there. Carmen, you're next to me. What time's the stripper booked to arrive?'

'I hope you're joking,' said Nancy.

'Never presume, sweetheart. Bloody hell,' Rennie exclaimed, gazing past Nancy in disbelief. 'Who's Zac brought along with him? Don't tell me that's his new boyfriend.'

Nancy turned. The man with Zac was a couple of inches shorter than him and a couple of decades older. Among the trendily dressed diners and baroque decor he stood out as they wove their way between tables, in his white shirt, brown corduroys and polished brogues. His grey hair was neatly swept back from a face that was oddly familiar.

'You know,' said Rennie, mystified, 'Zac has the weirdest taste in men. And my God, what does *he* look like tonight?'

Nancy gave him a nudge because Zac's fine blond hair was tied back in a ponytail and he was wearing a moss-green sweater over a paler green shirt and plain dark trousers. She knew who the older man was.

Clearly ill at ease, Zac approached her and said in a rush, 'Hi, Nance, I tried to reach you earlier but your phone was switched off. This is my father, William Parris. Dad, this is Nancy who works for me.'

'Zac's friend.' William nodded cheerfully, shaking Nancy's hand. 'I've heard all about you. Good to meet you. Many happy returns of the day.'

'Dad turned up unexpectedly this evening,' Zac went on hurriedly. 'Look, I know they won't be able to squeeze in another place, so we'll be off, but Dad just wanted to come and say hello before—'

'No problem.' Rennie indicated the waiter with whom he'd just had a word. 'All sorted, they can fit another chair at the table. William, let me introduce you to everyone. I'm Rennie, this is Carmen and this is Rose.'

'God, I'm sorry,' whispered Zac as William was whisked away to meet the others. 'The doorbell went and there he was. No warning, nothing! He just announced he'd come to stay for a week. I mean, what could I do? And I certainly wasn't planning on bringing him along tonight—'

'It's fine,' Nancy said, because Zac was sounding panicky. And notably un-camp.

'But I'd written it on my kitchen calendar and he spotted it. As soon as Dad realised it was your birthday there was no stopping him—'

'Really, it doesn't matter a bit,' Nancy patiently repeated.

'But it *does*,' Zac blurted out, 'because what if someone *says* anything? You know, about *me* . . .'

'They won't. I'll tell Rennie,' Nancy promised, because this was clearly who Zac was most bothered about.

'And it's not only that.' Zac gazed at her in anguish. 'I . . . er, well, I kind of let him think you're my, um . . .'

'He thinks I'm your girlfriend.' Belatedly realising what he was struggling to tell her, Nancy smothered the urge to laugh.

'I'm sorry. I told you I was a hopeless case.' Zac shook his head apologetically. 'But I'm sure I'd fancy you if I was straight.'

Which was quite flattering in its own way.

'OK, don't panic. We'll get through this. You'd better sit by me. We'll put your dad next to Rose. And don't worry,' Nancy assured him. 'Everything's going to be fine.'

'I only moved down here a few weeks ago myself,' Rose confided to William as their main courses arrived, 'so if you want showing around, I'd be happy to help. But only if you'd like me to,' she added hastily.

William's face softened. 'I'd love a hand with the underground—can't make head nor tail of it. And I've heard all about you too. Zac tells me you're the best knitter he's ever had working for him.'

'Och, you must be very proud of him, doing so marvellously, people from all over the world buying his clothes.'

'I am.' William nodded. 'I mean, I know it's a funny job for a grown man, but Zac always had it in his head to be a designer. And who knows what'll happen now that he and Nancy have got together?'

Not a lot, thought Rose.

'You and I could end up as in-laws,' William went on enthusiastically.

This last pronouncement was greeted with something of a startled silence. Nancy took a big gulp of wine. Everyone was looking at her.

Tabitha leaned across, almost setting fire to Nancy's sleeve with her cigarette. 'I must say, you're a dark horse,' she exclaimed. 'I didn't even realise you and Zac were an item! To be honest, I thought he was—'

'God, sorry, I'm a clumsy oaf,' Connor groaned, having managed to knock his cutlery into Tabitha's lap.

'I hope I'm not going to be making things awkward for the two of you.' William turned to Nancy, concerned. 'I won't be in the way, will I?'

'Absolutely not.' Shaking her head vigorously, Nancy realised she was going to have to have a private word with Tabitha. 'We're taking things very slowly; you won't be in the way at all. Um, Tab, you couldn't come out to the ladies with me, could you? I need to borrow some mascara.'

As Tabitha and Nancy left the table, William leaned sideways and whispered to Rose, 'I've been waiting so long for something like this to happen. Zac's never shown any sign of getting settled down before.'

Oh dear, thought Rose. Someone was going to have to tell him. It wasn't right that William didn't know.

'Sorry about earlier,' Tabitha murmured in Zac's ear. 'Nancy told me in the loo. I spend my life putting my big feet in it. Now listen, this bag of hers is fantastic. Can I ask how much it retails for?'

'Three fifty.' Zac didn't betray his surprise that someone who was got up like Tabitha should be interested in a bag that cost that much. Women and bags were an unfathomable law unto themselves.

'Is that your best price?' Tabitha was gazing longingly at Nancy's bag.

'You drive a hard bargain.' Zac smiled. 'OK, three hundred.'

'Any colour I like?'

'Any colour you like.'

'Waiting time?'

'Two weeks,' said Zac.

'Excellent. My boss is going to love this.'

That explained it. The bag wasn't for Tabitha at all. To show how generous and broad-minded he was, Zac said untruthfully, 'I like your top.'

Tabitha was wearing a sleeveless pink-and-white striped rollneck sweater with sparkly bits in it. 'Vintage. This came from Marks and Spencer twenty-five years ago. You'd never know it, would you?'

'Never,' Zac solemnly agreed. What had Nancy told him Tabitha did for a living? Financial journalist, that was it. That explained a lot.

Carmen was touched that Mia should be so indignant on her behalf.

'Forget him,' Mia declared between mouthfuls of asparagus. 'You're way better off without someone like that.' Putting down her knife and fork, she swished back her hair. 'Next time you meet a man you like, you could just say, now look here, the thing is I'm really rather rich but because I've been mucked about in the past you have to understand that you won't be getting your sweaty paws on a single penny of my money.'

Sweaty paws. Attractive.

'Right.' Carmen nodded solemnly. 'Is that what you'd do?'

'Maybe, I'm not sure. Depends on the man.' Mia was entirely serious. 'Or have you ever thought of getting rid of all that money? Give it away to charity! Then you'd be poor again and your problems would be over!'

'That's the worst idea I've ever heard.' Carmen shook her head, struggling to keep a straight face because Mia was so young, so idealistic. 'One, I give plenty of money to charity. Two, Spike earned that money, he worked his socks off for it. And three, I don't want to be poor again.'

'Oh, well, it was a long shot.' Mia shrugged.

'Any other ideas?'

'Find someone rich.'

Great. Back to Hugh Hefner.

'Rennie already had that idea,' said Carmen.

'Did he?' Mia speared a cherry tomato with her fork. 'Interesting.'

'Why is that interesting?'

JILL MANSELL

'Well, Rennie's rich.'

Carmen choked on her drink. Spluttering and feeling hot, she said, 'Rennie's my brother-in-law.'

'So? It's not illegal. Think about it. If you like one brother enough to marry him, why wouldn't you like the other?'

Carmen took a gulp of wine. 'I do like Rennie. As a friend. But he isn't like Spike.'

'OK. But he's still rich.' Mia was implacable. 'And I know he's almost old enough to be my father, but he's extra good-looking and even I can see he's a catch.'

Carmen couldn't quite believe they were having this conversation. 'It's not going to happen,' she repeated. 'He really isn't my type.'

Mia said interestedly, 'Have you ever slept with him?'

'No!' Carmen gazed around wildly, wondering if anyone would notice if she gagged Mia with a napkin.

'Fine, calm down, only asking.' Carrying on unperturbed, Mia said, 'Ever wondered what it'd be like?'

'Of course I haven't!' lied Carmen, beginning to panic.

'No need to go red. It's only natural to *wonder* things. I mean, Rennie's got millions of fans. They'd give anything to sleep with him—'

'And plenty of them have,' Carmen said bluntly, 'which could explain why the idea doesn't interest me.'

'Really? Gosh, now that *is* interesting.' Completely seriously Mia said, 'So who would you go for then, if you could choose? Cliff Richard?'

When dinner was over, everyone retreated to the bar downstairs to collapse into red velvet sofas. Having checked that Tabitha was happily occupied chatting to Mia and Nancy, Connor joined Rennie at the bar.

'Great evening,' said Connor, offering him a Marlboro and accepting a balloon glass of cognac. 'Thanks.'

'My pleasure.' Rennie nodded over at Tabitha, with her tousled blonde hair and merry face. 'So is this it, then? Could she be the one?'

'No,' said Connor.

'No? Really? I thought the two of you got on well.'

'We do. But she still isn't the one.' Shaking his head, Connor lit a cigarette and exhaled a plume of smoke. 'OK, you want the truth?' he continued. 'I've developed a system. It's called self-preservation. You see, Mia's desperate to see me settled down.' He pulled a face. 'And you know what my daughter's like when she gets an idea into her head. So I never let on when I really like someone, otherwise Mia just charges in like a rhino. The best thing to do is head her off at the pass, just state

302

categorically that whoever it is does nothing for me.'

Rennie grinned, only too easily able to imagine Mia in unstoppable matchmaking mode. 'She's a handful.'

'You're not kidding.' Connor stubbed out his cigarette. 'There's no way she's going to interfere with my love life. She encouraged me to go out with Tabitha and I'm going along with that to keep her happy, but there's no future in it. If I really like someone, the last thing I'm going to do is let Mia get wind of—oh, hi!'

'Hi,' said Nancy, breathing fast as Connor spun round to face her. 'Sorry, I didn't mean to—'

'Pinch your bum?' said Rennie cheerfully. 'Nance, you have to stop doing that. It's harassment.'

'Interrupt.' Flustered, Nancy attempted to make sense of what she'd just overheard. If it meant what she thought it meant . . .

'Hey, no problem, Nancy can pinch my bum any time she likes.' Connor grinned.

'I didn't actually pinch anybody's bum,' said Nancy. 'I only came over to let you know Mia doesn't want ice in her Coke.'

Connor sighed. 'And there was me thinking I was irresistible.'

Nancy gazed at him, wondering why he always had to make it so hard to tell whether or not he was joking. Oh God, so did this mean his assertion to Mia that he didn't find her remotely attractive *hadn't* been true? Could he actually—

'Of course he's irresistible.' Appearing at Nancy's side, Tabitha gave her a cheery nudge. 'Didn't I tell you that the first moment I clapped eyes on him? I said, that'll do for me!'

'Flattery'll get you everywhere.' Connor slid his arm round her waist.

'Ten out of ten, I awarded you. Of course, you've gone down to eight now.' Beaming up at him, Tabitha said, 'I've never known anyone take so long to order a round of drinks.'

'Ah, well, there are some things you shouldn't hurry.' Connor's eyes crinkled at the corners. 'Take as long as possible, that's what I say, and make sure you get it right.'

Nick looked up as Rennie appeared in the kitchen doorway. 'Hi. Can I help you?'

Friendly and without a flicker of recognition.

'I'm Rennie Todd,' said Rennie, causing the thin redhead currently washing up at the sink to whip round and stare at him, open-mouthed.

Nick's expression changed, grew less friendly. 'Carmen's brother-in-law. The big rock star.'

'Oh God, you're Rennie Todd,' gasped the redhead. 'From Red Lizard.'

'I am,' Rennie agreed.

'Pat, just get on with the washing-up.' Nick's tone was curt. 'We're going through to the office and we don't want to be disturbed.'

Once they were inside the office, Rennie said, 'This won't take long.'

Nick scowled. 'It certainly won't if you've come here to try to persuade me to change my mind. I suppose Carmen sent you, she's—'

'Yes, she sent me. And no, I haven't come here to try to change your mind. Far from it,' Rennie went on evenly. 'Carmen asked me to come here because she has something for Harry. Carmen said he usually comes in around now for his lunch. Is he here?'

'Yes. What has she got for him?'

Ignoring the question, Rennie said, 'I'll go and have a word with him.'

'I'll come with you, point him out.'

'No need.' Rennie remembered what Harry looked like. 'I can manage.'

Harry was sitting at the far end of the room, away from the blaring television. As before, he was buried in a book. When Rennie sat down beside him, he glanced up and—unlike Nick—recognised him. 'Hello.'

'Hi. Rennie Todd. I'm a friend of Carmen's. There's something she'd like you to have.' Rennie took a labelled key from the pocket of his leather jacket. 'She took a six-month lease on a flat in Battersea, but she won't be using it now. It's yours if you want it.'

Harry's hand began to tremble as he took the key. 'Why me?'

'Carmen thought you'd appreciate the peace and quiet. There's a word processor in the flat,' said Rennie, 'in case you feel like making a start on another book. You never know, things might turn out differently this time. No pressures. It's a decent little place. Furnished. Had a burst pipe recently, but everything's been dried out and redecorated.'

There were tears in Harry's eyes. Aware that he and Rennie were being watched by everyone else in the room, he wiped his face with his sleeve.

'Tell her thank you. You don't know what this means to me.' Harry shook his hand. 'This is incredible.'

'No problem. Look, I'm going to go now.' Before he attracted too much more attention, Rennie rose to his feet. 'Good luck with the writing.'

Nancy gazed in open disbelief at the newspaper's fashion section. 'That's my . . . that's *my* bag.'

It was her bag, there was no doubt about it. Under the heading MUST-HAVE BAG OF THE SEASON was a photograph of her very own bag. '"Zac Parris, London's best-kept secret."' Nancy read aloud: '"This fabulous custom-made bag sells for £299 and you get to choose your own colours. Just call 0207 blah blah or visit the website . . ." '

'This is fantastic.' Zac was delighted. 'How did it happen?'

'I don't know, but this is the paper Tabitha works for.' Nancy took out her mobile, into which Tabitha's number was programmed.

Zac frowned. 'I thought you said she was a financial journalist?'

'I did. But Tabitha was the one who took that photo of my bag. When we were doing our make-up in the loos at the Tipsy Prawn, she pulled out a digital camera and . . . hi, it's me.'

'Hi, you.' Tabitha sounded as if she was grinning from ear to ear. 'I wondered how long it would take to hear from you this morning.'

'So it *was* you. You told the fashion editor at your paper about Zac's bag.'

'OK. Guilty confession time,' said Tabitha. 'I'm the fashion editor.'

Nancy inwardly digested this information. It was like Princess Anne admitting that she'd whipped off her kit and posed for *Playboy*.

The silence lengthened. Finally Tabitha said gaily, 'Poor you, plunged into shock. I know. Hardly the usual kind, am I? The thing is, you don't have to be a great artist to appreciate great art. And just because I don't choose to dress like a fashion victim doesn't mean I can't put together decent outfits for other people and write convincingly about next season's pin-striped bikinis.'

Dumbstruck, Nancy said, 'But . . . but you said you were a financial journalist.'

'Well, wouldn't you? As soon as anyone finds out what I really do, they think I'm a complete airhead,' Tabitha protested, 'but I'm really not. I've got a first-class degree in economics. I always wanted to work in financial journalism, but the paper offered me a start in this department and I just, well, kind of got stuck here.'

'Right,' Nancy said faintly. She looked down at the fashion editor's by-line. 'Who's Kate Harris?'

Except, of course, it was all coming back to her now. Tabitha's surname was Harris.

'Kate's my middle name. Look, I'm sorry I fibbed to you, but I was desperate to impress Connor. Fashion editors can be downright weird and I didn't want to put him off.'

Doing her best to sound concerned rather than hopeful, Nancy said, 'Do you think it would?'

'Oh, he knows now. I told him last night,' Tabitha rattled on happily. 'He's absolutely fine about it. Thank God!'

'Well, um . . . good.' Nancy tried hard to quash the twinge of disappointment. She said hurriedly, 'What made you choose Zac's bag?'

'It's a great bag! Everyone in the office loves it! Besides, it's my way of thanking you for introducing me to Connor. You did me a *huge* favour! I thought it would be nice to do one in return.' Cheerfully she went on, 'After this, Zac's bound to give you a bonus!'

The phone on the desk began to ring. Zac, snatching it up, said, 'Hello, Zac Parris. Yes, it is. Oh, right. Great!' Waggling his eyebrows excitedly at Nancy, he listened some more and said, '*How* many? Hang on, let me just grab a pen . . .'

Rose felt like an old hand, showing Zac's father the sights of London. Having hopped off the bus at Trafalgar Square, she and William made their way down to the Thames and began walking across the Hungerford Bridge. On the other side of the river, the Millennium Wheel glinted in the sunshine. William's face fell when he saw it.

'What rotten luck. Not working.'

Rose, who had thought the same thing the first time she'd caught sight of the wheel, felt wonderfully superior. 'It is. Look, it's just moving really slowly. You expected to see it whizz round, didn't you?'

'I'm just an innocent country bumpkin.' William's eyes fanned into creases at the corners. 'I'll never be a smart city slicker like you.'

Rose experienced a warm glow in her stomach, not because of the compliment but because it was so nice to be in the company of such a gently humorous, genuinely nice man.

'More often than not, smart city slicker types don't have any manners. You have lovely manners,' said Rose. 'And you grow all your own vegetables. How many city slickers can say they do that?'

'How many city slickers can knit?' countered William.

'Heaven forbid.' Rose smiled.

'And how many have ever sneaked out of their fancy offices in the middle of the day to ride the Millennium Wheel?' said William. 'With homemade ham and pickle sandwiches and a Thermos of tea?'

'Probably none,' Rose agreed.

Linking his arm companionably through Rose's, William said with satisfaction, 'Country bumpkins win over city slickers every time.'

Rennie had a plan and it was about to be put into action. He'd waited long enough; now he had made up his mind to act. Rose had gone out for the evening with William. Thanks to the recent surge in demand for Zac's handbags, Nancy was working overtime at the shop and wasn't expecting to be home before midnight. The timing couldn't be more perfect. Carmen was upstairs in the bath. Any minute now she'd come down and be hugely impressed to find him preparing dinner.

Well, taking the just-delivered pizzas out of their boxes. And opening a decent bottle of wine.

Hearing the creak of her footsteps on the stairs, Rennie felt his throat constrict and his heart begin to quicken. Ridiculous; he'd never been nervous at the prospect of declaring how he felt about a woman to her face. Except, come to think of it, women had always made their own feelings so clear, it hadn't been necessary. But what if Carmen didn't feel the same way? What if she turned him down flat, or burst out laughing?

'My God, this can't be happening.' Having padded barefoot into the kitchen, Carmen stopped dead in her tracks. 'What are you trying to do, give me a heart attack?'

She was right. It was without doubt a startling sight. Out of sheer blind panic, Rennie had grabbed a cloth and a bottle of spray kitchen cleaner and was frenziedly scrubbing the worktop.

'I was just . . . um, cleaning up.'

Carmen narrowed her eyes suspiciously. 'Why? What did you spill?'

'Nothing! Just crumbs. All done now. Right.' Pulling himself together—Jesus, how could one small female with wet spiky hair terrify him more than a stadium packed with screaming fans?—Rennie said, 'Take the wine through to the living room. I'll bring the pizzas.'

'Stop!' shouted Carmen as he reached for the plates.

Rennie froze. 'What?'

'Kitchen spray, you idiot! You have to wash your hands after using that stuff or the pizza will taste of bleach. And probably poison us.' Tut-tutting, Carmen said, 'Honestly, you are *such* a hopeless case.'

Which, Rennie felt as she disappeared with the wine and he washed his hands, wasn't the most promising of starts.

Carmen's choice of TV viewing didn't improve matters. You couldn't call *EastEnders* conducive to seduction, and tonight's episode was an extra angst-ridden one.

'Hit him!' Carmen bellowed at the screen. 'Go on, wallop him!'

Rennie looked at her, stretched across the sofa with her legs resting on his lap. Five feet two inches tall, luminous dark eyes, expressive eyebrows and a complexion like Snow White. Dammit, she looked sexy. Even if she was currently yelling at the TV like a deranged wrestling fan.

At long last the end credits rolled and Rennie shifted Carmen's legs off his lap. 'OK, film next. I've got a great—'

'Oh no you don't.' Carmen grabbed his arm as he made to get up. 'You chose *Brigadoon* the other night, remember? Tonight I get to choose.'

Rennie's heart sank; he'd lined up *Brief Encounter* specially for tonight.

An all-time classic. All that erotically charged suppressed emotion—what could be more conducive to his cause?

'Ta-daaa.' Having rolled onto her side and groped under the sofa, Carmen resurfaced with a DVD in her hand and a look of triumph on her face. 'Mia lent it to me. I haven't seen it for years. We can join in all the songs, do the dances—now you can't say this isn't a brilliant choice!'

Bloody can, thought Rennie, because *The Rocky Horror Show* might be a cult classic but it wasn't what you'd call romantic.

Then again, a fight now wasn't likely to help.

'Wouldn't you prefer to watch *Brief Encounter*?' He gave it one last desperate shot.

'Hmm, let me think,' said Carmen, clambering off the sofa and heading happily over to the DVD player. 'Does everyone do the Timewarp in *Brief Encounter*? Do the men wear stockings and suspenders? Does *Brief Encounter* have Meatloaf on a motorbike in it? Excuse me, but I don't believe it does. So how about . . . *no*?'

Having completely geared himself up to the fact that Tonight would be The Night, Rennie was now feeling like a pressure cooker left on an increasingly high heat. How could everything be going so wrong?

Back in position on the sofa with her legs draped comfortably over Rennie's and her plate of pizza resting in her lap, Carmen jiggled her feet, wiggled her toes and sang raucously along while Rennie counted down the minutes to the end of the film. Since Rose was expected home at eleven, and he'd prefer to say what he had to say to Carmen without an audience, this meant he had a window of opportunity of an hour at most in which to say it.

'See? Didn't I tell you it was great?' Carmen demanded when the film ended. Reaching for her glass of wine, she spilt a bit on Rennie's denim-clad thigh. 'Whoops, sorry. Lucky it's only white. There now, you can't tell me you didn't enjoy that.'

Only Carmen could mean the film and not the fact that she was rubbing at the damp patch on his jeans with a tissue. Rennie heaved a sigh.

'What's the matter?' Carmen tilted her head to one side.

'It's too late now. It might have been . . . oh God.'

'*What?*' Carmen was by this time thoroughly confused.

He had to do it now, had to.

'OK, there's something I need to say to you. About how I . . . um, the way things have . . . well, it's just that . . .'

'Rennie, you're making no sense.'

Rennie closed his eyes. He was making no sense and time was running out. Terrific.

Actually, keeping his eyes closed was helping a bit.

'Right. The thing is, we've always got on really well. I've always liked you. But things have changed now. Since I've been back . . .'

'You don't like me any more?'

'No, it's not that.' Rennie shook his head.

'Your eyes are shut.' Carmen sounded worried. 'Open them.'

'I can't.'

'Rennie, you're scaring me. Tell me what's wrong.'

Rennie took a deep breath, wondering if she could hear his heart thudding against his chest. 'I love you.'

Silence.

Followed by more silence.

'Say something, for God's sake,' Rennie murmured when he could stand it no longer.

'I can't.' Carmen's voice was strained and distant.

When he finally opened his eyes, he saw that she was shaking her head. 'Sorry,' said Rennie. 'Bit of a shock.'

'You don't love me.'

'I do. Oh, I do. I've known it for weeks. Maybe long before that,' he admitted, 'but I never really allowed myself to think it because you weren't over Spike. You were so off-limits, it wasn't an option. But you're over him now, and I realised what was happening when you started seeing Joe. I hated it. I was so bloody jealous. Then when that ended and you got together with Nick, I was even more jealous.' Rennie was astonished to discover that now he'd started, he couldn't stop; the words were tumbling out. 'Because I knew you deserved so much better than him, and I wanted you to realise I was right, and—'

'You thought you were better than Nick? That I deserved *you*?' Carmen began to tremble. 'Rennie, don't you see? You're not better. You're a hundred times worse!'

Stung, Rennie said, 'How can I be worse? We know everything about each other. The money thing isn't an issue. I make you laugh. You can't tell me I'm not better-looking than that scruffy human scarecrow.'

'Like you just said, we know everything about each other. I know everything about *you*.' Carmen's dark eyes glistened as she met his gaze. 'And, yes, of course you're good-looking and funny and successful and rich, but you're also the last person any sane woman would risk getting involved with. All you do is sleep with them and leave them.'

'But that's because I didn't love them.' Rennie shook his head, willing her to believe him. 'I wouldn't do that to you because I *do* love you.'

A single tear slid down Carmen's cheek. 'Rennie, you *think* you

309

wouldn't do it, but you would. Sooner or later it would happen.'

'It wouldn't because I've changed,' Rennie insisted. 'How often do I go out now? Hardly ever, because I'm just not interested. Girls ring me and I don't return their calls. I get invited to clubs and I don't go. I stay here instead because I'd rather be with you.'

'People don't change just like that.' Miserably Carmen shook her head. 'You can't just wave a magic wand.'

For the first time, Rennie glimpsed a chink of light. All he had to do was persuade her that he could change his old ways.

'Warren Beatty led a pretty colourful life.' He nodded at Carmen. 'Then he married and had kids.'

'Oh, please. That's *one* person.'

'Paul McCartney. Look how he changed after meeting Linda.'

'Fine.' Carmen raised her eyebrows. 'Any more?'

'Um . . .' Damn, he couldn't think of any more.

'Oh dear,' Carmen sighed. 'Just those two then. I think that says it all, don't you?'

'Rennie Todd,' Rennie blurted out, daring at last to stroke her face.

'Stop it.' She turned her head away.

'I love you,' he repeated more bravely.

'We can't do this,' Carmen mumbled.

'Does that mean you'd like to?'

'It means we're not going to.'

'But you don't hate me?'

'Of course I don't hate you.'

Well, this was progress. She didn't hate him and she hadn't slapped his hand away from her face. Gaining in confidence Rennie said, 'So you like me a little bit?'

Carmen was quivering. 'This isn't fair. How much I like you doesn't come into it. It's still not going to happen.'

Rennie's other hand moved to the back of her head, his fingers trailing through her just-washed hair. She smelt gorgeous. He felt as elated as if he'd just climbed Mount Everest.

'*It* isn't going to happen,' he said, 'if that's what's scaring you. I've told you how I feel about you, and that's enough for now. This isn't about sex, believe me. We have the rest of our lives for all that. No hurry, no hurry at all. I can wait. You're in charge. The rest is up to you.'

Carmen lifted her head, gazed at him. In a voice barely above a whisper she said, 'What would Spike think?'

The nerves had lessened. Baby steps, baby steps. His mouth mere inches from hers, Rennie said, 'He'd think I was a damn sight better bet than those last two losers you got yourself involved with.'

'Oh God, I don't know.' Shaking her head, Carmen said, 'At the restaurant the other night, Mia asked me if I'd ever considered you.'

'For a flaky sixteen-year-old, that girl talks a lot of sense.' Rennie paused. 'And have you?'

No reply. Which was, of course, exactly the reply he wanted to hear.

'Right.' Breathing in the smell of her shampoo, Rennie inwardly marvelled at his self-control. 'We're stopping now. You can relax, I'm not planning to seduce you, OK? I'm not even going to try to kiss you.'

A spark of disappointment flickered in Carmen's eyes. Defiantly she said, 'Well, good.'

Rennie waited, idly stroking the side of her neck. 'Unless you want me to.'

Another spark, this time of relief.

'Why would I?' Carmen's tone was challenging with an undertone—a very faint undertone—of flirtatiousness.

'Well, it might be the sensible thing to do. Just to make sure we're compatible.'

Carmen nodded thoughtfully. 'That does make sense. You might not know how to do it properly.'

'Exactly. Could have been doing it wrong all these years. Better find out.' Rennie's green eyes glittered with amusement. 'Tell me if I have.'

Carmen closed the gap between them, her mouth seeking his. For the first time in his life Rennie experienced the sheer pleasure of a kiss in its own right, rather than as a prelude to sex. A warm, exhilarating sensation like electricity flooded his body.

So this was what he'd been missing out on all these years. This was what kissing was *for*. Then again, this was his chance to impress Carmen and he mustn't, *mustn't* blow it.

'Right.' Having made the effort to pull away, Rennie was delighted to see the look of disappointment on her face. 'Coffee? Or more wine?'

'Um . . . coffee, thanks.'

Heading for the kitchen, Rennie paused in the doorway. 'By the way,' he said lightly. 'How was I?'

Carmen smiled over at him. 'So-so.'

'Fine. More practice, that's what I need.' Rennie felt ridiculously happy at the prospect. 'Don't worry, I'll get the hang of it in the end.'

As he waited for the kettle to boil, Rennie thought his heart would burst. Carmen was in the living room wanting him to kiss her again. And he wasn't going to. If it killed him, he was going to prove to her that he could wait. Seconds later the kettle clicked off and the doorbell rang simultaneously. Clutching a jar of coffee, Rennie went to answer the doorbell. He found himself staring at a bespectacled tabloid journalist whom he vaguely recognised, having seen him before at various music awards ceremonies.

'Rennie, hi, how are you?' the journalist said. 'Eric Carson, remember?'

'What's this about, Eric? I'm busy.'

'Of course you are.' Eric glanced at the jar of coffee. 'And I won't hold you up, I promise.' Behind his spectacles his eyes gleamed. 'I just wondered how you're feeling about the news that you're about to be a father.'

Feeling sick, Rennie said, 'Who says so?'

'Biba Keyes.' Eric licked his lips. 'Remember her?'

Biba Keyes. Oh yes, he remembered. New York, last summer. Biba had appeared backstage after a concert. With her waist-length blonde hair, flawless figure and saucy sense of humour, he hadn't needed much persuasion. She had done a bit of Page 3 modelling, Rennie subsequently discovered; a spot of acting and a lot of turning up wherever the paparazzi were most likely to be, dressed in improbably skimpy outfits. They'd spent a weekend together.

'How pregnant is she?' Rennie forced himself to breathe slowly.

'Eight months.'

New York. Count back . . . Fuck.

'You'd think she might have mentioned it before now.'

Eric shrugged. 'According to Biba, she's tried. Phoned you, left messages and texts, but you never bothered to reply.'

Rennie's blood ran cold. Was this true? Sometimes he deleted texts and voicemail messages without reading them if they were from girls he had no interest in seeing again.

'So might we be hearing wedding bells in the near future?' Eric's tone was deliberately provocative.

'No comment.' Rennie made a move to close the front door.

'She's calling you the love of her life,' Eric shouted as the door slammed shut.

Wrong, thought Rennie. The love of his life was sitting twenty feet away, wondering what was keeping him out here. And he suspected she wasn't going to take it well when she found out.

Carmen didn't cry or yell or throw heavy objects at Rennie. What would be the point? He was Rennie Todd, always had been. It was a wonder this hadn't happened before. If anything, she should be glad it *had* happened, serving as a salutary reminder of how Rennie led his life.

'She means nothing to me!' Rennie was raking his fingers through his hair, scarcely able to believe this was happening. 'The baby might not even be mine!'

'But you slept with her,' Carmen said wearily.

'Well, yes, but—'

'What about safe sex? Didn't it even occur to you that something like this could happen?'

'Of course it did. We used condoms. It can't be my child, she's just—'

'Rennie, this girl is pregnant and she says it's yours.'

'But it doesn't have to change things between *us*,' he pleaded.

'It does.' Carmen couldn't look at him. 'It already has. You sleep with girls like other people eat biscuits, just because they're there.'

'But that was eight months ago.' Rennie's voice rose. 'I wouldn't do it now! *I love you.*'

'Sorry.' As she shook her head, Carmen heard a key turn in the front door. 'It would never work, Rennie. I was stupid to even think it might.'

'Coooeee,' Rose called out, signalling her return home and appearing moments later in the living-room doorway. Her eyes bright, she beamed at them. 'Had a lovely evening. You two?'

Carmen rose to her feet. 'You can tell her,' she said to Rennie. 'I'm going to bed.'

The double-page spread in the newspaper that had broken the story featured three photographs of Biba Keyes. The first was a reprint of an old page 3 photo, the second a casual snap of her and Rennie carousing at the party they had attended in New York on the night they met. The third and largest was a demurely posed portrait of Biba, eight months pregnant and gazing with wistful eyes into the lens of the camera.

Rennie had already left the house for an emergency meeting with his manager and agent. Carmen, who had barely slept, wondered if this was Spike's way of letting her know how stupid she'd been to even contemplate getting involved with someone as wildly unsuitable as his brother.

Nancy put a cup of tea on the kitchen table in front of her and gave her shoulder a squeeze. 'I've got to get to work. Will you be OK?'

'Oh, I'll live. *Again.* Third time unlucky and all that.' Having swallowed a mouthful of tea, Carmen said drily. 'I'm really getting the hang of it now.'

'And I'm not far behind you. Catching up fast.' Nancy pulled a face. 'Fine pair we are.'

Carmen managed a smile. 'Go to work. I'll be fine.'

Nancy gazed one last time at the photograph of Biba in her white Lycra top and hip-hugging pink jeans, displaying her distended belly with pride. 'It might not be Rennie's baby. We've only got her word for it.'

'It doesn't matter whether it is or not,' said Carmen. 'It's been a wake-up call for me. I must have been mad to even consider we could be happy together."

Chapter 11

DOREEN WAS IN THE MIDDLE of a dream. Mia hoped it was a happy one. She had been taking the little dog for a walk every day because Zac and Nancy were still rushed off their feet with the shop. Joining William on the sofa in the living room, she watched Doreen's paws twitch and her eyelids flicker, for all the world as if she was chasing rabbits.

William, careful not to disturb Doreen, sat comfortably beside Mia while he ate a bacon sandwich. Mia, watching him, thought how nice he was.

'You and Rose seem to be getting along well.'

'We are,' William agreed. 'Well, who wouldn't get on with a lady like that? What you see is what you get with Rose.'

Mia nodded. This was true, more or less. Apart from the fact that Rose knew something he didn't know. Quite a big something actually.

The beginnings of an idea began to unfurl inside Mia's head. It was so unfair that Nancy and Zac should have to pretend to be a couple purely for William's benefit. In fact, more than that, it was ridiculous.

Taking a sip of her drink, she said, 'Can I ask you a question?'

William shrugged and swallowed a mouthful of sandwich. 'So long as it isn't about quantum physics.'

'Do you think my dad seems like a kind of . . . forgiving person?'

'Forgiving? In what way?'

'OK,' said Mia. 'There's something I really should tell him, but I can't because I'm scared he'll hate me for it.'

William, watching Doreen's ears twitch, said easily, 'I can't believe that. Fathers don't think that way.' He tilted his head to one side. 'It's hard for me to judge if I don't know what it is that's worrying you.'

'OK.' Taking a deep breath, Mia said, 'I'm gay.'

William gazed steadily at her. Doreen opened one eye then closed it again as he stroked her head.

Finally he said, 'Well, that's not so terrible, is it? I've only met Connor a couple of times but I can't imagine he'd refuse to speak to you again. You're his daughter. He loves you. He just wants you to be happy.'

Mia took another swig from her glass. 'You think?'

'Definitely,' said William.

'Oh. Good. Well, thanks.'

'Don't mention it, love.'

'Actually, I was lying,' said Mia. 'I'm not gay.'

William looked at her. 'Why did you say it, then?'

'Because Zac is.'

William said nothing. He carried on stroking Doreen's head. Then he exhaled slowly, stirring the hairs on her silky ears.

'But you already knew that,' Mia said finally. 'Didn't you?'

'I didn't.' Shaking his head, William said, 'But I suspected he was. He never dropped any hints. It wasn't something that ever came up in conversation. We just aren't that kind of family. How could I ever ask Zac if he was gay? What if he wasn't? He'd never have forgiven me.' He frowned slightly. 'Does Nancy know?'

'Everyone knows,' said Mia.

'So there's nothing going on between them?'

'Nothing. It was all for show. To be honest, I had high hopes for Nancy and my dad, but she isn't his type. I've done my best.'

'Rose did mention that you were a bit of a meddler.'

'I don't meddle. I just try and help out.'

'Was Zac really afraid to tell me because he thought I'd hate him?'

'I don't know. But that's why people generally hide that kind of thing from their parents, isn't it? I just think it's better to get it out in the open,' Mia said simply. 'Then everyone can relax.'

'You what?' Dazed, Zac stared at Nancy.

'Your dad knows you're gay. He'd pretty much guessed anyway.'

'H-how does he know?'

'Mia told him. It's all right,' said Nancy. 'You don't have to worry.'

Anxiously Zac said, 'Are you sure Dad's OK?'

'Why don't you go and see for yourself? He's in the sitting room.'

Bracing himself, Zac went to meet his father. As he entered the sitting room, Doreen leapt down from William's lap and launched herself joyfully at Zac. Picking her up and cuddling her, Zac wordlessly met his father's gaze.

'It's fine, son. You don't have to say anything.' Rising to his feet, William made his way across the room to Zac.

'Dad, I'm sorry.'

'Nothing to apologise for.' Slightly awkwardly—they'd never been a demonstrative family—William rested his roughened hand on Zac's shoulder. 'I'm as proud of you today as I was the day you were born. No one could have asked for a better son.'

Zac's eyes filled with tears as the weight of keeping his secret all these years fell away. 'I've had a good dad.'

Evidently terrified that Zac might be about to hug him, William gave his shoulder a series of jerky pats, while Doreen licked Zac's face.

'Come on then, son. It's been quite a day. Let's go through to the kitchen, shall we? I reckon we could both do with a drink.'

Rennie stood in the kitchen and silently re-read the copy of the press release faxed through by his agent.

Biba Keyes had been rushed to hospital last night in excruciating pain and had undergone an emergency Caesarean. The baby, born five weeks prematurely, was a healthy boy—name yet to be announced. Biba was currently exhausted and recovering from the trauma of surgery, but delighted by the safe arrival of her beautiful son.

A boy.

Biba had a son.

Did *he*?

'All right, pet? You've gone pale.' Rose, busy making a plum crumble, looked anxious. 'Bad news?'

How could the birth of a child be bad news? His emotions scarily mixed, Rennie offered the fax to Rose, who held up her sticky hands.

'I'm all messy. You'll have to hold it, pet.'

Rennie's hand shook as she read the press release. Rose's expression changed and she said, 'Oh, sweetheart, and they didn't even ring you. Well, I suppose it all happened too fast. Thank goodness they're both OK.' Wiping her hands on a cloth and pushing the bowl of crumble away, Rose said tentatively, 'Am I allowed to say congratulations?'

'I don't know. It feels a bit weird.' The phone in Rennie's jeans pocket burst into life.

'Well, you'll be going to visit them.'

Would he?

'For Christ's sake don't visit them,' his agent announced without preamble. 'Don't go near the place. I've been in touch with the lawyers and they're arranging the DNA test.'

'She says it's mine.' Rennie watched Rose untie her floury pink apron and slip out of the kitchen.

'Ha,' his agent snorted. 'And her dad's Elvis. Innocent until proven guilty, remember. Just make sure you keep away from her and the kid.'

After an hour-long workout in the gym, Nancy was puce in the face and sweating profusely. As she made her way through to reception to pick up a fresh towel—yuk, Cyanide Sadie was there behind the desk checking bookings—the door to Connor's office crashed open. Connor, standing in the doorway, bellowed, 'What have I done to deserve this?'

He looked as if he should have steam shooting out of his ears. Zena, the new part-time receptionist, said apprehensively, 'What's wrong? Did I make a mistake?'

Raking his tousled hair, Connor said, 'I wish. The only mistake around here is the one I made when I said Mia could move to London. I've just had a call from Trudy Mulholland. One of our members,' he explained, because Zena was looking blank. 'She thought she should let me know that while she was stuck in traffic going round Trafalgar Square, she happened to notice my daughter sitting on one of the lions.'

'Oh,' Zena said anxiously. 'Is that not allowed?'

'She didn't have any clothes on!' roared Connor.

Sadie smirked.

'She had some kind of banner with her,' Connor went on. 'It said "Animals have feelings too", apparently. And there were police there, and paramedics, not to mention a crowd of people *gawping* at her. I'll have to get over there.' Patting his pockets, searching for his keys and cigarettes, Connor turned to Nancy. 'Will you come along?'

Perspiration was drying on Nancy's face, tightening her skin like a face mask. With no make-up and her hair tied back she felt clammy and disgusting and undoubtedly looked worse.

'Please?' said Connor agitatedly. 'She might listen to you.'

Sadie snorted with derision. 'That girl doesn't listen to anyone.'

Longing to slap her, Nancy moved towards Connor. 'Come on, let's go.'

'Hi, Dad.' Spotting him, Mia waved excitedly. 'Fancy seeing you here!'

'Oh *God*.' Connor winced and turned away.

'What?' said Nancy.

'She's my daughter. She's stark naked. I can't look at her.' Grabbing Nancy's arm, he said urgently, 'You tell her to get down.'

'She can't get down,' sighed a burly policeman. 'She's Superglued herself to the lion.'

317

Connor groaned and clapped his hands over his eyes. 'Can't you at least cover her up?'

'We've tried, sir, with blankets. But she keeps ripping them off. How old is your daughter, sir, may I ask?'

'Sixteen,' Connor said heavily. 'How are they going to get her unglued?'

'Some kind of solvent.' Burly pulled a face. 'But it's going to take a while. She'll be pretty sore afterwards.'

'Good,' said Connor.

It had been Nancy's idea to climb up and drape the banner around Mia's body. 'Your dad's embarrassed,' she told Mia. 'This way you won't be naked but you'll still get the message across.'

'Is he mad at me?'

'It's his job to be mad.' Nancy smiled as she tied the ends of the banner—a white sheet daubed with red emulsion paint—over Mia's shoulder. 'He'll get over it. In a few years.'

It took another ninety minutes to free Mia. During this time she had been interviewed by three journalists, offered a deal to pose for a top shelf magazine and had witnessed her father threatening to punch the guy who'd made the offer.

Pocketing a parking ticket and escaping being clamped by the skin of his teeth, Connor drove with Nancy to Charing Cross police station in Agar Street, where Mia, now under arrest, had been taken. They loitered outside the building and Connor smoked yet another cigarette. He saw that Nancy, drinking coffee from a polystyrene cup, was looking tired.

Connor, overcome with guilt, said, 'Look, you don't have to stay if you don't want to.'

Nancy pulled a face, her hand going up to her tied-back hair. 'Is that your way of telling me I'm too embarrassing to be seen with in public?'

'After Mia's one-woman show this afternoon,' Connor said fervently, 'I can promise you I'm beyond embarrassment.' A split second later, he realised his unintentional gaffe. 'Oh hell, I didn't mean you are embarrassing. You look fine, honestly. Very . . . natural.'

From the expression on Nancy's face he sensed that this was wrong too. Why did he always mess things up when he was with her?

'I'm a mess.' Nancy fiddled self-consciously with her fringe. 'Still, never mind. Anyway, I don't mind waiting. Mia shouldn't be long now.'

'I owe you one.' Eager to make amends, Connor said, 'Tell you what, why don't I treat you to dinner tonight, to make up for all this?'

There was an odd look in Nancy's eyes, one he was unable to read. 'It sounds as if you've forgotten you're seeing Tabitha tonight.'

Bugger, he had too. Connor reached automatically for his mobile. 'Look, Tab won't mind. I'll just give her a ring and—'

'The three of us can go out together?' said Nancy.

What? That wasn't what he'd meant at all. Connor opened his mouth to say so, then abruptly closed it again. Nancy wasn't remotely interested in him and the thought of the two of them having dinner together was, quite clearly, a chore.

'Of course,' Connor feigned delight in a last-ditch effort to redeem himself. 'Fine! Great idea.'

Nancy shook her head. 'No, thanks. You don't have to do that.' She shivered and took another gulp of coffee. 'Anyway, I'm busy tonight.' Balancing her coffee on a window ledge, she rubbed her arms.

'Here, put this on.' Removing his black suede jacket, Connor draped it round her shoulders. Standing in front of her, holding the lapels, he watched Nancy avoid his gaze.

His phone chose that moment to start ringing. Nancy fished the mobile from the pocket of his jacket and handed it over.

'Hi, it's me,' sang Tabitha. 'I've just got your message! How's Mia?'

'Unglued at last. We're at the police station now.'

'Don't worry, I hear Holloway's fab these days, better than any five-star hotel! Joking,' Tabitha said brightly. 'She'll be fine. So, are we still on for tonight? Great, I'll pick you up at eight thirty.'

As he ended the call, Mia emerged from the police station fully clothed and minus her banner. Spotting Nancy, she raced over and flung her arms round her.

'They let me off with a caution.' Mia was triumphant.

Relieved, Connor eyed the raw patch on the palm of her hand and said, 'They probably thought you'd suffered enough punishment.'

'Were you scared?' Nancy indicated the police station behind them. 'When they were questioning you there?'

'Nooo.' Mia looked scornful, then broke into a tiny grin and said, 'Well, maybe just a bit.'

Reaching for his car keys, Connor said, 'Serve you right.'

'But I did it for all the animals who have to endure appalling conditions while they're being transported from one country to another. I had a point to make and I made it.' Mia's silver-grey eyes shone with pride. 'And I tell you something, if I have to do it again I will.'

'Let *me* tell *you* something.' The note of paternal warning in Connor's voice prompted Mia and Nancy to exchange amused glances. 'You're my daughter, you're sixteen years old and you *bloody well will not*.'

JILL MANSELL

Biba's tabloid of choice had been running with the story for the last six days and Rennie was beginning to know how it felt to be a pantomime villain. When he ventured out, women of all ages narrowed their eyes at him in disgust and muttered sneering insults under their breath.

As he climbed out of the car in leafy Fulham, Rennie looked up at the second-floor apartment and saw Biba at the window. He rang the bell and she answered the door, looking pretty without make-up and wearing a simple emerald-green velour track suit.

Wordlessly, she led him through to the living room and sat down on the cream leather couch. Looking up at Rennie she said, 'Hi, babes.'

'I'm not the father.' Rennie had come straight from his lawyer's office. He held out his copy of the official result of the DNA test.

'I know. My agent just rang. Sorry.' Biba put her feet up on a sleek chrome-and-glass coffee table and gave him a sympathetic smile. 'Are you disappointed?'

Since there really wasn't any answer to that, Rennie said, 'You knew it wasn't me. You knew all along.'

Biba pushed back her long ash-blonde hair. 'Rennie, don't be cross. You know how this business works, right? If you can sell a story, you sell it. You'd be mad not to. Look at it from my point of view. I'm a single mother with a baby to support. Now, do I take some crappy little office job for five quid an hour and work my fingers to the bone to earn enough money to buy a pram? Or do I go to the papers for twenty grand and let *Hi!* magazine into my lovely home for another thirty?'

Rennie repeated, 'But I'm not the father.'

'You slept with me. You could have been.' Biba shrugged, blithely unconcerned. 'Don't worry, I'll put out a press release announcing it wasn't you. Oh, come on, babes, it's over now. Don't be grumpy.'

She was right, Rennie realised. There was absolutely no point in losing his temper because Biba genuinely didn't feel she'd done anything wrong. This was, effectively, how she earned her living.

Biba said cheerfully, 'Want to see him, then?'

Rennie nodded. For some reason he did want to see this child, who had, through no fault of its own, caused him such trouble.

Biba hauled herself upright and led the way through to the nursery. The baby lay in his ornately carved cot, asleep, with his chubby hands curled above his head.

'Isn't he gorgeous?' This time Biba spoke with genuine pride. 'I just love him to bits. Oops . . .'

At the sound of her voice the baby's eyes had snapped open. As he regarded them, Rennie found himself wondering how would he feel if this week-old infant had been his? How must it feel to have a child with someone you actually loved?

'Want to hold him?' Biba offered. 'Just for a few seconds, before he starts screaming the place down.'

Rennie lifted the baby out of the cot and held him in his arms. His heart swelled with emotion; it really was incredible.

As the baby opened his mouth to yell out in protest about the lack of food, Rennie passed him over to Biba. 'He's a pretty good weight, isn't he? Doesn't look premature.'

Biba, her eyes dancing with mischief, said, 'Now if you were selling your story to the paper, which would sound more exciting to you? Mother in labour rushed to hospital for emergency life-saving op? Or, mother turns up carrying suitcase, ready for pre-booked Caesarean?' She shrugged. 'Go on, pick one. Your choice.'

Of course. Why hadn't that occurred to him before?

Rennie turned to leave. At the door, he paused. 'What's his name?'

'Come on, you think I'm going to tell you that now?' Biba flashed him a triumphant smile. 'You'll have to read all about it,' she told Rennie, 'in next week's *Hi!*'

Rennie shook his head; he no longer had the energy to be angry. It was his own fault for tangling with a girl like Biba in the first place.

'Rennie? Can we still be friends?'

He looked over at Biba posing with her son beside the cot, supremely aware of the touching tableau they made. 'I don't think so.'

She kissed the baby's dark downy head, then hoisted him up to her shoulder. 'Oh well, never mind. No harm done,' She said chirpily. 'You can just carry on being you, having a ball and breaking hearts . . .'

No harm done. For a moment he was almost tempted to tell her just how much harm had been done. And that the only heart to have been broken was his own. But what would be the point of that?

'Bye,' said Rennie.

'He's miserable. He's been an idiot and he knows it. Dammit, he's making *my* life a misery,' Annie declared. 'He's no fun any more. Nick really is regretting what he did, Carmen. He misses you terribly. That's why I had to see you today. I thought you might want to know.'

Carmen laced her fingers tightly round her cup of coffee. Hearing from Annie out of the blue after all these weeks had come as both a shock and a relief. Terrified that Annie despised her as much as Nick did, Carmen had been touched by her former workmate's response.

'You twit,' Annie had chortled down the phone. Not many people could chortle, but Annie could. 'Of course I don't hate you!'

Now, ensconced with Annie in the steamy café a couple of streets away from the shelter, Carmen's stomach tightened as she wondered if she did want to know how much Nick was regretting what he'd done.

'So?' said Annie, greedily eyeing her second toffee doughnut.

'So what?'

'Don't give me that! Do you miss him too?'

Carmen's heart began to gallop. She and Nick had been so happy together. Of course she'd missed him. And then the thing had happened with Rennie—the thing that had first begun to make itself felt on Christmas night, if she was honest—and that had remained uppermost in her mind. But she and Rennie had no future together, she knew that.

'He was the one who ended it,' said Carmen.

'You were such a great couple.' Annie pushed up the baggy sleeve of her pink sweater. 'Look, it's twenty past six. Nick will be leaving work in ten minutes. How about if I give him a ring?'

'And say what?' Carmen began to scent a set-up.

'That we're here, you berk!' Delving into her bag, Annie eagerly whipped out her phone. 'That you'd like to see him again, and if he wants to drop by you could have a chat about . . . you know, stuff.'

Picturing Nick with his familiar face, scruffy hair and lamentable taste in clothes, Carmen realised how much she did want to see him again. She shook her head at Annie. 'You know what? You're shameless.'

'So is that a yes?'

Her stomach contracting with anticipation, Carmen said, 'Go on then.'

So this was how it felt to be stood up. Having packed Annie off home forty minutes earlier, because some reconciliations were definitely better carried out without an interested audience, Carmen had ordered a fresh coffee and waited. And waited.

When Annie had spoken to him on the phone Nick had agreed to join them at Luigi's. Clearly he'd had no intention of doing so.

It was almost seven o'clock. Nick wasn't coming and that was that. Wondering if anyone in London had a more disastrous love life than she did, Carmen said her goodbyes to Luigi and left the café.

It was a warm evening. When she emerged from the stuffy tube station, Carmen took off her navy sweatshirt and tied it round her hips. From a newsagent's she bought an *Evening Standard* and a Cornetto.

Five minutes later, rounding the corner into Fitzallen Square, the Cornetto slid from her hand and hit the pavement. Ahead of her, scarcely recognisable with his hair short, but otherwise deeply familiar in his old green jumper and dilapidated jeans, stood Nick.

'My God.' Carmen's hand flew to her mouth. She heard herself stupidly say, 'You're here.'

'I know.' Nick's smile was crooked, tentative. 'Amazing, isn't it?'

'I waited for you in the café.'

'Sorry. I wanted us to talk properly. I couldn't do it in Luigi's, in front of Annie.' With a self-conscious gesture he reached up to rub the back of his head. Close to, Carmen saw that it was a pretty terrible haircut.

'I sent Annie away. She wouldn't even have been there. I thought you'd stood me up.'

'I was nervous. And I wanted to impress you.' Ruefully Nick tugged at a stray asymmetric tuft of hair.

Taking a deep breath Carmen gestured towards number sixty-two and said, 'That's where I live. Are you coming in?'

'I rang the doorbell ten minutes ago. Your brother-in-law answered the door.' The expression on Nick's face indicated that he hadn't received the warmest of welcomes. 'Could we talk out here instead?'

Feeling nervous, Carmen led the way across the road and into the garden square. When they'd reached the wooden bench and sat down she said, 'Talk about what?'

'Me being the world's biggest idiot.' Nick heaved a sigh and avoided Carmen's gaze. 'Me realising that I should never have said those things to you.' Bowing his head he went on awkwardly, 'Me missing you more than I'd imagined possible.'

'Have you?' A lump sprang into Carmen's throat.

'Me wondering if you've missed me,' Nick continued.

Carmen nodded. 'Of course I've missed you.'

'Could you ever forgive me, d'you think?'

'Oh, I think so.' Managing a smile, she said, 'Do you think you could forgive me for being filthy rich?'

Finally looking at her, Nick reached for her hand.

'I wish you weren't, but I suppose I can tolerate it.' He gave Carmen's fingers a squeeze. 'Do you think we have a chance?' he said tentatively. 'Can we start again?'

How many times had she dreamed of him saying this? And now it was actually happening. Throwing her arms round him, Carmen whispered, 'Oh Nick . . .'

Rennie felt as though he'd been knifed in the stomach. Watching from his bedroom window, he experienced a surge of pain so acute it was almost physical, combined with more boiling jealousy than he'd known he possessed. That was it, then. He had lost. And Nick had won, not because he had the looks and the money, but because he was a genuinely decent, easy-going, *thoroughly nice bloke*.

When Nick had rung the doorbell earlier asking for Carmen, Rennie had been tempted to punch him.

Now he really wished he had.

Feeling sick, Rennie's fingers gripped the window ledge. Over in the square Nick and Carmen were still talking together, no doubt planning their shared future. He watched Nick in his manky green sweater stroking Carmen's arm as she spoke, then drawing her against him once more. Unable to bear it a moment longer, Rennie swore and turned away. This was his punishment for having lived the life he had. Worst of all, he knew that he would have to pretend to be pleased for Carmen when she waltzed into the house with Nick and announced that the two of them were back together.

Well, maybe he could manage that for a couple of minutes but there was no way he was going to be cracking open the champagne and sitting around toasting their future happiness.

After a long shower Rennie returned to his room and pulled on a clean white shirt and faded jeans, then splashed on some aftershave in the hope that it might make him feel better.

Checking out of the window, he saw that the square was now empty. Having dimly heard the front door opening and closing while he'd been in the shower, this meant that Carmen and Nick were here in the house. You lost, he won, sang an irritating voice in his head as he made his way downstairs. You lost, he won, you—

'*Shit!*'

The sound of Carmen's cry of anguish caused Rennie to halt abruptly at the foot of the staircase. Would it be too much to hope that she'd just accidentally trapped Nick's willy in his trouser zip? The curse had come from the living room. Rennie moved towards the closed living-room door. Maybe he could call the ambulance.

Innocently he said, 'Everything all right in there?'

He heard frantic scuffling, then Carmen yelling out in alarm, 'Rennie! Don't come in!'

Rennie pictured Nick, his teeth gritted with pain. Or maybe Carmen was hurriedly making herself decent.

'Fuck, *fuck*,' he heard Carmen gasp as a clattering sound ensued.

'What's wrong? Carmen, are you OK?'

'Oh, *I'm* OK.' Carmen sounded out of breath and panicky.

'Want me to fetch the first-aid tin?' Rennie offered, beginning to enjoy the fantasy of his rival in love losing his most prized possession.

Except he wasn't his rival in love, was he? Nick had won.

'Not the first-aid tin,' Carmen yelled. 'Fetch that squirty carpet-cleaner stuff. And lots of J-Cloths and kitchen roll. And stay outside,' she added distractedly. 'Just leave them by the door.'

Gallons of blood then. Excellent. Having located everything Carmen needed, Rennie returned from the kitchen and pushed open the living-room door.

'Can't you *ever* do anything I tell you?' Carmen let out a wail of despair. 'I *said* don't come in.'

She was on her knees in front of the TV, surrounded by a slew of videos and DVDs in and out of their cases, a snowstorm of damp scrunched-up tissues and a brown stain spreading across the carpet. An empty coffee cup lay on its side, coffee was dripping from the DVD player and there were wet patches on the knees of her jeans.

There was no Nick in the room, either mutilated or intact.

'What happened?' Rennie was referring to the absence of Nick.

'For crying out loud, what does it look like? I tripped over the sodding mains lead from the stupid DVD player and lost my balance and spilled my *buggering* cup of coffee.' Carmen's cheeks were hectically flushed, her tone defiant. 'It's gone into the DVD player and all over your precious videos and DVDs and I'll replace them, OK?'

Rennie watched her frantically shaking coffee out of his video of *The Asphalt Jungle*, before wiping it with a handful of tissues. Crouching down next to her, he silently inspected the damage. The DVDs would be fine but the videos were all coffee-logged and beyond saving. He picked up his favourite Humphrey Bogart video, *To Have and Have Not*, and lukewarm coffee seeped out onto the sleeve of his white shirt.

'I'm sorry,' said Carmen.

'Where's Nick?'

'Gone.'. Reaching for a J-Cloth and the aerosol can of foam carpet cleaner, Carmen turned her attention to the carpet.

Rennie's throat tightened. 'What was he doing here?'

'Saying sorry. Asking if we could get back together again.'

'And?' said Rennie.

'I said no, we couldn't.'

Yes, yes, yes.

Carefully he said, 'I was watching the two of you out in the square.'

'Well, that figures.' Carmen kept her head down. 'Allowing people their privacy never has been your strong point.'

Rennie ignored this. 'Why did you say no?'

'Because it would never work. Because I don't love him.'

'Why not?'

'God, you're nosy.' Leaning back on her heels, Carmen watched as Rennie reached for her right arm and firmly prised the J-Cloth from her hand. 'What are you doing?'

'I was watching at the window,' Rennie repeated. 'You were in his arms.'

'It was nice to be asked. Nick's a great person.' Carmen's eyes were bright. 'I hugged him and thanked him, then I turned him down.'

'So you changed your mind about Nick?' Rennie had no intention of giving up now. 'Does that mean you may have changed your mind about anyone else?'

'Give me back that cloth. If I don't scrub this stain out—'

'Carmen, just tell me.'

'We'll need a whole new carpet.'

'Sod the carpet,' said Rennie.

'Ha, that's easy for you to say! This cost thousands!'

'Sod the carpet and stop changing the subject.' Rennie gazed intently at Carmen. 'Why don't you tell me what's really going on here?'

Carmen felt the adrenaline zinging like sparklers through her body. As if bloody Rennie hadn't already guessed. Recklessly she said, 'Fine. OK. If that's what you want, I will.' She took a deep breath. 'Well, I realised I didn't love Nick because he could never make me feel like . . . I knew somebody else could make me feel. Even though the other person is the last person in the world anyone with any sense should get involved with.'

'I see.' Rennie nodded again. 'Tricky situation. How does this other person—feel about you?'

'God knows. He told me he loved me.' Carmen heard her voice begin to shake. 'But he's such a smooth-talking bastard, you can't believe a word he says.'

Rennie said, 'On the other hand, he could really mean it.'

'I hope so.' Carmen risked a smile. 'For his sake.'

'Or you'd punish him severely. Do something completely terrible,' Rennie pointed out, 'like destroy his entire video collection.'

'I really am sorry about that.'

'So you should be. I'm deeply traumatised.' Doing his best to look traumatised, Rennie reached for his sodden copy of *The Great Escape*. 'In fact, I shall probably need months of professional counselling.'

'I'll do that, it'll be cheaper. Are you going to shut up now,' said Carmen, 'and kiss me?'

He broke into a grin. 'You're the one who started all this. I'd say it was up to you to make the first move.'

Pushing aside the scattered DVDs and videos, Carmen shuffled on her knees through the white drift of carpet cleaning foam until she reached Rennie. She had loved Spike so much, but his descent into drugs had been hard to bear. It was a problem she would never have with Rennie, who had never touched drugs. Furthermore, she was sure Spike would approve of them getting together.

When Rennie put his arms round her, she breathed in the scent of his aftershave and felt the warmth of his body against hers. Sometimes these things happened and you just had to learn to go with them. No matter how much she'd fought against it, she had no control over her feelings for Rennie. Like it or not, for better or for worse, he was the one she loved and couldn't live without.

As his mouth closed over hers, Carmen realised that this was all she wanted. It was like coming home.

Chapter 12

'NANCY, COME HOME. *PLEASE*.'

Nancy gazed at the bouquet on the kitchen table—a rainbow of lilies, roses, long pointy blue foxgloves, glossy exotic leaves, curly twig things and, her all-time favourite, stupendously gaudy sunflowers. It was a vast arrangement, almost as big as the table itself.

'Nancy? Are you still there?'

'Of course I'm still here. And this is where I'm staying. Jonathan, I'm happy here. I'm not coming back. Our marriage is over.'

'But it doesn't *have* to be over.' Jonathan's tone was warm, comforting. 'Look, I know I hurt you and I did a really stupid thing, but I've *learned* from that. You don't know how much I've missed you, sweetheart. We had a great marriage. After this, we can make it an even better one. If you want kids, fine. We'll have as many as you like.'

Nancy smiled to herself. Oh, she wanted children all right. But not with Jonathan.

Aloud she said, 'What did you do with the sit-on lawn mower?'

'Nothing! It's right here.' Jonathan sounded excited. 'Waiting for you!'

Maybe that was why he was so keen to have her back, because the grass needed cutting. 'Jonathan, about these flowers.'

Eagerly he said, 'Do you like them?'

'Well, yes, of course I *like*—'

'I knew you would! And I told them to put sunflowers in, because I know they're your favourites. Remember the time—'

'Jonathan,' Nancy blurted out before he could get completely carried away, 'you can't seriously expect me to come back to you just because you've sent me a bunch of flowers!'

'It wasn't a bunch.' Hurt, he said, 'It was a bouquet. It cost two hundred pounds!'

'And you think that's what's needed to make me change my mind about divorcing you? Two hundred pounds' worth of flowers?'

'Sweetheart, listen to me, I'll come down to London and beg you on my knees, if that's what you want.' Sounding increasingly desperate, Jonathan shouted, 'Nancy, I love you, I'll do anything—'

'Really, you don't have to bother.' Smiling to herself, Nancy began hunting in the utility room for vases. 'I'm not going to change my mind, Jonathan. So I promise you, there's no point.'

The time had come, as it invariably did, to call a halt on a relationship that wasn't going anywhere. Connor sighed as he made his way across town to Tabitha's flat. He hated this bit, the telling-them-it-was-all-over bit, but he could no longer put it off. The other day Tabitha had rung to invite him to meet her parents this coming weekend. They were lovely people, she'd eagerly assured him, and they were so looking forward to meeting him.

Connor was sure he would have liked Tabitha's parents, but they would be mentally sizing him up as a potential son-in-law and that wasn't fair, on either them or Tabitha. She was a great girl. He didn't want to hurt her or string her along. So here he was, about to do the deed as gently as possible.

'Sweetheart, you're early!' Excited to see him, Tabitha gave him a hug and pulled him into the flat. 'Now, don't be cross. I know I said I was cooking tonight, but something's come up and I just haven't had time so we're going to be ordering in a pizza instead.'

'That's fine.' Finishing with someone over a pizza would be far easier than doing it during the course of some dinner it might have taken Tabitha hours to cook.

'Let's have a drink. We need to talk. God, everything's happened so fast.' Hurrying him through to the comfortably cluttered living room, Tabitha sloshed red wine into two glasses. All the better to throw at a man when he chucks you, thought Connor, watching her take out a cigarette. Her handbag and jacket were dumped on the blue checked sofa, indicating that she hadn't long arrived home from work.

'So what's all this about then?' Connor pulled a lighter from his trouser pocket and lit her cigarette.

Tabitha exhaled a long stream of smoke. 'I've been offered a new job. In financial journalism.'

'Tab, that's fantastic news!' He was genuinely pleased for her.

Taking a hefty gulp of wine, Tabitha said, 'In New York.'

Connor almost shouted, 'That's *brilliant!*' but sensed it wouldn't be appropriate. Over the rim of her glass, Tabitha was eyeing him intently.

Aloud he said, 'Well . . . that's a surprise.'

'I know. And I'm flattered, of course I am. But I don't know whether to accept.'

'I see.' Carefully, Connor said, 'And why's that?'

'Well, I was rather hoping you'd guess,' said Tabitha. 'How would you feel if I went to New York?'

'Well, I'd . . . um, I don't really . . .'

'Because if you'd rather I turned the job down and stayed here,' Tabitha went on hurriedly, 'I would. If you thought we had something worth hanging on to, I'd turn them down in a flash.'

There was a kind of hopeful yearning in her eyes, but it was tinged with sadness.

'Tab,' Connor said gently, 'you're a great girl and I think a lot of you, but you mustn't turn down an opportunity like this on my account.'

There was a long silence, then Tabitha heaved a sigh and said, 'Bugger. How did I know you were going to say that?'

'Sweetheart, it's not you. It's me.'

Tabitha rolled her eyes. 'How did I know you were going to say *that*?'

'I hope we'll always be friends,' Connor struggled on.

'*And* that.' She stubbed her cigarette in the ashtray.

'You deserve better than me,' said Connor.

'And *that*!' By this time half laughing, half crying, Tabitha picked up her packet of cigarettes and pretended to throw them at him. 'OK, I get the message.' She wiped her eyes and raised her glass. 'Let's have a toast, shall we? To my dazzling new job and my dazzling new life.'

They smiled at each other and clinked glasses. Overcome with relief, Connor gave Tabitha a hug, then they settled down together on the sofa. He reached for the bottle of wine and topped up her glass. 'It's the opportunity of a lifetime. You couldn't turn that down. You'll have the time of your life, and end up meeting someone who really deserves you.'

'How about you, then?' Tabitha eased off her pink high-heeled shoes and tucked her feet under her. 'Who deserves you?'

Connor pulled a face. 'Who'd want an old wreck like me?'

'Don't be flippant. Honestly, typical man. Any mention of emotions and you panic.' Taking a sip of wine, Tabitha said, 'Come on, you can tell me. Who do you like?'

Connor began to panic. As if he was going to tell her *that*. Banishing all thoughts of Nancy firmly from his mind, he said, 'Well, Michelle Pfeiffer's not bad. If you want to put in a good word.'

'See? You're doing it again.'

'Or that Penny Thingummy who reads the news on GMTV. Sparkly eyes,' said Connor. 'And a naughty smile. I like her.'

'How about Nancy?'

'What?' A breeze block landed with a thud on Connor's chest. Had he just said Nancy's name aloud instead of thinking it? And why was Tabitha looking at him like that?

'You heard.'

'I don't know what you mean.' The breeze block was pressing ever more heavily on his lungs. Was this how it felt to have a heart attack?

'Oh, come on, Connor, why don't you just admit it? Because I know,' said Tabitha. 'I *saw* you.'

'Saw me where? Saw me when? Doing what?'

'Your face.' Lighting another cigarette and taking fast, jerky puffs, Tabitha said, 'You should see yourself. OK, remember me ringing you from work after Mia glued herself to that lion?'

Rather than risk actually saying anything, Connor nodded.

'Well, I wasn't at work. As soon as I got your message I jumped into a cab and went down to Trafalgar Square, but you'd already left by then, so I guessed I'd find you at the police station. And I did,' Tabitha went on, her expression rueful. 'When I turned up, there you were. Outside the station with Nancy. I watched the two of you together from across the road. That's where I was when I phoned you. That's when I knew, really. Well, you'd have to be blind not to know. It was so obvious.'

Connor exhaled. Tabitha sounded resigned rather than angry. 'Was it?'

'Oh, yes.' Her smile was crooked. 'Well, I clung on for a bit, you know. Tried to pretend it hadn't happened. Deep down though, you know when you're beaten, don't you? But what I don't understand is why the two of you never got together in the first place. I mean, what was to stop it happening before I came along?'

Oh well, if Tabitha could be blunt, so could he.

'It hasn't happened because Nancy doesn't want it to happen,' Connor admitted. Now that it was finally out in the open, he felt a rush of relief. 'I'm crazy about her, but she just isn't interested. I asked her out more than once and she said no every time.' Resignedly he said, 'I suppose I'm just not Nancy's type.'

Two dimples appeared in Tabitha's cheeks. 'You berk.'

'I know. God, talk about embarrassing. To think you could tell, just from watching from across the street.' Closing his eyes, Connor sighed.

'You complete and utter berk,' Tabitha repeated, patting his knee and starting to laugh. 'You really don't get it, do you? When I was watching the two of you, it wasn't just you who was being obvious.'

'What?' Connor's eyes shot open in disbelief.

'You should have seen the way Nancy was looking at you when you weren't watching. I'm serious,' Tabitha insisted, stubbing out her cigarette. 'This was absolutely a two-way thing. Trust me, you are one hundred per cent *most definitely* Nancy's type.'

A letter had been pushed through the letterbox. Nancy, arriving home from work, bent to pick it up and carried it through to the kitchen. The house was empty. Rennie had whisked Carmen down to Nice for a couple of days and Rose was spending the weekend with William at his home in Weston-super-Mare. Nancy dumped her bag on the kitchen table, filled the kettle at the sink then messily tore open the envelope with her name on it.

Her name but no address, indicating that the letter must have been hand-delivered.

Except it wasn't a letter, it was an invitation. As the kettle behind her came to the boil, Nancy gazed at the thick white card and felt the first stirrings of annoyance. Bloody hell, this was all she needed.

Dear Nancy, said the invitation. *You are cordially invited to a picnic in Fitzallen Square on Friday at six o'clock. No need to RSVP. Just be there, please.*

It wasn't signed, but it didn't need to be. And it was already two minutes past six. Irritated, Nancy slapped the invitation down and stormed through to the sitting room. Bloody Jonathan, up to his stupid tricks again. She'd told him not to come down to London but that was Jonathan for you, he'd never been able to admit defeat. Now he was going that bit further, upping the stakes, making a more extravagant gesture that would no doubt include vintage champagne and smoked salmon. Checking her watch—ten past six—Nancy wondered what he would do if she simply ignored the invitation.

That was one possibility. The other was to march over to the darkening square right now and tell him in no uncertain terms that he was wasting his time. Which to do? Which to go for? Raking her fingers agitatedly through her hair, Nancy realised she couldn't bear the thought of Jonathan sitting out there all evening with his ridiculous picnic, waiting for her. She had to get rid of him now.

Dusk was falling as Nancy crossed the road and clicked open the gate. Reaching the wooden bench she turned left and saw the picnic. There were balloons tied to the lower branches of the trees in the mini-glade, candles flickering in glass holders, and a green-and-red tartan rug had been laid out on the grass.

No vintage champagne, no smoked salmon and no glittering crystal. No Jonathan either. Instead there was a cake. Moving towards the rug, Nancy saw Connor step out from behind the cluster of trees.

Evenly he said, 'You're late.'

Adrenaline zapped through her body. Nancy, her mouth dry, really wished she hadn't stormed out of the house without first combing her hair and repairing her end-of-a-long-day-at-work make-up. 'You didn't sign the invitation. I thought it was from Jonathan.'

A flicker of apprehension crossed Connor's face. 'Were you hoping it was from him?'

'In a way.' Nancy couldn't figure out what was going on. 'But only so I could march over here and tell him to fuck off back to Scotland.'

Connor almost smiled, and she realised it was probably the first time he'd heard her say fuck.

'Well, that's good. The reason I didn't sign the invitation was in case I lost my nerve and ran away. Then you wouldn't have known it had come from me.'

Lost his nerve? Connor was always so laid back and relaxed it was impossible to think of him as being nervous. Yet he *was* looking ill at ease scuffing the ground with the toes of his Timberland boots like a teenager. Her heart banging against her ribcage, Nancy said, 'Where's Tabitha?'

Connor shrugged awkwardly and said, 'It's over. Tab's fine. She's going to live in New York. This was kind of her idea, actually.'

Horror and shame seized Nancy. Had Tabitha finished with Connor and somehow managed to persuade him, against his will, to make some form of clumsy play for her instead? *Out of pity?*

'Look, there's no need,' Nancy blurted out, her skin crawling with embarrassment as she backed away. 'I don't know what Tab's trying to do here, but—'

'Ah shit, I've got this all wrong again.' His Irish accent becoming more pronounced, Connor shook his head in despair and said urgently, 'Wait, you can't go. Listen to me,' he pleaded, taking a couple of steps towards Nancy. 'It's not what Tab's trying to do here, it's what *I'm* trying to do.'

Nancy began to tremble. 'I don't know what you're talking about.'

'Tab knows how much I like you, but I told her you weren't interested in me because when I asked you out before you said no. Tab said I had to make more of an effort, do something . . . you know, romantic. So that's what I'm doing, but to be honest I've never tried anything like this before.'

OK, breathe, just try to breathe normally. Nancy said, 'I heard you telling Mia I wasn't your type. In your office at the club.'

'Oh God.' Connor slammed his hand against his forehead. 'I told her that to stop her sticking her oar in! You know what Mia's like. I wanted to do it by myself, without my bossy daughter scaring you witless.'

For the first time Nancy smiled, thinking of all the trouble Mia had unwittingly caused.

'So that was it,' Connor went on. 'I thought I had no chance at all. Until Tabitha told me otherwise.'

That wiped the smile off Nancy's face. Appalled, she cried, '*What*? How did Tabitha know?'

'Just did. Saw us together outside Charing Cross police station,' Connor shrugged, 'and that was it. According to Tab it was blindingly obvious. That was why I took her advice with this whole making-an-effort malarkey.' Scratching his head and pulling a face he said, 'Which just goes to show how bloody daft I am.'

Nancy felt her heart swelling. 'I don't think you're bloody daft. You made me a cake. That's the most romantic thing anyone's ever done for me.' Unable to hold back any longer, Nancy closed the distance between them and threw her arms round Connor and kissed him.

Oh yes, this was definitely, wonderfully, gloriously romantic.

Connor eventually pulled away. For several seconds he gazed down at her without speaking.

Breaking into a broad smile, Nancy kissed him again for good measure before dragging him over to the rug.

'We've got to try this cake,' she said. 'I haven't even seen it properly yet.'

She surveyed the lumpy white icing, thickly slapped on all over and studded with Maltesers and fruit pastilles. The cake itself was round, six inches in diameter and decorated with a red satin ribbon like a gaudy bride-to-be's garter. Struggling to keep a straight face, she said, 'What kind of sponge is it?'

'Oh, you know.' Connor shrugged modestly. 'The usual kind.'

Picturing him inexpertly weighing out flour and cracking eggs, Nancy's heart swooped with love. Since he'd forgotten to bring a knife along, she flipped open the Swiss Army penknife on her keyring.

'No, don't cut it!' shouted Connor.

'Don't be daft, we've got to see what it tastes like—*oh*.'

Taking the penknife from Nancy, Connor drew her to him once more. 'OK. I'm rubbish at cakes. But I do have other talents, I promise.'

Thank goodness for that.

'Don't worry, I'm still impressed.' Feeling she could afford to be magnanimous, Nancy said, 'You remembered that I like Maltesers.'

'I did.'

'And fruit pastilles.'

'Those too.' Connor looked pleased with himself.

Reaching up to kiss him, Nancy said happily, 'And no one's ever decorated a bath sponge for me before.'

JILL MANSELL

It's a grey and wintry day in London when I telephone Jill Mansell at her home in Bristol, but her warm and enthusiastic voice brightens the gloom as she chuckles about what triggered the storyline for *The One You Really Want*. 'I was writing about an art gallery for my previous novel, *Nadia Knows Best*, and I went up to Clifton in Bristol, where there's a lovely gallery, and was trying to pluck up the courage to go in. I hate saying, "Hello, I'm a novelist and I wonder if you can help me with some research," because I think it sounds so poncey, so I stopped and looked in the window of a jeweller's shop next door. And then I saw there was a jeweller's on the other side of the gallery, too! And I was just going backwards and forwards when I spotted the most gorgeous ring in one of the windows . . . and then another gorgeous ring in the other shop window. Well, of course, I tried both rings on and chose the cheaper one (although it wasn't that cheap!). When I came out, I decided I really wasn't brave enough to go into the gallery, so I went home.

'I'd been home for just ten minutes when my editor phoned to tell me that my most recently published book was going to be high up in the *Sunday Times* best-seller lists. I was so excited that I went straight back to Clifton and bought the more expensive ring as well! I've always been a bit bling-bling. When I was really poor I used to buy cubic zirconia rings from Argos and places. I've always loved having glitzy stuff on my fingers! Anyway, when my partner came home that evening he didn't notice the rings, and somehow

I couldn't bring myself to tell him I'd bought them—even though he doesn't care how I spend my money. This must have happened in the August, and by the time December came I'd forgotten all about it, until I opened a huge glossy Christmas card and it said "to a valued customer" . . . from the poshest jeweller in Clifton! And of course then I told my partner about the rings, but I thought: They shouldn't do that. What if a man has a mistress and he buys her a beautiful piece of jewellery and then the jeweller sends a card like that to his home address and the wife opens it? So that was the little hook of an idea that started me off on *The One You Really Want*.'

Once she has got her idea, Jill finds the hardest thing is not to introduce too many characters into each story. 'I just don't know where they all come from! I invented Mia about a minute before she arrived at her dad's door. And as soon as she arrived she was fantastic. I didn't mean to have her in there, but once she was I didn't know how I'd have managed without her. I think she's the kind of sixteen-year-old we'd all like to have.'

With a twelve-year-old daughter and a son of ten, Jill finds herself viewing the teenage years ahead with some trepidation. 'But they'll be a new set of experiences and I can write about them if I need to. I'm just finishing another book at the moment. As soon as I finish one I'm terrified that I'll lose the knack and not know how to write any more. So straight away I start searching for that hook, that one little idea that will set it all off again.'

Anne Jenkins

Goodbye, Ruby Tuesday

DONNA HAY

When sixteen-year-old Sadie Moon
discovers that she is pregnant she is
devastated. A baby will ruin her life and
destroy her dream of becoming a
singing sensation.
But when Sadie gives birth to her baby girl,
her Ruby Tuesday, she knows she can't give
up this precious little bundle for adoption.
Whatever the consequences may be.

Prologue

1970

SADIE MOON STUBBED out her cigarette in the rosebushes and climbed back in through the window of the Willow Lodge Diocesan Home for Unmarried Mothers.

Her room-mate Janey looked up, her baby clamped to her breast. 'You're taking a risk. Mrs Walcross would kill you.'

'I'd like to see her try.' Evelyn Walcross didn't scare Sadie. She called herself the home's moral welfare officer, but she was a sadistic bitch who made sure the girls in her care suffered for their 'sins'. They slept in chilly rooms and worked like slaves, cleaning the home and scrubbing shirt collars in the laundry until their hands were raw.

Janey stroked her baby's face, murmuring to him. She'd given birth three weeks before Sadie, the day before her eighteenth birthday. Her little boy had chunky limbs and a shock of black hair. Just like his father, Janey said. Her boyfriend played rugby for Wakefield Trinity. He'd wanted to marry her but her parents wouldn't allow it because he was Catholic and they didn't want their daughter to marry a papist.

Today was Janey's last day at Willow Lodge. Mrs Walcross had told her to be ready to leave by teatime.

'I am doing the right thing, aren't I?' she said.

Sadie shrugged. 'What choice did you have?'

Mrs Walcross had spelled it out when she gave Janey the adoption papers. If she didn't sign them, her baby would be taken away and put in a children's home. There was no way she would be allowed to keep it.

'It's going to be so hard to say goodbye,' Janey said.

'I know.'

Sadie looked into her baby's cot. She slept soundly, her long dark lashes curling on her soft round cheeks, her tiny starfish hands flung up on the pillow beside her. Seeing her made Sadie's stomach flip. No one told her it would be like this. No one warned her she would be ambushed by love.

It shouldn't have happened, not after the nightmare of everything that had gone before. Finding out she was five months pregnant—how could she not have realised sooner?—then having to break the news to her mum. And of course *she* told Sadie's brother Tom who, being the man of the house, decided Sadie should come to Willow Lodge. He would have sent her to hell if it might stop the neighbours gossiping.

At the time she hadn't cared what became of her. She didn't want a baby, especially not this one. She had other plans. She was going to be a singer, move to London and become as rich and famous as Shirley Bassey. She even had a stage name—Sadie Starr. She could almost see it, up there in lights at The Talk of the Town.

But then, a week ago, this thing she'd been carrying around inside her had become real. A little person who curled her tiny fingers tightly around Sadie's and stared up at her with dark, unfocused intensity, as if she was the only person in the whole world who mattered.

It wasn't her fault, she reasoned. The baby couldn't help how she'd come into the world, or who her father was. She was Sadie's and Sadie was hers. She'd even given her a name, although she'd never said it out loud. Only in her head. She knew she'd have to give her up eventually, but she tried not to think about it.

Mrs Walcross came into their room just before lunch. Janey's suitcase was on the bed. She'd dressed her little boy, Stephen, in the blue leggings and matinée coat she'd knitted. Now she was feeding him again, sitting in the hard armchair between their beds.

Sadie was on her third attempt at changing her baby's nappy. She still hadn't got the hang of folding all that bulky towelling, or where to stick the pins. But the baby didn't seem to mind. She kicked her little naked legs, surprising herself when they moved. She looked so funny Sadie couldn't help giggling.

But she stopped when Mrs Walcross walked in with a grim-looking social worker. She went across to Janey and said, 'Time to say goodbye.'

Janey looked up, startled. 'But you said teatime! Can't I just finish feeding him?'

'His mother and father are waiting for him.' Mrs Walcross nodded to the social worker, who lunged at Janey and roughly took Stephen from her. Janey screamed and Sadie yelled, 'Leave her alone!' but the social worker was already gone, her soft shoes squeaking down the corridor.

Sadie's scream startled her baby. Her tiny face crumpled and she wailed. Janey cried too, rocking in her chair.

'Shh, shh, it's all right, Ruby.' Sadie swept her into her arms and held her close.

Mrs Walcross turned. 'What did you call her?'

'Ruby. It's her name.'

Mrs Walcross gave her a look of pure spite. 'We'll see what her new parents say about that.'

Sadie sat on the edge of the bed as the door closed, holding her baby close, trembling with shock and rage.

Irene Moon sipped her sherry with a grimace and tried to listen as Glenys Kitchener droned on.

'You're so lucky to be able to get away with such a small do, Mrs Moon.' She was only twenty but looked and acted much older, in a prissy pastel-blue two-piece and white gloves. Her legs were buckling under the weight of the baby propped on her hip. He was trussed up in a sailor suit, his fat red face framed by a frilly bonnet. 'When little William was christened we had to go all the way to Leeds to find a place big enough. Such a fuss! But I suppose you have to expect these things when you're in public life, don't you?'

Irene fought to keep the smile off her face. Public life, indeed! Glenys might have come up in the world since she married Bernard Kitchener, a local councillor and ten years older than her, but it wasn't that long since she'd been playing hopscotch down their street.

She looked around at the small gathering in her front room. Her son Tom was parading around with baby Catherine in his arms, showing her off to everyone. At twenty-one, he looked too young to be married, let alone a father. Her daughter-in-law Jackie stood at Tom's side, smiling nervously. There were purple shadows under her eyes from all the sleepless nights she'd had. Now, as the baby began to cry, she reached up and took her from Tom, then carried her upstairs for a nap.

Glenys lowered her voice. 'I do think you're terribly brave, having a party at all in the circumstances.'

'And what circumstances would those be, Glenys?'

'You know. With your Sadie being . . . away.' Glenys glanced around then leaned forward confidingly. 'I did warn her about what would happen if she ran around with the likes of *him*.' Her mouth pursed. 'You did the right thing, Mrs Moon, sending her away.'

'Did I?' Irene was beginning to wonder. The only reason she'd done it was to silence gossips like Glenys. Now she felt disgusted with herself.

'Definitely. Think of the shame. And, besides, could you imagine Sadie caring for a baby? She can hardly look after herself, let alone a—'

They were suddenly aware that the room had gone very quiet. Irene turned round. There, standing in the doorway, was Sadie, her suitcase at her feet and a baby in her arms. She looked exhausted, but utterly defiant.

'Hello, Mum,' she said. 'We've come home.'

Tom reacted before Irene could summon her thoughts. Ignoring the guests, he grabbed Sadie's elbow and steered her out of the room into the kitchen. Jackie came downstairs and hurried after them.

Everyone tactfully started to leave. Glenys was the last to go.

'Are you sure there isn't anything I can do?' she said, craning her neck to catch a glimpse of what was going on in the kitchen.

'We can manage.' Irene hustled her towards the door and closed it firmly in her face. Then she headed for the kitchen.

Sadie sat at the kitchen table, still clutching the bundle in her arms. Her hair was damp with rain and she was shivering inside her pink mohair coat. Tom loomed over her, while Jackie looked helplessly from one to the other. Somewhere upstairs, baby Catherine was yelling.

'It's a little bastard. And you're not keeping it under this roof. Tell her, Ma!' But before his mother could speak, he went on. 'And I hope you're pleased with yourself, ruining my daughter's christening?'

'I didn't plan it, did I? I had nowhere else to go. What did you want me to do, sit in the bus shelter in the rain until you'd finished showing off to the neighbours?'

'I wanted you to do as you were told for once and leave that behind.' He pointed at the baby in her arms.

'I changed my mind.'

'You can't do that! We agreed—'

'She's my baby and I'm keeping her.' Sadie's face was thin and wretched, but her eyes blazed with determination.

'But—'

'That's enough, Tom.' Irene spoke up. 'We're not going to get anywhere by shouting, are we? Jackie, love, go upstairs and see to Catherine before she screams the place down.' Jackie ran off, relieved to have something useful to do. Irene reached for the kettle and filled it under the tap. 'Have you eaten?' she asked Sadie.

'Not since this morning. But I'm not hungry.'

'You've got to have something. I'll get you some sandwiches from the buffet in a minute.'

'What is this?' Tom demanded. 'She turns up with that . . . that thing,

342

and you treat her like she's the flaming vicar dropped in for Sunday tea!'

'Like I said, there's nowt to be gained by shouting.' Irene turned to Sadie. 'So what did the social workers say when you told them you'd changed your mind?'

Sadie fiddled with the baby's shawl. 'I didn't tell them. I just walked out. You don't know what it was like there. They were so cruel.'

Irene looked at the bundle in her daughter's arms. It was only a week old, just a few weeks younger than Catherine. She longed to see if the baby had her cousin's soft, fair colouring.

'You're in no state to be traipsing halfway across the country,' she said. 'Why don't you go upstairs and rest? I'll bring you up some food.'

Sadie shot a wary look at Tom, then left. Tom turned on Irene. 'I suppose you've said she can stay?'

'She's my daughter. And that baby's our flesh and blood, whether you like it or not.'

Tom's hands clenched at his sides. 'If she stays, we're going.'

'Don't be daft, Tom.'

'I mean it, Ma. It's her or us.'

Irene looked pleadingly at him. 'I can't put her out on the street, Tom.'

'Fine. We'll move out, then.'

'Where will you go?'

'We'll find a flat somewhere. Don't worry about us. Worry about *your daughter*.' Tom slammed out of the room. A moment later the bedroom door banged overhead and she heard him shouting something to Jackie.

Irene sighed. She felt torn. Tom had been so good since his father had died three years ago. But she couldn't turn her back on Sadie, no matter how much trouble she brought with her.

Sadie shivered in bed, the covers pulled up to her chin. It was strange to see her there, surrounded by all her teenage paraphernalia. It reminded Irene that she was only sixteen, barely more than a child herself.

The baby was tucked in beside her, sleeping peacefully. She seemed very contented, unlike her screeching cousin next door.

'Sorry, Mum,' Sadie whispered. 'I didn't mean to cause trouble.'

'You never do, do you? It just seems to follow you around.' Irene put the tray of sandwiches and tea on the bedside table.

Sadie looked down at the baby, tucked in the crook of her arm. 'Do you think I've done a stupid thing?'

'It doesn't matter what I think. It's done now, and we've got to make the best of it, haven't we?' She held out her arms. 'Can I?'

Sadie warily handed her over, as if afraid Irene might take her away.

Irene looked closely at her granddaughter for the first time. She was heartbreakingly beautiful, as dark as Catherine was fair. Just like her father. Sadie had stubbornly refused to tell anyone his name, but like everyone else Irene had a good idea who it was. Especially as the lad in question had left town just after finding out Sadie was pregnant.

Irene pushed the shawl back off the baby's face. She would never admit it to Sadie or Tom, but she was secretly relieved her grandchild was home where she belonged. 'So does this one have a name yet?'

'Ruby Tuesday.'

'What kind of a name is that?'

'It's a song by the Rolling Stones. I like it.'

'I might have known you'd come up with summat daft!' She looked down at the baby again, smiling in spite of herself.

Daft name or not, she couldn't have given her up either.

Chapter 1

Present Day

'HOW MUCH? And does that include free light sabres? How about the personal appearance by Darth Vader? I see, and that's how much extra?'

Ten minutes later Roo Hennessy put the phone down, feeling pleased with herself. In the past two hours, she'd fired off more than a dozen overdue emails, taken a conference call from Tokyo, and organised a *Star Wars* themed party for her son's sixth birthday. And it was only nine o'clock.

She opened her laptop and called up her notes on the Homeworks project. She'd been working with the DIY chain for four months, visiting stores, meeting the staff and management and generally seeing how everything fitted together. Now she was due to meet the directors the following day to present her report on how the whole operation could be run better and more efficiently. And more cheaply, of course. That was the bottom line for most of the companies that employed her.

And Roo usually delivered. She was good at her job, which was why she was now one of Warner and Hicks's senior management consultants, with a beautifully decorated office and a plate-glass wall that looked down the Thames as far as the Palace of Westminster.

But as much as Roo Hennessy told herself she deserved all this, there were still times when she felt like a fraud. What was she doing here, sitting at a big desk, telling corporations how to run their businesses? Didn't they know she was just a kid from the backstreets of a run-down Yorkshire town? She might be able to fool everyone else with her posh accent and designer clothes, but she didn't fool herself. Sometimes she could almost imagine Gerry Matthews, the principal consultant, coming in and telling her to clear her desk because she'd been found out.

The door opened and Gerry Matthews came in. Roo almost screamed.

'Got a good one for you.' He was in his early forties, Armani-suited and never wasted time on greetings. 'Failing business. The bank has asked us to take a look at it, see if we can do something.' He put the file on her desk. 'Three-month job. I've told them you'll be there on Monday.'

Today was Thursday. That gave her just three days to get up to speed, if she worked all weekend.

'And the bank wants us to try to turn it around?'

'Or close it down. It's up to you which way they go.'

'I'd better get started straight away.' She glanced at the name on the file and froze. 'Wait a minute. Fairbanks Fine Furniture? In Normanford?'

'Have you heard of it?'

'You could say that.' Roo stared down at the address printed in front of her. 'I was born in Normanford.'

'Great. So you'll have local knowledge?'

Oh, yes, Roo thought. I know it all right. Only too well. 'Can't you send someone else?'

'Why don't you want to go?'

'Personal reasons.'

Gerry considered it for a moment. 'Obviously you don't have to go if you don't feel you can,' he said. Then, just as Roo was letting out a sigh of relief he went on, 'There are other places. Funnily enough, I was talking to Iceman Frozen Foods the other day. They're still looking for someone.'

There it was. The unspoken threat. Take this job, or spend the next six months in eternal darkness on a fish-processing plant in Norway, away from her family and well out of the Warner and Hicks loop.

'I'll go to Normanford,' she said.

'Great.' Gerry beamed. 'Don't look so fed up. It'll be a good chance to catch up with your family and friends again.'

That's what I'm afraid of, she thought.

Roo decided she deserved to get home before Ollie's bedtime for once and headed for Wandsworth. Ollie was in the kitchen eating his tea while his nanny Shauna packed his lunchbox for the morning.

'May The Force be with you,' he intoned solemnly through a mouthful of food as Roo swept past, collecting the evening paper and the post that was crammed behind the toaster.

'Um, thanks.' Roo swooped down to kiss her son's cheek. She glanced at his plate and stopped short. 'What are you eating?'

'Chicken nuggets and chips.' Shauna looked defensive. 'He won't eat the stuff you left for him.'

Or you're too bone idle to cook it, Roo thought. Honestly, what was the point of stocking the fridge with healthy foods when her nanny poisoned him with junk?

She and Shauna eyeballed each other across the kitchen. She kept meaning to talk to her about her attitude, but she was terrified she'd leave. And, useless or not, finding a new nanny at short notice was a working mother's dread.

'You've got to hear my spelling words,' Ollie broke the silence. 'We're supposed to practise every day. Only you never do.'

'Doesn't Shauna do it?'

'Of course I do,' Shauna snapped. 'He just likes you to do it sometimes. It's important for him to know you're interested.'

'Everyone else's mummies listen to them,' Ollie piled on the guilt.

'Yes, well, other mummies don't have busy jobs like mine, do they?'

'Being a mummy is a job,' Ollie pointed out, as Shauna smirked.

Yes, but being a mummy doesn't pay wages, does it? Roo wanted to shout. It doesn't pay for toys, or school trips, or birthday parties. Or for nannies who seemed to think their only role was to stuff rubbish into their charges and swan around in the family Shogun.

But instead she smiled at Ollie. 'I'd love to hear your spellings.'

'Great!' The speed with which he rushed to fetch his book made her feel awful. Maybe she hadn't been spending enough time with him lately.

She peeled potatoes and defrosted chicken breasts as he struggled through his spellings. But then a headline on the front page of the *Standard* caught her eye.

'Mummy! You're not listening.'

She looked up sharply. 'I am.'

'No, you're not! You're reading the newspaper!'

'What's all the shouting about?' David wandered in.

'I was reading to Mummy and she wasn't listening.'

'I *was* listening. I can do more than one thing at once.'

'There you are,' David ruffled Ollie's fair hair and went to the fridge for a bottle of wine. 'Mummy's multi-tasking. She's a very busy lady, Ollie. We can't expect her full attention all the time, can we?'

Roo glared at him. He was being unfair, but she let it pass. She seemed to be letting a lot of David's comments pass these days. They'd be arguing all the time otherwise. She began chopping onions while David poured himself a glass of wine and Shauna read the Sits Vac column in the paper. Roo was convinced she only did it to make her feel insecure.

'You haven't forgotten Ollie needs to take his money for the school trip tomorrow?' she asked, dashing away a tear brought on by the onions. 'And you have to let his teacher know he has a dental appointment on Tuesday . . . Shauna, are you listening?'

'What? Oh, yeah.' Shauna looked up vaguely.

'Maybe she's multi-tasking.' David caught Shauna's eye and they both grinned.

'Very funny. And don't forget he needs to do his violin practice tonight. He's got a lesson after the school trip.'

'Bloody violin,' Ollie mumbled, kicking the table leg.

'Ollie!'

'I hate it!' Ollie's lower lip jutted. 'What do I have to learn the stupid violin for, anyway?'

'Because—' Roo opened her mouth and found she couldn't think of a single reason. Except that all the other kids in his class went to clarinet, junior astrophysics or preschool Japanese classes, and she didn't want to be a bad mother. 'You might enjoy it one day.'

'I won't. And I'm no good at it.'

'He's got a point,' David said. 'He's never going to be Yehudi Menuhin, so why put him through it?'

'I just don't want him to be left behind.'

'Heaven forbid!' David rolled his eyes. 'I don't know why you don't set him achievement targets, then you can sit down and have a monthly performance review. At least that way he might see you occasionally.'

Shauna hurried Ollie upstairs to do the dreaded violin practice, leaving them glaring at each other.

'Why do you have to be so hostile?' Roo demanded.

'Why do you have to be such a control freak?'

'That's not true.'

He refilled his glass. Roo regarded the bottle anxiously. He'd been drinking a lot more since he lost his job. But she didn't dare mention it. She didn't want him to fly off the handle again. Not now.

'Gerry Matthews has given me another project,' she said.

'So you'll be putting another bunch of poor sods out of work? I bet you'll enjoy that.'

She ignored the gibe. 'It's in Normanford.'

'Does that mean you're going away again?'

'Only for three months. And I'll be home every weekend.'

'Great. Just great. We never see you these days.'

'Look, I didn't want to take this job. I had to. It was either that or six months on a fish farm in Norway.'

'You could have said no.'

'Don't you think I tried? I haven't got much choice, have I? One of us has to earn a living.'

She could have bitten off her tongue as soon as she said it. She'd tried not to make a big deal out of them living off her income. But it was like treading on eggshells and sometimes she forgot to be careful.

'Great. Thanks for throwing that back in my face.'

'David, I didn't mean that—'

'I know what you meant. Don't you think I'm trying to get another job? Don't you think I feel bad enough, being chucked on the scrapheap before I'm forty?'

'Being made redundant wasn't a reflection on your abilities. It—'

'Spare me the pep talk. You're not talking to your clients now.'

No, Roo thought. If I was, I'd tell them to stop feeling so bloody sorry for themselves and sort their lives out.

They ate supper in silence. Afterwards David went off to watch television, leaving her to catch up with paperwork at the kitchen table. Roo wanted to talk to him about going back to Normanford, and how much she was dreading it. She wanted him to be sympathetic, to take her in his arms and tell her she didn't have to go, that he'd take care of her. But all he'd done was give her a hard time, as if she wanted to leave her home and family and go to a place that held nothing but bad memories for her.

It was raining on Sunday evening when Roo Hennessy returned to Normanford. She hadn't been home for nearly two years, and then it was only a quick duty visit.

Normanford had once been a thriving mining town in West Yorkshire, but the pit closures of the 1980s had torn its heart out. It depressed her to see how down-at-heel it still looked. The precinct was full of charity shops, cut-price electrical retailers and cheap boutiques. Some shop fronts were boarded up and covered with tattered flyposters.

She suddenly felt deeply miserable. It had only been a few hours but she already missed Ollie and David. She'd fought back the tears when she kissed her son goodbye, although he was more preoccupied with watching his favourite TV show than his mother leaving.

Usually the company would have put her in a hotel but Normanford only had a couple of b & b's, so they'd rented her a house instead.

'We could have found you a hotel in Leeds, but we thought this would save you all that commuting,' Tina, Gerry's PA, explained. But Roo would have gladly swapped twenty minutes on the motorway for the bliss of room service. Especially when she found out where she was staying.

She didn't need the directions from the letting agents to find the house the company had rented for her. By some sick irony, it was in the same street she and her mother had lived in before she went to university.

She hoped the residents had changed in the past twenty years. Sykes Street had always had a reputation in Normanford. It was where the problem families ended up. Barely a night went by without a fight breaking out or a police car screeching into the street.

She couldn't park outside the house because the space was taken up by a beaten-up Mini Traveller. Roo pulled up at the far end of the street. There, beyond a row of rusty iron railings, a steep grassy embankment ran down to the river. On the other side of the railings, a gang of youths were entertaining themselves lobbing rubbish into the water.

Roo remembered how she used to sit in that very same spot with her cousin Cat and Billy Kitchener. Sometimes she'd stay there until long after dark, not wanting to go home and watch her mother acting daft with her latest boyfriend.

She reached number sixteen and was searching in her handbag for her keys when the neighbour's door flew open and a blonde woman rushed out, pulling on her coat.

'Bastard!' she called behind her.

'Rachel, wait—' A man followed her, fair-haired, dressed in nothing but a pair of faded jeans.

'So who was she?' Her voice was shrill enough for the whole street to hear. Some things never changed, Roo thought.

'No one you'd know. Look, it wasn't serious—'

'And that makes it all right, does it? You shag some stranger and that's meant to make me feel better? Just answer me one question. Why?'

'I don't know. I'm an idiot, I suppose.'

'You know what your problem is? You're afraid to commit. As soon as a woman starts getting too close, you have to press the self-destruct button. I think you should take a long, hard look at your behaviour, because I really think you have some esteem issues to sort out.'

'And I think you've been reading too many self-help books.'

'Screw you!'

As she flounced away, the man turned to Roo and said, 'Hi, you must be my new neighbour. I'm Matt Collins.'

'Roo Hennessy.' Roo shook his hand, nonplussed. It was as if the last five minutes hadn't happened. Or maybe this happened to him all the time. He looked the type, with that bad-boy grin of his. 'Is that your car?'

'It certainly is,' he said with pride. 'Beautiful, isn't it?'

'It's also in my space.'

'Technically, it isn't. You see, contrary to popular belief you don't have any statutory rights to park outside your own house—' He caught Roo's withering look. 'But since you asked so nicely I'll move it, shall I?'

It took him ages. First he had to go inside and find some shoes. Then he couldn't get the damn thing started. Roo sat in her car, tapping her hands impatiently on the wheel. She was aware that the youths had given up their litter-lobbing and were watching with interest.

Finally Matt appeared at her window. 'Sorry, I can't seem to get it started. I think it needs some fine-tuning.'

Roo tutted, got out and slammed the door. She stomped round to the back and flung open the boot to get her luggage out. Matt watched her.

'Nice motor, by the way. You don't get many of those around here.'

'Audis?'

'Cars with hubcaps.'

'Alloys, actually.' She shut the boot and went to pick up her bags, but Matt got there first.

'Allow me.' They were heavy but he managed them easily. She opened the front door and he followed her in, looking around. 'Not bad. Better than the dump I live in, anyway.'

Roo had to admit it wasn't as horrible as she'd feared. The two living rooms had been knocked through, with a galley kitchen beyond. Upstairs, she already knew, there would be two bedrooms and a bathroom. The rooms were small, but the place had been newly refurbished, so at least it was all magnolia walls and plain carpets. The smell of new paint and pine disinfectant hung in the air.

Matt followed her into the kitchen. 'This is nice.' He ran his hand over the shiny worktop. 'Every place I've ever rented has smelt of boiled cabbage. Why do you think that is?'

'I have no idea. And much as I'd like to discuss it further, I'm afraid I have a lot to do, so—'

'I'll leave you to it.' He'd almost reached the front door when he turned back. 'I don't suppose you'd like to join me for a curry? I've just remembered I ordered a takeaway half an hour ago. For two. But my friend left unexpectedly.' He looked sheepish.

'No, thank you.'

'Are you sure? It's lamb bhuna.'

'Like I said, I'm rather busy.'

'I thought I'd ask. I suppose I'll just have to give the rest to Harvey.'

'Harvey?'

'My dog. Although he prefers Chinese.' He smiled. 'It was nice meeting you, Roo.'

As soon as she was alone she called home. David took a long time to answer. The first thing he said was, 'You're late.'

'The traffic was a nightmare. Can I speak to Ollie?'

'He's gone to bed. He waited up as long as he could, but he couldn't keep his eyes open,' he added reproachfully.

Roo glanced at the clock. 'But it isn't nine o'clock yet!'

'I can't help it if the poor kid's exhausted, can I? Today's been very stressful for him. He misses you.'

'I miss him, too.' Roo felt tears prick her eyes. 'Both of you,' she said. 'Oh, David, it's horrible up here. I wish I'd never taken the job.'

'You'll get used to it,' he said bracingly. 'And you'll be home at the weekend, won't you?'

'I suppose so.' There were a whole five days to get through before then. Not to mention a mammoth trek back down the motorway.

They chatted for a while. Then David said he had to go because there was a Tom Cruise movie on Sky he wanted to watch.

'Oh. OK.' Roo fought to keep the disappointment out of her voice. 'I'll call you tomorrow, shall I? To speak to Ollie?'

'You do that. Bye, Roo.'

'Bye, David. I love—' But he'd already hung up. Roo kept the phone to her ear, reluctant to put it down. It was strange, she spent half her life jetting everywhere from Stuttgart to San Francisco, yet she'd never felt so far from home.

Upstairs, the main bedroom was hardly bigger than her walk-in wardrobe at home, but it seemed like heaven. Exhausted after her journey, she dumped her cases on the bed and flipped open the first one. She was too tired to unpack everything, so she pulled out one of her suits and hung it up to let the creases drop out before the following morning.

She changed into her nightclothes. It was barely nine o'clock, but she hadn't worked out the heating and the radiators were stone cold. And she'd forgotten how chilly it could be in Yorkshire, even in June.

She got into bed, pulled the duvet up to her chin, and settled down to finish the Fairbanks accounts for the last financial year. Skimming through the figures she could see why the bank was so concerned. Fairbanks's sales were poor, and their overheads were far too high. The way they were going, they'd be bust within months. She made a few preliminary notes, then settled down to sleep. Lamplight seeped through the thin curtains, suffusing the room with faint yellow light. She could hear the teenagers outside laughing and scuffling with each other.

A chill prickled her skin that had nothing to do with the dead radiators. If she closed her eyes she could almost hear her mother singing along to her records as she dolled herself up for another night out.

Sadie Moon. Also known as 'Normanford's answer to Cilla Black', or 'that blonde husband-stealing slut', depending on who you talked to.

She glanced at her mobile phone on the bedside table, wondering if she should call her. She'd been steeling herself to do it all weekend.

It was too late now, she decided. She'd ring her in the morning. Or once she'd settled in properly. Or sometime.

Roo stared at her car in despair. She couldn't believe it. Fate couldn't do this to her, not on her first day. She felt her panic rising and took deep breaths to control it. Calm down, she told herself. It doesn't matter.

'Hi, there.' Matt greeted her from his doorstep. 'Lovely day.'

'Not from where I'm standing.'

He came up the road to where she stood gazing at the space where her alloy wheels used to be. At all four corners there was a neat pile of bricks. 'Oh dear. Someone's been busy.'

'You do realise this wouldn't have happened if I'd been allowed to park outside my house?'

'I hope you're not blaming me? I already told you, legally—'

'Spare me the lecture.' She pulled out her mobile phone.

'Who are you calling?'

'The police.'

'But you don't know who did it.'

'Surely that's their job? Anyway, I'm sure it was those kids who were hanging around last night.'

'I don't think it's a good idea to go around accusing people.' He snatched the phone out of her hand.

'Give me that back!'

'Not until you promise not to do anything stupid. You've got to live round here. And it won't just be bricks under the wheels next, it'll be bricks through the window.'

'I don't care.'

'I do. Suppose they get the wrong house? Anyway, I wouldn't feel happy about it, you being a woman on your own.'

'I'm not on my own.' She flashed her wedding ring at him. 'Anyway, I can take care of myself.'

'I'm sure you can. But I might feel obliged to rush to your rescue. And I'm not very good in a fight.'

'For heaven's sake, they were only kids.'

'Yes, but they have parents. Big ones, with tattoos and criminal records. And that's just their mothers!' He grinned. Roo refused to smile back. She was far too wound up. 'Look, I'll ask around. Give me until tonight and I'll see what I can find out, OK?'

She snatched her phone back. 'I don't have time to argue about this. I'm late enough as it is.'

'I'd offer you a lift, but I don't think my car's working.'

'Thanks, but I'll take a taxi.'

'I'll get you a number. Better still, I'll give them a ring for you. Where shall I say you're going?'

'Fairbanks. And tell them to hurry, please!'

He went back inside the house. Roo kicked at a tuft of grass growing through a crack in the pavement.

'It should be here in a minute,' Matt said five minutes later.

They stood together on the pavement, the silence between them stretching into awkwardness. 'Don't let me keep you, if you've got to be somewhere,' Roo said.

'I'm in no hurry.'

Lucky you, she thought, glancing at her watch.

'So you work at Fairbanks, do you? What do you do?'

Roo looked up the road, willing the taxi to appear. 'I advise them on how to run their business.'

'I bet you're really good at telling other people what to do.'

'I am, as a matter of fact.'

'Why doesn't that surprise me? Looks like your taxi's here.'

'Thank God.' Roo watched the Vauxhall Vectra turning with agonising slowness into the narrow street. At least something was going right.

She got into the taxi, slid into the back seat and slammed the door. 'Fairbanks,' she said shortly. 'And please hurry, I'm late.'

'What's your rush, our Ruby?'

She looked up sharply, meeting the driver's eyes in the mirror. Oh God. It couldn't be.

But it was.

'Uncle Tom?' She should have known that in a small town like Normanford she was bound to run into one of her family sooner or later. She just didn't expect it to be so soon.

'I knew it would be you, as soon as they said the fare was to

Fairbanks.' He'd put on weight. His face filled the rearview mirror. 'Looking forward to your first day, are you? Mind you, you'll have your work cut out sorting that place out. It's gone right downhill lately.'

'So I gather.'

'Still, it'll be all right now you're here. It says so in the paper.'

'Sorry?'

'You're famous, didn't you know?' He reached across to the passenger seat, picked up the folded *Normanford News* and passed it to her. 'Page three.' She flipped the page, and there she was.

'Troubleshooter To Save Fairbanks', the headline said, and the story told how the fate of the factory lay with top management consultant and 'local girl' Roo Hennessy. There was a quote from chairman George Fairbanks saying they expected great things from their new adviser. Oh hell, she thought.

But it was the final paragraph that turned her blood to ice. 'Roo is the daughter of local cabaret singer Sadie Starr. Says Sadie, "I always knew she'd do well for herself. I'm looking forward to having her back home."'

Roo put the paper down, feeling sick. Trust her mother to get her name in the paper! It was a wonder she hadn't insisted on a photo of herself. One of those tacky 'artistic' shots she used to keep in her handbag to hand out to talent scouts, all moussed-up hair and thigh-high skirts. Sadie Starr, indeed! Who the hell did she think she was? She was fifty years old, for heaven's sake! Didn't she ever give up?

'Your nanna's chuffed to bits,' Uncle Tom went on. 'She's already told all the neighbours. She's very proud of our Ruby.'

'Roo,' she corrected, without thinking.

'Eh?'

'I prefer to be called Roo these days.'

'Oh, aye?' He paused, taking it in. 'Well, I can't say I blame you. I always said it was a bloody silly name. Another one of your mother's ideas.'

Roo took a deep breath. 'How is she?'

'Just the same, goes from one disaster to another. She's back living with Nanna now, would you believe? Fifty years old and still can't keep a roof over her head.'

For the first few years of her life, while they lived with Nanna Moon in her terraced house on Hope Street, Roo had thought her mother could do no wrong. She looked like a film star, with her blonde hair, pink lipstick and platform shoes. It was Nanna who put the food on the table and made sure Roo always had clean socks for school, while Sadie flitted in and out of the house.

Then, when Roo was nine years old, everything changed. Auntie Jackie died, and Uncle Tom and her cousin Cat moved in with Nanna. It was a tight squeeze, but Roo didn't mind sharing her bedroom with Cat. They were like sisters anyway. The problem was that Sadie and Uncle Tom hated each other, which led to all kinds of rows.

In the end, Sadie and Roo moved out to a cramped flat over an iron-monger's shop. They had to share a bedroom, there were mice skittering behind the skirting boards and the roof leaked into the light fittings when it rained, blowing the lot. It was the first of many addresses.

Sadie wasn't like other mothers. Real mothers were like her friends' mums. They wore pinnies and baked cakes and had husbands. They didn't drink gin, wear hot pants or send their children down to the corner shop to beg cigarettes on credit. And they certainly didn't leave their kids to go off and sing in dodgy working men's clubs every night.

It was the only job Roo had ever known her mother stick at. They never paid her, except for the tips she collected, but Sadie did it because she was convinced she was going to be a star.

'You wait,' she'd say, as she stuck on her false eyelashes ready for her night out. 'One of these days some big-shot agent is going to walk into that place and sign me up on the spot. We'll be rich, baby.'

But somehow it never happened. In the meantime, Roo would spend most evenings alone. She'd go to sleep on the sofa with the light on and the telly blaring so she couldn't hear the noises in the street outside.

Then, as she got older, she found she didn't care so much. Sometimes it was a relief not to have Sadie around, with her singing and her music that always had the neighbours bashing on the walls. Then the place was quiet, and Roo could do her homework or read in peace, without Sadie telling her she'd get shortsighted—'And you know what they say, don't you? Men don't make passes at girls who wear glasses.'

As if Roo cared. She'd seen enough of men to last her a lifetime. Sadie had a never-ending stream of admirers coming through the flat.

'Be nice to him,' Sadie would say, 'he could be your stepdad one day!'

Some hope, Roo thought. She could see what they were after, even if Sadie didn't. And once they'd got it, they'd be off. Never mind that they'd promised to leave their wives, or marry her, or make her a star.

They argued a lot but their fiercest rows were about Roo's father.

'The less you know about him, the better,' Sadie insisted.

'At least tell me his name!'

'What's the point? It wouldn't mean anything to you anyway. Besides, I don't want to rake over old ground.' Which was all very well for her to say. But it felt as if part of Roo was missing.

Her uncle Tom was right: Fairbanks had gone downhill. The main factory building was surrounded by an ugly mishmash of outbuildings and was badly in need of new paint. Inside, the reception was even less promising. Roo's glance took in the drab paintwork, dilapidated seating and dried-up plants before coming to rest on the girl behind the desk.

'Yeah?'

'Roo Hennessy.'

'Oh! Right. I'll . . . um . . . let them know you're here.'

'Thanks, but I'd prefer to find my own way.' As she walked away she heard the girl pick up the phone and say, 'She's on her way up.'

Necks craned over computers and a tide of whispers followed her as she strode through the main office.

'Ms Hennessy?' Roo turned round and did a double take. There, standing in the doorway at the far end of the office, was her cousin Cat.

She blinked. No, it couldn't be. But the strawberry-blonde hair, freckled nose and mischievous green eyes were exactly the same.

'I'm Becky,' she said. 'Your new assistant.'

Roo frowned. 'Your name wouldn't be Kitchener, by any chance?'

Becky grinned. 'I wondered if you'd recognise me!'

Recognise her? It was like looking at a ghost. Cat's eldest would be seventeen now. Rebecca Jacqueline. Of course.

'Shall I show you to your office?' Becky said.

Roo's 'office' was a tiny annexe off the main room, with a desk, two chairs and filing cabinet. She looked round in dismay. 'I've seen stationery cupboards bigger than this,' she said.

'That's what it was. But at least you've got a view.'

That was a matter of opinion. Roo rubbed at the grimy glass and peered out. In the distance she could see the flash of cars streaming down the M62 and below her, the sluggish khaki river.

'You know, I always wondered what you were like,' Becky said.

'I'm surprised your mother didn't tell you.'

'She said you always thought you were too good for Normanford. She said all you ever wanted to do was get out of here.'

'And what else did she say?'

'Not much. Only that you stopped speaking years ago. She wouldn't say why, though.'

I bet she wouldn't, Roo thought. For a moment, she was tempted to tell Becky: how she and her mother had been best friends until Cat set her sights on the boy Roo loved and deliberately got pregnant so he'd have to marry her.

'It was a teenage thing,' she said.

She willed herself not to say any more, but as Becky turned to go she blurted out, 'How is your dad?'

'Don't you know? He's—'

'Ms Hennessy?' A tall, silver-haired man stood in the doorway. 'How do you do? I'm Frederick Fairbanks.' He shook her hand. 'I'm sorry my father isn't here to greet you. He's unwell at the moment. As finance director, I have my father's authority in the day-to-day running of the company.'

You haven't made a very good job of it, Roo stopped herself saying just in time. 'Then you'll know how grave the situation is?'

'I think that's putting it mildly, Ms Hennessy. I prefer catastrophic. Our trading figures for the last quarter were very poor indeed.'

Roo was surprised. He was taking the news very well, considering his family firm was on the skids.

He seemed to guess what she was thinking. 'I'm a realist, Ms Hennessy.' He perched on a corner of the desk. 'So how bad is it?'

'I'll know that when I've had a chance to look at the whole picture.'

'But the bank wants to foreclose? They don't think we have a chance?'

'They must think you have some chance or they wouldn't have asked me to come here.'

He smiled. 'Very diplomatic, Ms Hennessy.' He stood up. 'Let me know if there's any way I can help you, won't you?'

'I will, thank you.' As he turned to leave, she said, 'Do you know when I might be able to meet your father?'

Frederick's grey eyes twinkled. 'Oh, you'll meet him soon enough. I just hope you're ready for him when you do!'

Chapter 2

CAT KITCHENER LOOKED at the magazine clipping in her hand and back at the client sitting in front of her. 'Are you sure this is what you want?'

'Oh, yes.' Mrs March smiled back at her reflection in the mirror. 'I fancy something different.'

It was different, all right. The model in the photo had a spiky urchin cut tipped with acid blonde. It looked great with her killer cheekbones and sharp designer suit. Cat wasn't quite sure how good it would look on a middle-aged woman with crow's-feet and a sensible cardie.

She ran her comb through the greying curls. 'I don't know if it will work with your hair,' she said tactfully. 'But I could try something similar. Something that would really suit you.'

'I'll leave it to you, dear.' Mrs March settled back in her seat.

Cat sent her over to the basins for a shampoo with Natalie, the trainee, and glanced at her watch. Half past two. She'd sent Sadie out for a sandwich over an hour ago. She'd already been back late twice this week, and Maxine, the salon owner, definitely had it in for her. Maxine was right by the door, leaning on the reception desk chatting to Julie Teasdale, the other stylist.

'Great, isn't it?' Avril, the senior stylist, hissed as she whizzed past with a trolley full of rollers. 'We're working our backsides off while those two are gassing! If it wasn't my last day I'd walk out right now!'

Cat nodded in agreement. No one liked working for Maxine. She usually managed to drive stylists away with her tantrums. Or they took better-paid jobs in other salons, like Avril. Maxine was as mean as she was moody.

She set to work on Mrs March's hair, giving it a conditioning rinse in a warm coppery shade that suited her colouring. Then she snipped away at her curls, shaping them into a face-framing style that wasn't too far from the urchin cut she'd wanted, but flattered her face more.

'I haven't seen you in here before,' she chatted as she worked.

'Oh, I haven't got the money for hairdressers. My sister does it for me,' Mrs March smiled back. 'But just this once I thought I'd treat myself.'

'Special occasion, is it?'

'You could say that. I start chemotherapy next week.'

She said it so matter-of-factly, Cat almost dropped her scissors.

'They've already told me I'll probably lose my hair,' she said. 'So I thought I'd make the most of it while I still had it.'

Cat nodded. She was so glad she hadn't taken the lazy route and copied that model's hairstyle. Mrs March deserved better.

As it was, her client was delighted with the finished result. 'I look twenty years younger!' she exclaimed. 'How much do I owe you, dear?'

Cat glanced around to make sure Maxine wasn't looking and lowered her voice. 'It's on me. On one condition. That you let me do it for you again when the treatment's over and it's grown back.'

Mrs March smiled wistfully. 'Let's hope so,' she said.

Cat was sweeping up the hair from the floor when Julie sneaked up behind her. 'Letting customers off without paying?' she taunted. 'I might have to tell Maxine.'

'And I might have to tell her about you helping yourself to shampoo from the stockroom!'

They glared at each other. Julie was tall and scrawny with a nose stud, a lip ring and hair bleached to the texture of candy floss.

'What are you two gossiping about?' Maxine came over to them, her high heels clicking on the tiled floor. She was in her thirties with tiger-striped hair and far too much make-up.

Julie looked sideways at Cat. 'Nothing,' she muttered. 'I'll be outside having a ciggy if anyone needs me.'

'What's up with her?' Maxine asked, as she stalked off. 'I hope you haven't upset her. She's going through a bad time at the moment. Her Dwayne's been arrested again.'

'Now why doesn't that surprise me?' Julie's teenage son spent more time in youth custody than he did in his own home.

'Where's Sadie?' Cat's heart sank as Maxine asked the question she'd been dreading.

'I . . . um . . . think she had a doctor's appointment.'

'I don't remember seeing it in the diary.' She went over to the desk and flicked through the appointments book. 'No, it's definitely not here.'

'She probably forgot to write it down. You know what she's like.'

'Unreliable, you mean.' Maxine slammed the book shut. 'Right, that's it. She's had her last chance.'

'You can't get rid of her!'

'Why not? She's got to learn she can't turn up when she feels like it.'

'If she goes, I go too,' Cat said.

Maxine's eyes narrowed under the weight of her mascara, not sure if Cat was bluffing or not. 'Fine. I can replace you, no problem.'

'Are you sure about that? Avril leaves today, and you haven't replaced her yet. You wouldn't want to be two stylists down, would you?'

Before Maxine could reply, the bell over the door jangled and Sadie rushed in, her arms full of carrier bags. She stopped dead when she saw Maxine.

'Where the hell have you been?' Maxine hissed.

'I . . . um . . .' Sadie stared at Cat, who mimed furiously behind Maxine's back. 'I was at the . . . er . . . doctor's? That's it! I was at the doctor's,' she finished triumphantly.

'Hmm. Why don't I believe you?' Maxine drummed her nails on the desk. 'This is your last warning, Sadie. If you come back late from lunch one more time, you're out. Is that clear?' She snatched up her fake Gucci bag and stomped out of the salon, slamming the door behind her.

Sadie pulled a face. 'Someone's in a bad mood!'

'She means it.' Cat followed her into the staffroom. 'I can't keep covering for you, Sadie. She's got it in for you.'

'Don't I know it! But I couldn't help being late. I had to pick up some groceries for Nanna.'

Cat eyed the carrier bags. 'Just groceries?'

'Maybe not.' Sadie looked coy. 'I passed Dolcis on the way back, and I couldn't resist these—' she pulled out a pair of crimson stilettos. 'They'll go with that red dress I bought from the market last week.'

'Sadie! I thought you were still paying off your credit cards?'

'But they were such a bargain! Anyway, I felt like treating myself. I needed cheering up.'

No need to ask why. Sadie had been down since she found out Ruby was coming home and hadn't called her. She pretended she didn't care, but Cat knew different.

'And I got your sandwich.' Sadie handed her the brown paper bag. 'Tuna mayo and salad.'

Cat was picking out the lettuce when Julie came in. 'Shouldn't you two be out there doing some work?' she snapped.

'It's my lunch break, in case you hadn't noticed.'

'What about you?' Julie turned on Sadie. 'Why don't you make yourself busy? Go and straighten some towels or something!'

'She's got a bloody nerve!' Sadie said, as Julie barged out again. 'Anyone would think she was already senior stylist.'

'Maybe she is. She was getting very cosy with Maxine earlier on.'

'Rubbish, that job's as good as yours.'

'I don't know.' Cat tried not to think about it, but ever since Avril had announced she was leaving, she'd been hoping Maxine might consider her for the job.

They were distracted by the sound of shouting in reception. Cat recognised the woman's voice and groaned. 'Oh God.' She put down her sandwich. 'I'd better go and see what the old boot wants.'

Glenys Kitchener stood at the reception desk, her handbag swung over her arm, ready to do battle.

'You don't understand,' she said to Natalie, who was quivering behind the desk. 'I need a wash and blow-dry, and I need it NOW.'

Typical Glenys, Cat thought. She just waltzed in and expected everyone to bow down to her, just because her late husband used to be an MP. She fixed a smile on her face and went to meet her mother-in-law, Sadie following. 'Glenys, what a pleasant surprise.'

'Catherine.' Glenys's face twitched, but she couldn't bring herself to smile. 'I was just explaining to this—person here—' she glared at Natalie,

GOODBYE, RUBY TUESDAY

'that I need a wash and blow-dry. And *she* says you're fully booked.'

'She's right. As you can see, we're very busy.'

'Surely you could fit me in? I have a fundraising meeting at four.'

Cat was about to open her mouth when Sadie said, 'I could do it.'

'Aren't you busy with Mrs Weaver?'

'She hasn't arrived yet. Besides, she won't mind waiting. Poor old dear, she only comes in for a gossip. The longer she's here, the better she likes it.' She smiled at Glenys. 'Just a blow-dry, was it?'

Cat fumed as Glenys was whisked off to be gowned up. She didn't even bother to say thank you, acting as if she was doing Sadie a favour, allowing her to touch her precious curls.

Cat and her mother-in-law had never got on. Glenys made no secret of the fact that she thought Billy had married beneath him. Hers was the only long face on their wedding photo. Even his father had managed a smile.

She turned her attention back to her client. 'What can I do for you today, Pauline? The usual, is it?'

As she washed Pauline's hair she tried to listen to Sadie and Glenys's conversation at the next basin.

'You mean you haven't heard from your Ruby? How strange.'

'I expect she's busy.'

'Yes, but not to pick up the phone and call her own mother! It isn't right, is it? But you two were never really close, were you?' She glanced sideways and caught Cat listening. 'Do you remember how friendly she was with my William?' she said. 'Never apart, were they? You know, there was a time when I thought the two of them might—ow!' She sprang out of the chair, spluttering.

'Oops,' Sadie said. 'Sorry, the spray slipped.' Cat could see she was trying not to laugh.

Of course Maxine chose that moment to come back to the salon. 'What on earth's going on?' she demanded.

'She tried to drown me!' Glenys pointed at Sadie. 'I'm drenched! I can't go to my committee meeting like this!'

'Natalie! Fetch some towels for Mrs Kitchener.' Maxine snapped her fingers, summoning the junior. 'Come on, Glenys, let's get you dried off. Then I'll do your hair personally. I'll talk to *you* later.' She glared at Sadie as she hustled the dripping Glenys into the back room.

Cat watched them go. 'You've really done it now.'

'It serves her right, the old witch.' Sadie glanced at Cat. 'Take no notice of her. She doesn't know what she's talking about.'

'I know. She's just being poisonous.' But she had a feeling that where her husband and cousin were concerned, Glenys knew only too well.

361

Cat could still remember the moment she fell in love with Billy Kitchener. His mum and hers were friends, so they often came round to visit. He must have been about nine years old. He looked so out of place with his plastered-down hair and pristine trainers.

'Mother says I mustn't get my clothes dirty,' he'd said.

She'd risen to the challenge and pushed him in a mud patch. He'd gone home, filthy and fighting back tears. Cat was terrified of what her mum would do to her, but Billy insisted it was an accident, even when his mother smacked him for being careless. That day he'd stopped being a mummy's boy and become her hero.

Of course, she never admitted how she felt, not even to Ruby. She was afraid she might laugh and call her stupid. Cat had always preferred to hide her feelings behind a mask of indifference. She pretended she didn't care when she failed most of her O levels while Roo sailed through every subject with top marks. She even pretended to find it funny when her father said she'd never amount to anything.

But deep down she did care. Especially about Billy Kitchener.

Not that it did her any good. Roo was the one he wanted. You only had to see them together to know that. They even looked like they belonged together, both tall and dark and clever-looking. Cat always felt like the odd one out when she was with them. They understood about politics, read books and watched arty films with subtitles. They laughed at private jokes and talked about things Cat didn't have a clue about.

All the time, she told herself that one day Ruby would go to college and she would have Billy to herself. So when Ruby broke the news that she and Billy had decided to go to university together, her whole world collapsed. She felt as lost and abandoned as she had the day she'd come home from school and found her mother dead in bed with an empty bottle of pills. Everyone she loved left her in the end.

But she didn't plan what came next, whatever Ruby said about it. It just happened. Ruby was away, and Cat and Billy went out for a drink together. She dressed up specially, knowing it could be their last night alone for a long time, and she could tell straight away Billy fancied her. It felt good; she might not have her cousin's brains, but she could still get his attention. When the evening ended, they went back to his place, as his parents were away at some political do in Westminster.

They both knew what was going to happen, and even though she didn't plan it, she wanted it. She couldn't bear the idea of him going away and her never knowing what it was like to make love to him.

It was the first time for both of them. Afterwards, she'd fallen asleep in his arms, feeling special. His first time had been with her, not Ruby.

Whatever else her cousin took away from her, she couldn't take that.

But then the morning came, and Billy was full of remorse. No matter how much Cat tried to tell him she'd wanted it as much as he did, he blamed himself. She soon realised that it wasn't her he felt guilty about, it was Ruby. He'd betrayed the girl he loved.

When Ruby returned she and Billy were together again, making plans, talking about the future, shutting Cat out. That was when she came up with her plan. What if she was pregnant? Then everyone would know what had happened with her and Billy. They couldn't ignore her.

Of course, she knew she wasn't. She planned to leave it a few days, then tell them the panic was over. Except it didn't work out like that. Billy insisted he wanted to marry her, in spite of his mother, who said she should have an abortion.

Cat barely heard her. She had a sudden picture of herself married to Billy, living happily ever after in a wonderful home, surrounded by children and love. More than anything in the world she wished she really was pregnant so it could all come true.

She knew it was only a fantasy. She didn't really mean to marry Billy, or to ruin his life. But somehow as time went on she found it harder to let it go. Especially when Ruby confronted her. She told her Billy didn't love her, that he was only marrying her because he had to. She said if Cat really cared she'd get rid of this baby and set him free. She made her feel as if she would never be worthy of him. Between Ruby and Glenys Kitchener, Cat began to believe it.

The only one who didn't make her feel bad was Billy. He was always so sweet and caring, but Cat knew he was only going through with it because he felt sorry for her. The time had come to end the fantasy.

That was when she realised her period hadn't come. Panicking, she did a test. It was positive.

The news shattered her. She'd pretended to be pregnant, but the reality was different. In desperation, she tried to set Billy free. She told him she didn't want to marry him. She even offered to have an abortion.

'Is that what you want?' he asked.

She couldn't meet his eye. 'I don't want you to be tied down.'

'That wasn't what I asked.'

'I know you don't want this baby.'

'Who says I don't want it?'

'How can you? Your mum's right, it would ruin your future.'

'Maybe you're my future. You and our child.' Cat's heart leapt. He didn't know how much she wanted to believe that.

So they'd got married. His parents bought them a little starter home on the outskirts of town and pretended to be delighted about their wedding to keep up a front. Cat was thrilled to have a place of her own, and set about decorating and buying furniture and getting it ready for the baby.

Ruby didn't come to the wedding. And in spite of what Billy had said, Cat could see he was wistful as her cousin left for university. His future might be with her, but his heart had gone with Ruby.

Chapter 3

IT WAS A DARK, wet afternoon and the only sound in Roo's office was the steady drumming of the rain as she studied the balance sheets.

Then, suddenly, a shout from the main office jolted her back to reality. 'Where is she, then? Where's the woman who reckons she can run my factory better than I can?'

A moment later the door flew open and an old man stood there, leaning heavily on a stick. He was frail and stooped with age, but his gaze was fixed sharply on Roo. George Fairbanks, she guessed. 'So you're Sadie Moon's girl, are you?'

'Mr Fairbanks?' She plastered a smile on her face. 'I didn't think we'd be meeting today. Your son said you were ill.'

'Not too ill to fight for my factory.' He shuffled into the room and lowered himself into the chair opposite hers, wincing with effort. 'So how are you settling in? Office all right for you, is it? I chose it for you myself.'

I bet you did, Roo thought. 'It's fine, thank you.'

'Aye, well, I dare say you won't be staying long.'

'Just as long as it takes to make my recommendations,' she said.

'And we all know what they'll be!' He leaned forward, his face thrust closer to hers. 'I wasn't born yesterday! I know why the bank sent you sniffing round here. They're like vultures, the lot of them, circling round just because they think we're in trouble.'

'No, Mr Fairbanks, you *are* in trouble. And unless you make some serious changes to the way you do business, you're going out of business.'

There was a long silence. Then he said, 'Do you know how old I was when I started working here? Eleven. I served my apprenticeship on that factory floor, learned my craft from my father.' His voice wobbled.

'I have been working here for the best part of seventy years, Ms Hennessy. I've forgotten more than you'll ever know about making furniture. So why should I listen to some jumped-up accountant who wouldn't know a dovetail joint from a daffodil, telling me how I should run my business?'

They eyed each other across the desk.

'Because you don't have much choice. The bank has sent me here to do a job. It would be better for this factory if we could work together. But if you're not going to be able to do that . . . well, I'll just have to do it on my own. Either way, you're not going to stop me carrying out any changes I feel are necessary.'

'We'll see about that.'

That night Roo was too tired to cook, so she called in to the pizza place in the precinct for a takeaway. Pizza Paradise looked anything but. Unless paradise was decked out in Lego colours and as bright as a flood-lit football ground, with a whiff of stale grease and garlic in the air.

'Hello there. Fancy seeing you.' It took Roo a moment to recognise her neighbour Matt behind the till. He wore a yellow T-shirt, his bright red baseball cap at a rakish angle on his messy fair hair. 'What's a nice girl like you doing in a dump like this?'

'Would you believe, ordering a pizza? Do you have a menu?'

'Up there.' He pointed above his head at the row of illuminated pictures. 'A lot of our customers have trouble with the written word, if you know what I mean,' he explained.

Roo studied the photos. 'What do you recommend?'

'Personally, I'd recommend you go to the Star of Bengal. They do a very nice chicken Madras. Although you don't really strike me as a junk-food sort of woman.'

He didn't strike her as a pizza boy, either. Even in that lurid T-shirt he still managed to look like a Calvin Klein model.

'If you must eat at this hellhole, your best bet is the Margarita.'

'Fine. Whatever.'

'Regular or large?'

'Regular.'

'Garlic bread? I wouldn't recommend it,' he said, tapping the keys before she had a chance to reply. 'How about salad?'

'Well—'

'Definitely not.' He rang up the total and took her money. 'By the way, I've got some good news for you. I managed to get your wheels back.'

'You found out who stole them?'

365

'Let's just say I talked to a bloke in the pub and he retrieved them.'

'Great.'

'So you owe me fifty quid.'

'What? You're not serious?'

'That's the going rate.'

'It's outrageous! I'm not buying back my own property.'

'But I've paid for them. What do I do with four useless wheels?'

'You could try putting them on your equally useless car and driving it out of my parking space!'

'I take it you don't want them, then?'

'No, I don't. I'd rather claim on the insurance and buy new ones.'

'Suit yourself. So I'll take the old ones off your car again, shall I? I'm sure you wouldn't mind catching cabs to and from work every day while you wait for your insurance claim to be processed—'

'All right, I get your point.' Roo opened her purse and handed over the notes. 'But this is the last time I get involved in anything like this.'

The chef handed Matt a flat box and he pushed it across the counter to her. 'Enjoy your meal. And have a nice day,' he called after her.

Roo glared at him. 'Are you being funny?'

A *Question of Sport* was blaring from the sitting room when Sadie sneaked in just after seven. She closed the door softly behind her, wincing at the rustle of her carrier bags.

She hurried past the half-open door into the kitchen, dumped her grocery shopping on the table and had just reached the foot of the stairs when a voice rang out above her.

'And what time do you call this?'

'Mum!' Sadie clutched her chest. 'What have you been told about using those stairs? You could fall.'

'How else am I supposed to get up and down? Fly?'

'You're supposed to use that stairlift Social Services put in for you.'

'Stairlift! I don't need a stairlift.' Irene appeared at the top of the stairs. 'I can manage to put one foot in front of the other, thank you very much. It's my house and I'll use the stairs if I want to. Anyway, you haven't answered me. Where have you been?'

'One of the girls at work was leaving. I told you this morning I'd be late. Here, let me help—' She started up the stairs but Irene batted her off.

'Stop fussing, I can manage,' she grumbled.

Sadie retreated as her mother began her slow, awkward, sideways shuffle, her gnarled hands gripping the banister rail. Her knuckles were swollen and angry-looking, a sure sign her arthritis was bad today.

She reached the bottom, her chest heaving with the effort. Sadie tried to conceal her carrier bag behind her but her mother caught sight of it.

'What's that you're hiding? Been spending again?'

'Just a pair of shoes. They were a bargain.'

'They're not a bargain if you can't afford them.'

'It's my money and I'll do what I like with it. I'm not a teenager, Mum! I'm an independent woman and I can please myself.'

As she stomped up the stairs, Irene called after her, 'If you're so independent, what are you doing still living here?'

Bloody good question! Sadie slammed the door and threw the bag down on the bed. Turned fifty, and here she was still in the same bedroom she'd had when she was fifteen. No wonder her mother never treated her like an adult.

If only she knew the truth. Irene thought Sadie had moved back to Hope Street because her flat was repossessed for rent arrears. She never told her the real reason, that she didn't feel her mother could cope alone. She knew Irene would never have let her move back otherwise. And her mother did need help, even though she'd never admit it.

She went back downstairs to find Tom had arrived.

Sadie made some tea and carried the tray into the sitting room. Tom was reading the paper while Irene had switched to watching the snooker.

'I saw our Ruby today,' Tom said.

Sadie's hand wobbled as she poured. 'Oh, aye?'

'I gave her a lift this morning.'

'She hasn't been round yet,' Irene said.

'I expect she's busy,' Sadie murmured.

'Too busy to see her own mother?' Tom said. 'Says a lot, doesn't it?'

'Oh, yes? And when was the last time your daughter invited you round for your Sunday dinner?'

That got him. Tom liked to lay down the law, but his relationship with Cat wasn't good either. Not surprising, since he treated her with the same contempt as he did Sadie. No one was good enough for him. Sometimes she wondered if that was why Jackie had killed herself.

'All the same, she should have called. She is family, after all,' Irene said. 'Where is she living?'

'Sykes Street.'

'You're kidding!' Sadie laughed. Wouldn't her snobbish daughter love that!

'You should call round and see her,' Irene said.

Sadie stopped laughing. 'She hasn't bothered with me all these years, so why should I chase after her?' She stirred her tea.

'What about your grandson? Don't you want to see him?'

'That's up to his mother, isn't it?'

Sadie often wondered what she had done that was so wrong. She'd always tried her best for her daughter. And although she was the first to admit she wasn't too good at being a mum, at least she hadn't given her up to strangers.

Irene Moon had been looking forward to the snooker semifinal, but now she couldn't concentrate on Stephen Hendry heading for a 147 break.

She knew Sadie was more hurt than she let on about Ruby. She might pretend she didn't care, but she was proud and stubborn and she'd sooner go on hurting than make the first move.

Tom hadn't helped, rubbing it in like that. He never missed the chance for a dig at his sister, even after all these years.

She flexed her fingers gingerly, wincing at the pain. Sadie was a good girl; she deserved better than that. Irene knew she didn't always show her how much she appreciated her. The constant nagging of her arthritis made her short-tempered, and not being independent frustrated her. And sometimes she took that out on poor Sadie.

Wild applause filled the room as Stephen potted the final black. Irene came to a decision. As usual, her family weren't going to sort out their problems, so she would have to do it for them. Bang a few heads together, if necessary, just like she used to do when they were kids.

And she would start with Ruby.

'Doesn't look like anyone's coming, does it?' Becky said.

Roo looked around at the empty circle of chairs and felt slightly foolish. She'd had such high hopes when she'd arranged her first staff brainstorming session for that morning. But here she was, in the staffroom, her whiteboard and marker pens at the ready, all set to take down the wonderful flow of ideas, and no one had turned up.

'You might as well go back to the office,' she told Becky. 'There's no point in both of us hanging around. I'll tidy up here.'

She packed up the board and the marker pens, fuming silently. She'd done her best. She'd given them a chance to say how they felt things should be done. Now it was time to do things her way.

'Am I in the right place for the brainstorming?' a voice behind her asked.

Roo swung round. 'No, I was just—' She froze. The man in the doorway was smartly dressed in a suit but looked no different from when she'd last seen him eighteen years ago.

'Long time no see,' said Billy Kitchener.

She dropped the chair she was carrying. 'Billy?'

'Thank God for that. I wasn't sure if you'd remember me.' He grinned. 'Aren't you going to give me a hug? Or are you too grand for that kind of thing these days?'

Stunned, she went into his arms, feeling them wrap around her, holding her close. This couldn't be happening. 'What are you doing here?'

'Didn't Becky tell you? I'm Fairbanks's sales director.' He held her at arm's length. 'It's good to see you. You look great.'

'So do you.' She still couldn't believe it. Was this really Billy, the boy who'd broken her heart all those years ago? He was a man now, his dark hair flecked with grey. But those laughing brown eyes and warm smile were just the same.

'Sorry I wasn't here yesterday when you arrived. I had to go down south and sweet-talk a couple of customers.' He shook his head, marvelling. 'Look at you. Ruby Moon. What happened to the scruffy girl who used to skim stones in the river?'

'She's gone. And it's Roo now. I stopped being Ruby when I left here.'

'I thought you said you'd never come back to Normanford?'

'It was either here or a fish farm in Norway.'

'Put like that, I can see how this place might start to seem attractive.' He smiled, his eyes twinkling. 'So you're our saviour. Imagine that.'

She glanced around the empty room. 'I haven't made a very good start.'

'They just need time to get used to you. We're a bit set in our ways at Fairbanks. Look, why don't I take you to lunch? Catch up on old times.'

'I'm not sure I can. I have some notes to write up—'

'In your lunch hour?'

'I don't usually take lunch hours. I'm too busy.'

'Roo, this is me you're talking to. You know, the old friend you haven't seen for eighteen years?'

She smiled reluctantly. 'Put like that, I can't say no, can I?'

'The Ponderosa. Are you serious?'

'I told you you'd love it.'

'It's . . . unbelievable.' Roo stared around her. The restaurant was done out like an old Western saloon, its beamed ceilings hung with cowboy paraphernalia—saddles, bridles and, in the far corner, what looked like a hangman's noose. 'Please tell me you don't bring customers here?'

'Are you kidding? All Normanford's movers and shakers come here. And it's gone a lot more up-market since they got rid of the spittoons.'

'Oh, please!' Roo turned to the barmaid and ordered a mineral water.

'At least we stand a chance of getting a table,' she said, looking around the empty restaurant.

'It livens up in the evening, when they have a cabaret. In fact—' he stopped.

'What?'

'Your mum sings here sometimes. Sorry, maybe I shouldn't have mentioned it.'

'No, it's fine. Honestly. Shall we get a table?'

They found a place under a precarious-looking packsaddle. Roo studied the big laminated menu, with its coloured photos of food-filled plates. It made her think of Pizza Paradise. 'I think I'll stick to salad.'

'And I'll have the Rodeo Rib-Eye.'

As they ordered, Roo kept sneaking glances at him, drinking in the face she hadn't seen for nearly twenty years.

They made feeble jokes about the stupid Western decor and the impossibility of finding any vegetable in Normanford that wasn't oven chips. All small talk, as if they were strangers.

And all the time she was aware of what they weren't saying, how they were skirting around anything remotely sensitive. Like his marriage.

Their food arrived and Roo grabbed the chance to change the subject.

'I was sorry to hear about your father.' It had come as a shock to see the obituary in *The Times* a few years back, saying he'd died from a heart attack at the age of sixty. Not that she could remember much about Bernard Kitchener. He had always been away pursuing his political career. 'How is your mum these days?'

'Oh, you know my mother. She never stops. She's got her bridge club, and various charity committees she's on. It keeps her busy, thank God. Otherwise she'd never stop bothering me!' He speared a piece of steak.

'She must be proud of you. High-powered marketing man and all that!'

'Not exactly high-powered. Not enough for her, anyway. She'd much rather I was running some multinational corporation somewhere.'

'And what about you?'

'I'm happy the way I am.'

Are you? she wanted to say. Are you really?

They talked about their jobs, her life in London, her family. They swapped photos of their children—besides Becky, Billy had an eight-year-old daughter and a four-year-old son—and Roo raved about Ollie and David.

'You must miss them, being up here? I don't think Cat would like it if I had to work away for three months.' Roo didn't reply. 'It is all right to talk about her, isn't it?'

'It doesn't bother me. But I'm surprised you're still married.'

'Contrary to your direst predictions. And my mother's.'

They finished their meal and a waiter turned up with the dessert menus. Roo waved him away. 'Just the bill, please. I've got a lot of calls to catch up on this afternoon.'

'Don't you ever stop thinking about work?'

'Not often.'

He smiled. 'You always were single-minded. You knew what you wanted and went for it.'

It didn't help me get you though, did it, she thought. As if he could read her mind, he said suddenly, 'I missed you, when you left.'

She reached for her drink, not sure how to reply. 'Did you?'

'What do you think? You were my best friend. To suddenly cut all ties like that and not see each other . . .' He stared at his glass. 'You wouldn't believe how many times I nearly picked up the phone to call you.'

'Why didn't you?'

'I didn't think you'd want to hear from me.'

'I told you, I wasn't angry at you. I was angry *for* you. I didn't want to see you throw your life away.'

'I know. And you're right, it could have been a huge mistake. Getting married and becoming a father before I was twenty—it felt like a nightmare at the time.' He looked across at her. 'But it wasn't. It all worked out. My only regret was losing you as a friend.'

'You didn't lose me.'

'So how come I haven't seen you for eighteen years?'

'We drifted apart. It happens.'

'Not real friends. Not like us.' He paused. 'Cat missed you too.'

'I doubt it.'

'It wasn't all her fault, you know. I got her pregnant. I had to take some responsibility. I couldn't just leave her.' His eyes pleaded for her understanding. 'Nearly twenty years is a long time to stay angry, Ruby.'

As far as her cousin was concerned, Roo thought, it wasn't nearly long enough.

It was after ten when Roo finally left the office to go back to Sykes Street. The house was silent, apart from the sound of Matt's dog barking next door. Didn't it ever sleep?

She made herself some coffee, took a lukewarm bath, then left a brisk message on the letting agent's phone about her faulty boiler.

The dog was still barking when she came downstairs, wrapped in her dressing gown. It was too much. Throwing open the back door, she called out, 'For God's sake, will you shut that thing up?'

The barking grew more frenzied, followed by a clatter of falling dustbins. Roo tightened her dressing gown around her and stepped out into the darkness.

The houses in Sykes Street didn't have gardens. They had tiny yards that backed onto a narrow cobbled alley. As Roo stepped out, shivering in the drizzling rain, a dark shape flung itself against the fence separating their two houses. Roo leapt away from the flurry of gaping jaws. It would be just like her neighbour to own a crazed monster dog.

But then the barking stopped and she saw it wasn't a monster dog but an over-enthusiastic black labrador, his paws on the fence, tongue lolling in a friendly way.

Roo tentatively reached out a hand. 'Hello, er . . .' What was its name again? Henry? Herbie? Harvey! That was it. 'Hello, Harvey. Has that cruel man locked you out in the cold?'

There were no lights on in Matt's house. He was probably working, but that was no excuse for leaving his dog out in the freezing rain.

She scratched Harvey's velvety ears and thought for a moment. She couldn't just leave the poor animal shivering outside. She found the number for Pizza Paradise in the phone book.

No, said the weary voice on the other end of the line, Matt Collins wasn't working tonight. And no, he couldn't possibly give her his mobile number.

Roo put the phone down. Outside in the yard, Harvey had started whining plaintively at being abandoned again. Well, it wasn't her problem. It was Matt's dog, nothing to do with her.

'What the hell am I doing?' she wondered five minutes later as she lifted the latch to Matt's back gate. For all she knew, Harvey might be madly territorial and sink his teeth into her leg as soon as she stepped into his yard.

But he greeted her like an old friend, nearly knocking her flying. 'Come on, boy.' She curled her fingers under his thick leather collar and hauled him back into her own house.

As soon as she let him go she knew it had been a mistake. Harvey rampaged around like a hyperactive toddler, his tail swishing from side to side. As she followed him around, desperately trying to distract him, Roo began to understand why Matt locked him outside.

'Watch out for that vase. No, not on the chair!' She made a grab for him. 'Would you like something to eat? Let's see what we can find.'

That got his attention. He trotted after her into the kitchen and they both investigated the fridge. 'Don't look at me like that,' she said, as his reproachful brown eyes moved from the bare shelves back to her. 'I didn't expect guests, did I?'

Just at that moment the phone rang. It was David, calling to report that both he and Ollie were fine. After a brief conversation, Roo put the phone down and returned to the kitchen, only to find Harvey had got tired of waiting and helped himself to a low fat yoghurt and some tea bags.

'Right, that's it.'

She was seething with moral outrage as she rang the RSPCA. Matt couldn't be allowed to get away with treating dumb animals like that. And it wasn't her responsibility to look after them for him.

But as soon as she put the phone down she began to regret it. Perhaps she'd been a bit hasty? Especially now Harvey had settled down—admittedly taking up most of the sofa—and gone to sleep.

She felt even worse when the RSPCA inspector arrived, looking disturbingly like a police officer in his dark blue uniform. 'Did you report an abandoned dog?'

'Yes, but I've changed my mind.'

'You mean the owner's turned up?'

'Not exactly.'

'So the dog's still abandoned?'

'I wouldn't say abandoned. More sort of . . . home alone.' He lifted an eyebrow. 'Look, I'm sure it was just a mistake. Perhaps he got locked out accidentally—the dog's happy here until his owner comes home.'

He shook his head. 'We can't leave the dog. We have to take him away—' For questioning, Roo thought he was going to say. She imagined Harvey locked in a room with a light bulb shining in his trusting eyes. 'To the rehoming centre,' he said.

'You're not going to give him away?'

'Not until all the circumstances have been thoroughly examined. But if we think there's a case for neglect, we might have to prosecute.'

'But what will I tell his owner?'

The inspector looked ominous. 'Tell him we'll be in touch.'

It was nearly midnight when a car pulled up and she heard Matt's voice in the street. There was a woman with him, but not the blonde from two nights ago.

They let themselves into the house, laughing. Then Matt called out, 'Harvey? Come on, mate, I've brought you a burger.' His calls became more urgent as he flung open the back door. Then, 'Oh Christ!'

'What is it?' the woman said, coming out behind him.

'The back gate's open. He must have got out!'

For a second Roo thought about saying nothing and letting him think

Harvey had escaped. But he was bound to find out the truth once the RSPCA contacted him.

'Mr Collins?' Roo went outside, drawing her dressing gown tightly around her. 'Can I have a word?'

'Have you seen Harvey?' Matt looked distraught. 'He's escaped.'

'No, he's safe. He's . . . um . . . at the RSPCA.'

'But I don't understand. How did he get—' Realisation dawned. 'Please tell me you didn't.'

'It wasn't my fault. He was barking, and—'

'And so you decided to have him taken away?' Matt was furious. 'You had no right to do that! What did you think you were playing at?'

'I wasn't the one who locked him out in the rain,' Roo shouted back, forgetting her remorse. 'You're not fit to keep a dog if you treat it like that.'

'You have no idea what you've done! Harvey isn't even my dog. I'm looking after him for . . . a friend.'

'Then maybe you'd better tell your friend to take him home, since you're not capable of taking care of him.'

'I can't. She's dead.'

The woman appeared before Roo could reply. 'I've called the RSPCA. They want you to go in tomorrow morning.'

'Why can't I go tonight?'

'They won't release him until the office opens at nine.'

'Great.' He glared at Roo. 'I hope you're pleased with yourself.'

'Look, I'm sorry—'

'I don't want to hear it.' He held up his hand, silencing her. 'I've tried to be friendly but you've made it clear you don't want to know. So from now on, just stay out of my way, OK?'

Chapter 4

IT WAS FRIDAY AFTERNOON and the salon was in chaos, with everyone wanting their hair done for the weekend. Cat ran between Marjorie Prentice's wash and set, a full set of foil highlights, and old Mrs Wilmslow's perm. Meanwhile, on the other side of the salon, Julie was snipping at her solitary client's hair strand by strand, saying, 'Of course, just because they found my Dwayne with a box of matches and a can of paraffin doesn't mean he set fire to the school. Circumstantial evidence, our brief called it. Cat, could you mix my lady's colour for me?'

Cat skidded to a halt. 'Can't Natalie do it? If I don't get Mrs Wilmslow out from that dryer soon, those rollers will be welded to her head.'

'We're all busy, Cat.'

'I don't see you breaking your neck.'

Julie folded her arms. 'Are you going to mix that colour or not?'

'Do it yourself. Who do you think you are, giving me orders, anyway? You're not the senior stylist, you know.'

'That's what you think.'

Cat swung round. 'What?'

'Didn't Maxine tell you?' Julie looked innocent.

'When did this happen?'

'She told me this morning, before she went out to the cash-and-carry.' Julie smirked. 'Now, are you going to mix that colour?'

Cat went into the back room, too stunned to argue. It couldn't be true, could it? Surely Maxine must realise that Julie wasn't up to it?

She was still in a daze when she went to put Marjorie Prentice's rollers in. 'Are you all right?' Marjorie said. 'You're not your usual bouncy self.'

'Sorry. I've just had some bad news.'

'You're not the only one. I've just heard they're cutting my Alan's hours at Fairbanks.'

'No! When did this happen?'

'He got a letter this morning. Said they were putting all the staff on short-time working until the financial situation improved.'

'That's terrible.' Cat felt guilty. She might not like the idea of Julie being promoted over her, but at least she still had a job.

'I'll say this for your cousin. She doesn't waste much time, does she? She's barely been at that place a week, and she's already getting everyone's backs up.'

'That's Ruby for you,' Cat said. She was glad it was Sadie's day off and she couldn't hear what was being said about her daughter.

'But I suppose it's not all down to her,' Marjorie went on. 'Everyone knows Fairbanks is on the skids. This time next year there probably won't be a factory.'

Cat was thoughtful. Surely Billy would have told her if things were that bad? 'You should do something about it if you're that worried.'

'What could we do?'

'I don't know. Organise a petition. Talk to your MP.'

Maxine came back into the salon as Cat was putting the finishing touches to Marjorie's set. She watched Julie dart over and say something to her, then Maxine sent Cat a quick, panicky glance and disappeared into the back room.

So it was true. Julie was the new senior stylist.

She was so overcome with misery and disappointment that she hardly listened to Marjorie until she said, 'So you'll help, then?'

'With what?'

'This Save Fairbanks campaign. It was your idea.' Cat frowned. Since when had she come up with an idea like that?

'Oh, no, I couldn't. The only thing I've ever organised is the Infant School Summer Fair, and that was a disaster. Anyway, maybe it won't come to that. Maybe it will all turn out for the best.'

Marjorie looked grim. 'Maybe pigs will fly,' she said.

Roo sat in a traffic jam on the M25, heading south, glad that every crawling minute took her closer to home. She couldn't wait to get back, and not just to see Ollie and David. Normanford was a lonely place and it was about to get even worse once the news about the job cuts got out.

It had been a difficult decision to introduce shorter working hours, but she'd had no choice. She'd gone through the cash-flow forecast carefully, making savings where she could. She'd put a stop on company credit cards, cut back on sales bonuses and negotiated new terms with creditors. But in the end she knew she would still have to cut the wages bill somehow. And since production was already down owing to falling orders, it made sense to rationalise working hours. At least that way everyone could keep their jobs. And she could increase their hours once the orders picked up.

If they picked up.

The house was silent as she let herself in. She thought everyone was out until she heard laughter coming from the basement kitchen.

Shauna, Ollie and David were gathered round a shaky tower of Jenga bricks. David was trying to extricate a tricky one from the bottom, to the accompaniment of whoops of derision. They looked so happy that for a moment it felt as if they were the family and she was the outsider.

She dredged up a smile. 'Sounds like someone's having fun!'

'Mummy!' Ollie jumped up and ran to hug her, wrapping his arms round her waist. 'Have you brought me anything?' he demanded.

Roo smiled. 'As a matter of fact, I have. It's in the hall.'

Ollie ran off, dragging Shauna with him. David said, 'Do I get a guilt present too?'

Roo's happiness evaporated. He was trying to start a fight and he hadn't even kissed her yet. 'I didn't think you needed one.' She sat down.

'How was Normanford?'

'Awful. I don't want to talk about it.' What she wanted was for him to put his arms round her. But he didn't. 'How about you?'

'Same as usual.'

'No luck on the job front?'

His face darkened. 'No. But thanks for reminding me.'

Ollie rushed in, brandishing his new Millennium Falcon. He threw his arms round Roo's neck and kissed her. 'Thanks, Mum!'

'I'm glad you like it, darling.' She hugged Ollie tight. At least she knew how to put a smile on her son's face, if not her husband's.

'I'm going now,' Shauna announced from the doorway. 'You do remember I've got the weekend off?'

'Going somewhere special?' Roo asked.

'Just staying with a friend.'

Roo looked at her. 'Have you had your hair cut? It looks great.'

'Thanks.' Shauna put her hand up to stroke her shorn locks.

'So would this friend be male by any chance?' Roo said archly.

'No!' Shauna's face filled with colour. 'She's just a girl from college, that's all. Excuse me, I want to catch the eight o'clock train.'

'What did you have to say that for?' David said, as she scuttled off. 'You could see the poor kid was mortified.'

'I was only being friendly.'

'Roo, you haven't been friendly to her since she started here.'

She was hoping for a weekend relaxing but Shauna had set up a play date for Ollie on Saturday afternoon, which scuppered her plans for a family day out.

Sunday was better. They took Ollie to the park and Roo managed to forget about work and Normanford while they ate ice creams and took turns pushing him on the swings. They almost felt like a family. But that afternoon, as they cuddled up on the sofa watching *The Phantom Menace*, she stared at the clock, watching the minutes tick by and dreading the time she had to leave.

'Don't let us keep you, if you're desperate to get back to work,' David said, misinterpreting her anxious look.

At the door, Roo hugged Ollie tightly, breathing in the washing-powder smell of his *Star Wars* top. As they parted, he pressed a plastic figure into her hand.

'Anakin Skywalker,' he said. 'Before he went over to the Dark Side.'

A lump rose in her throat. 'Thank you. I'll take good care of it.'

'No,' said Ollie. 'He'll take care of you. May The Force be with you, Mummy.'

It'll take more than The Force to get me through this week, she thought as she drove away, tears blurring her eyes.

First thing Monday morning Roo had a meeting with Mike Garrett, the bank manager, and Frederick Fairbanks.

At first Mike was full of praise about the excellent start Roo had made to keep the company afloat. Then she said, 'I want to reinvest any savings back into the factory. Some of the machinery badly needs updating.'

Mike and Frederick exchanged wary looks. 'There's still a long way to go before we can talk about reinvesting,' Mike said.

'I know, but we've shown we're capable of managing our finances. We're no longer an unsound risk. And we need that new machinery.'

'What's the point in buying new machinery if we don't have any orders coming in?' Frederick asked. Roo stared at him. Whose side was he on?

'We'll get the orders,' she said.

'Show me the orders and you'll get the money,' Mike said.

'That's just it. We can't meet the extra capacity unless we have the equipment to deal with them. It's a chicken and egg situation.'

There was silence in the office while the two men considered this.

'I'm sorry,' Mike said finally. 'If we're going to forward any more capital we're going to have to see more commitment from you to saving money.'

'But we've already cut our overheads to the bone!'

'You could always lose a few jobs.'

Another silence.

'That's the situation. Take it or leave it.' Mike gathered up his papers.

'You could have backed me up,' Roo said to Frederick, when Mike had gone.

'It doesn't do to upset the bank manager. He tilted his head on one side. 'What's wrong, Ms Hennessy? Don't tell me you're losing your taste for wielding the axe?'

'I don't find any pleasure in putting people out of work.'

'Of course you don't. But if it's for the good of the company, you'll just have to bite the bullet, won't you?'

She went back to her office, fuming. She swept straight past Becky, who called after her, 'Roo? I've got—'

'Not now, Becky!' She slammed her door. Bloody man! If Frederick Fairbanks was so keen to put everyone out of work, let *him* do it. She was sick of everyone hating her just because she was trying to sort out his family's mistakes.

Becky crept in behind her. 'There's someone to see you.'

'Tell them to come back.'

'But, Roo—'

'Becky, please. I don't want to see anyone, OK?'

'Well, that's very nice I must say.'

Roo heard the voice from the outer office and froze. 'Oh my God. Is that—?'

Becky nodded. 'She was waiting in Granddad's taxi when I got here.'

Roo hurried to the outer office. Sitting at Becky's desk, her handbag perched on her knees, was Nanna Moon. She was dressed for an outing, her old brown coat fastened up to the neck, even though it was July.

'Nanna! Why don't you come through to my office?'

'No, thanks, I'm all right here. Anyway, this isn't a social call.' She fixed Roo with her beady gaze. 'Why haven't you been round to see me?'

Roo cringed. Suddenly she felt twelve years old again. 'Um . . . well, I've been really busy—'

'Too busy to see your family?' Nanna shook her head. 'I know what this is all about. It's to do with your mother, isn't it?' Roo darted an embarrassed glance at the women in the typing pool, who were listening avidly.

'It's time to mend this rift with your family. They're important. I should know, at my age.' She fumbled in her handbag for a handkerchief. 'I'm seventy-eight years old,' she sniffed. 'I don't have much time left on this earth. I should be spending my last few years surrounded by my loving family, not sorting out their fights.'

'Nanna, please—'

'I want you to come round for your tea on Wednesday,' she said, her tears mysteriously disappearing.

'I'll have to check my diary—'

'Wednesday,' Nanna said firmly. 'I'll get a nice piece of beef in.'

'Actually, I don't eat red meat any more.'

'Then we'll have lamb. I've invited your uncle Tom, Cat, Billy and the kids round as well. So we'll have a nice houseful.'

'Nanna—'

'Our Tom's waiting to take me to the Over Sixties club.' She eased herself out of her chair. 'Wednesday,' she said. 'We'll be expecting you.'

Sadie was in the middle of cooking when Cat, Billy and the children arrived. None of them looked happy to be there, but they all knew better than to ignore a summons from Nanna.

Cat wandered into the kitchen as she was fussing over the potatoes. 'How's it going?' She'd swapped her usual jeans and T-shirt for smart

DONNA HAY

black trousers and a low-cut red top that clung to her generous curves. Sadie had bought a black calf-length skirt and a soft, grey high-necked sweater from Marks & Spencer.

'Fine. You look nice.'

'So do you.' They gazed at each other and both burst out laughing. 'Look at us, done up like a pair of dog's dinners. Anyone would think she was visiting royalty.'

'Your nanna thinks she is. You should have heard her fussing.' But secretly Sadie was just as anxious to get everything right.

'Anything I can help with?' Cat asked.

'You could finish those carrots.' Sadie poked at the potatoes in the roasting tin. They sizzled and spat back at her. 'These are almost done. They'll be ruined if she doesn't come soon.'

The doorbell rang. Sadie jumped.

Cat smiled nervously. 'What do you know? Looks like the prodigal daughter decided to show up after all!'

She'd changed so much, Sadie hardly recognised her. Tall and elegant in a black trouser-suit, her dark hair glossy, she looked as if she'd just stepped off the pages of *Vogue*.

She had a bunch of flowers in her hand. Big showy gerberas in bright scarlet, Sadie's favourite colour. Her heart gave a little skip.

'Sorry I'm late. I had to go home and change. I brought you these.' She handed the flowers over to Nanna.

'They're lovely, aren't they, Mum? I'll put them in water, shall I?' Sadie's smile was fixed as she took them.

In the kitchen, Sadie found a vase under the sink and filled it with water. She told herself it didn't matter that Ruby hadn't even looked at her, apart from a quick nod of greeting when she'd first walked in. It was no more or less than she'd expected. Ruby might look like an adult, but inside she was still a sulky teenager.

She stuffed the flowers in the vase and got on with dinner. Cat came in as she was trying to beat the lumps out of the gravy. 'Where do you keep the corkscrew?' She opened a drawer and searched inside. 'Her ladyship's brought some wine.' She rattled among the cutlery. 'Are you all right? You seem a bit quiet.'

'The gravy's gone wrong.' Sadie suddenly felt near to tears.

'We'll strain it. No one will ever know.' Cat nudged her aside and took the pan from her trembling hands.

They sat crammed together round Nanna's best mahogany table, elbows touching. Sadie would have preferred to be at the far end with

380

Cat and the kids, but her mother had insisted she sit beside her daughter. As if it wasn't awkward enough.

Ruby kept up a forced smile and pretended everything was wonderful. But Sadie noticed the way she kept glancing around Nanna's little front parlour, as if she couldn't quite believe she was there.

The silence stretched between them. She couldn't think of a thing to say to her daughter. There were so many questions she wanted to ask, but somehow she couldn't bring herself to get a word out.

She topped up her glass and made a brave stab at conversation.

'So . . . um . . . how's the family?'

'Fine.' Her voice was so posh, no trace of Normanford in it at all.

'How old is your little boy now? Five?'

'He'll be six in September.'

She nodded. She already knew that. It was the first date she put in her new diary every year. 'I'd love to see him. Will he be coming up?'

'No plans for him to at the moment,' said Ruby, twiddling her fork.

It was so humiliating, Sadie just wanted to run away. She gulped her wine without thinking, to blot out the awfulness of it all.

'That was very nice.' Nanna pushed her plate away. 'Don't you think your mum's cooking's got better since you've been away, Ruby?'

'Definitely.' Was that why she'd left nearly all of it?

'The meat was a bit dry,' Tom commented, spearing it with his fork.

'Trust you to find something bad to say,' Cat muttered.

Sadie stood up, pushing her chair back. 'I'll fetch the pudding.'

She went into the kitchen, taking her wineglass with her, and drank deeply from it. Her head was beginning to feel fuzzy, but at least it took the edge off her embarrassment.

'Do you need any help?' She swung round, glass in hand. Ruby stood in the doorway. 'Nanna sent me. I think it was her less than subtle way of getting us alone together.'

'I expect you're right.' Sadie also knew if she sent Ruby away Nanna would find some excuse to send her straight back again. 'You'd better fetch the bowls and spoons. They're in that cupboard behind you.'

She took the trifle out of the fridge and set it down on the worktop, struggling for something to say. 'It must feel strange, being back in Normanford again,' she managed finally.

'You could say that.'

'Fancy you working at Fairbanks! Bet you never expected to end up there.'

'Life's full of surprises.' Ruby put the bowls and spoons on the worktop. 'Look, we don't have to do this.'

'Do what?'

'Try to be nice to each other. Nanna's not watching. Let's face it, neither of us wants to be here, do we?'

'Don't we?' Sadie said warily.

'I'm here because Nanna wanted me to come. She's got some stupid idea about us being one big happy family. But we both know that's never going to happen, so let's just get through it as best we can, shall we?'

'Fine by me.' Sadie shrugged. 'Like you said, I don't want to be here any more than you do.'

Roo picked up the bowls and spoons and carried them into the sitting room. Sadie followed with the trifle. Her ears sang from the pressure of keeping her temper under control.

What a high-handed bitch, making out she was doing them all a favour by being there! Sadie didn't want her there. She didn't want to play Happy Families any more than Ruby did.

She set down the trifle down on the table. 'Excuse me,' she said.

Up in her room, she pulled off the wretched skirt and jumper and flung them into the corner in disgust. It would take more than looking like a librarian to win her daughter's approval. Not that she needed it. She'd managed this long without it, and she wasn't about to break her heart over it now. She put on her favourite dress: low-cut and a defiant shade of flaming red. And just in case anyone didn't get the message, she added some lipstick to match.

Sadie Moon. Scarlet woman. It was what everyone thought anyway, so why disappoint them?

'Bloody hell!' Tom said, when she sashayed in wearing her highest heels. 'Where do you think you're going, dressed like that?'

'Out. Don't wait up, will you?'

'You see what she's like?' Uncle Tom said. 'Nothing changes, does it?'

'I don't blame her, the way you were all treating her. Especially you,' Cat turned on Roo.

'Me? What have I done?'

'Now don't go blaming our Ruby,' her father said.

'Why not? Sadie went to all this trouble for you, and you can't even be nice to her. You just sat there like you had a poker up your backside!'

The children giggled.

Roo felt her face burn. 'I didn't ask to come here.'

'That's obvious. You reckon you're too good for us, don't you?'

'I think it's time we left.' Billy stood up. 'Come on, Cat, before you say something you regret.'

'I haven't even started.'

Roo headed home shortly afterwards, determined never to go back to Hope Street again. This evening had lived up to her worst expectations. Nothing changed in Normanford. Especially not her mother.

Chapter 5

TWO WEEKS LATER, on a Sunday afternoon, Billy took Liam to kick a football around the park. Becky was shopping in Leeds with her boyfriend Dominic and Megan was absorbed with her Barbies while Cat tackled a pile of ironing in front of the *EastEnders* omnibus.

It should have been a peaceful afternoon, but then . . .

'Coo-ee! It's only me.' Cat and Megan exchanged a look of horror as Glenys walked in. Why had Billy given her a key?

'My dear, I'm so exhausted.' She plonked herself down on the sofa. 'What a day I've had. Judging the WI bake-off this morning, then lunch with the bishop. Where's William?'

'He's taken Liam to the park.'

'On his day off? Doesn't he ever get a rest?'

Cat rolled her eyes and picked up another of her husband's shirts to iron. Never mind that she came home from work every night, cooked supper, looked after the kids and did most of the housework.

Cat heard Billy's key in the door.

'We're home—oh, hello, Mum.' His smile dropped as he walked into the room and saw Glenys there.

'Sit down, darling. You must be exhausted. Let me get you a cup of tea.'

'I can get my own—' But Glenys wouldn't hear of it. As she rushed into the kitchen, Billy whispered to Cat, 'How long has she been here?'

'Too long,' Cat hissed back.

'So how's work?' Glenys asked, when she'd put a cup of tea into her son's hands and plumped up his cushions for him.

'Fine, thanks.'

'And how's Ruby?'

'She's OK. I think.' Billy shot Cat a wary look.

'It must be so difficult for her, sorting that place out. I'm glad she's taken a tough line. Those redundancies are just what Fairbanks needs—'

Cat looked up sharply. 'What redundancies?' she asked Billy.

'They've had to lay off some of the van drivers. It was cheaper to sub-contract for the amount of work they were doing. Look, can we discuss this later?' Billy glanced at his mother.

Glenys stayed for dinner and criticised everything as usual. Afterwards Billy insisted on taking her home. Cat knew he was trying to avoid her.

He came home as she was getting the children out of the bath. 'I'll put them to bed, shall I?'

He tucked them in and read them a story while Cat picked up the trail of damp towels and dirty clothes and put them in the laundry basket. She sensed he was hoping she'd forgotten about Fairbanks. But she tackled him the moment they were downstairs.

'Why didn't you tell me about those redundancies?' she asked.

'I didn't think you'd care. You don't usually take such a keen interest in industrial relations.'

'This is different. People I know are losing their jobs. How could you let that happen?'

'It's not up to me. I'm only the sales director, remember?'

'So it's all down to Ruby. I should have known.'

'She's doing her best. If someone doesn't do something we'll all be out of a job. Including me.'

He looked so tired, Cat forgot to be annoyed. 'You should have told me.'

'Believe me, Fairbanks is the last thing I want to talk about.' He pulled her into his arms. 'That's why I'm so glad to get home and forget about it all.'

Cat reached up and pushed Billy's dark hair back off his face and kissed his furrowed brow. 'You should share these things with me,' she said. 'I'm your wife. I want to help.'

'Just being with you is all the help I need.' He was reaching for her when his mobile trilled. He answered it, his expression darkening.

'What? Oh my God, when did it happen? Right, I'll talk to her.'

'What's going on? Billy?' Cat asked, as he reached for his jacket.

'I have to see Roo,' he said. And then he was gone. So much for sharing his troubles, Cat thought.

Roo arrived back from her weekend in London just before ten. She was so tired she hardly noticed the man approaching as she parked her car in Sykes Street.

'Billy? What are you doing here?'

'We need to talk.' He took her elbow and steered her into the house.

'Billy, what is it?'

'Someone's died,' he said.

Her mouth felt like it was lined with sand. 'Not Nanna—'

He shook his head. 'A man called Eric Pearson. He was a van driver at Fairbanks.'

'But I don't see—' She stopped. 'How did he die?'

'Suicide. They found him in his car this morning.'

'Oh my God.' She sank her head in her hands.

'Apparently the family had big debts. Then he lost his job. They were going to lose everything they'd worked for. He couldn't face it.'

'So why are you telling me all this?' Roo asked, already half knowing the answer.

'His family has issued a statement saying Fairbanks drove him to it.'

'By Fairbanks I take it they mean me?' She paused, taking it in. 'Maybe they're right,' she said. 'If I hadn't made those redundancies he'd still be here.' A tear rolled down her cheek and she dashed it away. 'I was so obsessed with making the figures add up I forgot they were real people with lives and families, and bills to pay.'

'It's your job.'

'Some job that drives people to kill themselves!'

She broke down in tears. Billy put his arms round her, pulling her to him. 'Don't cry. None of this is your fault. It'll be all right, I promise.'

But they both knew it wasn't going to be all right, not from now on.

Everyone was talking about Eric Pearson the following morning. Cat couldn't get away from it.

Billy hadn't come home until the early hours last night. 'Where have you been?' Cat asked him, switching on the light.

'I told you. I went to see Roo.' He looked shattered.

'Until this time? You must have had a lot to talk about.'

He sat on the end of the bed and pulled off his shoes. 'Please, Cat. Not now. It's been a long night and I'm tired.'

He fell into bed and switched off the light. For once he didn't reach for her. Cat lay stiff and unyielding beside him. So it was starting. They were shutting her out of their little private world, just like they used to.

'So that's good news, isn't it?'

'Sorry? What?' Cat looked up, brought back to the present to find Marjorie smiling at her.

'The newspaper's really interested in backing our campaign, especially after all this business with poor Eric Pearson. The reporter's coming to talk to us the day after tomorrow.'

'Great.'

'It was a good idea of yours, to get the ball rolling. We've already collected loads of signatures on our Save Fairbanks petition.'

'The list we put in the salon is filling up too. I'll let you have it soon.'

'Why don't you bring it on Wednesday? Then you can talk to the reporter.'

'Me? What would I say to a reporter?'

'You should be there. This campaign was your idea, after all.'

'Was it?' She still wasn't sure how that came about. 'I can't get involved. Billy wouldn't like it.'

'And you always do what your lord and master says?' Marjorie teased.

I do when my cousin is waiting to snap him up, Cat thought. 'I have my reasons,' she said. 'But I'll bring the petition from the salon round on Wednesday, OK? As long as I don't have to talk to any reporters.'

It had been a bad morning, starting with the story in the *Normanford News*. Even though it didn't actually say she was responsible for Eric Pearson's death, it mentioned the 'tough new regime' as causing stress among the workers.

There were quotes from other Fairbanks workers who'd been put on the streets. It seemed everyone had a tragic story to tell, from the single mum struggling to bring up her two children on the breadline, to the man who'd had to cancel his disabled daughter's trip to Disneyland. Every name was another barb in the heart no one thought she possessed.

The only one who had a kind word to say to her was Billy. He came in to see her just before lunch.

'I brought you this.' He put a sandwich on the desk. 'I had a feeling you'd be lying low.'

'Do you blame me? Have you seen the paper? All those people in trouble.'

'They'd be in a hell of a lot more trouble if this factory had to close.'

'You're right.' She managed a smile. 'What's in the sandwich?'

'Cucumber and salmon paste.'

She looked up. 'You're kidding? That was my favourite when I was a child! How did you remember I liked it?'

'You'd be surprised what I remember about you.'

Their eyes met. Roo suddenly found it hard to swallow her sandwich. 'Let's talk about work,' she said briskly.

They talked about Billy's ideas for changing the company's marketing strategy, refining the range and repositioning the brand. By the time he left, Roo was feeling more like her old self.

All the same, as she crossed the car park that night, she tensed when she heard a car approaching behind her.

'Bit jumpy, aren't you?' George Fairbanks said. 'Anyone would think you had a guilty conscience.'

'Why should I?' she said, pulling herself together.

'I dare say everyone's been giving you a hard time, have they? I'm not surprised. Eric Pearson was well liked here.' He looked at her shrewdly. 'No one would blame you if you walked away,' he said.

'And leave this place in a worse mess? I wouldn't be doing my job.'

'You've got some nerve, Ms Hennessy, I'll give you that.'

Cat had never seen the woman in the salon before. She was in her fifties, well-dressed, well-spoken and obviously well-off. Which was why Julie nabbed her as soon as she walked in. She could smell a big tip a mile off.

'I wonder what she's doing here?' Cat mused to Sadie, as they washed hair side by side at the basins.

'Just moved to the area, apparently. That's Elizabeth Montague. The Montagues have bought Bridge House.'

'Really?' Bridge House overlooked the only scenic part of the river on the edge of town. It sat behind tall, ivy-covered walls in its own grounds.

'It's funny, I swear I know her from somewhere,' Sadie said.

Cat frowned, watching Julie. 'I don't like what she's doing to those highlights. She's putting the colour far too close to the roots.'

'So?'

'So if she's not careful it'll expand and leak right out of the foil. It could end up a right mess. Maybe I should tell her.'

'Do you think she'd take any notice of you?'

'True.' But she felt sorry for Elizabeth Montague. From the look of her sleek ash-blonde head, she was used to the best.

She finished her client's hair and, as it was lunchtime, went off to deliver the salon list of signatures to Marjorie Prentice and the rest of the Fairbanks Action Group, as they'd called themselves. They were having their photo taken at the gates of Fairbanks factory when she arrived.

'Can't you at least smile?' the photographer pleaded, lowering his camera. 'Do you have to look so bloody grim?'

'We've nowt to smile about. That's the point,' Marjorie glared back.

'Yes, but you want some sympathy, don't you? You won't get it if you look like a bunch of scowling old—Hello!' He looked round as Cat ran towards them. 'This is more like it. Hi, darling, are you one of this lot?'

'No.' Cat rushed past him to hand over the list to Marjorie. 'Sorry I'm late, I had a client to sort out before I could get away.'

'Better late than never,' Marjorie replied, taking it from her. 'By the way, our MP's got back to us. He wants us to go down to Westminster and hand in our petition. Do you want to come?'

'I'd love to, but it's just . . . what's he doing?' She faced the photographer, who was lining her up in his lens.

'Trying to photograph your backside, I think.'

'No! I told you, I'm not part of this. I don't want my picture taken.'

She was still wondering how he'd managed to talk her into it as she posed with the others, clutching a corner of the petition.

She got back to find the salon in uproar. Julie was shouting at Natalie, who was on the verge of tears. And in the middle of it all, Elizabeth Montague sat quietly, her nylon robe wrapped round her shoulders, the picture of dignity despite the ugly streak of white blonde down the middle of her head.

'You put too much peroxide in that colour!' Julie screeched at Natalie.

'She didn't get it wrong. You did.' Cat jumped to Natalie's defence, putting her arm round her.

'It doesn't matter whose fault it is,' Elizabeth Montague said. 'The question is, what are you going to do about it?'

Julie looked blank. 'You could . . . um . . .'

'You could take it back to its original colour and start again,' Cat suggested.

'And how would you do that?' Elizabeth Montague asked. As Cat explained, she could see Julie turning more furious behind her.

'I don't think that would work,' Julie declared flatly.

'I do. And since you don't seem to be able to come up with a more useful idea, I suggest we try it, don't you?' Elizabeth's voice was full of calm authority. 'But not you,' she added, as Julie stepped forward. 'I want this young lady to do it.'

Cat was acutely conscious of the hate looks Julie kept sending her across the salon, but she forgot her nerves as she and Elizabeth Montague chatted like old friends. She explained how her family had moved back to her native West Yorkshire after years spent in London. She also talked about her daughter Charlotte's forthcoming wedding.

When she'd finished, Elizabeth insisted on paying, even though Cat tried to refuse. 'But you've done such a good job!'

'It was nearly a disaster,' Cat said. She was just relieved she'd managed to put it right.

'I insist. And this is for you.' She pressed something into Cat's hand.

Maxine arrived just as she was leaving. The door had barely closed before she pounced on Cat. 'Was that who I think it was?'

'I don't know. Who do you think it was?'

'You know! That actress. The one in the Bond film with Sean Connery. On the satin bed wearing nothing but a strategically placed python?'

'Lizzie Yorke! Of course!' Sadie cried. 'I thought I knew her from somewhere. Fancy you doing a famous film star's hair!'

But Cat wasn't listening. She stared down at the twenty-pound note in her hand. She'd never had such a big tip in her life.

'I'm definitely going to ask for her autograph next time she comes in,' Sadie was saying.

'I wouldn't hold your breath,' Cat said. 'I've got a feeling after today's disaster we won't be seeing her again.'

'**W**hat do you mean, you're not going?'

Roo held the phone away from her ear. Just because Nanna Moon was deaf she assumed everyone else was too. 'It's a funeral, you've got to pay your respects.'

'I don't think Mr Pearson's family would appreciate it in view of the circumstances.'

'If you don't it will look as if you've got something to hide.'

'But I didn't even know him.'

'No, but I did. His mother and I were old friends.' Roo wasn't surprised. Nanna knew everyone in Normanford. 'So shall I tell Tom to pick you up?'

'No, Nanna. I told you, I'm not going.'

There was an ominous pause. 'I'm disappointed in you, our Ruby.'

Roo put the phone down as Becky came in with the morning's post. As Roo picked it up a glossy magazine fell out. 'What's this?'

'That's mine.' Becky snatched it back but Roo caught the title. It was an up-market interiors magazine.

'I didn't know you were interested in interior design.'

'I like to look at the pictures.' Becky blushed. 'I've been reading about a new hotel in Leeds. The interiors have been designed by Salvatore Bellini. It's class.'

Roo glanced at the photos. The hotel was impressive in a cool, minimalist way. Lots of dark wood, white walls and moody lighting. 'It all looks a bit modern to me.'

'It's lovely,' Becky said, her face wistful. 'I wish I could see it.'

'Why don't you go and take a look?'

'What, me? In a place like that?' Becky shook her head. 'It's too posh.'

'Nonsense, you should go.' Then an idea struck her. 'Why don't you go today? Call it a research trip. And I'll come with you.' Today was such a depressing day, what with Eric's funeral, it had put her off working.

It was a strange, heady feeling, playing truant from work. Roo, who usually regarded a lunchtime sandwich at her desk as the ultimate in slacking, found herself tucking into Caesar salad and a cold glass of Chablis in the hotel bar, as if she'd always been a Lady Who Lunched.

Roo had to admit the photos in the magazine didn't do the hotel justice. It was a temple to modernism, with tinkling water features, vast, Zen-like white spaces and leather sofas you could lose yourself in. 'I was wrong about this place. It's fabulous.'

'Told you!' Becky looked triumphant as she finished her sandwich and pushed her plate away.

After lunch, Roo planned to go straight back to the office, but Becky persuaded her to take a detour for a meander around Harvey Nicks.

They both tried on clothes, something else Roo never had time to do. Becky persuaded her to try on a floaty Stella McCartney dress in a flowery print that she would never have considered before. It was nothing like the practical suits she wore. It was in a rusty, autumnal print that suited her dark colouring, making her look softer and more feminine.

'You should have that,' Becky said.

'I'd never wear it. But it is pretty.' Roo smiled reluctantly at her reflection. She hadn't seen herself looking like that for a long time. 'Maybe I will buy it,' she said, then added, 'but only if I can buy you something too.'

Roo woke up to her phone ringing. She groped for it blearily.

'Have you seen the paper?' George Fairbanks's voice shocked her awake.

'Of course I haven't seen it. I've only just woken up.' She squinted at the alarm clock. It was just before seven.

'Then I suggest you look at it before you come in to work. It's a bad business. Very bad indeed.' He slammed the phone down.

Roo thought about it as she showered and dressed for work. What could the newspaper have to say that was so dramatic George had to call her at the crack of dawn?

She soon found out. The front page leapt out at her from the newsagent's stand.

There was a photo of Eric Pearson's funeral, his flower-laden coffin being carried into the church, followed by his tearful widow and the Fairbanks family bringing up the rear. FAIRBANKSES' FAREWELL TO FAITHFUL ERIC, the headline read. Underneath, as a footnote to the story, there was another photo. A blurred, paparazzi-style snap of her coming out of Harvey Nichols, carrier bag in hand, grinning her head off, and next to it the words: 'while tough new boss shops till she drops'.

Roo clamped her hand over her mouth, feeling sick. She looked so cruel, so disrespectful.

She paid for the newspaper, avoiding the stony gaze of the woman behind the counter. As she hurried outside, she had the overwhelming urge to throw all her belongings into her suitcase and drive back to London. She didn't need this place and it certainly didn't need her.

She pulled herself together with an effort. That was the coward's way out and whatever else she was, she wasn't a coward.

Cat stared at page five of the *Normanford News*, horrified. How had she let herself get talked into appearing in that photo? If she'd known, she might have dressed up.

Becky was equally unimpressed. 'Oh my God, how could you? You might at least have brushed your hair!'

'I didn't know I was going to be photographed, did I? Anyway, no one will notice it.'

'Want to bet?' Becky shook her head. 'Dad'll go ballistic.'

'He'll see the funny side. It's only a photo, for heaven's sake!' But as Billy came downstairs she stuffed it guiltily into the bread bin. Which was where he found it five minutes later.

'Cat, why's the paper in— Bloody hell!'

Cat cringed. 'I know. I'm sorry. It's awful, isn't it?'

'Awful? It's disastrous!'

She glanced at Becky, who gave her an 'I told you so' look and went off to get ready for work.

'I can't believe it,' Billy said. 'Who the hell would be that malicious? It's not as if it was her fault!'

'Sorry? What are we talking about?'

'This!' Billy held up the newspaper and she saw the photo of Ruby on the front page. She'd been so desperate to see how dire her own picture was that she hadn't noticed it. 'As if she hasn't been through enough.' He slapped the newspaper down on the table. 'I'm going to ring her.'

'Why? You'll be seeing her at work in half an hour!'

'She needs my support, Cat. She needs to know she has at least one friend in this place.'

But why does it have to be you? Cat thought.

He hadn't even noticed her photo. He'd been so caught up with Ruby, she'd disappeared off his radar. As usual.

She got on with the children's breakfast and was refereeing an argument over whose turn it was to claim the free gift in the Rice Krispies when Dominic arrived to give Becky a lift to work.

He nodded at the *Normanford News*, lying on the table. 'All right, Mrs K? You've seen your picture, then?'

Cat groaned. 'Don't remind me.'

'You look fantastic for someone your age.' He saw Cat's face and added, 'Or any age, really.'

Billy came in, still brooding. Before Cat could stop him, Dominic said brightly, 'What do you reckon to your wife being in the paper, Mr K?'

'What?' Billy looked up, distracted. Dominic pushed it towards him. 'There, on page five. Doesn't she look sensational?'

Cat watched Billy's face as he snatched up the newspaper and scanned it, his brows drawing together in a frown.

He put it down without a word as Becky and Dominic left for work and Cat sent the children upstairs to brush their teeth. 'I'm sorry,' she said to Billy.

'Bit late for that, isn't it? Do you know what this could do to me? And to Roo?' His eyes blazed. 'Why did you get involved? It's not your fight, it doesn't even concern you.'

'It affects the whole community—'

'What do you know about it? You're a hairdresser, not a politician.'

She flinched at his cruelty. 'I'm still allowed an opinion.'

He glanced at his watch. 'We'll talk about this later.'

'Mustn't keep Roo waiting, must we?' Cat shouted after him as the front door closed. It was the first time he hadn't kissed her before he left the house.

So now she knew. Her own husband thought she was stupid. It was obvious from the contemptuous way he had looked at her.

The children were throwing their shoes at each other as she went into the sitting room and picked up the phone.

'You've seen the paper?' Marjorie Prentice said.

'I've seen it,' Cat said grimly. 'And I've changed my mind. I want to come to Westminster with you.'

Roo made sure she was home early on Friday night because David and Ollie were coming up to see her for the weekend. She rushed around cleaning the house, then showered and changed into white linen trousers and a T-shirt. It was a fine, warm evening. Perfect for sharing a bottle of wine in the garden. Or maybe not, she thought, as she stood at the kitchen window and surveyed the tiny back yard, the weeds growing through cracks in the concrete slabs. She wasn't quite sure what David would make of her new home.

As it turned out, David found it all highly amusing. 'You mean you actually live here?' he said, as he hauled their bags into the narrow hall. Quite a lot of bags, it seemed to Roo.

'I like it.' Ollie ran around, enjoying the novelty of it all. 'The toilet's got a chain hanging from the ceiling.'

'Very working class,' David remarked. 'Don't tell me, it's up the end of the garden, with cut-up pages from the *Racing Post*?'

'The *Guardian*, actually.' Roo glanced at the clock. Five minutes, and they were already getting on each other's nerves.

They had supper together in the tiny kitchen, which was surprisingly cosy. Afterwards Ollie played out in the yard under the setting sun while she and David washed up.

'By the way, I've got a job,' he announced as he dried a pot.

'David, that's wonderful! What? Where?'

'IT support manager at a precision engineering firm. The pay isn't that great, but it's interesting.'

'Congratulations,' she beamed. 'Why didn't you tell me sooner?'

'I only found out this morning.' He paused. 'There's just one problem. They want me to go on a week's induction at their head office in Bristol. Starting Monday.'

'So? I'm sure Shauna will cope if we offer her a huge bonus.'

'Ah. Well, you see, that's just it.' David looked awkward. 'Shauna's ill. She's had to go and stay with her parents.'

'So who's going to look after Ollie?' She saw his face and it dawned on her. 'Oh, no. You can't be serious!'

'He's your son,' David pointed out.

'But I'm working!' She thought desperately. 'Can't you find another nanny? There must be temp agencies—'

'Are you suggesting we leave our son alone in the house with a complete stranger for a week?'

Put like that, it didn't seem like a good idea. 'I wish you'd given me more notice—'

'Look, if you're too busy to look after your own son—'

'I didn't say that, did I?' Roo gazed out at Ollie, jumping from one paving slab to the other. 'Looks like I don't have much choice, doesn't it?'

The woman at the council offices laughed when on Monday morning Roo asked for a list of registered childminders who'd be able to take Ollie immediately.

'You are joking, aren't you? It's the summer holidays.'

Roo watched Ollie stubbornly refusing to eat his muesli in the absence of his favourite Coco Pops. 'So what do you suggest?'

'Don't you have any friends or family you could ask?'

'No,' Roo said. 'Look, I'm desperate. I'll pay anything.'

'I suppose I could give you a few numbers.'

Roo had told Becky that she wouldn't be in the office today but would definitely be in tomorrow. She had to find someone to look after Ollie before then.

She called the childminders, working her way down the list. The first five were fully booked for the whole summer. Three others said they might have vacancies. Roo bundled Ollie out of his pyjamas and into the car, roaring off as if she'd been told the last suit in the Dolce & Gabbana sale had just been reduced to a fiver.

The first answered the door with a howling baby in her arms. Before Roo could open her mouth she said, 'It's twenty quid a day, five days a week, and I charge extra for time after six.' Ash fell from the end of her cigarette onto the baby's rompers and she brushed it away carelessly.

She didn't even look at Ollie.

'We'll let you know,' Roo said.

'Don't wait too long,' the woman called after her.

The next, Angie, was more promising. Her house was bright and the children were busy making flapjacks in the kitchen. It seemed so comforting, Roo felt like asking if she could come there every day too.

Unfortunately, Angie could only take Ollie two days that week. 'It's all I can do at such short notice.'

'I really need someone full-time.'

'Then I can't help you. Sorry.'

Roo was sorry too. Especially when she had to drag Ollie away from the flapjack-making. He was subdued in the car as they drove to the final address.

'Don't worry, darling, we'll find somewhere for you to go.' She reached across and patted his knee reassuringly.

The last woman was called Liz. She seemed very nice, capable and obliging. 'What a piece of luck,' she said. 'My husband's been made redundant, so we need the extra money.'

A feeling of dread crept up Roo's spine. 'Where does he work?'

'Fairbanks. Do you know it?'

Roo and Ollie left.

She sat behind the wheel holding her head in her hands. She could feel stress building up like a pressure cooker inside her. This was rapidly turning into a problem she couldn't deal with.

'Don't cry, Mummy,' Ollie said. 'I'm sorry.'

'What?'

'I know you don't want me here. I could go back to Daddy.'

She suddenly saw the world through his troubled eyes. How she was so desperate to palm him off on someone else that she'd bullied him into the car when he'd barely had his breakfast and driven him round to strangers' houses, begging them to take him.

'Oh, Ollie, of course I want you to stay.' She hugged him fiercely. 'Come on, let's go home. And we'll pick up some Coco Pops on the way. How does that sound?'

'So I was wondering if you knew of any childminders in the area.' Roo looked out of the window at her son, who was playing in Nanna Moon's yard. The same yard she'd played in as a child.

After desperately trying every avenue, she'd finally taken the woman at the council office's advice and turned to her family. But it wasn't easy.

'Childminders?' Nanna bridled, as if she'd just suggested inviting the local paedophile round for tea. 'You don't want to send the kiddy to a stranger! Your mother can look after him. She'd enjoy it.'

'I doubt it. She's not interested in children.'

'But this is her grandson. You don't know how much she thinks of that boy.' She nodded towards the photos crammed onto the mantelpiece. 'Always bragging about him, she is, and yet she hardly knows the lad.' She looked severely at Roo. 'You've got your mother all wrong, you know. She was hardly more than a bairn herself when you were born, and of course she made mistakes. But she deserves a second chance.'

'Who deserves a second chance?' Sadie appeared in the doorway, laden with shopping bags. She spotted Roo, and her smile dropped.

'Our Ruby needs someone to look after her little lad for a few days,' Nanna said. 'I told her you'd do it.'

'Did you now? And what about my job?'

'You can take time off, can't you?'

Sadie looked from one to the other. Then said, 'No, I'm sorry, I can't.'

'Told you,' Ruby said, as Sadie left the room. Nanna was wrong to say her mother had changed. Sadie still looked out for number one.

Sadie dumped the carrier bags on the kitchen table, seething. Ruby had a nerve! After the way she'd ignored her over the years, she expected her to drop everything just because she'd decided she needed help.

She broke her nail and cursed. Then she realised she wasn't alone. A small boy was watching her shyly from the back doorway. Fair-haired, with dark, serious eyes like his mother's. When Sadie said hello he ducked away and hid.

She turned her back on him, knowing he was still watching. She talked out loud, reciting the contents of the shopping bags as she unpacked them. When she reached the variety pack of biscuits, she unwrapped them, selected a chocolate one and left it carefully on the corner of the table, within Ollie's reach. Then she moved away to put the kettle on.

He edged forward.

'Do you want a drink with that?' she said, still not turning round.

'Coke, please.' The hasty way he said it made her realise it was probably forbidden.

'Sorry, we don't have that in the house. How about a glass of milk?'

She poured it for him, then offered him another biscuit. He selected one with jam and cream in the middle.

'Who are you?' he asked.

'I'm your gran.' It felt odd, saying it out loud.

'No, you're not. My granny lives in the country.'

'That's your daddy's mum. I'm your mummy's mum.'

He eyed her suspiciously. 'You don't look like a granny.'

'I'll take that as a compliment.'

'So what shall I call you?'

'Most people just call me Sadie. So you're here for a holiday, are you?'

Ollie frowned. 'Sort of, but Mummy doesn't want me. She's too busy with her job to look after me.'

Sadie poured boiling water into the teapot, so Ollie couldn't see her shocked expression. And Ruby thought *she* was a bad mother!

A moment later Ruby walked in. Ollie turned to her excitedly. 'Look, Mummy, they have custard creams here. And pink biscuits. Why can't we have proper biscuits?'

Sadie glanced at her daughter. 'I've never known anyone get so excited over a chocolate digestive.'

'Be careful you don't get chocolate down your T-shirt.' Roo was instantly fussing, dabbing her son's chin with a tissue. Sadie wanted to tell her to stop, all kids got dirty, but she bit her tongue.

'Where's his dad?' she asked.

'On a course.'

'What happened to the nanny?'

'She's ill.'

Sadie arranged some biscuits on a plate and handed them to Ollie. 'Take these in to Nanna, will you, love? Tell her I'll bring her a cup of tea in a minute.' As he trotted off, she said, 'He's a nice little lad.'

'Yes, he is.' There was a long silence.

'What made you ask me to look after him?'

'I know you haven't seen much of him over the years. I thought you might like a chance to get to know your grandson.'

'Nothing to do with the fact that you couldn't get anyone else?'

Ruby looked flustered. 'Well—'

'Let's face it, the only reason you came here is because you're desperate. You wouldn't let me anywhere near him otherwise. You'd rather pay a stranger to look after him than his own grandmother!' She shook her head. 'And you wonder why I said no.'

'Actually, I would have been amazed if you'd said yes. I stopped expecting you to help me a long time ago.'

'What's that supposed to mean?'

'Think about it. When was the last time you did anything for me? Even when I was a kid, it was always you first. You, you, you. Never mind that we couldn't afford to pay the gas bill because you'd spent the money on a new dress. Never mind that I had to go to bed in the cold and dark because you were out getting drunk with your latest boyfriend and we didn't have fifty pence for the electric meter. As long as you got what you wanted, that's all that mattered!'

Sadie felt the colour drain from her face. She'd never been that bad— had she? 'If you feel like that, I don't know why you bothered asking.'

'Like you said, I was desperate. But I'll sort out my own problems. I've had a lot of practice, living with you all those years!'

It rained all the way down the motorway on Friday night, and Roo began to regret her impulsive decision to take Ollie back to London a day early instead of waiting for David to pick him up the following day.

'It'll be a lovely surprise for Daddy, won't it?' she told Ollie, full of excitement. She was looking forward to immersing herself in some domestic bliss after such a stressful week. In desperation she'd taken Angie's offer of part-time child care, which meant working late into the evenings to catch up. But at least she felt she was getting somewhere at Fairbanks. After the last round of job cuts she was well on the way to convincing the bank to lend them the extra money they needed. And with Billy and the sales team chasing all possible new avenues for orders, she hoped they could get the factory workers back to full-time soon.

They got home just after six. As Roo bundled through the door with an excited Ollie and all their bags, she heard a noise upstairs. A moment later David appeared on the landing.

'Roo! What are you doing here?'

'It was meant to be a surprise. I thought your course didn't finish until tomorrow?'

'The last speaker didn't turn up, so . . . where are you going?' He swung round as Ollie cannoned past him up the stairs.

'To his room, probably. He's desperate for a reunion with his *Star Wars* DVDs.' Roo smiled. 'How was Bristol?'

'Great. Very . . . enlightening. Look, why don't you go and pour us a drink? You probably need one after that journey.'

'I've got a better idea. Why don't you get the drinks while I take these bags upstairs?' She moved to pick them up, but David had already bounded down to meet her.

'Let me take them.'

'You're very edgy, what's—' She was interrupted by Ollie on the landing above them, his face quizzical.

'Daddy, what's Shauna doing in your bed?'

A moment later Shauna emerged from the bedroom, wearing David's bathrobe and looking sheepish. 'Hello,' she said.

They all looked at each other, frozen. Then Roo said, 'Excuse me, I think I need that drink.' She dropped her bags and went into the kitchen.

Someone had spilt red wine on the table. She grabbed a cloth from beside the sink, ran it under the tap before scrubbing away at the sticky patch, wondering all the while at her unnatural calm. She'd just discovered her husband *in flagrante* with the nanny and all she could think about was whether the wine would stain the wood.

She was still scrubbing when David came in. 'Where's Shauna?' she asked, not looking up.

'Upstairs, with Ollie.'

'Nice to see she still remembers what she's paid to do.'

He sighed. 'Don't be like that, please.'

'Like what?' She stopped cleaning. 'I'm sorry, David, how should I be? What's the appropriate response for someone who comes home and finds their husband in bed with the hired help?' He stared at his shoes. 'So how long has it been going on?' she demanded.

'Not long. A few weeks.'

'Since I've been away?' He didn't answer. 'I see. So all the time I've been working, you've been shagging the nanny. And you had the nerve to make *me* feel guilty!'

'I'm sorry.'

'Is that all you can say?' She threw the cloth in the sink, went to the fridge and poured herself a glass of wine. 'Shagging the nanny, for God's sake. Couldn't you think of anything more original?'

He flinched. 'It wasn't like that.'

'Then what was it like? Come on, David, there must be a reason why you'd go to bed with her?'

'Yes, there is!' Anger flared in his eyes. 'For a start, she isn't a control freak. She doesn't tell me what to eat, or where to live or what car to drive. And she doesn't make me feel like a pathetic loser just because I don't have a six-figure salary. You want to know why I slept with her, Roo? Because she isn't perfect.'

For a second she was shocked, then anger reasserted itself. 'Then you make a good couple, don't you? Because you're not perfect either!'

'I've been trying to tell you that for years,' he said.

She raged around the room, picking things up and putting them down again, fighting the urge to throw them at his head.

'Do you want me to go?' he asked.

She stared at the plate in her hand. It was discontinued Villeroy & Boch, too precious to smash. 'I don't know what I want.'

'That makes two of us.'

'David?' Shauna stood in the doorway, white-faced. She couldn't bring herself to look at Roo. 'Is everything all right?'

'What do you think?' Roo snapped.

'You'd better wait upstairs,' David said, but Shauna stood her ground.

'This affects me too. I want to stay.'

'Stay? You think I'd let you stay under my roof after this? I want you to pack your bags and leave now. I paid you to look after my son, not sleep with my husband!'

Shauna looked at David. 'Do you want me to go?'

'I think it might be best,' David said.

He went upstairs with Shauna. Roo gulped her wine and listened to the muted hum of their voices. Shauna sounded upset, and David was reassuring her. How dare he comfort that bitch, she thought. Shouldn't he be down here with her, trying to save their marriage?

Finally she heard them thumping down the stairs with Shauna's bags. Roo went out to see them, feeling strangely calm. Shauna looked as if she'd been crying. She flinched as Roo held out her hand.

'Key,' she said flatly.

Shauna handed it over. 'You won't stop us seeing each other.'

'No? Have you ever heard the expression, "Out of sight, out of mind"?'

'That's enough!' David said. 'Your taxi's here. I'll call you,' he muttered to Shauna.

Roo went straight upstairs and ripped the sheets off their bed, still fighting not to lose control. It was all she had left.

David followed her. 'I've put Ollie to bed. I'll sleep in the spare room.'

'No, *I'll* sleep in the spare room. Do you honestly think I could sleep in the same bed when you and she—' She bundled the sheets up and threw them into the corner.

Neither of them slept much. As she lay awake, she could hear David prowling around downstairs. What was going through his mind? she wondered. Was it anything like hers, veering wildly from despair to disbelief and back again, encompassing every emotion in between?

She finally drifted to sleep just before dawn and awoke four hours later, disorientated. For a split second she couldn't remember what had happened, then it all came flooding back in a sickening rush.

The house was silent. David was gone. Roo panicked until she found the note on the kitchen table saying he'd taken Ollie swimming. It seemed so normal, just like any other Saturday morning. All that family stuff she'd taken for granted. She longed for it back.

And she could get it back. Now some of the shock and pain of last night had worn off, she realised her marriage was too important to throw away because of a fling.

David came home just before lunch. 'I took Ollie to play with a friend,' he said. 'I thought it would give us a chance to talk.'

'Good idea.' They sat on opposite sofas. For a long time neither of them could think of anything to say. Then they both started talking at once. 'You first,' David said.

Roo took a deep breath. 'I've been thinking about last night.'

'Me too.'

'I want you to know I don't blame you for what happened. It was my fault as much as yours. I've been working too hard and neglecting you.'

'I haven't been very easy to live with, either.'

'You couldn't help it. I should have been more supportive. I should have realised your self-esteem was damaged when you lost your job.'

He frowned. 'Sorry?'

'But we can put things right. I've been thinking about it, and I reckon we should spend some time together as a couple.' She smiled. 'Which is why I've booked us a holiday.'

'You've done what?'

'A holiday. I called the travel agent this morning. After I finish in Normanford, we're jetting off to Tuscany for two weeks.'

David's brows drew together. 'I wish you'd asked me first.'

'I thought you'd be pleased.'

'I hate Italy.'

'But we always go there!'

'I know, and I've always hated it.'

'You've never said.'

'Oh, I have. Many times. But you never listen.'

'That's not true. You're just saying that because—'

'There, you see? You're not listening now. Why does it always have to be about you? Jesus, I can't even have an affair without it being something you've done! When are you going to stop telling me how I feel and actually listen to what I want?'

'OK, I'm listening,' Roo said. 'What do you want, David?'

His eyes met hers, serious and direct. 'I want a divorce.'

Chapter 6

ROO FELT AS IF she'd been punched in the solar plexus. 'You don't mean that.'

'There you go again, telling me what I'm feeling. I've been thinking about it for a while. Before all this business with Shauna happened.'

'But I thought we were happy!'

'We haven't been happy for a long time and you know it. When was the last time we talked? Laughed? Stayed in the same room for longer than five minutes without arguing?' She was silent. 'You see? There's nothing holding us together. Nothing really important, anyway.'

'We've got Ollie. Isn't he important?'

'You know he is.' A shadow passed across David's face. 'But he'd be better off if we weren't getting at each other all the time.'

'All couples go through bad patches,' she said.

'This isn't a bad patch, Roo. We want different things out of life. You want a career man, someone as driven and ambitious as you are.'

'And what do you want? A thick teenager?'

'Leave Shauna out of this.'

'How can I? You brought her into it when you jumped into bed with her.' She stood up and paced the room. 'I can't believe this. She's half your age, David. You'll be a laughing stock.'

'It's better than being lonely,' he said.

His words struck her like a blow. 'Thanks a lot. I had no idea marriage to me was such torture.'

'It isn't. It wasn't.'

'So why do you want to throw it all away?'

'Because it isn't what I want any more.'

She stared out of the window at the common opposite. For the first time in her life she didn't know what to say.

Finally she took refuge in bitterness. 'You're not having this house.'

'I don't want it. I never liked it much anyway.'

'But you chose it!'

'No, *you* chose it. Just like you chose everything else. I went along with it for a quiet life.'

Roo was shocked. She had no idea he'd been so resentful all these years. Her happy family life was built on a fantasy.

'All I want is Ollie,' David said. Roo swung round to face him.

'No way. You're not having my son!'

'He's my son, too.'

'But I'm his mother.'

'So what? You might have given birth to him but you haven't shown that much interest in him all these years.'

'That's not true!'

'OK, tell me, what football team does he support? Who's his best friend at school? You don't know, do you? You don't know the first thing about your own son. And you call yourself a mother!'

His words haunted her as she drove to pick up Ollie. Of course she loved him. And she did her best for him. He never wanted for anything, not like her when she'd been growing up.

And she couldn't lose him. She could already feel David slipping away from her; she couldn't let Ollie go too.

David was waiting for her, in a far more subdued mood. 'I've been thinking,' he said. 'Perhaps it would be better if you took Ollie back with you, just for a couple of weeks. It's bound to be unsettling for him here, especially if I'm moving out. But that doesn't mean I'm handing him over to you permanently,' he added quickly. 'I'm still his father. And I won't have him used as some kind of emotional football.'

'Of course not!' Roo was shocked. 'I'd never do that.'

'I know. I shouldn't have said that. I'm sorry.'

'So what made you change your mind?'

He looked wary. 'I spoke to Shauna,' he admitted reluctantly. 'She convinced me it was for the best—'

'Shauna! What the hell's it got to do with her?'

'It might surprise you to know she understands our son a lot better than we do,' David said. 'Anyway, you should be thanking her.'

'For ruining my marriage?'

He smiled sadly. 'I think we managed that all by ourselves, don't you?'

She didn't see what was waiting for her in Sykes Street until she'd almost driven into it in the darkness. Ollie stirred and woke up. 'Mummy, what's that smell?'

'It's . . . um . . . compost, darling.' A great steaming mountain of it, right outside her house. 'For the garden.'

'What's it doing outside your house?'

Good question. She parked her car down the street and sat behind the wheel, staring straight ahead of her. Under her tough exterior she could feel all her strength sapping away.

Just let me get inside, just let me get through the night and in the morning I'll be strong enough to deal with it, she thought as she and Ollie marched past the offending mountain of manure to their front doorstep. But as soon as she put her key in the door Matt appeared.

'What do you think?' he grinned.

He was smiling all over his face, so pleased with himself. Roo opened her mouth to retaliate and appalled herself by bursting into tears.

Matt's smile vanished. 'It was only a joke—to pay you back for what you did to Harvey,' he stammered, as Roo fumbled with her key. She opened her door and fell through it, dragging Ollie and all her baggage behind her, then slammed it in Matt's face.

Once she'd started crying she couldn't stop. She sat on the sofa, rocking gently as the tears exploded out of her like the rush of a broken dam. Ollie pressed a scrap of toilet paper into her hand, wide-eyed at the sight of his fearless mummy dissolving in front of him.

She heard a man's voice. Matt stood over her, his face grave.

'How did you get in here?'

'The last tenant gave me a key so I could feed his goldfish while he was away.'

'You had no right to use it.' She covered her dripping nose with the shredded tissue. 'Can I have it back, please?'

'In a minute.' He crouched down so his face was level with hers. 'I just wanted to say I'm sorry. I didn't realise it would upset you so much.'

A hysterical laugh bubbled out through the tears. 'You think you've upset me? You really think that's why I'm in this state?'

'Isn't it?'

'I'll tell you what's upset me, shall I? I'm the most hated woman in town, I'm snowed under at work, and I can't find anyone to look after my son. Oh, and I've just caught my husband in bed with another woman. And he wants a divorce. I'd say next to all that a pile of horse shit is nothing, wouldn't you?'

'Bloody hell. I had no idea.'

'Well, now you know.' She stood up, mustering her dignity. 'Now I'm going to put my son to bed. See yourself out, would you? And leave the key.'

She went upstairs, washed her face and managed to pull herself together for Ollie's sake. He was still anxious as she tucked him into bed, but he was so tired he fell asleep straight away. Roo knelt beside his bed, stroking his fair hair off his angelic face. Poor baby. He didn't deserve to be caught up in this mess.

Matt was waiting for her downstairs with a large bottle of brandy and two glasses.

'I thought I told you to leave.'

He handed her a glass. 'Brandy. It's good for shock.'

'I don't drink spirits.'

'Now might be a good time to start.'

'If I start now I might not stop.'

'Does that worry you? Not being able to stop?'

She looked at him sharply. 'What do you mean?'

'You keep a lot of stuff bottled up, don't you? Why are you so frightened of losing control?'

'Because I'm a control freak.' That's what David called her. The thought of him made her down her brandy in one gulp.

'Blimey,' Matt said. 'For someone who doesn't drink you can really put it away.'

'Shut up and pour me another.'

'That's more like it.' He refilled her glass. 'So what happened?'

She hadn't meant to tell him. The last thing she wanted was to drag the whole sorry mess up again. But the brandy loosened her tongue and somehow, bit by bit, he managed to coax the story out of her.

'I don't know how it happened,' she said. 'It was never meant to be like this.'

'No one ever means these things to happen. They just do.'

'Not to me they don't.'

'What makes you so sure?'

'That's why I chose David, because we were totally compatible and I knew he'd never cheat on me.'

Matt was amused. 'You make it sound like picking out a kettle!'

Roo couldn't see why he found it so funny. 'The principle's the same.

Whatever you choose has to meet all your criteria, otherwise you end up with something totally unsuitable.'

Matt looked at her, not sure whether to take her seriously. 'I'm surprised you didn't run a credit check on him.'

'I did.' She was totally serious.

Matt spluttered with laughter. 'You're unbelievable, do you know that? Do you always let your head rule your heart?'

'It's the only way, unless you want to end up like—'

'Who?'

'My mother. And before you say anything, I don't want to talk about her,' she added warningly. 'Anyway, it worked for David and me. We were very compatible.'

'Maybe he decided he needed more than compatibility,' Matt said. 'Maybe he wanted chemistry.'

'I don't know what you mean.'

'You really don't, do you?' Matt shook his head in wonder. 'Haven't you ever seen someone across a crowded room and thought you had to have them there and then?'

Roo blinked at him. He seemed to be sitting a lot closer now, lounging on her sofa. He reminded her of an Australian surfer, all lean, tanned muscle and sun-bleached hair. Even his eyes were blue like the ocean.

'Absolutely not,' she said tartly. 'Although you obviously have.'

'Meaning?'

'Meaning I've seen all those women you bring home. You're obviously some kind of serial shagger.'

He laughed. 'I think you'll find the term is "commitment phobic", so I'm reliably informed.'

She twisted round on the sofa to face him. 'So why exactly do you find it so hard to commit, pizza boy? Did you have a difficult relationship with your mother? Are you secretly afraid you might be gay?'

Matt wasn't smiling any more. 'It's not complicated,' he said shortly, refilling her glass. 'I like women, that's all there is to it.'

'Maybe that's what I need,' Roo said.

'A woman?'

'A revenge shag.'

Their eyes met. It was a knowing look that spoke volumes.

'I don't think that would be a good idea,' he said. He finished his drink and stood up. 'I'd better go. It's getting late.'

'Don't you want another drink?' Roo was absurdly disappointed.

'No. And neither do you.' He picked up the bottle. 'Look, things will sort themselves out. Just try to relax. Life's too short.'

'That's an easy philosophy for someone who doesn't have the worries of the world on their shoulders.'

He sent her a long look. 'You'd be surprised,' he said.

She woke up on Sunday morning with a hangover and a deep sense of shame. Had she really made a pass at her next-door neighbour? Worse still, had he really turned her down?

She would have preferred to avoid Matt, to spare her blushes. But he called round that afternoon while she was cleaning.

She threw herself behind the sofa, panicking. But as she lay sprawled out on the carpet, praying he wouldn't look through the window and see her, she heard voices at the back. Ollie had wandered into the yard and was talking to Matt over the fence.

There was no way she could avoid him. She had to brazen it out.

'Oh, hello.' Ollie was playing with Harvey, throwing a rubber ball which Harvey leapt up and caught.

'I knocked round the front but there was no answer.'

'Sorry. I was . . . um . . . on the phone.'

'Funny, your son said you were hiding behind the sofa.' He looked amused. 'I hope you weren't avoiding me.'

'Why should I?' Her blushing face gave her away. 'Look . . . um . . . thanks for last night. For listening, I mean.'

'Not at all. It was an interesting evening. We must do it again some-time.' Oh God, now he thought she was after him! She immediately saw herself through his eyes—newly separated and desperate.

'I just wanted to let you know I've got someone to get rid of the . . . er . . . you-know-what from the front of your house. And I came round to give you this.' He handed her a square box.

Ollie recognised it before she did. 'A PlayStation!'

'It's not the newest model, but there are a couple of games with it. I thought it might help keep Ollie amused. Although it looks like he's already found a friend to keep him company.'

'Perhaps they'll keep each other out of trouble.' They both laughed as Harvey misjudged a catch and the hard rubber ball hit him squarely between the eyes. 'It's very kind of you to let us borrow this. Are you sure you don't need it?'

'Absolutely not. In fact you'd be doing me a favour taking it off my hands. I need to get on with some work and it's far too distracting.'

She frowned. 'Work?'

'My dissertation. Didn't I tell you, I'm doing a PhD in clinical psy-chology?' He grinned. 'Maybe you won't feel so bad now.'

She frowned. 'About what?'

'Propositioning me.' His brows lifted. 'Let's face it, it's got to be better than making a pass at a pizza boy.'

Cat had made it to the front page of the *Normanford News* this time. She and her Fairbanks Action Group friends were clustered around the shiny black front door of 10 Downing Street clutching their petition.

Becky handed the paper to Roo with her morning mail. 'Honestly, you'd think Mum could have bought something decent to meet the Prime Minister. That suit's ages old,' she groaned. 'By the way, we've had a letter from them. They're organising a public meeting and they want to know if you'll come along and put Fairbanks's case.'

'Tell them I'll let them know.' Secretly she didn't relish the prospect. Public meetings had a habit of turning into public slanging matches.

She tried to say as much to George Fairbanks later that morning, when they met in his office. 'Nonsense, you've got to go,' he insisted.

'Even if I get lynched?'

'If you're so sure you're doing the right thing by Fairbanks and its workers you've got nothing to fear, have you?'

Roo glared at him. He didn't care if she was torn apart by an angry mob. Anything that might send her scuttling back to London with her tail between her legs. But she wasn't going anywhere.

'I'd be glad of the chance to put my case,' she said through gritted teeth.

'That's the spirit.' George Fairbanks chuckled.

Billy caught up with her as she was walking back to her office. 'Penny for them?' he said.

She looked up, distracted. 'Sorry?'

'Your thoughts. Let me guess, it's only Monday morning and you're missing Ollie already?'

Roo suddenly realised that he thought Ollie had gone back to his father in London. 'There's been a change of plan. He's staying with me,' she explained. She couldn't bring herself to talk about her marital problems, not yet. It was embarrassing enough that she'd confided in Matt.

'So have you got your child care sorted out?'

'I managed to find someone in the end. A woman called Angie.' Although it had cost her dear. After bribing her with double rates Angie had finally agreed she could fit Ollie in full-time.

'I've got some good news for you,' Billy said. 'I've been talking to Roger Fleet, the MD of the Park Hotels group, about contract furniture. It turns out he's carrying out a major revamp of some of their older hotels and he's looking for a new supplier. It all looks pretty hopeful. I wondered if you'd like to come along to the meeting.'

'Yeah, sure,' she replied, her mind elsewhere. 'Get Becky to put it in the diary.'

'Of course, us winning this contract would depend on you sleeping with him.'

'No problem.'

Billy snapped his fingers in front of her face. 'Hello? Anyone there?'

'What? Oh, sorry. I've just got a lot on my mind, that's all. I take it you've seen this morning's paper?'

'Oh, that.' His face fell.

'Apparently they're organising a public meeting. George wants me to go along.'

'What for?'

'Sacrificial goat, I think.'

Billy sighed. 'Why did Cat have to start all this?'

'I think she's getting at me.'

He looked shocked. 'She wouldn't do that!'

'Maybe not. I just wonder if she'd be taking such an interest if it was someone else doing this job.'

'Do you want me to talk to her about it?'

She shook her head. 'This is something that Cat and I have to sort out for ourselves.'

Cat was surprised to see Elizabeth Montague back in the salon. There was a young woman with her, fair-haired and ethereally beautiful in designer jeans.

Maxine fell over herself to get to her. They spoke for a few minutes, then she called Cat over.

'Mrs Montague would like a word with you,' she said, her lips stretched in a fake smile.

'It's more of a favour, really.' Elizabeth turned to the young woman beside her. 'This is my daughter Charlotte—you know, the one I was telling you about? She's getting married in a month's time. I was telling her how terrific you are and she wondered if you'd be interested in doing her hair for the wedding.'

'It's just me and two bridesmaids—and Mum,' Charlotte said. 'My usual hairdresser was going to come up from London but he's off to Cuba for a month. Mum reckons you'd be perfect.'

'Are you sure you wouldn't prefer Julie to do it?' Maxine interrupted, unable to contain herself. 'She is our senior stylist—'

'I wouldn't trust your senior stylist to trim my garden hedge.' Elizabeth smiled sweetly. 'I know it's short notice, but we'd be terribly grateful,' she said to Cat.

'I—'

'Of course she'll do it,' Maxine stepped in quickly. 'Why don't you come through to the office? We can talk about fees and so on.' As Maxine guided them past, she heard her say, 'So what's Sean Connery actually like close up? Is he a good kisser?'

'I'm sorry, Roo, I really am. But it's the bank's decision and there's nothing I can do about it.' Mike Garrett looked regretful. 'We can't approve any more funds.'

'But you've seen the cash-flow forecasts. Now we've made all those savings to the overheads and tightened up our credit controls, our financial picture looks a lot healthier.'

'We're all delighted with what you've done. But we still don't consider Fairbanks a good financial risk.'

'What about the potential new markets I've outlined?'

'That's all they are. Potential. They mean nothing until they're translated into solid sales.'

'So that's it. Fairbanks is finished.'

'Don't take it so personally,' Mike said. 'No one said you had to make this work. Your job was to find out if the company had a viable future, not to save it from ruin. You've already done more than enough.'

Maybe Mike was right. Maybe she should just wind things up and leave. No one would blame her if she did.

But she couldn't. Somewhere along the line, it had become personal. She'd broken her own golden rule and got involved.

She felt like going straight home but she wanted to go and break the news to George Fairbanks. She wasn't looking forward to it, but knew she wouldn't sleep that night if she left it until the morning.

It was early evening and the sun was out for once as she drove through the factory gates. George Fairbanks was still in his office. He gazed out of the window, watching the workers leave.

'There they go,' he said. 'I wonder how long it'll be before they're leaving permanently.' He turned to look at her, the shadows casting troubled lines on his face. 'That's what you've come to tell me, isn't it?'

'The bank wasn't as helpful as I had hoped.'

'And you couldn't wait to come and tell me the good news.' He turned to look out of the window again.

'That's not fair!' Roo protested. 'I've worked hard to keep this factory going. OK, so maybe you didn't approve of some of the things I did, but at least they gave this place a fighting chance. Which is more than it had before.'

'I know.' To her surprise, George backed down. 'I'm sorry if I've given you a hard time. I suppose I was just blaming you for everything going wrong.' His eyes were sad. 'I do appreciate what you've done. I'm just sorry you didn't get here a year ago, then maybe you could have made a real difference.'

'So am I,' Roo said, and was surprised to realise she meant it.

He turned to gaze at her with respect. 'You're a fighter, I'll give you that. And I haven't made it easy for you. I know that I'm a stubborn old fool. But this factory's been my life since I was a young lad, and it broke my heart to see it being torn apart by you and that son of mine.' There was a faraway look in his eyes. 'I just wish I could have done something about it, before—' he broke off.

'Before what?' Roo asked.

He averted his eyes. 'Before I die,' he said.

Roo laughed uneasily. 'You've got years yet!' But George shook his head, his face sombre.

'Cancer,' he said. 'The doctors found it last Christmas.'

'Can't they do anything?'

'It's too far gone. I've surprised them by lasting this long. They thought I'd be dead by Easter!' He smiled wistfully. 'I've hung on because I've been waiting for a miracle. Not for me, for this place. But it doesn't look like it's going to happen now, does it?'

Roo suddenly felt overwhelmingly sad. Against all the odds, she'd grown to like George Fairbanks.

'Do you know what hurts most?' he said. 'That I've let them all down. The workers, my father, my grandfather. They trusted me to keep this place going and I failed them all.'

'You can't say that.'

'Why not? It's true.' He turned away from her. 'I've been looking out at this same view for thirty years. It's changed a hell of a lot in that time. All that land over there used to belong to the pit. Now look what's hap-pened to it.'

She followed George's gaze out of the window. Across the river, JCBs were churning up the ground to put in foundations for new houses.

'Would they be allowed to build on this site?'

'Try stopping them,' George said grimly. 'I've already had offers from property developers.'

'Is that right?' Roo gazed across the river. An idea was beginning to form in her mind. 'Mr Fairbanks,' she said. 'What if I told you I might be able to save this factory?'

'I'd say you were a flaming miracle worker,' George said.

'**S**ell the factory?' Frederick Fairbanks stared at her. 'Have you been drinking, Ms Hennessy?'

'It's the answer to all our problems. This site is prime development land. It's worth a small fortune. And the factory itself is a liability. It's too big and needs too many repairs. If we were to try and put everything right we'd be in the red for years.'

'I agree. Our heating bill alone is astronomical.'

'So why don't we sell it? We could use the money to lease a smaller, purpose-built unit, which would be more efficient and cost less to run. And we'd have enough money left over to pay off our existing loan and buy the new machinery we need.'

Frederick Fairbanks looked tempted. Then he shook his head. 'My father would never agree to it,' he said shortly.

'I talked to him last night. He thinks we should do it.'

Frederick gazed at her in admiration. 'How the hell did you manage that? I've been trying to talk him into it for years.'

'I have my ways.' It had been a long, emotional conversation. But in the end George Fairbanks had reluctantly agreed that even his father would have approved of getting rid of the building if it meant keeping the family firm in business.

Roo smoothed her Stella McCartney dress over her hips and twisted to catch her back view in the full-length mirror. It gave her a slight shock to see herself looking so sexy. When she'd bought it, she'd never imagined she'd be wearing it to save her marriage.

She still had a chance, she thought. David had called every night this week. Admittedly it was to speak to Ollie, but they'd had a few words, and she sensed he was missing his family.

Tonight he was coming up to Normanford, and she was going to try to convince him to give their marriage another go over a romantic dinner. Matt had agreed to baby-sit to make up for the manure incident.

Ollie was glued to the sitting-room window, watching out for his father's car, when the phone rang.

'There's been a change of plan,' David said. 'I won't be able to make it.'

'No!' Roo looked at her son, his nose pressed to the glass. 'What am I going to tell Ollie? He's been looking forward to this.' And so have I, she thought.

'I know, I'm sorry.'

'What's so bloody important you can't come up and see your own son?'

'It's a bit difficult. I just need to be at home at the moment, that's all.' Something in his voice sent warning signals up her spine.

'David, what is it? What's wrong?'

There was a long silence. 'Shauna's just found out she's pregnant. Roo? Are you still there?'

'Yes, I'm here.' She took a deep breath. 'I don't know what to say.'

'Neither did I, when she told me.'

There was a long pause. 'So what are you going to do?'

'I don't know yet. Shauna's in a bit of a state, which is why I have to stay with her. I'm sorry, OK? Believe me, I'd rather this wasn't happening! Tell Ollie I'll be up next weekend.'

She glanced at Ollie and lowered her voice. 'He'll be heartbroken.'

'Now you know how I felt all those times I had to tell him you weren't coming home,' David said shortly, and hung up.

'Was that Daddy?' Ollie demanded as she put the phone down. 'When's he coming? Has he brought me a present?'

'Sorry, darling.' Roo steeled herself. 'Daddy can't come today. He's . . . um . . . had some bad news.'

She hugged him as sobs shook his little body. She tried to say all the right comforting things about how his daddy loved him and hated to let him down, but all the time she kept thinking what an utterly selfish bastard David was.

Ollie still hadn't calmed down when Matt turned up half an hour later, laden with popcorn and crisps. 'All ready for our boys' night in?' he said cheerily. 'I've brought a few provisions; I had a feeling your mum wouldn't be a junk-food fan—' He stopped when he saw Ollie's tear-ravaged face, his head buried in Roo's lap. 'What's wrong?'

'David's not coming,' Roo explained through tight lips.

'Ah.' Matt read the unspoken message in her eyes and immediately took charge of the situation. 'There's no reason why we shouldn't still have our fun. Why don't we take this lot next door and watch a video? We could even order a pizza, if you like. And Mummy can come too. She can be an honorary lad for the evening.'

'I don't know—' Roo began to say.

Ollie looked up tearfully. 'Have you got *Star Wars*?'

'Have I got *Star Wars*? I've got the lot. And *Lord of the Rings*.'

'*Star Wars* is better.'

'I don't know about that. I reckon Gandalf could beat Darth Vader any day.'

'But Darth's got a light sabre. Gandalf's only got a stupid old stick!'

'We'll see about that!' Matt winked at her. 'Everyone round to my place, then!'

Matt's house was messy and lined with books. More books and papers were strewn all over the table. 'Sorry, I didn't know I was going to be having guests.' He collected them up in an untidy pile.

Roo glanced at one of the typed sheets. 'Are you really doing a PhD?'

'No, I only say that to impress women. Of course I'm doing a PhD. My thesis is in non-verbal communication.' He swept last Sunday's newspapers off the sofa, clearing a space for her. 'Make yourself comfortable. Ollie and I will order the pizza.'

'Don't I get to choose too?'

He frowned, mock severe. 'Excuse me? Are you a man?'

'No, but—'

'Then stay out of it. Ordering pizza is men's work.'

She smiled to herself, listening to them in the hall bickering over the takeaway menu. Matt was just what her son needed.

She examined the photos on his mantelpiece. Lots of studenty groups of lads in wacky poses. A couple of family shots. But only one girl. Surprising, considering the number of lady friends he seemed to have.

Roo studied it. She was red-haired, green-eyed, freckled and pretty. 'I haven't seen this one before,' she said when Matt came back from phoning his pizza order.

'No, you wouldn't have.'

'Don't tell me, she was the one that got away?'

'You could say that. Ham and mushroom all right for you?' he changed the subject, his smile flashing into place. Roo put the photo back, wondering if she'd touched a nerve.

When the takeaway arrived they all huddled on the sofa and watched *Star Wars*. Roo tried not to mind when Ollie absent-mindedly shared his pizza with Harvey. She was too tense to concentrate on the film, which she'd already seen a million times. She couldn't stop thinking about David and Shauna.

By the time the film finished Ollie had fallen asleep, propped up against Harvey. 'He missed the end,' Matt said.

'He knows it off by heart anyway.' Roo got up. 'Thanks for a lovely evening. It was just what he needed—'

'Don't go.'

'I need to get Ollie to bed.'

'He's OK there for a bit longer. We haven't had a chance to talk.'

'Are you sure I'm not keeping you from your work?' she asked as Matt fetched a couple of beers from the fridge.

'Believe me, you're a welcome break.' He snapped the top off one of the bottles and handed it to her. 'Sorry, did you want a glass?'

'This is fine.' She eyed the bottle warily, then sat with it on her lap.

'Why didn't your husband show?'

'His girlfriend's pregnant.'

'No way!'

'So it looks like there isn't going to be a reconciliation after all.'

'I'm sorry.'

'To be honest, I didn't really think there would be. But I had to try, for this one's sake.' She pushed Ollie's fair hair back off his brow. She'd thought he might stay fair like David, but it was already turning from pale straw to the colour of golden syrup. Reminders of David were slowly slipping from her life. 'It's Ollie I feel sorry for. I feel like I've failed him.'

'How do you work that out?'

'I should have tried harder,' she said. 'I could have held it together if I'd done things differently.'

'This is a marriage, not an exam. You don't get a better grade by putting in more effort. Not if the chemistry isn't there.'

'Chemistry! You mean your "eyes across a crowded room" thing?'

'That's what it's all about.' Their eyes met and held. Roo could instantly see why he was such an expert in non-verbal communication. His body language was sending her all kinds of messages.

And then the doorbell rang.

'Where the fuck have you been?' She heard the girl's voice, shrill with anger. 'Eleven, you said. Outside Ritzy's. I've been waiting hours!'

'I'm sorry.' Matt muttered something she couldn't make out. Seconds later the girl barged her way into the room. She was a tall, Scandinavian blonde with ice-blue eyes that raked over Roo like an arctic storm.

'This all looks very cosy,' she snapped. 'Who the hell are you?'

'This is Roo, my next-door neighbour.'

'I'm just leaving.' She gathered Ollie up in her arms.

'Let me.' Matt stepped forward to take him, but Roo held on.

'No, it's fine. I'm sorry if I ruined your evening,' she said in an undertone.

'You didn't,' Matt whispered.

As she left, she heard the girl say, 'Bit old for you, isn't she?'

She didn't hear Matt's reply. She didn't need to. Her face flamed as she let herself into her house, still with Ollie bundled in her arms.

Chapter 7

'MUM, I DON'T feel well,' Ollie said, pushing his cereal around his bowl.

Roo, in the middle of browsing the foreign markets in the *Financial Times*, putting another load of washing in and looking for his missing trainer, suppressed a sigh. 'Again? What is it this time?'

'My tummy hurts. Can't I stay at home?' he pleaded.

'You know Mummy has to go to work.'

'You could stay off too.'

'I can't, darling. I'm meeting Uncle Billy at a furniture show in—oh hell!'

She snatched Ollie's half-finished breakfast bowl away, found the missing shoe hidden behind a cushion in the sitting room and bundled him, still groaning, into the back of the car.

'I thought you'd stood me up,' Billy said as she roared into the car park of the exhibition centre half an hour later.

'Don't.' She reached into the back of the car, stuffing papers into her briefcase. Billy watched her with amusement.

'Surely this isn't Roo Hennessy, super-organised businesswoman?'

'No, this is Roo Hennessy, working mother on the edge. So don't push it, OK?' She slammed the car door shut and straightened her shoulders. 'Right, let's go.'

'Not until I've done this.' He moved towards her and for one alarming second she thought he was going to kiss her. But he reached up and tucked a strand of hair behind her ear. 'There. Can't have you less than perfect, can we?'

'Heaven forbid.'

He was still standing very close to her, so close she could smell the lemony tang of his aftershave. Then Billy moved away hurriedly.

'We've, um, got quite a full day ahead of us,' he said, straightening his tie. 'There are lots of buyers I want you to meet. I'm hoping you can win them over.'

'With your looks and my brains how can we fail?'

The hangar-like building was already packed. Buyers thronged between lavish room sets displaying sofas, chairs, tables, beds and wardrobes, each manufacturer vying to catch the eye of the retailers.

By contrast, the Fairbanks stand was subdued and uninspired. It stood out among their slick, modern competitors like a middle-aged maiden aunt at a disco.

'I know,' Billy said, seeing her look. 'But we were lucky to get this. Frederick reckons it's a waste of marketing budget.'

They spent all morning luring potential customers over to the stand and giving them the big sales pitch. Roo had never talked so much or thought so fast in her life, trying to convince customers there was life in Fairbanks yet, and they should take a chance on them. Unfortunately, it didn't make people want to place any orders.

'It's not you, it's the furniture,' she kept hearing again and again.

Then Roger Fleet arrived. He was MD of the hotel chain Billy had been talking to about supplying contract furniture. Even he seemed less than impressed with what they were offering.

'Our hotels are exclusive and up-market, and the styling should reflect that.' And your furniture doesn't, his look said.

'We are working on a new concept at the moment,' Roo said, ignoring the quizzical looks Billy gave her. 'It's something totally new for Fairbanks. And frankly it's going to blow this lot out of the water.'

'Really? Can I see it?'

'I'm afraid not. We're keeping it under wraps.'

Roger Fleet was intrigued. 'If this new concept of yours takes off, we could be in business,' he said.

'What new concept?' Billy asked, as soon as he'd gone.

'I've no idea,' Roo admitted. 'But I couldn't just let him walk away, could I?' She put down the sheaf of brochures she'd been trying unsuccessfully to offload. 'Let's have a coffee. I need to think.'

There was a long queue in the cafeteria. At the head of it, a foreign man was holding everyone up, trying to pay for his coffee with euros. 'What do you mean you can't take them?' he kept saying to the blank-looking woman at the cash desk.

In the end Roo lost patience and marched to the head of the queue. 'Here, let me.' She handed over cash for all their coffees to the unsmiling woman at the till. 'And next time go to the bank.'

She regretted being so sharp as soon as the man looked at her, his wicked smile lighting up his inky black eyes. 'I only flew in from Milan two hours ago.' He looked disreputable and sexy in a rumpled dark linen suit over a black T-shirt. 'I'm Sal.' His voice was as rich and smooth as espresso.

'Roo Hennessy.'

'Shall we sit down?' Billy hissed behind her.

To Billy's chagrin, Sal joined them at the only available table.

'So what do you do?' she asked. 'Are you a buyer, or a designer?'

'I make furniture. I have a stand over there.' He pointed vaguely towards the far end of the hall.

'Really? I must take a look.'

'Yes, you should. I'm very good.'

'So modest,' Billy muttered, toying moodily with a packet of sugar.

'You should come over and see us, too,' Roo said. 'Stand 207. Fairbanks Fine Furniture.'

He stifled a yawn. 'Your British furniture lacks—how you say?— imagination. Just like your food.' He put his cheese roll down with a grimace. 'And your men, maybe.'

Billy bristled beside her. 'And you think you can do better?' Roo asked quickly, before he could respond.

'Better than your furniture? Or better than your men?' He gave her a grin that could scorch a woman's underwear at fifty paces. 'I can show you my furniture. The rest you will have to find out for yourself.' He pushed a card across the table towards her. Roo glanced down at the name and recognised it instantly.

'Salvatore Bellini. You designed the interior of the Wharf Hotel in Leeds.'

'You've seen it?'

'I certainly have. And I was very impressed.'

'Of course.' He shrugged. 'My furniture is very beautiful.'

'And bloody expensive,' Billy said. Sal regarded him coolly.

'Money is not important. Beauty, that is what drives men to distraction.' He looked at Roo.

Billy pushed his cup away. 'We'd better get back to the stand.'

Roo stood up. 'It's been nice meeting you, Signor Bellini.'

'*Ciao, bella.*' He reached for her hand and planted a kiss on it. 'And if you want to see how furniture should be made, come and see me.'

'He was a bit bloody full of himself,' Billy said as they left.

'He was Italian.' And very charming, she thought. She couldn't stop thinking about him. Later that afternoon, when Billy was busy with a potential client, she slipped away to take a look at Salvatore's stand.

Roo spotted it straight away among the crowded room sets. A single chair, crafted in slices of cherry and walnut, sitting on a raised plinth. Moody low-voltage lighting picked out its exquisite lines.

'I knew you wouldn't be able to resist.' He lounged in the shadows at the edge of the stand. 'Is it the furniture you've come to see, or me?'

She nodded towards the chair. 'There isn't much to see.'

'I prefer quality to quantity. Every piece is flawless.'

Roo felt an idea stirring in her mind. Not just any idea. The big one. 'It's a shame more people can't enjoy your beautiful furniture,' she said.

'We can't always have what we want, can we?'

'We could if we combined our talents.'

His eyebrow rose. 'That sounds tempting.'

She ignored the suggestive look he gave her. 'You could design a capsule collection for Fairbanks. We'd make it in our factory and sell it under our joint names. And it wouldn't affect the exclusivity of your own range,' she went on, seeing him frown. 'There will always be people willing to pay premium prices for something exclusive.'

Sal pulled a face. 'I am not sure.'

'Our furniture is very well made.' Her mobile rang and she switched it off quickly. 'At least come and look round our factory, meet our production team. Then you can make your mind up.'

'Will you be there?'

Didn't he ever let up? 'If it would help,' she laughed.

'OK, I will meet your people. But if I do not like what I see, that's it.'

'That's all I ask.' She could hardly conceal her delight and excitement.

He nodded past her shoulder. 'I think your boyfriend wants you.'

Roo glanced behind her. Billy was pushing his way through the crowd towards them. 'He isn't my boyfriend!'

Sal smiled enigmatically. 'If you say so, *cara mia*.'

Billy was surprisingly lukewarm about her idea. 'It would mean changing all our production methods.'

'That will be easy once we get our new machinery. I think it'll be just the shot in the arm we need. And it would be something different, something special. The stores would definitely go for it.'

'How do you know the Italian Stallion can deliver?'

'Oh, he can deliver. Ask your daughter. She's a big fan of his.'

'You too, by the look of it.'

As he stalked off to his car, Roo wondered if Sal was right. Billy certainly seemed to be acting like a jealous lover.

She was still on a high about her idea when she rang Angie's doorbell. Angie greeted her with a bemused smile. 'Hello, what are you doing here?'

'I've come to pick up my son. You know, about this high? Fair hair? Thinks he's Luke Skywalker?'

'Hasn't your mum spoken to you? Ollie wasn't too well earlier on, so I rang her to take him home.'

'You rang my mother?'

'I tried calling you but I couldn't get through,' Angie said defensively. 'Sadie said she'd let you know.'

'She probably didn't think.' That was Sadie. She didn't think. God only knew what she was doing with her son now!

'Higher! Higher!' Ollie squealed with delight as Sadie pushed him on the swing, up and up until her arms ached. He'd made a miraculous recovery since she brought him home from the childminder's.

On the way home, she began to wonder if she'd done the right thing. Ruby wouldn't thank her for getting involved. And Ollie didn't seem half as sick as Angie had made out when she had called her. He was well enough to pester Sadie for a detour to the park.

She gave him one last push and massaged her stiff arms. 'Come on, we'd better head home. I've got to let your mum know where you are.'

'Can I have a lolly?'

'I thought you felt sick.'

He stared at his shoes. 'I'm better now.'

'That was quick.' She caught his blushing face. 'Maybe I should take you back to Angie's.'

'No! I don't want to go back there! I don't like it.'

She took him to the ice-cream kiosk, where he stared into the fridge as if his life depended on it. Finally he chose a Cornetto.

'So why don't you like Angie?' Sadie asked as they headed home.

'She's all right. It's the other children I don't like. They make fun of me because they say I talk posh, and . . . they say things.'

'What kind of things?'

'They say my mum's horrible and we don't belong here.'

'Have you told your mum about this?'

'She won't listen. Anyway, I don't want to make her sad.' He unwrapped his Cornetto carefully. 'She and Daddy are getting divorced.'

Sadie nearly dropped her lolly in shock. 'What?'

'I think it's a secret,' Ollie said. 'Mummy doesn't know I know. But I listen to them on the phone. He's got another woman.'

'I'm sure you've got that wrong, love.'

'I haven't! Her name's Shauna. She used to be my nanny but now she's Daddy's girlfriend. What's pregnant?' he asked suddenly.

'Ask your mum.' Sadie's mind reeled as she struggled to take it in. So Ruby was getting divorced. Why hadn't she said anything to her about it? Because you're the last person in the world she'd confide in, a small voice inside her head reminded her.

419

As they turned the corner into Hope Street, Sadie saw Ruby's car parked outside her mother's house. They'd barely reached the gate before Roo ran down the path and gathered Ollie into her arms as if he'd spent the last six months held captive by white slave-traders.

'Where the hell have you been?' She glared at Sadie over his head. 'I've been worried sick.'

Sadie's hackles rose. 'Let me see. We played a quick game of hop-scotch in the middle of the M62, then I taught him how to juggle with hand grenades.'

Ollie looked at her, a frown creasing his angelic features. 'No, you didn't. We went to the park and I had an ice cream.'

'You could have let me know,' Ruby said.

'If you're that worried, try answering your phone next time.' Sadie stalked past her into the house, all her sympathy forgotten. That was absolutely the last time she ever tried to be helpful to her daughter!

She'd put the kettle on and was starting on supper when Ruby appeared in the kitchen doorway.

'Sorry,' she muttered. 'I didn't mean to snap. I was just worried, that's all. When I got here and you weren't back—'

'You assumed I'd done something daft? Thanks a lot,' she said bitterly.

She expected Ruby to go but she didn't. 'Ollie seems to like you.'

'Don't sound so surprised. Not everyone thinks the same as you.'

'Look, give me a chance, I'm trying to apologise!'

Sadie glanced across at her daughter. She'd lost weight. In the early evening light, her face looked gaunt and tired. She fought the urge to put her arms round her.

'I wasn't interfering,' she said. 'I told Angie she should wait for you, but she insisted he wasn't well—'

'I know. You did the right thing,' Ruby said shortly.

'He's a lovely little boy. So bright. He's a credit to you.'

'Thanks.'

There was a long silence. Then Sadie said, 'He must miss his dad.'

Ruby looked up sharply. 'What makes you say that?'

'Being away from home for so long. It must be hard on him.'

'David's coming up this weekend.'

There was something in the way she said it that made Sadie realise Ollie was right. If Ruby's marriage hadn't broken up yet, it was heading that way. Kids knew more than their parents gave them credit for.

The kettle came to the boil and to Sadie's surprise Ruby offered to make the tea.

'I don't know,' Sadie said. 'You know how particular Nanna is.'

Ruby nodded. 'Always loose, never bags. Warm the pot first and let it stand for exactly seven minutes.' She smiled. 'You can't grow up in this house and not know how Nanna likes her tea.'

It was strange seeing her there in her chic clothes, sluicing Nanna's old brown teapot out over the sink. Strange but nice. Sadie wondered if she should risk ruining the mood by mentioning what Ollie had told her about being bullied at the childminder's. In the end she knew she had to say something; she couldn't let her grandson go on being miserable, even if her daughter did bite her head off.

Ruby was dismissive at first. 'What do you mean, not happy? How can he not be happy? Angie's lovely.'

'It's the other kids he doesn't get on with.'

'He'll be fine. He's just taking a bit of time to adjust.'

'I think it's more than that. He told me the other kids tease him and call him names.'

'He's never said anything to me.'

'I don't think he wants to worry you. He reckons you've got enough on your plate.'

She expected some smart reply. But Ruby sat down at the kitchen table, her head in her hands. 'Oh God. Why didn't I notice it before? All those times he pretended to be ill, I had no idea—What am I going to do?' Ruby said.

'You could let me look after him.'

'You?'

'I managed to take care of him this afternoon without killing him, didn't I?'

'But I thought you didn't want to do it.'

'I've changed my mind. It'd be better than sending him somewhere he's unhappy.'

'It might not be for long,' Ruby said. Her mascara was smudged under her eyes, making her look less terrifyingly perfect, more vulnerable. 'Just a couple of weeks. And I'd pay you, of course.'

'There's no need for that.'

'I want to.'

Sadie saw her daughter's determined expression and realised that the only way Ruby could allow herself to accept her mother's help was by turning it into a business transaction. 'Suit yourself,' she said.

Ruby finished making the tea but politely refused Sadie's offer of supper. This far but no further, her cool look said. Sadie was disappointed, but at least they didn't part screaming at each other for once.

It was a start.

The draughty church hall was packed for the public meeting the following day. Roo stood at the back, watching people shuffling down the rows looking for empty seats, knowing none of them were on her side. There was no sign of the Fairbanks family. They'd left her to face the ordeal alone.

'Ready?' She jumped as Billy touched her arm. 'No need to ask if you're nervous!' He smiled.

'I'm OK, honestly. You don't have to do this, you know.'

'You don't seriously think I'd let you face this on your own, do you?'

'What about Cat?'

His face clouded. 'Cat's got enough people on her side. She doesn't need me. You do.'

Up on the platform, Cat was suffering a crisis of nerves. She gazed over the rows of faces and felt daunted. What the hell was she doing? She didn't belong up here. She was no public speaker. Beside her, Marjorie Prentice was white-faced as she shuffled her notes.

Cat glanced through her prepared speech. The words, which she'd worked on carefully for the past week, sounded clumsy as she read them through in her head. She could feel damp patches of perspiration under her arms, and prayed they weren't showing through her top.

There was a stir at the back of the hall as Ruby walked in. Her heels clicked on the tiled floor as she calmly walked the length of the hall to take her place on the platform. She looked composed, and Cat was almost ready to throw in the towel there and then—until she saw Billy.

She had no idea he was going to be there. And she certainly didn't know he'd be with Ruby!

It couldn't have been a more public taunt. She felt everyone's gaze go from him to her, waiting for her reaction. Ruby caught her eye and nodded a greeting, but Billy stared straight ahead of him.

'Take no notice,' Marjorie whispered. 'That Fairbanks lot probably made him come to put you off.'

If they had, it hadn't worked. Anger sent a surge of adrenaline that chased her nerves away, and before she knew what she was doing she was standing at the microphone addressing the crowd.

'Ladies and gentlemen.' She stumbled through her opening address, constantly looking down at her notes because her brain had gone blank and she couldn't remember a word. All the time she felt Ruby watching her, waiting for her to make a berk of herself. When she did look up briefly, she saw the reporter from the *Normanford News* stifling a yawn, his notebook unopened in his lap.

She quickly finished her opening speech and handed over to Ruby for her presentation. As she took her place at the microphone, the reporter woke up and reached for his pen.

Her voice was full of cool authority as she began her speech. 'Ladies and gentlemen, thank you for allowing me the opportunity to come here and explain what's really happening at Fairbanks—'

'We know what's happening!' someone shouted. 'You're closing the place down!'

'That's where you're wrong. It's true we've had to implement certain measures over the past few weeks, to ensure the company's survival—'

'To ensure bigger profits for you lot, you mean!'

Ruby turned on the heckler with an icy smile. 'When I arrived at Fairbanks, the factory was facing insolvency. We were in danger of not being able to meet the following month's wage bill.'

'Management toady!' someone shouted halfheartedly. Everyone ignored him. They were all listening to Ruby now. Cat could feel them warming to her. She didn't know if what she said was true, but it was certainly convincing.

'Now we've made the necessary savings, hopefully we can start to rebuild the company,' Ruby was saying.

'Why should we believe you?' A voice came from the back of the hall. 'What do you care if Fairbanks goes down the drain?'

'I care because Fairbanks is part of my history too.' Now she was playing the local hero card. How sickening. 'I was born and brought up in Normanford—'

'Yeah, and you couldn't wait to get out of the place!' Everyone laughed. Cat looked round to see who'd shouted and realised to her horror that it was her.

The people at the back took up her cue and began a Mexican wave of jeering.

'Capitalist pig!'

'Filthy scum!'

'Fairbanks fat cats!'

Ruby tried to stay composed, but the heckling and cat calls went on, growing louder and more ferocious. Some members of the crowd were turning on the troublemakers. Scuffles broke out, and people were beginning to surge towards the stage.

Cat saw him before Ruby did. A yob in an Adidas hoodie pushed his way to the front. Cat saw him raise his arm, caught the glint of something in his hand. 'Look out!' she screamed. Ruby turned towards her, just as the bottle flew through the air and struck her on the head. She fell. Cat dropped her notes and ran to her, but Billy was already there. He knelt beside her, cradling her in his arms, saying her name over and over again. Her blood was all over his shirt.

'I've got to get her to hospital,' he said.

'Shall I call an ambulance?'

'No, I'll take her.'

Cat looked down at her cousin. 'Is there anything I can do?'

Billy glared at her. 'I think you've done enough, don't you?'

'**H**onestly, Billy, you don't have to make such a fuss, it was only a cut!' Roo reclined on the sofa, propped up with cushions.

'You still had stitches. And blows to the head can be dangerous. You heard what the doctor said; you have to rest in case of concussion.'

'He also said I was absolutely fine.' Roo sipped her tea and grimaced. 'Ugh! Did you put sugar in this?'

'It's good for shock.'

Roo put her cup down. His over-protectiveness was beginning to trouble her. 'Shouldn't you be going home? It's after ten. Cat will be wondering where you are.'

'I don't really care.' Billy's jaw was clenched. 'After tonight I don't think I want to be with her.'

'It wasn't her fault it turned into a riot!'

'She shouldn't have started this bloody protest in the first place.' He reached for the phone. 'Do you want me to ring David?'

'I don't think he'd be very interested.' She saw his quizzical expression and added, 'You might as well know. David and I have split up.'

'What?' He stared at her. 'When?'

'A couple of weeks ago. Although to be honest things haven't been right for a long time. He's met someone else. And she's pregnant.'

'And you didn't think to mention it? I thought we were supposed to be friends.'

'It was my problem. I had to deal with it.'

'Christ, Roo, why do you have to be so independent all the time?'

'Who else have I got to depend on?'

'You've got me.'

'Cat would love that. She's bad enough about us working together. God knows what she'd do if I started crying on your shoulder.'

'You're probably right. I don't know what's got into her these days. She used to be so kind and loving but lately she's changed so much I hardly recognise her.'

He looked so confused, Roo wanted to shake Cat. She had a good man and a good marriage, and she risked throwing them away for the sake of some stupid feud.

'Perhaps you should be telling Cat, not me?'

'That's just it. I can't say anything to her without her flying off the handle.' He looked rueful. 'Listen to me going on. It's you we should be worrying about. I really wish you'd told me about you and David.'

'Like I said, it's my problem.'

She shifted against the cushions and Billy was instantly solicitous, reaching over to plump them up for her. 'Better?' He lifted his eyes to meet hers, dark and intense.

'Thank you.' He was very close to her. If she reached up, she could kiss him. And she realised that he was thinking the same thing.

She turned her face away, breaking the spell, just as the doorbell rang.

'I'll go.' Billy stood up. 'It might be a reporter.' They'd already called twice, begging for a quote about the evening's events. Roo listened to the voices on the front doorstep, trying to make out who would be calling at that time. Then Billy came back.

'It was some boy called Matt. He said he's a friend of yours.' He looked unconvinced. 'I told him to come back tomorrow.'

Roo felt a pang of disappointment. Suddenly the one person she wanted to see was Matt, if only to relieve the charged atmosphere between her and Billy.

Then he was there, shouldering past Billy into the sitting room.

'How the hell did you get in?' Billy demanded.

'I used my key.' He turned to Roo. 'I heard what happened. Are you OK?'

'I'm fine,' said Roo.

Billy loomed behind them, waiting for an introduction. 'Billy, this is my neighbour Matt. Billy's an old friend of mine,' she explained.

They nodded coolly, eyeing each other up. 'I can take over the patient now, if you need to go home,' Matt said.

'That won't be necessary.'

'I don't need anyone looking after me, thank you very much!' Roo said firmly. They collided with each other to get to her as she stood up. 'And Matt's right. You should go home, Billy.'

He looked as if he might argue, then gave up. Roo saw him to the door. She felt guilty dismissing him after he'd been so kind. But she had a feeling he might never go home otherwise, and she didn't need another reason for Cat to hate her.

'He didn't seem in any hurry to leave,' Matt said. He was in the arm-chair, his long legs stretched out in front of him.

'He and his wife are having problems at the moment.'

'Let me guess. You're the problem?'

She looked up sharply. 'What makes you say that?'

'I've spent three years studying non-verbal communication, remember? I get the feeling you two have a history.'

'You could say that.'

'Want to tell me about it?'

'Do I have a choice?' Matt had a way of getting her to open up. Perhaps it was all that psychology training.

She gave him a brief summary of her complicated relationship with Billy and Cat. 'But like you say, it's history,' she said.

'Are you sure? I reckon you could have him back any time you liked.'

'What makes you say that?'

'Because he's vulnerable, and his marriage is in a mess. And now he's beginning to wonder if he made the right choice all those years ago.'

Roo was silent. Matt was right; something could have happened between her and Billy earlier on, if she had given him the slightest encouragement. But she wasn't sure she felt that way about Billy now. He was still wildly fanciable, but the spark wasn't there any more.

'It would be a big mistake if you did,' Matt said.

'Why's that?'

'Because deep down he still loves his wife.'

'How can you say that? I don't know if he's ever loved her. She forced him to marry her, remember?'

'She couldn't force him to do anything he didn't want to,' Matt said. 'And even if he didn't love her when they married, that doesn't mean he hasn't grown to love her.'

'What about your instant chemistry thing?'

Matt shrugged. 'It doesn't always work like that. Sometimes it takes a while for people to realise how they feel about each other.'

He looked at her, and Roo felt alarming little prickles of electricity shoot up the back of her neck.

The phone rang, distracting them. It was Sadie, sounding frantic. 'Tom just called,' she said. 'Is it true? You've been attacked by a madman? Are you badly hurt? Why aren't you in hospital?'

It was weird, Roo thought as she reassured Sadie she hadn't been shot, or stabbed, or lynched by a hysterical mob. She sounded concerned. Almost like a real mother.

'Is there anything I can do? Shall I come round?'

'No, really. But it would help if you could keep Ollie with you tonight.'

'Of course. He's dropped off on the sofa with Nanna anyway.'

Matt smiled when she put the phone down. 'I thought your mum was a selfish cow.'

'So did I.' Roo was thoughtful. 'She was different when she was younger.'

'Weren't we all?'

'Even you?' Roo curled up on the sofa, tucking her legs under her.

'Even me.'

'Are you seriously trying to tell me you weren't always the habitual womaniser you are today?' Roo teased.

He gazed into the empty fire grate. 'Actually I used to be a one-woman man.'

'That girl in the photo?'

He nodded. 'Emma.'

'Don't tell me, she broke your heart?'

'In a way.'

'So what did she do? Run off with your best friend? Grow a beard and become a lesbian?'

'She died.'

'Oh Lord, I'm sorry. When did it happen?'

'Three years ago. We were going to get married after we graduated, but then Emma found out that she had leukaemia. I wanted to bring the wedding forward but she was determined she wasn't going down the aisle in a wheelchair. She really thought she was going to beat it, right up to the end.' His voice was flat. 'We buried her in the same church we were due to marry in. Now the only thing I've got left of her is Harvey.'

No wonder he'd been so angry when his dog was taken away. 'Is that why you don't want to commit to anyone now? Because you're still in love with Emma?'

'Possibly,' he agreed. 'Or maybe I just don't want to get hurt again.'

'What about all those girls you go out with? Don't you care about hurting them?'

'I don't set out to hurt anyone. They know the score. They know I'm not interested in anything long-term.'

Roo suddenly felt very sad and tired. Matt caught her stifling a yawn. 'Are you OK? Can I get you anything?'

'I'm a bit tired. I think I might go to bed.'

'Let me help you.' Against her protests, he insisted on waiting on the landing while she took off her make-up, brushed her teeth and changed into her pyjamas. 'And before you argue, I'm spending the night here,' he said. 'You shouldn't be left alone for twenty-four hours after a blow to the head. Surely the doctor told you that?'

'He mentioned something about it. But I'm sure it's not necessary—'

'I'm staying, and that's all there is to it.' He noticed her wary face and laughed. 'Don't look so terrified; I'll sleep on the sofa. I'm not going to try anything while you're weak and defenceless.'

'The thought never crossed my mind.'

'Didn't it? It did mine!'

Billy hadn't come home until gone midnight the previous night.

'Before you start, I left Roo's two hours ago,' he snapped before Cat could speak. 'I just couldn't face coming home.'

Cat bit her lip. 'I'm sorry.'

'It's not me you should be apologising to, is it?'

'Is she all right?'

'Just about. No thanks to you. I'm going to bed.'

The following morning, as Billy got dressed, he said, 'And you might as well know now, I have to go to Birmingham to visit a hotel next week. It'll mean an overnight stay. And Roo's going.' He sent her a defiant look.

'Fine,' Cat said humbly, not daring to argue. As Billy left, she added, 'I can't help the way I feel, Billy. You two have always been so close.' Closer than us, she thought.

'But I married you,' Billy said. He didn't look happy about it.

What are you doing here?' Becky looked up from her computer when Roo walked into the office. 'Aren't you supposed to be resting?'

'I'm not an invalid! Life has to go on. Anyway, we've got an important meeting today. Salvatore Bellini's coming in.'

'You mean *the* Salvatore Bellini? What's he doing here?'

'He's meeting George. If everything goes well he might be designing a capsule collection for us.'

'That's fantastic! How did you pull that one off?'

'I haven't yet. That's why I had to come in this morning.'

They'd already started the meeting by the time she got there. Roo was pleased to see they were all getting on famously. Salvatore and George made an unlikely pair, Sal with his flowing dark locks and leather jacket, George in his shabby, ancient suit and walking stick, but they impressed each other with their shared love of furniture-making. And even Billy was beginning to thaw towards the charismatic Italian as he realised the impact their new designer range could have on sales.

After the meeting, Sal invited them all to dinner that night at his hotel in Leeds. Roo called Sadie to check if Ollie could stay the night.

'Again? You didn't see him last night either.'

'I could hardly help that, could I?' Roo bridled. 'Anyway, I'm not going out to enjoy myself. This is a business dinner.'

'I'm sorry, I have to go to work. It's my cabaret night at the Ponderosa.'

'Mustn't miss that, must we?'

'You're not the only one who has to work, you know. Look, if you tell me what time you'll be back I could see if I can start later.'

'Don't bother. I'll find someone else to look after him.'

But there was no one else. She'd already promised Becky she could go to the dinner and meet her idol, so she couldn't disappoint her. And Matt was working at the pizza place. She was in a foul mood when she went to collect Ollie that night.

'What's the matter with you?' Sadie stood in the doorway, watching her throw Ollie's things into a bag.

'If you must know I had to cancel dinner. We could lose this deal.' Although she knew that wasn't true. Salvatore could see the advantages of going into partnership with Fairbanks, even without her being part of it. She was just pissed off at missing out.

'You should have checked with me first, shouldn't you? Anyway,' Sadie added, 'it will do you good to spend some time with Ollie.'

'I'm sorry?' Roo stared at her in disbelief. 'Are you trying to tell me I'm neglecting my own son? That's rich coming from you. How many times did you abandon me to go off and do your own thing?'

'And how many times did I stay with you when you needed me?' Sadie snapped back. 'But you forget about that, don't you?'

'At least I make sure my child's properly cared for. He doesn't have to put himself to bed in the dark because there's no money for the meter.'

'You're lucky, aren't you? Some of us didn't have a choice. You seem to think I was out having a grand old time, but I was working to keep a roof over our heads.'

'By singing in some poky nightclub for a couple of quid?'

'What else could I do? I didn't have a bunch of exams like you.'

'You could have got a proper job, like—' She broke off.

'Like everyone else's mother? Is that what you were going to say? Well, I'm sorry, but I wasn't like all those other mothers with their nice homes and their nice husbands. Believe me, I wish I had been.' Sadie's voice shook. 'Don't you think I used to lie awake at night and wish I could give you what all the other kids had? A proper home, a family?'

'It's a pity you didn't give me away when you had the chance then, isn't it?'

She saw her mother's eyes fill with tears and immediately wished she could take the words back.

'Isn't it?' Sadie said, and walked out.

She was still packing up Ollie's things when Nanna shuffled into the room. 'You shouldn't be so hard on her, you know,' she said. 'She was a good mother. As good as she knew how to be, anyway.'

'She wasn't interested in me.'

'If she wasn't interested, why did she fight so hard to keep you? Why didn't she just leave you at that unmarried mothers' home, instead of running away with you?'

'I wish she had left me there,' Roo muttered truculently.

'How dare you talk like that!' Nanna rapped her walking stick hard on the floor. 'You don't know the half of what she went through for you. Oh, she was young and stupid, I'm not denying that. But do you think it was easy for her, bringing you up on her own? She was sixteen years old! And it wasn't like it is these days, I can tell you. Folk round here made her life a misery, gossiping about her behind her back.'

'That didn't stop her enjoying herself, did it?'

'And why shouldn't she have a bit of fun? God knows, she didn't have much to laugh about. Sometimes she'd be up at dawn cleaning offices, then off to work in a shop all day, then back to office-cleaning at teatime. Anything to put food on the table.'

Roo thought about her mother flitting out of the house, done up like a film star. 'She never kept a job for more than five minutes.'

'They all took liberties with her, just because she was young and desperate. And they usually ended up sacking her because she needed to take time off to look after you.' Nanna sent Roo a hard look. 'They made her choose between you and the job, and she chose you every time.'

'Except for her singing,' Roo said bitterly. She still needed a reason to resent her mother. 'She never gave that up for me.'

'That was the only dream she had left,' Nanna said. 'She needed her dreams. She's not perfect, Ruby. But she's always cared, in her own way.' Nanna looked thoughtful, then beckoned to her. 'Come with me. I want to show you something.'

It took a long time to get up the stairs. At least Nanna used her lift, though she grumbled all the way up.

They ended up in Sadie's room. It was typical Sadie, clothes were heaped up on the bed, make-up scattered over the dressing table.

Nanna gestured to a table. 'Under there,' she said. 'The box.'

Roo pulled it out. 'What's in it?'

'Have a look.'

It took her a moment to recognise the contents. 'My old schoolbooks!'

'Not just the books. There's every school report you ever had in there. And your GCSE certificates. She never threw anything away.'

Roo rifled through the papers. Deeper inside, there were old school photos, and a couple of clumsy, handmade Mother's Day cards.

'She was always there, you know,' Nanna said. 'At all those school concerts and prizegivings.'

'I never saw her.'

'You wouldn't. She used to sneak in late and stand at the back.'

'Why?'

'Because she didn't want to embarrass you.' Roo had a sudden flash of herself as a teenager, refusing to acknowledge her mother at a parents' evening. It only occurred to her now how much it must have hurt. 'She was so proud of you.'

Roo felt hot tears sting the back of her eyes. She had started to put everything back when a photo fluttered out of her English book.

It was a tall, handsome boy with dark curly hair and laughing eyes. He looked like a young David Essex in faded jeans, T-shirt and leather jacket. He also looked like trouble.

On the back, scrawled in her mother's writing, were the words, 'Johnny Franks. November 1969.'

The year before she was born.

'What have you got there?'

'Nothing.' Roo stuffed the photo back in the book and put it with the rest.

But she did have something. After all these years, she had a name.

Chapter 8

'DADDY'S HERE!' Ollie bounced up and down at the window. 'And Shauna's with him.'

'What?' Roo looked up. Her neck and shoulders ached from where she'd been hunched over her laptop for several hours.

Shauna looked pasty-faced and sullen. She hung on to David's arm so tightly he had to prise her off before he could hug his son. Roo, who'd been steeling herself for this moment, was amazed at how little it bothered her.

'Shauna, what a lovely surprise,' she greeted her, determined to be utterly charming. 'How are you?'

'Shauna's suffering from morning sickness,' David answered for her.

'All day bloody sickness,' Shauna mumbled.

David surprised Roo with a hug. 'You look . . . different,' he said.

'It's my new image.' The new, slim-fitting Earl jeans were a departure for her—she hadn't owned anything denim since she left university—as was the pink T-shirt with a sequinned heart on the front. 'You're not the only one who fancied something younger-looking!'

David's mouth fell open, then he laughed. Shauna looked grumpy. 'Can we sit down?' she whined. 'My ankles are swelling up.'

It was a surreal situation. Ollie sat with David on the sofa, Shauna next to them, as if she couldn't bear to let him out of her reach.

'What's with the computer?' David asked.

'I'm trying to do some research on the Internet.'

'Maybe I could help.'

She smiled. 'I was hoping you'd say that!'

'So what is it you're looking for?' he said, as he sat at the keyboard.

'My father.'

'Really?' His brows lifted. 'You've found him?'

'That's what I want to find out.'

'Let's see what we can do, shall we?'

'What shall I do?' Shauna said.

David glanced over his shoulder. 'You and Ollie can amuse each other for a couple of minutes, can't you?'

It felt very strange, her and David busy while the nanny entertained their son. She kept having to remind herself that Shauna wasn't the nanny any more, but her husband's girlfriend.

And just when she thought the day couldn't get any more bizarre, Matt arrived.

Roo was shocked when he let himself in. When was he going to give back that wretched key? But she was completely amazed when he took her in his arms and kissed her. 'Sorry I'm late, darling, I had some research to finish.' He glanced past her ear. 'Oh, hi. You must be David.'

'Who are you?'

'This is Matt—'

'Her boyfriend,' he added, squeezing her shoulder.

She felt she'd entered the twilight zone. Matt stretched out in the armchair opposite David, who was surreptitiously sucking in his stomach.

Roo slipped away to get more drinks. Matt followed her. 'Alone at last,' he murmured suggestively.

'What are you playing at?'

'Trying to make your husband jealous, what do you think? I saw them pull up and I guessed you might be feeling outnumbered, so I came to lend you some moral support.' He grinned.

Matt insisted on staying for a drink. Roo cringed as he chatted to David, all the while keeping his arm firmly round her shoulders.

'Didn't know you were fond of toy boys,' David grunted after he'd gone.

'You can talk.' Roo stared at the door, absurdly disappointed that Matt hadn't kissed her goodbye. 'At least he's out of his teens.'

Shortly afterwards, Shauna nagged David into taking her back to their hotel in Leeds, saying she felt tired.

'Can I come?' Ollie asked. David and Roo looked at each other.

'Would you mind?' he asked.

'I don't see why not.'

As Roo followed Ollie upstairs to pack his overnight things, she heard Shauna grumble, 'You could have asked me if I minded!'

They were all smiles again by the time Roo and Ollie returned, although Shauna's appeared to have been nailed in place. 'I've called the hotel and it's all arranged,' David said. 'They're putting an extra bed in our room.'

As they drove away, Roo could see Shauna's mouth moving in a constant litany of complaint. She almost felt sorry for David. Almost.

But she didn't want him back. She was still fond of him, but more as a friend than a husband. So Matt had been wasting his time, trying to make David jealous. But it was nice of him to try.

David brought Ollie back on his own the following afternoon. 'Shauna's back at the hotel. She isn't feeling too well.' He smiled wanly.

'Coffee?' she offered.

'Please. Lots of sugar.' He grimaced. 'Shauna thinks it's bad for me.'

So did I, but it's not my problem any more, she thought, ladling in an extra spoonful.

As they drank their coffee he said, 'When is Ollie coming back to London?'

It was the question she'd been dreading. But she'd promised herself she would be utterly fair about it when the time came. 'When do you want him?'

'I'd like to take him home with me tonight.'

'No!' So much for being utterly fair. 'It's far too short notice.'

'It would mean you could get on with your work without worrying about child care.'

'I can manage, thank you.' Funny how the thought of coping with child care wasn't nearly so terrible as the thought of coping without her son these days. 'Sadie's looking after him.'

'Your mother?'

'What's wrong with that?'

'Nothing. I just thought she's the last person you'd ask for help.'

'I didn't ask. She offered. And I pay her, so it's a business arrangement.' She stirred her spoon around her mug, scraping the milky froth from the rim. 'Anyway, she's got quite close to Ollie. She'd be upset if I just sent him away without giving her a chance to say goodbye.'

'Why don't we ask Ollie what he wants?' David suggested.

'That's not fair. You can't expect him to choose!'

'What's wrong? Worried he might not choose you?'

As David called Ollie and put the question to him she prayed silently. Ollie looked from one to the other. 'I want to stay with Mummy.'

Roo, who'd been steeling herself not to get upset, looked up sharply. So did David. 'What?' they said together.

'I'd miss Harvey,' Ollie said.

Roo smiled. That was honest. 'Matt's dog,' she explained to David.

'Ah.' She saw his disappointed face and felt sorry for him.

'Why don't you stay here for another week and then go and visit Daddy?' she said. 'That'll give you a chance to play with Harvey and see Sadie and then you can say goodbye to them properly before you go.'

'And will you come with me?' Ollie asked.

'I can't, sweetheart.' She was amazed at how sad she already felt at the prospect of him going. 'But I'll only be here for a couple of weeks longer and then I'll be coming back to London too.'

'And then you'll be going somewhere else,' Ollie said in a small, accusing voice. 'You're always going somewhere.'

'We'll see.' Now it was just her and Ollie she was going to have to cut back on travelling. And if Gerry Matthews didn't like it—tough.

As David left, she said, 'By the way, just in case you were wondering. Ollie's best friend is called George and he prefers cricket to football.'

David smiled. 'Very good. You'll make a mother yet.'

He was halfway to his car before he turned back. 'I almost forgot. I did a bit of digging on the Internet when we got back to the hotel last night.' He pulled a scrap of paper out of his pocket and gave it to her.

'What's this?'

'Your father's address and phone number.'

'A lap-dancing club?' Matt said.

Roo was instantly defensive. 'We don't know that for sure. It says it's a "private gentlemen's establishment".'

'Roo, the place is called *Babes*. They're hardly going to be passing the port and swapping war stories, are they?' Matt was highly amused. 'Fancy that. Your long-lost dad is Peter Stringfellow!'

'Don't.' Roo groaned. She was still trying to get used to the idea herself. She'd sort of hoped Johnny Franks might turn out to be a doctor, or a bank manager. She never in her wildest nightmares thought he'd be a medallion-wearing nightclub owner.

'If you feel like that, maybe it would be better if you didn't find out any more,' Matt suggested.

'I can't leave it now. I've spent my whole life wondering who my father is. Now I finally get the chance to find out. Do you really think I'm going to give up just in case I'm disappointed?'

'I suppose not. Are you going to tell your mother about this?'

'I don't see why I should.'

'She might not want her past dragged up. She might have a good reason for wanting it to stay buried. You ought to give her the chance to prepare herself, at least.'

'She's had over thirty years to prepare herself. Now I have a right to know and I'm going to see this Johnny Franks.'

Roo sat in the bar of the Park Solihull Hotel, feeling pleasantly drunk. It was rare that she allowed herself to indulge, but this was a special occasion. Earlier that day, she and Billy had secured a contract with Roger Fleet to supply the furniture for the refurbished Park Hotels.

Now they were celebrating, although neither of them could quite believe they'd pulled it off.

'I wonder what swung it in the end?' Billy mused as they started on their second bottle of Pinot Grigio.

'Salvatore,' Roo said. 'If that new range wasn't generating such a buzz Roger Fleet might not have been interested.' Everyone in the industry was talking about their partnership. People were beginning to look at Fairbanks with new respect.

Billy gazed into his glass. 'It was a good idea to get him on board.'

'I thought you didn't like him.'

'Only because I thought he was after you. I didn't want to see you getting hurt,' Billy went on.

'And there was me, thinking you were jealous.'

'Maybe I was. A bit.'

There was a second's charged silence and then suddenly they were both talking about something else.

They finished the bottle and headed up to their rooms, drunk and happy. 'Fancy a nightcap?' Billy asked as they said good night outside his door. 'I could show you the new website we've set up.'

Roo hesitated. Every iota of common sense told her it was a bad idea. But lulled by alcohol and euphoria, she didn't want the evening to end. 'Why not?'

The message light was flashing on his bedside phone. 'Aren't you going to listen to that?' Roo asked.

'It'll only be Cat.' He peered inside the minibar. 'What can I get you? Whisky? Vodka? Gin?'

'Vodka and tonic would be nice.' She glanced back at the phone. 'Have you two had another row?'

'We can't seem to talk without it ending up in an argument these days.' He added tonic to her glass. 'Sorry, there's no ice.'

'It doesn't matter.' She took the glass from him. 'Is it because of this protest?'

'Not any more. It's gone beyond all that.' He took his laptop out of its case. 'Now, about this website. You've got to remember, it's just a work in progress . . .'

They lay side by side on the bed, their shoulders touching. Roo tried to concentrate on the screen.

'I wonder what Cat would say if she could see us now,' she said.

'She'd probably go mad, as usual.' Billy didn't smile as he tapped in his password.

'She's still jealous, then?'

'You could say that. I don't understand it. I've never given her any reason not to trust me. I've never even looked at another woman since we got married.'

'Lucky her,' Roo said. 'Mine did a lot more than look.'

Billy glanced at her. 'I'm sorry,' he said. 'I wasn't thinking. How are things between you two?'

'It's strange, we seem to get on better now we're apart than we ever did when we were together. I don't know why we ever got married,' she said wryly.

'Presumably you must have loved each other.'

'Like you loved Cat when you married her?'

'Touché.' His mouth twisted. 'So are you saying you didn't love him?'

Roo considered for a moment. 'I thought he was what I wanted. And so did he. But we were both wrong.'

'So what did you want?'

She looked at him. You, she wanted to say. Surely he knew that. 'Something I couldn't have,' she said.

Their eyes met and held. A second later he rolled away from her and stood up. 'I think I will get that ice after all,' he said. He grabbed the ice bucket and left.

Roo rolled over onto her back and covered her eyes. What the hell had she done? She didn't even fancy Billy any more. It must be the alcohol, she decided.

The phone rang on the bedside table. Without thinking, Roo reached across to answer it. 'Hello?' The line went dead.

Billy came back as she was hanging up. 'Who was that?'

'They hung up. Must be a wrong number.' She sat up, straightening down her clothes. 'Look, Billy, I don't think I can finish this drink. I'm tired, and I'm going to be wrecked in the morning.'

'To be honest I'm not really in the mood either.' He put the ice bucket down, not meeting her eye.

As she headed for the door he suddenly said, 'Roo?'

'Yes?'

He looked at her. 'I do love Cat, you know.'

Cat put the phone down, shaking. And to think she'd called Billy to try to apologise for their row! He hadn't wasted much time getting Ruby to console him, had he?

She'd been doing her best to keep her jealousy in check, telling herself she was being paranoid. Of course Billy couldn't ignore Ruby, he had to work with her. Just because they were friends it didn't mean he loved Cat less.

And he'd betrayed her. Not only that, he'd had the nerve to make her feel bad for suspecting them!

She went to bed but couldn't sleep. The bed felt too big without Billy, and she kept hearing Ruby's voice on the other end of the phone. Every time she closed her eyes she saw them entwined in each other's arms. All night she lay awake, wondering what to do.

The following morning she had a thumping headache from lack of sleep. Her neck muscles were like knotted ropes of tension. Megan and Liam, sensing her mood, ate their breakfast like lambs for once. They even went off to brush their teeth without her nagging them.

Maxine wasn't pleased when she called in sick, but Cat didn't care. It would do Julie good to cover for her clients for once; Cat was constantly covering for her while she took Dwayne to his juvenile court appearances.

She was on her third cup of coffee when Billy came home. Cat's heart lurched as she heard his key in the front door.

He must have seen her car in the drive because he came into the sitting room looking for her.

'Cat? What's wrong? Why aren't you at work?' As he swooped to kiss her, Cat turned her face so he caught her cheek instead.

'I wasn't feeling well.' She wasn't feeling well now. Her stomach was churning like a ferry in a force nine gale.

'Poor you. Why don't we go upstairs and I'll make you feel better?'

'As good as you made my cousin feel?' Cat shrugged him off. 'Don't touch me!'

His face fell. 'Not this again.'

'So what were the two of you doing in your room at eleven o'clock last night? Playing dominoes? Or was it another one of your "business meetings"?'

He couldn't hide the fleeting look of guilt. 'We were having a drink.'

'Very cosy, I'm sure. Do you think I'm stupid or something?'

'At this moment—yes.'

'Thank you. It's nice to know what you really think of me.'

'I didn't mean it like that. There's nothing going on. I didn't sleep with her.' He sounded weary. 'All right, maybe I could have. But I wouldn't.'

'Why not?'

'Because I'm married to you! And believe it or not, I take those marriage vows seriously. If you don't trust me, I might as well not be here.'

So that was it. He was still trapped, tied to her. It wasn't that he loved her, he just couldn't bring himself to break a sacred promise.

She took a deep breath. 'Fine. You'd better go, hadn't you?'

He stared at her. 'You don't mean that.'

'Like you said, what's the point in staying if I can't trust you?'

'Fine. I'll go and pack my things.'

Cat listened to him overhead as he opened and closed cupboard doors, and felt a chill creep around her heart. It was all she could do not to beg him to stay. She kept thinking that he wouldn't really go through with it. However bad things were, he wouldn't leave her.

The next thing she knew he was standing in the hall with his bags.

'You know, you're right,' he said. 'Maybe it is better if we're apart. I don't know you any more. You're not the woman I married.'

'You mean I've stopped being a doormat?'

'No,' he said. 'You've started being a bitch.'

She flinched as the door slammed shut. He was gone. The nightmare she'd always dreaded had come true. She was alone.

From the outside, it was very discreet. So discreet Roo walked past the doorway three times before she noticed the tiny brass plaque bearing the words: 'BABES—MEMBERS ONLY.

Down the narrow stairway that led from the street, it was a different story. Even in the middle of the afternoon the place was dark, hot and sleazy, with deep-plum-coloured walls and leopardskin sofas. The room was dominated by a long catwalk surrounded by tables and chairs. A big-breasted blonde wearing a G-string and a set of handcuffs was gyrating around a pole, watched by a group of bored-looking businessmen.

As Roo stared, a leggy black girl loomed out of the shadows towards her. 'Can I help you?'

'I'm here to see Johnny Franks.'

'He's in the VIP lounge.' She pointed to a door.

The VIP lounge had fuchsia-pink walls, white leather sofas and heavily shaded lamps. Roo spotted Johnny Franks straight away. He was lounging on one of the sofas, flanked by a pair of heavies.

His curly hair had greyed to the colour of pewter, but it was definitely the man in the photo. He had an aura of menace and power, from his heavyset body in his well-cut suit to the thick gold jewellery that adorned his deeply tanned wrists.

He looked up as she approached, his wolfish eyes sweeping over her.

'Mr Franks,' she stammered. 'Thanks for seeing me.'

One of the brawny men spoke for him. 'Get changed in the back,' he said brusquely.

She looked at him blankly. 'I'm sorry?'

'Into your gear. I take it you don't want to audition in that get-up?' He looked her sober navy suit up and down.

'Audition?' Suddenly it dawned on her. 'Oh, no! I'm not a lap-dancer!'

'Thank Christ for that!' Johnny Franks muttered. They all laughed.

'So if you're not here for the audition what do you want?' the man asked.

'I . . . I'm . . .' Her brain deserted her. She hadn't expected to get this far, and had no idea what to say. So she just said the first thing that came into her head. 'I'm your daughter,' she told Johnny Franks.

At least it got his attention. Those silvery eyes fixed on her.

'My name is Ruby,' she said. 'Ruby Tuesday Moon. You might remember my mother—Sadie Moon?'

There was a long silence. The two henchmen glanced at each other then at their boss, like Rottweilers awaiting their master's command. Finally he said in a deep, gravelly voice, 'Get rid of her.'

Five minutes later she was back on the street. She headed back to her car, so furious she barely noticed the black limo gliding to a halt along-side her, until the electric window slid down and a voice said, 'Get in.'

'Fuck off,' Roo said, not breaking her stride.

'I see you've got your mother's way with words.'

She stopped. 'So you admit you know her, then?'

'Oh, aye, I know her all right. Now will you get in this car before I'm arrested for kerb crawling?'

Inside the warm, musky-smelling interior of the car Johnny Franks seemed even more intimidating.

'What makes you think I'm your father?' he said. 'Did Sadie tell you?'

'No, but I found a photo of you.'

'I've got a photo of the Queen, but that doesn't make her my mother!'

'It was the only photo she had. I thought it might mean something.'

'Is that right?' He scratched his chin thoughtfully. 'And did your mother tell you where to find me?'

Roo shook her head. 'She doesn't know anything about this.'

Johnny gazed out of the smoky window. 'Sorry, I'm not your father,' he said finally.

'You would say that, wouldn't you?'

'I'm saying it because it's true!' He turned on her. 'Do you think I'd walk out on my own kid? If Sadie had been carrying my baby I would have married her.'

'But how do you know you're not my father?'

'Because she told me.' A muscle worked in his jaw. 'And because on the day you were conceived I was doing time in Armley jail.'

'So do you know whose baby I was?'

'If I'd known that I would have killed him.' He signalled to the driver to stop the car. 'This is where we part company,' he said.

Roo didn't argue. As she got out of the car Johnny said, 'Your mother never got wed, then?'

She looked at him bleakly. 'Would I be here if she had?'

'I can't believe you did that,' Matt said.

'I know.' She was still shaking two hours later. 'I confronted a bunch of gangsters.'

'No, I can't believe you went to a lap-dancing club without me. You knew I was looking forward to it.'

Roo smiled in spite of herself. 'Be serious!'

'I am.' He grinned. 'Did they really mistake you for an exotic dancer?'

'Not for long. I think I'd flunked the audition without needing to take my clothes off.'

'I find that hard to believe.' Matt sent her the kind of look that might have turned her to a quivering heap if she didn't know he was joking.

'Anyway, I'm no nearer to finding out who my father is,' she said. 'Johnny Franks is certain it's not him.'

'Perhaps he is your father and he just needs some time to get used to it,' Matt suggested.

'Maybe. But how do you explain the bit about him being in jail?'

'There's only one person who can answer that. Your mum. You're going to have to ask her.'

'I suppose so,' Roo agreed heavily.

Roo waited until the following evening, when she picked Ollie up.

'I met an old friend of yours yesterday,' she said, as they stood in the back doorway waiting for Ollie to finish playing in the garden.

'Oh, yes? Who was that?'

'Johnny Franks.'

Sadie was silent for a moment. Her face, fixed on Ollie, gave nothing away. Then in a neutral voice she said, 'I can't say I remember the name.'

'So why do you keep his photo in that box of yours?'

Sadie turned on her. 'You've been going through my things? You had no right to do that!'

'Is he my father?'

'What? No!' Sadie's face was blanched with rage.

'So why do you keep his photo?'

'I don't know. I forgot I even had the bloody thing.'

'You're lying. Why can't you be honest with me?'

'I am. Johnny Franks isn't your father, all right? Oh God, why did you have to go and dig all this up?' She twisted her hands in agitation.

'Because I've got a right to know. If he isn't my father, who is?'

'He wasn't worth knowing.'

'You must have thought so once, or you wouldn't have got pregnant.'

Sadie flashed her a look and for a second it seemed as if she was about to say something. Then she went into the yard and called Ollie in.

Frustrated, Roo had no choice but to end the conversation. In clipped voices they talked about arrangements for dropping Ollie off the next day. Then, as they were heading for the car, she said, 'You might as well tell me the truth, because I'm going to find out anyway.'

Not if I've got anything to do with it, Sadie thought as she watched them drive away. Why couldn't Ruby leave well alone? Why did she have to keep digging up the past?

And now she'd found Johnny. Hearing his name again after all this time had been a shock. She'd closed the door on that part of her life over thirty years ago.

And yet she hadn't. There was still a part of her that was wretchedly in love with him. No man she'd met since had ever come close.

She made a start on her mother's supper, still thinking about Johnny and the time they'd first met. Everyone adored Johnny Franks. Especially the girls who hung around the fairground where he worked. They all wanted to tame the boy with the dark, Gypsy good looks and wild reputation. But Sadie didn't. She was the only one who didn't want him to settle down and find a steady job. Which was probably why she was the only one he didn't want to love and leave. She took the trouble to see beyond his arrogance, to the frightened boy who kept moving to escape his troubled past. While everyone else thought of him as a tough street-fighter, she knew those scars on his face were the result of having his skull fractured by his drunken stepfather while trying to protect his mother from another beating. Later, when his mother died, he'd run away from home at the age of thirteen and taken his younger brother on the road. Sadie was the only one he'd ever confessed to about his past. He'd trusted her.

And she'd let him down.

Johnny was twenty-one when he was sent to jail. His kid brother Darren had fallen in with the wrong crowd and got involved with a burglary, and Johnny had taken the blame to keep him out of prison. He got six months. Sadie said she'd wait for him, of course. They'd already started to make plans about their future, and Johnny had promised to stop travelling and settle down once he got out.

But one night had changed all that.

The worst moment of her life was getting pregnant. The second worst was breaking the news to Johnny. Even now she could clearly remember the hurt and pain that flashed across his face when he found out.

He left town the next day. She never saw him again. She let everyone think he'd left her alone and pregnant because it was easier that way. It meant there were no more awkward questions about who the real father was. But she felt guilty when Tom and her mother refused to have his name spoken in the house, because she knew she was the one at fault, not him. He would have done anything for her, and she'd let him down.

Salvatore Bellini's drawings had been couriered overnight from Milan and were waiting for her when she got into the office the following day. Roo could hardly contain her excitement as she looked at them. Even to her untrained eye, they were something special. Simple but stunning designs, just as they'd asked for.

She wished Becky was there to see them. But she'd taken some time off to deal with 'personal problems'.

No need to ask what they were. Billy had told her about his row with Cat and that he was staying in a hotel in Leeds.

'I'm going up to show these drawings to George Fairbanks,' she told the girls in the main office.

They all stopped typing. 'You haven't heard, then?' one of them said.

'Heard what?'

'Mr Fairbanks was taken to hospital this morning.'

Frederick was talking on his mobile phone outside his father's room in the private hospital. He hung up abruptly when he spotted Roo approaching down the corridor.

'How is he?' she asked.

'Holding on. Mother's with him at the moment.'

Before Roo could say anything, the door opened and a tall, silver-haired woman emerged, dabbing her eyes. Frederick rushed to her side.

'How is he, Mother? Is there any news?'

She looked straight past him to Roo. 'Are you Ruby Moon?' she said in a voice full of quiet dignity.

'I . . . yes,' Roo nodded, not wanting to quibble over her name.

'He's asked to see you.' She touched Roo's arm as she passed. 'Be careful, my dear. He's very weak.'

George Fairbanks was as white as the sheet he lay on. He seemed to have shrunk and shrivelled inside his skin.

He turned his head slightly to look at her, a smile lighting up his eyes. 'I told Agnes you'd be here,' he whispered.

'How are you?'

'I'll live to fight another day, lass.'

Roo could hardly speak. She kept thinking of the spirited old man she'd first met, who was so determined to save his company he'd staggered off his sickbed to confront her. They'd had some bitter arguments since then, but she'd never lost her respect for him.

'I've got something to show you,' she said, taking Salvatore's drawings out of her bag. She had to hold the papers up in front of his face because he was too weak to hold them for himself. But he studied them carefully, asking questions, not missing a single detail.

'You can tell he's Italian,' he said finally.

Roo laughed. 'Is that good or bad?'

'Bit flashy. But I reckon we can make a good job of it. And Billy says it'll sell, does he?'

'We've already had loads of interest and they haven't even seen the designs yet. We're planning a big marketing launch for a couple of months' time.'

'I'll have to put it in my diary,' George said.

'And we signed the Park Hotels deal three days ago,' she went on, feeling tears sting her eyes. 'We should be in production again by the end of the month. We'll have all our staff back on full-time. We might even have to offer them overtime, to cope with retraining once our new machines arrive!' Suddenly all she wanted to do was please him, to bring a smile to that gaunt face.

'New machines, eh? That should make a big difference.' He lifted his head from the pillow, struggling to nod his approval. It took all his strength to do it. 'You did well, lass.'

Roo's heart swelled inside her chest. Those words meant more to her than any incentive bonus Warner and Hicks could come up with. 'I was just doing my job,' she said.

They talked a little more, until she could see George was getting tired. 'I'd better head back to the office,' she said.

'Aye. Thanks for coming in. I'll see you on Monday morning—if I can get them to unhook me from this bloody machine,' he growled.

Roo smiled. 'See you on Monday.'

But as she left the room she had the feeling that was the last time she was ever going to see George Fairbanks.

There was a good crowd in the Ponderosa tonight. Beyond the dazzling footlights, Sadie could make out dim shapes at the tables surrounding the stage. They were chatting, but as Dennis, the keyboard player, played the first bars of her opening number, everyone stopped to listen.

Sadie scanned the room, making eye contact with the crowd. She took a deep breath, opened her mouth to sing—and then she saw him. At a far corner table was Johnny Franks.

As his eyes met hers, direct and piercing as a laser beam, Sadie felt as if she'd been shot through the heart.

Behind her, Dennis was coasting into his third intro, still waiting for her to take her cue. Somehow she managed to pick up the microphone and sing 'You Don't Have To Say You Love Me'. She'd been doing the old Dusty Springfield number for so many years, thank God, she didn't have to think about the words. She was in such a blind panic she would have been hard-pushed to remember her own name.

She managed to struggle through the set by pretending he wasn't there. Then, when she finally plucked up the nerve to look back at the corner table, she was horrified to find he wasn't.

She lurched from panic-stricken to poleaxed with disappointment. Bastard! He'd put her on edge and nearly wrecked her act, then he couldn't even be bothered to stay to the end!

Or maybe he'd seen enough? Maybe he'd turned up expecting to see the sexy Sadie he used to know, and instead he'd found some tired old bag trying to look twenty years younger.

She hardly noticed the appreciative applause as she fled back to her dressing room. She stripped off her dress, pulled on her old silky robe, then noticed an enormous bouquet of red roses with a note. *Meet me by the back door in ten minutes*, it said. No 'hello' or 'please' or 'what have you been doing for the past thirty-odd years?' Not even a name.

Arrogant sod! Who the hell did he think he was? 'Meet me in ten minutes', indeed!

She'd dressed and was by the back door in five.

He was waiting for her in the back of a limo. 'Hello, Sadie Moon,' he said softly. 'It's been a long time.'

Sadie got in, determined not to be impressed. 'I can't stop,' she said. 'Mum will be expecting me home.'

'Some things never change.' He looked every inch the successful businessman in his cashmere overcoat and polished shoes. Only his wicked smile reminded her of the Johnny she used to know.

'Thanks for the flowers,' she said. 'You didn't have to send so many.'

'There was a rose for every year since I last saw you.'

She blushed. 'A bunch from the petrol station would have done.'

'Not for you.' His eyes crinkled at the corners. 'How about a drink? Or, better still, let me take you for a meal.'

'At this time? You won't find anywhere open.'

'I know somewhere.' Johnny gestured to the driver.

She looked down at her denim skirt. 'I'm not dressed for going out!'

'You look fine.'

The limo was warm and smelt of leather and Johnny's musky aftershave. The sound system played a sexy, soulful Aretha Franklin number.

'Nice car,' Sadie commented, trying to break the seductive mood. 'Did you hire it for the night?'

He laughed. 'It's mine.'

'You've done well for yourself.'

'I have, haven't I?'

She peered out of the window. 'So where are we going?'

'You'll see. Somewhere very special.'

'Not too special, I hope?' She didn't want to go anywhere she might not be able to afford to pay her share.

'You call this special?' she said ten minutes later, as they stood in the queue at The Friendly Plaice fish-and-chip shop.

'Don't you remember? This is where I brought you on our first date.'

How could she forget? 'You really know how to show a girl a good time, don't you? Is this all I'm worth? A portion of haddock and chips?'

'I didn't want you to think I was being flash.'

'You? Flash?' she grinned as they got back into the limo with their fish and chips. 'Why would I think that?'

Johnny reached into the minibar and took out a bottle of champagne. The real thing. The best Sadie ever got was sparkling wine at Christmas.

'I suppose you keep a bottle handy just in case?'

'No, I put this one aside for you especially.'

'What made you so sure I'd come?'

'You never could resist me, Sadie.'

It wasn't fair that he'd got more attractive with age when all she'd got were crow's-feet. 'So how come you can afford all this?'

'Like you said, I've done all right for myself.'

'And what is it you do?'

'Oh, you know. A bit of this, a bit of that. All strictly legit. I run a club in Sheffield, and I've got a sideline in limo hire. You know, for hen nights and race days? Very popular these days.'

Sadie licked grease and vinegar off her fingers.

'I met your daughter.'

She took a deep breath. 'I'm sorry she came to see you. I had no idea.'

'She seemed to think I was her father.'

'She didn't get that from me.'

'So you've never told her who her father is? Just as you never told me?'

Sadie sighed. 'I've never told anyone.'

'You broke my heart,' he said. 'I never got over it.'

'It didn't stop you getting married, did it?'

He looked shocked. 'How did you know?'

She nodded at his hand. 'You might have taken your ring off, but the mark's still there. Where is she? Back home in Sheffield, I suppose?'

'Actually, at this precise moment she and her toy boy are probably on their third bottle of sangria at our villa in Spain. We divorced last year,' he explained. 'After she'd taken me to the cleaner's, of course.'

'You don't seem very upset about it.'

'To be honest, I shouldn't have married her. I knew she was only after my money. But she was younger than me, and I was flattered, so . . .'

'How long were you married?'

'Five years. She was my third.'

'Not a very good track record, is it?'

'I never found anyone to match up to you.'

'You should have come back,' she said.

'I was tempted.'

'So why didn't you?'

'Because I was scared of what I might find. I thought you'd be married with loads of kids.'

'I never got married.'

'Why not?'

'Probably the same reason as you had three wives.'

'Why didn't you marry him? The baby's father.'

'I couldn't. It wasn't possible.'

'Is that why you kept the baby, hoping he'd marry you?'

'No!'

'So it was just a meaningless fling?' His face was bleak. 'You threw away everything we had for a one-night stand?'

'It wasn't like that.'

'Then what was it like?'

She stared at him. 'You wouldn't understand,' she said.

They were silent as the car drove her home. But as Johnny dropped her at the end of Hope Street he suddenly said, 'Can I see you again?'

She was wary. 'Not if you're going to keep talking about the past.'

'Fine,' he said. 'We'll talk about the future.'

Chapter 9

BRIDGE HOUSE WAS in chaos the following Saturday, the day Charlotte Montague was marrying Daniel Hetherington.

Cat felt as if she was on a production line. Her fingers hurt from making pin curls and weaving tiny silk roses into intricate plaits. Her feet ached and she longed to sit down.

But the atmosphere made up for her weariness. Everyone was very high-spirited and giggly, thanks to a bottle of champagne one of the bridesmaids had smuggled upstairs.

'I wonder if the caterers have remembered the candles I asked for?' Elizabeth Montague gazed out of the window. She looked serene in her dove-grey couture coat dress, but Cat could tell she was fretting.

'Don't panic, Mummy. Have some champagne! It'll help you relax.' Charlotte handed her a glass. Unlike her mother, she seemed to have no worries about the day ahead.

Her mother eyed her severely. 'When are you going to get dressed, Charlotte? I'm afraid Daddy will wear a groove in the hall floor if we leave him pacing for too long.'

'Calm down, Mummy. The wedding isn't for another half an hour.'

'It takes twenty minutes to get to the church.'

'So? I can't possibly be on time for my own wedding.'

'How do you know he'll wait?' one of the bridesmaids said. She was already dressed in a narrow sheath gown of gold raw silk.

'Of course he'll wait. I'm worth waiting for, aren't I?' Charlotte smiled complacently.

Cat felt a pang of envy. She couldn't remember feeling like that on her wedding day. All she'd felt was that she was lucky to be marrying Billy, and she'd better snatch him up quick before he came to his senses and realised he was throwing his life away.

'How do I look?'

Cat looked up from threading roses into the other bridesmaid's hair. Charlotte stood in front of her, transformed into a radiant princess in an ivory silk gown that shimmered with iridescent beads.

'What do you think? Will I do?' Beneath her perfect make-up she suddenly looked young and anxious.

Cat nodded. 'Daniel's a lucky man.'

'I know!' Charlotte laughed delightedly.

Cat finished the last bridesmaid's hair. 'There. All done.'

'Thanks, Cat, we couldn't have managed without you.' Elizabeth smiled.

'It was my pleasure.' She meant it. It had taken her mind off her problems, and it had felt good to share in someone else's happiness.

Billy was looking after Megan and Liam for the day, but Cat didn't mind the thought of going home to an empty house. She used to be afraid of being alone but now she found she quite enjoyed the peace and quiet.

And then she spotted Billy's car in the drive.

Becky opened the door before Cat had a chance to get her key out. 'Dad's here,' she said.

He was waiting in the sitting room, perched on the edge of the sofa. He seemed ill at ease, like a visitor. 'I brought the kids back.' He sounded defensive. 'I know I said I'd keep them longer but Mum had a migraine so we had to come home.'

'You should have called me. I would have picked them up on my way back.' Cat headed for the kitchen. 'Would you like a coffee?'

'If you're making one.'

He followed her into the kitchen and lingered in the doorway, watching her. The children, she noticed, had beat a tactful retreat upstairs, leaving them alone. 'Becky says you've been working today.'

'I had a wedding. At Bridge House.'

'Really? That big place? What's it like inside?'

'Incredibly glamorous.' She told him all about the wedding, and about Elizabeth Montague being a Bond girl. Billy seemed impressed. More than that, he seemed interested.

Feeling bold, Cat decided to tell him about a plan that had been going through her mind for a few days. 'I'm thinking of branching out on my own,' she said.

'You mean open your own salon?'

'Nothing quite that ambitious. Not yet, anyway. I thought I'd start with mobile hairdressing. You know, going round to people's houses to do their hair? It would mean I could work my own hours.'

'Do you think you could handle it?' Billy asked.

'I don't see why not. I'm a pretty good hairdresser, and I know a lot of the customers would come to me.'

'There's more to it than that,' Billy warned. 'What about your accounts? And maybe VAT. And you'd have to think about pricing to cover your costs—'

'I've thought about all that. I'm not stupid, you know!'

'I'm sorry. I was only trying to help.'

He looked so crestfallen, Cat felt sorry for him. 'I know. Maybe I'm just over-sensitive.'

They finished their coffee and Billy got ready to leave. 'Are you sure you're OK?' he said. 'There's nothing you need?'

'I don't think so.' Except you, she thought. Although she didn't need him, not any more. She wanted him. There was a big difference. The past few days had taught her she could stand on her own two feet. But she still missed Billy. 'I'm coping fine on my own, thanks.'

'So I see.' Was it her imagination, or did he seem hurt?

On impulse, she said, 'Why don't you stay for supper? I'm sure the kids would like it,' she added quickly.

'I wish I could, but I've arranged to have dinner with one of our retailers.' He looked regretful. 'Why don't we have dinner sometime this week?'

'OK,' she agreed. 'But it'll have to be Pizza Paradise. Megan's gone off burgers since someone told her they put horses in them.'

He hesitated. 'I was thinking of just the two of us. Maybe we could go somewhere a bit more up-market.'

Cat was puzzled. 'You mean, like a date?'

He smiled. 'Exactly like a date.'

Roo wasn't impressed when she went round to collect Ollie from Nanna's house on Hope Street the following Friday and found him getting out of Johnny Franks's limo.

'Mummy!' He launched himself into her arms. 'I've been for a ride in Uncle Johnny's car. It's got a telly in it and everything!'

'That's nice.' Roo glanced at Johnny Franks as he came towards them.

'Hello again,' he said. He still looked menacing, even in jeans and a polo shirt. Thick gold chains nestled around his tanned neck. How on earth could she have imagined he was her father?

'I didn't know you were back.'

'After you came to see me I decided to renew an old acquaintance.'

At which point Sadie came out of the house, wiping her hands on a tea towel. 'Hello, you two, I didn't hear you—Oh!' she spotted Roo. 'You're early.'

'I'm taking Ollie back to London tonight, remember?'

'Yes.' She looked embarrassed. 'You've, um, met Johnny, haven't you?'

Johnny put his arm proprietorially round her mother's shoulders. Roo felt sick, remembering all the other men who'd mauled her like that over the years.

'Come and have a look, Mummy!' Ollie dragged her towards the big black car. 'It's huge inside. As big as a house! And I can go for a ride in it any time I like. Uncle Johnny says—'

'He's not your uncle!' Roo shouted. Ollie's chin wobbled.

'There's no need to yell at the kid,' Johnny said quietly.

Roo whirled round to face him. 'Did I ask you to interfere?'

Johnny stared at her for a moment. Then he turned to Sadie and said, 'I think I'll leave you to it, love.' He kissed her cheek. 'I'll call you.'

As soon as he'd gone, Sadie turned on her. 'What did you do that for?'

'I don't like him.'

'That's obvious. What's he done to upset you?'

He's your boyfriend, Roo thought. Even now, at her age, she still couldn't look at her mother with a man and not feel ill. 'He's a thug,' she said, as Ollie wandered inside.

'No, he isn't. He's a legitimate businessman.'

'Oh, come on, even you can't be that naive. Do you think he got that car by putting money away in a post-office savings account?'

'Johnny's my friend,' Sadie said quietly. 'It would be nice if you two could get along.'

'I'm not twelve years old. I don't have to be nice to your boyfriends.'

'I don't recall you ever being nice to anyone at that age!'

'And didn't you ever stop to wonder why?' Roo shot back. 'What do you think it was like, watching you parade all those men through the house? It's not easy, growing up knowing your mother's the town tart—'

The slap took them both by surprise. Roo stepped back, putting her hand to her stinging cheek.

'Don't you ever call me that again!' Sadie turned and stalked back into the house. A moment later Ollie came out. 'Why is Sadie crying?' he asked. 'And why are you crying too?'

'I'm not.' Roo blinked fiercely and opened the car door for him.

It felt odd being back in her own home, and yet it didn't feel like her home any more. When she went to unpack, she half expected to find Shauna's clothes in her wardrobe.

'Shauna hasn't moved in,' David said cagily, when Roo asked him about it. Then added, 'Actually, she isn't pregnant. Not any more. She had an abortion last week. She's spending some time with her parents.'

They didn't talk about it until Ollie had gone to bed. The story finally came out as they sat at the kitchen table, eating quiche and baked potatoes washed down with a bottle of Sancerre. Apparently Shauna had decided she couldn't face the idea of having a baby at her age, and booked herself in for a termination. But she hadn't told David about it until afterwards, when she called him to pick her up from the clinic.

'I don't understand it,' he kept saying, his face desolate. 'I mean, I know she was fed up about being pregnant, but not to tell me what she was going to do . . . It seems so unfair.'

'Maybe she thought you'd try to change her mind.'

'I would have liked the chance. It was my baby too.'

Roo felt desperately sorry for David, who seemed to have aged ten years in as many days. He'd lost everything.

As she left on Sunday evening, David said, 'Sorry for screwing it all up.'

She shrugged. 'It takes two.'

She headed home, feeling shattered. The weekend with David had depressed her. And after the exhausting row with her mother on Friday, she didn't think she could handle any more bad news.

When she got home she found a message on her answering machine. It was from Frederick Fairbanks, telling her his father was dead.

It looked as if the whole of Normanford had turned out for the funeral the following Tuesday. The dull, grey day matched everyone's mood. People lined the streets to watch as the carriage, weighed down with flowers and drawn by a plumed black horse, travelled down the High Street towards the tiny modern church of St Pauline. Roo spotted Nanna and Sadie on the kerbside. Nanna nodded at her; Sadie looked away.

George's widow Agnes, tall and stately behind her veil, followed her husband's cortege, next to her son.

In the church, before a packed congregation, Frederick delivered a touching eulogy praising his father's contribution to the town's fortunes.

Later they ended up at the Fairbanks family home for the ritual of the funeral tea. Roo had never understood why someone who had just lost a loved one should be forced to go through the ordeal of hosting a party straight afterwards, but everyone seemed to expect it.

Glenys, as the widow of another prominent Normanford resident, had naturally wangled herself an invitation. She spent a few minutes offering her condolences, and the rest surveying the Fairbanks home and then examining a Staffordshire figurine on the mantelpiece.

'Reproduction, of course,' she sniffed. 'But it's so easy to get caught out if you don't have a trained eye.' Roo saw Billy on the far side of the room, and wished she was with him.

'He looks tired, doesn't he?' Glenys followed her gaze. 'Poor boy, I keep telling him he should come home. He doesn't have to stay in that dreadful hotel.' Her mouth pursed. 'Still, at least he's got away from her now. They were never happy, you know.'

Behind her, Roo saw Billy wander over but stop short to listen.

'All she ever did was drag him down,' Glenys went on. 'I mean let's face it, she's nothing special—'

'That's where you're wrong, Mother.' Glenys swung round. Billy's face was dark with anger. 'Cat is special. She's kind and beautiful, and no one in this whole bloody world makes me feel the way she does. But do you know what's really special about her? She loves me.'

Glenys glanced nervously around, aware they were being watched. 'We all love you, William.'

'No, you don't. You all wanted me to be something I wasn't. The top student, the captain of the rugger team, the head of some multinational company. You loved me as long as I was living up to your expectations. Cat was just happy to love me for what I am.'

Roo glanced at Glenys's pinched face but knew she was just as much to blame. She'd always assumed Billy was as ambitious as herself. But now she realised she was just the same as his ghastly, overreaching mother, wanting him to be something he wasn't. Cat hadn't held him back; the truth was, he didn't want to go anywhere.

'Y—your father and I only wanted the best for you,' Glenys stammered.

'But you never stopped to ask me what I wanted, did you? You want to know the real reason I married Cat? To get away from you!'

'And a fat lot of good it's done you,' Glenys fought back. 'She doesn't want you now, does she?'

'No,' Billy admitted bleakly. He put down his drink and stormed off.

Roo caught up with him in the garden. He was sitting on a stone balustrade, his head in his hands. 'I've really done it now,' he groaned.

'It needed to be said.' She hesitated. 'I'm sorry, Billy.'

'Me too. I'm sorry I didn't show Cat how much I loved her when I had the chance.'

'Look, why don't we go out for a meal to cheer ourselves up?' she suggested. 'I don't know about you, but I don't fancy going home.'

Billy looked doleful. 'You're lucky to have a home to go to!'

Johnny listened in grim silence as Sadie told him about her row with Roo. She'd held off telling him for days, not wanting to burden him with her problems. But he'd noticed how depressed she was and had finally got it out of her.

'Do you want me to talk to her?' he asked.

'No!' The last thing they all needed was another confrontation. 'I don't know why I did it,' she said. 'I've never lifted a hand to Ruby before.' But her remarks had been so cruel, so cutting.

'She'll get over it,' Johnny said. 'She can't hold a grudge for ever.'

'You don't know Ruby.' Whoever said time was a great healer had obviously never met her daughter.

Johnny gave her a lift to the Ponderosa. As usual, she felt like a film star stepping out of the limousine. 'I feel like we should be going to The Talk of the Town, not the pub.'

'So you should,' Johnny said. 'You've got a terrific voice. You're wasted in this place.'

'I might not be here for much longer.' She told him that the owner had plans to sell up. 'It'll probably end up as some fast-food restaurant. And even if it doesn't, they won't want an old crock like me on stage.'

'Don't put yourself down.' He kissed her, sending the old familiar shivers down her spine. Then he got back into the limo.

Sadie was disappointed. 'Aren't you coming in for a drink?'

'Sorry, sweetheart, I've got some business to sort out in Sheffield. But I'll call you later. You've got your phone with you, haven't you?'

'That thing,' she grumbled, reaching into her bag for her brand-new mobile. 'I don't know why you bought it.'

'I like to check up on you,' he said proprietorially. 'And it's useful if your mum needs to get in touch in an emergency.'

'Don't put that idea in her head or she'll be ringing every five minutes!' Sadie was pleased Johnny and her mother were getting on so well. They'd had a frosty start, but since Johnny had let slip that he was a personal friend of Jimmy White and offered to get her front-row seats for the snooker final at the York Barbican, Irene had softened towards him.

'Keep your chin up.' He winked at her, and then he was gone. Sadie stood on the pavement, watching until the car disappeared down the road. Johnny Franks. She still couldn't believe he was back in her life again. She didn't care what Ruby thought. She deserved some happiness, after everything she'd been through.

Her happiness stayed with her until the moment she stepped on stage and spotted her daughter and Billy Kitchener at a table holding hands.

The red message light was winking at Roo when she got home. It was Ollie, wishing her good night. Hearing him brought tears to her eyes. She missed his little arms wrapping fiercely round her neck as he hugged her good night. But much as she missed him, she knew David was in need of those hugs more than she was at the moment.

The doorbell rang as she was watching the ten o'clock news. Roo hit the mute button on the TV remote control and went to answer it.

It was Sadie. She must have come straight from work. Roo caught a glimpse of her pink spangly dress under her coat.

For a second she thought Sadie might be feeling as fed up as her and had come round to sort things out between them.

'Is he here?' She pushed past Roo and stepped into the hall, looking round.

'Excuse me? Is who here?'

'Don't play games with me!' Sadie swung round. 'You know who I mean. Billy Kitchener.'

'No, he isn't. Although I don't see what it's got to do with you—'

'You've got to stop seeing him.'

'I beg your pardon?'

'I mean it. Whatever you two have got going, you've got to finish it. Right now.'

Roo's surprise hardened into anger. 'You can't just barge in here and tell me what to do!'

'OK, I'm asking you. I'm begging you. Don't see him any more.' She looked so anguished for a moment Roo felt afraid.

'What's all this about?' she demanded.

Sadie faltered. 'I can't tell you. I'm just asking you, for once in your life trust me and do as I say. Please?'

'Not until you tell me why. Why shouldn't I see him?'

'Because it isn't right.' Sadie couldn't meet her gaze. 'He's a married man—'

'That's got nothing to do with it, and you know it. So why don't you tell me the truth?'

Sadie put her head in her hands. 'I can't.'

'You're not leaving here until you do.' Roo moved against the front door, barring her way. 'Well? I'm waiting.' Her mother was silent. 'Maybe I should call Billy and ask him.'

'No! Don't say anything to him. He doesn't know—'

'Doesn't know what?' Roo grabbed Sadie's hands and dragged them away from her face. 'What doesn't he know? Tell me!'

Sadie looked up at her. The expression of utter defeat on her face frightened Roo so much that suddenly she didn't want her to speak.

'That he's your brother,' she said.

Suddenly everything went so silent they could hear the steady drip of the tap down the hall in the kitchen.

'You were never meant to find out,' Sadie whispered.

Roo couldn't take it in. 'Bernard Kitchener is my *father*?'

Bernard Kitchener.

All kinds of questions scrambled over each other in her mind, wanting to be let out. 'Did you have an affair? How long did it go on for? Did Glenys know?'

'No!' Sadie held up her hands, trying to ward off the barrage of words.

'Did he know I was his daughter?' She thought of all the times he'd turned his professional politician's charm on her, asking her about her schoolwork. Was he just making polite conversation with his son's friend, or was he genuinely interested because he was her father?

And if he did know, why hadn't he done more to help them?

'Ruby?' She'd almost forgotten her mother was there. Sadie's voice sounded as if it was coming from a long way away. 'I'm so sorry. I know you must hate me, but I never meant for you to find out. If you and Billy hadn't got so close—'

Her and Billy. Her brother. If things had been different, they might even have . . . oh God! Bile rose up in her throat and she just made it to the bathroom before she threw up.

Afterwards she sat on the bathroom floor, hugging herself, the chill of the tiles creeping through her clothes.

'Ruby?' Sadie was outside the door, her voice anxious.

'Go away.'

'I can't leave you like this.'

'I need to be on my own.'

There was a long silence. Then Sadie said, 'I'll go, then. If you're sure. I'll ring you later, OK?'

Roo said nothing. A moment later she heard her mother's footsteps on the stairs, and the door closing softly behind her. She relaxed slightly. She couldn't face anyone. After all this time of trying to find out the truth, suddenly she wanted to shut it all out, forget it.

But she couldn't. Disjointed thoughts kept coming into her mind, linking together and then coming apart again.

Billy was less than a year older than her. Which meant Glenys must have been pregnant when she was conceived. A horrible picture rose up in her mind. Surely Sadie couldn't have seduced Bernard while her friend was having a baby? She'd always been willing to think the worst of her mother, but even she couldn't believe her capable of that.

The insistent chirp of a mobile phone interrupted her thoughts. Roo got to her feet and went to look for it.

She tracked the sound down to the hall. Just inside the front door, under the hallstand, she found it. It must have fallen out of Sadie's bag.

She answered it without thinking.

'All right, love?' Johnny Franks's voice was deep and warm.

'It's Roo,' she said wearily.

Johnny was instantly guarded. 'Where's Sadie? Is she all right? Has something happened?'

'Something's happened, all right. I've just found out who my father is.' She gripped the phone. 'You'll be pleased to know it's not you.'

'And?' he said gruffly.

Roo hesitated, then disconnected. She couldn't be the one to tell him.

Matt didn't react when he found her in a sobbing heap on his doorstep. Without another word he put his arm round her and drew her inside. Then he poured her a large brandy and let her talk.

'I did try to warn you you might not like what you found,' he said when she'd finished.

'I never thought it would be like this! And don't try to tell me there are two sides to every story.' She glared at him over the rim of her glass. 'I don't feel like being reasonable, OK?'

'So what do you want me to say?' he asked.

She gazed at him. 'Nothing,' she said. 'Just hold me. I don't want to be on my own tonight.'

She woke up early the following morning with a thumping headache, staring at a poster of Sigmund Freud in a dress. It took her a moment to work out where she was, and when she did a wave of embarrassment washed over her.

Oh Lord, what had she done? She had a horrible feeling she'd just become Matt Collins's latest conquest. And the worst thing was that after so many glasses of brandy she couldn't even remember it.

She found Matt in the kitchen, watching Harvey in the garden while he waited for the kettle to boil. His fair hair was rumpled, and his dressing gown hung open, revealing an Adonis-like body—broad, smooth, muscular chest, a rippling washboard stomach and endless legs.

Roo diverted her gaze sharply away from his boxer shorts as he turned to look at her. 'Coffee?'

'Not for me, thanks. I don't want to be late for work.' She glanced at her watch. It wasn't yet seven.

'About last night . . .' she said.

'What about it?'

'It probably wasn't the best idea, in the circumstances.'

'No.'

'Not that it wasn't really good,' she added hastily, not wanting to offend him. 'I just don't think we should repeat it, that's all. We've got a good friendship, and—'

'And you think sex could spoil it?'

'Exactly.' She sat down at the kitchen table. 'Couldn't we just pretend it never happened?'

'That might be difficult. I'd have trouble forgetting a night like that.'

She gulped. 'Really?'

'But you're probably right,' he agreed.

Roo's shoulders sagged with relief. 'Good.'

'It's not like we're going to be secretly lusting over each other, is it?'

'Of course not.' She fiddled with the neckline of her shirt. 'I'd, um, better go home.'

'You're sure you wouldn't like that coffee?'

'Some other time.'

He turned away to open the door for Harvey, who bounced in, tail wagging joyfully. 'Have you thought about what you're going to do yet? About your mother?'

'I've no idea.'

'You've got to sort it out with her sometime, you know.'

'I know.' She just wasn't sure if she could face it.

'Don't forget, my door's always open if you need to talk. Or anything.'

'Er, thanks.'

As she fled, he called her back. 'Roo?'

'Hmm?'

His mouth twitched. 'Last night—it *was* pretty good, wasn't it?'

Sadie was surprised when Johnny turned up unexpectedly that evening. Tom had taken their mother to bingo, leaving her alone in the house.

'Thank heavens you didn't arrive ten minutes later, I would have been in the bath with a face pack on!' She saw his grim face and tensed. 'Is something wrong?'

'I spoke to your daughter last night.'

A knot of dread tightened in her stomach. 'You'd better come in.'

Sadie poured a whisky for Johnny and a large gin with a splash of tonic for herself. She had a feeling she'd be needing it.

'So you told her, then?' Johnny said.

Sadie nodded. 'I had to.'

'And you couldn't tell me?'

'I was going to.' She dreaded dragging it all up again. But now Roo knew the truth she felt she owed it to Johnny. She'd been steeling herself to phone him but he'd beaten her to it.

He sat down on the sofa. 'I'm waiting,' he said.

Sadie perched on the armchair across the room from him, wondering where to begin. 'His name was Bernard,' she said quietly. 'Bernard Kitchener. He was a local councillor, a lot older than me. I didn't know him that well. Not until he married my friend Glenys—'

Johnny sat up. 'You slept with your friend's husband?'

'It wasn't like that,' she said in a rush. 'It only happened the once; it was a mistake.'

'Pity you didn't think about that beforehand, isn't it?'

Sadie couldn't bring herself to look at his face. It felt as painful as it did when she first broke the news to him that she was pregnant, more than thirty years ago.

458

Johnny stood up and paced the room. 'Do you know how much this has haunted me? All this time I've spent wondering what kind of man would make you break your word and turn your back on me.' His hand shook as he took a gulp from his glass.

'Johnny, please.' She put out her hand but he turned away from her.

'I shouldn't have come back,' he said gruffly. 'I was wrong. There's no way we can turn back the clock. There's too much bitterness.'

He put down his glass. Panic shot through her. 'Johnny, don't go,' she pleaded. 'Don't let him ruin my life again.'

'No one made you sleep with him.'

Sadie looked at him, and realised the time had come to tell the truth.

'That's where you're wrong,' she said.

'Glenys had just had the baby. I went round with some flowers for Bernard to take to her in hospital.' Sadie was aware of Johnny watching her intently, but she couldn't bring herself to look at him. If she did, she knew her courage would fail her.

'I knew straight away he'd been drinking. Wetting the baby's head, he called it. He wanted me to have a drink with him. Most insistent, he was. Wouldn't take no for an answer—' She swallowed hard. 'I should have dumped the flowers and gone home, but he kept on and on at me to stay. So in the end I thought I'd have one, just to shut him up.'

'Go on,' Johnny said.

'He kept talking. He was saying all this stuff about how he'd always fancied me. And all the time he kept trying to touch me. Putting his arm round me, and all that. I said to him, "What about Glenys?" But he laughed. He reckoned she hadn't let him touch her since she got pregnant. Then he said—'

'What? What did he say?'

'He said, "I bet you're missing it too, with your fella locked up."' Her voice was flat. 'I tried to laugh it off. I told him not to be so stupid. I started to leave, but he wouldn't let me. That was when he turned really nasty.' She wrapped her arms round her body, shielding herself. 'I'd never seen him like that. It was like the drink had turned him into a monster. I tried to fight him off but it just seemed to make him worse. So in the end I just lay there.' She could still feel his wet mouth, reeking of alcohol, plundering hers, his pale, sweating body on top of her. 'I should have fought him off. I should have done something. But I just wanted it to stop.'

'And then what happened?' Johnny's voice was gruff with emotion.

'Then it was all over. The next thing I knew, he was throwing my clothes back at me and telling me to go. I got home, ran the bath as hot as I could, and scrubbed every inch of my skin with carbolic soap until it was red raw. But I could still smell him on me.'

'Why didn't you go to the police?'

'What was the point? He'd only deny it. And who do you think they'd believe? Anyway, I just wanted to block it out, pretend it never happened.'

'You should have told his wife.'

'I was going to. But when she came out of hospital, I couldn't bring myself to do it. She was so happy, you see. She had her baby son and her husband—the perfect family. And she probably wouldn't have believed me, either.'

Johnny lit up a cigarette. His hands were shaking.

'Did you ever speak to him again?'

She nodded. 'He came round when he found out I was pregnant. He was worried I'd try to make trouble. He thought I might try to damage his political career. He denied the baby was his, but he gave me money to keep quiet. Five hundred pounds. More than I'd ever seen in my whole life. He said it was to help me out because I was Glenys's friend,' she said bitterly.

'And you took it?'

'Of course I took it. But I never spent a penny of it.' It was still upstairs, hidden away in the back of her wardrobe. 'There were times when we desperately needed that cash, I can tell you. But I didn't want his blood money. I thought if I spent it I'd be exactly what he thought I was—a cheap whore.'

'I'm surprised you could go on living here, go on facing him.'

'What choice did I have?'

Johnny took a long drag on his cigarette and watched the smoke curl towards the ceiling. 'You should have told me.'

'And what good would that have done?'

'I would have killed him,' he said flatly.

'And you would have ended up straight back in jail.'

'Maybe. But it would have saved me a lot of hurt.'

Their eyes met. 'So who else knows about this?'

'No one. And that's the way I want it to stay.'

He frowned. 'What about Ruby? Doesn't she have a right to know?'

'To know that she was born because of a cruel, brutal act? How do you think that would make her feel?' She shook her head. 'No, she must never know the truth.'

'Too late,' said a voice from the doorway. 'I already do.'

460

Chapter 10

SADIE STARED AT HER. 'How long have you been there?'

'Long enough.' Thank God Nanna had given her a key to let herself in because she couldn't always hear the door when she had the TV on.

Roo looked at Johnny. 'Would you leave us alone, please?'

He turned to Sadie. 'Do you want me to stay?' She shook her head. 'Are you sure you'll be all right?'

'I'm fine. This is between Ruby and me.'

Outside, the sun was going down and the room was filling with shadows, but neither of them moved to light the lamps.

It was Sadie who spoke first. 'Whatever else has happened,' she said slowly, 'I just want you to know that I've always loved you.'

'How can you say that?' Roo felt sick. 'Every time you looked at me you must have remembered him.'

'I thought I would too,' Sadie said. 'When I first found out I was pregnant all I could think about was giving you away. I didn't want you anywhere near me. And then I saw you.'

'And it was love at first sight.' Roo's lip curled.

'That's exactly what it was. They put you in my arms at that hospital and from that moment I knew you were mine. My Ruby Tuesday. Nothing to do with him.' She looked at her daughter with tear-filled eyes. 'If anything good could have come out of something like that, it was you. I ran away so they couldn't take you from me. I waited until they were all in the chapel then bunked out through the window with a suitcase full of nappies and the clothes I stood up in. I was terrified they were going to send the police after me.' She smiled wanly. 'Now does that sound like someone who didn't love you?'

'I didn't make it very easy to love me over the years,' Roo admitted.

'You and me both. You were right; I've not exactly been the perfect mother, have I?' She looked rueful. 'I was young and daft. But I was angry too. I'd been saddled with this reputation through no fault of my own, and instead of living it down I decided to live up to it. I thought if everyone reckoned I was a brazen hussy then that was what I'd be. I wanted to show everyone I didn't care.'

Roo looked at her mother, the picture of defiance in her bright yellow jumper, still done up to the nines even though her mascara was smudged and she'd chewed off most of her lipstick. For the first time she felt proud of Sadie, not embarrassed. She was filled with a sudden burst of outrage. She wanted to put it all straight, right all the wrongs, make up for every bit of pain and humiliation Sadie had ever suffered.

'We can't let him get away with it,' she said. 'We'll go to the police—'

'He's dead, Ruby.'

'We'll go to the press, then. We'll tell them what he was really like.'

'And what good would that do?'

'They might stop naming hospital wards after him, for a start. And it would show Glenys what kind of a monster she was married to.'

'Glenys is a daft cow, but she doesn't deserve to be hurt,' Sadie said gently. 'And it wouldn't just be her everyone was gossiping about. It would be me, and you. And Billy.'

Oh God. Billy! She'd forgotten all about him. 'We should tell him, at least,' Roo said.

'Why? What good would it do?'

Roo opened and closed her mouth. 'He ought to know the truth,' she said finally.

'What, that his father was a rapist? Or that you're his illegitimate sister? Honesty isn't always the best policy, Ruby.'

'But Bernard shouldn't get away with it,' she said.

'He didn't. He went to his grave knowing he'd done wrong. And I never let him forget it. Every time he turned round I was there, large as life, right under his nose. He lived in fear I was going to tell the papers and wreck his career.'

'Am I anything like him?' Roo caught a glimpse of her reflection in the polished brass fireplace and flinched.

'No! He was a weak, selfish man. You're brave and strong. You're a Moon.' She reached across and laid her hand on Roo's. 'I've got over this and so must you. You've got too much to be proud of.'

They heard a key in the door and sprang apart as Nanna shuffled into the room, followed by Uncle Tom. 'I don't know, three numbers short of the National jackpot . . . what's this? Why are you two sitting in the dark?' She flicked on the light switch, took one look at the pair's tear-stained faces and said, 'Put the kettle on, Tom.'

'What?' Tom looked at the scene and backed away. As he went, Roo heard him mutter, 'More bloody women's troubles, I suppose.'

Nanna looked sharply from one to the other. 'Have you two had a row or have you sorted things out finally?'

Roo and Sadie looked at each other. 'Sorted things out, I think,' Sadie said.

'About time too. I don't suppose there's anything you've got to tell me? No, I didn't think so,' she said when they were both silent. 'Oh well, I've been in the dark for this long, I don't suppose there's any point in knowing now.' She shuffled to the door. 'I hope Tom's not using tea bags. They're never strong enough.'

After the traumatic events of that evening, it felt strange sipping tea and making conversation with Nanna and Uncle Tom.

'I hear Frederick Fairbanks has gone abroad, is that right?' Nanna shook her head. 'And his father barely cold. He's no respect, that lad.'

'I've no idea,' Roo answered. 'I wish someone would tell me where he is. He's supposed to be running the company.' Or she assumed he was. The official will-reading wasn't until the following week. 'I need his permission before we can get moving on our new orders.'

'I expect your nanna could find out for you,' Uncle Tom joked.

'I dare say I could.' Nanna looked serious. 'I could ask at the Over Sixties club. Or I expect you could find out something at the hairdresser's, couldn't you, Sadie?'

She nodded. 'Frederick's secretary, Barbara, often comes in for a blow-dry. I could ask her.'

'Good luck with that,' Roo said grimly. 'She won't tell me anything.'

Uncle Tom winked at her. 'Never underestimate the Moon mafia,' he said.

A man was hitching Matt's car to a tow truck when she arrived home.

'Don't tell me. Off to the garage?' she said.

'Off to the scrapyard, actually. It wasn't quite the vintage classic I thought it was.' He peered at her. 'Have you been crying?'

'Well spotted, Einstein.'

'Let me guess. You've been to see your mother. How did it go?'

If she was going to share Sadie's secret with someone, it would have been Matt. She knew he'd understand more than anyone. But she'd promised never to breathe a word and she had to respect that.

'We've reached an understanding,' she said.

'I'm pleased to hear it.'

She had a bath, changed into her pyjamas, then searched through the freezer for something to eat. She'd just selected a tuna-and-pasta bake when the doorbell rang. It was Matt, a bottle of wine in one hand and a couple of pizzas in the other.

'Can I come in?'

'Why?'

'I don't know. I just thought you might need some company.'

She was about to turn him down when she realised that was exactly what she needed.

They sat on the sofa together, sharing the pizza and watching an action thriller on TV.

'The only thing missing is Ollie,' Matt said. 'How is the little guy?'

'He's fine. Which is more than I can say for his father. David and Shauna have split up.'

'What about the baby?'

'There is no baby.' She explained about Shauna's decision to have an abortion.

'That's tough.' Matt chewed on his pizza thoughtfully. 'So there's nothing to stop the two of you getting back together?'

'I suppose not. Except I don't want to.'

'Really? Why's that?'

'I think we've both realised we're better off apart than together.'

'Good.' He reached across and nabbed a piece of mushroom from her pizza. 'He wasn't right for you.'

'How come you're such a relationship expert, when you avoid them like the plague?'

'Talent, I suppose.'

They sat in silence, staring at the television.

'I need to talk to you,' Matt said. 'About last night.'

Oh God. Roo twisted round to look at him. He was still staring at the screen. 'I thought that subject was closed.'

'I know, but I can't just leave it like this.'

'Why not? Look, I told you, you're sensational in bed but I don't want it to happen again.'

'Sensational, eh?' He looked pleased with himself. 'So what bit did you like best?'

'Sorry?'

'Oh, come on, you must remember. If I was that good . . .'

Roo felt herself blushing. Then she saw his smile twitch. 'What's this about?'

'I'm afraid I have a confession to make. You know that sensational night you remember so well? It didn't happen.'

She stared at him. 'But I woke up in your bed.'

'And I woke up on the sofa. With Harvey. Come on, do you really think I'd take advantage of an emotional wreck like you were?'

'You bastard! And you let me think—'

He shrugged. 'You seemed to think we'd had such a fabulous night, I didn't like to disappoint you.'

'I dare say I would have been disappointed,' she said tartly.

'Why don't you find out?'

Suddenly the air seemed charged with a million tiny crackling particles of electricity. Roo felt her mouth tingle in anticipation, seconds before Matt leaned over and kissed her. He tasted of mouthwash and pizza. His teeth gently raked the softness of her lips, his tongue probing. Roo felt herself turning liquid with desire.

They went to bed, and this time she remembered every glorious moment. His gorgeous body with its lean, hard muscles. The way his warm, smooth, golden skin felt against hers, the tender way his lips explored every inch of her, making her arch with pleasure. Then the joyous concentration on his face as he slid into her, his body moving with hers until they both convulsed with ecstasy.

The following morning she got a call from Sadie.

'I spoke to Barbara,' she said. 'You know, Frederick's secretary?'

'That was quick.'

'I know which bus she catches in the morning, so I made sure I just happened to be passing. Anyway, she was very talkative about old Freddie. She's expecting him back tomorrow. Apparently he's promised her a bottle of perfume from Duty Free.'

'Did she say where's he's been?'

'Now where was it? Somewhere I don't think I've heard of . . . ah, I remember. Croatia. Wasn't there a war there not long ago? Seems a strange place to go on holiday, don't you think?'

Roo gripped the phone tighter. 'I've got a feeling he isn't on holiday.'

Agnes Fairbanks didn't seem too surprised to see Roo.

'I hoped you might call,' she said. 'I didn't get a chance to speak to you at the funeral. I wanted to thank you for all you've done for the company.'

'I was only doing my job.' Roo looked around the stately sitting room.

'This place is so empty without him,' Agnes said. 'I know he could be an old curmudgeon sometimes, but we were together a lot of years. I got used to his funny ways.'

'So did I.'

Agnes regarded her thoughtfully. 'He had a lot of respect for you.'

'He didn't always show it.'

'That was just George. Always thought he knew best, especially when it came to that factory of his.' She turned her eyes to the ceiling. 'I wonder if he's looking down here now.'

'If he is, he's probably wondering why we haven't got that Park Hotels order started.'

Agnes didn't reply as she poured them both a cup of tea from a bone china pot.

'I suppose you're here about Frederick,' she said finally.

'Well, yes. I—'

'I just want you to know I don't approve. And neither would his father. Poor George would be turning in his grave if he knew what was going on.' She handed the cup to Roo. 'I've tried to talk to Frederick, of course, but he insists it's for the best. Biscuit?' She held out the plate.

'No, thank you.' Roo shifted uneasily in her seat. 'Excuse me asking, but what are we talking about here?'

Agnes looked at her blankly. 'Frederick's plans to sell the factory, of course. What do you think I'm talking about?'

'What? He's selling Fairbanks?'

'Not selling. A merger. At least that's how he puts it. But I suppose it amounts to the same thing. All our production would move to Eastern Europe. Apparently they can do things a lot cheaper over there.'

'And what would happen to the factory?'

'Oh, it would still be here.' Agnes stirred her tea. 'I don't know much about the details, but it would be more like a marketing and retail operation, Frederick says.'

A glorified warehouse, in other words. Roo closed her eyes. 'I didn't know any of this.'

'Frederick wanted to keep it all under his hat until he was sure of closing the deal. That's where he is at the moment. And of course he had to wait until he took control of the company. There was no way his father would agree to it.'

'And now the company's his he can do what he likes?'

'I'm afraid so.' Agnes nodded. 'Sidney Pennington is going through the will with us formally at the factory on Friday. That's also when the buyers are coming over to take a look around.'

'And what do you say about this?' Roo asked.

'I'm opposed to it. George would have hated to see his factory run by foreigners. But what can I do? It's Frederick's factory, not mine.'

Cat put down the phone on another mother, eager to book her for her daughter's wedding. It was only Wednesday, but ever since the glossy colour spread of Charlotte Montague's wedding had appeared in *Hello*

Yorkshire magazine the previous Saturday, they hadn't stopped ringing.

'I hope you don't mind,' Elizabeth had said when she called to tell her it was being featured.

How could she mind? *Hello Yorkshire* was her mother-in-law's bible, full of articles about wealthy, famous people in the area, and lots of glossy estate agents' ads, featuring grand country homes.

And there, among the photos of rich people at York races and the Great Yorkshire Show, were Charlotte's wedding photos. And a photo of her, pinning Charlotte's hair up. Underneath, the caption read: 'Top local stylist Cat Kitchener puts the finishing touches to the beautiful bride'.

'I thought it would be a good advertisement for you,' Elizabeth said. And she was right. She'd already been booked for three more weddings. Even Glenys had been impressed, and had boasted to everyone about her 'clever daughter-in-law', much to Cat's surprise. The only one who wasn't delighted was Julie, who seethed every time one of Elizabeth's posh friends rang up for an appointment. And Maxine, who was furious the salon hadn't got a credit.

'Another wedding booking,' Cat said as Becky wandered in.

'You'll be as famous as Nicky Clarke soon,' Becky replied, and for once she wasn't being sarcastic.

It was something else for her to tell Billy when she saw him that night. They'd been out a couple of times since they split up. It was a weird experience, going on a date with her own husband. But it gave her a good excuse to dress up. They talked, they laughed, and they had fun—something else that had been sadly missing from their marriage.

The only thing she didn't like about it was saying goodbye at the end of the evening. Cat still fancied him like mad, and it was all she could do not to drag him off to bed. Unfortunately Billy seemed to be resisting the urge too. Cat was beginning to wonder if he was still interested in her.

Megan came in. 'Liam's covered in spots,' she announced.

'Oh, no, you haven't been using Becky's lipstick on him again?' Cat sighed. Then her son appeared and she realised at once they weren't the kind of spots she could scrub off with soap and a flannel.

'Jesus, what's wrong with him? He looks like he's got the plague.' Becky grabbed her cereal bowl and slouched off into the sitting room.

'More like chickenpox.' Cat counted Liam's spots.

'If he dies, can I have his bedroom?' Megan asked, helping herself to a bowl of Frosties.

Julie answered when Cat called the salon to say she wouldn't be coming in. 'You can't keep being unreliable like this, you know,' she said. 'It's very unprofessional.'

'I'm sorry. I'm not leaving my son if he's ill.'

'I don't know why you bother coming in at all,' Julie grumbled. 'We could get a dozen stylists better and more reliable than you are.'

Cat had heard the same thing many times a day, and usually she ignored it. But today something inside her cracked. 'Fine,' she said. 'Why don't you?'

'What?'

'You heard. I quit.'

'You can't do that!' Julie spluttered. 'You're fired!'

'Whatever. Either way, I'm not coming in today. Or tomorrow,' she added, glancing at Liam's face, crammed with spots.

Five minutes later Maxine called back. 'I think there's been a misunderstanding,' she said in a wheedling voice.

'I don't. Julie's sacked me.'

'She had no authority to do that.'

'You made her senior stylist, remember? Anyway, I've resigned.'

'But you can't do that.'

'Why not? You're always telling me I can be replaced, so why don't you do it? If you can find someone to work for the slave wages you pay!' she added, and slammed the phone down.

'Way to go, Mum,' Becky grinned from the doorway.

Cat smiled back, feeling heady with her own power. She must be a good hairdresser after all, if Maxine was so desperate to have her back.

Her euphoria evaporated when she realised she didn't actually have a job any more, but she forced herself to stay positive. When Becky had taken Megan to the childminder's on her way to work, and Cat had settled Liam on the sofa, wrapped in his duvet in front of *The Tweenies*, she sat at the kitchen table with a notebook and started to work on the ideas she'd had about starting up on her own. She'd been thinking about it for weeks, but had never got round to doing anything practical. Perhaps this might give her the boost she needed.

She was sketching out some ideas for ads, and wondering if she could ask Billy to help her with marketing, when the doorbell rang.

The person she least expected to see was Ruby. Cat was instantly on her guard. 'What do you want?'

'Can I come in?'

Reluctantly she stood aside to let her in. The hall was littered with the kids' bikes, Liam's skateboard and Megan's riding paraphernalia, but Cat refused to apologise for the mess.

She led the way into the kitchen. 'I rang the salon and they said you were off today,' Ruby said.

'As a matter of fact I've resigned. I'm going into business on my own.'

'Really?' Ruby picked up the notes she'd been scribbling. 'You've spelt "professional" wrong,' she said.

'Oh, fuck off!' Cat snatched the notebook away from her. She should have known better than to expect anything nice from her cousin. 'What do you want, anyway?'

'I need your help.'

'Yeah, right.' Cat filled the kettle. 'Since when have you ever needed my help?'

'I need it now.' Ruby laced and unlaced her fingers. 'Is that action group of yours still going?'

'We wound it up a few days ago. There didn't seem to be any reason to carry on now the factory's out of danger.'

'That's just it. It isn't out of danger. It's going to be closed down if we don't do something.'

Cat made coffee while Ruby explained how Frederick Fairbanks planned to sell the factory off to the highest bidder.

'He has a buyer all lined up,' Ruby said. 'They're due to come in and sign on Friday. Frederick's getting the company then, so he wants to sign the contracts straight away.'

'But what about all your hard work?' Cat asked. Much as she hated to admit it, Ruby had done a fantastic job getting Fairbanks back on its feet.

'All for nothing,' she shrugged. 'But that's not what bothers me. It's the thought of all those workers being put out of jobs for no reason.'

'So why can't you do something about it?'

'There's nothing I can do. The bank's happy about it; they don't care who owns the place. Besides, you've got all the contacts. People will listen to you. They'd never listen to me,' she admitted.

They drank their coffee in silence. Cat wondered how much desperation it had taken for Ruby to come and ask for her help. Suddenly she didn't seem so confident or all-powerful after all.

Finally Cat said, 'It's only two days away. That doesn't give us a lot of time to organise anything.'

'I know.' Ruby put down her cup. 'I've made a few notes. I thought perhaps if you got your old action group friends together, you could—'

'Hang on a minute. Who's organising this, you or me?'

'You are, but—'

'Then we do it my way, OK?'

They stared at each other for a moment. Then, to Cat's amazement, Ruby backed down. 'Sorry.' She smiled weakly. 'It's just my natural bossiness taking over.'

'Tell me about it,' Cat muttered.

Just then Liam wandered in, still wrapped in the duvet. He was suck-ing his thumb, his dark hair sticking up on end. Ruby took one look at his face and said, 'No need to ask what's wrong with him!'

'It's better when they get it young.' Cat pulled him into her arms, smoothing down his hair. 'Luckily the other kids have already had it or it would go through this family like wildfire.'

'Ollie got it when he was eighteen months old.'

'Was it very bad?'

'I don't know.' Roo gazed down at her hands. 'I was in Madrid at a conference on Integrated Performance Management.'

'Sounds very important.'

'Not as important as being there to look after your little boy.' Her face was bleak. 'I envy you.'

Cat laughed. 'Me? Why?'

'Because you've got your priorities right. Maybe if I'd done things dif-ferently I'd still have a family.'

She looked sad. How could Cat have been so in awe of her for all those years? She was just Ruby, the cousin who'd shared a bedroom with her, listened to all her secrets, laughed and cried with her. Cat sud-denly felt sorry for all the years they'd wasted hating each other.

'You're not the only one who's made mistakes, you know,' she said. 'Look at me and Billy.'

She steeled herself, waiting for a smart comment about them never being suited in the first place. But Ruby just said, 'Yes, but Billy loves you. And it's breaking his heart, you not being together. So it's about time you stopped being so pig-headed and took him back.'

Cat's hackles rose. 'What gives you the right to tell me what to do?'

Ruby glared at her. 'Because I love you too, you silly cow!'

Roo still wasn't convinced Cat was going to help. She wasn't even sure how much use she could be in just two days. What they really needed was a miracle.

Matt did his best to help her relax. 'You really should try to chill out,' he said, as he massaged her tense shoulders.

'How can I chill out when Fairbanks could be sold down the river tomorrow? I should be doing something constructive.'

'I can think of something constructive.' He kissed the back of her neck, his breath warm against her skin.

Roo relented, knowing she couldn't resist him for long. She was becoming seriously addicted to him, she thought later as they lay in bed. And like most addictive things, he was incredibly bad for her.

Their relationship, if she could call it that, had lasted a whole week. Not too long for most people, but a lifetime for Matt Collins. He hadn't shown any signs of wanting to move on. Just the opposite, in fact—he'd even taken the drastic step of leaving his spare toothbrush in her bathroom. But that didn't stop her waiting for him to tell her it was over.

And the worst thing was, as each day passed she was growing closer and more dependent on him. Falling in love with him, in other words. It was scary. Especially as it was exactly the kind of behaviour guaranteed to drive him away.

She'd made up her mind not to push him. But the following morning, as she watched him munching toast, she said very casually, 'I'll be going back to London when this is all over.'

He looked up. 'How soon?'

'I don't know. It depends how this protest works out. If Frederick sells the factory there won't be much more for me to do.'

'I expect Ollie will be pleased to have you back.'

'I'm looking forward to seeing him.' She waited. No reaction. 'David's found a flat, so I'll have the house to myself when I get back.' Still no reaction. 'You could come and visit me?'

'I could.' He fed a toast crust to Harvey. 'Or I could come with you.'

She almost dropped her mug. 'What?'

'I could come to London with you. My research is almost finished. All I have to do is write it all up, and I could do that anywhere.' He frowned. 'Unless you don't want me to come.'

'No! I mean, yes. I'd love you to come. It's just a shock, that's all. Isn't that a bit too much like commitment for you?'

'All I know is that I want to be with you.' Matt stood up and cleared his plate into the sink. Then he dropped a kiss on her forehead. 'I'll see you later, OK? Good luck with the protest.'

'Aren't you coming?'

'I'll try, if I can get away from college early.'

'I'd like you to be there.'

'Like I said, I'll try. But I can't promise anything.'

Typical Matt, she thought as the front door banged shut. He couldn't even commit to something two hours away, so how could she seriously expect anything long term?

She wasn't sure what to expect as she drove to work that Friday morning. But she certainly didn't expect the crowd that greeted her as she turned the corner. It was a fine, sunny day and it seemed like the whole of Normanford had turned out to enjoy the sunshine. She couldn't see the factory gates for the people gathered there, all waving their placards and chanting. Not just the factory workers themselves, but hordes of local shopkeepers, mums from the school gates and office workers.

And in the middle of it all was Cat. Roo caught her eye as she drove past. Neither of them smiled, but the slightest nod of acknowledgment passed between them.

There was huge excitement in the office. Becky and the other girls had their noses pressed to the glass, trying to see out. 'I don't understand,' Becky was saying. 'Why is Mum doing it? Why would she want to cause trouble now?'

'I'm not sure,' Roo replied coolly, sifting through the morning's post. 'But I think it's got something to do with Frederick Fairbanks selling the factory to a company in Eastern Europe.'

They all exchanged horrified looks. 'Will we lose our jobs?'

'Probably. Unless you're fluent in Croatian.'

Next she went to see Billy. He was standing at the window too, staring down at the protesters. Or at one in particular, Roo guessed.

'I wonder how they knew those buyers were coming today.'

'I've no idea.'

'Are you sure about that?' He gave her a quizzical look. 'You didn't tip them off, did you?'

'Me? And risk losing my job? Where's Frederick, by the way?'

'Holed up in his office, fuming. Serves him right, the scheming little shit.' He turned back to the window. 'I should be down there with them, showing Cat some support.'

'So why don't you?'

'You're not the only one who could lose their job.'

'You'll lose it anyway once this new bunch takes over.' She looked at him. A pair of brown eyes startlingly similar to her own stared back at her. How could she have failed to realise he was her brother? 'Billy, there comes a time when a man has to stand up for what he believes in. The question is, do you want to save your marriage, or your job?'

Once Billy had gone, Roo went back to her office. It was deserted, apart from Becky, who insisted on giving Roo a running commentary on what was going on down in the yard.

'There must be hundreds of them now. The town's rugby league team, the Normanford Gorillas, has just turned up. Ooh, and a brass band.'

Roo glanced out of the window, where the Normanford and District Darby-and-Joan club were mustering by the gates. Then something else caught her eye. A flash of black as Johnny Franks's sleek and sinister gangster limo glided slowly into the fray like a prowling shark. Hanging out of the sun roof were Sadie and Nanna, the latter waving her walking stick with gay abandon.

All the Moon women were there. Except her.

'Where are you going?' Becky said, as she grabbed her bag.

'You don't think I'm going to miss out on the fun, do you? Are you coming, or not?'

There was a carnival atmosphere by the factory gates. The local brass band were leading everyone in a rousing chorus of 'Roll Out the Barrel'.

Cat shouldered her way through the crowd to Roo. 'What are you doing here? You'll lose your job if Frederick catches you.'

'Like I said to your husband, there are more important things in life than work.' Could that really be her saying that?

Suddenly the crowd parted like the Red Sea as Frederick Fairbanks bore down on them across the yard, looking furious. The brass band burst into a spontaneous chorus of 'Colonel Bogey'.

'You have no right to create a disturbance,' he shouted. 'I'll have you all arrested for causing a breach of the peace!'

'Try it,' someone called back. The policeman who'd been sent to keep an eye on the situation looked up guiltily from having his palm read by one of the Darby and Joan ladies.

'You have no right to sell this factory from under us!' someone yelled.

'If you think this is going to put off our new buyers, you're sadly mistaken. I've already telephoned them to put off their visit.'

'So we'll just come back on Monday,' Cat shouted. 'And the next day, and the next, until your buyers finally get the message!'

A roar of support went up from the crowd. Roo tried to lose herself behind a wall of rugby players but Frederick spotted her. 'Can't you do something to get rid of this lot?' he demanded.

'Why should I? They're exercising their democratic right to protest. Besides, I fully support them.'

Frederick was apoplectic with rage. 'We'll see what your boss has to say about *that*. I'm dispensing with your services.'

A jeer went up from the crowd. Roo stood her ground.

'It's not up to you. I was brought in by the bank, remember? Besides, you don't own this company yet.'

'I wouldn't be so sure about that.' Frederick pointed to a silver-grey car pulling up at the gates. 'If I'm not mistaken, this is our lawyer with my father's last will and testament.'

Sidney Pennington looked around apprehensively as he got out of his car, clutching his briefcase. 'Have I come at a bad time?' he said.

473

'It couldn't be better,' Frederick said. 'Perhaps you'll tell these good people exactly who is in charge of this factory?'

Sidney looked nervous. 'Shall we go inside and discuss it?'

'I'd rather do it out here, if you don't mind.' Frederick scanned the crowd in triumph. 'I want everyone to hear who my father trusted to run this place after his death.'

'Judas!' someone called out.

Sidney Pennington took off his spectacles and polished them. 'I have to say this is most irregular—'

'Just do it, man!'

A hush fell as Sidney broke the seal on the thick white envelope containing George Fairbanks's last will and testament. He glanced through it for a moment, then intoned gravely, 'I, George Arthur Fairbanks, being of sound mind—'

The first section was all about his estate and how it was left to his widow Agnes. Frederick stood at his shoulder, twitching with anticipation.

'The company, man! What does it say about the company?'

Sidney sent him a severe look. 'You are aware your father had me draw up a new will shortly before he died?'

'Of course I know. He showed it to me, remember?'

'Not that one. He ordered another to be written after that.'

Frederick frowned. 'Why would he do that?'

Sidney Pennington didn't answer. His gaze swept the crowd. 'Is there a Ruby Moon here?'

Roo lifted her hand. 'That's me.'

Sidney smiled benignly over the top of his spectacles. 'Congratulations, my dear,' he said. 'It seems you've just inherited a factory!'

Chapter 11

ROO PACKED HER BAGS, marvelling at how much she'd managed to accumulate over the past months. But at least she was leaving behind a lot of other baggage.

'I've never seen you wear this.' Cat held up a strappy top.

'I haven't. It's never been warm enough.'

'Southern softy.'

'Take it, if you like it.'

'Are you sure? It's Dolce and Whatsit.'

'I'm sure. Unless you're too posh for my castoffs these days?'

'Are you kidding?' Cat stuffed it in her bag before Roo had a chance to change her mind.

'I suppose you'll be buying your own designer labels once you're a rich and successful businesswoman?' Roo teased.

'Don't,' Cat blushed. 'I'm strictly a chain-store girl. Anyway, I've only got a bag full of brushes and scissors to my name so far. That hardly makes me millionaire material, does it?'

'It's a start. This time next year you'll have your own thriving business.'

'Yeah, right.' Cat sat on the bed, hugging her knees. 'It feels so weird, going it alone. Even Glenys hasn't stopped bragging about her daughter-in-law, the businesswoman!'

She tried to sound self-deprecating, but Roo could see she was chuffed that someone was proud of her.

'You might not be the only one starting out on your own,' Roo told her. 'I'm thinking about it myself.'

'You mean leave that posh job of yours? Never.'

'That posh job takes me away from home and makes me live out of a suitcase,' Roo said. She'd done some hard thinking and had begun to wonder if her future was at Warner and Hicks.

'You could have had a job here,' Cat said. 'You had a factory to run, remember?'

'I know, but it wasn't really my factory. Anyway, I've got to get back to London.'

'Billy will be sorry to have missed you,' Cat said. 'He had to fly to Milan to see Salvatore this morning about the final details for the capsule collection.' She picked up a pair of Roo's shoes. 'I never thanked you properly for making him managing director and giving him those shares.'

'I gave them to both of you. In joint names,' Roo reminded her. 'And I expect you to get in there and make some decisions too!'

'I couldn't do that. I don't know much about business—'

'Then you'd better learn, hadn't you?' Roo smiled. 'Don't do yourself down so much, Cat Kitchener. If it wasn't for you organising that brilliant protest, there might not even be a Fairbanks now.'

'It was more to do with George leaving you the factory. I still laugh when I think of Frederick's face. I thought he was going to explode!'

'He nearly did.' He'd also threatened to contest the will on the grounds of his father not being of sound mind. At least they'd managed to reach a compromise. She'd agreed to buy Frederick out.

After two weeks of thinking about it, Roo had handed a large number of her shares over to Billy and Cat. He deserved a chance to show what he could do, and she could trust him to do his best for the company.

'Anyway, thanks again for giving them to us,' Cat said.

Roo shrugged it off. 'Call it the wedding present I never gave you.'

They looked at each other. 'Billy really is lucky to have you, you know,' Roo said.

Cat twisted her wedding band on her finger. 'I don't know about that.'

'He is! And I think he's just beginning to realise it.'

'We're getting there. Slowly.'

Roo smiled. They hadn't seemed that slow off the mark when she'd spotted them kissing passionately after the protest. And when she'd looked for Billy later, and his secretary had told her that he'd gone home, she didn't need to imagine what they were doing.

She was pleased for them. She couldn't have chosen a more loving wife for her brother. She just wished she could be as happy as they were.

Roo gazed out into the street. It was deserted, apart from a couple of kids playing football with an empty beer can.

Cat watched her. 'What are you waiting for? Or should that be who?'

'What do you mean?'

'Oh, come on. You've been rushing over to that window every five minutes, looking out for someone. Who are you expecting, Brad Pitt? Or your dishy next-door neighbour?'

Roo smiled. 'I think Brad's more likely.'

Matt wasn't coming. Right up until two days ago he'd insisted he was. But since then she hadn't seen him. There was no answer from his house, not even Harvey barking. He'd taken off and now she guessed he was lying low, too scared to face her and tell her he'd changed his mind.

She let the curtain drop and picked up her case from the bed. 'Come on, then,' she said. 'I want to miss the traffic.'

She'd allowed for a quick fifteen-minute visit to Hope Street to say goodbye. But she'd reckoned without her family. Johnny Franks was already there, his limo taking up most of the street.

Nanna had insisted that Sadie make Roo up a flask of coffee and a carrier bag full of food. 'For the journey,' she explained.

'They do have food on motorways, you know,' Roo pointed out.

'That rubbish! You might as well eat your own tyres.'

'How would you know? You've never been on a motorway in your life,' Sadie teased.

'I read, don't I? And I watch *Watchdog*.' Nanna briskly wiped a tear from her eye. 'Now I hope you're not going to make a fool of yourself saying goodbye, Sadie. Our Ruby doesn't need you having hysterics.'

'She's my daughter, and I'll make a bloody fool of myself if I want to. Don't leave me with her,' she begged Roo. 'She'll drive me mad.'

'You can always change your mind and come with me.'

Four months ago she could never have imagined asking Sadie to move down to London to live with her. And she was actually disappointed when her mother refused, saying her life was up in Normanford.

'I'm too old to uproot myself now,' she said. 'Nanna needs looking after and all my friends are up here.'

And she had her own business to run now. Johnny had bought the Ponderosa, so Sadie could sing to her heart's content, every night if she wanted to. He even planned to rename it The Talk of the Town, after the famous London nightspot where Sadie had always dreamed of topping the bill.

Sadie's expression softened. 'Thanks for the offer; you don't know what it means to me. But somehow I don't think the big city's ready for Sadie Moon yet!'

'Besides, I wouldn't want to be without her, now I've found her again.' Johnny put his arm round Sadie.

'But you will come and visit, won't you? Both of you,' Roo added, looking at Johnny. They'd made their peace since she realised how much he adored her mother. If only they'd managed to stay together thirty-odd years ago, it could have saved them all a lot of heartache.

'Try and stop me. I have to see that grandson of mine, don't I?'

There was a screech of brakes as Uncle Tom's taxi came to a halt outside. Johnny rushed to the window. 'Your bloody brother!' he cursed. 'If he scratches my paintwork—'

But Roo wasn't looking at the limo. She was looking at the black labrador bounding out of the back of the taxi.

She rushed to the door, fighting her racing heart, and tried to stay calm when she saw Matt standing there, holding Harvey's collar.

'I thought we'd missed you,' he said.

'Come to say goodbye?'

'No way. We're coming with you. Harvey's looking forward to London. I can't disappoint him, can I?'

'But your house was empty. I thought—'

'You thought I'd changed my mind?' He shook his head. 'I've been working all hours to get the last of my research done. You didn't think I'd let you down, did you?'

Roo stared past him as Uncle Tom began pulling luggage out of the boot of his taxi. 'I wasn't sure.'

He held her at arm's length, his warm turquoise eyes meeting hers. 'I told you, I want to be with you.'

'For how long?'

'For as long as it takes to convince you I love you.'

Their kiss was interrupted by her family, spilling out into the street to say goodbye. Uncle Tom tutted. 'Just like your mother,' he grumbled.

'Ignore him. Miserable old goat.' Sadie hugged her. 'Goodbye, Ruby Tuesday,' she whispered. 'Take care of yourself.'

'And you, Mum.' They stared at each other, both realising at the same moment that Roo hadn't called her that since she left junior school.

As they got into the car, Matt said, 'Ruby Tuesday, eh? No wonder you kept it quiet. What kind of a name is that?'

Roo glanced in the rearview mirror at her mother, who was waving frantically on the doorstep.

'A bloody good one,' she said.

DONNA HAY

For Donna Hay, writing *Goodbye, Ruby Tuesday* was therapeutic because, like her heroine in the novel, Donna has spent years wondering about the circumstances surrounding her own birth. For much of her childhood, she had what she thought was an ordinary family: Mum, Dad, a brother, and a sister eighteen years older than her. Every so often, a family friend called round and would single her out for treats and outings, but when Donna reached thirteen she began to ask questions about him. 'He must have picked up on my growing teenage unease because one Sunday in May, just as he was leaving he told me that he was my father,' Donna told me. 'My whole world tipped sideways. Thoughts and images whizzed through my head: my mum, so much older than any of my friends' mothers; the neighbour who had always referred to her as my nan; day-trips with my "sister" . . . I didn't have to ask who my mother was. The pieces fell into place so quickly I wondered why I'd never put them together before.' But Donna did not want to accept the truth and she and her 'parents' never discussed it. 'Looking back now, I see that denying the truth was my only way of coping. For a while, that was how I wanted it. But things like that don't just go away.'

It wasn't until Donna was in her late twenties and about to get married that she told anyone the truth about herself. She was amazed by how many people had similar stories to her own. 'But the truly amazing part has just

happened,' she told me. 'The Daily Mail recently interviewed me about *Goodbye, Ruby Tuesday* and my history, and "my father" saw the feature when sitting in a doctor's waiting room. First of all he thought it was just another sob story, but then he saw a family photograph in the corner of the article and realised that it was the same one he'd carried in his wallet for forty years.'

Her father sent a letter to Donna via *The Daily Mail*. 'It was really, really moving. It turned out that he and my sister/mother had been teenage sweethearts and for the first four years of my life he saw me regularly and I called him Daddy. He then joined the army and was posted to Indonesia for over two years. When he came back I didn't know who he was and by then I was calling my grandparents Mum and Dad. They persuaded him not to confuse me by telling me the truth and my father agreed. But by the age of thirteen I still hadn't been told and he just blurted it out that Sunday in May.' In the letter her father went on to tell Donna that he had never forgotten her and had always wanted to get back in touch with her.

'Being a writer, I've composed endless scenarios about my past, but I feared I'd never know the truth. My parents—the people who I've always called my parents—are dead, and my biological mother and I parted company ten years ago after a family dispute. But now, having established contact with "my father" again after thirty years, I might finally fill those blank pages.'

Jane Eastgate

Printed and bound by Maury Imprimeur SA, Malesherbes, France

601-029-1